KISSED BY BRIMSTONE

BOOKS
1-3

LEIGH KELSEY

THREE FREEBIES FOR YOU

Fancy some freebies? I'll send you three when you join my newsletter! I promise never to spam you, and I rarely send more frequently than once a fortnight so you won't be overloaded with emails.

Join here: http://bit.ly/LeighKelseysNL

HELLBORN ANGEL

LEIGH KELSEY

BLURB

Hell hath no fury like a demon psycho scorned.

The first thing you should know about me is I'm completely cuckoo. Two hundred years ago, a monster of abusive proportions killed my fated mates. And me.

Don't ask how I've been reborn. All I know is I still have my memories, my rage, and the power to make blood boil in someone's veins. Both literally and because I'm a sarcastic little shit.

Emlyn, Malakai, and Harveil held me together, and without them, I've hit breaking point. Probably when I stole that porcupine demon's quills and made them into a tiara. (Looks cute; tragically impractical.)

But in positive news, my insanity helped me become Lucifer's best assassin. Now, I spend my days taking out hell's enemies and my nights scouring every forsaken city for my mates.

Because if I've been reincarnated, they have too. And someone thought it was a good idea to keep me from the men I love.

Hellborn Angel is a paranormal romance with psycho men, a

For one of my favourite authors
Sarah Rees Brennan
who encouraged me to keep writing
when I was young and very bad at it.
You probably don't remember, but I've never forgotten that kindness.

And I'm still in deep, obsessive love with
the Ryves brothers.

I'm pretty sure my demon addiction
is your fault.

ruthless revenge-driven FMC, twisted romance, and lots and lots of bloodlust. Deadly archdemons, cutting sarcasm, epic reincarnation romance, and gruesome murders fill these pages, so get ready to laugh, cringe, and swoon.

This book is medium burn, with moderate heat, and multiple love interests, and set in the same world as Lili Kazana - but this series stands completely separate.

NOTE

This book contains mentions of past abuse and sexual assault that could be incredibly triggering for some readers, plus it deals with infertility, so please proceed with caution. Don't hesitate to skip this book if it's safer for your mental health.

As always, don't recreate any sexy times in this series without doing your research, communicating with your partner, and discussing aftercare.

This series also contains some spoilers for the Lili Kazana trilogy, which takes place a year before this series, but nothing too major that doesn't appear in the books' blurbs.

Oh, and this series will break your heart. Fair warning.

Leigh x

P.s. don't forget to read the footnotes for added hilarity!

PART I - MERCENARY

CHAPTER ONE

"Of course it's fucking raining," I grumbled, taking my frustration out on a puddle.

This town was a shitheap of crumbling houses, worn-down shops, and as many pubs as you could squash onto two dirt roads. Sometimes I hated my job. But I was a single woman in her twenties with no family, few friends, and an empty purse. If I wanted to eat this month, I had no choice but to be here.

It was slightly worrying that no one else had taken the job, though. Usually mercenaries clamoured for anything with this hefty a reward. Not to mention it didn't require a murder —it was a simple retrieval mission.

"It's probably nothing," I dismissed, checking my weapons before I approached the squat cube of an inn. Warped windows threw squares of light on the ground, catching yet more puddles. "Just think of the ten thousand gold crowns."

Inside, the pub was as delightful as I expected. A heavy scent of stale beer filled my lungs, accompanied by the familiar sensation of my boots sticking to the floorboards as I let the door fall shut behind me.

Rough voices and coarse language came from people sitting at chipped tables a week away from falling apart, and every liquid behind the bar was cloudy, brown, and unpalatable. But at least there was a fire roaring across the room, so a wall of pleasant heat sank through layers of travel-dirty clothes and into my body.

It sucked that I couldn't let it bleed the tension from my bones; I needed to be alert while I searched for my mark.

I'd been given a shitty amount of information about Wane Van Khama, the man I was here to take back to my client. All I knew was a vague description—he looked to be in his late twenties, though my client had notably left out his true age; he was a demon with bat-like black wings, spiralling black horns; and deep bronze skin. And I knew he was an experienced fighter, so I needed to be on my guard.

I didn't know what he'd done, or what my client would do with him. But *fuck*, ten thousand gold crowns. That would set me up for a whole year. Maybe two if I was clever about it.

Maybe I could get a house, buy myself a sweet husband and a family. The devil knew I wasn't getting one without paying for them—I was a foulmouthed, bad-tempered bitch who preferred stabbing to singing and combat to cooking. Men wanted a sweet, romantic girl, not one who came home dripping blood and got into fights on a Friday night because she was bored.

But hey, if I *paid* a guy to like me, problem solved.[1]

I hopped onto a bar stool and flagged down the portly, moustachioed man currently cleaning a cloudy glass with a rag.

I didn't make the mistake of asking after Wane in a place like this; everyone would close ranks, maybe even throw me out on my ass. My ass was already too cold to land in a muddy puddle, so I asked for a beer and canvassed the place while I waited for my drink.

The single room was filled with the usual assortment of scowling and sneering demons in grungy clothes. Some stared into their pints while others scanned the pub like I did, although for entirely different reasons. In the back, a woman in a frothy purple dress sat energetically in a man's lap, leaving little question about what was happening under her skirts. There were a number of winged, horned men, some with brown skin and others pale, ruddy, or crimson, but I knew which one was Wane Van Khama when my eyes skimmed over him, and a clang went through my chest.

"What the fuck?" I hissed under my breath, jumping when the bartender set my beer in front of me. I *never* got jumpy on a job. But what the hell *was* that clang? I still felt it echoing through me, like someone slammed a fist into my chest. Only instead of hitting skin, muscle, and bone, they hit my vulnerable insides.[2]

There's still time to turn around and leave, I told myself.

But I accepted the job, and fuck knows what would happen if I returned emptyhanded. I might have been a vicious bitch with very few hard lines, but my client was powerful—and a total psycho. I couldn't predict what he'd do. One thing was for sure: if I walked away from this, I'd have to find a new career.

But let's be real, there's no chance in Hell I'm walking away from this.

Ten thousand fucking credits.

So I sipped my beer and discreetly watched the slim, black-winged man. His lithe body was wrapped in shadows like a huge fur coat, and my gut cramped as I watched him. My chest fluttered. It was alarming as fuck. It wasn't a flutter of fear, but *excitement*, and my heart needed to get its head in the game.

Sure, his bronze face was carved by the gods, and there

11

was a visible corona of power around him, but come on! *You're working, Halwen, get your shit together.*

Retrieval. Probably fisticuffs. Definitely trouble with capital T.

Wane van Khama wasn't alone; he sat with three other men that gave me the same deep, resonating clang in my chest. These three looked every bit as intimidating and deadly as Wane, with an assortment of horns, claws, wings, and tattoos. I almost slipped off my stool.

Whatever that warning clang was, it was not. Fucking. Good.

I needed to get Wane alone, because his buddies were *massive*. Muscle wrapped around muscle, and bulged from shoulders, arms, chests, and *thighs*. One was so thick his arms were like tree trunks. I briefly entertained the thought of climbing him like he really *was* a tree, and hissed at the immediate pounding between my legs.

So what, they were hot? They were still trouble. Still in my way.

When I next glanced their way, the oldest (and biggest) man watched me.

Oh, shit!

I panicked, and batted my lashes, covering up my reconnaissance with pathetic flirting.

This bastard was every bit as hot as Wane, his features more rugged and his jaw covered in a salt and pepper beard to match the hair that curled slightly at his shoulders. The grey, long-sleeved shirt he wore hugged muscles my hands were desperate to trace, and the fabric clung to the unmistakable shape of weapons. *That* dunked cold water over me; I spun back to the bar and my pint.

Okay, I reasoned. *Just go over there, flirt with them, get Wane alone, and cuff him. Easy.*

I had enhanced metal cuffs that would bind even a furious,

magical rhinoceros, but something told me Wane wouldn't *let* me snap them around his wrists. There'd be a fight.

Why did my blood spark?

Why did my stomach change from churning nerves to excitement?

Oh, because I was crazy. Yeah, that explained a lot.

Like why I took another sip of beer[3] and sauntered over to the table of four clear predators, swishing my hips and channelling the woman getting lucky over in the corner. *Good for her.*

"Hello, boys," I purred, my voice already raspy enough to be sultry. No one had to know it turned that way by screaming while my 'trainer' hurt me to make me a good little soldier.[4]

Interest lit in the eyes of the older man, and he leaned back in his seat, grey feathered wings spreading as he eyed me up and down. I doubt he saw much; I'd been on the road for days, and my leather trousers were caked in as much dirt and dust as my heavy jacket. Fuck, I hadn't thought this through. I needed to be alluring.

But the interest in his vibrant blue eyes only flared, as if I was attractive to him even covered in the grime of travel. Yet his arms remained crossed over his chest, and he wasn't the one to reply.

"And who might you be?" a shaggy-haired, bronze-skinned Adonis asked, his chin tilted at a cocky angle and molten silver eyes meeting mine in a sultry look. I'd never seen eyes like that before, otherworldly and shining like mirrors. I fought a shudder.

"Jynn," I answered, curving my mouth in an inviting smile. I could play sweet and flirty if I wanted to; mercs had to play so many roles that I'd lost count. It was all part of the job.

"Pretty name," the bronze god replied. "But I think I'll call you sugarplum."

I couldn't control my reaction; my mouth fell open. "You fucking *won't.*"

"Try and stop me," he taunted. "Now, are you joining us or going back to your lonely seat by the bar?"

I was tempted to go back to my lonely seat by the bar just to spite him. But my eyes drifted to the other two men—to Wane, who was a near identical copy of the smirking bastard —and a man who sat a head taller than the others, with ultra-pale skin, deep red eyes and matching crimson hair, and a body *covered* head to toe in scrawling ink—writing. He watched me like he'd enjoy cutting my body apart to see how it ticked, so I avoided his gaze and met the challenge in the smug bastard's.

"Fine." I shrugged, "I suppose you're not the worst company in this place."

The big guy grunted, his beard twitching with a smile.

"*So*, sugarplum," the cocky bastard said, taking great pleasure in the glare I shot his way, "what brings you to our little town?"

I came to kidnap your brother. But I couldn't exactly tell him that.

"I'm here for work," I replied expertly. "What about you? Do you live here? And you haven't even told me your names."

"We live here—ish," he replied. "As for names, I'm Harvey; this is my brother, Wane; the stern, silent bastard is Emlyn; and this is Malakai, our resident psychopath. Don't make any sudden moves," he whispered. "Kai tends to get a little twitchy and choke people until their heads fall off."

"It's really good to meet you all," I bullshitted. "Thanks for letting me sit with you."

Malakai grinned, a slow spreading, chilling thing. "Little liar."

He gave the others a meaningful look and angled his horned head at me. "She's from the guild; it stands out a mile."

Uh-oh. The guild as in the guild *of mercenaries.*

"What guild?" I asked, my eyes big and innocent.

The look Malakai gave me could have scalded iron. My heart skipped when he shoved his chair back, throwing it to the sticky floor.

I jumped automatically to my feet—my instinct wouldn't let him tower over me. But I gave myself away with my fast response.

"For fuck's sake," Harvey spat, silver eyes flashing. "We've barely been here a week. What did he offer you?" He dropped his hand, giving me a loathing look. "Fame? Fortune? A city?"

I snorted. "You're way off the mark, buddy."

"She's struggling to survive," Emlyn, the big, bearded guy spoke, and I gasped at the low thunder of his voice. I was having inappropriate thoughts again, and it couldn't have been worse timing. "They offered money or food."

"Ding, ding, ding," I replied, and *shrieked* when Malakai launched at me

He moved so fast, I had to pump my wings to leap out of his path.

The rest of the pub's patrons jumped to their feet, but not to help me. Not even to help Wane and co.

Wane hadn't spoken a single word, and only stared at me, half wrapped in shadows.

People moved out of the way, clearing space for Malakai to throw himself at me. Generous of them.

I dodged, scanning for an exit that *wasn't* blocked by a crimson-haired psychopath. This job was impossible with Wane's entourage around him. I'd have to leave, and later follow them to get him when he was alone.

I pumped my wings and reached inside my jacket for my knives. They were old and mottled, but I sharpened them regularly and they could cut as well as any new, pretty blade. I slashed one at Malakai when the pale, inked bastard hurtled at me again, moving faster and far more graceful than he looked. That was the benefit of being a demon; we were faster, stronger, and with magic in the mix, *anything* was possible.

"Fine," I growled, throwing my hands up and giving the red-haired man a scowl. "You win; I'll leave you alone. Happy?"

Judging by the way he slammed into me, wrapped both hands around my neck, and squeezed until my eyes almost popped out of my head … no, he was not happy.

"Kai!" a raspy voice called, gravely and raw like my own voice.

My gaze snapped to Wane as the bronze-skinned, sleek-haired man came toward us. His face was the only visible feature, his shadows wrapped around him like a shield. Or like a child's comfort blanket.

"Stop," he ordered tiredly.

I took advantage of the pause to angle a knife up into Malakai's gut, but when I tried to slam it home, my hand refused to budge.

"What the fuck?" I spat, trying my other knife to the same effect. "Who enchanted my knives? Undo it *now!* These are my best pair, you salty cumrags."

Malakai scoffed and glared at me, his eyes dark crimson and *seething* with murder. "*You're* the one who's enchanting."

"Aww, thanks, that's so sweet of you," I preened, batting my lashes. Sometimes I thought I had a death wish.

"Whatever you've done to my hands," he hissed, deep and throaty as he snapped sharp teeth at my face,[5] "I'm going to kill you for it."

His scent of amber and crackling firewood invaded my senses, annoyingly pleasant.

"Stop," Wane said in that same quiet but forceful voice, footsteps approaching us and the other two guys right behind him. "It's not an enchantment, it's *nature*. Instinct. You can't kill each other, because you're mates."

I laughed.

Malakai's upper lip curled back.

"Didn't you feel it?" Wane went on, looking at *me* now. My stomach squirmed at the eye contact, and I was a little embarrassed when my heart skipped. "When you first saw me? I know *I* felt it, like a bell rang through my entire soul."

That clang...

A chill went down my spine.

"You're—you're our mate, Jynn. You're mine, and Malakai's."

"And mine," the burly, older man grunted.

Harvey flashed me a blinding grin. "Guess that explains why I want to fuck you into submission so badly."

"You wish," I hissed, trying to stab Malakai and failing miserably. "I wouldn't touch you if my life depended on it."

Wane sighed, his shadow-wreathed shoulders drooping an inch. "It might, actually. You can't kill any of us, but the man who sent you to hurt me? When he finds out you haven't done the job, he'll do unspeakable things to you. It's worse than death."

I frowned, unable to get a read on what kind of person Wane was. Something about him registered as genuine. And it made me think he'd personally experienced those unspeakable things.

"Son of a goat-fucking whore," I muttered, and removed my knife from Malakai's stomach.

I had four soulmates.

CHAPTER TWO

"My name is actually Halwen," I told the guys on a sigh. We'd righted the pieces of furniture that got pushed over when me and Malakai tried to kill each other, and the ambience of the pub went back to normal. Now, we sat at the same table with refreshed drinks in front of us—I sipped my beer, but it still tasted like a pig's bathwater—and my knife was openly in my hand instead of hidden inside my mud-splattered jacket.

Malakai still glared at me, his unnaturally pale face twisted with hatred. Fair enough—I was pissed that some law of nature had stopped me killing him, too.

"What does this mate shit mean, exactly?" I asked, some bitterness leaking into my voice even as I tried to mask my emotions. I was in a full scale panic, my heart hammering my ribs, my breathing jagged, and my black wings refused to stop twitching with nerves.

I looked to Wane, who'd broken the news of me being their mate in the first place, but he'd retreated into the dark corner and was now so wrapped in shadows that I couldn't make out his hands or even his face.[1]

Harvey, the bronze Adonis, wasn't smirking anymore, but this was worse. *Oh, so much worse.* Mercury-silver eyes tracked my every movement in awe, like I was a goddess. But this was Hell and there were no gods here, only Lucifer ruling us in his fancy-ass city.

"You're telling me you've never heard of a soulmate?" Harvey drawled, but the bite in his voice was drowned out by the way he propped his chin on his hand and *gazed* at me.

I made a throaty sound and sipped my beer—and wished I hadn't. Gods, it was gross. "Of course I've heard of a soulmate. But how does this *work?* What power does it give you over me?"

Emlyn snorted, his beard twitching as he smiled. The giant was a man of very few words, but he noticed *everything*, and the way he kept scanning the room for threats told me he was used to fighting. Maybe was used to protecting his friends from people like me.

"You can't use it to control us, Halwen," Emlyn said with gruff amusement, instantly figuring out the true root of my question.

Dammit.

"Bonds don't work that way; they're a link forged between souls. We can sense each other anywhere, find our way back together, and it's ... a comfort. A feeling of safety like no other."

I tapped my knee with the flat of my knife. "I make you feel safe?"

Malakai's vicious grin grew, red eyes flashing with the promise of another tussle. To my horror, my blood heated in eagerness.

"You were sent here to kill us; you're hardly safe," the psycho breathed, his voice sending a chill down my spine.

"Not kill, just pick up and deliver," I replied flippantly, my heart drumming faster. Antagonising Malakai came as easily as breathing, and gave me the same rush as a bar brawl.[2] "But it's a shame I can't kill you; I had so many pretty plans for you."

"She's just winding you up," Harvey told Malakai, reaching out to ruffle the psycho's wine-red hair.

Malakai turned slowly enough to make even *my* stomach squirm, but Harvey only smirked and patted his head before letting go. It was impossible to believe this upbeat, golden nuisance was Wane's brother, but the resemblance was undeniable. Well, when my mark wasn't wrapped in shadows and trying to disappear into the wall, that was.

"You still think you can finish the job," Emlyn rumbled.

I stiffened unconsciously in my seat, swallowing at the deep thunder of his voice. "Well, obviously I can't with all this mate business."

Malakai's upper lip pulled back from his teeth—sharp, deadly rows of teeth— and he hissed so viciously that a few patrons slipped out the pub door behind us.

"You even *think* about touching him, and you die."

I leaned back in my wooden chair, giving him a lazy stare. Like I gave a shit about his threat. I'd been threatened too many times, almost *died* too many times, that it had lost its edge. If I died, so what? My life wasn't exactly sweetness and light; I wouldn't miss it. And no one would miss me.

"If Wane's right, you can't kill me," I taunted, giving Malakai a wink that had him shooting out of his seat. Harvey and Emlyn dragged him back down.

"*Enough*," Emlyn growled, and again I responded with a base, primal instinct. A deep shudder worked through me, my breathing abruptly short. The man might have been quiet, but he was dominant as hell, and *powerful*. Demons didn't have a hierarchy of power per se, but we had damn good instincts, and all my warning sirens were flashing and screaming, telling me to back the fuck down.

"Halwen, you can feel the pull to us as much as we can feel it to you; stop trying to convince yourself you can't."

I grumbled and glared at the table, but there was no ignoring the clang I felt through every part of me.

But just because I felt the bond didn't mean I had to be all in with this *soulmate* shit. They still hadn't properly answered my question. *No power over me, my ass.*

"You're a part of us now," Emlyn went on, scowling at the table even though we all knew his scowl was meant for me. "We're part of you. Live with it."

Well. That was a bit harsh. Then again, I'd come here to kidnap his friend. It was a wonder I was still alive, honestly.

"You're not taking Wane," Harvey warned me, the awe wearing off his mercury gaze. He crossed his arms over his chest, and I noticed for the first time the homespun but sturdy clothes they all wore. Nothing fancy or expensive. Weird; criminals usually paraded their riches in front of people's noses.

"Look," I sighed, "it's not my fault he pissed someone off and they hired me to hunt him down. Whatever he did—"

"*Nothing,*" Malakai snarled so fiercely that his red eyes flashed and power trembled around him, making my bones quake. The inn windows rattled in their frames; a few pint glasses vibrated off their tables and shattered. Malakai didn't flinch. "He did *nothing.* You don't know a damn thing about him."

In the corner, Wane vanished entirely. I knew he was still there, but I didn't want to examine why and *how* I knew that too closely.[3]

"It's fine, Kai," a barely-there voice whispered.

But Malakai was too angry to back down. His nostrils flared, the ink scrawled across his skin shifting, *moving.* I jerked back in surprise—and cursed when I found my arms bound to the chair arms by invisible chains, my torso simi-larly wrapped.

Well, that answered *that* question. We might not be able to kill each other, but the space between life and death was a big playground. And I couldn't wait to play with this mean bastard.[4]

"Whatever you're thinking," Harvey said, his eyes once again fixed on me but with an intensity that made me squirm, "you're wrong. Look at Wane. *Look* at him."

I frowned, wrenching against the invisible bindings tying me to the chair, sweat dripping down my forehead. "Fuck off, Harvey."

"Actually, I've changed my mind about that," he fired back, his cheerful persona stripped away to reveal something that made me nervous. "Only my friends call me Harvey. You can call me Harveil."

My eyes widened; my breath hitched. Oh no. *Ohhhhh no.*

"Yeah," he laughed, entirely devoid of humour. "*That* Harveil."

The Harveil who slaughtered his way through a whole town, decimating their council and leaving buildings in rubble? No one knew what kind of demon he was, or the limits of what he could do, but he left destruction in his wake. And then he vanished.

"Maybe my client meant for me to kill *you*," I mused.

"No," a soft, raspy voice disagreed, and I startled, my eyes shooting to the corner where a swath of shadows unwrapped from Wane van Khama. "It's me he wants."

"He's not getting you," Emlyn swore, something like protectiveness threaded through the violence of his voice. It rattled me to my core. "She won't hand you back to him."

Oh, wouldn't I? Emlyn had *clearly* never been promised ten thousand crowns before.

"You think I'm a criminal, don't you?" Wane asked, catching my attention again with his soft, husky voice.

I shrugged. "Most people are criminals, buddy. I'm not gonna judge you for it."

"Your client, it's—it's Cassander Locke isn't it?"

"I don't know his name," I admitted, my voice gentling on instinct, my bravado and attitude softening around the edges. There was something broken about Wane. Hiding in his shadows, speaking in murmurs, his voice as raw and husky as my own.

Had I completely screwed up, coming here? My stomach twisted up until I was nauseated.

"I know it's him," he replied, his eyes lowered, the same molten silver as Harvey's. "It always is. And whatever he told you about me—"

"Not much, to be honest," I murmured.

"Let him *speak*," Harvey snapped, every bit as protective of his brother as the other two were.

I made a show of sitting back in my seat. Not that I could go anywhere with Malakai's magic trapping me. Should I have been more worried about that? It bound me but didn't hurt. The psycho could have squeezed the air out of my throat, or cut off the blood circulation to my feet, rendering me unable to walk. He did neither.[5]

"Whatever he told you about me," Wane began again, shadows wrapping around him until I could see only his shining silver eyes, "it's a lie. He wants to drag me to his council and force me to tell everyone I lied. But I *didn't*."

I blinked. "What didn't you lie about?"

Wane shook his head, visible only as a scatter of inky shadows and chestnut hair a few shades darker than his brother's.

"He hurt you," I guessed.

He mentioned a fate worse than death; maybe he told

everyone what my client had been up to. Was it an experiment? Everyone knew there were fucked up labs and cages in Hell's seedy underbelly, where people experimented to make faster, stronger, weaponised demons. They called them a new breed of alphas—the unnatural variety.

"Yes," Wane hissed. "And I told everyone what a fraud he was. What he's *really* like. Now he wants me to lie to save his reputation."

I blew out a hard breath, tightening my fingers around my knife.

Fuck.

"I'm not a good person," I told him unapologetically. "I don't usually give a shit what my marks have done to deserve being grabbed or killed or whatever. This is Hell; we do whatever screwed up shit we need to survive. And that's what my client is offering me; survival. It's not personal, and I'd rather *not* haul you in, but I need the money."

Malakai and Emlyn exchanged a glance.

"How much is he paying you?" Malakai demanded, leaning across the table. Dark ink scrolled in words I couldn't read across his skin, and I stiffened, waiting for the magic trapping me to cinch tighter. It didn't.

"Ten thousand," I replied.

Malakai spat a curse I hadn't heard in a long while. I smiled, reminiscing; when I was a teenager, I knew a red panda who used to use it constantly. Of course, no one spoke her language so they didn't realise how colourful her words were. Man, I missed her. Dad and I had been forced to move out of that neighbourhood and into a shittier place when it cost too much.

"But," I sighed, wondering what the fuck was wrong with me, "if you're thinking of paying me off, I'll take half."

That would set me up for six months. And all I had to do

was walk away from this pub and never see these people again.[6]

"Five *thousand?*" Harvey demanded, his face slack with disbelief. "Do you think we're loaded, sugarplum?"

"Of course not, buttercup," I replied, heavy on the sickly sweetness. I even batted my long lashes at him, and wished I had a hand free to twirl a strand of pale pink hair around my finger. "But you could *get* the money, if you were really determined."

"But I'm your mate," Wane breathed, the words striking the vulnerable squishy flesh of my heart like he'd gored me with a spear.

I swallowed hard.

"Three hundred," Emlyn muttered, disapproval clear in his eyes.

Three *hundred?* Was that a joke?

"Two thousand," I countered, flexing my fingers around my knife and ignoring the sickly twist in my chest at Wane's hurt.

"He'll kill you if you don't bring me to him," Wane said abruptly, leaning closer. "You won't ever be safe; he'll find you like he found me."

"A thousand," I sighed before they could even shoot down my demand of two.

I was hot and clammy and miserable, and I was pretty sure it was because I planned to walk away from these bastards. Well, these bastards and Wane. Wane wasn't a bastard; he hammered at my protective instincts like no one ever had.

"Five hundred," Malakai spat, nostrils flaring and power thrumming around him. He was thinking about killing me again; it was obvious.

"Fine," I groaned. "Five hundred and I'll leave you alone."

"*No*," Wane blurted, his shadows scattering until I saw him —*all* of him. He was remarkably like Harvey, his features the same and his clothes similar, but the rest of him was covered in pale, overlapping scars, and my stomach turned over at the sight of them.

"He did that to you?" I whispered, my heart slamming against my ribs.

Wane nodded, dark chestnut hair tumbling into his strikingly elegant face.

I'll kill him.

I couldn't explain where the thought came from, or why the need to exact blood and vengeance beat at my chest like a war drum.

Because he's your mate, dumbass, an inner voice drawled.

My shoulders slumped in defeat. I flicked a glance at Malakai and watched his pale face tighten with a threatening snarl.

"Set me free; I'm not gonna hurt any of you," I murmured.

Malakai's head tilted in an unnatural swoop, crimson eyes scanning me. I had the unnerving sense that he saw through my skin to the red, sinewy bits inside.

A line of text spun around his pale, muscle-corded forearm and he nodded. The restraints fell away, and I could *finally* drag in a full breath, finally move my damn body. When I looked at Wane next, he was wrapped in his shadows again. It was like he wasn't even there.

Emlyn dug his purse out of his jacket and threw a pouch of coins on the table. But my heart was tight with compacted pain, and I kept glancing at the shadows in the corner.

Gods fucking dammit, I growled at myself as I stood and backed away from the table.

"Keep it," I grunted, and could have cursed myself. Since when was I a selfless bleeding heart? "Use it to get as far away from here as possible."

"What?" Malakai spat.

Yeah, I shocked myself, too. I was broke, and hungry, and I

needed that money. But like a complete idiot, I turned and walked away.

"You're serious?" Harvey demanded as I weaved across the room, tucking my knife back where it lived.

"Yup," I replied without turning, and tried to ignore the pain that carved itself into my chest as I took one step after another.

I tried to tell myself it was because I was walking away from the money, but I knew that wasn't true.

Maybe they really were my mates, and I was a complete bloody idiot for leaving them behind.

But like I said, I wasn't wife material—and I certainly wasn't soulmate material. It was better this way.

CHAPTER THREE

Sixteen days later

I'd like to say I slept deeply and dreamt of happily ever afters, but like the paranoid, jumpy woman I was, I slept with my hand wrapped around a knife under my pillow, and woke at the slightest creak of the house beneath me.

I was back home in Sarishon in East Hell, barricaded in my second-floor room in a building tucked between a *delightfully* perfumed butcher's shop and a rowdy pub. The other rooms in this building were rented by a single mother, a drunk, and three guys who were either brothers or lovers. Not the place anyone would expect to find a merc. It was almost always safe.

Even so, I never slept easy, and tonight I was glad for it. I knew beyond a doubt I'd locked the window, so the low, sultry creak it made when it opened had me shooting out of bed.

My covers ended up tangled around my legs as I assessed the bastard climbing into my room. Tall, slim, and moving quietly and competently enough to tell me we were in the same field of work.

Great. Someone had been sent to kill me.

The second his feet touched my floorboards, I kicked out my leg and threw the covers at him, momentarily blinding the merc. He was distracted long enough for me to kick him into the middle of my living room/kitchen area.

He sprawled onto my table, snarling as he ripped the covers off his face, but I was already jamming my knife into his ribs and angling up into his heart.

"Bye bye," I taunted, a little breathless.

He dropped heavily to the floor, and I had a moment of relief before I spotted the blood spreading across my rug. It was a rare impulse purchase I made in a market town a few months ago while hunting a mark, and it was my favourite damn possession. I wanted to kill this bastard all over again for daring to stain it.

I was so consumed with the blood crawling across my rug that I missed the second assassin climbing through the window, and the *four* that snuck through the door I'd also locked when I got home.

Five against one. Wonderful.

I wasn't overly attached to my knife, so I threw it into the skull of the man who dropped from my window.

I needed to get better locks. If I'd been paid ten thousand crowns, I could have had better locks.

I exhaled a hard breath and dove into the kitchen. Well, kitchen was a stretch; it was two cabinets and a stove in the corner of my room. Two cabinets, a stove, and a *knife block*. I grabbed two knives out of it, measured the weight of them in my palms, and threw them with force. One hit a black-clad woman in the shoulder and the other downed a man with a blade to the dick—my favourite move.[1]

While they were distracted, I lunged across the sofa to the

box of weapons I stored under it—one of three in this room. I crossed my fingers that no one found the stashes under my bed or in the bathroom. Dragging the wooden box out, I threw up the lid and closed my fingers around my beloved dagger. It had seen much, much better days but it was special to me.

Rough fingers ensnared my hair before I could use the dagger, and pain tore across my scalp. I spat a clever insult about the man's father as the bastard wrenched my head back.

Cold steel kissed my jaw as he angled it for my throat.

The good thing about being clinically insane was no one could ever predict what you were going to do next.

"Harder," I purred. "Lower."

His grip faltered in surprise, and I laughed as I shoved the knife easily away.

"Boring," I critiqued with a pout, spinning and burying my knife in his gut.

It was a nasty, slow death I dealt him, but in my defence there were two women and four men running at me and—

Wait, there shouldn't have been that many.

"Where the hell did *you* come from?" I demanded as a tall, brawny woman barrelled into my right side, slamming me into my small kitchen counter, wrapping her hands around my throat.

"Now *this*," I croaked, "is more like it."

The good news was my breath play kink was satisfied. The not so good news? I was going to be murdered. Life was cruel sometimes.

I rammed my knee up into her ladybits, slashing with my knife at her arm for good measure. Holy shit, she didn't budge. The tanned woman only grinned, her mean face lighting up like I got on one knee and asked her to marry me.[2]

But she didn't know I had a secret talent, a party trick I liked to pull out on special occasions. Like, when someone was trying to murder me. I could make the blood boil in someone's veins until it roasted them alive.

I matched my attacker's crazy grin, and reached for the well of cruel power that burned inside me, slamming it into her body and—

"What the hell?" I croaked, my mouth parting. My power couldn't touch even a drop of her blood. That had never happened before.

"Nothing can hurt me," she took great pleasure in informing me.

Well, wasn't that just *typical?*

Black spots crowded into my vision, blotting out my attacker's satisfied smile. My arms were getting weak, and I was too woozy to correctly aim my knee into her vagina. My knife barely glanced off her stomach instead of burying deep in her gut.

Great, was I actually going to *die?* That was annoying.

But then, what did I have to live for, really? A rug I was emotionally attached to and a job that paid in as much violence as it did coin?

The black spots wrapped around my vision like a blanket of menacing death.[3]

"I curse you," I croaked as the other intruders began breaking my shit. If I was going to die, I was at least going to scare the shit out of everyone here. It sounded like they'd ripped my door off; they deserved a curse. "I curse *all of you.* You'll never know sleep, never know peace—"

In my head it sounded profound. Aloud, it was a slur of syllables barely pronounced, but the intention was the same. The woman choking me snorted—and then gurgled.

Uh. What?

Her hand tore away from my throat. I learned, quite suddenly, it was the only thing holding me up.

My knees slammed into the hard wooden floor—not the

rug, because I had shitty luck—and I groaned as I collapsed onto my side.

Yay, not dead.

Nay, I didn't know what the fuck was happening.

"Halwen," a soft, breathy voice rasped.

I groaned unintelligently in reply, falling into a warm body when they lifted me off the floor. I felt liquid, like my body forgot how to be solid; I poured over whoever had grabbed me, and jumped when a soothing cold wrapped around me. It was like going outside at night when you were too hot. I wilted into the sensation, even if the more intelligent side of me was screaming, *you're being attacked, you woolly yarmouth.*

"Are you okay?" that whispery voice demanded, soft and sharp at once. "Are you hurt? Where did they cut you?"

I made a throaty sound of protest as the cold seemed to surge, sweeping over my legs, my stomach, my back, and my chest, before pausing on the trickle of blood at my throat—and what was already no doubt a nasty ring of bruising.

"Harvey!" he hissed.

I groaned for a whole new reason, trying to drag myself out of the comforting cocoon. "Not you lot."

The floor shook as someone slammed to their knees beside me. Oh, were we still on the floor? That was nice.

A new set of hands grasped my face, ignoring the teeth I snapped. I needed to open my eyes, but they'd glued together when the world started going dark.

"This might hurt," Harvey said, sounding more concerned than smug. It was the only thing that kept me from killing him as fire blasted through my face and down to my throat. I clenched my teeth on a scream as the burn travelled lower, finding all the places I'd slammed into furniture.

"Bastard," I gasped, forcing my eyes open.

Harvey leaned over me, gloriously handsome with his

bronze skin and wild brown hair, his eyes flashing as he scanned my face.

"I was completely fine without your help," I muttered, which was a total lie, but my pride wouldn't allow me to thank him.

I scanned my body for wounds and jumped when I noticed both the thick shadows wrapped around me and the scarred, dark gold arms around my waist. Fuck, I really wanted to relax into that hold and take a nap. Oh no, my eyelids were fluttering.

"It's okay," Wane said in his comforting rasp. "You're safe with us."

I fought the closing of my eyes, managing to glimpse Malakai storming through my small living room, throwing his hands at my assailants and doing something evil and invisible until they dropped dead. I didn't see Emlyn anywhere, but something crashed in my room behind us, and I swore I heard wings beating.[4]

"You break shit, you pay for it," I slurred and passed out.

CHAPTER FOUR

"*H*alwen." An unfamiliar voice stirred me from the dream I'd been having about a donkey heist. Not riding into a heist *on* a donkey—stealing six of them. They were my beloved family now. "Haley."

I groaned, batting my hand at the scalding hot body splayed against my front. "Not now, I've got donkeys to save."

A snort stirred my hair, and I realised all at once that I should have been alone in bed.

"Mother*fucker*," I gasped, snapping my eyes open and lurching up and out of bed.

At least I was in my own bed, and I was still dressed in my pyjamas. I could have done *without* the arrogant bastard splayed on my mattress like he owned it, a cruel smirk on his mouth and inked fingers tapping on his knees.

Malakai was hot as sin, and I despised him for it. His crimson hair looked incredible against my pillow, but the sharp tips of his horns left a scratch on my headboard, and my eyes narrowed at the pale slice.

"You're buying me a new headboard," I growled.

Malakai shrugged, lines of ink winding around his

arms. I waited for him to strike me with magic, but nothing happened. Maybe the tattoos were alive? Fuck if I knew.

"Get off my bed, you cockroach."

He made a contemplative sound, and then said, "I like the name."

I made a throaty noise. Of course he did. Bastard.

A glare was glued to my face as I reached out and grabbed his arm, surprised by the thick layer of muscle I could feel under his skin *and* by his scorching temperature. I had a sleepy memory of being surrounded by delicious heat, and tried my hardest to stamp that memory out. But fuck, it had felt good.

"Out," I ordered, hauling on his arm. It was a tiny bed, and he looked damn near comical splayed across it. He also didn't budge until he threw a crooked grin my way and deigned to climb off the bed himself.

I realised far too late that he'd boxed me into the corner of my bedroom—well, the sad space I *called* my bedroom. He loomed a head above me, his curved black horns adding another seven inches, and menacing dominance coming off him in waves. Crimson eyes narrowed, his mouth pressed thin, and his shoulders blocked out the light from the window.

I shuddered.

"Here's the deal, Halwen," he said in a voice that oozed danger. "Fourteen assassins broke into your room with a single intention."

"To kill me," I agreed, stealing his thunder.

By the twitch in his jaw, he'd been about to say the exact same words. I tried not to preen in satisfaction.

I froze when he reached out to tuck a wayward strand of pink hair behind my ear.

My heart sped.

Dammit, now we were even. He didn't even *try* to hide his smirk.

"Exactly," he agreed. "And they're going to *keep* trying to kill you, because you pissed off a man with limitless power, dangerous connections, and zero morals. The guys and I are what you might call morally grey, but we *do* have morals unlike the bastard who hired you. You're a loose end."

Yeah, I realised that in the middle of fighting the intruders. But I shrugged. "I'll go on the run, set up somewhere new."

"Good plan," Malakai agreed, watching me too intensely for comfort. Like a viper fixed on its prey.

My stomach squirmed; I glanced over his shoulder at the rest of my home, planning my escape. Emlyn and Harvey were laid on my sofa, cuddled close like kittens. Aww, cute. I didn't spot Wane or his shadows anywhere, though, and a pang of worry went through my heart.

"I'm sensing a *but* coming," I sighed to Malakai.

"*But* you're alone, and easily overpowered."

"Hey!" I snarled, teeth bared and my feathers ruffled. Literally—my wings twitched angrily. "I was not *easily* overpowered. I'll have you know I killed *five* of those bastards before they got to me."

"At which point, you were easily overpowered," he drawled, red eyes glittering in his harsh face.

"Fine," I muttered, my ear tingling with warmth where he'd brushed my hair back. I viciously ignored the heat. "But only because she was indestructible. What's your point?"

"Our souls are the same," he replied, which was not what I expected to come out of his cruel mouth. "The idea of you getting hurt makes me want to set the entire realm on fire and toast marshmallows over the embers."

"I've never had marshmallows," I told him, my mood brightening.

Malakai snorted, but his lips lifted in a genuine smile. "You're fucking crazy."

"Takes one to know one, psycho."

He snagged another strand of my hair, giving it a hard enough tug to make me hiss; I snapped my wing at him in warning. "I'm trying to have an actual conversation here."

"You're pretty bad at it, aren't you?" I taunted, my whole body lighting up when he released the strand of hair only to grab a fistful, gripping tight enough that sparks leapt down my body.[1]

"Would you shut the fuck up?" he groaned, exasperation flattening his gaze.

"Dubious," I quipped, and let out an embarrassing whine when Malakai slammed his mouth onto mine.

He kissed me so fiercely I could barely catch a breath. When I *did* draw air, his fingers tightened in my hair until it hurt. My hands shot up, grabbing fistfuls of the black tunic he wore.

The wicked man distracted me from the sharp hurt by sucking on my tongue.

Holy fucking fuck.

I could count on one hand the number of good kisses I'd had in my life. Good sex was easier; all you had to do was pay attention to your partner and you were gold. But good *kisses?* Holy *Hell*, they were rare. And this was better than good; this was explosive and violent and for a second I forgot how to breathe.

"Better," he grunted, releasing my hair to glide his hand down my spine, pressing his hot palm to the small of my back. "Now be a good girl and stay quiet while I explain our proposition."

All I heard was he thought I was a good girl.

"More assassins will be sent after you, because you dared to disobey Cassander Locke. By happy coincidence, those same assassins are being sent after *us*, and we've learned a few tricks over the last year. You took us off guard, but that's the first time an assassin has gotten that close."

"Technically, it was a retrieval mission," I murmured, wondering if I could con Malakai into more kisses.

"No," he argued, but his anger was directed elsewhere, "trust me when I say you'd kill Wane by dragging him back there."

I had so many questions, but my head was too mushy to sort through them.

"Have you got to the proposition bit, yet?" I asked sassily.

Malakai groaned, dragging me flush against him. Heat and pleasure pounded through my clit when a hardness pressed against me. "Here, grind on this and keep quiet."

"Maybe I'll keep *you* quiet," I threatened.

"Maybe I'd like it," he whispered, his face close to mine.

I should probably be stabbing him and running away, shouldn't I? He was an obvious threat, and clearly crazy. Anyone else, and I'd have been out the door before they could touch my hand, let alone kiss me senseless.

"Come with us," he urged. "Instead of fighting off the assassins on your own, come with us. There's safety in numbers."

I made a face. "I'm not a people person."

Malakai chuckled, the sound vibrating into my chest. "And we are?"

Eh, he had a point.

"How do I know you won't stab me in my sleep?" I asked, squinting suspiciously.

"Because we're your mates, stupid woman," he groaned.

"Call me stupid woman, and I'll make you infertile for the rest of your life," I threatened. I controlled blood; it wasn't an idle threat.

I went still when he jerked forward, dragging his tongue up my cheek and groaning at my taste.

"I almost want to," he breathed against my wet skin. "But that would deprive us both of a delicious future."

Oh man, he was *really* crazy. I thought he was a little insane, but this was asylum-worthy.

"We can't hurt you," he echoed his point, drawing back to look at me and flicking his tongue against his lips, as if there was still a taste of me there. My pussy clenched hard. I wished, not for the first time, I had a normal, safe taste in men. Sadly, this level of sheer madness did wicked things to my body.

"Because of the mate bond?" I guessed. I'd heard of mates, but never met anyone who had one.

It was like marriage, friendship, kinship, and unconditional love rolled into one magical fusion of souls. It was the stuff of legends and fairy tales, and I highly doubted a fairy tale would choose four coarse, psycho bastards and a mercenary to play out its fabled story.

"Can you feel it?" Malakai asked, his focus honed on me and sharp enough to make my belly squirm. "The bond?"

In a rare moment of sense and logic, I disentangled myself from the six-foot-tall package of unhinged violence and stepped back. Not that I had far to go; my place wasn't exactly roomy.[2]

"I can't feel anything. Sorry, cockroach."

The flash of challenge in his eyes made my stomach twist into an even tighter knot. I slipped across the room away from him, pulling clearer air into my lungs. His heady scent of amber and crackling firewood muddied my common sense.

I sighed when I looked at Emlyn and Harvey on my sofa, feeling a strange combination of emotions. Like a kitten had destroyed my room, clawed up my curtains, pissed on my favourite rug ... but then fell asleep in the cutest possible way.

I was alarmed by the soft feelings in my chest, and even

more unsettled by the cannonball that hurtled against my ribs from the inside.

"What the fuck?" I demanded, my hand flying to my chest.

Malakai laughed. "Good. You felt it."

I shot him a seething glare which intensified in heat when I saw he'd helped himself to my bed. *Again.* He sprawled across it like a lazy prince. At least he'd taken his boots off; if shoes had met my covers for even a second, he'd be dead, mate or not.

"And since you felt it," he went on with a crooked grin, "you can stop denying the bond's existence."

My expression went flat. I let him see all my exasperation. "I want you out of my home."

"That's nice," he murmured, getting comfier in my bed. His horn left another scratch on my headboard.

I took a threatening step towards him, but paused when he spoke.

"You'd be dead if we hadn't been watching you. You're lucky we got here in time; you were thirty seconds from death. It would be a shame if we weren't there to save you again." He met my glare from across the room, his red eyes urging me to agree with his madness. "Come with us. We're setting up a permanent safe house so we don't have to run forever. As our mate, you have a place there."

I ground my teeth. "I'm not settling down with you fuck-ers. I'm no sweet housewife."

"More like a panther," he teased.

I raised my eyebrows in agreement, trying to hide how he'd poked at my insecurities. "So you agree. You're better off by yourselves, and I'm perfectly fine alone."

"Who said being a panther was a negative, sweetheart?"

"Well, that's a step up from *stupid woman,*" I muttered, but his meaning finally processed and I blinked. "So you're into women who want to scratch your eyes out?"

Malakai gave me a cocky grin. "I bet I can have you clawing my back instead."

"Don't antagonise her, Kai," a quiet voice murmured, and I jumped in surprise.

Wane had materialised out of his shadows; I watched him climb to his feet in the corner of the room and understood *exactly* why he slept over there. It had a good view of the door, and with both walls behind him no one could sneak up on his vulnerable back. My heart thumped with sympathy.

"Not antagonising," Malakai replied, crossing his ankles on my bed. "Just convincing her to come with us."

Wane's silver eyes flared with panic, and he snapped his attention to me as shadows bound tighter around him. "That's up for debate. We *have* to stay together. Locke will get you, and he'll—he'll—"

Malakai shot off my bed and stormed across the room, reaching through the blanket of shadows for Wane.

Shit. What the hell had Wane been through, to be so traumatised? My instincts battered at me, urging me to approach the shadows and haul him into a tight hug. I took a step forward, but logic held me back. My client, this Locke, had obviously hurt Wane; he'd hardly want a mercenary like me touching him.

I sighed and dragged a hand over my face, rubbing the crust of sleep off my eyelashes. Malakai was right; Locke would keep sending people after me, and it would get tedious real fast. I'd almost been strangled to death, and I might have had the inflated bravado of a housecat, but it had rattled me.

These four could be biding their time, playing me, but if they *were*, I had my weapons and my magic. I could take them down before they hurt me.

And yet ... two of them were asleep on my sofa, one of them was in the midst of a panic, and the other was trying to calm him. They were pretty unlikely murderers. And there was no ignoring the soulmate thing.

"Fine," I sighed quietly. "I'll come with you. But the second any of you lays a finger on me, I'm cutting body parts off."

The shadows around Wane's face thinned enough for me to see the relief there. "Thank you. You'll be safer with us."

Malakai tilted his red head, considering me in a way that made me nervous. "What about a finger *inside* you?"

I rolled my eyes and went to wake the cuddling demons. They could help me pack up my shit.

CHAPTER FIVE

Two months later

*E*verything was rosy and rainbows for two months, if you didn't count clashing with Kai and getting scolded by Emlyn for stealing shit, starting fights, and taking on dangerous jobs.[1] It turned out the gentle, bearded giant wasn't quiet because he was mild mannered, but because he measured his words carefully. And when he went on a rant, he went on *a rant*.

I sensed him building up to one now as he shot Harvey an *I told you so* look. To be fair, he had warned us this job was too good to be true. The posted info only said we needed to pick up a package and drop it off on a street corner uncomfortably close to Akstrang. Five thousand silver for an afternoon's work? Of course we signed up.

But Akstrang? I'd only spent two years in the children's home when I was sixteen, but it was long enough to leave its scars. I'd left enough scars on other kids—and adults—too, but I still preferred to stay away from his place.

Harvey edged closer, brushing my arm. He'd been finding little excuses to touch me for weeks, and I was growing more used to it each time. I was starting to crave the touches, which was dangerous as fuck. They kept looking at me like I was their perfect woman, and I kept waiting for them to wake up and see what I really was: not a beautiful doll but a wolf with bared teeth.

The only issue was they'd seen me fight, and even seen me kill an assassin that hunted us last month, and their eyes *still* followed me when I walked into the room.[2] I was so used to not forming connections because men usually preferred their women meek and submissive, or at the very least *polite*. This was … strange.

"Are you okay?" Harvey asked, his voice dipped low and stripped of its usual laughter. He was always more serious, less himself, when we went on jobs. At least until the fighting started, and he seemed to thrive in the chaos of violence. Especially with Kai goading him; those two bickered like an old, married couple.

"Fine," I replied, and jumped when his fingertips skimmed mine where they were curled into a fist at my side. "I'm just uncomfortably acquainted with this part of Hell," I added, and patted myself on the back for sharing something personal.

"You're safe with us," Wane's raspy voice came from my left, making my heart jump out of my chest. Fuck, he was so quiet and so completely covered in his shadows that he was a talented sneak. "Always, Haley."

"I know that," I replied, dismissive. It wasn't that I didn't feel *safe*. They were being dramatic.

But Harvey's fingers skimmed my knuckles, and a knot I didn't realise had formed in my chest unwound a fraction. "Anyone who even *thinks* about hurting you will die instantly," he assured me.[3]

"Thanks," I replied gruffly, and hoped he didn't notice the

heat that flooded my face when Wane's shadows brushed my other hand, filling my head with all kinds of indecent ideas. Sandwiched between them, sunlight and shadow on either side of me, two cocks filling me—

Nope. Bad Halwen. Bad, bad Halwen.

"You know we care about you, don't you?" Wane asked, shadows thinning over his face so I could see his big, silver puppy eyes. I fought a groan, my heart softening. "You're our mate, Halwen."

"You can call me Haley," I said, disturbed by the emotions fluttering in my chest. "If you want," I added quickly, and internally cursed myself. *A little handholding and you're acting like a bashful teenager?*

"What about me?" Malakai demanded, stopping where he walked with Emlyn on the dirt road ahead of us and spinning to face me. His jaw clenched; he crossed his arms over his chest. I waited for his red tail to start swishing like an angry cat, but it was sadly still, hanging behind him. "Do I get to call you Haley?"

Unlike the others, Kai refused to give me space and time to get used to the whole *mate* thing. He seemed to think that little M word gave him permission to touch me whenever he wanted, climb into my bed in the morning, and kiss me even if I was busy reading, or training, or even defending myself from the mercs Cassander Locke sent at us.

"No," I replied just to piss Kai off.

Crimson eyes flashed and glowed. He stalked closer. My heart skipped, instincts blaring that a predator had me in his sights.

Harvey snorted and let go of my hand. "You're in for it now, Sugarplum."

I shot him a sharp look when he went to stand beside Emlyn. "Traitor. Wane, you'd never leave me, would you?" I asked his brother, matching his wide, pleading look with my own.

Wane wrapped a tendril of shadow around my wrist and—and brought my hand to his mouth. When he kissed my knuckles, my heart legitimately skipped. Wane never touched anyone. Ever. I didn't know why, or what had happened to him, but I knew touch triggered him into violent memories.

I was so stunned by the kiss that I missed him stepping back.

"Kai isn't going to hurt you," he said, eyes flickering with amusement. "He's more likely to push you to the ground and rut you."

My mouth fell open in shock as Wane went to stand with the others, that glimmer of amusement growing in his eyes. "Hey—"

I drew a knife when Kai grabbed me, but I was a little distracted when instead of pulling my hair or choking off my air, he thrust his hand inside my leather trousers and cupped my pussy.

"Ah—" I gasped, fingers white around the knife when he buried a finger inside me.

We were out in the open, on a dirt road surrounded by low hills. There were houses only a minute away. Anyone with sharp eyes and magic would be able to see where his hand was.

"Tell me I can call you Haley," Kai demanded, his face hard but a gleam of obsession in his crimson eyes. The ink wrapped around his body moved, restless.

"Fuck you," I breathed, and threw a scowl over his shoulder. "And fuck all of you for just watching."

Even Emlyn didn't intervene, his arms crossed over his chest and curiosity on his face. His blue eyes were a shade darker, hunger barely hidden there. Great, he was enjoying the show.[4]

"Who made this pussy wet, my rose?" Kai asked, stroking his finger in and out of me as much as he could with my trousers in the way. That was another thing—he kept calling me that. *My rose.* He hadn't explained why, and refused to stop even when I cut him a teeny, tiny bit with my knife. I'd given up trying.

"Like I said," I spat, my face hot and the heat spreading to the rest of me. My knife slid a little lower, less threatening. Dammit. *"Fuck you."*

Kai leaned into my personal space, his lips finding my neck—a spot he'd found through relentless study of my body these two months. "Was it Harvey? Wane? Or—was it both of them, together?"

I stifled a groan, my pussy clenching around his finger.

Kai laughed against my throat, grazing sharp teeth in a threat. My heartbeat jumped. "I felt that, *Haley.*"

"Fine," I gasped when he adjusted his angle. He loved the noise if his grin was anything to go by. "You can call me Haley."

"I know I can. That's old news." He wrenched my body into his with the finger he had inside me, putting pressure on a spot that made me moan. Loudly. "Let's talk about you wanting two cocks at once."

"Never said at once," I panted, glaring at his sharp, infuriating face.

Kai tilted his head, crimson hair spilling over one shoulder. "So you *don't* want your mates to fill your needy holes at the same time? To fuck you until all you can do is tremble and moan as we give you so much pleasure that you forget how to breathe?"

"Kai," I warned. Pleaded.

His finger curled inside me, moving faster. I wanted another, and like he could see the plea in my eyes or sensed it through the bond, he glided a second finger into me. My hips jerked into his, pushing them deeper.

"One in this needy, dripping pussy," he went on, putting his lips to my ear so every breath sent a shiver through me. "One in your filthy, swearing mouth. But that's only two—where should the others go?"

I was going to kill him.

"Make me come, or take your hand out of my fucking pants."

"Is that a threat, my rose?"

"Yes," I snarled, my whole body wound tight.

"Fuck, I love it when you threaten me," he groaned, dragging his mouth down my neck and nipping my throat. His fingers moved faster, and my face burned at the wet sounds his palm made when it ground against my clit.

I swore at the added stimulation, frantically sheathing my knife so I could clutch him with both hands. I hoped my fingernails drew blood; he deserved it.

Footsteps scuffed the ground and made me jump, but it was only Emlyn, Wane, and Harvey. Coming for a closer look. I groaned and dropped my head on Kai's shoulder, heat pounding through me.

"I think," Emlyn said, his deep voice making my inner muscles flutter, "our mate would like a cock in her pussy and another in her ass."

I shuddered hard, digging my nails into Kai's arms, my bottom lip caught between my teeth as his fingers drove into me faster.

"That was a big one, my rose," Kai purred. "Your pussy's gripping my fingers so tight. Is Emlyn right? Does your greedy ass need to be stretched around my cock while Em fills this dripping pussy, Harvey fucks your mouth, and Wane strokes himself, watching you be our pretty whore?"

I was a mercenary and a tough bitch; why was I whimpering?

I swallowed, nodding. My whole body was red hot under my clothes. I could only pant and cling to him as he fucked me with his fingers better than most men had with their dicks.

"Good girl for admitting it," Kai praised, kissing my neck and drawing back to look at me. I knew what he'd see; red-faced, wide-eyed, breathless desperation. His free hand curved over the back of my head as he laid another kiss on my cheek. "We'll give you everything. Won't we, guys?"

"Everything and more," Harvey promised, edging closer so he could touch me. Knuckles glided softly over my cheek and down my jaw, and I bit my lip to trap a whine, leaning into the touch.

"Everything you can dream of," Emlyn added, catching my eye as he walked around me, pressing his chest against my back. Broad, hot hands slid up my stomach to cup my breasts until my pussy throbbed wildly around Kai's fingers.

Kai flicked a glance to my left, and my heart lurched in my chest when I saw the hunger in Wane's expression. The angles of his bronze face were tighter, sharper, his silver gaze fixed on me. He stood a few paces from us, but his shadows had thinned enough that I saw the hands fisted at his sides and the way his stomach hollowed with a rough breath.

"There's nothing I don't want to do to you, Haley," he rasped, holding my gaze.

The heat in my belly coiled tighter, my toes curling in my boots. I didn't take my eyes off Wane, but it was Harvey who tipped me over the edge when his fingers shoved their way into my trousers and grazed my clit.

"*Fuck*," I cried, digging my fingernails into Kai's arms and holding on desperately as pleasure slammed into me like a hammer. The waves were so forceful and all-consuming that I didn't stand a chance of holding in my moans. Anyone with their window open right now must have heard every breathy noise, and I did not care. It felt too incredible to stop.

"That's it," Kai breathed fiercely, stroking me through each spasm. "Come all over our fingers, Haley. This pussy knows who it belongs to; it's time you realised it, too."

That should not have made me come harder. Fuck, I was in trouble with these men.

It took a long, long minute for the shudders to die down. My head spun, strangely light. My lungs filled with blissful air.

"Beautiful," Emlyn sighed, his voice deep and rough as he wrapped both arms around my waist. "So beautiful."

I was a stab-happy, filthy-mouthed mercenary with a dark grey moral compass, but for the first time I felt feminine and desirable and—good. I felt really fucking *good*. I wanted to feel this more, and it wasn't just the orgasm. It was them, their words, the way they looked at me.

Harvey slid his fingers out of my pants first, licking my arousal from them instead of wiping them clean. The man was insane, or insatiable, or both. He groaned, eyes darker as they flicked to me. "I want more."

"Not now," Emlyn disagreed, stroking my stomach. "We're going to be late picking up the package; we don't have time for more."

He dropped a kiss on my head, almost like an apology. I never wanted to leave his arms. It was the safest I'd felt in months. Maybe years.

Who knew what I needed more than anything was for Kai to shove his hand down my pants and give me a grand awakening?

I'd been tolerating the mate bonds these two months, but possibilities opened up now, and they were endless. So many orgasms, so little time.

"Here," Kai huffed, stroking my pussy one last time before

he withdrew his fingers. Harvey literally *skidded* across the ground to grab Kai's hand, sucking them clean.

My pussy throbbed again, more in curiosity than any pressing need. The sight intrigued me, too. These men had been together a long time before I found them. Had they ever been intimate with each other...? Gods, they'd be beautiful together.

"Shit!" Wane hissed so suddenly that I jumped.

I was still dazed and relaxed enough that I forgot to reach for a weapon, though. He threw himself at me, a whirlwind of shadows brushing my skin, wrapping around my body and feeling like *heaven* on my wings. Before his fingers could touch me, too, a solid cage of orange magic slammed down around us. It sizzled hot enough to tell me I'd blacken my fingers if I dared to touche it.

"Great!" Harvey snarled, pacing as much as he could in the cage, his tawny wings tense at his back. "Now we're fucking trapped!"

"I knew this was a bad idea," Emlyn growled, his softness gone and the gruffness back in his voice. He didn't let go of me, though, and Wane's shadows pressed up against me too.

"I wouldn't say *bad* idea," Kai disagreed, giving me an impish smile. "I'd say it's time for round two."

"Oh, no you don't," I argued, holding up my hands when Kai pressed his body back to mine.

"Oh, yes I *do*," he countered, and kissed me hard, making any argument impossible.

His tongue made my head spin, my breathing non-existent, and my underwear soaked all the way through. Now I knew the pleasure he could offer, I wasn't opposed to more. I just liked bickering with him.

When his mouth dragged down my jaw, I looked at Harvey and Wane for backup. This was the worst time for sex, and an even worse time for an orgy. We needed to get out of the trap before the mercenaries found us. Or worse—*him.* Locke's favourite hunter whose intense stare chilled even my blood.

I should have known better than to expect sense from Harvey.

He already had his cock in his hand.

CHAPTER SIX

Ten years later

I couldn't say for sure what woke me up, but the four bonds wrapped around my soul were my number one suspect.

Wane was innocent—he was tucked against my chest, warm breaths puffing over my skin. His shadows were the thinnest I'd seen them in a while, only a light mist draped over his back. It was a sign of how safe he felt here with me.

It had been two years since the last attack, and I had to admit things were starting to feel steady and secure. I still slept with a knife on the bedside table like I did ten years ago, but at least I'd stopped putting it under my pillow. Mostly because Harvey nicked his ear on it one night and whinged about it for three weeks. It was no bigger than a papercut. Big baby.

I jumped when the dull smack of flesh meeting flesh came from downstairs, my wings ruffling in surprise—one splayed behind me and one draped over my mate, our feathers overlapping. Ink and blue-black merged into one.

"Zivai," I murmured to wake Wane, though if anyone ever witnessed me being so soft and calling him *my heart*, I'd firmly deny it.

A breath caught in his throat; his arms tightened around me and a velvety shadow caressed my cheek. "Is it morning?"

"Mm," I confirmed, enjoying the feeling of Wane holding me close. He was taller than I expected when he first dropped his shields for me to fully see him, but nestled so close to me he seemed worryingly small and fragile. I ran my fingers through the long, messy strands of his chestnut hair and was rewarded with him melting into me like he was made of liquid night instead of flesh and bone. "Someone's fighting downstairs."

He jerked like I had when I heard the noise, rubbing his eyes as he pulled away and smiling at my noise of complaint. "You don't sound worried."

"There's no panic in my bonds," I replied, sinking deep into my soul where the others were entwined around me. Emlyn was busy but distracted, and Harvey and Malakai thrummed with determination and satisfaction. No panic, no alarm, no stress.

"Come back here." I opened my arms, taking this rare chance to study Wane in all his beautiful glory.

A soft green shirt hung loose over his torso but it clung to the defined curves of his upper chest, and his long hair tumbled over his shoulders, mussed by sleep. A vein in his forearm caught my attention, and I wished I could trace it with my tongue. I wished I could kiss all the pale scars that made a callous canvas of his body.

But it was a miracle and a gift that he'd sleep in a bed with me, and let me *hold* him. As badly as I wanted more, wanted *everything*, I couldn't push him. The idea of hurting my mate, triggering him, made me sick.

"You're not wearing a shirt," he murmured, as if he'd forgotten during the night.

I waggled my eyebrows, stretching on the bed. "Enjoying the view?"

He laughed, silver eyes averted from my gaze but trailing the muscle, curves, and scars of my chest and stomach.

"Always, itzaia," he said, husky and sweet.

Itzaia—*my soul.*

When he was so adoring and lovely, could you blame me for being a complete sap in return?

He snuggled back against me, his hands tracing a raised slash on my lower belly. I ignored the way my gut squirmed, his fingers on my stomach reminding me of the emptiness inside it. We'd been together for ten years, safe for two, and trying for a baby for most of that time. And ... nothing.

Sensing the turn of my mood, Wane pulled me flush against him, his arms tight around me and shadows caressing me.

Another loud smack came from downstairs a minute later. Wane drew back with a frown.

His features were softer than Harvey's up close, his eyes the same quicksilver but heavier, more haunted. I knew some of his past now, knew he and his brother had been raised in true and total darkness and only saw light when they killed their jailor uncle and fled their abusive father. I couldn't imagine living my entire childhood in the dark, never seeing the sun for twenty years.

I kissed the curve of Wane's jaw as he frowned at the door, as if he could see what our family were up to through the wood.

"I bet they're trying the Devil's Tornado again," he mused, amusement in his soft, raspy voice.

I jolted back, eyebrows slamming down over my eyes.

"They better fucking *not* be. The last time they did that, they broke my good knife display and put a hole in the wall."

Wane laughed, and as gruff and annoyed as I was at the thought of our home suffering more idiotic destruction, my heart went all soft and squishy at the sound.

Before I climbed out of bed, I trailed my fingertips along his jaw and brought his face to mine for a quick kiss. It wasn't easy to judge how much contact he was okay with, so I tried to be as gentle as possible. But sometimes he surprised me, like now when a hot hand grasped my thigh and pulled it over his leg so he could fit closer, kissing me deeper, harder.

"Fuck," I groaned against Wane's lips, my hands tingling with the need to feel more of him, to sink my fingers into his hair, to hold his face as he kissed me like a starving man. But I held back, not wanting to ruin the moment. Heat and liquid built between my legs, my clit throbbing hard, and I arched into his body, desperate and flush and sensitive.

"Touch me," he rasped, his hands wandering down my bare back until I was shuddering and moaning into his mouth. His taste overwhelmed my senses with the sweetest wine until I was drunk on him, and I wasted no time in touching him.

I tangled fingers in his hair, and slid my other hand under his shirt and across sleep-flushed skin. Wane kissed me hard, rough with the same urgent passion I felt as I caressed his body, loving every single inch of him.[1]

We only drew apart when something crashed downstairs.

"Fuckers," I spat, but breathlessly. My head spun, need pulsing in my pussy and my skin on fucking *fire*.

"Should I kill them for you?" Wane asked, silver eyes bright with happiness.

"Depends what they broke," I muttered, stroking my fingers across his stomach. I drew them from under his shirt when he shuddered, and brushed his brown hair back into place before letting go. "I suppose we should go see the damage."

"Haley," he breathed when I climbed out of bed and hunted down a shirt.

"Mm?"

"I'm sorry I can't—"

I snapped upright, tunic in hand. "Fuck that. You're completely perfect. Don't *ever* think you're not. You give me *everything* I need." I waited for him to look at me, but he didn't. "Wane. *Zivai.*"

His breath hitched; he lifted his head and met my steady gaze. Kneeling on the bed, his wings slumped behind him, he looked like the broken man I met ten years ago. Sometimes, I thought I was still the snarling, broken woman they met, too. Healing took time.

"You give me everything I need," I said emphatically. "You are enough."

A corner of his mouth flicked up; he ran his hands down his face. "Ten years, and you're still telling me that."

"And I'll *keep* telling you," I replied, opening my arms and wings in an offer.

He scrambled off the bed and practically dove into my embrace, bending over so he could touch me everywhere. I wrapped him up in my arms, and bound my wings around him in a protective cocoon.

The distinct sound of someone being slammed into a wall echoed up the stairs, and I tilted my head back to yell, "Stop breaking my shit!"

"Get down here and stop us then!" Harvey shouted back.

I laughed, laid a kiss on the side of Wane's head, and let him put space between us. Through the bond, I felt the itchiness of his discomfort approaching. He'd almost reached his quota for touch this morning.

"Tea?" I asked, angling my head in a *follow me* gesture as I headed into the hall.

The guys planned this house long before we met, but I swore they'd looked into my head and built my dream house. It was everything I ever imagined, from the huge attic bedroom to the round windows on the landing to the bright, airy kitchen and living space downstairs.

I hoped there was still something left of my beloved kitchen, but I wasn't too optimistic.

"Alright, fuckers, what did you break?" I demanded, stalking into the open plan room on the ground floor, and scanning it with a keen eye.

My sofas were intact, and my replacement weapons cabinet was still standing. There were three logs scattered across the room, though, and in the kitchen ... *godsdammit.*

"Devil's tornado?" I demanded, watching Malakai and Harvey grapple with each other, circling so fast they'd be dizzy if they weren't so demonic.

It had been a shock to find out they weren't regular demons, but long-lived *arch*demons. They weren't as immortal as Lucifer and his inner circle, but they'd last a good five hundred years. As their mate, I still wasn't sure what that meant for me—being bound to them could extend my life, too.

"Two plates and a mug," Emlyn answered my question, nodding at a pile of shattered pottery that had been swept into the corner, likely by him. My other mates didn't clean up after themselves. Spoiled brats.

"I warned them they'd knock them off," he added, lifting a mug of coffee to his mouth and glancing at me over the top of a leather-bound book with a gold tree stamped in its centre. "Any chance you can rein in your brother, Wane?"

"Zero chance," Wane replied with a long-suffering huff that did little to cover up his fondness.

He approached the kitchen via the long route, avoiding the whirling mass of limbs to grab the coffee press and pour dark liquid into a mug.

I frowned, watching the floor so I didn't cut myself on any wayward shards of broken crockery as I approached. Wane didn't drink coffee; he'd gone through a phase of drinking herbal tea but was now firmly in his black tea era.

I swear, my entire body, heart, and *soul* softened when he added milk and honey, and I realised he'd made the coffee *for me.*

I let all my love show when he handed me the mug. My heart legitimately skipped when he bent to kiss my brow even though he was at his limit.

"Hey, you don't look at *me* like that," Harvey complained, tossing shaggy hair out of his face.

I took a drink of sweet, bitter coffee and smirked. "Stop smashing up my house, and I will."

"*Our* house," Malakai corrected, shoving wine-red hair off his forehead. Damn, he looked good all sweaty and worked up, his eyes gleaming with excitement and inked scripture swirling on his bare chest.

"*My* house," I corrected right back. "Em, whose house is it?"

Emlyn set down his book and steepled his big hands. "On paper, it's ours. But in reality? It's yours, Hales."

I stuck my tongue out at Malakai. A thrill made butterflies burst in my stomach when his red eyes flashed. I'd pay for that comment later, and enjoy every damn second of it.

"We need to go shopping," Wane murmured, opening cupboards with one shadow-wrapped hand while the other held a mug of steaming tea. I was pleased to know him, and his drink of choice, so well.

If I could go back in time and tell myself I'd be here, living in an amazing house, with four men I loved so much my heart exploded, in domestic fucking bliss? I'd check myself into an asylum for delusion.

"There are spiced cakes," Emlyn replied, stretching his arms over his head, either because his muscles were stiff or because he wanted my eyes on him. I trailed a hungry stare over every bit of bulging, tempting muscle, and the heat Wane had started upstairs pounded again in my pussy. "We can heat those up for breakfast, and later—hello, Halwen," he laughed when I plopped onto his lap, straddling him.

His arms settled around my back, reassuringly strong.

"Don't mind me," I murmured, resting my hands on his big shoulders. Em was still a man of few words, but his deep, rumbly voice was addictive as hell. Especially when I felt it vibrate on a certain area...

"Are you in heat?" Malakai asked with a laugh.

"Yes," I deadpanned, resting my head on Em's shoulder to give Kai a sulky look.

"I propose a change of plans," Harvey said, his voice lower, softer as he prowled around the table. I bit my lip. "Spiced cakes can wait; I know exactly what I want to eat for breakfast. Up on the table and spread your legs, sugarplum."

I laughed in surprise, but heat razed through my body and I swallowed. I looked from Emlyn to Harvey to Kai and Wane. If I hadn't glanced at Wane, I'd never have seen the shadowy figures in the garden outside the window—or the ball of fire streaking from the forest right at us.

"Wane!" I screamed and threw myself out of Emlyn's lap, slamming into my shadowy mate.

I knocked him away from the wall just as the unnatural fire hit our house and spread faster than a wildfire.

CHAPTER SEVEN

" *I*tzaia, *itzaia,*" Wane breathed, running panicked hands over my face and down my neck to my shoulders.

"Are you hurt?" I demanded, my head rattled but my instincts kicked in instantly. "Did the magic touch you?"

"No," he rasped, grabbing my waist and rolling us further into the kitchen. "I'm fine."

"Guys?" I demanded, my voice screeching.

"We're okay," Emlyn rumbled, loosening the knot in my chest.

"Apart from being under attack," Kai hissed.

Shadows blasted around me and Wane as he crawled to the couch where the others sheltered. "I'll kill them," he seethed.

"I'll fucking help," Harvey spat, looking remarkably like his brother when they were both raging with protectiveness. "It's him again."

The assassin we'd tried to kill six times and failed, the smug, evil bastard who taunted and gloated. He broke Em's arm the last time we fought.

"Neither of you are doing anything," Emlyn growled,

nostrils flaring in his bearded face as he took charge. "Get out the back door. We're not fighting."

"Like *Hell* we're not," I spat, peering around the side of the sofa. Through the fire and smoke, I glimpsed shadows, figures. I knew which one was his—talk and commanding, his hair sleek and pretty. That beauty hid a deep, wicked ugliness. "They just sent a *fireball* at my house! I'm not letting them destroy what's left of it."

"The next one could hit *you*," Emlyn hissed right back, his teeth bared and sharp behind his beard. "Out—all of you. *Now!*"

I didn't argue, but I made my displeasure known with a glower as we crawled towards the back door, only faltering when the house shook as more magic hit it. Not fire this time. This was *him*, I knew it. All the fine hairs on my body stood on end, my stomach churning and soul flinching like he'd struck me and not the house.

I jumped when another fireball hit the front of the house, thrown by whatever merc Locke paid this time. Kai and Wane both had shields around the exterior, but the fire burned through them like cobwebs. Emlyn was right, as much as I didn't want to admit it. And I couldn't let one of my mates be burned next.

I gazed longingly at my weapons cabinet, but it was all the way across the room. Instinct wouldn't let me leave my mates' sides to arm myself.

"Wane," I breathed, glancing around for my mate. I could feel him beside me, and his heat met my side, but he'd vanished entirely. Not even his shadows were visible. "It's alright; no one's going to hurt you. I won't let them."

Fierceness bled into my voice with that promise. Harvey had grown up in the dark too, but he'd filled himself with light and humour in defiance of those horrors. Wane had taken the dark *into* himself. He'd been through worse, unspeakable nightmares. Even Harvey wouldn't tell me what had been done to him, but Wane's scars gave me a good guess.

Even years later, my bastard client, his monster of a *father*, was still hunting him. The man who abused his children and let his brother do the same, who made Wane into a terrified man—he would never let them live in peace.

Two fucking years, that's all we had. And now the tentative peace we built crashed and burned around us.

"Fuck!" Kai exploded, rage in his voice when the exterior wall in the kitchen came tumbling down. But there was pain there, too. This was our home, our sanctuary. We were *happy* here—and it was on fire. *"Shit!"*

"Keep it together," Emlyn growled as we crawled faster, the voice of reason. "Kai, go out first and take out anyone who's out there. Then Hales and Wane will follow. Me and Harvey will take the back. Defensive position."

My ears hunched by my shoulders at those two words. For years, I'd heard them every few months. In the beginning, I'd drilled and practised for hours every day until I learned the manoeuvre, until it was second nature.

We'd been *safe!* We were supposed to live happily ever after here. My throat burned. My eyes stung ruthlessly.

"Kai," I choked out when he reached the back door. He snapped his attention to me, his crimson eyes livid. "Don't do anything stupid. Please."

He blew out a hard breath at what I didn't say—*don't leave me*—and nodded. He was still shirtless from sparring, so nothing covered the thick lines of text wrapped around his chest as they began to spiral faster and faster.

"I'll stay safe if you will," he agreed.

I nodded, my throat too tight to speak.

We were supposed to be safe! I was terrified someone would get hurt, but equally terrified that any progress Wane had made these past two years would be lost. He worked so fucking hard, had healed *so much,* and it felt like I already lost him with the first blast.

"Hales," Emlyn murmured, and I dragged my eyes away from the door Kai disappeared through. I couldn't hear sounds of a struggle outside, but I felt the thrum of Kai's power and imagined invisible whips choking off our attackers' air. Snakes, every bit as alive as Kai. *"Breathe."*

"I'm fine," I dismissed. But there was a pit in my stomach, and I couldn't catch a breath, and I was going to be sick.

I didn't miss the look Emlyn shot at the space beside me, where heat wafted from Wane's body. Em could sense what was wrong, what I needed. I shook my head at my protective mate. I'd be fine as long as we all got out of this unhurt.

I noticed no one spoke about defending the house; we were abandoning it like we'd abandoned so many houses over the years. But this wasn't just a safe house; it was our home.

My bottom lip wobbled when a shadow wrapped around my wrist, the ends tying together so I wore a soft, velvety bracelet.

"We'll be okay," Wane murmured.

I nodded, and choked down the lump in my throat.

It was running and fighting time, not breakdown time. I needed to get my shit together.

A grunt came from outside, and I took that as my cue to jump to my feet and burst through the door.

There were seven people in our vegetable garden, most in the standard black uniform of all assassins and mercenaries, but one in dark crimson leather. Ah, shit, not an Islavian warrior. There were three of them in the mercenaries' guild and every single one of them hated me. There were even more who *weren't* part of the guild, and they hated me more.

"Traitor," the warrior woman spat, her saliva burning a hole in my lawn as I paused in the garden.

Angelfucker!

The air shimmied behind me, telling me Wane followed. Emlyn and Harvey wouldn't be too far behind us.

"Flavia," I greeted, subtly nudging Wane towards the mercs trampling my rose bushes. "Delightful to see you again. And look, you've made friends. I'm proud of you."

"Is now a good time to be taunting her?" Kai demanded from deeper in the garden, whipping his hands through the air at lightning speed. Mercenaries were struck down or knocked aside wherever his invisible power lashed.

I watched one man smirk as he brought a knife down on the power, cutting himself free. I snorted. Malakai's magic wasn't ropes or cord; he wielded *snakes*, and like the mythical Hydra, whenever one was cut, two grew back.

"Halwen," Flavia spat at me, abandoning her attempt to free one of her buddies to give me her full focus. Lucky me. She looked the same as ever, snotty and sneering, her tanned face and golden hair pretty but the rest of her dripping in hideousness. "I wondered where you crawled off to."

We'd been friends until we got into a minor disagreement about a shared job. The orders had been to kill a crime family, and I'd been completely on board until I found out that included a five-year-old boy. Flavia tried to assassinate the kid. I tried to assassinate *her*.

I tilted my head, circling her and aware that my two other mates crept into the garden, their panic and adrenaline thumping through my body like it was my own.

Blood roared in my ears, mine and that of everyone else here. Locke's favourite Hunter came leisurely closer, content to watch. His blood pounded the same rhythm as mine—fast and violent. *Bastard.*

I focused on Flavia, heat like a wall behind me as fire raged. "Crawled off to? I've been living in the lap of luxury in a giant house, with my every need attended to by my servants."

"Mates," Kai bit out, grappling with a massive mercenary.

"Same thing. Where have *you* been, Flavia? Miserable and alone as usual? Last I checked, even rats ran from the sight of you."

She bared her teeth—needle-thin and silver—in a semblance of a grin, and drew her long, serrated knives. Those knives were a declaration of murder in themselves.

From the corner of my eye, I saw a giant, green-skinned fucker charge at Harvey. Without taking my attention from Flavia, the biggest threat, I lifted my hand and flicked my wrist. Most demons had elemental magic, or flight or strength —something normal. But I could feel the thump and flow of blood in someone's veins.

Right now, the blood leaking from someone Wane killed sang to me, and I felt the slowing heartbeat of whoever Kai was choking out. But it was the panicked thrum of my mates' pulses that called to me, that reminded me why everyone here had to die. The exhilaration in the mercs' blood just wound my fury to a fever pitch.

It was scarily easy to grab control of the green guy's bloodstream and give it a little tug. His heart seized; I felt it even across the garden and my own blood shuddered in response.

Flavia rushed at me, sensing what I was doing or just bored of waiting to fight.[1]

"Really, Sugarplum?" Harvey groaned when the green guy exploded, covering him in goop and gore. Ah, I might have tugged a little too forcefully.

"Sorry," I called, but my attention was fixed on Flavia as the golden woman hurtled at me, flickering light limning her red leathers in fiery orange. My poor, burning house.

Hurt and wrath fused inside me; I used them to launch across the lawn and slam into Flavia before she could gain the upper hand.

"I've had plenty of company, for your information," Flavia

bragged, lethal teeth bared as she aimed her knives at my chest. I grabbed her wrists, digging my nails into her golden skin. "Thanks to you, I've been busy this last decade and paid handsomely for it."

"Happy to be of service," I replied, teeth gritted against the force of keeping her back, my biceps burning. Fuck, I'd forgotten how strong the Islavian warriors were. They trained in a volcano at the heart of Hell, for Lucifer's sake. *I'd* trained in a children's home in shitty Akstrang, and then in a war camp in even *shittier* Jinsevia. I was outmatched.

But I had more to lose.

Even all these years later, Cassander Locke was still trying to repair his fucked up reputation and get Wane to lie that his statement was false. I desperately wanted to know what was in that statement, and at the same time I was terrified of it.

"Cassander doesn't like you much," Flavia told me, pushing her knives closer until the tips touched my skin. Now would be a good time for me to grasp control of her blood and stop her heart, but like all the Islavian warriors, I couldn't touch her with magic.

"Yeah, I got that impression," I spat, slamming my knee between her legs and knocking her back an inch. "The feeling's mutual."

"He's set on your murder," Flavia taunted as if her vagina wasn't screaming in pain. She wrenched her arms back, and used my surprise at her surrender to swipe a blade across my stomach. *Son of a—*

"He's not killing *any* of us," I snarled, grabbing the blood of two of her buddies and melting their veins. They hit the lawn and collapsed into blood, the thick stuff running down the slope towards the forest that encircled our home.

We should have been safe here.

Rage made me faster, stronger. I might have been without a weapon, but I had my mates with me and I had power.

"He's paying anyone five times the usual amount if we bring him your head," she laughed, and something inside me froze, going very still.

"When you say Cassander wants 'you' dead, you mean me? Just me?"

"Mhmm." She snapped her needle teeth at my throat, laughing when I dove under her fist and spun around her back, my heart crashing when I saw the embers of our home. "Just you; you're special like that."

If he only wanted me dead, that meant he was trying to capture Wane *and* the others? Like fucking Hell he was taking a single one of them.

A woman screamed, but I couldn't take my eyes off Flavia to see which of my mates caused it. The sky grew darker, the sun disappearing as the moon came out—Wane's power, his control of the dark. And whether he realised it or not, he had power over light, too.

I shuddered as the warmth of the sun was replaced with burning, icy cold. The roar of the hunter's blood quickened. Even Flavia's eyes widened with fear when colour bleached out of the world. I could still see if I squinted, but the world was cast in greys and blacks.

"You're not killing my mate," a quiet, *furious* voice spat, and warmth heated my front as Wane stepped in front of me. He was visible now but only as a swarm of ink and shadows. "And you're not taking me back to *him.*"

Flavia snorted.

Rage blinded me. Power seethed like a battle in my blood; I grabbed the heart of every enemy and crushed them until they all collapsed. The hunter—was gone, out of reach like he knew what I planned. Thuds told me the rest of them hit the ground, but it wasn't enough. I speared my magic at Flavia's blood—and hit a brick wall. It jarred my magic, my soul, clanging through me like a punch.

"You think you can outrun him forever? He's practically a god," Flavia laughed, doing a good job of hiding her panic at Wane's darkness.

"He's a monster!" Wane shouted, louder than I ever heard his raspy, broken voice. "He's a monster, and a rapist, and a *fraud."* He quieted his voice, the darkness growing thicker around us. "I won't go back to him, and I won't lie for him. He can rot in the Damned Realm for all I care."

Flavia chuckled, diving at Wane, but all I could hear was one word on repeat in my head. All I could think about was my mate hiding in shadows most of his adult life, shut in the dark for his entire childhood, jumpy at sudden movements, triggered by touch, and unable to be intimate with his mate even though I felt the desperate need in him.

Locke ... he ... he raped my mate, my soul—my Wane?

Through the near-pitch darkness I saw Wane's shadows wrap around Flavia's throat. I saw her angle her knives up at his ribs, and my wings snapped out at my sides as a growl of lethal, unending rage shook my ribcage.

The thump of my mates' hearts filled my senses until I could almost taste blood, the pulse of their beats shivering over my skin. But it was *hers* I focused on, so furious, so *consumed* with my magic that I could finally sense it.

I clenched my fist, seizing control of her body, forcing her still for Wane to land the killing blow. Her death was *his*, not mine, and through whatever instincts came with our bond, I knew he *needed* it. He needed to reclaim the power, needed to be in control of himself instead of the fear that had taken over him.

Shadows shoved down her throat—not just to suffocate her I realised, as the thick tendril ripped out again, her heart in its clasp. Holy fuck. I'd never seen Wane like this before. He squeezed the organ in his power, his veins pumping faster, until her heart splattered into blood and matter.[2]

It took me too long to realise the darkness was now absolute, and I couldn't glimpse a single shape around me—because the fire had gone out. Our house—*fuck*. I almost didn't want Wane to pull his shadows back, didn't want to see what was left of it.

"He'll never stop hunting me," Wane rasped, so quiet I almost missed the words.

I stumbled towards the sound of his voice, but hesitantly. Touching would be out of the question right now. Even the sound of my voice could be like salt in a wound.

"He'll stop," I whispered. "I'll make him."

"So will I," Harvey swore, somewhere to my right.

"You know I will," Emlyn rumbled, sounding like a grizzly bear.

Malakai let out a soft hiss, the bond between us like a fierce current. "It's about time we eviscerated that bastard."

The darkness peeled back slowly, a glimmer of sunlight peeking through until I could make out the rough shape of my mates around me—there were Em's broad shoulders and big arms; there was Harvey raking his hands through his shaggy hair; there Malakai stalked closer, his figure tall and foreboding; and three feet in front of me, his head ducked and fists clenched at his side, faint light outlined Wane's body.

"The house ... it's gone," Em said in shock.

I didn't follow his line of sight, didn't want to see. "Where do we go now?"

"Back to Sailas," Harvey murmured.

Wane spun to face him with an explosive hiss. "We *can't!*"

"We need to kill him before he kills *us,*" Harvey snapped back.

I sucked in a surprised breath, cold all over. Harvey never shouted at his brother. Not once in the ten years I'd known them.

"He'll keep coming at us," Harvey went on, his tone harsh

and fear in his silver eyes as he drew closer. "You said it your-self, Wane, he'll never stop hunting us. So we turn the fucking tables; we hunt *him*. We kill the bastard."

"It's so easy for you. You were his favourite; he didn't scar you."

"Didn't scar me?" Harvey laughed, something cruel and sharp in his voice, something—

Broken.

Oh god.

I covered my mouth with a bloody hand, backing up a step as I realised—not just Wane. Locke hadn't hurt one son; he'd hurt both. And not with fists and knives like I'd thought all this time.

My stomach roiled and heaved.

"Didn't *scar me?* I might not wear them on my body, but they're here." Harvey screwed his finger into his head. "You think I came out of that place unscathed after everything he did?"

Wane's throat bobbed; he didn't say anything. But I sensed the vicious edge of his fear turning to brittle, shaky misery.

"You think because I don't wake up screaming, covered in shadows, that I sleep *easy?* That I don't dream of the darkness, never knowing who moved within it, or if someone was going to grab me, throw me onto my stomach and—"

He heaved for breath, and with every word I watched them land like knives in Wane's chest.

Wane staggered back. His soul splintered with pain; I felt it as clearly as I felt Harvey's mania, his deep-born terror.

I twisted aside as my stomach clenched, and vomit rushed up my throat, splattering what was left of the vegetable garden.

"He'll kill her," Harvey whispered, pain thick in his voice. "He'll kill our mate, Wane."

"I know," Wane breathed. The tears in his voice took a dagger and slammed it right into my heart.

"Stop," I rasped, wiping my mouth on the sleeve. "Just—stop. You've hurt each other enough. We need to get out of here before the hunter returns. Em, where's our closest safe house to Sailas?"

"I'm not going back there," Wane hissed.

"I know," I assured him. Kai's hand found the small of my back to support me. If I were him, I'd have kept my distance; I could easily throw up again. What Casander Locke did and allowed to be done by others to my mates, his own—his own *sons*—

I clenched my fists, fighting the cramp and roil of my gut.

"But Harvey's not wrong. We need to stop him." I held up a hand when Wane began to argue. "Let's get out of here and find somewhere safe for now."

I allowed myself one glance at the blackened rubble of our home.

We could search the ashes for anything salvageable ... but it hurt too much to even try, so I took a step towards the forest. It didn't have an official name, the forest that shielded and protected us for years. My mates jokingly called it the Forest of Halwen. It hurt to leave it behind.

"There's nothing left of the house," Kai realised, his voice tight and devastated.

"*We're* left," Emlyn disagreed. "That's all that matters."

I knew he was right, but it felt like we'd lost everything. And I didn't know what we were going to do now.

CHAPTER EIGHT

*T*he safe house was in a little village between Sailas and Iarlon—the home of Lucifer and his all-powerful inner circle. I preferred to stay away from this swath of Hell; too many power players. Too many guards and enforcers. Not a comfortable place for a criminal like me. But at least the villagers were sweet and welcoming cat-demons with badass spikes on their tails and ears that twitched.

The neighbours were the only silver lining as we moved in. Harvey went straight to the punching bag in the basement; Wane wrapped himself in his shadows and hid where we couldn't find him; Kai started opening and slamming cupboards, looking for food; and Emlyn hovered on the threshold, staring at the unfamiliar street.

My eyes stung as I tucked myself into his side, wrapping my arms around his big frame. I was exhausted and emotionally drained after the journey; I'd lost all my fight hours ago.

"We can build another home," I whispered, not brave enough to say the words any louder. "I'll take on more jobs; Kai can help, and you and the brothers can find work here in the village. We'll get it all back. I promise."

Emlyn's chest moved with a huge sigh. He settled his arms around me, his chin resting atop my head. "I hope so, Hales. But I can't see that future for us right now."

I was bullshitting and he knew it, because I felt the exact same way. We were back on the run. It was like two years ago, when we barely spent two months in a place before fleeing it for somewhere new, always outracing the endless mercs Locke sent after us. And that damned hunter—always him.

"We've got each other," Emlyn said eventually, watching two small kids playing down the street, their furry tails swishing through the air. I didn't look at them; it was just another reminder of how miserable our lives were.

Em kissed the side of my head and then guided me inside. "We'll be—*for fuck's sake*," he spat.

My eyebrows shot into my hairline when I saw the state of the small, dated kitchen. All our safe houses were stocked with non-perishables and long-life food in case we needed to move in at a moment's notice, and I presumed those non-perishables had been *inside* the cupboard when we arrived. Now, tins, boxes, and jars were discarded all across the countertops and the kitchen table, and there were even lentils strewn on the floor.

"Malakai," Emlyn hissed, his nostrils flaring and shoulders rounding.

"Em," I said when he took a determined stride across the room. "Don't. He's stressed, we're all stressed. Just—don't start a fight. Please."

Emlyn huffed a breath through his nose like a raging bull, his hands flexing at his sides, but he nodded.

"I'll clean this up. Go—go check on Wane?"

"If I can find him," Em replied, but he stiffened when a crash came from downstairs—where Harvey was beating the shit out of a punching bag. "Leave the mess; you find Wane, and I'll check on Harvey."

I nodded, my heart tight and painful at my mates' suffering. Didn't we deserve to live in peace? Sure, I was a criminal and I'd killed people, and the guys were ruthless when it came to survival, leaving a string of bodies in their wake, but come on! It was *enough*. All these years, and now thinking we were safe only for our home to be razed to the ground...

I'd had enough.

I loved Wane more than life itself, but I had to go against his wishes this one time. Cassander Locke needed to die.

CHAPTER NINE

*I*t was easier than it should have been to sleep alone that night. Normally, all my mates piled into bed with me, but after a day like today, I told them I needed space and that wasn't a lie. I practically vibrated with rage about losing our home and the life we'd built there, and especially our peace of mind. It was easy to let the guys think I was pissed at them, too.

I'd apologise for it tomorrow, when Locke was dead. Or I'd never come home, and they'd believe I was angry with them for the rest of their lives. *Fuck!*

I raked a hand down my face, my conviction wavering as I stood in our temporary living room. The furniture was different here, and the whole place smelled of stale air and disuse, but there were already signs of my mates scattered around: a pint glass Em left on the coffee table and the jacket Harvey found in the drawers upstairs thrown across the sofa.

We couldn't keep doing this. A life on the run was no life at all, and I was *done*. Happily ever after or not at all.

So I dragged my stare from the house and left through the

back door, the hinges oiled earlier tonight to let me sneak out soundlessly.

I made it three streets away before hairs rose on the back of my neck and my skin prickled with warning. I was being followed.

I tucked my wings in tight, my body on high alert, senses sharpening. Thank Lucifer all our safe houses were stocked with weapons; I missed my beloved knives and daggers, but at least I had *something* to draw. The weight of iron in my hand was comforting. So was the whoosh and thump of my power when I reached for it.

Blood chugged sluggishly within the houses around me, but thrummed much faster in my stalker.

I sighed, my pale pink braid flying as I turned, scanning the darkness. I didn't see him—he was well hidden—but I knew he was there.

"What are you doing, Malakai?"

"What are *you* doing, my rose?" he threw back, his tone sharp. But the term of endearment told me he was in a good mood. Excitement and eagerness explained the fast rhythm of his heart. It was a welcome change from him trashing our new kitchen.

"You know what," I muttered, watching him peel away from the shadow of a house and cross the road to me, dressed head to toe in black with his red hair slicked back and a scarf pulled over his chin. He walked with a swagger and confidence that suited him too damn well, his crimson eyes pinned on me.

"I do know," he agreed, reaching me on the pavement. "Which is why I had these brought from my safe in Iarlon."

A furrow cut between my brows as he lifted his hands and I saw twin long daggers, both with viciously sharp tips and wavy shafts. Lovingly wrapped in pale pink, the handles beckoned me as Kai flipped them in a flash of a movement, gripping the blades as he held them out to me.

I took them in a daze, trailing my gaze over the etchings down the centre of each dagger. I didn't speak or read this particular Hell language, but I knew the whorls and loops by heart. Every year, on the anniversary of our meeting, Kai bought me flowers—small, white soulcaps from the forest around our home, picked by him personally—and hand-wrote a message that vowed *I will always be your shadow and light; you will always be my rose and life.* He wrote it in both his native dialect and mine.

I'd kept every note in a box in our room.

They were cinders now, I realised.

"Fuck, Kai," I choked out, swallowing down emotion. I was too raw for thoughtful gifts like this.

"They're forged from the first volcanic eruption of Hell."

"Just casually?" I laughed, thick with emotion. The eruption had shaped Hell into the landscape it was today. "How the hell did you do this?"

"It's our tenth anniversary in a month," he replied, sliding closer, his hand gliding possessively across my waist. "I've been planning this all year."

"Romantic bastard," I teased, leaning up to kiss his smooth jaw. "I love you."

"I love you, too," he replied, his voice serious and rough but a ripple of awe going through our bond. "I have since the day we met."

"When you tried to kill me?"

"Yes," he confirmed, red eyes flashing. "Since that exact moment."

I angled my new beloved knives down so he didn't spear himself on them—he was dumb and romantic enough to not care about bleeding out as long as he was close to me.

Kai's hand closed around my throat, a reassuring warmth

that *shouldn't* have relaxed the stress from my body but somehow did, and he slammed his mouth into mine. He kissed me with a rough, uncontrolled passion until we were both breathless and shaking.

It killed me not being able to touch him, but I was too attached to my knives to put them away just yet.

"Soft bastard," I breathed against his lips when he rested his forehead against mine.

His mouth flattened into a thin line. "Tell anyone that, and I'll mutilate every part of your body."

I snorted, drawing away. "Sure you will."

He narrowed his gaze, baring sharp teeth I usually glimpsed just before they sank into my skin to heighten my pleasure.

"I love you," I told him again, just to watch his viciousness melt.

His eyes grew bigger, lips softer, and a sigh left his now-smiling mouth. I never tired of seeing that effect on him, and he never tired of hearing *I love you.*

His fingers flexed around my neck; he leaned even closer until his words brushed my lips. "Who do you belong to?"

My pussy throbbed; my breath caught. "You."

"And who do I belong to?"

"Me," I whispered fiercely.

"Always," he swore, and kissed me before drawing back. "Now let's go use your pretty knives to behead a snake, shall we?"

I moved my weapons around until I could sheathe one of my gifts and held out my hand, confidence and determination filling me when Kai wrapped his fingers around mine.

"We need to find the fucker first," I said as we set off walking. "But I have an idea where to look."

CHAPTER TEN

*I*t took us three hours, but we finally found a hint to Cassander Locke's location. I'd never hated anyone as much as I did that bastard, so I didn't even baulk when a bald guy in a seedy pub told us he'd done a job for Locke in Iarlon. If that was where he was, that's where we'd go.

Kai and I borrowed a horse and sprinted for the capital, following the rough description Baldy gave us. Every time I came, I always expected there to be guards with swords and killer magic on the gates into Iarlon, but Hell was civilised in this part of the realm.

Here, people went about their daily business with a calm and ease I envied, not glancing over their shoulders or jumping at the sound of a cart rattling down the cobbled streets. Or a kamikaze horse bolting after we climbed off his back.

"We should move here," Malakai murmured, his eyes on a landlord closing the stained glass doors of a classy-looking inn, laughing with the last of his customers as they left. "It's a fucking paradise."

Everything was so well kept and *clean;* even the village

we'd moved to was a little unkempt and raw around the edges. Here, the cobbles shone and lush trees lined the streets; the houses were pristine and all the shops were inviting as we strolled past them, looking like two ne'er do goods scouting for trouble.

"We wouldn't fit in," I replied, looking at the flowers over-flowing from a pale fountain in the middle of the road. It was the prettiest damn roundabout I'd ever seen. My covetous heart wanted to steal it; the rest of me wanted to take a hammer and shatter it to pieces. After the dark ugliness of the day we had, it felt like salt in the wound.

"Good point," Kai murmured after a while, leading us past the fountain and down a pale street full of banks and businesses. "Two weeks and Harvey would be chased out of the place for doing something dumb."

I slid a look at Kai. "Two *days,* and your smart mouth would get you thrown in a cell."

Sharp teeth flashed as he grinned. "You'd be right there with me."

Okay, he had me there. We were a troublesome duo. Emlyn had more grey hairs than ever, and as a near-immortal archdemon, that took a lot.

A shadow passed overhead, and without a word we flattened ourselves to the side of a pale newspaper printer. I held my breath, my head tipped up, eyes scouring the sky for—

"It's a pigeon," Kai groaned, dragging an ink-wrapped hand down his face.

Okay, so we were a little jumpy. But in our defence, someone had burned our house and tried to kill us. And the mastermind of that was right here in this city.

"On the plus side," Kai added, squeezing my arm as we set off again, "no one's followed us yet. We got farther than I expected."

I made a noise of agreement, spotting the steep golden

staircase Baldy had described. It was right where he said it would be, its stone columns and railings wrapped with ferns and evergreens. This place was so damn pretty. Who told a Hell city it could be pretty?

"I can't tell if the guys know we're gone," I told Kai as we headed side by side up the staircase, elegant streetlamps guiding our way. "We're all stressed already; I doubt I'd even notice the change."

The houses up here were grander, older. Definitely the sort of place Locke would live. He might have raised my mates in the dark, and hurt them unspeakably, but above the basement where they'd lived for twenty years had been a palatial manor house.

There were no words strong enough to describe how despicable he was.

"You'd notice it in Emlyn," Kai chuckled, gliding his hand up the railing. "He'll lose his absolute shit when he finds you gone."

I winced.

"He might even break my nose for helping you," Kai added, his red eyes scanning the street we emerged onto.

The roads were wider up here, with flagstones rather than cobbles, and pale brick arches joined both sides of the street overhead, strung with colourful lanterns to brighten the dark.

"There," I hissed, pointing at the biggest house at the end of the street and barely noticing the way Kai's jovial smirk fell. "That's the house Baldy told us about."

"Jesus, *look* at it," he breathed, staring at the arches, columns, and exterior staircases. It was like a mini castle, and it was pretentious as hell. Pretty, but pretentious.

Maybe we should liberate it; it fit my personality.

"How do we get in?" I murmured. "We should probably hide; we look suspicious."

"We *are* suspicious," Kai quipped, but I felt a ripple in the air—his magic was ready to play.[1] "There's an alcove there."

I hurried into it, glad to be hidden in the shadows as I squinted at the windows and doors of the palace. "That fence there could probably reach that window if I jumped."

And didn't fall six feet and crack my head open...

"Not a chance," Kai growled, his hand finding my hip and holding protectively. Like he thought I'd run off and attempt it now. If I was going to do that, I wouldn't have told him beforehand. I wasn't an amateur.

"You got a better idea?" I asked, raising an eyebrow.

His lips twisted to one side as he assessed the house, his clever eyes flickering. Fuck, he was handsome like this, all competent and devious. I leaned close, dragging my lips up his pale, inked throat to kiss his jaw.

"Either you stop that or I rail you right here in this alcove," he hissed, his hand flexing on my hip.

"Tempting," I murmured. But I couldn't hang onto a single good emotion today; it all came back to our house burning and Wane terrified and Harvey snapping because panic pushed him to breaking point. "But I think I'd rather kill that bastard and fuck you as a celebration."

"Good plan," Kai agreed, and proved he was perceptive as fuck because he laid a lingering kiss on my temple to soothe the raw edge of my hurt.

"I need him dead, and I need us to be safe," I confessed, my voice uneven.

"I know," he murmured, pulling me into a too-brief hug. "So let's go kill the bastard. And to answer your earlier question, my rose, I *do* have a better idea."

I gave him a questioning look.

He just jerked his chin at the gates, and my breath caught as his invisible power surged, filling the air with a charged ripple.

"Holy fuck," I breathed, almost reconsidering the alcove fuck when his snakes tore the gates completely off their hinges.

The quiet night was splintered by the loud grating of tearing metal, the shriek as the gates skidded across the ground even louder.

"Let's go," Kai ordered, serious-faced and all business as he flicked his hands, hauling open the big front door of the house. "I'll go first and take out any guards; the second you see Cassander, use your magic on him. Don't fuck about; we get in, we kill him, we get out."

I nodded, calm settling over me, clearing out all my emotions. It wasn't natural but this calm had been with me for years now. I used to get excited by jobs like this, but with my mates at stake, all the fun was gone.

I fell in behind Malakai as he stormed through the broken mouth of the gate, my mate blowing up the steps like a sand-storm. I drew one of my long daggers and reached for the blood around me as we crossed the threshold. There were three sluggish heartbeats, but none of them were Locke's particular rhythm.

"Fuck," I snarled, glaring at the pretty ivory foyer we found ourselves in. It smelled of roses and lilies, and I wanted to steal this house *so* badly. "He's not here. We'll have to wait until—"

"Until what?" a familiar—and highly unwelcome—voice growled.

"Ah," I breathed, turning to the door slowly, like I was facing a firing squad. "Hi, Em."

Emlyn's nostrils flared, colour high on his cheekbones and his salt-and-pepper hair wild. "Don't *hi, Em* me, Halwen Vakhara."

Oof, full name.

Okay, he was pissed all the way off.

Harvey followed him into the house, his stare jumping from the pale marble walls to the pots overflowing with greenery to the art hanging on the walls. I'd never seen his bronze face so wan, or his posture so tight and edgy. He looked around like he was waiting for his father to jump out and throw him back in the basement where he was raised, and bile hit my throat in a burning rush.

"You're not supposed to be here," I breathed, my voice tight as I took a step towards them. "You're supposed to be home, *safe*—"

"*So are you!*" Emlyn exploded, throwing up his big hands and stalking closer.

"Can we at least kill the fucker while we're here?" Kai muttered, his hands flexing at his sides.

"I told you," I huffed, giving him a glare he'd done nothing to deserve. "He's not here—"

But another heart beat thumped, unfamiliar and fast— exhilarated. Wane was beside me, close enough to touch but invisible to my eyes, but just beyond the front door there was another person.

Fury exploded through my blood. I grabbed hold of my magic and speared it towards his heart to collapse the rotten thing in his chest. But the second I touched my magic, the building rocked.

"What the fuck?" Harvey breathed, the whites of his eyes showing.

"Shields," Kai growled, teeth bared and his bands of ink coiling faster around his body. "Fuck!"

I grabbed Harvey's arm, and threw him behind me so I could shield him. "Wane, get behind me," I ordered, cold spreading through my whole body. "Em, Kai, beside me."

My tone must have told them how deadly serious I was because they moved instantly into formation as footsteps came up the front steps. We barely entered the massive house, so we could easily see the tall, slim, black-haired man who paused on the top step and assessed us. He wasn't what I'd pictured, but I should have known better; he was a politician, so of course he'd be slick and slimy and smug.

I could see my mates in his features and it sickened me, the reminder of what he'd done to them making me shake with rage.

The calm I slipped into was gone, replaced with bone-deep terror. *I'd* done this, brought them into a trap their abuser set.

"I'm sorry," I choked out. "I'm so fucking sorry."

No one spoke.

Cassander Locke assessed us with a smile, his hands in the pockets of his long, expensive coat. "I knew you'd fall into one of my traps eventually, but breaking into Lucifer's spare home?" He tsked.

My stomach crashed.

This was Lucifer's home—*the devil's* home? We'd blown the gates off and broken in. Fuck. *Fuck.*

I was going to be sick.

"Very naughty," Locke laughed.

Wane shook so hard the air shivered over me. I fumbled blindly and grabbed his wrist, squeezing tight.

"I'm going to cut you into pieces," I hissed at Locke, the sound coming from deep in my throat.

His mercury-silver eyes sparkled. "I doubt that. You're trapped in these shields, and until a member of Lucifer's guard comes to free you, you're going nowhere. I'll be long gone before that happens. But so will my treacherous son. The shields can't hold a shadow—so come here. *Wane,*" he barked, a clear order.

"Don't say a single word to him!" I hissed. I bet Locke looked respectable and trustworthy to anyone who didn't know the vile things he'd done, but all I could see was poison and ugliness, and *no* fucking way would I let him touch my mates again. "He's not taking you anywhere," I swore to Wane, to Harvey. "You're mine."

Locke snorted, toeing the solid barrier that apparently trapped us inside the house. The barrier he knew would come down. He must have paid Baldy to send anyone who came asking after him here. Motherfucker.

"You were idiots to fall for it," he taunted, bragging of his own cleverness. Piece of shit. "I knew as soon as you ran, you'd follow one of my trails. What was the plan? Kill me?"

I bared my teeth.

"Shut your fucking mouth," Emlyn growled, his hand thrown behind himself, resting on Harvey's arm. "Kai, get us out of here."

"I'm trying," Kai breathed, his panic a sharp spike in my chest. "Whoever put these shields up is stronger than me."

"A pity," Locke murmured. "Wane, *come here.*"

I tightened my hand around Wane's wrist.

"If you don't come here *right now—*" Locke began, spit flying from his mouth.

"You'll what?" a blunt voice asked—a new voice.

Clawed, lilac hands locked around Cassander's arms, and it was satisfying to see a tall, purple woman with short, dark hair slam that monster into the wall beside the door.

"These five criminals broke into Lucifer's home; I was just making sure they didn't escape before the guards got here," Locke lied.

I hissed. Em snarled.

"Shut it!" the woman barked, rattling Locke's body with shockingly strong hands. "I heard every word you said, so don't try to talk yourself out of it. From where I'm standing, six people broke into Lucifer's house; you were the ringleader."

"No!" Locke sputtered. "I'm a politician, not a criminal. Talk to the devil, I was the mayor of Jast."

"Fascinating," she deadpanned.

I jumped when Cassander threw something back into the woman's ribs, making her grunt. When they broke apart, I saw it was a knife shining with red blood. Fuck!

"Wanker!" the woman hissed.

"Kai, try something!" I breathed while they were both distracted.

Kai threw me a sharp look that said he'd tried fucking everything.

"No," Wane breathed beside me, going rigid. "He's going to—"

I snapped my attention back to the open door in time to see Locke bolt through the broken gates and disappear into the shadows of nearby buildings.

"Don't let him get away!" I screamed at the woman. "He's a *monster; go get him, kill him, whatever—just don't let him go!*"

The stranger straightened, her hand slapped over her bleeding side. It wasn't a deep wound, but it had been enough to distract her, and now Locke was gone.

"Don't go anywhere," she growled. "Lucifer will want to question you."

My stomach dropped, but Wane's wrist was still solid under my fingers and Harvey was still behind us. Locke hadn't touched them.

But it wasn't much of a victory.

CHAPTER ELEVEN

*M*y knees slammed into the marble floor of Lucifer's throne room, flinching away from the terrifying demon on his dark throne above us. My whole body shook. His power pressed on me, and I had a sick feeling he wasn't even using his magic—he was just *that* powerful.

Renna, the purple woman whom Locke stabbed, wasn't an unlucky bystander or even a guard—she was one of Lucifer's inner circle.

No part of being carted into the palace—the *actual* palace, not just the giant house we broke into—by a woman who was besties *with the devil* was a positive experience.

Neither were the gold ropes wrapped around our wrists— binding even Wane. I scowled at the floor, not brave enough to show any attitude to the man on the throne.

"These are the people who broke into my home?" Lucifer asked Renna, his terror-inducing bestie.

"Found them trapped in your shields," she grunted, strong arms crossed over her chest as she lurked beside us. Like we'd try anything stupid with our hands bound and *the ruler of hell* watching us.

Although … Kai might. I gave him a warning look. If we kept our mouths shut, we'd get thrown in a prison cell. If we gave Lucifer snark, we'd get ourselves killed.

"There was another guy," Renna added, giving Lucifer a significant look. "Slimy bastard, said he's the mayor of Jast."

"Former," Harvey spat, his chest rising and falling fast. I watched him, a knot of worry in my chest. "He hasn't been the mayor since everyone found out what he did."

I dared a glance at Lucifer, and tried not to get distracted by the fact he was actually kind of hot. Alright fine, he was drop-dead gorgeous and it was confusing. His long, black hair hung loose around his shoulders, his mouth pressed into a flat, serious line behind his beard, but there were smile lines around his red eyes, and the way he sat on his impressive throne, clothed in elegance and riches, *screamed* power.

I quickly glanced away. I didn't know what I'd been expecting but not … that.

At least he didn't look murderous at Harvey speaking.

"I've heard of his crimes," Lucifer replied after a moment, distaste or disgust in his voice. "What did he want with my house?"

I jolted when four pairs of eyes fixed on me.[1] "What're you looking at *me* for?" I hissed at my mates.

Kai gave me a pointed look.

Oh goody, *I* was the mouthpiece. Shouldn't they have picked someone smarter and calmer? Shouldn't it have been Em?

I darted a glance at the shockingly handsome devil, and to the best of my ability, answered with respect and calm.

"He didn't want your house; he used it as a trap for us. He's been hunting us for ten years. Your house was a convenient cage for us."

Lucifer glanced at Renna, who nodded her dark head.

"I heard the bastard say something similar, bragging about

how fucked they were. And then he stabbed me," she growled, staring at the blood still trickling from her.

"Where is he now?" Lucifer asked, a thread of emotion—anger, maybe—entering his even voice. I'd pictured him as emotionless and uncaring, but he was definitely a person and not a robot. That was a good sign for us, right?

"Bolted," Renna muttered. "I chased him as far as the river park, then lost the bastard."

Lucifer let out a slow breath, fingers flexing on the arms of his throne. "So Cassander Locke set a trap for you using my house, and he wanted you to be brought here. Why?"

"He wants us dead," I replied, losing all calm. My words were bitten off; rage poured through my whole body. "If you know what he's done, you know he's a monster who—"

I couldn't say it. The words wouldn't come out. I swallowed hard.

Lucifer shifted in his throne; I watched from the corner of my eye, waiting for him to smite us like he himself had been cast from heaven. "Who are you?"

I licked my bottom lip, my mouth dry. The marble grandeur of the throne room pressed on my chest until I could barely gasp. "I'm no one; Halwen Vakhara, orphan and nobody."

I glanced at my mates, trying to covertly ask if I should use their real names. Emlyn nodded, encouraging.

"This is Emlyn Johahn, Malakai Virex, and Harvey and Wane van Khama."

"It was—" Harvey added haltingly, his breathing splintered and rough. I reached my bound hands across and squeezed his, holding tight. His tawny wings sagged to the floor. "We changed our names, didn't want *anything* associated with that piece of shit. But it was—it used to be—"

He couldn't say it. My heart broke.

"Locke," Wane said from within his cocoon of shadows, the

inky tendrils not visible but covering him entirely. My heart ruptured with pain; I expected it to collapse.

Lucifer sat back in his throne with a sharp inhale. "I see. Does he believe everyone would forget his crimes if you're dead?"

"If I tell everyone I lied," Wane breathed, so quietly I feared Lucifer wouldn't hear him.

But the devil nodded, rage crossing his tanned, bearded face for a moment before it was swept behind calm and patience.

"He wants the rest of us dead," I added, my eyes on my mates, frantic to help them, to heal them. But their wounds were inner, and there was nothing I could do. "We've been on the run for years, and we thought we were safe. This morning —he sent mercenaries to burn down our house. It was my last straw."

I looked Lucifer dead in the eye and ignored the squirm of my stomach. "I'm sick of running, sick of being terrified that bastard will find us and take my mate from me."

Lucifer inhaled so quickly I'd have called it a gasp on someone less terrifying. "Your mate."

I nodded, my throat swollen. I wanted my daggers, wanted the comfort of them in my hands, but they'd been confiscated.

"These are my mates. They're mine, all of them, and I—I couldn't let this happen again. We lost our fucking *home*," I spat, and wasn't calm enough to modulate my language even for the devil. "We lost everything we built for two years and— I decided to stop running. To go after *him* and take out the bastard. So if you're going to kill anyone—"

"No," Harvey choked out.

"It should be me," I finished, not daring to look at my mates. "I was the idiot who thought I could hunt him down. *I* walked us into a trap. I broke into your home—but I thought it was Locke's. So don't ... don't hurt my mates. Please. It was all me."

"She's lying," Kai growled, straining against his ropes. "I went with her. I ripped off your gates."

I shook my head, tears building. I didn't want to leave them, but the thought of them being snuffed out of the world was unbearable. "That was all me." I blinked back tears, holding Lucifer's stare. "It was all me."

Lucifer sighed. Not a tiny wisp of a breath but a huge, heaving sigh. "I'm not killing anyone. You were obviously set up, and this is far more complicated than a normal break-in."

He rubbed his face, looking tired. I stared, confused where the terrifying leader had gone. He looked normal and human, and—real. This was weird. Why wasn't he ripping off wings and horns, throwing our innards to his terrifying bestie?

"I can't let this go unpunished, or everyone will get ideas about breaking into my home."

"The gate's wide open; no break-in necessary," Kai drawled.

Renna let out a guttural growl. I didn't speak *Terrifying Purple Woman From Hell,* but even I understood it was *keep your mouth shut.*

Emlyn knocked his hands against Kai's leg, echoing the order. They'd had to wrap the gold rope around Em's hands three times, they were so big and powerful. The ropes must have been soaked in magic; I couldn't feel a single heart pumping blood around me. Not even my mates'.

Renna cleared her throat and gave Lucifer a meaningful look. The devil sat back in his throne with a little smile that made me nervous.

"I have a proposition for you," he said, meeting each of our eyes. Something in his face flickered when he looked at Wane, writhing in shadows, only parts of him now visible through the tendrils, but Lucifer didn't make a comment.

I stiffened. Proposition? This did not sound good.

"What kind of proposition, sir?" Emlyn asked as courteously as I'd ever heard him.

"Isn't the correct term of address, *your majesty?*" Kai whisper-hissed.

"I thought it was *your highness,*" Harvey added.

"Shut up," I barked at both of them. "He's the fucking devil; let the man speak."

For a moment, I wasn't waiting for an axe to fall, and it was just a normal moment of being exasperated by my mates —and so entirely in love with their nonsense.

"Thank you, Halwen," Lucifer drawled, almost amused, and I stiffened at *the devil* speaking my name. "The last custodian of the Damned Realm died five days ago."

"Sorry for your loss," Emlyn murmured.

If Kai had said those words, it would have had a snarky undertone, but Em genuinely meant them. I wanted him to wrap his arms around me and give me one of his signature bear hugs that made everything feel alright for a little while.

Lucifer nodded in acknowledgement, light catching the silver and gold embroidery on his fancy tunic. In comparison, mine was washed-out blue and had dirt crusted on the hem and sleeve. I didn't even know how it got there.

"If you agree to take on the role of custodians of the Damned Realm, I won't punish you for this crime. Even better —if you keep the souls there in line, I'll leave you alone. You'll never have to see me again in your whole lives."

My eyes shot to Em, then Harvey, Kai, and Wane. *I say we go for it.*

Kai widened his eyes emphatically. *But it's the fucking* Damned Realm, *where the worst of humanity are sent to suffer when they die.*

Wane averted his eyes, but he nodded. He thought we should accept the offer.

"Hell no," Harvey hissed. "It's a place of misery and suffering."

"But Locke will never find us there," Em breathed, looking at all of us.

And that was a strong enough point that we couldn't argue against it.

I faced Lucifer, my stomach in knots, and said, "We'll do it. Proposition accepted."

CHAPTER TWELVE

*T*here should have been a cautionary phrase about jumping to conclusions without any proof. You know, *be careful what you wish for,* but more along the lines of *be careful what you assume about the maniacal abuser determined to kidnap/kill you.* That would have come in really handy right now.

The move to the Damned Realm went without a hitch, if you ignored the fact we'd moved to a realm within Hell that was the home of misery, suffering, and nightmares come to life.

I didn't know where to start with being the custodian of this place and keeping the souls of the damned in line, but that was a problem for tomorrow. Now, they were nicely locked inside the realm, burning in their fiery pits or screaming from caves deep down in the rotten earth. So we ignored them and focused on scoping out the huge manor house that came with the job. The past custodian had left all their shit in it, so on the plus side it was furnished.[1]

"Home sweet home," I sighed, leaning against the admittedly gorgeous black island in the kitchen. For a second I forgot my mates were furious with me, but then I met Emlyn's gaze and flinched.

"What were you *thinking?*" he demanded, stalking across the cold grey tiles, seeming even bigger than usual with his muscles strained and arms crossed.

"I'm sorry," I replied in a small voice.

"We're lucky we were only sent to the Damned Realm—we could all have been *killed!*"

I wrapped my arms around my middle, my stomach knotted up tight. "I know."

"Of all the stupid things," he growled, grinding his teeth. "We're struggling to stay one step ahead of Locke, let alone surviving the bastard head-on!"

Sour saliva filled my mouth. I was going to throw up.

"Enough," a quiet voice rasped.

"You should have stayed in the safe house—" Em growled.

A tear burned in the corner of my eye. He was right—every single word. This was all because of me. I was a fuck-up.

"I said *enough!*" Wane yelled, his hoarse voice loud and forceful. He unravelled his thick blanket of shadows and stalked across the kitchen—but to *me,* not Em.

A cry caught in my throat when Wane pulled me into his arms, holding me so tight he might actually hold the broken bits together.

His lips skimmed my temple and quieter, gentler, he said, "Can't you see Haley already knows everything you're saying? You're hurting her. If you keep pushing, she's going to break."

I was already there, breaking into little pieces, but I didn't correct him.

"It's not like we set out to get ourselves killed *or* exiled to the Damned Realm," Kai muttered, the blood in his veins thumping fast with anger. Or, if I knew him, helplessness—his least favourite emotion. "We can't keep running. Running has one outcome: Wane and Harvey back in their own personal hell and the rest of us dead."

Wane tightened his arms until I grunted, and I wasn't sure if it was at the idea of him being at his father's mercy—or lack thereof—or at the thought of me dying.

"It was reckless," Em argued, but gentler, and I heard the exhaustion in his voice now. He was as scared as the rest of us, but masking it better.

"It was *desperate*," Kai corrected, his voice as sharp as the knives he'd gifted me.

The knives … my bottom lip shook; my eyes burned and blurred. They'd been confiscated when we were marched into the palace in Iarlon, and Renna hadn't given them back.

My breath caught, broke, and emerged as a sob.

"You've made your point, Em," Harvey sighed, no sarcasm or smart remark on his tongue. "There's no going back now; it's done. Maybe they did us a favour sending us here. Kai's right—if that bastard finally caught us, there's only one way that would end."

"It's okay, my rose," Kai murmured, suddenly behind me. He wrapped himself around my back, hugging Wane in the process.

Safe between them both, I lost even more control of my emotions, and a rush of broken cries escaped my clenched teeth.

"My daggers," I gasped out, burying my face in Wane's soft shirt. "Kai, Renna *took* them."

His fingers ran through my hair in a slow, soothing stroke. "I can have more made."

A laugh strangled me. "Where are you going to find more volcanic metal?"

"Don't underestimate me, Haley," he murmured, kissing the top of my head. "I'm capable when I put my mind to it."

But they were gone—our tenth anniversary gift, the sign of

Kai's love and commitment. And Emlyn was angry at me. And we were stuck here for the rest of our lives, in the realm of eternal fucking suffering. And ... it was all my fault.

"I should have listened to you, Wane," I whispered, ignoring my sobs. "I'm so sorry."

"Shh, itzaia. You have no reason to apologise; you were trying to keep us safe." He said the last part in a sharper tone, his eyes fixed on someone over my head.

I swallowed the huge lump in my throat. My good intentions didn't seem to matter now.

"We'll be fine," Harvey input, muscling in on my right, his heat sinking into me. "If we've been fine in the thirty other hellholes we've stayed in, how's the Damned Realm gonna be different?"

"When did you get all sunshine-y and optimistic?" Kai drawled, tightening his arms possessively around me.

"Shut up," Harvey muttered, shoving him. "Asshole."

"Love you, too," Kai replied and made kissy faces.

A tiny smile curved my lips and some of the brutal heaviness lifted off my chest. They were acting normally, like this was any other day, and it made everything easier to bear.

Except for Em being angry. *Nothing* could make that bearable. I squeezed Wane, turned to kiss the angry line of Kai's jaw, and rested my forehead against Harvey's, giving him a deep, apologetic stare.

"Nothing to forgive, Sugarplum, so stop looking so pitiful," he said, quiet and just for me. "Or I might forget how vicious and stabby you really are."

It was a little easier to smile. A little. But it didn't make it easier to detach my body from their arms and force myself to meet Emlyn's stare.

"I'm sorry," I choked out, using up all my courage to face him. "I didn't—I didn't mean for this to happen. Worse case scenario, I thought I'd die killing the bastard and you'd be safe.

I-I *hate* seeing you all scared, watching you j-jump at noises outside, feeling how tortured you are through the bonds. I just..."

I wanted to fix it. But now I saw how fucking stupid that idea had been. Cassander Locke wasn't the sort of man you caught off guard. He wasn't even the sort of man you survived.

"No," Emlyn breathed, and I froze as he rushed across the space between us. He caught my face in his warm hands and brushed the tears off my cheeks. "I made you cry."

"It's not all you," I replied, my voice thick. "I'm fine."[2]

I began to shake when Em pulled me against his body, hugging me tight.

"Fuck, I'm sorry I snapped, Hales," he murmured, guilt heavy in his deep voice. "The thought of you in danger drives me crazy. I keep thinking about what would have happened if we hadn't shown up, all the things he could have done to you."

Growls rose from behind me, one low and raspy—Wane. He knew first-hand all the vile things Cassander Locke could do to me. So did Harvey. I bit my lips together as they wobbled again.

"It's okay," Em murmured, tucking me closer with his hand on the back of my neck. "We're still alive, and we're together. We can figure everything else out."

"Quite the change of heart," Kai muttered.

"Don't," I sighed. "No more arguing today."

"Forgive me if the sight of my girl crying is a wakeup call," Em huffed at Kai. His voice was placating enough that I squeezed him tightly in gratitude.

But a chord of alarm spiked through my chest. A sharp intake of breath echoed the alarm, making cold race through my blood. It took me a second to realise it was Wane, and panic was spreading in our bond like ink through water.

"Wane?" I breathed, peeling away from Emlyn to watch my

mate wrap himself in layer after layer of shadows, his terrified silver eyes the last thing to disappear.

"That's not my shadow," he rasped, gesturing with a tendril of darkness at a patch of shadow in the corner of the kitchen between the black cabinets and the wall. "It's not mine. *Harvey, it's not mine!*"

All the blood drained from Harvey's face, leaving him wan. He jumped in front of Wane, backing him up to the marble counter, and the rest of us reacted instinctively even if we had no idea what was going on.

"It's an inherited power," Harvey explained breathlessly, his eyes wild. When I pressed into his side, his whole body was shaking. "Wane's shadows—they're inherited."

And if that mass of shadow in the corner wasn't Wane's, and it certainly wasn't natural by the way it ebbed and flowed...

I bared my teeth, my voice deep and guttural. "Get the hell out of my house."

I was almost sick when the shadows peeled back, layer by layer, until the sleazy, smirking asshole within was revealed.

He looked too much like my mates for comfort, with his sharp, defined features, his hair the same chestnut brown. He resembled them even more closer up, not separated from us by a barrier of Lucifer's power. But he was a monster and an abuser, where my mates were caring, protectors through and through.

"You touch anyone," Kai hissed, throwing his hands out, "and you *die.*"

Cassander Locke laughed, a quiet murmur of sound. Quietly confident and sinister enough to send a chill down my spine. I reached back and grabbed Harvey's clammy hand, gripping tight.

"Actually," Locke replied casually, inky darkness pooled in his hand, "you're the ones who'll be dying."

We pushed tighter together, growls all around me. I waited for Locke to unleash the shadows in his hand; I realised too late that the darkness wasn't the threat, but *hiding* it.

I'd never seen a shotgun up close before, never heard the devastating sound of gunpowder exploding.

A piercing shriek filled my ears when it went off, ringing like a bell. When Emlyn fell, I didn't even hear my own scream.

CHAPTER THIRTEEN

*E*m hit the kitchen floor so hard his head bounced, a red stain spreading across his chest from the hole blown through his middle.

"No!" Malakai roared. I didn't hear the sound; numbly, I watched his lips form the words, watched devastation twist his pale face.

Harvey launched across the kitchen at his father, his tawny wings snapping with a vicious gust of air and his head ducked low to ram his horns at the bastard. Locke evaded the blow expertly, grabbing Harvey's spiralling horns to keep them out of his gut. Barely even exerting himself.

My ears kept ringing. My soul was frozen, numb, until my terrified stare dropped from the gun to my mate, bleeding on the floor.

"Em," I breathed, crashing to my knees and touching his face, his shoulders, his neck, avoiding the mess the gun made of his chest. He was still warm, but so frozen that I knew instantly, and denied it.

"Emlyn, come on, wake up."

I shook his shoulders, only making his hair flutter and

wings ruffle. Nothing else moved. Not his chest or his heart. It didn't pump at all because—because he was—

"No," I gasped at my own thoughts. He wasn't. He couldn't be. It made no sense; he'd been holding me a minute ago, warm and reassuring and *whole*.

But there was too much blood, and the shot hit at a close range. My whole body shuddered. The wound was smoking, but not with ordinary grey smoke—this was black.

Shadows.

Fuck—

No!

If the gun wasn't loaded with normal ammunition, the rules of human weapons didn't apply, and he didn't have to reload it—

"Harvey!" I screamed, throwing myself to my feet. *Too late, too late.* I reached my mate in time to catch him as shadows blasted into his chest and out through his back.

"It's okay, you're okay, it's okay," I babbled uselessly as we collapsed to the floor, hot blood soaking my hands when I pressed them against the wound. His wings splayed over my legs, heavy and drenched red.

"Sugar—plum," he choked out, silver eyes fluttering. His hand pressed weakly to mine—and fell limply away when his eyes turned dull, all the life gone from them.

Nonono. This wasn't happening. This wasn't *happening.*

"*Harvey!*" I screamed, my throat so raw I tasted blood. Or maybe some of Harvey's blood had splashed my face. I shouted his name, like I could bring him back if I was loud enough. "You can't—can't leave me. You can't!"

But he didn't move. He didn't smirk at me or make a smart-tass remark. He didn't even blink, his eyes open, still fixed on me, but empty.

"Harvey," I gasped, bowing over him, my chest cracking open from the inside. "Harvey, please."

A wail built, loud enough that I heard it even over the ringing in my ears. I sounded like a siren, a banshee. My mates were dead. Emlyn and Harvey were dead.

Shadows slammed down in front of me, and I no longer cared what Locke did to me. Harvey's blood covered my hands, his wings draped over me, but the blood that soaked into my pants was Emlyn's. My Em, my protector and safe space.

I keened louder, the sound coming from deep in my soul. I was close enough to wrap my shaking fingers around Emlyn's.

They were already cold.

The air shuddered, and I snapped my head up, horror closing off my air and silencing my wail. Kai—that was *Kai's* magic.

Oh gods, it wasn't Locke's shadows walling me in but Wane's; he'd wrapped himself around me, tears soaking the back of my shirt and his fingers knotted with Harvey's.

"Kai," I rasped, staring at the bubble of darkness, gasping in panic and shock. *"Kai!"*

Where was he? I couldn't see through the thick dome all around us. I needed to see. I needed him safe, *alive*. Em and Harvey were dead. Really dead. I choked down vomit. Kai was going to take on Locke alone. Kai would be ripped away from me, too. I struggled in Wane's arms, blood rolling down my hands as I reached for the dome.

"No one," Kai seethed, too close—to us *and* Locke. I couldn't see him but I felt the iron poker of his horror and fury like a brand on my skin. Another part of me broke as I struggled to reach him. "Fucking *no one* hurts my family."

"Let him in the dome," I gasped, frantic as I pawed at the shadows. "Wane, let him—"

A boom as loud as any explosion rocked the floor beneath us as Kai called up a snake bigger than any I'd felt before. I tried to scramble away from my dead mates to get to Kai, to pull him back, to protect him.

My magic—fuck, *my magic!* I seized the slow, steady blood pounding through Locke's body and sank inner claws into it, burning with the need to splatter him into a million pieces and—

No, I really *was* burning. Where my power met Locke, my magic *scalded.* I gritted my teeth, screaming, crying. Em and Harvey were dead. I would follow them soon; this pain was *nothing.*

But the longer I held on, the harder it became to sense Locke's blood. It scorched and slipped through my fingers. I lost my grip entirely when another gunshot blasted through the room.

I flinched so hard, Harvey's wings slid off my legs.

Wane's whimper filled my ears, his arms wrapping around my waist and squeezing so tight, I couldn't draw enough air to scream.

The slam of a body hitting the ground was unmistakeable.

Kai, my Kai—my secret romantic, my steadfast friend, my heart and soul and—

I couldn't breathe, and I no longer *cared* about drawing breath. I laid Harvey gently on the ground and turned in Wane's arms.

I knew how this would end. We both did. I was too numb to fight. I didn't even want to.

I wrapped my arms around Wane's shoulders and gripped as tightly as numb arms would allow.

"I love you," I rasped, choking on air. "I love you so much. I'll never stop loving you, no matter what."

Tears streaked down Wane's face, shining as bright as his mercury eyes. He blinked and another rush of tears rolled down his cheeks. I leaned forward to kiss one away, then the other, and his bottom lip wobbled.

"You are every bit of light in my world, itzaia," he choked out, his arms shaking but viciously tight around me.

"And you're mine, zivai," I rasped, burying my face in his shoulder and holding him tight. "I want you to run. The second the dome comes down—"

But death came on the fifth gunshot, when Wane's shadows finally buckled. He didn't get a chance to run, or even scream. After that, there was nothing.

PART II - HUNTRESS

CHAPTER FOURTEEN

A hundred years later

*T*here was nothing … until there was *something*.

There was dirt on my face, pressing on my mouth, my nose. It was everywhere, penning me in like a cage. Its earthy scent was all I could smell, all I could taste. A wordless scream shook my throat as I clawed at the cold dirt above me, forcing my weak, trembling hand through, carving with my claws until I saw daylight.

Someone … buried me.

I scrabbled more frantically, pushing the Earth away until I could breathe, until I could see more glimpses of light.

I sat up with a desperate gasp when I cleared enough space, pawing at the ground under me, the ground I'd been *buried* in.

Oh gods, oh gods.

I swivelled my head, sucking down air and tasting my own grave dirt as I searched frantically for Harvey, Em, and Kai.

My mates—*where were my mates?*

The marble floor had gone from under me. Instead, my fingers sank into loose dirt, cold and shocking as it crumbled.

"What...?" I rasped, my voice thick with disuse.

A panicked breath scraped up my throat. I wavered, nearly falling back to the ground when I saw massive, thick-trunked *trees* around me instead of the kitchen in the Damned Realm house.

What the fuck?

"Guys?" I choked out, crawling unsteadily to my feet. I had to grab a tree to stop myself face-planting the ground, and my wings snapped clumsily out at my sides. It was too dark to see much except the rough shape of trees and the cloying darkness around me. How did I get out here? And where even *was* here?

There wasn't a forest around the house in the Damned Realm. I'd never actually seen a forest this old; the trees were *massive*. They reminded me of the forest around our home before those bastard mercs razed it to the ground, but these were far taller. Far older.

One thing was for sure: I was on my own. No more shallow graves dug in the dirt. No mates in sight.

The last thing I remembered was darkness wrapping around me as gunshot after gunshot ricocheted through our new home. Light broke through after repeated shots, and then something slammed through my body—and that was it.

Locke *killed* me...

So where the hell was I? Human souls went to Hell after they died, but I was already a demon, and I was ashamed to admit I'd never really thought about where demons went after death. Nowhere. If anything, I thought we were snuffed out of existence and there was nothing left.

"Guess this is the afterlife," I groaned, finally finding my feet and taking a step without the tree's assistance. I scrubbed the muck off my face as much as I could, but I could still taste it.

Fuck, every part of me hurt. Walking was not a fun experience. But staying here was out of the question unless I wanted to live in the forest.

"This hurts too damn much to be the afterlife," I hissed, hardly daring to voice my suspicion. I felt *alive*—hot and pulsing with pain, not cold and numb.

I hesitated with my fingertips over my wrist, but forced myself to check for a pulse and—

Holy shit, I *was* alive.

I was so confused and relieved and stressed, I wanted to curl into a ball on the forest floor. Mostly, I wanted to find my mates, hunt down a bed, and snuggle with them for the world's longest sleep.

My chest tightened, pain rupturing through my soul. I brushed it tentatively, and hissed at the fractured mess, the frayed threads of each bond, greyed with death. They died— really, truly died.

But I was alive, I was back somehow. And if *I* was, they had to be, too. They *had* to be.

I could find them, wherever they were. No matter how long it took me.

But first, I'd hunt down Cassander Locke and make him wish he'd never been born.

CHAPTER FIFTEEN

I walked for hours, numbly putting one foot in front of the other until a cluster of lights flickered on the edge of the horizon. I groaned in relief, my whole body aching from dying, being reborn, and walking miles through forest and farmland. My wings dragged along the floor, my shoulders too weak to hold them up. When the lights became a village, I could have cried.

In the fading light, I finally dared to peer down at my body, noticing with a twist in my stomach, I still wore the clothes I'd been shot in. Blood was crusted all down my front, the crimson almost black, dirt muddied my trousers and —*what the fuck?*

I'd been a badass bitch before, but I'd never had ink on my arms. Now a tattoo spanned the length of my right forearm in a strange combination of lines, arrows, dots, and a half circle that looked like a crescent moon.

"Oh, *fuck* no," I hissed, clenching my teeth as I stared at my new tattoo. I'd seen something like this before, on a mercenary who'd picked up a curse from a mark in the south of Hell. This was a *curse* mark.

Some bastard buried me alive and cursed me.

I pawed at my clothes, pulling up my shirt, ripping my bloody pants down, twisting to see my back, bending to scan my legs. The good news was my legs were curse free. The bad news: a *massive* curse mark was inked up my stomach.

I had two curses. Someone fucking *cursed* me!

Anger fuelled the last of my journey down the hill into the village. I lifted my wings back into place and stormed right up to the first person I found—a farmer herding his cows into the pen for the night. The sun was setting behind the farm, crimson and blood-orange, an appropriately violent backdrop for my current situation.

"Hey," I called in my new scratchy voice. The farmer turned in surprise to see me, or maybe to see anyone out here on the edge of the village. "Weird question. What's this village called?"

"Wenthai," he replied in a brusque accent that reminded me of home. I faltered, the familiar accent unexpected. "Where did you come from?" he asked with faint amusement. "You're not local; I don't know your face."

"I came from that damn forest," I muttered, stabbing a finger at the trees I'd woken up surrounded by. Bastards had tripped me up at every opportunity with their roots, swung branches into my face, and filled the air with biting, irritating insects. Plus, the canopy was so thick that I couldn't risk flying.

"Ah," he said with a knowing smile on his ruddy face. "The Forest of Halwen's been known to swallow people and cough them up again. It's all the magic in it."

"The..." I stumbled back, emotion making my voice break. "What did you just say? The Forest of Halwen?"

"Yeah," he confirmed, giving me a strange look as he wiped sweat from his brow. "Where did you think you were?"

I shook my head. *The Forest of Halwen.* The name my mates

gave to the woods around our house. The house Cassander Locke's cronies burned down. My chest pulled tighter, but there was something fragile to the emotion now instead of anger. I wanted to burst into tears.

My mates were still alive. This was a message.

"Thanks," I said gruffly, and turned away from the farmer. I didn't need directions to the nearest city; this was my home. I knew the way like the back of my hand.

"Hey, are you in trouble?" he asked, hurrying after me. "Come inside, my husband can make you a spiced tea. We've got paper you can use to write a letter. No communication stones, I'm afraid."

"I'm fine," I replied, and cleared my throat when it came out thick and harsh. I turned to him and pasted on a smile. "Really. You're kind; that's pretty fucking rare and I appreciate it. But I'll be fine. I know where I'm going."

Back to the capital, to the mercenary guild headquarters. What else was I going to do? I had no home, no mates, and no money.

I needed a job.

CHAPTER SIXTEEN

"*Y*our name's not on the list; you're not coming in," the six-foot-three guard on the guild's double doors rumbled.

"What a cliché," I muttered, my eyes narrowed and sharp fangs bared. "Look, I'm a guild member. Check my name—Halwen Vakhara."

He crossed dark bronze arms over his considerable chest, leathery brown wings ruffling in irritation. "I checked. There's no one currently registered with that name, only an inactive membership that's been dormant for years. And I mean *years.*"

Well, how many years were we talking? Three? *Ten?*

I gnashed my teeth and spelled it out for him, slowly, "That's me. Haley Vakhara; how many damned Halwen Vakharas do you think there are in Hell?"

He shrugged, giving me a no-nonsense look with beetle-black eyes. I suppressed a growl of frustration.

"Someone killed me, which is why I haven't been an active member. Kinda hard to do jobs when you're six feet underground."

He snorted, shifting to stand clear in front of the big door, barring my entrance. "You don't look so dead to me."

"That's because I'm *not*," I growled. "Look I understand it as much as you do, but I'm back from the dead and I need a damn job. I'm a registered member; you can't pull this shit with me."

When he said nothing, a stoic wall of leather and muscle, I threw my hands up in exasperation. He reacted to the movement like he would a threat, and I released a scream of rage when he grabbed my arm, spun me, and slammed me face-first into the wall beside the door.

In positive news, I was closer to the door than I'd been before. I could have done without the little stones biting into my cheek and the burly guard's hot breath fanning across the back of my neck, though.

I suffered the indignity of him patting down my body, searching my ragged, bloodstained clothes for weapons. He grunted in confusion when he came up empty.

"Like I said," I growled against the brick wall, "someone killed me, buried me, and now I'm reborn. No weapons, no fucking clue what's going on. So I need *a job*."

He grunted again and flipped me around when I bucked in his hold. He released me with a little shove into the road. "You'll have to reapply for a position."

"I'm Haley Vakhara, you giant lump of stupidity! I *have* a position."

But I might as well have been talking to the guild's sturdy brick wall.[1]

"Fine," I growled, and gave him my meanest glare. "I hope a wasp stings your asshole."

"Just doing my job," he muttered, affronted.

I shrugged and pretended I looked badass and intimidating when I stormed away, and not like a once-buried corpse that had been dug up. Or rather like I'd punched my way out of my own damn grave.

Hatred and rage burned in my heart, but I curled my hands into fists and forced myself to calm as I walked down the steep road, no clear destination in mind.

Find a job first, buy weapons second, hunt Cassander Locke third.

I could steal knives, but people who owned their own personal armouries tended to be the people you wanted as friends, not enemies. Turn my back, and there'd be a dagger, a throwing star, a sword, *and* an axe buried between my shoulder blades.

I scanned the street as I walked, searching for somewhere that might accept me for a job, surprised at how gleaming and *new* everything looked. Had they rebuilt the city? A bakery was out of the question—Emlyn was the baker. If I tried anything in the kitchen, houses tended to burn down. The florists were a hard no. Not because I couldn't tend to flowers or make an arrangement; because they reminded me of the soulcaps Malakai picked every year on our anniversary.

How many anniversaries had I missed? I'd have to make it up to him when I found him again. I'd have to make it up to all of them—Kai, Harvey, *and* Emlyn.

An ache burned behind my ribs where my bonds used to live, but I gritted my teeth. My brain throbbed in my skull, along with the haunting sense that I'd forgotten something, but when I examined it more closely, a sharp bolt of pain made me stumble into the pretty iron fence of a café.

Fuck!

I clutched my head, waiting for the pain to pass, and eyed the sweet little café in front of me.

"I can't cook for shit, but I can move plates from the kitchen to tables and back again," I mused.

I'd take a pot washer's position, for Lucifer's sake.

Ugh, that phrase had a little more meaning thanks to actually *meeting* the guy. He hadn't been a total bastard, and I supposed he'd been fair, but still. Sending us to the Damned Realm? He couldn't have thrown us in a jail cell for a few years? Not that I thought we'd have been safe from Locke—or his hunters—there, either.

"Enough," I rasped, pain stabbing my chest, my head, and my soul. "Enough."

It was done. I couldn't go back and change it; I had to live with the consequences of my actions that night.

I reached for the gate to the café at the same time the glass-inlaid wooden door swung open, and I came face to face with a black-haired, purple-skinned woman I never thought I'd see again.

"You!" I snarled, and launched myself at Renna.

CHAPTER SEVENTEEN

*S*he dodged my first blow, snapped up a gauntleted wrist to deflect the second, and caught my fist on my third. Okay, so I was a little rusty.[1]

"Excuse me?" she snapped, her eyes hard. "Care to explain why you're trying to rearrange my face?"

I laughed, the sound coming from low in my chest and *oozing* with bitterness. I ripped my fist out of her lilac hand and bared sharp teeth.

"You don't remember me? You exiled me to the fucking Damned Realm, and you don't even *remember* me?"

I slammed my fist into her shoulder, pretty sure the blow only landed because shock bloomed across her sharp face and she stared at me with sudden comprehension.

"You're—but that's impossible. There are reports of your death. I've seen the sketches; you were blasted into three pieces."

I winced. "I could have lived without knowing that, thanks Renna."

She shook her head, her sharp black hair cutting through

the air around her jaw. "You're supposed to be dead," she snapped. "What deal did you make to come back?"

"Don't you think I'd have asked to not die in the first place if I was going to make a deal?" I snapped right back.

"You broke into Lucifer's house; you're an imbecile."

"I didn't *know* it was his house," I threw back, shoving her shoulder.

She shoved my hand away hard enough that my wrist ached.

"Whatever is happening here," a soft voice put in, and both Renna and I jumped when a pink demon in a bonnet and pinafore peered through the doorway, "can you take it away from my café? You're terrifying my customers."

A glance through the door showed her customers were watching, looking more eager for a show than terrified, but she was right that this wasn't the right setting.[2]

I backed up, keeping an eye on the purple woman and waiting for her to draw one of the many knives on her person. I cursed myself for not swiping one when I had the chance, and then ground my teeth when the word 'cursed' proved too sensitive.

"How are you alive?" Renna barked, as sharp and curt as I remembered. Her whole body was sharp, from her figure to her features to her personality.

I swept my arms out at my sides and shrugged. "I don't know. I woke up in the Forest of Halwen last night. A name that no one should know, by the way, because it was a private name between me and my mates. But apparently everyone calls the forest my name now.

"Oh, and when I say 'woke up,' I really mean I dug myself out of a shallow grave and nearly choked on dirt. I don't know what happened, or how I'm alive, or where my mates were."

If knives could soften, Renna did just that. Her mouth pinched a little less, maybe. "They're not with you?"

She cast a look around the street, like Kai would sneak out of the shadows with his snakes poised to strike, Emlyn would creep along the rooftops and leap off, his feathery grey wings spread in flight, or Harvey would blind the street with his sunlight, a smirk on his face, or—

Or what? I gritted my teeth when pain exploded through my tender skull. Renna didn't miss it but she must have thought it was the pain of missing them.

"Come with me," she sighed, her eyes narrowed. "Lucifer will be able to figure out what happened."

A laugh bubbled up my throat. I rose to my full height. "You're not taking me to Lucifer."

The last time I saw the devil, he made us custodians of the Damned Realm. The realm of suffering and eternal misery. The last thing I wanted was to be sent back there, and this time without my mates at my side.

So I had to get sneaky and clever.

"Holy shit!" I exclaimed, my mouth falling open as I stared at something non-existent at the bottom of the road. "Look at that!"

"What?" Renna snarled, turning.

The second she moved, I spun and sprinted up the road, aiming for a snicket between the florist's shop and a three-story house with a weathervane on top, the metal bright silver against the purple Iarlon sky. Fuck, I was out of breath. I shouldn't be panting already.

I made it all of seven steps, barely reaching the little side street before Renna's fingers hooked in my tattered clothes and she yanked me back.

"It's for your own good," she huffed, and locked her arms around my struggling body.

My stomach dropped hard when I felt the disorienting pinch and tilt of transportation. Shit, she could sift?

This is not fucking happening.

I lost control of my breathing as the street vanished around us, replaced by an endless black void tinted the slightest violet.

When we flew out the other side, I managed a single glimpse of a formal reception room with a roaring fireplace, a desk full of papers and files, and a sofa that held two people— a pretty young scarred woman with soft brown hair and black wings, and Lucifer, the devil himself.

When Renna's magic released me, I collapsed to the floor, claws scraping a fine rug, and I could do nothing to stop myself throwing up bile all over the devil's expensive, black shoes.

CHAPTER EIGHTEEN

I'm dead, I'm so dead.

"Renna, didn't we agree no more kidnapping people?" the pretty woman sighed, getting off the sofa to hand me a tissue. "Are you alright?"

"Me?" I groaned, wiping my mouth and darting a quick glance at Lucifer. He looked exactly like he had the last time I saw him, from the long black hair that flowed over his shoulders, the bearded, dark gold face, the fine clothes he wore, and the dark eyes that watched me with an intensity that made me squirm. I quickly glanced away. "I was fine before this madwoman abducted me."

Renna crossed her arms over her chest, and gave Lucifer a wry look. "You don't recognise her, either."

Lucifer, in the process of wiping my vomit off his shoes, glanced up in surprise. He looked from Renna's smirking face to me as I got to my feet, helped by the winged woman I was ninety percent sure was Lucifer's queen. He certainly hadn't had a queen the last time I was dragged here—by the same damn woman—but fond murmurs around the capital spoke of a queen who helped save everyone and end a war. Impressive. The Justice of Hell they called her.

I wanted my own fancy title, but that could come after I found my mates and killed anyone responsible for keeping them from me. Why bury *me* in the woods, but not them? *Where are they?*

Lucifer was still scrutinising me, no doubt noticing the tattered clothes, the blood visible underneath, and my general sorry state. I sketched a bow that was more ironic than respectful and said, "Halwen Vakhara. You might remember sending me and my mates to be custodians of the Damned Realm. Great idea, by the way, ten out of ten, definitely didn't get us murdered."

Lucifer shot to his feet, shock widening his dark crimson eyes and parting his mouth behind his beard. "But you're dead."

"That's what I said," Renna remarked, dropping into an armchair and stretching out her legs like she owned the place.

"I'm missing something," the queen said, glancing between the three of us. "She can't be dead if she's here. Luc?"

Damn, she called Lucifer *Luc.* The man was terrifying, and brimming with power; she was brave as fuck. No wonder the people loved her.

Lucifer didn't respond straight away; he narrowed his eyes and walked a circle around me, like he was waiting for my arms to decompose and drop off.

"This is weird," I muttered. I wanted to shout *boo!* but the shudder that went down my spine at his close inspection kept my tongue in check. "Hey!" I gasped when he snatched my arm, fingers pressed to my wrist.

"Luc," the queen repeated, her tone different—exasperated. A deep V cut between her eyebrows. "What are you doing?"

"Checking if I'm corpselike," I supplied when he stayed silent, focusing on my pulse. It was still there. I was still alive.[1]

Lucifer dropped my wrist, picked up my other, and gave it the same treatment.

"Nice to meet you," I said to the queen over the devil's bowed head. "I'm Halwen—Haley. I've only been in Iarlon a day, but I've heard a lot about you."

She ducked her head, blushing. Cute. "A lot of the stories are exaggerated," she replied, casting a sharp look at Renna, who innocently cleaned her fingernails with a sharp knife.

"But well-deserved, sweetheart," Lucifer replied, releasing me from his intimidating study to give his partner a sickeningly affectionate look.

My stomach whirled like a tornado, a fist squeezing my heart. I missed my mates so fucking much. I swallowed down my pain and asked, "So. Any ideas how I'm not dead, sir?"

I used my most respectful tone, and mentally patted myself on the back.

"None," he sighed.

"I was shot, probably multiple times. It ripped me apart; I definitely died. My—my mates died, too."

Don't cry, Haley, don't fucking cry.

"And they didn't wake up with you?" the queen asked, her brown eyes big with sympathy. I shook my head, my jaw clenched against a torrent of emotion, and she softened even further. "I can't imagine how much pain you're in. I'm so sorry."

"It's fine," I ground out, swallowing the lump in my throat. "Could be worse, right? I could be dead." I tried to laugh, but I sounded like a donkey braying. Awkward.

Even Renna was eyeing me with sympathy now. Fuck, I must have sounded *really* pathetic.

"Anyway, I'll get out of your seriously beautiful hair," I told Lucifer, heading towards the door beside the sofas. "I don't know why your stabby friend kidnapped me, but nice seeing you."

He stepped into my path, because of course he did. My stomach dropped, dread crawling up my spine like an insect.

"The only way you could come back from being dead is with a god's or goddess's power."

"Which is a non-issue," I said slowly, "because the gods have been gone for years." I laughed nervously when they all exchanged a look. "Right?"

"Not ... exactly," the queen replied, and bit her lip.

"They recently became more involved in our lives," Lucifer explained, and for a moment the terrifying aura around him dimmed, making him more mortal. "Angels and alpha demons conspired to end my reign, destroy most of Hell, and rebuild it as something far more horrific."

I winced. "Parts of it are horrific enough as it is."

Renna snorted.

"It's not out of the question that a god would be watching Hell and moving game pieces around, but why resurrect *you?*"

All my respect and fear flew out the window, and I snapped.

"First of all, that's incredibly rude, Lucy. Don't talk to me like I'm worthless; I'd be pretty damn useful to a god. Second, I am no one's damn game piece. *No one's.*"

"Lucy," Renna choked out, tapering into a deep, guttural laugh. "I like her; let's keep her."

"I'm not a pet, either," I snapped, teeth bared and wings ruffling in agitation.

Lucifer began to speak, but he paused when his queen—I really needed to learn her name—crossed to the far end of the room. With her back to us, I couldn't see what she was doing, but I took advantage of the distraction to edge a little closer to the door. It wasn't like I could elbow *the devil* in the gut and run, though. Anyone else, I'd have already done it, but this was Lucifer. The big bad, the guy who ran the whole realm, the King of Hell.

When the queen turned back to us, she was holding a glass with a decent amount of amber liquid in it. A woman after my own heart. Wait, she was crossing the room, holding it out— she'd made the drink *for me?*

Fuck, she was impressive *and* sweet. She reminded me of my mum, or what I could remember before we moved from Earth to Hell and I never saw her again. I had a faint memory of singing, fierce laughter, and feeling safe in her arms.

"Thanks," I rasped, accepting the drink and downing half of it in one go.

"We're not saying you're a pawn," she said kindly, "just that a god or goddess might want to use you as one. Do you have any new powers?"

I shook my head, the alcohol burning down my body. "None. I do have these, though."

I held my arm out, and twisted it into the light so they could see through the dried blood to the black inked curse on my arm.

"Shit," Renna hissed, flying to her feet.

"Yeah. Also this." I lifted my shirt, showing the biggest, nastiest curse down my middle. "I don't know what these curses do, but I can tell you I never had them before I died. Someone must have tattooed them after I died, and then buried me in the woods."

"But why bring you back now?" Lucifer growled under his breath, eyes narrowed on my curse marks. "After a hundred years?"

I laughed.

No one else laughed.

"After *how many* years?" I demanded, my voice a little high, a lot screechy. I threw back the rest of the drink, my breathing turning frantic. "A hundred years?"

"I thought you knew," Lucifer murmured, an apology in the look his red eyes settled on me.

"You couldn't have told me?" I snapped at Renna, ignoring the sympathy and confusion on her sharp, lilac face.

"How was I supposed to know you were so clueless?" she snapped right back.

I snarled, hating that she was right. "I thought it'd been a few years, ten tops. Not a fucking hundred. But that's—I don't even know—I—"

"Oh, Halwyn," the queen breathed, and shocked the fuck out of me by swallowing me into a floral-scented hug that worked wonders on my jagged emotions.[2]

When she let me go, I noticed Lucifer watching me with that apologetic look again. That's how you knew your life was depressing; the devil himself thought you were pitiful.

"You know it's Halwen, like *the Forest* of Halwen, right?" Renna drawled, watching me closely. "A forest that was named a hundred or so years ago."

I shot her a panicked look, my hands shaking where they still held the tumbler. *No.* Just … no. "That's—that can't be right."

"Why not?" Lucifer asked, tilting his head in a preternatural way.

"It's what my mates called the forest around our home before Cassander Locke burned it down. I thought—maybe they told everyone to call it that as a message to me that they're back, too. But if it was named a hundred years ago—my mates have been back, alone, for a hundred years."

I covered my mouth, feeling sick.

"Someone kept you apart," the queen guessed angrily. "If your mates were reborn a hundred years ago, why wait until now to bring *you* back?"

"Good question," Lucifer muttered. "But not an easy one to answer. Someone went to a lot of trouble to do this; they won't be easy to find."

"I don't care," I snarled, putting the glass down on a nearby surface a little too heavily. "I'm going to find them, rip their intestines up their throats, and choke them with them."

The queen's eyes blew wide. "That's ... graphic."

"I like it," Renna remarked. "I'll help; I've been bored lately."

"You will not," Lucifer disagreed sharply. "I have a job for you."

"Oh, goody," she replied flatly, and dropped back onto the sofa. The two of us were kindred sarcastic spirits; if she stopped kidnapping me and dragging me to Lucifer's palace, I might even become friends with Renna.

"What do you need, Halwen?" Lucifer asked abruptly, like he'd been keeping it inside for a while. "It's my fault you were taken to the Damned Realm. It might not be my fault you were killed, but—I share some of the blame."

"She did break into your house, boss," Renna pointed out.

I ignored her. "I need a job. Badly. I need money so I can find my mates. I'm good at tracking—I used to be a mercenary before I settled down with my mates—but getting information out of people costs a pretty penny."

Or a hefty pouch of gold crowns, the most valuable coin in Hell's currency. Every pouch I handed over broke my heart a little.

"Positions in my palace are few and far between," the devil said, sympathy in his red eyes. "There's one job, but everyone I've offered it to has turned it down. It's too dangerous—"

"Danger is my middle name," I cut in, my heart leaping, racing. Who cared how dangerous it was; if it paid, I could get everything I needed to track my mates. I knew it would be a long search, and it might take months, but the sooner I could get started, the sooner I found them.

"What's your real middle name?" the queen asked, a flicker of laughter curling her lips. Her brown eyes glimmered.

"Danger," I insisted.

"Bullshit," Renna spat, pointing her dagger at me. "Tell us your actual name, and I'll give you this knife."

"You just cleaned your nails with it; do I look like I want your nail cleaning dagger?"

"It's free," she pointed out.

"Siybella," I muttered, and snatched the dagger from her outstretched hand. I'd need to deep clean it, but at least it was sharp. I felt more like myself with a weapon in my hand; my panic settled. Renna smirked deeper, like she noticed. "So what's the job?"

"I need someone to track alphas, and infiltrate their community," Lucifer answered, almost … tired? "Most of them were dealt with in the war, but there are some left, quietly stirring up trouble. The last thing Hell needs is another battle, so I want them found and brought in."

"Alphas," I repeated.

The biggest, baddest, most powerful and *feral* of demons. They were more animal than man, and impossible to reason with. Get on their wrong side, and they'd start tearing limbs off and ripping out eyes. I usually gave them a wide berth, and avoided jobs with them. Of course, no one told me the job to hunt—uh? Harvey?—would involve archdemons. They were practically alphas themselves, but with a *few* extra brain cells.

"How many alphas?"

"It's hard to say," Lucifer replied cagily.

"So you have no idea," I sighed, dragging my teeth over my bottom lip.

But it was paid work, and work I was good at—tracking, hunting. It would get me one step closer to Emlyn, Kai, and Harvey, and while I was out hunting the alphas I could search for my mates, too.

"I'll take the job," I told him, ignoring the flare of surprise in his eyes. "Consider yourself the proud employer of a new tracker. I'll report to you in the morning, shall I? Or do you want me to start now?"

Please don't say now. I was so exhausted I could fall asleep sitting upright in the middle of a raucous bar.

The devil waved his hand, looking as knackered as I surely did. "The morning's fine."

"Where are you staying?" his queen asked, something unsettlingly knowing in her gaze.

I hesitated a moment too long.

"Right, you'll stay in the palace. No, no," she cut in when I tried to argue. "I'm not letting you sleep on the streets. I'll show you to the guest wing. Follow me."

I gave Renna a wide-eyed look. "Is your queen always this bossy?"

"Always," she confirmed.

Lucifer chuckled, watching his queen with sweet, sickly love. My chest pulled tight again. I missed that. I missed it so damn much, and I'd only been alive for a day and a half. The weeks or months it took me to find my mates were going to kill me.

But I had a job, and somewhere to sleep. That was more than I had this morning.

"This way," the queen called, leading the way down the bright, airy corridor outside. "I'm Lili, by the way. Lili Kazana."

"Nice to meet you, Lili Kazana," I replied, distracted by the architecture, art, and the sheer *size* of the palace around us.

"We'll figure out what the marks mean," she said gently, watching me as she led the way through a courtyard full of statues and wild greenery. "We've got the biggest library in Hell; there must be something in there about curses like yours."

The smile she gave me was probably supposed to be comforting, but all it did was remind me of the curses inked on my body. What were they for? What if I was cursed to die again in a week? What if I was cursed to never find my mates?

For a moment, I felt optimistic that things were going to work out.

My mistake.

CHAPTER NINETEEN

*I*t felt like yesterday when I slept in our bed in the house by the forest, before Locke's minions set it ablaze and forced us to a safe house. I hadn't slept in that bed; I snuck out before unconsciousness could take me. The difference between this huge, four-poster, cloud of a bed in Lucifer's palace and our worn, five-sleeper mattress at home was crazy. It was too comfortable, too soft, swallowing my body whole. Where were the springs digging into my back? Where were the dips caused by sleep-heavy bodies?

It took me hours to settle, to stop scanning the cream and gold walls of the room, or staring obsessively at the shadows playing on the wardrobe and chest of drawers. I kept waiting for those shadows to come to life and attack me, for Cassander Locke to appear.

"It's been a hundred years," I whispered to myself in the dark. But I climbed out of bed to tug the curtains open and let more silvery lilac moonlight flood the room. I gave the furniture and pale bed another sweep, my heart clanging when movement chased through the big mirror above the dressing table across from the bed.

"It's *you,* you daft bitch," I groaned at myself, and climbed back under the nebular covers. "And Locke's probably dead by now; he was already fifty when he killed you. No way did he live to a hundred and fifty."

Cassander was a slimy bastard, though. Maybe he prolonged his life somehow.

"Stop it," I hissed at myself pulling the covers over my head and poking a hole so I could breathe cool air.[1]

I finally drifted to sleep when the sky began to lighten and exhaustion took over my body, dragging me down.

It seemed like as soon as I closed my eyes, they were blinking open again. But there was no stress wrapped around me here, no fear tightening my chest, only a warm weight pressed to my back and a pleasant heaviness resting in the dip of my side.

I groaned a wordless question, and the arm tightened.

"Go back to sleep, Hales," Emlyn muttered, grazing his nose against my shoulder and inhaling a long breath.

I drifted off again, safe and comfortable.

But then Em startled, his whole body jolting, and I came awake in response, scanning the room for threats.

"Is this real?" he rasped, staring at me while I assessed our room—the room back at the house that had burned down. My beloved bedroom. "Tell me this is real."

"It's a dream," I realised, a furrow between my brows as Emlyn gathered me so close to him that I grunted, his arms squeezing me so hard.

"But you're here. You're here." He scattered kisses across my shoulders, throwing his leg over mine to—to kick Harvey awake. Harvey was here? A small, choked sound escaped me. "Wake up. Now!"

Kai flew awake too, a flurry of swear words on his tongue until he spotted me. My heart thumped when Kai stared at me. I waited for him to rant or laugh or kiss me. Instead, he burst into shaking, wretched tears, burying his face in inked palms.

"Fuck," Harvey breathed, staring at me with disbelieving silver eyes. "You don't look hazy like you normally do in my dreams."

"She's here," Emlyn grunted, and pulled me up until I was sitting.

Somehow we ended up in a giant cuddle pile, with Kai sobbing and clutching me tight, Emlyn kissing every bit of my skin he could reach, and Harvey staring at me like I was a star given life—a miracle he never expected to see.

I hugged them all close to me, and ignored the sharp twist of pain through my chest. I knew something was off, something was missing, but for now I had my mates in my arms and I didn't care about anything else.

CHAPTER TWENTY

I woke in pain, clutching at my chest. Unable to breathe. Unable to process the vicious sensation that sliced through my soul and radiated to every part of me. I threw back the unfamiliar covers and stumbled out of bed, scanning the airy white room as if I'd find them here. My mates. My whole, goddamn everything.

"W—" I choked out.

My fingers flew to my throat as it closed, strangling the word before I could utter it. A name? I tried to recall it, but pain exploded through my skull with sudden cruelty, and I staggered into the windowsill with a cry.

"Fucker," I whimpered, digging my nails into the wood of the sill and staring out the window as I panted to catch my breath. Pain burrowed through my ribs and made a home in my heart. I gasped for air, resting my head against the cold window pane and waiting for it to settle.

Something very, very bad happened to my mates. Worse, I thought, than me being buried and having to claw myself out of a grave in the forest.

"I'll find you," I swore to them, reaching through my chest

for the bonds that tied us and finding only tatters and shreds. "I swear. No matter who I have to blackmail, threaten, or kill, I'll find you."

But I didn't know where to start, and the thought of returning to the Damned Realm sent a shiver of warning down my spine. My instincts screamed never to return.

There was no point trying to sleep again despite the early hour and the fact I was normally dead to the world before noon. Or just dead if you considered anything before yesterday. I shuddered, crossing the room to grab my new coat. It was red velvet and fancy and *so* not me, but I wasn't about to complain to Lucifer and his queen when they'd been crazy enough to clothe me in the first place.

It wouldn't have hurt them to give me a suite with a bath, though. I had to walk halfway down the quiet, sun-filled corridor to a bathroom where I could do my morning ablutions and soak in the tub.

I hoped a bath would cleanse my panic and hurt, but nope, the remnants of the dream were still there when I was clean, dressed, and hunting down breakfast.

Had my mates really been there, like Emlyn said? I wanted to believe that was true, that we'd connected in a mystical, mate-ish way, but it was too good to be true.

I slumped into the dining room when I finally found it, feeling weird in my velvet coat. I wanted my leather back, but I didn't know what happened to the safe house when we got caught breaking into Lucifer's second home. It was probably stolen years ago. A *hundred* years ago.

Fuck, I'd been dead a hundred years. I wasn't just reborn; I was a relic.

There was a demon slumped over a table, snoring so loudly the quills all over her black-and-white body rattled. I smiled when I saw a few of them scattered on the floor around us, and my eyes lit up as an idea struck.

Careful not to wake her, I crept over and scooped up the four quills from the floor, sliding them into my hair and wrapping a few strands around them to hold them in place, sticking straight up. Hell yes! Porcupine quill tiara!

My mood was boosted, and I looked cool as fuck, but I was still drained.

"Thank fuck," I breathed when I spotted a carafe of coffee, but when I tilted it towards a cup, nothing came out. I shook the glass. Empty. Fucking typical. I growled and put it down on the table hard enough to knock the quills out of my hair. Nooo!

My mood plummeted.

A different, deeper growl answered me in a long rumble, and I startled, spinning around to see—holy shit, a red panda as big as an elephant, with black horns spiralling off their head and red smoke wafting dangerously from their fur. The porcupine demon shot up from her nap, took one look at the panda, and bolted.

I tried to back up, but the table stood in my way, and when I reached for a knife I came up empty.

The panda rumbled at me, their big jaw unhinged like they wanted to swallow me whole. A whimper caught in my throat and the panda—laughed? Mammoth teeth bared and their big, furry chest shook with a rumble of undeniable laughter.

I stared into their eyes, searching for murderous rage and—

"Wait a fucking second," I blurted, stumbling forward a step as my heart took off beating like a frantic bird. "Tali?"

Her giant, furry head bobbed, and a laugh of disbelief shot from me. I hadn't seen her in years—a hundred and twenty years thanks to being dead. We were friends when I was a kid and we lived next door to each other. After my mum abandoned us on Earth, and Dad and I came to Hell to escape the pain of her walking out on us, Tali got me out of that darkness. She gave me something good when everything else sucked.

We'd been inseparable. People struggled to understand her because she spoke in growls, purrs, and grunts, but I always understood her perfectly. And unless something dramatic had changed, she had one of the fiercest eye-rolls known to demonkind. It spoke far louder than any words.

She used to take a running jump and dive into my arms; she'd been roughly the size of a housecat, so catching her was easy. But when her big butt wiggled *now* and she launched across the room, I squeaked and threw up my hands.

"You can't jump up, you're bigger than a horse, Tal-Tal!"

But she didn't stop running, so I braced for impact—and shrieked when her head butted the entire side of my body and a giant, slobbery tongue covered me in drool.

"Tali," I shrieked.

Before I could process the pressure in my chest, it bubbled up as laughter and filled the whole dining room.

Fuck, it felt good to laugh. It felt good to have a friend, too. I was so alone, and even though I tried not to think about it last night, it was impossible to feel lonely this morning. I should have lived a long, happy life with my mates, but now I was here and they weren't.

But I had a friend. I had Tali.

"I'm so fucking happy to see you," I choked out, wrapping my arms as far as they'd go around her giant neck.[1]

She nudged me with her head, questions in her eyes even as she vibrated with happiness.

"You're probably wondering how I'm still alive, and how I'm as gorgeous, glamorous, and mind-bendingly beautiful as I ever was."

The flat look in her eye when she drew back assured me she was not.

"Let's sit down; I'll tell you everything," I said, turning to glare at the coffee pot. "But first, I need coffee. Please tell me you can—"

I jumped when a strange cube of metal began to steam, and slanted a look at Tali to see the red smoke on her fur fade. "Well, someone's learned a new trick."

And so had coffee. Why was it pouring out of a hole in a metal box? *Shit, I'm losing my coffee!* I scrambled to put a cup under the flow, and when it shut off, I added milk and I couldn't hold back a groan at how damn good it was.[2]

Holding my ambrosia protectively to my chest—and slightly mourning my quill tiara—I sank into a chair at one of the dining tables, and tried not to laugh at the sight of Tali shoving chairs aside so she could sit her giant, furry butt opposite me.

"It started when I was sent to hunt someone. Only it turned out my client was an abusive bastard, and my target was my mate."

"No," I argued when Tali jutted out her furry red chin and fixed me with a hard look.

I told her everything that happened since we last saw each other, finishing with my new hunter job. I knew that look on her face—*I'm going with you.*

"I'm doing this alone; I can hunt, Tali. I've been doing it for years."

The dry look she shot me said, *you've been dead a hundred years.*

"Yes, thank you, I know that."

She huffed through her nose. *I'm going with you, and nothing you can say will convince me otherwise.*

"Fine," I groaned, and drew out my winning card as I

sipped the last of my coffee.[3] "But you're asking Lucifer for permission."

And no way was the devil going to allow my friend to come with me on a secret mission because she was worried I'd get a little stabbed.

And yet ... the smug look she shot me made nerves tumble through my belly.

"Wait," I protested when she lumbered to her feet. "You can't just go ask Lucifer *now*."

She made a throaty sound that assured me she could.

"But he's Lucifer!"

She shrugged and uttered a groan. *He's my friend, too.*

"Wait, *what?* Get back here and tell me your life story too, Tali!"

I sped into the hallway after her, empty coffee cup in hand, but she was already bounding down the corridor with huge strides. I groaned a curse. Even with wings, there was no chance I'd catch up with her.

"Halwen Vakhara?" someone grunted, their voice low and gravelly.

I froze between one step and the next, apprehension crawling down my spine.

Anyone knowing my name when I'd been gone a century was not a good omen.

CHAPTER TWENTY-ONE

I turned slowly to face the bald, muscular man who spoke. Fuck, he was tall; I had to tip my head back to meet his scowling gaze.

"Yes?" I asked as calmly as possible. He gave off unfriendly bulldog vibes, and I didn't want to be bitten.

"General Callahan is looking for you," he replied, his scowling expression telling me he'd rather be anywhere but here, talking to me. "I'll take you to him."

I laughed, crossing my arms over my chest, and didn't take a single step. "Sure, I'm just going to follow a strange man I don't know to an undisclosed location."

He already turned to guide me down the hall, but he paused— and growled as he faced me again. "I'm Bernard, *your commander.* But you won't get your orders from me unless they're extremely sensitive, so Callahan can deal with you. Follow me."

"You have a lovely way with words," I replied, probably foolishly given he was a powerful commander. But telling Tali everything that happened had raked up all my pain again, and I wasn't in the best mood.

"You met my girl. Lili."

My mouth dropped.

"Holy shit, *you're* one of her men? You?" I winced. "Sorry, that was rude. It's just ... she's all sweetness and sunshine and you're—growly," I finished when he bared his teeth.

"Do you want to die?" he asked casually.

"Actually, I was gonna ask for tips. My mates are missing, but one of them is a bright, optimistic fucker, too."

Talking about Harvey made my heart hurt, but I refused to stop talking about my mates. If I did, it'd be like they didn't exist. "I'm a growly bastard like you; how do you put up with it?"

Bernard snorted, some hostility leaving him. "Pretend it's annoying when it's actually your favourite thing."

"Genius," I breathed, shaking my head in awe.[1] "So who am I hunting? I'm guessing that's why this Callahan's after me? I've got a job."

Bernard gave me a stern look that didn't have as much impact as it had a minute ago. "He'll brief you on your roles. But there's one thing I wanted to talk to you about."

"You? Want to talk? You don't strike me as the type."

He barked an abrupt laugh. Hell yes, I was making friends everywhere in this palace.

"On paper, your job is to hunt and retrieve alphas." He lowered his voice and checked we were alone in the corridor. "But we only need one alpha from each group to mine for information."

"Cute way of saying interrogate and torture," I quipped. When his huge shoulders stiffened, I added, "No, I mean it. It's cute; I'm going to use that. And don't worry, on the moral scale I'm far closer to black than white. I'm a hunter, thief, and assassin. It's not the first time I've been sent to kill someone."

"These aren't ordinary jobs," Bernard replied, his brow furrowed. "These are alphas."

"How many alphas are we talking?" I asked, and followed him down the hallway.

"This first job is seven."

"Seven?" I demanded, my voice shrill. The man had lost his mind.

Seven alphas against one angel-demon hybrid?

Fuck, those were depressing odds.

CHAPTER TWENTY-TWO

Kalador was a truly *beautiful* city, so sweet-smelling that it was like perfume on my senses, with blooming trees and delicate flowers dripping like diamonds from balconies—and children ran through the streets with tinkling laughter.[1]

At least, that's what Tali told me it was like fifty years ago.

Now, I sidestepped a bull demon with a beer gut, the man brandishing a cutlass as he charged after a teenager with a clearly-stolen bottle of ale in his hand and a grin on his face. Neither of them cared that they sloshed through a question-able brown puddle, splattering their worn shoes.

I jumped out of the path of the 'water' and slumped into the leaning wall of a grimy inn. Inside, people yelled and sang off-key. Honestly, it was nostalgic.

"I love cities like this," I sighed. I'd had so many amazing nights in places like Kalador, all of them fuzzy with both age and ale.

The look Tali shot my way said, *this is a town and you need your sanity tested.*

"I could do without the river," I added, leading Tali down a snicket to an even grimier pub. "That thing stinks."

Try having advanced panda senses. I can pick out the individual notes of piss, shit, and vomit.

I wrinkled my nose. "Delightful."

She chuffed a laugh through her nose.

Tali got a few looks as we jogged down the cobbled road and onto the riverside path where our targets were said to be staying. Callahan, my truly *charming* commander, received word of alphas staying at a halfway house called the Cock and Claws. I snorted, remembering his face as he told me the name.

Cock is the name of an ale, Tali said with an eye roll, bursting my amused bubble.

"I refuse to accept that," I replied, and spotted the three-storey brown structure down the road, its top floor hanging over the bottom two and black beams criss-crossing the stone walls. "Oh look, it's a brown cock. I have one of those."

Tali's expression flattened, her furry brow heavy over vivid eyes.

"He's called Harvey," I told her cheerfully, "and he's very talented with it. By *it* I mean his—"

Yes, thank you, Tali cut off with a deep sigh. *Got it. Dick puns galore.*

"You know me, Tal-Tal. I can't let a good dick pun go unspoken."

I wish you would.

"If wishes were horses, beggars would ride," I quipped, and leaned my shoulder into the heavy wooden door of the Cock and Balls.[2]

"Wait outside," I told Tali with a scratch under her chin. "I won't be long. That looks like a lovely alley, don't you think?"

She rolled her eyes again, and headed around the back of the pub. We never hunted together[3] but even after all these years, there was a deep bond between us and she must know what I had planned. Or she'd been on these kinds of jobs with other people. I pushed down the friend-jealousy that rose, and strode through another heavy door into a cramped little tavern that smelled of beer and sharp cleaning solution. Well, at least it was clean.

Sadly, the same couldn't be said for some of the patrons. But I'd worn shredded clothes and smelled like death for two whole days, so I wasn't about to judge.

I scoped the place out as I strode to the bar, dismissing three clusters of men before I found a group of demons with bulging muscles and massive shoulders sitting at the back, involved in a card game with a pile of money on the table. A flash of excitement went through me, fluttering my belly.

Oh, hell yes.

"Pint," I said to the grey-haired purple man behind the bar.

"Pint, *what?*" he barked back, barely lifting his head from the clean glasses he was organising into straight lines."

"Pint, pretty please," I said sweetly, and fluttered my lashes.

He flicked a look at me, and grabbed a glass, pulling a pint. Callahan had given me an allowance; I gladly handed over someone else's money and sipped the foam of my beer. Huh, not bad. At least it was somewhat cool.

"Thanks," I told the barman, who vaguely grunted in my direction and went back to straightening his glasses.

I made a beeline for the alphas in the back. There were only five of them, three men and two women, not seven alphas like I'd been sent to track,[4] but something told me a ruckus would bring the other two running out of the woodwork.

"Hi," I said shyly, letting my gaze linger on each of the alphas, cataloguing their appearances. I kept the reason why I was doing this in the forefront of my mind, holding onto my mates' faces as I batted my lashes at a muscular woman with rich brown skin and tight curls of hair. "Can I join you? I haven't played stress in years."

A green man with long tusks snorted but made no comment. Two others stayed silent, the two of them like reflections—both as pale as ice with short hair and the same face despite their difference in sex. But a slim, winged man assessed me with a critical eye, and the woman I'd batted my lashes at leaned back in her chair to give me an appreciative glance.

"No amateurs," the winged man grunted, scowling.

"Oh, don't be so glum, Ken," the black woman teased, giving me a sultry look and patting her knee.

Please let my mates never find out about this, I whispered to the gods and climbed into the woman's lap, setting my pint on the table. She was annoyingly comfy. Maybe I should browse for a female mate, round out my little family with some softness. Not that destiny took requests.

I'd done my research this afternoon, cramming all the recent history I could into my head, memorising the events of the war that only ended five months ago. Alpha demons made an alliance with angels—demons' natural enemy, of which species I was half—in order to bring Lucifer down. They wanted to end his wicked ways of keeping Hell peaceful, preventing mass murder, punishing rapists with eternal suffering, and providing a safe, generally clean place to live with actual *houses* instead of huts made of shit and mud. *How dare he!*

Alphas felt their rights had been breached by Lucifer keeping the peace; like spoiled children, they threw a tantrum. But their tantrum killed hundreds, and brought war on two sides to Hell. If it hadn't been for alphas, Heaven would never have gained an inch here, let alone destroyed so much.

There was also a whole thing with corrupt angels and evil gods, but I skimmed that section since it wasn't relevant. I knew enough to give the brawny people around the table a knowing smile and murmur, "I haven't seen any alphas in months. Where did you guys all go? I missed seeing your pretty muscles."

I played the role a little too well, squeezing the powerful bicep of the woman whose lap I sat on. She let out a pleased growl, sending a rush of warning down my spine.

This woman could rip you in two and eat your innards, my instincts screamed.

But she was an easy target, and alphas' main weakness was flattery. I took a drink of beer to bolster my courage.

The two pale twins laughed in unison at my question, low cruel sounds that made my blood run cold. They'd be harder to find a weakness in; everything about them screamed *apex predator* and *total psychopath.*

"Curious, aren't you?" the pale woman asked, tracking my every movement.

"Too curious," her male counterpart added, snapping his cards on the table.

The woman under me laughed so hard she rattled my whole body.

"She's not a spy; she's an alpha chaser." She ran her hand up my right wing, and I shuddered, primal terror shooting through me. I played it off as arousal, forcing out a soft gasp. "Aren't you, pretty thing?"

I swallowed and glanced aside, faking embarrassment. The twins laughed, believing the act.

Their game of cards was forgotten in the face of something far more interesting.

The big, green man leaned forward, parting his mouth in a grin around his tusks. "You need some real demons to show you a good time?"

I swallowed, and purposely licked my lips. Gave a nod in reply. If Kai found out about any of this, he'd go on a murderous rampage and then spend hours, maybe days, reminding me who I really belonged to. And don't even get me started on Em's possessiveness, or what Harvey would do to me.[5]

"I don't even know your names," I pointed out, casting a curious glance at the winged, dark-haired man who'd called me an amateur. "I'm Acacia."

"Pretty name for a pretty girl," the black woman purred, and stroked my wing again to elicit another shudder. My stomach cramped, instinct warning me to fight, that I was vulnerable. "I'm Micola."

"Ronald," the green guy said, eyeing me with unveiled hunger.[6]

"Ken," the winged man muttered, but despite his gruffness, his eyes kept returning to me, trailing my body. If he wondered why a shy, curious girl like me was decked out in leather, he showed no sign of it.

"Nice to meet you," I said, forcing myself to lean back into Micola and relax like I wanted to be here. I glanced at them through heavy-lidded eyes. Sex eyes. Ugh.

"Bria," the pale woman introduced herself, baring rows of thin teeth. Fuck, those were sharp-looking teeth.

"Bevan," her brother murmured, looking at me less like he was thinking of fucking me than dissecting me.[7]

Micola petted my wing, close to where it connected with my back under my coat, and I shuddered hard.

"Shall we skip the *getting to know you*s and get straight to the part we all want?" she asked, her voice low and husky.

I swallowed, flicked a shy glance at the rest of the alphas, running quick calculations of how I'd take them all out. I had three small knives, concealed so they wouldn't be noticed, and I had my magic. I could take control of the alphas' blood and either slow it so they passed out, or quicken it so they exploded; I'd be fine. Why was I so nervous?

"Gods yes," I breathed, turning my head to give Micola a coy look. "Are you—sure you want me?"

"Oh, pretty thing," she purred, stroking her hand up my back. "The things I want to do to you will make your toes curl."

Promises, promises. Shame I was here to kill her; if I'd been single, I might have explored those promises. The rest of the bastards didn't interest me, but I didn't let that show as I hopped off Micola's lap and secretly ran through how I'd kill them in my head.

"Our rooms are upstairs," she told me, resting a proprietary hand on my back. I calmed myself by picturing how Malakai would react to her hands on me. First, he'd cut her hand off, then he'd unleash his snakes on her until she screamed and begged for mercy. He wouldn't give it, obviously, but that wouldn't stop her begging.

My heartbeat calmed, and I kept my shy, sensual persona in place as Micola led me away from my drink and towards a tight staircase at the back. *Farewell, beloved pint. May we meet again.*

Ken and Ronald—exceptional names—followed, while the twins gathered up the money from the table. I didn't miss that they pocketed it, despite not winning the game.

"Here, pretty thing," Micola said when we reached the top, pushing open a door on a surprisingly nice little room. Two single beds were pushed against opposite walls with a small window between them and matching bed-stands. The floor was clean, and the place smelled fresh, not sour with sweat. This was nicer than most places I'd stayed while hunting as a merc.

It was a shame to paint it with blood.

The second the door closed behind us, I slipped the knife from the slitted pocket in my leather trousers and spun, driving it into Ken's thick neck. Throwing more weight behind it, I dragged the blade until his throat split and the light left his eyes.

"What the fuck?" Micola exploded, a shock of betrayal on her face for a moment before she recovered.

I was already moving to counter Ronald, who threw himself at me with a roar, launching over his dead friend's body and raising massive green hands. Maybe to throw me back, maybe to break my face. The only problem with his plan was I'd placed myself in front of the little window, so when he came barrelling at me, I simply stepped aside and his momentum carried him through the glass.

It shattered on impact. He fell to the ground with a scream.

There you go, Tali. Don't say I never give you anything.

I didn't wait for the thud of collision below before I spun to deal with Micola and the twins.

Wait. Shit, where did they go?

"You deceitful bitch," Micola spat from the doorway. Well there *she* was, but where were Bria and Bevan?

"It's nothing personal, just a job," I said with a shrug, taking a step after her as she moved into the hall.

I slammed into a solid wall, rebounding back with a gasp. Pain slit my stomach, and I stared in surprise at the sudden stab wound on my stomach, blood soaking through my shirt.

"You deserve everything you get," Micola called from the corridor. "Kill her."

Shit. I wasn't alone in the room, even if it looked empty.

When another arc of pain slashed across my back, *just* missing my wing, I realised the psycho twins were still here. I just couldn't see them.

The door swung shut; the lock snapped into place with a clang. Trapping me in a room with two invisible threats with orders to kill me. And a dead body.

CHAPTER TWENTY-THREE

*W*hen locked in a room with two invisible people dead set on murdering you, my first tip is to run for the smashed window. *Ideally,* clear the path between you and the window, but if the assailants are invisible you might end up like me.

"Son of a five-titted bitch!" I swore, spinning blindly away and slamming my palm over another slash on my stomach. Blood soaked down my side, staining my clothes, but they were shallow cuts designed to inflict pain, not slow me down. The twins were definitely psychopaths.

"Come out, come out, psychos," I sang, turning, trying to sense a disturbance in the air at the same time I grasped my magic.

I expected to feel the heat and rush of blood in two bodies but instead I felt … nothing. Not like when I was attacked by an invincible woman in my flat; I didn't hit a block, there was just nothing there.

The core where my magic normally sat was empty.

I was powerless.

Air puffed out of me in a shallow gasp, my chest tightening. How was I supposed to win a fight against two invisible attackers with no magic?

Don't, I reminded myself.

I spun to the window, slashing the space in front of myself as I moved, slamming my wings down to propel myself faster. Paranoia made my skin tingle as I waited for another blow.

A low laugh warned me of another blow. I dropped to the floor with a grunt, flattening myself to the bare floorboards. Air shifted above me, and I used it to place the twin who'd tried to stab me again. Rolling onto my back, wings pinned uncomfortably, I slammed my booted feet into a solid body. Ha! The air flickered, Bevan's body visible for a moment. I adjusted my angle and slammed my heavy soles into his dick, dropping him to the floor with a screech. Fun.

Bria could have been anywhere, hidden by her magic, watching me. The awareness made my breathing short as I shot to my feet and dove for the window.

My skin prickled, little hairs standing on end. I made it two feet, then four.

I slashed my knife in front of me, clearing my path. Five feet.

Bria didn't laugh like Bevan had. She hooked her arm around my neck with no warning, and I screamed in surprise and frustration as she pressed mercilessly on my windpipe.

"Dick," I choked out with my last remaining air.[1]

She had my throat pinned, but there was nothing to stop me driving my knife down into her thigh, so I did, over and over. The muffled scream she let out was satisfying, even if it was right by my ear and drowned my hearing in sharp ringing.

Her grip weakened. *Promising.* I slashed up in an awkward motion that strained my muscles, but I managed to carve my dagger through her forearm. I earned a splash of blood on my chin and a howl of rage in my ear.

I gritted my teeth and tore her forearm from my neck while she was distracted. The floorboards creaked as I twisted unsteadily on my feet, jamming my dagger into where I guessed her chest was. The blade met bone first, but I angled it upward and thrust it under her ribs and right into her heart.

Thank fuck for that. My head spun a little, and I was bleeding from two shallow wounds. The last thing I needed was a long, gruesome fight.

Bria sagged, suddenly visible, and crashed to the bare floorboards with a glassy look in her eye.

I wrinkled my nose and wiped the blood off my face, staring at her body.

Killing stopped leaving a stain on my soul years ago; it was a necessary thing when you were a young woman with no family or home, and survival was essential. The first kill haunted me, my second brought me nightmares, but by my twelfth I got used to the shaky rush of adrenaline and horror.

This was my job; it would allow me to find my mates. I did what I needed to do, and if I enjoyed the fight and the thrill, that was just a nice bonus.

I meant what I told Bernard; on a morally grey scale I was far closer to black. I didn't have a tragic backstory, didn't have murdered parents or a brutalised sibling to drive me to darkness. When my dad died when I was seventeen, I found my way to the streets and met darkness the usual way: in people. Spend enough time in the shadows and the shadows start to take form inside you.

A whole swarm of them lived in my soul now; sometimes I swore I felt them brushing against me in a cold, pained wave.[2] I sidestepped the pool of blood forming under Bria's body and swung my leg over the windowsill, casting a glance down at the alleyway.

Oh, lovely, there was a huge pile of trash at the end of the little path, perfuming the air with rotting food and shit. We were lucky Lucifer had introduced toilets; otherwise the streets would be full of *actual* shit like they used to be. Another reason the alphas hated him. He brought change and progress and *cleanliness.* The horror!

Hovering on the ledge of the window, and careful to avoid the jagged edges of broken glass, I peered down and saw the splayed form of Ronald, his green skin sickly and a pool of blood under him. Aww, his blood pool matched Bria's. Something told me Bevan would be so pissed off about that.

Wait, where *was* Bevan? I only kneed him in the dick; he shouldn't be dea—

Rough hands slammed into my back, propelling me off the window frame and into a fall so sudden I screamed.

Well, that answered the Bevan question.

Tali roared in panic from the alley below. I didn't dare look down to see if she was okay or under attack herself. I wasn't scared of heights[3] but falling was still terrifying.

Screaming at the top of my lungs, I snapped my wings out as much as I could in the cramped alleyway. I barely had enough space to flutter them enough to slow my fall, but in positive news I landed on the cobbles on my feet and not my face.

Halwen! Tali rumbled, bounding down the alley towards me. If she'd been anyone else, the sight would have been petrifying. A massive, six-foot-tall red panda with horns and smoking skin raced towards me with her jaw parted and sharp teeth showing. But I read the distress in her fast pants, and her green eyes overflowed with worry.

"I'm fine," I said breathlessly. "Someone thought it was a good idea to *throw a winged woman out of a window!*"

I yelled the last bit at the window and hoped Bevan heard.

Tali butted her head against me, dragging her raspy tongue over the slashes on my stomach.

Movement drew my eye to a shadow leaning out the window, checking if I was dead.

"Next time, pick someone who can't fly, you stupid fucker!" I yelled at Bevan, which was probably not smart but it was incredibly cathartic.

"I'm fine," I insisted again when Tali made a low, trilling rumble. I patted her big head and cracked a grin. "At least I still have my pretty face."

She huffed. *When did you get so confident? And sarcastic?*

"What can I say? I've made some improvements over the years. Did any alphas come out this way?"

She shook her head.

"Great. That means there are still four left. We need to take out three and capture one. Bernard said you'd know how to call him to come and collect them."

Tali bobbed her head, about to convey something with her big eyes when her attention shot behind me. She growled so low my ribcage shook.

I spun, lifting my hand and mildly surprised to see I still held my dagger. Nice. I hated losing my toys. I reached for my magic on instinct, my stomach sinking when it slipped away like a ghost instead of responding to me.

Fuck, what happened to my power? Had death done this? Or were one of the curses inked on my body to blame?

Micola stormed down the alleyway, her brown face twisted with rage. Fair enough, I'd seduced her and then killed her friends; I'd be pretty pissed off, too. She was flanked by two alphas I hadn't met, one in russet hellhound form with glowing yellow eyes, snarling jaws, and a body almost as big as Tali's. The other was horrifying, a type of demon I'd never seen before. They were seven-feet-tall, thinner than was natural, and completely naked, with pale, translucent skin on display for all to see. Oh, and they didn't have a face.[4]

I shot Tali a quick look. *Remember we need one alive.*

She dipped her head and charged at the three alphas. Nerves twisted me up at the sight of my only living friend charging at three powerful, murderous alphas. But I reminded myself she was giant, had sharp teeth, and her claws could probably gut them in a single swipe.

I futilely grabbed for my magic, but at least I drew another, longer knife at the same time. I was still totally powerless, and getting more frustrated about it with every second. I'd become too reliant on my magic over the past few years[5] when dealing with Locke's hunter and mercenaries. If I had my magic, I could have exploded all of these alphas right here and now.

Minus one for Bernard, obviously.

Instead of handling it quickly, I was forced to race after Tali and jump into the fray. When she dove for the slender, pale alpha with her maw open, I went for the hellhound.

It's not a real dog, I reminded myself as I arced my knife at its body. *It's a man in disguise.*

I was glad when the hound snarled and dove aside, evading the sharp edge of my blade. Less glad when he swiped out with his claws and raked a burning, fiery path across my thigh.

"Alright, puppy, *that's it!*" I snapped, kicking out with my heavy boots and landing a footprint on his ribs, knocking the hound back a few paces. Up close, he smelled of brimstone and weeds. His yellow eyes narrowed as he assessed me for weaknesses.[6]

Tali growled in sudden pain, but when the hellhound launched himself at me, I couldn't spare even a second to check on my friend. Shit. I had no choice but to drop my weapons when the hound collided with me hard and sent me to the ground.[7]

Cold bled through the cobblestones and into my body as the hound snapped his sharp jaws at my face, slobber dripping from his sharp teeth. A drop landed on my cheek. I wrinkled my nose at the feeling of cold fluid dripping down my face.

"Gross," I gasped as I fought to keep those jaws as far from my face as possible. I got the sense the hound wanted to rip my head off with his massive fangs.

Why couldn't I have got a nice, normal job and saved up for weapons the safe way?

Because you're not nice, normal, or safe, my inner voice responded. She had a point.

Heat from the hellhound's panting breaths fanned across my face, and I gritted my teeth, straining to keep his snarling head away from my throat. A knee rammed into his ribs did nothing to dislodge him. My arms ached, struggling to hold back his full weight. Ah, fuck. I'd have to do something stupid and desperate, like letting go so I could snatch up a knife. But the chances of me burying steel in his skull before he ripped my head off was pathetically slim.

My arms buckled. A breath expelled from my lungs in a panicked rush. *Now or never.*

I loosened my grip, but the hellhound was torn away from me before I could risk my neck to find my knives.

Tali, I thought, my heart soaring. Instead, my stomach plummeted when I watched *Bevan* tear the hellhound off me. He grabbed one side of the hound's jaws in each hand and wrenched them apart until there was a sickening crack and the light left his yellow eyes.

"You just ... killed your own friend," I breathed, cold drenching my whole body as I scrambled to my feet, frantically scanning the ground for my knives.

They were behind him. Of course they were.

"You killed my sister," Bevan replied in a glacial, utterly dead voice.

"Fair point. No need to take it out on your frien—"

I cut off with a shriek when Bevan came at me with his

pale hands outstretched, claws as long as my fingers extended to slice me to ribbons. Well, I knew what cut me earlier. Not knives after all.

He didn't turn invisible. No, he wanted me to see him as he killed me. I knew that rage, and guilt twinged in my chest. I'd have tried to kill me in his position, too. But I had a job to do, and I didn't know how else to find Em, Kai, and Harvey.

"I'm going to bleed you dry, and make you scream during every second of it," he said in a cold, flat voice that sent shivers down my spine.

We circled each other, me keeping a distant eye on the silver sheen of my knives on the ground, Bevan's pale eyes fixed on me like he could kill me with a single stare.

"While we're chatting," I said airily, like I wasn't scared shitless, "I'd like to know where you came from. Where are the remaining alphas? I know you're still planning Lucifer's death."

"You don't know anything," Bevan replied emptily and threw himself at me.

I had a split-second choice between fleeing down the empty end of the alley and isolating myself, or racing towards the strange, faceless man and Micola—and Tali. I had to hope my friend would be enough backup, and Micola didn't get her hands on me. I knew she'd be far worse than Bevan.

"Tali, I've got a slight issue," I called, and bolted in her direction. My heart slammed into my ribs in a fast rhythm as Bevan's wicked fingernails sliced my back. He missed causing serious damage, though. I pumped my legs, quickly assessing the situation.

The faceless man was dead on the ground, missing an arm and half his shoulder. Had Tali ... *eaten* him?[8]

Micola swiped at Tali with a rusty pole she got from gods knew where. My heart plummeted when my friend was only able to avoid the pole enough to lessen the damage, not escape the blow.

"Hey!" I shouted, because one murderous maniac wasn't enough, apparently I needed two. "Leave my friend alone, you bitch."

Micola turned to face me slowly enough that my blood ran cold, and all the hairs rose on the back of my neck when her attention snagged on something behind me. It gave me a split second warning, enough to throw myself to the right, thumping into the wall in time to watch Bevan thrust his clawed hands through the air.

He'd have ripped out my spine. *Fuck, fuck, fuck.*

Tali snarled in my direction. *Be careful, you stupid cow.*

"Be careful yourself," I snapped back, shoving off the wall and inhaling sharply when Bevan threw himself at me too fast for me to evade him.

With the wall at my back, Tali grappling with Micola on my left, and Bevan throwing himself at my right, there was nowhere to go. No escape.

I tried to duck, but Bevan's claws slammed into the brick on either side of my shoulders, pinning me. A slow grin twisted his sharp face. His prey was caught. He knew I was dead.

I tried the old faithful and kneed him in the balls, but he was ready for me now and evaded my knee. *Fuck a duck, I'm dead.*

"You'll die slowly for what you did to my sister," he swore, mania in his sharp eyes.

"That makes no sense," I replied, because I was scared and physically *could not* shut up. "I killed her quickly. It should be tit for tat."

His eyes drifted to my chest. He heaved his right hand from the wall, claws loosening mortar. *Not that tit, not that tit!*

Panic stole my breath. I threw up my hands, sacrificing my hands to protect my chest, my heart drumming my ribs.

Pain didn't slash across my palms, and a surprised breath froze in my lungs when Bevan tore his other hand from the wall and stumbled away from me. When I lowered my hands enough to see him, he was even paler than before, his black eyes wide and mouth parted as he stared at me. No, at my arms, where the ink on my forearm *glowed.*

The tattoo was black, but the power that glowed from it was eldritch and red. *What the fuck?*

"Cursed One," he gasped, stumbling back, horror shortening his breaths.

I was lost, reeling, baffled when in the next moment he pissed himself, a dark stain bleeding through his trousers. He couldn't take his eyes off me.

Cursed One. Great, now I had a title? I wanted to be a princess or a lady, not a *cursed one.* Life was so unfair.

At least Bevan wasn't attacking me now. I took advantage of it and demanded, "Where are the other alphas?"

I expected resistance and cold, icy rage. Instead he blurted, "A border town that was abandoned in the war. It's near the Bend of Boraven in the river."

"Why there?" I pressed, wondering if he'd snap out of this fear if I went for one of my knives. I didn't risk it. I'd come here for information and to kill alphas, and I wasn't going to pass up this chance.

"There's a collector, Lord Wynvail. He lures us there and traps us with magic and binding vows."

Well, shit. All the people I just killed might have been acting against their will. Murder didn't leave a sour taste in my mouth, but this did. Regret burned in my belly and tasted like guilt.

"Collector," I echoed, watching the pale alpha for any signs of deceit. He looked terrified; he shook so hard his claws rattled, his eyes glued to my curse mark. "What is he collecting them for?"

Bevan's throat bobbed. "I'm not supposed to say." But he must have been more scared of me than this Lord Wynvail because he whispered, "I don't know for sure, but I've heard whispers he's collecting us for someone else. Someone more powerful, who gave him the magic to bind us."

Fuck. That was just what I needed—a Lord and someone even *more* powerful. Queen Lili's gang of boyfriends would want to know all about this.

"Is he collecting them to kill Lucifer?" I pressed, casting a quick look Tali's way when there was a sudden movement. She swiped a big, furry paw through the air and knocked the pole from Micola's hand, snapping her jaws around the woman's hand in the next moment and crunching down. Gross. She was definitely eating them.

"No," Bevan gasped, breathless and shaking, his eyes never leaving me even as Tali tucked into her four course meal.[9] "I'm loyal to Lucifer. I swear!"

"And your Lord? Is he loyal?"

"I don't know," Bevan breathed. "Please spare me, Cursed One."

I glanced around the alley. Everyone else was dead.

"It's your lucky day, Bevan, I'm feeling merciful. You can live."

When Bevan collapsed to his knees and uttered endless thanks, I decided to leave out the part about Bernard torturing him.

CHAPTER TWENTY-FOUR

$\mathcal{I}$ was exhausted when we got back to the palace, and my thighs ached like crazy from my bumpy ride home.[1] Cuts still stung across my body, gradually healing, and all I wanted was a hot bath to ease the aches. The last thing I wanted was Renna storming down the pale gold hallway, barking out my name.

"Not now," I groaned, my shoulders slumped and feet dragging on the floor.

"You'll want to come with me," she replied in a steely tone, her lilac face giving nothing away.

Did I have another job? Had she decided I was too annoying and she was going to murder me? Was she leading me to a thank you banquet as a reward for catching the alphas? Or rather, catching *one* while the others fought us and 'ran off.'[2]

"Fine," I groaned, salivating at the thought of a banquet. If it *wasn't* a banquet, I might kill this woman.

Renna seized my arm before I could second guess my decision, and hauled me bodily down the hall. Her legs were longer than mine; she practically dragged me across the castle while my boots skidded. Anyone who saw us must've had a right laugh.

"Damn woman, what were you in your past life? A debt collector?"

Renna snorted, not slowing her pace. "If I let go, you might face-plant the floor. You look awful."

"Please tell me you're leading me to a bed," I groaned, using all my focus to keep my feet under me, the palace passing in a blur.

Renna gave me an arch glance, her black eyebrows raised. "You're not my type. And I'm married."

I gave her the middle finger. I'd already fake-flirted with a woman today; I didn't have the energy left to do it again.

But I still had enough self respect to protest, "I'm everyone's type."

Her snort was dismissive. "Sure, sweetheart."

If I had any strength in my arms, I'd have elbowed her in the ribs. Instead they flop-shimmied at my sides, and I gave up after two attempts.

"Here," she said, pushing open a heavy gold door that flickered with black magic in response to her touch. Nice shields. Very nice.

Inside were three more doors, each sealed.

I groaned. "This is overkill."

"You won't think that when you see what's inside," she replied knowingly, digging out a key to unlock the fourth door and swinging it open on—

Heaven. Pure, steel heaven.

I let out a tiny whimper. "It's beautiful."

Renna shot me a look that questioned my judgement, and drawled, "It's an armoury."

"I want it," I said dreamily.

"Well, you can't have it," she shot down instantly, flicking sharp black hair out of her face as she led me to a specific area of the armoury.

Swords of all shapes and sizes hung from the walls, yet more rested in velvet-inlaid boxes on tables. I wanted everything. With this, I'd be strong enough to obliterate Cassander Locke. These weren't piddly little knives like I'd taken on the last job with me; these were *real* weapons. Even without magic, I could hold my own with these, and I wouldn't have to rely on my cursed marks scaring the shit out of my assailant next time.

They'd stopped glowing now, and looked like ordinary tattoos, but it was ingrained in my memory. Tali had been just as baffled to see them glow. Neither of us had a clue what had happened.

"Here," Renna grunted and held a closed wooden box out to me. My heart raced. It was big enough to contain a short sword. "I wanted to make sure I could find it before I said anything, in case the box had been lost during the destruction and rebuild."

The builders had done such a good job, I kept forgetting the whole city had been levelled a year ago.

"If you were trying to bag yourself another wife," I breathed, accepting the mahogany box, "this is definitely the way to do it."

Renna laughed coarsely, shaking her dark head. "Just open it."

I used my weak arms to lift the lid on the box, not prepared, nowhere remotely *near* prepared, for the contents. When I saw the two long, wavy daggers inside, the inscription still carved on the fuller of the blade, I burst into horrible, gut-wrenching tears.

My volcanic blades. My anniversary gift from Kai. I hadn't lost them.

"I love you," I choked out to Renna, cradling the wooden

box to my chest as tears veiled my vision. "We're friends forever now."

"Calm down." She looked disturbed at the thought.

But she'd given me a priceless treasure, and I would never forget it or stop being grateful.

I sniffled, and said, "You're stuck with me. Just accept it."

"Gods save me," she groaned.

CHAPTER TWENTY-FIVE

I tossed and turned in bed, my daggers clutched to my chest. I'd never let them out of my sight again. I don't know how long it took me to fall asleep, but the day's events played through my head over and over, keeping me restless. I kept returning to the name Bevan had called me— Cursed One. It was a strange name even if he'd seen the curse mark on my arm. Cursed One suggested a title, a reputation.

How the fuck did I have a reputation when I'd been dead for a hundred years?

I'd either been mistaken for someone else, *or* someone knew I'd been reborn and told assholes like Bevan about it.

I needed to go to that Bend of Boraven and find out who else knew about this title. Someone might know what curses I actually had, and might know how to break them.

There was another possibility, but I wasn't brave enough to admit that was why I wanted to go to the alphas' town. Someone remembered me, and named the Forest of Halwen after me. What if that same someone created this Cursed One reputation so people would be too afraid of me to hurt me?

"You're thinking too hard, my rose," a soft voice murmured, a warm breath fanning across my cheek.

My heart jolted, tripping into my ribs, and I whipped my head back to stare—at Malakai, his tall body stretched out on the bed beside me, *here.*

My eyes burned, but I didn't take my eyes off him for a moment. He looked so damn good, with his dark red hair mussed by the pillow and his sharp, elegant face softened by sleep. Even the texts that wound around his body scrolled sluggishly, lulled to sleep too. He wore no shirt, every bit of flesh and ink on his toned body exposed, and my heart skipped.

My Malakai, my night, *here.*

"I'm dreaming," I breathed, and was surprised to find my voice scratchy with sleep.

Warm fingers brushed my cheek and traced the shape of my face. "Who cares if we're asleep or awake? I'm back where I belong."

Before I could reply, he rolled closer and stole my breath in a kiss. It wasn't a forceful or demanding kiss, but the passion in it made me weak. It had been so damned long since we'd been together. It didn't feel like a hundred years, but my body had experienced every minute of distance between us, and it reacted with a fierce need that made me gasp against his lips.

A hundred years—that's how long it had been since we last kissed, in the middle of the road in a town on the edge of Iarlon.

When his hot mouth dragged down my jaw to my throat, his forked tongue flicking over my skin, I groaned.

"Renna kept my knives. She gave them back to me. I didn't lose them, Kai."

"Knives," he huffed against my skin, raising goosebumps.

"Knives don't matter. *You* matter. Us being here, together, matters."

"They matter to me," I replied defensively, trailing my fingers through his long hair to grab a fistful of the wine-red strands. "You spent a lot of time, thought, and money getting them made for me."

"I told you I would get you more," he murmured, scraping his teeth down my throat and making my body flash hot.

"And did you?" I'd been gone a hundred years, but how long had Kai been?

"I ... don't know," he replied, pausing between kisses. "I only remember my dreams."

"Dreams?" I pushed on his shoulders, getting him to lean back so I could see his face, beautiful and deadly and sharp. "What dreams?"

"Like this one," he said, peering up at me with ruby eyes full of softness. "But you're not normally so ... here."

I blinked, processing that. "How long have you been dreaming of me, Kai?"

He shrugged, climbing up my body to kiss my cheek. "As long as I can remember."

"A year?"

He shook his head with a wry laugh. "Far, far longer."

My stomach dropped, a lump closing off my throat. Fuck. I reached for him, wrapping him up in my arms. "I think you were brought back before me. *Long* before me."

"Brought back?"

"We died, Kai. Cassander Locke killed us all. I dug myself out of a shallow grave four days ago, but I don't know where you guys are."

"Here," he said, pulling back a few inches to meet my gaze, something sad and longing in his expression. "We're right here, always waiting for you."

Fuck. My throat swelled with a bigger knot, my bottom lip suddenly weak.

We're right here, always waiting for you.

Fuck. *Fuck.*

"Sometimes we're together, sometimes I'm alone. Sometimes you're here, but never like this. I can feel the texture of your skin now; I can taste you when we kiss."

As if to reassure himself of that fact, he surged down over me and claimed my mouth in a rough, demanding kiss, forcing a gasp so he could taste me. A groan filled his throat as his forked tongue stroked mine, vibrating through his chest into my body, and he pressed his fingers into the softness of my thigh, curving my leg around his waist.

"I can call them sometimes," he said against my lips, pressing his body down into mine and devouring the expression on my face with hungry eyes. "I should call them now, but I want to be selfish and keep you to myself. When I wake up ... all of this is gone, I think. It only exists here, in my dreams."

I licked my bottom lip, my lower belly tightening with hunger at the look on his pale face. "Call them after."

"Yess," he hissed, almost snakelike as he returned to my lips with a fierceness that made my stomach jump. The air tingled with his power, as if he was right on the edge of control, and I arched up into him in response, giving up my own control.

"I missed you so fucking much," I groaned into his mouth, a soft moan escaping when he sucked my bottom lip, grazing with his teeth, a constant edge of danger and pain. "I love you."

Kai shuddered, a catch in his breath, and he kissed me so hard my head spun and I forgot how to breathe. Need pounded hot and fast through my pussy, and I rolled my hips up into his, the hardness there only encouraging my feverish desire.

Nights and mornings like this flashed through my head,

sometimes in bed, sometimes on the sofa or the kitchen table or against a wall down a quiet alley, too needy and desperate to wait until we got home. Sometimes we were alone, sometimes my other mates watched, sometimes they were all involved. Every time, Kai was almost feral with need, his control over my body and pleasure was both obsessive and ruthless, and I came so hard I saw stars.

"Who do you belong to?" he asked, panting as his fingers climbed my thigh, slipping under the soft shirt I slept in and brushing the sensitive seam between hip and leg.

I pulsed with hot need, my hips unable to stay still, bucking with a pointed suggestion to Kai's warm, teasing fingers. "You."

"Fuck yes, you do," he groaned, his red eyes almost black with desire as he drew back and slid down my body. He pushed my shirt up so he could kiss my belly, then my ribs, and then fasten his hot mouth around a nipple, teasing with his tongue.

I threw my hand over my mouth and bit my palm, my body so neglected it was oversensitive. Or maybe it was just the dream heightening everything. This was both real and not. He was here, but somewhere else too. He could have been anywhere, could have been on Earth or Heaven, wasting away in the too-pure atmosphere.

He caught my nipple between his teeth and pulled until an electric sensation shot straight to my clit, making it throb wildly. I breathed shakily when he released my nipple and gave the same treatment to my other breast before asking, "And who do I belong to?"

"Me," I hissed, twisting my fingers in his hair as he kissed, licked, and bit his way down my body. My nipples throbbed, wanting him back. "You're fucking mine."

"Always, my rose," Kai groaned against my stomach, his breathing a wrecked mix of panting and gasps. Cold rushed into the places his kisses left empty, but he always found a new bit of skin to lavish with attention. My whole body tingled and buzzed. "I'm yours for life, death, and whatever else there is."

"My night," I promised, biting back a groan when he widened my thighs and sank lower over me.

"Fuck, you smell like I remember. I can taste your pussy on the air, too. This is real."

"It's real." I softened my grip on his hair, stroking strands back from his face, brushing gentle touches over the ridges of his sensitive horns.

I gasped when his hands slid under me and wrenched me possessively closer, adjusting the angle of my hips so he could stare at me. A growl built in his throat.

"Beautiful. Just as beautiful as I remember."[1]

I shuddered at the soft, careful touches he drifted around my pussy, his eyes rapt on me as I throbbed, dripping wetness.

"Mine," he snarled, and darted forward to lick up the drop, his forked tongue stroking from my ass all the way to my clit, both ends wrapping around it. "This pussy is mine."

His magic crackled through the air, invisible but so damn powerful, and I jumped at the tentative brush of something velvety and soft over my calf. For a delirious moment I thought it was his power touching me, but when it stroked higher, I laughed in surprise.

"Holy shit, I forgot you had a tail."

He grunted against my pussy, his tongue making rigid circles around my clit, teasing, heightening my need so I dripped for him and his greedy mouth. He sucked up every drop with a satisfied rumble.

"It's going to get you nice and ready for me," he said in a guttural voice, his tail gripping my leg when I rubbed my thumb over the grooves in his right horn—the more sensitive one.

"I'm ready *now*."

Kai's ruby stare flicked up to me with enough warning to fill my belly with butterflies. "I decide when you're ready."

"Yes, my night," I groaned, and watched satisfaction flare in his eyes.

"Beautiful," he murmured again, but stared at my face, not my pussy, this time. The compliment hit deep and bloomed with warmth, comforting a broken place inside me.

His tail grazed my upper thigh, and I tightened in anticipation, my blood boiling with a need that was so familiar to me but strangely new too. My mind knew it was only days since I'd been with Kai, but my body insisted differently.

When Kai swirled his tongue around my clit and his tail brushed a soft stroke over my throbbing entrance, I twisted my head and sank my teeth into my shoulder, needing something to ground me.

"Does that feel good, my rose?" Kai asked with a casual flick to my clit.

I could only whine in response as his tail thrust into me, not as thick as his cock but certainly big enough to stretch me. I wrapped my fingers around his horn and gripped until the grooves bit into my palm. Kai snarled, teeth bared.

When his tail glided deeper, overwhelming my senses with the sudden fullness, my other hand fluttered, desperately searching, needing a tether while my body was overwrought with sensation. Kai's fingers entwined with mine, squeezing tight, the gesture sweet. But he smirked and drove his tail deeper, wrenching a tight, whining sound from me when it curled back on itself inside me, the head now twice as fat.

"Too much?" he asked, and kissed my clit.

"Yes," I cried.

"Good," he snarled, and drew his tail out a few inches, fucking me with it until my whole body shuddered. I was so overwhelmed with pleasure and fullness, I didn't know *what* I felt. "I want to consume every one of your senses. I want to own every single part of you. When I'm finished, there'll be no part of you that won't be aching for me, throbbing, begging for more."

I gripped his hand so tightly it must have hurt, wet sounds filling the room—our old room? I couldn't tell—as his tail drove its bulbous end into me, gathering speed until my body twitched with every thrust.

"I missed you so much," Kai said tightly, moving his tail faster until I struggled to speak, to find meaning for the words he uttered. "I missed your voice and your laugh and the feel of your hand in mine. I missed the way your cunt grips my tail so perfectly, and the way you throb around me, desperate for more but too afraid to admit it."

I shook my head fast. No more. Too much.

"Oh, I should *stop?*" he asked, and uncurled his tail inside me, gliding out quickly.

The unbearable sensation slipped away, but I cried out. No, I—I needed it back. It was too big and too much, but I *needed* it.

"Malakai," I pleaded, my eyelids heavy over my eyes as I gave him a desperate look.

"Hmm?" He smirked and ducked his head, tracing a maddening circle around my clit with his tongue, making my throb harder, so swollen it ached.

"Please. Give me your tail again."

"I thought it was too much," he replied, flicking an arched, amused glance at me as he pressed a feather-soft kiss to my clit. A loud cry tore from my lips, the touch making my need worse and offering no relief.

"Kai," I snarled, the sound a pure command this time.

"Yes, my rose?" he asked casually, his tail grazing my inner thigh, taunting me with my own arousal slicking the velvety skin.

Need pounded through me like a drum. I wanted his tail to overwhelm me with sensation again. My pussy was achy and so damn wet I felt it drip out of me.

"You're lucky I love you," I told him, the decree half a threat. "Give me your tail or give me your cock. Please, I'm empty." I gave him a sulky look, sure I was pouting. "A *good* mate would fuck me sensel—"

I didn't finish the question. His tail drove inside me, stroking every taut, sensitive spot until I was sighing in relief.

"You're going to come for me," Kai said in a hard voice. scraping his teeth over my thigh. "And you're going to scream my name. *Then,* I'll give you my cock."

I nodded fast, heat rushing to my face as his tail broadened at the tip and stretched me until the ache was pleasant, fulfilling instead of frantic. When he withdrew and slammed back inside me, setting a punishing pace, my eyes rolled back and my legs shook.

He fastened his mouth to my clit in slow, sucking pulses, and pleasure blasted through me like an explosion, my mouth hanging open on a cry. I forgot to scream his name, forgot what his name even was as he pounded pleasure through me, hitting the spot he knew would undo me.

Stars burst around me, my eyes rolled all the way back, and I trembled as wave after wave of pleasure hit me, unmade me, and left my soul in tatters.

I barely felt when his tail uncurled and withdrew, but my body hummed with every soft, loving kiss Malakai placed on my thighs, my stomach, my breasts, and finally my lips.

"You are my life," he breathed against my lips, his voice reverent.

I blinked my eyes into focus, a smile curving my mouth at the awed look on his handsome face. I lifted my fingers to trace the sharp lines of his cheekbones, the curved edges of his eyes, all the way up to his horns. His hips jerked where they rested between mine, somehow naked when I knew he'd been wearing loose sleep pants before.

"You'll always be my night and light," I breathed, reciting the words he said to me every year on our anniversary, the words etched down the centre of my swords.

His whole face softened, red eyes wide, blinking fast. "You'll always be my rose and life," he finished, his voice thick.

I tugged him to me, kissing him slowly, letting the emotion bursting from my chest soar through the kiss, hoping he could feel it in my soul even in the dream. We were still unnervingly distant in the bond, souls still in tatters. Maybe it'd be that way until we found our way to each other outside these dreams, too.

"Haley," he sighed against my lips, a soft expulsion of air that spoke of relief and weakness.

"I'm here. Really here."

"Never leave me again," he hissed, and reached between us, grasping his cock and slamming into me so suddenly, my back arched. "I want to stay like this forever. You're not allowed to leave."

A soft puff of laughter left me, and I kissed him. "You can't live with your cock inside me."

He bared his teeth. "I can."

He punctuated the statement with a rough thrust, making me gasp. I was already so sensitive thanks to his tail, but feeling his cock inside me was fulfilling on both physical and soul levels. I threw my arms around him, digging my nails into his back. My skin buzzed as the scrolling ink moved on his skin, power thrumming just under the surface.

I knew he wanted to set a slow pace and make love to me, but we were both too desperate for that, and emotions ran high. He crushed his mouth to mine in a brutal kiss and fucked me so fast we both gasped, moans filling my mouth and his, tongues gliding and forceful.

"My rose. Mine."

"My night," I groaned, wrapping my legs around him and rolling my hips up to meet each demanding thrust. Pleasure built fast and suddenly, and judging by the tension in Kai's back and the low, menacing snarl he let out, he wasn't far behind.

His power finally erupted, brushing me everywhere, curling around my wrists, squeezing my thighs, brushing my nipples. Making good of his promise to make me feel him everywhere.

"Kai," I gasped into his mouth, slamming my eyes shut as my release built, my body already clenching, trembling. "Oh, shit."

"Mine," he replied in a growl, echoing the word with every slam of his hips to my inner thighs. "Mine. Mine. *Mine.*"

Fuck. I sank my fingers into his hair and gripped tight, arching up into him, my breathing fast and sharp. My pussy gripped him tightly, clasping his cock so possessively that every thrust touched my most sensitive spots and made my toes curl.

"Kai," I choked out, legs locked around him, a guttural whine tearing up my throat and making his eyes flash.

"Yes," he hissed, his hands finding my hips and pressing marks into my skin as he watched me fall apart, never once letting up his feral pace. "Look at me, see exactly who owns this body." He brushed his lips across mine, soft and sweet, a complete contrast to his thrusts. "Give me your climax, my rose. Let me taste it, feel it. I want to be consumed by you."

I moaned, burying my face in his shoulder, and stiffened when my release tore through me with the force of a burning sun. I choked out his name, my breath throttled in my throat and eyes blown wide as pleasure charged through me like fire and lightning.

"Take me," Kai gasped, his hands trembling on my hips. "Take all of me, my rose. Every part of me is yours."

My pussy gripped him in a brutal fist, demanding he find release too, and Kai grunted and came hard, jolting madly inside me. Heat spilled through me, filling me with every drop of him, and I gasped at the deep throbs of his cock against sensitive inner flesh, wringing more pleasure from me.

"Haley," he groaned, shudders moving through him as he clung to me. "Haley."

I held him as I came down from the high, deep pleasure making me limp and satisfied. When I ran my fingers through his long red hair, he shuddered and relaxed atop me, nestling his face against my neck.

"Don't leave," he whispered.

"I won't. I'll stay as long as I can."

If I could have never woken up, I'd have stayed there forever, holding him, ignoring the fractures in our bond to pretend we were whole again.

"My whole life," he murmured, his breathing deepening.

I waited until he was asleep to let my heavy eyelids close, knowing if I slept here, I'd wake up in the palace.

I resisted as much as I could, luxuriating in the feel of his skin under my fingertips, the weight of him pressing me into the bed. But finally exhaustion tugged my eyes shut, and I woke up, heartbroken and alone.

CHAPTER TWENTY-SIX

$\mathcal{F}$or two days, nothing of consequence happened and it was fucking weird. No one had attacked me, Callahan hadn't got a new job for me, and even Renna didn't turn up to bark orders at me. I didn't like it.

I'd spent a few hours with Tali yesterday, catching up after years spent apart, getting to know each other as adults.[1] But when Tali had to leave the city, I was left with nothing to do. Restless. Bored.

The devil and his inner circle were busy organising a new batch of souls who'd come from a mass shooting on Earth. I shut down my thoughts at the mention of guns, my own death and my mates' murders rearing like a cruel vision around me until I could almost taste the gunpowder.

Alone, I had no distraction from missing my mates. Nothing to keep me busy so I didn't stress about not dreaming last night. What stopped me connecting with my mates in my sleep? Where were Em and Harvey? Did Kai hate me for waking up and leaving him alone in his dream?

I also couldn't shake the feeling of darkness wrapped

around me. The sensation was so vivid, cold but nowhere near threatening—soothing.

I shuddered, pain lancing through my chest. My hand shot up and I clutched the painful spot, a frown tugging my brows together. I obsessed over the strange sensation for hours, but I couldn't sit still and let my own thoughts torture me.

So I hauled myself out of my room and went in search of the library Queen Lili mentioned. The pain in my chest followed.

The library was bigger than I'd been expecting, although maybe I was naïve for not realising *Lucifer's palace* would have a magnificent, three-level library filled with pale bookshelves, gilded edges, warm lighting, and *thousands* of books bound in soft brown leather. I paused in the doorway, my mouth hanging open.

I might have been in Hell, but this was something straight out of Heaven.

I'd only been to Heaven once, to the beautiful garden-like city of Wisteria where my mother was born. The bastards who lived there had taken one look at my black wings—the mark of a demon or Fallen angel—and bullied me out of the place. Funny, demons who knew I was an angel-demon hybrid had never made me feel any less for having an angelic side.

"Either come in and shut the door, or piss off and close it behind you," a low, female voice barked, snapping my attention to a grand, golden desk to my right where a woman with shining onyx skin and soft brown ringlets sat, glaring daggers at me.

I met her scowling stare, held eye contact, and slowly closed the door. "Happy?"

"Thrilled."

I smirked, strolling over to the gilt desk, lilac light filtering through a huge window on the far wall to give the whole room a dreamy cast. The fifty-something, narrow-lipped woman scowling at me was far from dreamy though, even if she did wear a soft beige gown and was beautiful enough to be the heroine of a legend.

"Since you're so sweet and willing to help," I said, giving her a troublemaker's grin, "can you direct me to a book on curses?"

The librarian looked down her nose at me—impressive, given she sat below me. "So you can curse me and Lucifer's whole empire? I think not."

I glanced at the wooden block on her desk that pronounced her AGATHA AVONLEA, CHIEF LIBRARIAN. "Why would I curse the empire when I live here, Agatha?"

"Aggie," she corrected through gritted teeth.

"I want a book on curses so I can figure out what the hell *this* means," I replied in the same tight tone, shoving up the sleeve of the violently pink dress I'd found in the wardrobe in my room.[2] "Any ideas, Aggie?"

Aggie rolled her thin lips into a flat line, the dark skin on her cheeks pulling taut. "That's a nasty looking curse."

"I had no idea," I drawled, shoving my sleeve back into place. "Your insight is truly mind-boggling."

"Try in that corner," she replied, picking up a book she'd left page-down on her desk, and not sparing me another glance as she waved towards the left of the big window.

"Thank you *so much* for your help. You've been delightful, Aggie."

She shot me a flat look over the top of her book. "It's nine a.m. on a Monday. Sorry I'm not bubbly and chipper."

"Try being dead for a hundred years, and see how chipper you are then," I huffed, and strode away from the woman. Showing impressive restraint by disappearing into the stacks instead of biting her head off.[3]

It took me a good half hour to find the section darling

Aggie directed me to, but the sun was warm on my back and at least I wasn't thinking about the pain in my chest or lack of mates in my dreams. I was in no hurry, so I sat cross-legged on the polished floorboards and leisurely browsed the bottom shelf, picking out books with *curse* in the title and perusing their pages.

I wasn't surprised that none of the designs matched my marks, and that nothing referenced being killed and brought back to life. Of course it couldn't have been that easy.[4]

But at least I'd spent the morning distracted. A few hours later, I climbed to my feet and stretched out my arms, muscles dully aching from being in one position. I turned to pick up the last book and return it to the shelf—and shrieked at the dark face too close to mine, eyes bright gold and eerie as fuck.

"Holy *shit*, Aggie," I cried, slamming my hand over my racing heart. "You nearly scared me back to death."

"You've been here for five hours," she huffed, making me jolt in surprise. Fuck, had it been that long? "Idiot girl, you're probably starving."

She thrust a warm, buttery bread roll stuffed with bacon at me and stalked away before I could recover from the gesture. With a shrug, I replaced the book and bit into my bread roll, groaning at the explosion of flavour on my tongue.

I waited for Harvey to warn me against making noises like that unless I wanted to be bent over the breakfast table. My heart plummeted fast when I caught the reflexive thought. Harvey was gone, lost to me. But I refused to think he was dead. My mates had to be alive and resurrected like me. My dreams were *real*, not just trauma-fuelled delusions.

"I'll find them," I whispered to the watchful books around me, making the vow real by giving it a voice.

I finished the warm roll and left the library—and the *enchanting* Aggie—to head out of the palace, my beloved daggers slapping my thighs as I walked swiftly. I expected a guard to step into my path and haul me back to General Callahan or maybe even Lucifer himself, but no one batted an eyelid as I strode out the main doors and down the pale gold steps into the city.

I shouldn't torture myself, but I couldn't fight the compulsion to return to the scene of the crime. Or rather, the house we'd broken into and been trapped in by Locke. The house that had made us custodians of the Damned Realm, ultimately murdered by the abusive bastard.

It took me three hours walking around the city, searching every corner for the steps that had led Malakai and I up to Lucifer's second home, to realise it was no longer here. It must have been destroyed during the angelic attack on Iarlon.

Like my mates, there was nothing left in the city to show it had ever existed.

The pain in my chest grew, festering into anger and a foul mood.

"The fuck are you looking at?" I demanded of a [bald,] red-skinned demon with a forked tail and a naked penis swinging around. I tried not to look, but it was *right there*, whirling like a windmill.

"My eyes are up here, darlin'," he replied with a warm laugh. But he winced when a furious man roared, "Get back here, Travis, I'm not done yelling at you!"

"Arguing with the husband," the red guy laughed with me, quickening his steps as his husband's voice grew louder. "You know how it is."

"Actually, my mates are probably dead," I replied flatly.

It was hard to hold onto hope right now, even if I'd kick myself for saying that later.

Ugh, his red face turned all sympathetic. It made my skin itchy and stomach even tighter.

"Good luck with the husband," I told him and quickened my footsteps.

When I reached a high ledge, I snapped my wings out and dove off the edge, air slicing at me as I took a wide arc around the capital. Seeing what remained and what was new.

From the air, it looked almost entirely different. The angels had really done a number on the city. Probably to weaken Lucifer so he'd be an easier target. Obviously that didn't work—he was every bit as intimidating and powerful as I remembered him.

I tried not to remember that day we became custodians of the Damned Realm, kneeling on the cold marble floor of the throne room beside my mates, terrified we were about to be sentenced to a gruesome, grisly death. The memory was blurry in places, but I remembered the panic in Em's eyes, the sharp fear in Harvey's voice, and the tension gripping Kai's body.

I angled my wings, catching a gust of wind and flying around the golden dome of an elegant, intricately carved building. A park encircled it, perfumed with honeysuckle. I got a strange memory of Wisteria, my mother's homeplace. Had someone built a piece of Heaven here in Hell? Two, if the library was angelic like I suspected. Weird.

I shook off the strange feeling crawling down my spine and followed the arch of the river, the water gleaming silver-lilac. The bird part of me wanted to freefall into the water and ruffle my wings in the world's largest bath, but I squashed the impulse and kept flying. I had no direction or plan, only an aimless urge to escape my past. As if murder and grief was something I could outpace.

I flew high to avoid a tall cluster of trees around a monument, and for a moment it wasn't a cushion of air that wrapped around me, caressing my wings, but shadows.

I jolted so hard I nearly fell from the sky, my heart slamming in my ribs. I could still feel the phantom touch of shadows wrapped around me, not strangling or threatening but almost ... protective.

I saw Cassander Locke's cruel, slimy face down the barrel of a gun and suddenly those shadows were all I could feel.

I doubled over, my stomach twisting violently, and I plummeted towards the trees fast, struggling to draw a sharp breath into my lungs. I flapped my wings like a madwoman to slow my descent, but the second my feet touched the golden flagstones under the trees, I dropped to my knees and vomited.

My throat burned and stomach cramped, and even as I was sick, I didn't know *why*.

I'd ... forgotten something. I couldn't shake the sense that something had been taken from me, and that was true of my mates, but there was more, I knew it. I just didn't know *what*.

I didn't know why there was a crack in my chest, why I felt deeply, irreparably heartbroken.

I spat the taste of vomit from my mouth and dove into my memories of the day I died. That was the trigger somehow, thinking about that day. It was as blurry as when we knelt before Lucifer, but brilliantly sharp in places—Emlyn's cry when he was shot, Kai throwing himself at Locke with his magic shuddering through the air, Harvey's blood soaking into my trousers.

But when I tried to focus on myself, my screams, my fear, it was covered in an opaque haze like someone had thrown a veil over it. I eyed the curse mark on my forearm as I pushed up to my feet. Something important had happened that day, and all the other blurry days, too. And if one of these marks was why I'd forgotten it, those memories had been *taken* from me.

"Fucking curses," I snarled, and stalked around the tall monument for the demons lost in the war. Flying was out of the question with my stomach sloshing like a ship on a stormy sea, so I got my anger out by slamming my boots to the ground with dirty stomping step through the park.

I riffled through my memories as I trekked through the city's clean, leafy streets towards the palace. In every memory from the last ten years I was alive, there was a sheen obscuring something. Whatever I'd been cursed to forget, it was entwined with every one of my memories since I met the guys.

I needed to find my mates, right the hell now.

CHAPTER TWENTY-SEVEN

*C*allahan was busy in a meeting with Cerny, Lucifer's spymaster, and the rest of their team. At least the ones high up enough to warrant an invite.[1] I tried to hunt down Bernard, but a scowling, grey-bearded soldier warned me not to bother him and Queen Lili during their date night. I gnashed my teeth, bristling with impatience and panic and the need to *do something,* but I took the man's advice.

I needed a job, needed a new place to search for my mates. I'd gone around every inn and pub in the last town, but I'd come up empty.

I'd spent too much time doing nothing these past two days while I waited for Cerny or whoever else to interrogate Bevan. We needed to know what we were up against, to formulate a plan for maximum impact, but the longer it took the less I cared about waiting.

I was a mercenary; I wasn't known for tact and patience.

Restless, I stalked to the training room. The shadow of my empty memories followed me there, moving around the high-ceilinged room like a spectre, haunting pieces of metal and padded cushions that were as alien to me as the little black phones everyone was using. Tali had given me hers—she didn't have the opposable thumbs to work it anyway—but I had no clue how to use it.

Ugh, I was out of date. And old.

I approached a rack of weights along the side of the room because at least I knew what a weight was, and grabbed a small one while I stretched out the tension in my arms and legs. I watched what the three other people in the room did with the equipment, pretending I was admiring their form instead of completely hopeless. When a man with huge bull's horns spotted me staring, I gave him a thumbs up.

"Great job, man."

He snorted and glanced away, but I imagined he was pleased by the compliment. Even surly bull demons loved compliments.

After another voyeuristic minute, I'd got the hang of how the apparatus worked, so I approached an empty seat and plopped down onto it, grabbing the padded bars on either side of my head. I grunted at the pull in my muscles, but I'd once carried a small pony on my back, so this was nothing.[2]

Fifteen minutes later, I was aching all over, drenched in sweat, but my head would *not* shut up thinking and the phantom grief in my chest had transformed into a living, endless rage. Something that belonged to me had been stolen. Someone had cursed me, went into my head and rearranged my memories. They were *my* memories.

I left the weights and approached a punching bag hanging from the ceiling, not pausing to wrap my knuckles before I slammed my fist into it. Impact vibrated up my arm, and I caught my breath. *Yes.* This was what I needed; pure violence and messy rage unleashed on an unsuspecting punch bag.

These things had changed since I'd last used one, sturdier and stiffer, but it absorbed punch after punch without tearing off the chain it hung by, so I had no complaints.

Copper filled the air, the scent wrapping around my taste buds, but I didn't stop hammering blows on the bag, my hands throbbing and my breathing shot apart.

Memories flashed—the scent of gunpowder, the blistering heat of gunshots, the visceral, lancing fear of watching my mates crash to the floor of our new kitchen. Locke's smirk; the satisfaction and revenge in his eyes.

Why? Why did he hate us so much? He was Harvey's father, and I knew he was an abusive piece of shit, but when I reached for the memory of *why* Locke hunted us, I hit another hazy wall. Whatever lay beyond was firmly hidden.

"Fuck," I hissed, driving my bleeding knuckles into the bag again, my stomach hollowing with rough breaths, my whole body starting to shake.

"Woah, woah, stop before you do serious damage to yourself," a warm, honeyed voice called, swift footsteps rushing in my direction.

Soft hands caught my wrists and pulled me away from the punching bag. Curved eyes widened in a pretty, freckled face when I bared my teeth in a snarl.

"Get fucked," I spat at the pretty man, registering a tight outfit on a long, slim body and long red hair, scanning him for weapons and finding none—only white wings. Shit, how did he have *white* wings in Hell? They were pearly and untainted by a Fall.

"Halwen, I presume?" he asked, releasing me instantly and taking a step back like I was feral. Smart man.

"You're like me," I blurted, my rage faltering for a moment, "aren't you? You'd wither in Hell otherwise. You're part angel."

"I am," he agreed, his red brows tugging into a furrow. "I didn't realise you were."

I shrugged, pulling my black wings tighter to my back. "I know I don't look it, but my mother was an angel."

He smiled, like the threat had passed.[3] "Lili's like us, too. She mentioned meeting you."

I blinked—and then realisation hit. "You're not another of Queen Lili's harem, are you?"

How many did she *have?*

The pretty man gave me a crooked smile. "I certainly am. Speaking of, Cerny's looking for you. He sent me to find you; he has a job for you."

All the tension drained from me, and I let out a rough breath. "Thank *fuck* for that."

Right now I'd take any distraction. Even if it didn't lead me to my mates, hunting alphas was a perfect distraction. I couldn't think about the aching absence in my soul if I was fighting for my life against a city full of violent, brutish demons.[4]

CHAPTER TWENTY-EIGHT

"*C*overt," I breathed to myself as I flew through the darkening night along the river. "Subtle."

Those were Cerny's words—the *spymaster's* words. Riding into the alpha city on the back of a giant red panda wasn't going to cut it for this job. I had to pose as a rogue demon myself; I had to seem as unhinged and vicious as possible, and I needed to go alone.

I was fine with everything except the alone part. Alone, my thoughts ran wild, returning to those vacant spots in my memory, poking them like broken teeth and waiting for the throb of pain. It came every time, lancing through my head and chest.

"Leave it," I snapped at myself, keeping my gaze fixed down on the river, searching for a cluster of buildings. I'd already investigated three ordinary villages and an empty town demolished by the war, and found no alphas in either. Bevan had only given Cerny's team a twenty-mile area, not a specific location, so I'd been flying along the Bend of Boraven, circling in search of a city *all day.*

I was ready to land, find a tree to sleep in, and admit defeat for tonight. Bevan might have been 'mined for information' but there was no telling he'd been honest. Maybe if *the Cursed One* had been present to scare him shitless, he might have been more open. So far, there'd been nothing along the river to show an alpha city was nearby. It was quiet, peaceful—and grating to my prickly soul.

I reached up to check the bone pin securing my pink hair into a knot on my head, releasing a quick breath when I found it still in place—and letting go quickly when its power lit my veins on fire.

"To pose as an alpha," Cerny said, his rugged face ultra serious as he watched me from the other side of his heavy desk. The office behind him was full of weapons, paintings, books, and a small topiary bush carved into a shocking likeness of the queen. "You need power."

"I had power," I muttered, scowling at the curse on my arm as I dropped into the green leather chair opposite the spymaster. "I used to be able to boil the blood in anyone's veins. Make their whole body explode."

Cerny blinked bright topaz eyes, the only sign of his surprise. "That would be useful."

"But since I died, it's gone," I muttered, and then gave Cerny a canny look. "You have a plan for that, though, don't you?"

"I do," he agreed, sliding open a drawer beside him and producing a small velvet jewellery box.

"I'm spoken for," I protested before he could open the box.

"So am I," he replied, the expression on his tanned face flattening. With his soft golden colouring, he looked more angelic than demonic, but that grumpy disposition was a hundred percent hellborn. "Very spoken for. Open the box, Halwen. And just know, the second you touch it, you'll experience a severe reaction."

I scowled, sliding the box towards me. "This better not kill me. I have a pretty good track record with coming back to life, and the second I do, I'm coming right for you."

"It won't kill you; it'll give you power. A lot of power."

"So I can pose as an alpha," I surmised, and snapped the box open, spying not a ring inside but a hair pin. The end was made of bone and sharp enough to draw blood, but the head caught my eye and made my heart pull tight. There were small, white enamel flowers decorating it, so similar to the flowers around our home—the ones Kai picked a bunch of every anniversary.

I reached out to brush my finger over those enamel flowers—and my whole body locked. My eyes flew wide, my mouth open on a scream of surprise as fire and ice filled my body.

My hair lifted off my shoulders, floating around my face, and my wings snapped wide, knocking things off the shelves of Cerny's office. I waited for the thud of them hitting the rug, but it never came. Oh fuck, everything was floating—from books on the bookcase by the window, to the knives and strange, unfamiliar weapons on the walls, to the knickknacks and objects decorating the room. Even the little topiary hovered.

"Help," I croaked to Cerny, my head thrown back as more power rampaged through me. I could taste the sparks on my tongue, sharp and bitter. My nose stung; my eyes streamed, stinging like I had needles embedded in them.

Glass cases rattled to my left, bookshelves lost their books on my right, and the room filled with the acidic bite of magic. Even Cerny reacted, a strange red mist hovering around his shoulders for a second before the whole thing cut out and I sank back into the chair, heaving for breath as things fell back into their places.

My head spun. I felt weird in my body, my limbs unwieldy.

"Good," Cerny rasped. "We know it works. Put it in your hair; only touch it if you need it."

"You," I panted, gripping the table's edge, "are completely insane."

The spymaster straightened the papers on his desk while I snapped the velvet case closed and shoved it away. "How do you feel?"

"Like I got struck by lightning," I spat, scrubbing tears off my face. My heart raced too fast, my skin tingling all over.

"Any pain?" he asked, lifting his gaze to give me a worried look.

I paused to answer that and—I didn't hurt at all. Actually all my aches had gone from the trek through the city and from throwing up earlier, not to mention beating the shit out of a dummy. If I ignored the ever-present pain in my soul, I felt good.

"No. That's weird."

Cerny smiled, a cunning thing that made me nervous. "This will work. And if you're lucky, this new power might unlock your old magic."

Now, that sounded too good to be true.

I dropped my fingers swiftly from the bone pin when power burned through me, coating my tongue with sharp magic, filling my veins with freezing lightning and scorching lava. A steady current of air was the only thing keeping me airborne for a moment as my wings locked.

Fuck, that thing was potent. There'd be no mistaking me as anything but an alpha if I drew on its magic. I panted, my whole body pounding with the remnants of its ferocity, and—

"What was that?" I breathed, excitement making my heart leap.

A cluster of lights flickered as I angled my body to the left, but when I veered back, they were hidden. No wonder I'd missed them all afternoon; the city was camouflaged.

Now, I was focusing, there were scents of alphas on the air, and power thrummed like a static charge through this valley. A few trees had been felled, probably in an alpha rampage. I grinned, my heart beating faster, full of sharp magic as I swooped and landed on the road below.

"Found you."

CHAPTER TWENTY-NINE

I laid on my belly in the grass, using the tree cover to hide me as I scoped out the city that was cleverly hidden—unless you were looking for it, like I'd been. A sign driven into the ground proclaimed it Alphaven. That took a lot of thinking about; alpha haven.[1]

There wasn't a wall or iron fence ringing it to ward off outsiders; the whole thing was open. But I had no doubt if I waltzed into the city, someone would know my every movement.

I was counting on it.

My plan wasn't elegant, but it would work. I had insane power with the pin, enough that there'd be no doubt I was an alpha with extreme power. *Far* more than any regular demon. Alphas tended to get overwhelmed by their power and go on mad, destructive rampages. That was my whole plan: go on a rampage, draw attention to myself, and get snapped up by this lord who collected alphas.

It didn't need to be fancy; I was supposed to be an intellectually challenged alpha after all. Alphas lived to feed, fight, and fuck, and little else. I could play that role. Hell, back in my mercenary guild days, most of my allies lived for those three things. I knew the type of person I had to become.

I watched for another twenty minutes, looking for a guard patrol, sussing out the houses at the edge of the city. If this was anything like other cities, the better houses would be in its heart and the outer edges would be for the people struggling to feed themselves. I'd lived on the edges for most of my life, my dad doing his best to keep us alive.

Sometimes it pissed me off that we were in Hell, we were *demons,* and here we were working and acting like humans. But it was thinking like that that made rebels start an uprising against Lucifer.

I wasn't a fan of working, but I *did* like not pissing in a bucket, and clothes were nice. So was food that wasn't a leg ripped off another demon and roasted over a fire.

I glanced at the tattoo on my arm, letting it fan the flames of my rage, and watched the road ahead for another few minutes. Only a few people were about, but they'd be good enough witnesses to an alpha outburst.

"Let's do this," I breathed, and pushed off the ground.

The back of my neck tingled as I pulled the pin out of my hair—catching my breath at the power that electrified me—and slid it up the sleeve of my jacket so it had full contact with my skin.

Fuuuuck.

My tongue burned, my eyes prickling viciously, and for a moment I thought my body was going to explode at the sheer power that erupted through my system, frazzling everything from my eyelashes to my toenails.

I'd swallowed a star, my body lit up and frantic, and for a moment I was so consumed with magic that I didn't realise there was a big, clawed hand wrapped around the back of my neck and someone was shaking my body.

"Get the fuck off," I growled, my voice deeper and more resonant, echoing off the tall trees I'd used as cover.

I threw my elbow back and whoever had grabbed me howled with pain like I'd stabbed them.

"Don't know—what the fuck she is," a man croaked, my hearing as sharp as a razor. He released me and staggered back.

I spun, inhaling a sharp breath at the sight of four big, burly fuckers—three older men and a silver-haired woman around my age. Their clothes were made of leather and aged, dirty, all in shades of brown.

The woman's face split in a grin. "Looks like we'll be eating like kings tonight, boys. Wynvail will reward us for this capture."

Capture? *Son of a bitch.* I couldn't get captured for some Wynvail guy when I needed to get taken to the lord's collection.

"Back off," I warned, my deep voice making me jump. I held my hands in front of myself and blinked when long, bone fingernails grew from mine, my wings itching too. A quick glance showed my feathers were now tipped in bone. I gave the raiders a slow grin. *Come at me, fuckers. See what happens.*

I'd heard of raiders—they;d been around when I'd last been alive. They were a poorer, meaner version of bounty hunters and mercs, and would grab anyone and anything for a price. It wasn't far off what I'd done by going to grab—

Who did I go to grab?

My head flashed with pain as I tried to remember, and my knees buckled.

In that split second of weakness, the raiders swarmed in around me. I growled when someone slammed a hand over my mouth, crammed my wings tight to my back, and took my hands in a tight, restrictive grip.

"Dead—all of you," I threatened, ignoring the sweaty hand

pressed to my face, muffling my voice. "You're all fucking *dead.*"

The silver-haired woman snorted, two of her cohorts echoing it. "You shouldn't have come so close to Alphaven, darling. Anyone stupid enough to wander out here is fair game."

I snapped my teeth, the only thing I could move on my body. "I came here because I heard it was a safe place for alphas. My mistake."

"Big mistake," a huge, half-naked man agreed, something bullish about his face. "You'll wish you'd never been born in this city."

"Talking from experience?" I asked sweetly. "Because I can make things so much better for you, no problem at all."

The woman snorted, her muscles bulging as she slapped the guy on his shoulder. "Think she just offered to be your whore, Jhonna."

"She offered to kill you, imbeciles," the biggest alpha snapped, his long, pretty black hair flowing as he stalked towards me. Huge *and* intelligent? Someone call Iarlon's reporters; I had a ground-breaking story for their newspaper. "And I'll have to decline on his behalf."

"Pity," I replied, and tried to kick off the ground so I could use my legs to attack them. The second my legs swung up, someone kicked them from under me and I tipped back into the bastards holding me, utterly at their mercy, not even my feet on the ground.[2]

"You'll regret this," I growled through the hand muzzling me. "By the time I'm done with you—"

"Someone shut her up," the big, clever bastard barked, and a fist slammed into my skull.

Everything went scarily black.[3]

CHAPTER THIRTY

*J*jerked awake with a yell, metal rattling and my arms stretched above my head. I tilted my head back with a groan, my stomach already cramping with dread, knowing what I'd see. Yup, my hands were chained to the wall above me. An experimental kick proved my legs were chained, too.[1]

I squinted at the room I was in, surprised to find a dusty attic with short, sloped walls instead of a grimy basement. Huh, guess times were changing. It was nice to mix things up a little.

"Pretty," I murmured, watching fat dust motes float through a beam of sunlight before falling into the shadowy parts of the room. I was the only person up here, but there were chains on two other walls, so clearly this was a regular occurrence. I admired the set-up, but I'd admire it a whole lot more if I wasn't chained to a wall with my shoulders pounding from the awkward position.

I tilted my head against my shoulder, watching more dust spin through the air, the sun beginning to set beyond the short, angled window opposite me. It was the nicest place I'd ever been strung up, honestly. I couldn't complain about the view; I could see all the way across the flat rooftops of Alphaven to the rolling hills and the forest I'd hidden in earlier. There was a fire burning in the heart of the city, in the middle of an open-top building, the flames so high they almost touched the sky.

I watched the fire dance, curious to know if it would catch and spread to the buildings on either side, but steady footsteps on wooden stairs drew my attention back to the attic. Panic caught in my chest, but adrenaline raged faster, drowning out my nerves. The magic that burned through me from the hair pin up my sleeve seemed to pulse higher, fiercer, and I gasped as my bone nails lengthened, my body jolting, rattling the chains.

I couldn't see the staircase from where I was chained to the wall, but the pin's magic made every sense razor sharp. I knew it was a single set of footsteps, a single person, not heavy-set but strong. Normally I'd say male, but with alphas it was hard to tell. A woman could just as easily break my ribs as any man here. They weren't breathing heavily despite the climb to the attic so they must be fit. None of which were good signs for me getting out of this place and finding the damn lord.

"Hello again, Halwen," a low, cultured voice said, the steps reaching the top of the staircase, echoing into the attic.

Again. Hello *again*.

I bared my teeth. The only people I'd met in a hundred years were Lucifer's circle, which meant this bastard was a traitor in the palace.

"I don't know why you're stupid enough to come here and spy on me," the voice went on, echoing steps carrying him into my line of sight.

Every thought fell out of my head. The magic in my system rampaged, making my fingers twitch, my tongue burn cold like I'd swallowed ice.

"I know you," I breathed, staring at the handsome, cruel bastard when he came to stand in front of me, his mahogany hair short and his sculpted face full of sickening satisfaction. He wasn't a traitor to Lucifer. I didn't know him from the palace. He'd tried to kill me—a hundred years ago.

He hunted us from safe house to safe house. He burned our house down. He should be dead. But here he stood, gloating at having me chained in his attic.

"I should hope you know me, Halwen," the hunter laughed, coming closer and raking a slow stare down my chained body. "I'm your mate."

CHAPTER THIRTY-ONE

I jerked away from the hunter when he reached a bronze hand toward me, my chains rattling violently in the empty attic.

"No," I hissed, not even contemplating it.

No fucking way. I'd remember him if—but there were gaping holes in my memories.

No.

This was a lie. My body shook, terror and rage meeting the bone pin's blistering magic in me, burning all the way to the tips of my canine teeth.

"Of course you don't remember me," he said smoothly, something in the way he looked at me making my stomach churn. "The last time we met was so traumatic, your poor mind must have blocked it out."

"You," I snarled, breathing faster, "are not my mate."

I'd know; I'd feel it. All I felt were the tatters of my broken soul, *nothing* that linked me to this creep.

"It'll take some time to remember me," the hunter told me, mild and smug as if I wasn't snarling at him. He stroked the backs of his fingers down my cheek, and my stomach revolted. Serves him right if I threw up on his face. "But we have all the time in the world now I've found you."

I spat in his face.

He reared back, nostrils flaring, his true, cruel face showing for a moment before he hid it behind a veneer of smug calm.

"You tried to kill me and my mates; you're not one of them."

He wiped the spit from his face with an unsettling calm. "You think that because someone tampered with your memories. I'm Wynvail. Your mate."

I shook my head, but those hazy spots in my memories taunted me. "I remember you perfectly. You hunted us, you hurt my Emlyn."

"That's the curse playing with your mind," he murmured, reaching out to stroke my face and ignoring the way I recoiled. "Your mates are Emlyn, Malakai, Harvey, and me. Harvey and I are brothers, remember?"

I shook my head. Ignored the catch in my breath. His touch burned, disgusted me. But it felt so *right*.

"You have two Locke brothers as your mates," he went on, a strange light in his eyes. "Both of us."

I wanted to snarl in his face, but I froze. He was right. I couldn't explain how I knew, but he was right. I ... I did have two brothers as my mates. Harvey and—this asshole?

"Then who cursed me?" I demanded, pulling on my chains.

"I don't know, honey," he replied, his cruelly handsome face trying to be soft, and failing.

"Don't call me that," I snapped.

Mercury eyes glowed at my defiance, and a quiet, animal part of me squeaked in terror. "Behave, or I'll leave you chained here all night."

"Why chain me at all if I'm your mate?" I challenged, my heart pounding.

Wynvail laughed, a corner of his mouth curved into a wicked slash. "I know you, Halwen. At the first chance, you'd bury a knife in my throat and run."

He had a point.

He brushed my cheek with a thumb, and I tried to push down my nausea at the soft touch. He couldn't be my mate. No fucking way. But I couldn't deny that what he told me made sense, and it felt right. Everything fit.

"Prove it," I growled at him, hiding the way my hands shook. Had I found them? Had I really found my mates? "If you're my soulmate, prove it."

He was an asshole, and a creep, and I wanted to break his nose, but I'd wanted to break Kai's nose in the beginning, too. Hope strangled me until I couldn't breathe.

"Look at me, Halwen," Wynvail murmured, his voice dropping as he came closer, his face so near to mine. His scent overwhelmed every sense, cloves and sugar and blood.

I swallowed and looked into his eyes, my heart skipping because—I *knew* those eyes. Memories tried to break out, to push through the drugged haze over my mind, and I flinched with a cry as pain pierced my head from all directions. It burrowed deep until I was sure my skull would burst.

"Stop!" Wynvail commanded, genuine panic in his voice. "Stop, or you'll break your mind, Halwen."

I bared my teeth, but he was right. I reluctantly retreated from those memories, panting, the pin's magic rising like fire and ice in my veins until my eyelashes tingled and I couldn't feel my face.

"Careful," he murmured, his cool hand cupping my cheek.

I remembered days like this, cool skin on mine, softness and care. My bottom lip wobbled. "Whoever made me forget you will die. Horribly."

"I'll make sure of it," he promised, and reached up to unhook my chains from the ceiling.

He was my mate; he really ought to have known I would wrap the chain around his throat and strangle him the second my arms were down. My muscles screamed, weak and painful from hanging above me, but the pin's sharp power erupted through me and gave me strength.

Wynvail laughed, the sound chilling, and reached up to—to snap the chains apart with a flash of white light before I could choke him.

What? How did he do that?

I shook my head at the pain that cracked my skull when I tried to remember his magic. I thought ... part of me had been waiting for shadows, like the darkness I remembered cushioning me when Locke killed me.

"I warned you to behave," Wynvail rasped, rubbing his throat as we stared at each other across the attic.

I shrugged, panting and pained. "Where's the fun in behaving?"

He grinned, a sudden flash of something in his eyes. Interest.

I held up my hands in warning as he edged closer, my claws long and made of viciously sharp bone. Power slashed through the chains around my ankles, the magic in the pin horrifically intuitive, and I took a step towards the staircase.

"You *know* me, Halwen, you just can't remember," Wynvail urged.

"Where are the others?" I asked, my stomach knotting at the thought of seeing them again, of all of us being together. *Please, please.*

But part of me was so scared it would never happen, and my throat closed up.

"Breathe, honey," Wynvail murmured, sliding closer to stroke my cheek. I shuddered, and couldn't tell if it was in relief or revulsion. I needed to get these curses broken as soon as fucking possible; I hated feeling disgusted a my own mate's touch.

I know those eyes, I thought again as I stared up at him, my heart thumping fast. He was so damned tall, I was going to develop a crick in my head looking up at him.

"I'll take you to them," he offered, and reached for my hand before remembering my huge claws. He grasped my wrist instead, his fingers cool and calming.

I laughed, fluttering my fingers. "Not a fan of the killer claws?"

"I don't remember them," he replied, guiding me to the staircase and down a tight, narrow hallway to the floor below. The house smelled of pine cleaning solution and coffee, an unpleasant combination. The decor wasn't much better. "Something new?"

"I woke up with them," I lied, unable to explain why I did. "What—what happened when you were reborn? Where were you?"

Wynvail's thumb stroked my pulse, making my heart beat faster as he led me to the bottom floor of the house. It was in pretty good condition, not falling apart like I'd expected the alpha city to be. To say these alphas wanted civilisation destroyed, they lived pretty comfortably.

"I resurrected ninety years ago, not too far from here. I've been trying to figure out what happened ever since." His silver gaze slid to me and lingered. "Trying to find you."

"I only just—came back," I replied, pain tightening my chest. They'd been back so much longer than me. "I'm sorry, Wyn."

The name came naturally—a fluke or a memory?

He pulled me closer when we reached a landing on the bottom floor, laying a kiss on my temple. My throat swelled, a strange blend of unease and comfort buzzing through me. "You have nothing to apologise for Halwen."

I elbowed him lightly, pushing off my pain. "I'm going by Haley now. Halwen's weird since there's a whole forest by the same name."

"You're welcome," he replied dryly, and I jolted, staring at him. This smug, attractive bastard with his perfect hair and straight teeth and expensive clothes.

"You..."

The mate who'd left me a message to say they were all still alive. The mate who never forgot me, who named a whole damn forest after me. Wynvail Locke.

"Me," he agreed, and squeezed my wrist, tugging me towards an open door that led into darkness. "Your mates are this way. The tunnel leads across the city."

My heart soared even as I felt like I'd throw up. I dredged up a smile for the mate who never forgot me and said, "Lead the way, Wyn."

CHAPTER THIRTY-TWO

When Wynvail said the tunnel led across the city, he meant it. We'd been walking for twenty minutes before any light flickered in the tight space. If it wasn't for Wynvail's soft breaths and his fingers on my wrist, I'd think I was alone down here. Being guided to my death.

"What *is* this place?" I whispered when the flickers of light broadened, casting a glow over arches carved into the walls ahead, and limning the bars across them gold. They were cells, but for who?

"The city was built over fifty tunnels like this," Wynvail replied, his voice low. "They were used to hold prisoners centuries ago. Now, they're for our most volatile alphas. The ones who can't follow rules."

I shot him a look, apprehension tight in my belly. "That sounds ominous."

He smirked. "It should. It's the only thing that keeps a lot of these beasts in line."

Beasts. But wasn't he a beast too? Wasn't I? We were both demons but a little bit *more*. I could sense it in him—the heavy throb of power, the dominance.[1]

"Fresh meat," a raspy voice whispered from somewhere to my right, and I flinched into Wynvail. The fingers he'd locked around my wrist felt far more protective than restrictive now there was a new threat. "Come closer, you smell so clean, so sweet."

"Back off," Wynvail growled, so much power and wrath in his voice that the man skittered away. He tucked me closer against him, his body as tense as iron,

"Sorry, Lord, sorry, Lord," the man whispered.

I swallowed the words on the tip of my tongue, resisting the urge to stare at Wynvail.

Lord? Fucking Lord? So *he* was the psycho collecting alphas?

Also, I'd killed six of my mate's minions...

Ugh, why could my life never run smooth?

I'd been sent to infiltrate the alphas so I could feed information about *my mate* to Lucifer's spymaster. I resisted the urge to bang my head against the bars of the next cell. When I looked into it, green eyes glowed back at me, and I inhaled sharply.

"They won't hurt you," Wynvail promised, watching me.

"Because they're scared to death of you," I replied dryly, but—warmly. This didn't scare me; the rest of my mates were maniacs too. "I'm jealous; I want people to be scared of *me*."

Wynvail lifted my wrist and kissed the back of my hand. "All you have to do is slaughter everyone who tries to hurt you, and they will be."

I laughed. "I'll try."

Wynvail didn't laugh, didn't even smile. He gasped, a shudder moving through his body, and—and I realised he'd kissed my hand to distract me while he removed the hair pin from my sleeve.

"Give that back!" I snapped, reaching for it.

He held it above my head, a gleam of insanity in his silver eyes. Covetousness. Greed.

I growled in frustration, cursing myself for not being a six foot Amazon. I jumped, trying to snatch the pin from his aloft hand.

"Seriously, Wynvail, I need that."

"Why?" he laughed, an eyebrow raised on his sculpted face. He shuddered with a groan, the power razing his body from within. "So you can pretend to be an alpha? We both know you're not, honey."

"Yeah, well, I'm a reborn hybrid, so I'm probably more powerful than an alpha."

He grinned abruptly, and my heart skipped. He was completely and truly mad, wasn't he? "I wonder if you're more powerful than three."

"What?"

"You can survive," he murmured, his eyes smoky when they trailed down my body. "You're my mate, after all."

I hissed and dove at him when he tore away from me, stealing my pin, but a metal grate slammed down from the ceiling and I jumped back with a gasp, narrowly avoiding being impaled.

"You're insane!" I cried, staring at my bastard mate. Thief and lunatic. *Sexy, sexy lunatic.*

He tipped his brown head in acknowledgement and tucked my bone pin into his pocket. "Just like you, Halwen."

"What are you playing at?" I screeched, riling up the alphas in the cells along the tunnel, and momentarily deafened by growls and snarls. Why did solid bars separate us? What the fuck was he doing?

Wynvail gave me a long, scorching look. "Make me proud."

I bared my teeth, wrapping my fingers around the grate that refused to budge even an inch. My stomach dropped when I saw my claws were normal, not bone. The power had left me entirely—Wynvail had it all.

"I'll make you pay for this, you sick bastard," I threatened, but when I looked up from my claws, he was gone.

PART III - MATE

CHAPTER THIRTY-THREE

A sudden roar of stone had me spinning, breath catching and dying in my throat when I saw the solid rock door behind me was sliding open. Dread shuddered down my spine; I stared at the door, reaching for my weapons —and coming up empty.

Fuck. He'd disarmed me before he strung me up in his attic.

My mate was a goddamn psychopath. If I didn't know better, I'd say he wanted me dead. And I'd lost my volcanic blades again. I was going to stab Wynvail after this, mate or not.

I faced the archway that had opened, taking a tentative step towards it and squinting at the space beyond. It took me a moment to place the bright orange glow and when I did, I cursed violently. There was an enormous fire burning in the centre of the rectangular arena, and rows upon rows of seats were arranged around the edges, the roof open to the night.

It was a godsdamned fighting pit, and I had no interest in fighting alphas—let alone three like Wynvail suggested.

But the bars behind me wouldn't budge, and ahead the

audience of alphas roared, a sudden rise of sound that made my heart jolt into my throat. *Oh gods, why are they cheering?*

It didn't take me long to spot why, or hear the grate of stone on stone as three more doorways rolled open, one on each side of the arena. Wynvail wanted me to fight, but why?

And if he'd stolen my pin, did he want me to lose?

I took a tentative step into the ring, the concrete cold even through my boots as I scoped out my competition. The crowd roared louder, not excitement so much as hunger—for blood, for violence. I hated places like these. The pit already smelled of blood, probably from the last suckers to be forced into the ring.

How many people had died here? More than a few, I'd bet.

I wasn't about to be the latest smear of blood on the concrete. I hadn't risen from the dead just to die again. Besides, Wynvail wouldn't let me be hurt too badly. His instincts wouldn't let him.

I patted down my body again, searching for *any* weapon, even a clam shucking knife, and hissed in victory when I found a tiny, thin blade tucked into a pocket in my leather trousers. So slim, it would have been missed. I drew it out and held it like it was precious, ignoring the pathetic size of it. It was meant for throwing, not grappling with massive, instinct-driven alphas, but beggars couldn't be choosers.

Another yell went through the audience hulking in their seats around me, and I gritted my teeth as I peered around the doorway to see what caused it: a huge shadow stalked out of one of the other archways.

For a moment, a memory surged to the surface and stabbed my brain with agony. Indistinct but sharp and brutal. I knew it wasn't real, but the flicker of flames in a fireplace filled my ears, and someone turned a page in an old book. I gasped, clutching the wall, blinking until my eyes focused on the fighting ring, grinding my jaw as I absorbed the pain.

This was the worst timing for a memory to try to resurface, especially as the huge alpha took a step.

My heart jolted violently in my chest. There was something about that gait, something about the way they moved. I took a step into the arena without thinking about it, an uproarious chant going through the crowd.

Kill her! Kill her! Kill her!

"Fuck you very much," I yelled at them, but only succeeded in drawing the attention of the hulking alpha. Oh gods, he was *huge*, his shoulders twice the breadth of mine and his thighs as thick as tree trunks.

I caught my breath when he came at me, faster than I expected for a man of his size. I didn't know how I knew he was male when he was still in shadow, the only lights coming from the stands above. As if Wynvail wanted us to be even more unsettled, in the dimness. Psycho bastard.

I didn't stand around gawping at the alpha. I sprinted around the edge of the fighting pit, angling my tiny knife for maximum damage and assessed the way the alpha ran towards me, hoping he had a cock because my knife was going straight in his crown jewels. The closer he came, scarily fast even as I dodged out of his path, the more familiarity and alarm blared in my head. It throbbed like a broken tooth, pain in each pulse.

The crowd kept up their cheery, supportive chant,[1] and I did the smart thing by not taking my attention off the alpha to give them my middle finger. But it was a battle.

The alpha didn't talk, didn't taunt or threaten; he just growled like he was feral and hurtled at me. He was bigger and more muscular than me, but I ought to have been faster. I ought to have been able to outrun him, but I could feel his breath on the back of my neck, lifting all my fine hairs and sending a rush of chills down my back.

"Shit," I gasped out when the growl grew loud enough to block out the crowd's jeers.

I pushed my legs harder, racing aimlessly away from the alpha, nowhere to escape except back into the tunnel I'd come from. And no way in hell was I trapping myself between an alpha brute and the metal grate. I was stupid but not *that* stupid.

The scent of leather and old books hit my senses, the only warning I had before a massive, scalding body slammed into mine, tackling me to the ground.

My front slammed into the concrete, pain crashing through my hip and making me cry out. The growl became a deep, throaty sound that made me tremble.

That scent dominated my senses, raking up so many memories that I couldn't breathe. Even as I waited for the alpha to tear out my throat with his sharp teeth, even as my hip screamed, memories drowned out everything.

Lazy mornings waking up to Emlyn tracing his fingertips over my ribs. Hectic afternoons watching him run around making us dinner while I planned a hunt, the scent of roasting meat and buttery bread filling the kitchen. Sumptuous nights where Em would lay me out in our bed and cover every bit of space on my body in kisses, rolling me onto my front so he could lavish my back in kisses too, only stopping when he reached my pussy, unable to resist tasting the arousal pooled there.

I jerked back to the present with a gasp, bucking suddenly enough that the alpha gave me enough space to flip onto my back.

The beast looming over me was a stranger, his salt-and-pepper hair long and grizzled, his beard so thick it consumed most of his face; the only parts I could see were golden and scarred. The scars were unfamiliar, the feral rage in his eyes was new and terrifying, but the eyes themselves, sharp and blue—I knew those eyes.

Even as a hand wrapped around my throat, lifting my head only to slam it into the unyielding ground, I reached up and brushed my fingers over his beard.

"Em. Emlyn, it's me, it's Haley." But I could see in his eyes my words meant nothing to him. Maybe words altogether meant nothing. I surged for him through the bond, reaching out my soul and—touching nothing but wind-blown tatters. He was right here, but he might as well have been miles away.

"It's Halwen, your Hales, remember?" I rasped, my throat in his too-tight grip, threatening to buckle. My heart collapsed, too.

I stared up at him, my mate, and knew I was a stranger to him. All I saw in his eyes was murder. Nothing to suggest Em was in there at all. He wasn't just an alpha—he was an animal.

"Emlyn," I rasped, holding his gaze. My heart jumped when his mouth parted, hoping he'd say my name. But he snarled, sharp teeth bared, and didn't speak a word. "Emlyn Johahn!"

Kill her! Kill her! the crowd chanted. Did they know he was my mate? Did they know Wynvail had sent me here to—to kill them? What the fuck was his game?

My heart soared when Em tore away suddenly, his hand ripped from my throat. He remembered. He—

"No," I whimpered, my voice so small. I shook my head over and over, crawling backwards until my spine hit the stone wall beneath the arena seats. "No."

Em hadn't had a sudden awakening; he'd been wrenched away from me so another alpha could take his place. They snarled and hissed, fighting over who got to kill me. Emlyn didn't shift into his giant, feathered form. Did he even remember he could fly?

I couldn't take my eyes off the second alpha even as I fell apart. He wasn't as big or physically intimidating as Emlyn, but I knew every bit of cruelty and violence he was capable of. I'd stood beside him while we dealt that violence to our enemies, revelled in watching him unleash that crazed darkness to protect me.

But when Kai shoved Emlyn aside and prowled towards me, I knew I'd receive the full brunt of his madness today.

I scrambled to my feet, my hand shaking around the pathetic little knife I had to defend myself.

"Kai," I breathed, my voice hitching, collapsing.

Unlike Em, he looked exactly the same. His dark red hair was flawless, flowing down his back, maybe a little longer, and his neck was inked with flowing, tiny scrolls of text that carried on down his body, brutality etched into the sharp lines on his face as he stalked me.

"This isn't you," I rasped, shaking too hard to properly defend myself, my soul shattering in my chest all over again. I'd watched him die, and now he would kill me. It was breaking me, severing my soul in even more places. "Kai. Look at me, listen. It's Haley, your rose."

His eyes flashed, and hope choked off my air. He remembered the name, he would remember me—no, he'd just seen the knife in my hand. Fuck. A sob choked off the rest of my air. I needed to fight; they didn't really want to hurt me, not deep down. It would ruin them if they woke up and realised what they'd done. But I wasn't sure I was strong enough to fight them.

Not when just the sight of them made me want to curl up into a ball and sob.

I kept my back to the wall, moving in tiny steps to put space between us, and this time I recognised the flare of light in his eyes—the pleasure of the hunt.

Goddammit, I am not your prey, Malakai Virex.

My heart pounded in my throat as his crimson eyes tracked me. *Please don't let me die for this.* I shut down every survival instinct and forced myself to stop moving. I wouldn't let him chase me. If I engaged Kai's hunter instincts, there'd be no hope for me.

"Why are you doing this?" I screamed at the stands above my head, knowing Wynvail sat in the seats above this wall. What kind of man threw their mate into a fighting arena with three unhinged alphas who were also her mates? There were only two explanations—he wanted me to kill them, or he wanted *them* to kill me.

You can survive. You're my mate, after all.

He was unhinged. If I survived, I'd kill *him.*

"Malakai," I snarled when invisible magic slammed me into the wall, bruising my already tender skull and dragging my attention back to him. "You love me, for fuck's sake."

More like he was obsessed with me, and completely and utterly devoted. He'd *never* hurt me like this. That was proof more than anything that there was nothing left of my mates.

His snakes coiled around my upper arms, dragging a cry from my lips at the sudden pain, and my vision wavered when fangs grazed my skin. Kai was a tall, dark-clad blur as he stalked closer, his tail lashing the air behind him. I remembered the loving way he'd looked at me in my dreams, and my eyes burned with tears.

I knew I couldn't get through to him, knew he was too animalistic to hear what I said, but it still *killed* me. It tainted my soul a little darker to lift my arm as far as I could while pinned and flick my fingers to send the knife flying.

It buried in his shoulder, drawing a grunt of pain from the man I loved with all my fucked up heart.

My tears overflowed at the sound, pain splintering through my chest as more cracks formed in my soul. After this, I'd be lucky if there was anything left of me to put back together.

When Kai grabbed the knife and drew it out, hissing with

renewed pain, I threw myself against the cage of his invisible snakes and stumbled free.

I didn't look back; I ran as fast as my shaky legs would carry me, firing straight across the arena, my lungs burning as I gasped for air. A dozen places ached and screamed on my body, slowing me down.

I wanted to yell more obscenities at Wynvail, wanted to denounce him as my mate, but I didn't have the breath to spare.

Air hit me from below, and I gasped, pushing myself faster, harder. Kai chased me, sending his snakes to capture me again. Only this time, I knew I wouldn't get free.

"Shit," I cried when my knee buckled and I slammed into the concrete on my side, momentum throwing across the arena like a twisted bowling ball.

A roar of noise swallowed my senses, making me cry—the crowd screaming, frantic.

A massive clawed hand grabbed the back of my neck and flipped me mercilessly onto my back, snarling in my face when a crack of pain made me scream.

I cried, staring at the monster looming over me in pure terror. My blood ran cold. The beast was death incarnate, a thing of shadows, nightmares, and fangs. My whole body rattled, shaking uncontrollably. My lips parted to plead for my life but I couldn't breathe, couldn't make a single sound as huge jaws parted and he roared in my face.

My heart skipped when I saw the beast's face. I didn't know the dark fur, didn't recognise the darkness that bled from bright silver eyes, or the clawed paws that crushed my chest. He smelled like brimstone, not sun-warmed earth. But I knew it was Harvey. His black, spiralling horns were the same, his molten eyes the same metallic shade.

But my Harvey was pure sunlight—merciless and bright but *warm*. This monster of shadows and teeth held no light.

I knew without being told that this was the Harveil whose name drew base terror, who destroyed a whole city when he and—when he and his brother fled their father. *Wynvail.* No wonder he was fucked up enough to send me into a fighting pit with my mates; Cassander Locke was an abusive, evil piece of shit. I didn't want to think about the things he'd done to him. Wynvail was a black spot in my memory, but Harvey—I *knew* everything that monster had done to my sunshine mate.

Locked in the dark, shut away for his whole life, never seeing the sun, never breathing clear air. Hidden in a basement beneath a glittering, socialite house like a dark secret.

"It's okay," I breathed, inhaling sharply at the pain in my ribs as I reached up to sink my fingers into Harvey's fur. I shuddered as I stroked the heated skin underneath, my heart breaking. "It's okay, my Buttercup. Everything's going to be okay."

But his silver eyes bled darkness. And I tasted magic in the air before power charged through my body strong enough to black out the entire arena.

My scream drowned out the crowd's feral cries, and for a moment all that existed was the empty rage in Harvey's silver eyes—

And then my back arched as the pain crescendoed, swallowing my awareness of the arena, the crowd, and my mates. It shattered me into nothing but agony, and I screamed until my voice gave out.

CHAPTER THIRTY-FOUR

HARVEY

The doll's screams grated my ears, sounding like suffering instead of the usual victory. It didn't stop me pressing my clawed paw to her ribs and letting the destructive force of my magic burn through her.

Above, in the stands, my captor and master watched with a frown on his face. He always frowned when I killed. Never smiled. But if I performed well, he'd throw a whole leg of meat into my cell and the guards wouldn't shove their torture sticks into my body, lighting me up with pain.

I always performed well. His pet monster.

I didn't know who he was, didn't know when I got here or who I was. It didn't matter. Drawing blood and ending lives mattered; they bought me food and a reprieve from the pain.

So I pressed harder on the fragile creature under me, not looking too closely at her face. She didn't look like an alpha, but some of them didn't. Some of them were like pretty dolls —too breakable for a place like this.

Noise roared. The watchers, screaming as the doll's death neared. I felt it, brushing my side like a familiar friend, and wished it would come to claim me, instead. To end this.

I didn't know how long I'd been here. How long I'd been killing. I only knew it never ended.

The doll gasped something, a word that had no meaning. I only knew the ones my master taught me; everything else was gibberish.

I looked at her and wished I hadn't, a blade of horror slicing through my chest. I tore my gaze away, my heart pounding. It didn't matter what she said or how she looked at me; she had to die. If she didn't, I would.

Her defiant gasps reached my ears, her lungs fighting for breath. It would be soon—her death.

Ruddy light flared along her pale arm, coming from dark marks tattooed on her forearm, but the crimson glow died in the next moment. I caught my breath. What *was* that? The light had touched my paw; had she infected me with venom?

"Enough," my master shouted, and I whipped my head around to growl at him. Enough? She was still alive. *"Enough,"* he repeated firmly. It was one of the few words I knew. "Back down, *all* of you."

I lifted my foot off the doll's chest, not sure why panic gripped my chest when she lay still. She didn't rise to fight me, didn't even roll her head to the side to look at me with that unnatural stare again—like she saw me and wasn't afraid. She should have been afraid; she was stupid not to be.

I flexed the paw her crimson light had touched, claws extending and retracting, and was surprised to find my fur and flesh the same. I was unhurt. What kind of alpha was she, to not fight at all? Her light should have crucified me. Instead, the pads of my paw tingled.

"Return," my master called, ignoring the disappointed noise from the watchers. I wanted to kill all of them, but I'd tried that nine times before and each one ended with me in my cell, the guards jabbing sticks into my body until magic erupted and I screamed.

So I only bared my teeth at them as I dragged myself back to the doorway and through it into my cell. My paw still tingling, I curled up on the pallet on the floor and waited for the next fight.

Maybe this one would finally put me out of my misery.

CHAPTER THIRTY-FIVE

HALWEN

a soft touch on my forehead roused me, and I jerked upright with a cry, remembering the emptiness in Emlyn's eyes, the pure murder on Kai's face, and Harvey—I didn't know what happened to him. What had *been done* to him.

"Get the fuck away from me," I snarled at Wynvail, my heartless mate leaning over me, brushing hair from my eyes.

"How do you feel?" he asked as if I hadn't spoken.

"Like I was just almost killed by my mates."

He sighed, sadness in his molten eyes, cut into his bronze face. I curled my aching hand into a fist and slammed it into that face, breaking his nose with a crunch of cartilage.

"How *dare* you?" I seethed, crawling off the bed and refusing to admit how wrecked and weak I was. "What's your game, Wynvail? Kill me and get rid of a mate you can't stand, or kill all my mates so their deaths break me? Enlighten me; I can't *wait* to hear this explanation."

A muscle ticked in his jaw, but he didn't rise from where he perched on the edge of the mattress I'd slept on, his short hair mussed and expression tight. Tired. "I thought—they'd see you and recover."

He dragged his hands through his hair, but they were a little too steady. His voice was a little too fake in its tremor.

"They're beasts; you *saw* them. There's nothing left of the men we knew. Nothing left of our family."

The words arrowed into my heart and carved a piece out. I bled, where no one could see. But I shook my head, a cruel smirk on my face, mostly encouraged by the pain ravaging my ribs and shoulder. I'd healed while I was passed out, enough to walk around without screaming in agony, but not much.

"The only issue with that, Wynvail," I replied tightly, my eyes glued to him, "is I don't buy it. Cut the crap. Tell me the truth; I'm a big girl, and I assure you I can handle it."

After being trampled by Harvey, choked by Em, and bruised by Kai in the fighting pit, there was nothing I couldn't handle.

Wynvail pinched the bridge of his nose to stem the flow of blood and cut a glare at me. "You can't even *pretend* to believe I have noble intentions?"

"No."

"Fine," he muttered, licking blood off his lips. "I hate them, and the feeling is mutual. I hated them a hundred years ago, and now they're mindless beasts? They're a nuisance. They're in the way of what I want."

My stomach plummeted when his gaze dragged to me. "They're my mates," I breathed, wanting to wrap my hands around his throat and suffocate him.

"Not if they're dead," he replied, tilting his head to watch me when I snarled. "Then, you'd be all mine."

"You're insane," I laughed, shaking my head and ignoring the flash of dizziness. "Killing them will kill me."

"Not necessarily," he disagreed. "You already died once; there's no telling the effect their deaths could have on you."

"So you thought you'd experiment with my life and sanity by throwing me into *a fighting pit* with them."

He shrugged. "I knew you'd be fine. I was watching you the whole time."

"There's something broken in you," I said, my lip curling in a sneer.

For a moment, something real slashed across Wynvail's face, like I'd hit a nerve.

"No doubt there is," he replied flippantly, the moment over.

"You shouldn't be able to tolerate seeing your mate hurt," I spat, my throat sore thanks to screaming as Harvey brutalised me with magic. Fuck, he'd never forgive himself when he realised what he'd done. "But you're fine with me being beaten as long as they die and you get to win? Am I even your mate, or your prized toy?"

He tilted his head, considering that. "Can't you be both?"

"I'm out of here," I hissed, heading for the open gate in the cell. Oh, how nice of him. He'd locked me up with the rest of the beasts down here.

"If you want them to survive," he called, halting me on the threshold, "you'll have to offer me something I want with equal measure."

A low, burning laugh caught in my throat as I turned back to him. Here we finally had the crux of the matter. I wasn't what he wanted; I was just a pawn, leverage to be used.

"Go on, then," I laughed, empty and joyless. "I'm sure you're dying to tell me what it is you really want."

Wynvail rose, his movements calculated and elegant but hiding so much power that, for a moment, it rippled through the tunnels and robbed my breath. I held still as he crossed the cell to me, brushing a knuckle over my jaw.

"Archdemons are harder to kill than regular demons, you know that."

I nodded tightly.

"They can be killed an infinite number of times, in many different ways, and as long as there's a tether to bring them back, they never truly die."

"Why are you telling me this?" I demanded, baring my teeth and tucking my black wings tight to my back. Instincts screamed that I was in danger, that I needed to *run*.

"It's incentive to return," he replied mildly, and I froze as he leant closer to kiss my cheek, his lips burning hot. "They've survived so much, your mates, but I know the ways they can be really, *truly* killed."

I inhaled sharply and jerked away. "Keep threatening my mates, and I'll find a way to really, truly kill *you*, asshole."

He grinned, true pleasure in his silver eyes. "I welcome the attempt."

"Just tell me what you want," I said through gritted teeth, retreating into the tunnel to escape the power and desire surrounding him like a dark miasma, threatening to pull me under.

"There's a tiara in the bowels of Lucifer's palace. It belonged to an ancient goddess and holds untold power."

"Forgive me if I don't want to give a total maniac untold power," I drawled, my heart pounding fast as I scanned the tunnel, weighing my chances of successfully escaping.

But I'd be leaving my mates here. To fuck knows how many more deaths. To unspeakable suffering. To whatever made Harvey a bestial shell of himself.

Wynvail shrugged and leant against the bars of my cell, looking like an arrogant, repugnant prince with his short chestnut hair and that cruel, devastating face. "It's your choice, of course. Just know you'll be leaving your mates with *a total maniac*. And I have very little patience and mercy."

"No shit," I said under my breath. My skin itched, the feeling of a trap closing around me. "What's this tiara look like?"

"Like a tiara," he replied flatly. "Pretty, with white and red gemstones, intricate silverwork—I'm sure you know what a tiara looks like."

"I'm sure the palace has more than one tiara," I threw back in the same heartless tone.

He sighed, but there was no hiding the heat of obsession on his face when he looked at me. "Most tiaras will be powerless; you'll know it when you find it."

Speaking of powerless...

With a tight smile I pointed out, "It'll look suspicious when I return without my bone pin."

Wynvail didn't miss a beat. "You're a resourceful woman. I'm sure you can come up with a clever explanation."

"I'll have to tell them everything I know about Alphaven," I told him, the conversation like a battle. The whole tunnel was silent, like the demons were afraid the apex predators would notice them. "I'm sure you understand."

"Of course. As long as you understand whoever comes to breach the city will die painfully." He gave me a faux-sad smile. "Their deaths will be on your head, honey."

My wings ruffled, giving away my anger. "If I get caught stealing from Lucifer, my death will be on *your* head."

"He'll exile you to the Damned Realm. Home sweet home."

I jerked toward him with a snarl, wrapping both hands around his throat and squeezing tight. Wynvail grinned, grabbing my waist and wrenching me close, our hips brushing so I could feel the hardness under his trousers.

Ugh, he loved this. I let go of him like I'd been burned.

"I'll get your tiara, but I have conditions."

"Don't murder your mates?" he asked dryly, reaching down to readjust himself in his pants.

"Don't hurt them *at all*," I corrected, my voice biting. "If I find out anyone has touched them, I'll keep your damned tiara for myself."

He shrugged. "Then I'll keep your mates."

Bastard. I snapped my teeth at him. "Second condition. Whatever the fuck you did to them, undo it. Whatever made them..."

"Beasts?" he supplied.

"Yes," I spat.

"You did that, honey," Wynvail said, watching my face like he was delighted by my horror. "With you dead, and your mates returned to life so long before you—a mere five months after being shot—they went mad. Poor creatures. It must have been torture to know you were dead and they were returned to life. To feel the absence of you in their soul every day. To know you'd never come back because you're not an archdemon like them."

I wanted to carve Wynvail's heart out of his chest with my claws. But I was going to be sick, and suddenly all my anger drained, leaving something weak behind.

They were like that—mindless and feral—because I died?

"How do I fix them?" I asked, my voice raw.

Wynvail sighed and crossed the tunnel to me, sliding his hand along my jaw in a soft caress. But his voice was as sharp as a sword when he answered, "You can't. They're gone."

"You're lying," I snapped and shoved him away, not caring that his sharp fingernails opened lines of fire on my cheek. "You just want me to think that because you want them out of the picture."

"If that's what you need to think, honey," he agreed, licking my blood off his claws. "Are those all your conditions?"

"When I bring you this tiara, you let us all go. Em, Kai, Harvey and me."

His silver eyes flashed, his expression tightening. "That was not our deal."

I knew he'd argue, but I had a quick response thought out already. "And here I thought you'd enjoy the hunt of finding me again."

A low sound rumbled in his chest. "And what prize do I get when I catch you again?"

"Your teeth punched out of your face."

He laughed abruptly, his head tipped back and the rich sound filling the tunnel.

"I'm serious," I growled.

"I hope so," he replied, dropping his head to stare at me. "You're delicious, Halwen, and even more so for being deadly and poisonous."

He took a predatory step towards me but I evaded him. "I don't think so. I want your promise—your word."

"My word counts for very little, as I'm sure you've realised."

I swallowed. I knew what I had to do, I just really, *really* didn't want to do it. But I couldn't see another way to make sure he didn't kill my other mates while I was gone. I needed a guarantee. So I surprised Wynvail by sliding closer to him, laying my hands flat on his stomach before I glided them down to his hips.

That low rumbling sound came from his chest again and he grabbed my ass, squeezing and grinding my hips into his as his mouth slammed down on mine.

Pretend, I ordered myself. *Make it convincing.*

But when he bit my bottom lip, drawing blood, and his tongue claimed my mouth, it was hard to pretend. A shudder chased cold through my body, but my pussy was red hot, pounding a frantic beat as Wynvail growled into my mouth and kissed me thoroughly. Blood coated my tongue and his, but it tasted like need and satisfaction.

He dragged his mouth from mine and grazed my jaw with his sharp teeth, breathing fast. "Take as many knives as you like, honey. If I get to kiss you like that each time, you can strip me of a hundred weapons."

Shit. I tore away from him with a knife in my hand, the blade feeling less like a prize now. He knew what I was doing; he *let* me kiss him. Even when I made the first move, I felt like a pawn in his game.

"I want a blood vow," I told him, clearing my throat when it came out husky.

"I thought you would," he agreed easily, holding out his arm as if a blood vow was nothing. As if it didn't lock both people into a promise until death.

I licked my dry lips, hating that I tasted blood, tasted *him.* Shuddering—definitely with revulsion—I slashed my forearm, and then Wynvail's, and fought back a shudder when his fingers intertwined with mine after zero prompting.

"I, Lord Wynvail Locke, vow no harm upon the mates of my mate, and upon receipt of a tiara, Emlyn, Malakai, and Harveil will be released from their cells." He met my hard gaze. "To whatever end."

I swallowed. What did that mean? "I, Halwen Vakhara, vow to retrieve the tiara from Lucifer's palace in return for my mates' freedom."

Wynvail grinned as power roped around our forearms, lashing them together for a long, long moment. It was barely visible as a shimmer of opalescence in the air, but it was as strong as steel rope. My stomach knotted, foreboding crawling down my spine.

"Shall we seal it with another blistering kiss?" Wynvail asked, his molten eyes gleaming. "I think another will send me over the edge, I'm so fucking hard from the taste of you."

The second the magic released us, I tore my arm away. "Fuck you."

"Your body wants to," he taunted.

"It wants to kill you," I corrected in a snarl, scanning my arm. The vow was barely visible with the curse mark already on my forearm; there was just a cluster of promise dots above the moon at the centre of my tattoo.

"That's your mind, honey," Wynvail replied with a laugh, squeezing his cock through his trousers. "Your body wants something *very* different."

"I assure you, my body also wants to stab you in the eye."

"I'd fuck you better with a single eye than all those brutes put together."

I turned and stalked up the tunnel without bothering to reply. My whole body was on edge. Violence, bloodlust, terror, and explosive desire made me shaky.

Wynvail followed me like a shadow.

I flinched away from the thought, remembering the shadows wrapped around me when Locke killed us. Wynvail was broken and cruel now, but those shadows had been protective and kind—loving. Was this cruelty the start of his deterioration? Would I become a stranger to him, like I was to the others?

I was alive now, but what if it was too late to stop Wynvail's descent? What if there was no way to reverse the others' either?[1]

Wynvail didn't talk the whole walk down the tunnel, but he followed closely enough that I felt the heat and intensity of him against my wings. He only spoke when we reached the stairs back up to the house where I'd woken up, chained to an attic wall.

"Wait, Halwen."

I paused only because he didn't snarl the order and it felt more like a request. I watched, my arms crossed over my chest, as he ducked into a kitchen and retrieved—my swords.

My heart stumbled; I snatched them out of his hands and held them to my chest.

"They mean so much to you," he observed, his eyes narrowed. Jealous.

"Yes," I bit out, driving them into their sheaths where they belonged. I felt better with their weight on me, like I was carrying my mates with me. I'd find a way to bring them back to themselves. As long as they were out of the cells, I'd find a way to reverse what my death did.

"I'm keeping the pin, though," Wynvail told me, remorseless. "And this is for luck."

I was too emotional to realise he'd sidled closer. His lips pressed to my forehead; I felt his smile against my skin.

I slammed a fist into his stomach, and when he doubled over with a grunt, I fled.

CHAPTER THIRTY-SIX

*P*aranoia burrowed under my skin and made me itchy as I strode down the tall, bright hallways of Lucifer's palace. I had every right to be here, but I was so scared someone would take one look at me and know *why* I was here.

I held my breath every time I rounded a corner, expecting cruel gods to throw Callahan or Cerny into my path. I didn't know how I'd explain losing the bone pin. I could get thrown in the dungeons for all I knew, and I didn't have that kind of time to waste.

My mates were suffering, traumatised and abused, forced into a fighting pit regularly. I needed to get them out of there. I'd figure everything else out when they were free. And fuck Wynvail. Just ... fuck that guy.

Your body wants to.

I shut out his words, struggling for breath as I walked deeper into the palace. I didn't know where to find an all-powerful tiara, but the vaults seemed like a good place to start. Thank fuck for Tali's guided tour; I sent a silent apology to my friend for abusing the information she gave me.

But this was for Kai, Em, and Harvey.

I inhaled sharply when images shattered through my mind; Em's feral eyes, the new scars on his bearded face; Kai's complete and utter lack of humanity, his hunger for my death; and Harvey, a beast of nightmares made of fur, claws, and teeth. The pain he'd inflicted on me...

I had to get them out of those damn tunnels. Had to get them somewhere safe.

I didn't know where we'd go, but getting out of Alphaven was more important. I'd figure everything else out later. At least we'd be alive, and together again.

"Hey," a male voice called from behind me, and my stomach turned over even if his tone was friendly, not furious. "You're Halwen, right?"

I turned slowly, dread blooming from my gut to the rest of my body. My hands shook as I assessed at the brown-haired, thirty-something man opposite me; I pressed them flat to my thighs.

"That's me," I confirmed, frowning. He didn't strike me as a threat, but appearances could be deceiving.

He pushed his glasses up his tanned nose and said, "I'm Russ; my brother, Cerny asked me to talk to you about—"

"Look, I'm really sorry, Russ, but I'm in a huge rush. Can we talk about this later? I'll be free in a couple hours."

When I'd be safely out of the palace.

"Uh, yeah sure." He frowned at me, his brown eyes pinching. "Are you okay? You look sick."

I gave him a thumbs up, because my awkwardness was at an all-time high.[1] "I'm great, thanks. See you later."

Ugh, gods smite me.

I turned and hurried away before Russ could question me further.

I wasn't great; I was cold and clammy and close to passing

out. But I wasn't about to tell a stranger that and rouse suspicion.

The vaults were next to the armoury where Renna had brought me to return my knives, but neither Renna nor Tali's tour had told me how to get *in*. I paced down the hallway, staring at the spot of solid, white brick where the vaults lay, and didn't know how the hell to open it. Where even was the door? It was just pure brick, no handle, nothing.

If I still had the pin, I had no doubt I'd be able to force my way in with brute power alone. But without it, all I could do was skim my hands over the wall in search of a seam.

"What are you doing?" a husky female voice made me jump.

I spun, my hand going to the hilt of a knife as awareness of being caught sent shivers down my arms.

Shit. Queen Lili stood there with her lips in a flat line and her eyes darting between me and the wall, like she knew exactly what I was doing.

"I'm lost," I blurted, dread crushing the air from my chest.

When her dark wings snapped tight to her back in clear disapproval, my stomach dropped hard. "No. You're not."

I shook, turning halfway to look at the wall. I needed to think fast or I was dead, Wynvail would win, and my mates' suffering would never end. I couldn't bear it, everything that was happening to them. The emptiness and harrowing rage in their eyes. There was nothing I wouldn't do to get them out of there.

"Renna told me to meet her here," I breathed, nowhere near strong enough to be believable. "She needs to give me something for my next job."

Lili took a slow step forward, her dress barely rustling, the expression on her face frozen with wrath. "Are you stealing from us, Halwen?"

"No," I argued, putting enough force into it that it *might* be believable. I backed up a step when she advanced, power bleeding into the air. It was enough power to make my bones ache and my skin tingle with warning.

I caught my breath, the aches in my body flaring a thousand times worse than when I'd woken in the cell with Wynvail.

"After we took you in and gave you a job, and a *home*. After we made you our friend and ally—you'd betray us like this? *For what?* Money? Status? To brag that you could break into Lucifer's vaults?"

"No!"

I trembled harder, the sensation of being caught, trapped making my head spin. The emotion that had been ravaging me since I realised it was Emlyn who attacked me blazed through my chest, pressing against my weak spots. Everything that had happened in the last twenty-four hours was too much. It pressed on me until I felt something in my soul collapse.

I *needed* this damn tiara; without it, Wynvail would do fuck knows what to the others.

Lili advanced on me, and I was so busy falling apart I didn't get away in time. She grabbed my arm and dug her fingers in.

"You better start explaining yourself, Halwen, or I'll show you why I'm known as the Justice of Hell."

"I can't," I gasped. What would Wynvail do if he found out I told the queen of Hell about him? "I can't tell you why, but I *need* to get inside the vaults. *Please.*"

Lili shook her head, a glint of ruthlessness in her brown eyes. "Not good enough, Halwen."

"I found my mates!" I blurted.

Her pretty face swam as the pain in my ribs and shoulder flared, my soul copying the sudden surge with a sharp slice, making me gasp. A surge of cool shadow crashed through me in response, and it felt like worry, like blinding fear.

"They're captive," I went on breathlessly, her grip painful, "and I can only free them with a tiara in these vaults. *Please.* The psycho who has them will *kill them.* He's been torturing them for a hundred years and—and something's wrong with my mates."

A sob broke up my throat, and I lost complete control of my voice, my breathing. Tears blurred my vision until all I could see were smears of light.

"They attacked me. They shouldn't even be able to hurt me, but they wanted to *kill me.* Something broke them, and I don't even know if they can be saved, but I need—I need to try—"

I hated breaking down in front of other people, but I couldn't stop now I'd started. My chest collapsed with cries, my heart breaking out in the open for anyone to see.

"Which tiara?" Lili asked, releasing my wrist, a deeper frown blurring her golden face.

"I don't know, it used to belong to a goddess," I rasped.

Lili nodded and stepped around me, pressing her palm flat to the seamless wall. I wiped my eyes to see a ring on her finger glow faintly, like it was a key. Or maybe a master key for every door in the palace.

She didn't say anything else, silently ducking inside the room. Tall ceilings made her soft footsteps echo.

I pushed my way through the door as dread swelled to fill my chest. But my breath caught with a gasp of awe at the huge, golden shelves that spanned from the floor to three storeys high, filled with so many different things that I couldn't begin to imagine what they were.

Lili strode right for a glass cabinet, her skirts trailing on the ground. She was terrifying. Soft spoken, elegant, and kind, but terrifying. I hesitantly followed her past three dozen waist-high bookcases that bowed with the weight of globes, astrolabes, and objects of unknown power. I eyed the strange and varied collection like it would grow teeth and bite me. For all I knew, it would.

My heart slamming against my ribs, I kept a hand on my knife as Queen Lili opened the cabinet. I waited for the axe to fall. Would it be handcuffs? A cursed bracelet? A crown of rusty nails to punish me?

She was right; they'd taken me in and given me a home, given me kindness and friendship, and here I was driving a knife into their backs.

I turned for the door. What had I been thinking, following her in here? She had every right to murder me.

"Halwen." She stopped me before I could leave.

I swallowed the lump in my throat and turned, instinct burning at having my back to the most powerful woman in Hell. I jumped, what breath I had left abandoning me when I saw what she held out to me:

A tiara with glimmering white and red gems and beautiful, scrolling silverwork.

I swallowed, wiping tears from my cheeks and looking from the tiara to her face. "You know giving me that could put its power in the wrong hands, right?"

Oh, my voice was so not sexy. The word *clogged* came to mind.

Queen Lili crossed the room to me, nothing but understanding in her brown eyes. "I would burn down the whole world for my men. It probably makes me a bad person for putting them above everyone else, but I would. So go get your mates."

The metal was cold when she pressed the tiara into my numb hands, the pain ravaging my shoulder and soul easing, like the tiara's magic already seeped into me.

"Was it really owned by a goddess?" I whispered, my heartbeat loud.

Lili nodded, sweeping soft brown hair over her shoulder. "Eos. Lucifer's mother."

I blinked. Wait..."His mum's *a goddess?*"

"I know," Lili laughed, a smile rounding her cheeks. "Crazy, right?"

"Definitely," I agreed, staring at the tiara in my hand. The tiara that had been worn by a goddess and had her power still within it.

The thought of Wynvail having all that power made me sick. He already had the bone pin, and control over demons. What would he do with this? Something far worse than fighting pits and tunnels full of prisoners forced to fight.

"Do you need anything else to free your mates?" Lili asked, nothing but understanding in her husky voice. She looked one move away from pulling me into a hug.

I turned the tiara over in my hands and swallowed. I had an idea—a very stupid, reckless, suicidal idea.

"Actually," I replied, "I need one more thing."

CHAPTER THIRTY-SEVEN

This time, I approached Alphaven with so much steel and iron on my body that I rattled with every step. I didn't crouch in the trees to scope out the road into the city; I blew into the place like a storm and snarled at anyone who got in my way.

"Well, well," a sneering voice remarked as I strode up the road, fixed on the giant fire burning in the middle of the fighting pit until four people stepped into my path. "Look who's back."

The raiders who grabbed me the last time I was here crowded around me, obviously thinking they could cage or intimidate me. I didn't bother with conversation; my heart had slowed to a sluggish beat and a cold, brutal calm filled me. It had been a long, long time since I'd felt this lethal calm.

By the time the raiders reacted to me drawing my beloved blades, I'd slashed the throats of two of them and buried a dagger in the stomach of a third, leaving them to a painful death. The fourth—the biggest, smartest one—stumbled back, but I slammed a dagger back into its sheath and grabbed him.

"Take me to Wynvail."

"And you won't kill me?" he asked.

Yeah, something like that.

I kept my other dagger as an incentive for him not to piss me off, but the ice cold wrath in my expression must have been enough because he didn't even look at me. He scurried quickly across the city, leading me through the warren of streets, past houses too intact, too perfect to show the rotting underbelly of Alphaven.

A rotten core my own mate was responsible for.

I was starting to think whoever had cursed my memories had been doing me a favour.

"Thanks," I told the raider when he led me to the door I'd fled eight hours ago. I'd have been back faster if the cloud cover hadn't fucked with my visibility in the skies. I'd had to *walk*, and I wasn't happy about it.

I slashed my knife at his throat, fully meaning to kill this asshole too, but he dodged the move like he'd been expecting it. Without looking back, he sprinted away, kicking up a cloud of dust on the dirt road.

I shrugged. I'd let him live; with any luck, he'd live in terror for the rest of his life. Serves him right for working for a twisted psychopath like Wynvail.

I adjusted my grip on my dagger, reached for my blood magic—swearing when I failed to grasp it—and then kicked in the front door with my heavy boots.

"Hey, asshole, I'm back!"

WYNVAIL WAITED FOR ME IN THE KITCHEN. HE DIDN'T GET UP from his seat at the table when I crashed through the door or stalked down the hallway. Cold spread deeper through me, icing my emotions until every part of me felt sharp like broken ice. With mechanical movements, I swapped my volcanic dagger for a regular blade.

The little smirk on his face made me want to slam my knuckles into his nose and draw blood, but I locked down that rage and just stared at him. He stared back with unflinching silver eyes, cocking his chin in invitation.

"Take a seat," he ordered, that smirk growing.

My expression went flat. There was only one chair and he was sitting in it. All the others had been removed; he'd planned this.

I wasn't about to drop onto his lap, so I gave him a psycho, little smile that should have made him piss himself in fear, and stalked to the countertop by the small window, hoisting myself up.

I swung my feet back and forth, satisfaction beating in my heart when a vein throbbed in Wynvail's bronze forehead.

"So you failed," he said after a long pause, his fingers knitted together on the tabletop, knuckles white. His irritation threatened to show. It seemed he was trying to get a rise out of me, and my icy calm was driving him mad. Good. "You didn't bring me the tiara."

I tilted my head, assessing him with a cold gaze. "I'll give it to you when you release my mates. That was our deal."

His smile was sudden and as sharp as a razor's edge. "Why would I free them without evidence?"

I didn't look away from his cruel, sharp-planed face as I reached into the leather satchel at my waist and pulled out the tiara. I settled it on my head, inhaling a sharp breath like I had when I first touched the bone pin. My hands visibly shook; I curled them into fists.

"Its power corrupts," Wynvail said, rising from his seat like a predator marking its prey. "It takes over its host entirely, until they're nothing but mindless magic."

He drew closer, hands gliding up the outside of my thighs

until I jumped, my heart slamming fast. "How does it feel, honey? To hold unlimited power?"

That was as good a time as any to drive my dagger all the way through his shoulder. It took more force than I expected to bury it deep, like I punched through a shield as well as skin.

Wynvail cried out in pain, staggering back in surprise. Nostrils flaring, his face frozen with rage, he lifted his hand where blood poured freely from his shoulder. It darkened his white shirt, ruining the fabric. *Aww, so sad.*

"Like I said. Release my mates."

Wynvail stared at me with an intensity that scared me, his chest rising and falling fast. Like he wanted to own me, *devour* me. "I could slit your throat and rip that tiara off your head right now."

I bared my teeth in a smile. "So do it."

His eyes flicked up to the tiara, burning bright silver, and returned to my face. His stare lingered dangerously on my mouth. "I'll return your mates to you."

My heart pounded faster. I couldn't let my relief show.

He grabbed my chin in a vicious grip and tilted my head up while I shook, overcome with power. "They're waiting in the pit. But I warn you, Halwen, they're wild beasts. If I release them, they might kill you."

They're my mates; they can't kill me. Unless they were too far gone to even feel our bond…

"Maybe they'll kill you instead," I replied, matching his viciousness. I wrapped my fingers around the knife's hilt and tore it free; he drew back with a hiss but there was no concealing the obsession in his eyes.

His smirk hooked deeper. "I can't wait to watch them tear you apart."

"Likewise," I spat, and shoved him away so I could jump down from the counter. "I'll meet you at the pit. No fucking way am I walking those tunnels with you again."

He laughed, standing in the kitchen like a god, unaffected by the blood pouring from him.

"Brave of you to turn your back on me," he taunted when I stormed from the room, ripping the tiara from my head, "when I want to break you so badly."

"As if you could," I threw over my shoulder, crushing the terror that tried to form in my gut. He wanted me alive for whatever reason. He'd have killed me already if he didn't.

I shoved the front door open—and sucked in a sharp breath, stumbling into the wall when a long, carnal touch stroked down my soul.

Fuck, was that—?

Wynvail's low laugh behind me confirmed it.

Oh, gods.

I knew he was my mate all along; everything about his story made too much sense, and felt *right,* but I didn't want to believe it.

I'd hoped I was wrong.

"Safe flight, honey," he called from behind me.

I scrubbed a hand down my face and pulled myself back together, but it was impossible to grasp the emotionless ice from before. My temper was too hot, emotions too fiery. I grabbed a throwing knife and spun, judging his location by the sound of his voice.

I grinned when it sank into his existing wound. I might have been dead for a hundred years, but I was still a damn good shot.

Wynvail grunted, his eyes flashing. But he pulled the knife from his shoulder and ran his tongue along the blade suggestively.

"I can almost taste your fingerprints," he purred.

"I hope you die in the tunnels," I spat, and kicked off the ground, pumping my wings to carry me across the city.

Something was going to go wrong. I could sense it,

warning prickling my skin even though I had the tiara safely stashed in my bag. The feeling grew, throbbing behind my skull, instincts *screaming* at me to turn back, to run, to—to find something. *Find what?*

The feeling grew, making my heart race and sweat prick my palms. I was missing something, and I didn't know what. And the longer I ignored that gnawing sense, the bigger it grew.

I needed the icy calm back, but I struggled to grasp even *regular* calm as I raced across rooftops, weaving in a manic path to the open-roofed arena at the heart of the city. The bonfire blazed high enough to leave scorch marks on the highest edges of the roof; I avoided them as I flew closer.

I was so focused on the flames, I didn't see the arrows firing right at me until one lanced through my wing. I screamed, a mingled sound of pain and fury that made my throat hoarse. Another arrow tore my shoulder apart when I tried to twist out of its path, and a third slashed a burning line across my chest.

I filled my lungs with air and did the most reasonable thing a person could do when they'd been impaled by three arrows. I threw my head back and bellowed, *"Cock-sucking motherfuckers!"*

My wing was pierced. The dishonourable bastards had *shot my wing.* My breath shattered in panic when my next wing-beat faltered, too much pain slicing through the delicate membrane beneath my feathers.

"No," I whispered, trying to catch enough air to slow my descent, but the sky tore at me as I plummeted.

I flung my arms out, as if they could stop my fall, but they were useless. I plummeted straight through the fire, screams bruising my throat. It took me a long, terrifying moment to realise they didn't burn my skin, didn't make my flesh bubble and melt. Oh.

I caught my breath, snapping out my good wing to gain some control of the descent, but I was *far* closer to the ground than I realised. I only had two seconds to twist my body so I landed on my shoulder and not my face.

When I slammed into the fighting pit, a piercing scream ripped up my throat, sounding utterly foreign. The arrow in my wing had torn on a jagged angle, and the one in my shoulder pushed deeper.

"Ouch," a smooth voice remarked high above me. "That looks painful, honey."

I snarled, trying to push to my feet.[1] "I'm going to kill you."

"I look forward to it," Wynvail replied. "Bring me her bag."

Hands reached for my bag and snapped the strap; I kicked out, but my leg was too weak to land a blow.

I took a tight, stabbing breath and shoved my body off the floor, baring my teeth at the pale-skinned demon who crossed the arena to give my bag to Wynvail who ... *fuck*, who sat on a throne like a dark king.

I wanted to cry. Instead, I panted for breath and summoned a sneering laugh from beneath my pain.

"Who do you think you are, Wynvail? You're *nothing*. Nobody. The son of a dirty politician that no one knows anymore. You look—ridiculous on that throne."

I panted by the time I finished talking, but it was worth it for the dark, livid expression on his bronze face—and for the way someone snorted in the crowd.[2]

"Hold her down," the psychopath snapped at the pale guy who'd stolen my bag. Oh, no, wait, there were three more of them. Quadruplets? They all had the same damn face. "I want her forced still for this punishment."

He rifled through my bag as his eerie goons came for me. I was forced to drag my stare away from the cruel bastard to defend myself. No way would I let them grab me and hold me down for—what? What would Wynvail *do?* Were there any lengths he wouldn't go to? Any lines he wouldn't cross?

A hush went through the audience, and for a moment I thought it was because the bastards had reached me, but from the corner of my eye I watched Wynvail raise the tiara to his head.

"I'm not sure it's your style," I remarked breathlessly, and slid a knife from my leather trousers, jamming it into my pale assailant's throat before his hands could touch me.

Shit! He landed *on* me, blood pumping hot from his throat until I was drenched. I was too weak, pain scorching through all the places I'd been shot, to push him off.

"Did I say you could touch her?" Wynvail asked in a calm, still voice. It was the sort of quiet rage that carried across an entire arena.

A sudden rush of movement to my right preceded the dead man being hauled off my bleeding body. I groaned, arrows shifting in my flesh.

My abhorrent mate paused above me, seeing the dagger in his goon's throat, realising I'd been buried under dead weight. He stared at the pale man with such hatred, his chest rising and falling, like he wanted to reanimate him so he could kill him himself. "She's *mine.*"

Wynvail tossed the man aside and reached for me.

I reacted on instinct, throwing my palms out, sweat dripping down the side of my neck and temple. A deep crimson light exploded from the tattoo on my arm, glowing through my jacket and lighting up my hateful mate in shades of blood and violence.

The formerly hushed crowd erupted into sudden noise, and I flinched, striking my head against the floor.

Cursed One...

She's cursed...

Cursed marks...

She'll kill us all...

Great, these bastards knew me as well as Bevan and his little band.

Even Wynvail staggered back, staring at me like he'd never seen me before. "You..."

"Me," I agreed with a grin that was—easier to fake. Huh? What happened to my agony?

I wasn't sticking around to find out answers. I vaulted off the floor and drew a dagger, driving it into Wynvail's unmarked shoulder. *Might as well make them matchy matchy.* I gouged a nice, deep line before tearing the blade out and plunging it under the ribs of another pale bastard when he lunged at me. The tip pierced his heart; I watched the light leave his eyes.

"I suppose I should be grateful you didn't stab *me* in the heart," Wynvail mused, his arms locking around me from behind. Shit, how did he sneak up on me?

I kicked off the floor, throwing all my weight into him to dislodge his grip. It didn't work. *Fuck.*

"I should warn you," he said, lips brushing my ear in a warm caress that made my toes curl. "Physical combat turns me on."

I turned my shudder into one of revulsion. "Gross."

He laughed, breath tickling my ear. "You *ache* for me, don't you, honey? You need this cock stretching you out, filling you up with every inch of me. I can feel your need, throbbing in your soul. Does your cunt throb, too?"

I gritted my teeth and stretched my arm down, panting fast as I reached for a concealed knife. The second my fingers connected, I drove it into his thigh and—felt his cock throb against my ass. Shit, fighting really did turn him on. Injuring him earlier had been little more than foreplay.

"Let me go," I hissed when he dragged his teeth up the line of my throat, his tongue hot and wet on my skin. Everything tightened inside me, my clit pulsing even though I was so close to being murdered by him.

"Give me one good reason I shouldn't thrown you down on the floor and fuck you in front of all these people. I could make you scream my name, Halwen. I could make you come harder than you ever have, until the only cock your body craves is mine, until you exist only for the pleasure *I* can give you."

Cool fingers stroked my wing, grasping the arrow piercing it and tearing it free.

I screamed so loudly it echoed around the arena. His cock jerked madly against my ass.

But both my cursed marks flashed red, burying my pain until I had enough strength to elbow Wynvail in the gut and hurl myself out of his arms. I could barely breathe.

I brought my knife up to kill the remaining pale demons but—they were already dead. Their eyes were nothing more than burned red sockets, mouths hanging open in pain. Had he done that ... or had my curse?

"I'd rather die than touch you," I hissed at Wynvail, turning to face him, my heart pounding at the predatory, intense way he watched me. I clenched my jaw, panting, and tore out another arrow before he could do it himself.

"Gods, I love the way you fight me," Wynvail groaned, a bright fanaticism on his face as he pulled out the knife in his thigh and tucked it into his pocket, blood spurting to the ground. "Will you fight me when I'm buried in that sweet, aching cunt? Fuck, I hope so."

"Where are my mates?" I snarled, the back of my neck burning as the crowd stared at me. I reached for the last arrow and yanked it free. The magic in my curse marks soothed the pain as soon as they were out.

"I'm the only mate you'll ever need," he replied, but there

was a bite in his voice and his face tightened. He was angry that I had other mates?

"Where are they?" I demanded, my nostrils flaring. "That was our deal. You release them if I bring you the tiara."

He tilted his head, observing me in a way that made my skin crawl. "Kneel, and I will."

My breath stuttered. I glanced at our audience, and quickly looked away from the hunger in their faces. They didn't chant for Wynvail to kill me, but I could see the desire for blood in their eyes.

"What?" I breathed.

"You heard me," Wynvail replied, a smirk on his cruel mouth. "Kneel."

I licked my dry lips. My heart thumped so hard I felt each beat through my body and—no, that wasn't my heart. That was *magic*. It pulsed in time with the glow in my curse marks.

"Kneel before your master," Wynvail purred.

I gave him the middle finger, and focused on that ebb and flow of power, my breath syncing with the magic. Five answering thumps went through my blood, shocking my soul with power and—life.

I jolted back a step, magic unlocking inside me that had no right to be there. I didn't have the pin, and my blood power was locked down, cursed away, so—where the *fuck* was this magic coming from?

Wynvail laughed, strolling towards me, covered in blood. "Well, isn't that interesting?"

"Fuck you," I hissed, keeping my eyes on his face as I grasped that power. What the hell was happening?

Rage filled my soul, blisteringly hot; I flinched away from the sudden intensity. I felt clawed hands curl around cold iron bars, and a muscular shoulder slam into a cell wall, and invisible snakes coil protectively around frail shoulders, and a body curl into a tight wall, fresh cuts throbbing on an arm already littered with scars, and cold, cutting rage swell to fill a chest as—as Wynvail stalked closer to me.

Shit! I twisted aside, throwing up my glowing arm to ward him off, but he only grinned.

"That won't hurt me, Halwen. You can't harm your mate."

"You can't harm me either, then," I panted, the ache that had bruised my soul ever since I climbed out of a grave growing viciously, making my legs buckle.

Wynvail made a contemplative noise, his boots stopping in front of me as I bent over myself. "I suppose I can harm you, but not kill you. The same goes for you killing me."

I made a throaty sound, my curse marks pulsing faster, the light casting further. I could feel the cold bite of cells, feel the strength of stone walls, the suffocation of being trapped, always trapped.

"I don't need to kill you," I breathed to Wynvail, wrapping fingers around those bars like they were my own. Magic throbbed faster, power sinking through my fingers into iron. It made no sense, but I wasn't about to question how the curse mark's power travelled down my soul to my mates.

"They can kill you," I rasped, and felt the bars collapse—not just in my mates' cells but *every* cell under Alphaven.

"What did you do?" Wynvail demanded, grabbing my arms and dragging me to him.

I grinned, snapping my teeth at his face as alphas and beasts burst through the tunnels into the arena. "Your move, *honey,"*

CHAPTER THIRTY-EIGHT

*M*y victory was undermined by the pain that ravaged my chest and weakened my legs, but it was satisfying to watch the blood drain from Wynvail's face.

"They'll kill you, too," he hissed, already storming away, leaving me to the mercy of alpha beasts.

I gave his retreating form my middle finger. "Coward!"

He spun with a hiss, teeth bared, ruining his smug, aristocratic mask. He opened his mouth to retort, but his attention caught on something behind me and panic widened his eyes.

I spun, throwing my hands out in front of myself, not sure how to wield the power of my curse marks. But I had no doubt this glow was magical. The curse had blocked my blood power, but there was no way I'd be able to unlock all the cells without magic.

Who the fuck cursed me?

"Shit," I gasped when I spotted the giant running straight at me, his meaty fists outstretched like he was going to grab me up.[1]

He wasn't deterred by my curse marks, but the next crea-

ture—a snarl of shadows, black fur, and vicious teeth—
flinched away when the light spilled over him.

"Harvey," I breathed.

He didn't even look at me.

"We're getting out of here, Buttercup," I told him, shrieking
as I threw myself out of the path of the giant's hairy hand
before it could crush my bones. Harvey paused at the sound,
his head tilted.

"This way," I yelled over the sudden snarls, growls, and
roars filling the arena. A muscular body jostled me; a huge
woman with tusks shoved me aside. I kept my eyes on Harvey
the whole time, not letting my heart sink at his lack of recog-
nition. "Where are the others? *Harvey!*" I shouted when he
stalked away from me.

He didn't know his own name. A lump rose in my throat.

"Stop!" Wynvail yelled from above. He must have made it
into the stands without being murdered. Fucking pity. "All of
you, *enough!*"

A bull-demon beside me chuffed viciously through his
nose. I didn't think he thought it was enough; quite the
opposite.

Someone else shoved past me, knocking my shoulder so
hard I went flying to the ground, pain cracking up my wrists
as I landed awkwardly. Shit, I was gonna get trampled down
here.

"*Get up*, Halwen!" Wynvail roared, a sudden yank on my
soul making me gasp. "I want to kill you myself, not watch
you get murdered in a stampede."

My heart skittered. The crimson glow of my curses illumi-
nated boots, bare feet, and hooves, all running frantically,
coming too damn close to my face.

When a shapely leg landed beside me, I used it as a crutch
to heave myself back to my feet—and came face to face with

Kai's livid face, his nostrils flaring and crimson eyes bright with murder.

"There you are," I sighed, grabbing his shoulder to keep him from running off.

He stared at my arm, and inhaled a sharp breath when he saw my curse marks. "Yeah, this is a whole thing."

For a moment I thought he recognised me and he was worried because his mate was cursed, but the next moment he tried to wrench himself out of my grip, his invisible snakes brushing over my skin with a mix of sparkling pain and soft familiarity. Kai didn't recognise me, but he was *afraid* of me.

"Stop fighting," I barked, hauling him away from a sudden brawl, blood spraying the air. "I'm trying to rescue you, you difficult fucking damsel."

He bared sharp fangs.

"Yeah, yeah, whatever," I muttered, scanning the melee for Harvey and finding him on all fours not too far away, snarling in the face of any alpha that came too near to him. "Harvey! *Hey!* Fucker!"

I swallowed down the lump of emotion in my throat when he didn't even look my way. He really didn't remember me at all.

None of them did.

"Well, I remember *you*, you bastards," I snarled, and dropped my arm to Kai's hand, linking our fingers to haul him across the arena to Harvey, craning my neck for Em's broad-shouldered frame and salt-and-pepper hair. "And I'm not leaving you here to Wynvail's mercy."

Kai's snakes tried to harm me and failed. He hissed, deep and throaty at my touch.

"Yeah," I agreed. "Wynvail needs to suffer. But not now; we need to get out of here."

He threw me a wary look, trying to extricate himself from my grip and failing. *Nice try, buddy, I'm as clingy as an octopus.*

"Em!" I screamed, finally spotting him rolling on the floor, knocking ten lumps out of a demon that looked like a gorilla.

It was bizarre to see my quiet, introverted gentle giant fighting like a wild animal. His anxiety must have been going crazy right now. I reached for him in the bond and—found nothing but shreds of our tether. Pain cracked through my middle.

"Stop!" Wynvail boomed again, some of the alphas responding with snarls but others pausing with their fists and paws frozen.

I shoved past them, hauling Kai with me, and grabbing Em's shoulder. When he growled in my face, I bared my teeth and growled right back, my wings ruffling and giving away my nerves.

"You need to come with me. We'll be safe."

Em pulled away, using his superior strength, but Kai let out a foreboding hiss and Em's blue gaze snapped to me, finding the curse mark on my arm. Were they ... communicating?

My bottom lip wobbled, but I shoved the vulnerability behind an iron wall. I didn't have time for it, even if I was *so damn relieved* they could talk to each other, that they might have been together all this time, as our family—not alone in their cells.

"We need Harvey," I shouted over the noise, surprised Emlyn wasn't running anymore. I grabbed him again, just in case he got any other ideas. "Harvey!"

Wynvail's laugh had me turning, my breath catching in my throat. He ruled over the chaos and violence like this had been his grand plan all along, a smirk on his gloriously arrogant face.

I tried to connect with the ruddy power in my curse marks, to push it out towards Harvey. It had worked once; it had to work again.

I staggered as a heavy boot slammed into my stomach, rearing back to crunch something in my chest, then drive into my face until my nose broke and blood flowed. Every hit made my head spin, my body throbbing and howling.

I stumbled where I stood, my knees buckling, but a hand tightened around mine, ripping me out of the vision.

"Harvey's in trouble," I breathed, which was such a familiar statement that I nearly sobbed.

I wrinkled my nose and found it unbroken, not bloody. Not mine, then. Harvey's.

I wish the wounds were dealt to me. My chest cinched tight at the realisation he was being beaten at this very moment.

Emlyn rumbled something in my direction, his brow low over his eyes and gaze darting to my forearm, then to where I touched him, and back to my face.

"This way," I barked, tucking my wings in tight and towing both my mates across the arena.

The handy thing about them being mindlessly violent was they punched everyone out of our path. The less handy thing was they kept trying to escape from me, and they looked at me like I was a bigger monster than the man with lobster claws for arms and crab legs. He scuttled sideways to escape a wolfy woman; actually, it was kind of cute.

Em grabbed a winged demon that looked shockingly like me and—and tore her wings off before casting her side like she was rubbish. Phantom pain sliced down my back, stealing a gasp.

"He's this way; I can feel it," I breathed, which was useless to them, so I tugged Kai and Emlyn left. They moved like obedient horses under my reins, but I knew it was because they were afraid of my glowing arm and not because they remembered and trusted me.

Fuck, how was I going to get their memories back? I didn't

care if they stayed like this, driven by base instinct instead of rational thought, but I needed them to *remember* me. If I had to live as a stranger to them for the rest of my life, it would kill me.

I gasped when an elbow jammed into my throat, my steps stumbling as I fought for breath. Mother*fucker,* that hurt.

"Careful, Halwen," Wynvail barked—closer but still in the seats ringing the arena. Fucking coward.

"Fuck you," I shouted back. Oh no, my voice was hoarse and low. My voice better not be forever changed.

Emlyn rumbled his agreement. He might not have known his name or who I was to him, but he certainly seemed to understand the sentiment of *fuck you.*

A cruel smile lifted my lips when Kai's snakes tore into the man who elbowed me, dropping him so fast he didn't even scream.

Hope isn't dead, I promised myself, forging on through the violence around us. *I'll get them back. I just have to get out of this place first.*

Wynvail had his damn tiara. He was vow-bound to let us go. It wasn't my fault if he didn't realise I'd faked the whole *overcome by uncontrollable power* thing. He'd bound me to fetch him *a* tiara. So, I had.

A sudden stench of sulphur and brimstone made me recoil on my next step. Lucifer, someone *stank.* Please don't let it be Harvey...

The first thing I'd do when we were safe would be find a bath if that gross smell was coming from—oh, thank fuck, it was coming from the gorilla he fought.

Well, the gorilla currently turning him into mincemeat.

The growl that burst up my throat was deep and furious and not entirely under my control. Instincts buried for a hundred years erupted.

"Stay here," I ordered Kai and Em, not expecting them to listen.[2]

"Hey, asshole!" I roared at the huge black gorilla, charging right at him and drawing my long daggers in each hand.

He—I presumed the beast was a *he* because of the giant balls dangling between his legs—didn't blink at the blades, but his attention caught on the red light coming from my arm.

"What the hell are you?" he demanded, shocking the hell out of me.

"Holy fuck, you can talk."

He bared his teeth in a blunt grin. "I'm new here."

So the longer you stayed, the more of yourself you lost. And my mates had been here for a hundred years. *Gods.*

"Good for you, buddy." I jumped between him and Harvey, ignoring my mate's low complaint, probably at my proximity. "You're beating the shit out of my mate."

"He started it. He grabbed me and punched my nose.

To be fair, that did sound like Harvey.

"Find another punching bag," I replied, a hard edge to my voice.

"I like the one I've got, thanks," the gorilla replied, matching my tone.

I sighed. Here I was thinking it would be easy.

"Dakarh," Wynvail yelled from the crowd.

"Oh, fuck off," I shouted back without looking at him, hoping it pissed him off. I wasn't connected to him beyond that first flash of emotion so I couldn't know for sure.

"Kill the monster and I'll reward you," he told Dakar. Whoever Dakar was.

"He's not a fucking monster," I snarled, turning despite myself to bare threatening teeth at my evil mate. "You're the only monster here, Wynvail."

He shrugged, standing at the edge of the seats in a dusty

suit, his eyes fixed on me and gleaming molten silver. Harvey's eyes.

You have two Locke brothers as your mates.

I wished he wasn't my mate and felt sick for the wish. I *wanted* to love him, wanted him to love me back, but whatever memories I had of our epic love were gone. All I knew was the cruel, heartless man I wanted to stab in both eyes.[3]

Harvey sucked in a short, pained breath, and I knew his ribs were at least bruised, probably broken. I twirled my knives to warn the gorilla off, refusing to let anyone close. When Emlyn and Kai slunk closer, their eyes full of violence, my stomach flipped. But they only protected Harvey's vulnerable back.

They knew him, and still acted like a family unit. I swallowed the lump in my throat, and slashed at the gorilla when he dove at me with a low, warning sound. Wait, should gorillas have had seven-inch claws? And fangs that were half the size of my arm? Those hadn't been there before; now he spoke with a lisp.

"Nothing personal, sweetheart."

I stabbed him for that remark, more because it was cliché and clichés pissed me off than any offence caused. Also, he left his left side right open, swinging his arms around like that; it was his fault I stabbed him, really.

The roar he let out when I tore my dagger out of his body made my ears ache. I winced through the discomfort and followed up the first cut with a second and third, my training kicking in. It was as if I hadn't been rotting underground for a century.

Harvey let out a pitiful sound on the ground, wheezing with each breath.

"Stay down," I barked at him, distracted long enough for the gorilla to get a solid, blunt blow against my jaw. "Bastard!"

"Like I said," he grunted, intelligent eyes following my

movements, "it's nothing personal, but I need to kill that thing behind you."

Thing?

All my anger stilled. Froze over. It drowned out everything except the whoosh of blood in my ears. The red glow splashed higher on my arm as I dove at the gorilla—apparently Dakarh—driving the full force of my strength into the blow. My body might have been aching, but rage gifted me strength.

I kicked off the concrete floor and slammed my wings up and down, jumping above the gorilla and driving a long dagger straight down.

I missed. Shit, how did I miss?

"Another! Don't let her leave me," Wynvail yelled, his voice reaching right into my chest and gouging my heart.

Heat and fire flashed through my wings, and I caught my breath, losing height. What the fuck? I twisted, scanning my dark feathers until—a wooden shaft stuck out of my tender membrane. I'd been shot again.

Son of a bitch!

I gritted my teeth, a sound of deep, unyielding rage building in my throat as I snapped my wings open, clawing my way higher.

"Up here, asshole," I panted at Dakarh.

He laughed, dismissive of the half-angel demon flying around his head, refocusing his attention on Harvey. *Big mistake.* I didn't miss this time; I gripped the pink hilt of my dagger and drove the wavy blade through his hairy skull until it met his chin and forced its gruesome way out.

No one screamed or raced towards him. No one mourned him at all, and instead of satisfaction, sadness filled my chest when I landed unsteadily.

"Watch my back," I breathed to Em and Kai, hating that the familiarity and camaraderie between us was ruined. But as long as we were alive, we could rebuild it.

I sawed at the wooden arrow in my wing and ripped it out, beyond glad I hadn't been shot *twice* despite Wynvail's barked command. That fucking bastard. What was I supposed to do with a mate I hated, who wanted me dead every bit as much as I wanted to kill him? I threw the arrow aside, blood spilling down my feathers.

"Come on," I gasped, ignoring the rough pants of my own breathing and focusing on Harvey's rough, wheezing breaths as I sheathed my knives. I bent and grabbed him under his shoulders, trying to heave him up. I couldn't do anything for his injuries here, but if I got him somewhere safe he could heal them himself.

I'd have struggled to lift him in his other form, but his beast was even more muscular and damned heavy. I couldn't pick him up. I couldn't get him out. All of this was for *nothing* because there was no way I could leave him behind, even to get Em and Kai to safety. A sob escaped my clenched teeth.

A sudden growl made me flinch; my hands were knocked away.

My vision wavered in shades of blood red, and suddenly I was staring at myself with narrowed eyes, confusion and unease beating against my chest.

I staggered back when the vision released me, knocked aside when Emlyn scooped Harvey into his arms.

Either my mates realised I was their ticket to freedom, or they were just too afraid to go against me. Whichever way, I was so fucking relieved when Em picked up Harvey, both of us glancing up at the open sky at the same time.

"Stay with me," I pleaded, hoping he understood, hoping he'd listen, but holding absolutely no hope. His eyes darted to the curse mark on my forearm and he swallowed.

"There's nowhere you can go that I won't find you," Wynvail shouted from the stands, leaning against the barrier with the tiara clenched in his fist. Judging by the rage on his face, he'd figured out it was a fake. "Do you hear me, Halwen? You are *mine*. You don't get to leave. Launa, get them! Don't let her escape!"

"Shit," I hissed, and reached for Kai, gritting my teeth against the sharp lance of pain through my bloody wing when I moved.

I didn't know what attack would come next—more arrows? another ferocious beast?—but I braced for pain as I wrapped my arms around Kai, my contrary mate already struggling to free himself. He hissed, eyes flashing and magic twisting in tattooed text around his throat.

"Stay still, or I'll drop you to your death," I snapped at him, tightening my arms and exchanging a glance with Em—who was already in the air, flying away with Harvey.

Fuck, *fuck*. So much for us being a family unit; they'd straight up abandoned Malakai.

"Stop fighting," I growled at Kai, unable to take off with him wriggling and hissing.

Fuck it.

I slammed my mouth into his and kissed him hard, willing him to *remember* with every press of my lips. He parted his mouth to hiss at me, and I jumped at the vicious zap of his snakes as he wrapped them around me, constricting my chest, shocking sparks into my tongue. I kissed him deeper, forcing Kai into submission, and leant into his magic's touch as if it was pleasure and not sharp, biting pain.

I missed you so much.

When I drew back, his ruby eyes were wide, stunned. Good. That was all the distraction I needed to kick off the ground and pump my wings in a rapid beat, catching enough air to shoot a few feet into the air, then more, and more.

My nostrils flared as wicked-edged shards of pain travelled down my nerves, cutting through muscle and membrane until I was gasping with every wingbeat. Kai hung limply in my hold, not fighting but not helping me carry him either. Couldn't he use his snakes to make a damn sail? *Anything* to catch the air and help us fly faster.

"Good luck finding safety," Wynvail shouted as we passed him, his voice carrying easily. Wicked cleverness filled his tone, along with something cruelly amused. "You're cursed to kill each other, Halwen, and if my calculations aren't wrong, you only have thirty days of mated bliss before you all murder each other."

He paused, enjoying my gasp, watching my wings falter for a moment before I flew faster, dragging my body and Kai's through the air. A low growl of pain shook my throat, the sound constant.

"Of course, mated bliss will be difficult when they don't even know your name," he added, wholly unnecessarily. "But you don't need them when you have me. I'm all you need."

I didn't have any breath to spare on calling him delusional, so I just panted and slammed my aching, bleeding wings through the air, hauling us higher. I avoided the fire as much as I could, but its heat licked my skin like a threat.

Kai dragged in a sudden breath, his arms latching around my middle when we reached the top of the arena.

"Oh yeah, vicious fear of heights," I gasped out, wasting air I didn't have to spare.

I groaned, forcing my wings to keep flapping, Kai's body so heavy in my lead-weight arms that I came dangerously close to dropping him. But now he held me back, and it was enough for me to carry us out the open roof and down to the other side of the arena.

I stumbled when my feet touched down, my knees buckling. Wynvail's voice filled my head like a nasty echo.

The curse marks—one to nullify my power and memory, but the one on my arm? The one they all kept staring at? It cursed me to kill my mates?

We were free, but a far worse and painful threat loomed like Cassander Locke's shadow.

"Where are the others?" I rasped, holding onto Kai and refusing to let go even when he released my waist, looking decidedly less green-faced on the solid ground outside the arena.

He hissed at me, his forked tongue lashing out, which was not helpful but did throw me back into a dozen different memories. I clutched his shoulders, wavering on my feet.

"Harvey. Emlyn," I reiterated. "Where are they?"

The names meant nothing to Kai. I wasn't sure the words did; he gave no indication if they did. I let my head fall on his shoulder with a groan. How was I going to do this? With three mates who didn't know me, didn't remember how to speak, and who I was cursed to kill?

"One foot in front of the other, Haley," I breathed to myself, patting Kai in thanks for not shoving me off him. I'd needed that moment of physical contact. Of course, when I drew back he was staring at my curse mark with narrow, wary eyes.

I turned and picked a direction at random, hoping my instincts were guiding me. I opened my mouth to tell Kai to follow, but he was already jogging up to me and—catching my arm to slow my stumbling steps. The physical contact made my bottom lip cave in.

His brow knitted, lips pressed thin as he let go of me and reached for the hem of his shirt.

"Now's not the best time for a—striptease," I finished with a gasp, instantly spotting what he was trying to show me: the exact same curse mark sprawled over his too-defined ribs. I knew that body, and knew his ribs had been covered in a massive, inked raven surrounded by roses. But now it was the same brutal mark I had on my arm.

My eyes stung as I looked at it, awareness of its power burning through my bloodstream.

"You're cursed too," I choked out, Wynvail's words repeating in my head like a taunting echo.

You're cursed to kill each other, Halwen.

Each other—not me cursed to kill them. We were cursed to kill *each other.*

"I can't do this," I sobbed, reaching out to trace that mark on his ribs, his hot, velvety skin so damn familiar.

He inhaled sharply, and I tore my fingers away, eyes burning.

"Does it hurt? When I touch you?"

Kai only watched me intensely, the same expression he wore when he was either thinking about skinning someone alive or stripping me naked. I didn't know which one it was.

"Let's find the others," I breathed, turning back to the road —and flinching when a shadow dropped from the sky with a growl of warning.

I skittered back, narrowly avoiding being crushed by—by Emlyn, carrying Harvey.

A weight fell off my shoulders; I drew a full breath. But relief was a double edged sword. I became more aware of the injuries burning across my body, pain driven like arrows through my skin.[4]

"You're both okay," I breathed, staring at Em and wondering why he had two heads. That was weird. Maybe because I'd lost a scary amount of blood? "I'm not, by the way. Someone should probably catch me."

No one caught me when dizziness dropped me, but I did successfully slump into Malakai so I called that a win.

"Got my daggers back," I told him, annoyed that my voice was thick and clunky. "They weren't lost. Renna preserved them."

The words were meaningless to him.

We all jumped when a sudden chorus of roars and barks warned the rest of the alphas were breaking free of the arena.

"Time to go," I slurred, forcing myself to stay conscious. I couldn't pass out. Not yet. Not until we were safe. "The forest," I told them, pointing at the trees at the edge of the city.

Em followed my line of sight and nodded. He quickly rumbled something at Kai, but I was too busy passing out to see if they broke into a fight.

Warm arms caught me before I could hit the floor. Aww, did Em tell him to catch me?

That was so sweet.

I tried to tell him he was sweet, but blackness snapped shut around me like a trap. Safe in my mate's arms, I didn't fight the tug of a deep healing sleep.

Everything else could wait until I woke up. Sure, we were cursed to kill each other, they didn't know me at all, and I had no idea where we were going to go, but that could wait.

I did it. I found them.

CHAPTER THIRTY-NINE

WANE

The shadows were whispering her name again. The woman I refused to forget, the woman *he* tried to torture from me. It had been a hundred and two years, three months, and twelve days, and he hadn't given up. I broke years ago, probably when he had me held down while two of his cruellest warriors snapped my horns off. I didn't know the name of the titan who held my leash, who called me his wicked pet. People whispered *he* and *him* and *the titan.*

Titans were supposed to be dead. They weren't supposed to have warrens below the earth or cells so pitch black it was easy to forget your own name. I'd forgotten mine so many times, but not hers.

I felt for the shard of metal I was using currently. Before, it had been glass or broken pipe or even a claw ripped off my wings during torture. Both wings were gone now, the wounds still hot and bleeding decades later. *He* didn't let them heal.

The cuts pulsed in time to the name I repeated over and over, refusing to let *him* take it.

My shadows whispered again, holding onto her name with a ruthless possessiveness. Her name was mine. *She* was mine. A hundred years of torture hadn't stolen her from me—not like the curse written on my back, ringing both severed wings, had stolen me from the memories of everyone else.

Only the titan and his servant knew me now.

I dug the metal point into my skin, writing her name over another scarred slash of her name. I wrote it deep, so it wouldn't fade easily. My whole body was covered in that name, scarred flesh overlapping scarred flesh. The titan called me a freak, called me ugly, a monster.

As long as I never forgot her name, he could call me anything he wanted.

A memory of a lazy morning chased through the true darkness of my stone room, and my fingers tingled at the remembered feeling of silk-soft skin. My mate had let out a soft, sleepy sound and curled into me, like a flower seeking sun. But my brother was the sun; I was cold starlight and shadow.

My mate was fire and rage.

I fell into the memory as I wrote her name on my body. I wouldn't forget.

I wouldn't forget.

I jumped, a gasp torn from cracked lips when metal clanged against metal. I was broken beyond repair, but there was no denying I was still alive. I was afraid of more pain, and scared of the fear itself.

Would I give in one day?

No, the shadows whispered. *Halwen.*

Yes, I agreed as the door to my room swung open with a low creak.

"Come on, pet. He wants to see you."

See you. That meant hurt. It meant *tear apart,* meant *push to exhaustion* so he could laugh at my misery.

Halwen, I reminded myself as I was grabbed and hauled through the warren. *Halwen.*

MIDNIGHT
DESCENT

LEIGH
KELSEY

BLURB

I have four soulmates, but we're a match made in Hell...

I found my fated mates, but they're mindless beasts who don't remember me at all. On a good day, they ignore me. On a bad day, they eye me with suspicion and fear. Every blank look fractures my soul more, until I'm ready to break.

I'll need a miracle to restore my mates' memories, let alone undo the curses inked on my body. But with my psycho mate Wynvail hunting me, determined to claim me at all costs, I'll be lucky to survive to the end of the month—when I'm cursed to kill Harvey, Emlyn, and Kai.

And the final nail in my coffin? There's a black pit in my memory. Every time I try to remember what I've forgotten, pain explodes through my skull.

Being crazy, violent, and ruthless might not save me this time.

Midnight Descent is a paranormal romance with psycho men, a ruthless revenge-driven FMC, twisted demon romance, and lots and lots of bloodlust. Deadly archdemons, cutting sarcasm, epic reincarnation romance, and gruesome murders fill these pages, so get ready to laugh, cringe, and swoon.

This book is medium burn, with moderate heat, and multiple love interests, and set in the same world as Lili Kazana - but this series stands completely separate.

NOTE

This book contains mentions of past abuse and sexual assault that could be incredibly triggering for some readers, so please proceed with caution. Don't hesitate to skip this book if it's safer for your mental health.

This series also contains some spoilers for the Lili Kazana trilogy, which takes place a year before this series, but only minor spoilers for the events of the story (nothing character-wise is spoiled.)

Oh, and it contains MM, because I'm queer as fuck and my books are lacking in that representation. (Time to fix it!)

Leigh x

PART I
MISSING

CHAPTER ONE

*M*y mates were trying to kill each other again.

I pinched the bridge of my nose and stalked around the fire I'd built with zero help this morning, flinging my arms out at Harveil and Malakai. The black tattoo that spanned the length of my arm from elbow to wrist wasn't glowing, but the curse inked on my skin was enough to give Kai pause, at least. Harvey was a whole other matter, his sharp claws flashing in warning.

"Harvey, Kai, knock it off!"

At least they'd learned to respond to their names. They *chose* to ignore them.[1]

Kai cast a glance in my direction, his red eyes dark and wary, but he still aimed a blind punch at Harvey and nailed him on the shoulder.

Harvey was less bestial than when we fled the fighting pit run by my villainous bastard of a mate, Wynvail. His chestnut hair was shaggy and long, though, his shoulders usually hunched, and his bronze face was etched with a hundred years of suffering. His molten eyes were lifeless except for when he was beating the shit out of the others.

"No," I warned him, seeing that gleam in his silver eyes as he glanced at Kai. "No more—*annnd* you punched him."

I sighed. That was another broken nose Kai would sulk about later. At least Harvey didn't use his claws.

Emlyn snorted where he sat by the fire, warming his grey wings. Like I said, housecats.

"Let me see it," I huffed, pointing my finger in warning at Harvey as I stalked across the shitty forest camp to Kai. He let me grasp his chin and tilt it, but he hissed fiercely.

"It's not bad; you'll heal this overnight."

Their advanced healing worked wonders on their injuries from the training pit. So had mine. Harvey was still shaking off the worst of it though, and hissed in pain whenever he moved too fast. That damn gorilla had beaten the shit out of him.

Kai's ruby eyes simmered as he watched me, standing still for my inspection. When I let go and turned to Harvey, I felt his eyes on me. I told myself it was because, deep down, he remembered his mate, and not because the tension grew higher between all of us with every night we spent in the same small area.

They were beasts driven by nature, and fighting would only go so far. Beasts needed to fuck, too. They needed to breed, but I wasn't thinking about that—about all the failed conceptions and the uselessness and despair I felt for years.

Emlyn let out a low, warning rumble; I turned towards him in time to catch his hard look at Kai. A moment later, a charge filled the air, shivering over my skin, and I realised Kai was fighting dirty.

"No!" I barked, tempted to draw my daggers since they only listened to violence. "No magic."

Kai hissed, nostrils flared. Snapping his teeth at me, he let it disperse.

I assessed Harvey, as familiar with his body as I was with

my own. It was different now, thinner, not as strong, but still familiar. He remained still, curious and suspicious, as I pulled him into a quick hug. I kept hoping it would grind down the walls between them and their memories, that the touch would bring them back to me.

But after a week in the forest, I was almost ready to accept they'd never come back.

Almost. But not entirely, not yet.

"AND THEN YOU HIT KAI SO HARD HE FLEW INTO THE KITCHEN counter," I told Harvey, the four of us gathered around the fire under a light drizzle, the cold and wet already slicing through my clothes and into my skin.

They watched me warily, not understanding my words but at least used to the sound of my voice. It had been a week since we fled Alphaven, and as much as I kept hoping they'd open their eyes each morning and remember everything, a hundred years of abuse and suffering wasn't undone overnight. But at least they were a tiny bit less feral.

Emphasis on *tiny*.

"His snakes hit the cupboard, and the wood shattered completely," I huffed, still pissed off about my cupboards.[2]

Kai's eyes burned my face, never wavering from me as I recalled our past. Emlyn stared at the fire as it popped instead, Harvey more focused on the blood on his bronze knuckles.

"You're a nightmare when you get competitive," I told Kai, holding his gaze, waiting for him to look away.

He never did; I broke eye contact first.

"You once got in a bar fight with a six-foot-seven man because he told you you couldn't take him." I shot him a wry look and glanced at the others to see if they remembered. My heart sank when they weren't even paying attention. "He broke both your arms, because you're an idiot who can never back down."

Kai flicked out his forked tongue with a little hiss, and my stomach flipped. Did he understand?

I rushed on, "I had to force you to stop taking on jobs while you healed, but you were so stubborn you kept unfastening the bandages I wrapped around your arms, and you drank twice as many healing tonics as you were supposed to. I found you in the bathroom, even worse than before." I held his gaze, a smile on my face. "Because you're an idiot."

Kai's attention lifted to the sky, his tongue flicking out again and—and I realised he just sensed the weather growing worse.

Thunder cracked, because of course it did. Why *not* add shitty weather to my general misery and despair? I shrieked when a cloud burst above us, a sudden downpour sinking its cold claws under my jacket and into my skin. Kai hissed and shot to his feet, racing for cover under a leafy tree.

I snorted, watching him fondly as I got to my feet. "You always hated the rain. Scaredy snake."

I pulled my jacket over my head but the damage was already done, and I was *freezing*.

"I wish we had a tent," I sighed, ducking under cover and frowning at Harvey who flopped onto his back in the wet grass and let out a deep chittering noise .

"What's he doing?" I asked Em as my big mate lumbered to his feet and approached us, sliding a wary look at my curse mark. His brow furrowed, like he was puzzling the question.

"Come here," I sighed. "You've got a leaf in your hair."

I reached up to brush it out of his damp silver-black hair, but Emlyn growled gutturally deep and jerked away from me like I'd burned him.

I let my hand fall, tipping my head back to stare at the sky and blinking fast as my eyes heated.

Fuck this. Just ... fuck this.

"We need to get your memories back," I said, ignoring the lump in my throat and the tears stabbing my fragile eyes. "I thought I could handle this as long as we were all together but —it's too fucking hard. I can't stand it when you look at me and see a stranger. Or worse, a threat."

With every hiss and snarl and glare, they were breaking my heart. Breaking me, full stop.

Harvey let out another high, jagged noise, and I jumped. I was too damn fragile for this.

"Wait," I breathed, my chest cracking apart as I watched Harvey wriggle on the grass, his skin pelted by rain, chestnut hair soaked through. "Is he ... laughing?"

I'd caught him staring at the sun for hours every day, and no matter how many times I told him *you'll lose your eyesight*, he kept staring. The man who'd grown up shut in the dark, who'd only known eighteen years of sunlight and warmth before being locked in a tunnel for a hundred years, only let out to fight to the death.

No wonder he was rolling on the ground, laughing like a lunatic because of something as simple as rain.

With a lump in my throat and rain streaming down my cheeks.[3] I carefully crossed the distance and laid down a few feet from Harvey. The dry spots in my clothes drenched instantly, but I didn't care. Hypothermia would be a merciful death compared to how I was killed.

My chest ached and my eyes burned viciously, but I stayed there with Harvey until he rose minutes or hours later, shook the rain from his shaggy hair, and loped off into the trees like a wild wolf.

CHAPTER TWO

I dreamed of a night a hundred years ago, when we pretended to be normal, civilised people and went to the pub for a couple pints and some quality time together. We'd just finished a rough job chasing down a murderer who didn't want to be found, and we'd been paid handsomely by our client for handing him in.

"I hate this place," Emlyn grumbled, both hands wrapped around his pint and a sulky look on his face. He'd worn his biggest coat so he could pull the collar up and hide in it.

"You hate anywhere there's people," I teased him. Emlyn might have been big, bearded, and winged, but he was a shy man and a complete softie.

He grunted in answer.

"Oh cheer up, Em," Harvey teased him, knocking his shoulder into him. "You never know, something *exciting* might happen."

"Like a murder," Kai agreed, pointing with his dagger like that was a good point. Where the hell did he get a dagger? We were supposed to leave all weapons at home.

I cleared my throat, and all their stares snapped to me. "What's that in your hand, Malakai?" I asked mildly.

"A prop," he replied easily, an incorrigible grin on his pale, sharp face. I jumped when an invisible snake glided over my shoulders and down my chest, its invisible tail flicking my nipple.

"Malakai," I warned, my voice low. Our table was far too close to three other tables for any sort of shenanigans.

"What?" he asked innocently.

I grabbed the snake before it could go lower than my stomach, squeezing its slippery body tight. I shouldn't have been able to touch his magic, but I was his mate and apparently that allowed me to break every rule of power.

Kai choked out a deep, throaty sound and grabbed the table, leaning forward with a strained expression on his face. Anyone might think he was in pain. I stroked my thumb over the snake's head. Kai's mouth dropped open.

Harvey snorted. Even Emlyn cracked a grin between gulps of his pint. The shadows in the corner of the booth pulsed like they, too, were amused by Kai's jagged gasp and wide eyes.

I squeezed the snake again, and Kai dropped his forehead to the sticky table with a low grunt, breathing fast. His tail shuddered, giving him away.

"Don't play with fire, my night," I said sweetly, releasing my grip on the snake. "You'll get burned."

When he lifted his head, his nostrils flaring as he breathed fast, I knew I was in for it when I got home. But here, surrounded by non-killers in a normal pub, Kai couldn't punish me for making him come in his pants.

So, I sat back and sipped my beer, turning to the pocket of shadow in the corner, a name on the tip of my tongue and happiness bubbling through my veins for the first time in weeks. Before I could speak, pain arrowed through my head and I dropped my pint with a gasp, clutching my head.

What had I been about to say? I couldn't remember.

I gasped in the dream, and flinched awake in the forest, shivering and cold—

No, wait, I was *warm.* I should have been freezing, should have caught a chill with how long it had rained, the leaves above offering scant cover. Plus my clothes were completely soaked, threatening me with illness.

But I was *warm.*

For a moment I didn't take a single breath. I had to suck up the courage to crack my eyes open, hope making my heart race.

I nearly sobbed when I saw the slim back in front of me, the head of damp wine-red hair. His chest rose and fell, each inhale making him brush my chest.

Kai was sleeping close to me.

It's just so we don't freeze to death, I told myself. But there was a weight slung over my side and a hot hand on my hip. How many mornings had I woken up like this, with Em's hand in the exact same spot, his chest warm and broad behind me, keeping me protected. In front of me, it was either Kai, Harvey, or—or Wynvail? I tried to remember how he fit into our lives, but I couldn't reconcile the poison-filled monster with my past.

We might all be bastards, killers, and thieves, but ... we weren't cruel. We fit together, and shared so much love, and Wynvail felt like the antithesis to that.

He's ruined, too. Cassander Locke did this by killing us.

What was Wynvail like before death made him a rotten, heartless man? Was he smartmouthed like Harvey, or a secret romantic like Kai, or a stern protector like Emlyn? Was he quiet and full of fierce, defiant love like—

Pain speared my skull again, and I bit my lip hard to trap a gasp, so scared of waking my mates. Scared to ruin this rare moment of peace and normalcy, where no one was trying to kill each other and they didn't stare at me like I was—like I was going to kill them by the end of the month.

Because I *was* going to kill them, and they'd do the same to me. We were cursed.

My teeth ground as rage at Wynvail built, but I forced my jaw to unclench and let out a long breath. I kissed the back of Kai's head because nothing could stop me, and laced my fingers with Em's at my hip. Harvey was asleep on Kai's other side; I could just make out the splay of russet hair over his shoulder.

We needed to break this curse; that was more important than getting their memories back. As soon as they were awake, it was time to leave the forest. It had offered a modicum of safety for the past seven days, but it was time.

No more hiding. We were cursed, and on borrowed time.

I had an idea of where we could start looking for a solution, but bringing three instinct-driven alphas with me was going to be challenging.

Em's chest rumbled in his sleep and he pulled me closer, his nose brushing the back of my neck. On his next breath, with my scent in his lungs, he settled.

I meant to stay awake and take advantage of this intimacy while I had it, but the warmth and closeness of all my mates around me seduced me back to sleep, and this time it was dreamless and deep.

CHAPTER THREE

I woke up to a pile of wet leaves being dumped on
my face.

A sudden snarl tore across the forest, and for a moment it
was so familiar for Em to be growling at the others to stop
being pains in his ass, or to let me sleep longer, or to be careful, that I smiled.

Harvey's low, sulky rumble was familiar too, as was Kai's
dangerous silence. That was a silence that plotted, that bided
its time.

"Whatever you're thinking, Malakai," I said, throwing the
leaves off me and sitting up, "don't."

Em threw them both a look to say, *look what you've done
now.* As if he was worried about me getting a few more
minutes' sleep. The old Emlyn would have been that thoughtful, but the new one was just less concerned I'd murder him
when I was asleep.

I brushed off my clothes and got to my feet, ignoring the
stale scent of fabric that had been soaked in rainwater and
dried by body heat. I peeled my shirt off my skin, making a
face at the crunch in the fabric, and shot Kai another warning

look when his stare lingered a little too long to the bare skin of my stomach.

Light flashed in the edge of my vision, and for a moment I didn't understand what I was seeing. A sunbeam cut viciously through a gap in the trees and aimed right for Malakai.

"Harvey!" I yelled, but it was too late. He became a thing of black fur and claws and dove on top of Kai, whimpering when Kai retaliated with his own forceful magic.

This was the magic that destroyed a whole town, and he was using it on *Kai.*

"No!" I snarled, raising my voice as I ran across the clearing. "Harvey, *no!* Stop!"

Harvey's molten gaze darted to me before returning to Kai. Why were they so determined to kill each other? What had happened in those cells?

"Can you stop them?" I asked Emlyn, storming over to tug on the tuft of furry skin behind Harvey's neck like he was an unruly kitten.

Emlyn returned my question with a flat look, crossing his arms over his chest.

I tried an old tactic, fluttering my lashes at him. *"Pleeeeease,* Em?"

He did nothing. I groaned, heaving on Harvey but failing to budge him more than an inch. Fuck, he was heavy in his beast form.

"I'll give you a blowjob," I offered Emlyn. "A really, really good one."

He didn't even glance my way. I groaned, thumping my head against Harvey's furry back. He was massive in this form, and terrifying to anyone he was trying to kill. Except Kai, who lived for drama and danger; he only grinned and sent power shivering through the air.

Harvey fell back with a low, pained sound, nearly toppling onto me.

When he whined, my heart skipped.

"Shit," I breathed, running around his huge body so I could see his face, my stomach dropping to my feet at the pain clouding his silver eyes. "What is it? Where do you hurt, Buttercup?"

I searched his chest with gentle hands, moving up to his neck until my fingers came away wet. Harvey must have been in intense pain because he held still enough for me to part his fur and look for—two puncture wounds.

My back went ramrod straight. A seething, lethal hiss slashed the air, and I spun to Kai, stalking right to him and shoving his shoulder hard enough to knock him back.

"Give him the antidote, you absolute bastard."

I shoved him again, pushing him back a step, my wings high above my shoulders and teeth gritted. "Antidote. *Now.*"

Emlyn gave Kai a deep growl, and my heart leapt. Did he understand me? Was he translating?

But Kai just rolled his eyes and gestured at Harvey as his front paws buckled and he collapsed to the grass.

"No," I choked out.

My whole body flashed cold. I couldn't breathe.

I was back in the house in the Damned Realm, watching my mates get shot, watching them die one by one. I flung myself towards Harvey, landing hard on my knees beside him and—nearly collapsing with a sob when I saw that he was breathing.

Kai could use his venom to kill or put someone to sleep, and it was impossible to tell which kind his snakes would pump into someone until they dropped dead or fell asleep.

"You're okay, you're okay," I breathed to Harvey, to myself. I sank my shaking fingers into his thick fur and buried my face in his shoulder, dragging his scent of sun-warmed earth into my lungs.

"You ... care?" a soft, raspy voice asked, and I jumped back from Harvey like my heart had been shocked by lightning.

Kai—that was *Kai's* voice. He was using words, talking, asking me a question.

My bottom lip wobbled as I nodded. I couldn't see him with tears welling in my eyes, but I knew which smear was Kai and which was Em.

"He's my mate; I love him."

Kai made a low, thoughtful sound and turned away.

"I love you, too," I breathed, not knowing if my voice would reach him. But he understood language, at least to some extent. "Thank you for not killing him."

Kai didn't say anything else, but I didn't care. My mood went from shattered to dizzyingly hopeful. If Kai was speaking, maybe the others would, too. Maybe they'd understand me when I told them about our past life and—and maybe they'd remember me.

"Right," I said, clearing the lump from my throat as I stood, and scrubbing the tears from my face. "Time for breakfast, and then I need to see a man about a curse charm."

Em narrowed his eyes in an obvious question. *What the fuck is a curse charm?*

"No idea," I replied cheerfully. "I just made it up."

CHAPTER FOUR

*B*arnakon was a fragrant little town on the way to Iarlon, half in the shadow of the mountains and full of dodgy deals, crime, and booze. It was one of my favourite places in Hell, especially great for finding jobs. And once upon a time, I actually met Barnak, the guy the town was named after.

Barnak had a brother who was sweet and kind and good-looking, but sadly their shared wife named the place for Barnak, who was kind of a dick but who had the biggest ass she'd ever seen.

"You know," I told my mates as we walked down the dirt road into the town, passing dubious inns and halfway houses, "they call this place the Shapely Bum of Hell."

I waited for laughter, but didn't get even a chuckle. *Fine, be boring.*

"I brought you fuckers here once for a job. You met the guy we're going to; Foster. He's a bit of a snarly bastard, but he's got a good heart—and an even better stash of dark magic shit. All illegal, of course, but that's the fun part."

Not even Malakai cracked a smirk. Shame; he used to *love* illegal stuff.

"I'm starting to think you're ignoring me just to be a prick, Kai," I told him, grabbing Harvey by the scruff of his neck before he could run after a street dog. He was still in his beast form, and acting like a pure animal. "You can understand some of what I'm saying, I know you can."

Kai slid a narrow glare at me, but said nothing.

"Fine, be surly and mysterious. Harvey, stop struggling, I'm not gonna let you go fight a damn dog. Em, backup please."

Emlyn, at least, had the good sense to give Harvey a warning growl. Harvey bared his teeth and struggled harder, but at least he'd tried.

"Hi," I called to a man with a horseshoe tattooed on his face who was eyeing us with obvious curiosity as he passed us. "Don't mind my mate; he's the type to pick a fight with anything."

The horseshoe man snorted. "My husband's the same. All muscle, no sense."

"Tell me about it," I laughed, my soul literally *soaring* at having someone to converse with. I almost reached out and grabbed the man as he headed down a street away from us, almost begged him to stay and *talk*. I'd been going mad talking to myself these past seven days.

Rough fingers grabbed my hair and jerked my face away from the horseshoe-tattooed man. I raised an eyebrow when I realised it was Kai, bodily stopping me looking at another man.

A zip of delight went down my spine.

"Well, well, well, look who's being all possessive and sexy again," I teased.

He tightened his grip on my hair until shivery cold splashed down my spine and I caught my breath.

Emlyn rumbled a warning; Kai ignored it. Harvey slipped

from my grasp while I was distracted, chasing after a demon in spiked porcupine form.[1]

"Get back here, you little shit!" I yelled at Harvey, annoyed that it came out breathless. "The shop's right here!"

I flung my arm towards a dingy little shop with peeling dark purple paint on the window frames and door, and a wooden sign with a bow tie painted on it. Huh. The bow tie was new; maybe Foster was rebranding.

"Harvey!" I yelled, surprised when he lifted his head and stared at me. "Back here. Now!"

He snarled at the porcupine who slid a glare in our direction, and loped back to our side.

"Sorry, he's newly trained," I called to the porcupine who strode off in a huff. "Harvey, you can't just—oh, you idiot," I groaned, spotting the spines sticking out of his mouth. "You bit the porcupine, didn't you?"

I reached back and tapped Kai's hand, surprising him enough that he loosened his grip on my hair and I slipped free. Amused and exasperated, I gently tugged the three spines from Harvey's lips. At least he had healing magic and these punctures were clean enough that they'd close in minutes.

"You moron," I sighed, and kissed his snout.

His big, furry ass slammed down on the pavement, and his stubby little tail wagged like crazy, as if he was a dog. I stroked his head, careful of his new cuts, and met his stare. He didn't attack me for once, but there was nothing but confusion in his silver eyes, like he was unsure why I was caring for him.

Exactly like Kai. They kept waiting for me to make good on the promise my curse mark made. I had to keep proving that I was safe, and I'd *never* hurt them.

I held onto the porcupine spines; Foster would find a use for them, so they'd be good bartering chips.

"This," I told them, pushing the door open and surprised

by the tinkle of a little bell, "is the greatest illegal magic shop in—"

I froze at the rails of coats, the piles of soft tunics, and stacks of boots. It was a godsdamned clothes shop.

"Hell," I finished with a curse.

CHAPTER FIVE

"Where's all the dark potions, the crystals of death, the piles of stolen knives?" I demanded, my mates crowded behind me. It was far too much muscle and testosterone for a tiny shop like this, but I liked how close they were. I shoved the quills into my pocket; I wouldn't be needing those now.

The dapper, blue-skinned man behind the counter gave us all a wide-eyed stare, his throat bobbing. "You're thinking of the shop my dad ran. Foster's hasn't sold any of *those* things for forty years."

"But I need *those* things," I complained, giving the fifty-something man a beseeching look. "There's really nothing useful left here?"

He straightened, his blue chin lifted in offence. "This is a clothes shop; everything here is useful, *unlike* the dangerous tat my father filled it with."

"Oh, fuck you very much, Foster Number Two. Your father ran the best shop in all of Hell, and I won't have you besmirch the memory of my friend's pride and joy. You have no idea how much love went into the *dangerous tat* of this shop."

Foster Number Two's shiny eyes went even wider. "You were friends with my father?"

"Yes," I replied emphatically. "Kai, put that down, orange is not your colour."

He hissed and clutched the orange scarf to his chest, probably just to be a defiant little shit.

"But he died forty years ago," Foster Number Two said, baffled. Looking at a thirty-something woman, AKA me.

"I've been dead a hundred years," I replied flippantly. "And now I have two curses tattooed on me, so you can understand why I might need some *dangerous tat.*"[1]

Foster Number Two sucked in a breath and nodded, easily believing I was the sort of person to get cursed. Rude. "You could try the alchemist's on the corner of Ulrich Crescent."

I kept an eye on Kai, who put back the orange scarf and picked up a dark green one shot through with metallic silver. He ran the soft fabric against his face, and the air rippled with his magic.

"Ulrich Crescent was a no-go back in my day," I replied, unease twisting through me. "Too many murders happened down there, and that's coming from a mercenary. Unexplainable shit, creepy and bloody. *But* you're gonna tell me it's all changed and completely harmless now." The shopkeeper was silent for a beat too long. "Right?"

Foster Number Two winced. "That's your best bet for anything curse-related."

"Thanks," I groaned, and then forced my tone to something genuinely grateful. "Really, thanks. Sorry I insulted your shop."

He let out a relieved breath, like he'd been holding it since we stormed in here. "Sorry I couldn't help more."

I grinned. "That's something your father would never have said."

"No," he agreed with a chuckle. "I'm glad there are people who still remember him. There's just me left."

I nodded, my throat suddenly tight. I didn't want to think about my friend being dead, or my favourite shop being repurposed, or everything being new and different and unknowable.

I *hated* it. I hated that I'd been in a grave for a hundred years while the world brutally changed around me. The only thing left that was familiar were my mates, and they didn't even know who I was.

"We'll take this," I told the man, snatching the green scarf from Kai and putting it on the counter. "Em, do you want anything?"

Emlyn gave me a blank stare, which I took as a no.

"Harvey? You might shred anything we get you into ribbons, so don't choose anything expensive."

Harvey tilted his big, furry head. I scanned the shop, looking for an item the old Harvey would have liked and spotted something luminescent and gold. His eyes followed me as I crossed the small floor, picking up the black leather gloves, each painted with a violent slash of gold paint.

"What do you think?" I asked, holding them up. "You'd need hands, obviously."

He tilted his head again, but didn't growl. I took that as an assent.

"These too, thanks," I told Foster Number Two, and handed over a third of the coins I had left from the allowance Callahan gave me. I tried not to wince at the price; as long as they were happy, everything was fine.

"Come on, you lot," I sighed, trying to keep my heart light as we left the shop even though grief and depression hovered like a dark cloud.

I thought I'd be reunited with my friend. Instead, he was dead.

Kai stayed close to my side; I flicked a glance at him, my stomach squirming at the intense way he watched me.

"Here, this is yours." I handed him the green scarf, and swallowed when he didn't take his eyes off me as he wound it around his neck. His black pupils slitted with happiness, and my heart did a giddy little flip.

"Ulrich Crescent is this way," I told my Kai and Harvey and —where was Emlyn?

"Oh, for fuck's *sake!*" I yelled, watching Em race down the street to a fountain filled with gross brown water. "Don't you dare, Emlyn Johahn!"

Oh, he dared. Em plunged apologetically into the dirty fountain and splashed the water all over himself with a loud rumble of pleasure.[2]

I pinched the bridge of my nose. "And here I was thinking you were becoming more civilised."

CHAPTER SIX

*T*he alchemist's shop was painted ink-black with midnight blue accents, and looked to have been cleaned ... well, never. A black film of grime covered the windows, and the whole place pulsed with magic. *Stay the fuck away,* the aura warned.

I covered my hand with my sleeve and reached for the doorknob, pushing it open and coughing at the plume of dust and power that burst out.

"Wow," I choked out as I stepped inside, scanning the cramped room.

Every shelf lining the dark walls was filled with knick-knacks I couldn't begin to name; scales and phials and scientific apparatus were cluttered all over the place. Liquid bubbled over a fire on the long table at the back of the room, and a bespectacled man with deep brown skin and a tuft of silver hair bent over it.

He snapped upright at the sound of my voice. Shrewd eyes narrowed behind his glasses as he lowered a vial of questionable silver liquid.

"What do you want?" he demanded in a nasal voice, eyeing me and my mates suspiciously.[1]

"I'm looking for something that can undo a curse," I told the man, carefully manoeuvring around the shelves and cases full of alchemy shit. "I'm willing to pay handsomely for help."[2]

He snorted. "Piss off."

I sucked in a long, calming breath and counted to ten. Killing this bastard wouldn't solve my problems.

"You've got a shop full of magical items, and you expect me to believe nothing can undo a curse?"

"I've a thousand things that can *give* a curse," he disagreed, setting the silver vial in a stand and propping his hands on his hips. He was tall as hell, well over six-five, impressive for a man who looked past seventy. "But take one away? That's beyond my ability."

I drew another calming breath. *Do not lash out, be calm, Haley, be calm.* "What about lost memories, then? Anything you can do for that?"

The alchemist pushed his glasses up his dark nose and peered at me closely. "Maybe."

Wow. *So* forthcoming, *so* helpful.

"These are my mates; guys, say hello."

Em and Harvey ignored me, more bothered about a stuffed magpie hanging from the wall. Kai hissed, flicking out his forked tongue. That counted as a hello.

"They can't remember me, or our life at all. And there's a gap in my memories, like something's been removed."

"Hmm," the alchemist mused, tilting his head so the silver tuft on his head jiggled. "Two different charms, then. Not necessarily curses."

I rolled up my sleeve and held out my arm. "This is a curse."

"Oh yeah, that's a bad one," he agreed with nowhere near

the appropriate amount of gravity to his voice. "Not seen a curse like this in years. It's nice work."

I bared my teeth when he came around the table and clasped my wrist. One moment, the alchemist's clammy fingers were on me, the next he was thrown across the dingy shop, slamming into a shelf full of vials. He crashed to the floor, followed by shattering glass.

"Shit," I hissed, rushing to help the old man. "Sorry about that, my mates are a little insane when someone else touches me."

It was such a normal thing to say, I didn't even realise Kai'd had a normal-Kai reaction.

"You'll pay for this," the alchemist spat, and for a moment I thought he was swearing revenge. But he just meant we'd pay for all the shit Kai broke.

"Of course we will," I agreed, and shot a look over my shoulder. "And we won't break anything else. *Will we,* Malakai?"

Kai bared his sharp fangs, not promising anything.

"If your mates take that magpie down, their bollocks will shrivel. It's doused with a nasty potion," the alchemist huffed, accepting my hand to help him back to his feet.

"Harvey! Em! No!" I barked. "It's dangerous."

Kai rolled his eyes. It was such a Kai gesture that my throat choked up. When he hissed something at them, they drew their hands back like they'd been burned. Harvey sat on his big, furry beast ass and ducked his head to check his balls were still there.

The alchemist snorted, strolling down the side of the room, gazing at his crazy collection of wares. "Have they always been like this? More beast than man?"

"No, that's a recent thing. We were murdered a hundred years ago and—I came back recently, don't ask me how. But they've been back for years, without me."

"Their souls decayed while you were apart," he mused. "That's nasty business. I knew a woman, hundreds and hundreds of years ago, whose soul severed into two pieces when she lost her mates. She went completely mad, of course, but I think she's still knocking around."

"Well, at least I know *that* won't kill them. Being cursed to kill each other, on the other hand..."

The alchemist nodded, his tuft of hair shivering. "What's your name? I'm Ashboren the Terrifying."

I blinked. Twice. "I'm Haley. Just Haley. Well, technically Halwen."

"Like the forest?" Ashboren the Terrifying made a noise in his throat. "Fascinating. Well, Just Haley, I can tell you whoever drew that curse on you was no amateur and knew exactly what they were doing. There's no loophole to exploit; you'll definitely kill them when the moon above Hell burns red. That's in twenty-three days, by the way."

"Great," I muttered. No way out. No way to stop killing the men I loved. "You're just full of good news, aren't you?"

I jumped when Kai brushed close to me, something tight and ... upset in his expression. He grunted at Ashboren and lifted his shirt, baring his own curse mark.

"Well..." the old man murmured. "This is a pickle, isn't it?"

A bitter laugh clawed up my throat. *A pickle?* Yeah, you could say that.

"You'd need a curse expert to get a proper opinion, and there haven't been any young'uns studying curses for years. You'd have to find someone really old."

"Like you?" I asked hopefully.

Ashboren's dark brow flattened. "I'm in the prime of my youth."

"Sure you are," I agreed, watching Kai drop his shirt back into place and scowl at the alchemist's unsatisfactory response. He stroked a hand over his new scarf, like the texture calmed him.

"I'm not an expert," Ashboren said after he'd recovered from the slight to his age. "And I don't know anyone who is. But I can tell you that curse is intricate and exact."

"And this one?" I asked, pulling my own shirt up to show the one that started at my belly and travelled up my ribs in a collection of curves, circles, and arrows.

Ashboren narrowed his eyes, a knot in his brow. "I've never seen these exact marks before. This half circle suggests a disruption of some kind, the full circle shows it's preserved but the rest of the marks make me think something has been blocked from you."

"My magic," I snarled. So one cursed my magic away from me, and one made me kill my mates.

"Back," Kai hissed.

I turned, ready to intervene when he attacked Ashboren again, but I jumped when he grasped my shoulders and turned me—and dragged a finger from the top of my spine to the base. "Curse."

A laugh bubbled up, full of denial and delusion. Nope. No way. I didn't have a third curse; Kai was wrong.

But Kai had stared at me whenever I bathed, and had seen *all* of me. I'd never looked into a mirror to see my back since I resurrected. My stomach plummeted with dread.

"Let me see," Ashboren muttered.

I spun and took a step back, not wanting to know. If I did have a third curse, I wanted to be in full denial about it.

Emlyn let out a deep, rumbling sound and stalked across the shop to stand at my shoulder. A weight fell off me to have him so close his grey wings brushed my arm, almost like everything was normal.

Ashboren the Terrifying made a throaty sound of surprise. "To say they don't know who you are, they're certainly protective of you. If their memories aren't lost but *hidden*, I have something you can try to unlock them. But first, stop being a coward, Haley, and show me your back."

I groaned, but womaned up and threw off my jacket, lifting my shirt over my head. When Ashboren sucked in a sharp breath, I knew it was bad. The first curse had made him gush like a fan seeing work from his favourite author, but this? This unsettled him.

"That's not a curse. Put it away. Show no one."

I dragged my shirt and jacket back on and turned, hesitantly, to see the alchemist's expression. "What is it?"

"A different sort of mark. An old, old kind that hasn't been seen for years—even with all the upheaval of angels invading Hell, demons battling Heaven on Earth, and the children of gods returning from their hiding places to help us. That prophecy mark on your back means something bigger and far bloody worse is coming."

"Then why the fuck is it on me?" I demanded, shoving my shaky hands in my pockets and leaning into Emlyn's comforting heat. I needed him, needed *all* of them.

"There's greatness meant for you," Ashboren replied, striding around his table to inspect a shelf. "Something terrible and grand and probably traumatic."

"I don't want it."

"I don't blame you; I wouldn't either. But the gods have chosen you."

"The gods can go fuck themselves," I snarled.

"They often do. Here, take this. I imbued it with a memory enhancing elixir fifty years ago when I was trying to find my glasses. It worked like a charm."

I numbly accepted the dark red gem he dropped into my hand, surprised that the stone was warm, not cold.

"Fifty gold crowns, thank you very much," he said, annoyingly upbeat considering he'd just told me I was meant for terrible greatness.

"You're robbing me," I grumbled, but closed my fingers around the stone. If this could help my mates remember me, I'd stand a better chance of fighting this damn curse. No way would they actually hurt me if they remembered me. I wouldn't hurt them, either.[3]

"I'm giving you a good deal. Returning your soulmates to you? Priceless."

I narrowed my eyes, but the bastard was right. "Twenty crowns."

"Fifty."

"Twenty-five."

"Forty," he countered begrudgingly.

"Twenty-six," I offered, summoning the little shit I'd been before I died, giving the grumpy alchemist a sharp grin.

"Thirty-nine, and I'll go no lower," he muttered, crossing his arms over his chest.

"Thirty-five, and I'll pay for the shit we broke," I haggled, not flinching when he stared at me, trying to get me to break.

"Fine," Ashboren growled. "But only if you remember me when you're on your path to greatness, and you stay the hell away from Barnakon."

I shrugged. "Done."

I wasn't going to go looking for this traumatic greatness. If I never found it, that was fine by me. I had enough to contend with having three mates who didn't remember me and one who'd done his damnedest to kill me.

"Hold that stone too, and you might find your own memories returning," Ashboren told me. "But it won't be overnight."

"Nothing ever is. What does the mark say? On my back. You can read it like the curses, can't you?"

"It's in the old language, not curse glyphs, but I'd rather not say it out loud," he replied, looking decidedly wan.

"I'd rather you did," I fired back, gripping the memory stone so hard the sharp edges bit into my palm.

"Something about gods and—worse than gods. Now, it's been nice meeting you, but I need to get back to my work."

I pressed my lips into a flat line, but dumped a pile of coins on his table and rounded up my mates. Wait—

"Where's Harvey?" I asked, a furrow between my brows. He was an enormous, black-furred creature with claws and vicious teeth; how had I lost him in a shop this small?

"The sun soul?" Ashboren asked with a low laugh.

"The what?" I breathed, lethally soft. Emlyn backed me up with a growl, bristling beside me.

"He's a sun soul—that dark creature is what happens when they're starved of light. They go mad and feral; some of them even go rabid, but your mate seems to have avoided that."

My heart compacted into a knot. I had to clench my jaw to fight back tears, my eyes stinging viciously. "Where is he?"

"He licked a potion he shouldn't have," Ashboren the Terrifying chuckled, and jerked his chin towards the door where ... where a frog hopped around. "He might be easier to manage that way."

He had a point, but I could hardly let my mate stay a frog.

"Let me guess," I sighed, giving Ashboren a wry look. "You expect us to pay to turn him back."

Ashboren the Terrifying grinned and picked up the vial of silver liquid, resuming his work like he wasn't bothered at all.

"The issue is I don't want to pay," I replied slyly, propping my hip against the counter and shoving back my dread about the curses and prophecy marks on my body for the moment. "And I'm not leaving until Harvey's turned back. So I guess we'll just hang around here, right guys?"

I threw a smile at my mates, and fought a wince when I saw Kai prowling over to Harvey. "Don't eat him!"

He glanced at me over his shoulder, something flickering

in his red eyes. If he was the old Kai, it would have been amusement.

I stretched my arms over my head and forced a smile at Ashboren. "Yeah, me and my prophecy mark will stay right here. Nice place you've got. I can imagine myself being comfy here for a long, long, *long—*"

"Alright, you've made your point," the alchemist growled, and made a sulky show of grabbing a box of tiny potion bottles from a heavy drawer, selecting a vial of emerald liquid. I tensed when he poured it over Harvey, but my big, furry beast of a mate was back a moment later, knocking shit off the shelves. "Now *get out.*"

I sketched a bow. "With pleasure. Thanks for your help."

I ushered my mates out the door, and tucked the stone away for safekeeping. I'd need to figure out how to get them to hold it long enough for their memories to unlock, but that was a problem for when we found somewhere to sleep tonight.

I closed the door behind us and—slammed into Emlyn's muscular back.

"What's the hold up, Em? Move your big butt—oh."

I swallowed when I saw why he'd stopped, why all three of them had.

All the way down Ulrich Crescent, alphas stood shoulder to shoulder on the cobblestones. Meaty hands gripped axes, maces, swords, and some things I didn't even know the name of.

I struggled to draw my next breath, reaching out to touch Em for reassurance that barely penetrated my panic.

"Wynvail found us."

CHAPTER SEVEN

*M*ates couldn't kill each other, but Wynvail may have found the work-around for that. The alphas he'd sent after us could certainly kill us.

I remembered his rage when the pale demon hurt me in the fighting pit, but I shut it out. His unsettling duality of wanting to hurt me but refusing to let anyone else hurt me made no difference. He'd sent alphas after us, and he wanted Em, Harvey, and Kai dead. That was as good as murdering me.

"Kill them all," I told my mates, and drew my volcanic knives with a soft ring that made my heart swell with love. Kai had spent *months* having these made for me; with them in my hands, I felt capable of anything.

Even if fighting fifty plus alphas was *a bit* of a stretch.

Kai glanced at me, his eyes lingering on the wavy daggers, but the furrow between his eyes told me he didn't remember them. But did he get the strange uncanny sense he'd forgotten something like I did when I looked at Harvey, or Wynvail, or —or shadows?

I tried not to think about what Ashboren said about

Harvey, but it kept racing around my head, vicious and hurtful.

He's a sun soul—that dark creature is what happens when they're starved of light.

I kept close to my mates as we moved down Ulrich Crescent, a solid, unbreakable unit just like we were before. If I hadn't spent a week trying to remind them who I was, I'd have thought nothing had changed.

"Kai, stay beside me," I said under my breath, scanning the rows of alphas storming to meet us, fangs bared and weapons raised, light catching their vicious spikes and sharp edges. "Emlyn, shift into your bird form."

When he gave me a blank look, I asked Kai to translate, which he did, begrudging with a low, guttural hiss. Emlyn's brows slammed down; he cast me a strange look.

"You have another form," I told him quickly, watching the alphas storm closer, bringing with them a stench of sweat, steel, and violence. "You can shift into an eagle, and a fucking massive one. You usually hit threats from above while Kai and I fight on the ground, and Harvey does his usual kamikaze shit."

Emlyn's eyes flashed, sharp blue lighting up from within. I lost all the breath in my lungs when he grinned, all viciousness and bloodthirst. I wanted to grab him and kiss him so badly, but that would probably get my face ripped off.

Kai hissed a warning; the alphas were close.

Emlyn nodded to me—actually nodded, like I was an equal and not a threat—and seemed to pause as he contemplated how to shift. If our bond had been intact instead of shredded, I could have shown him the place where his eagle lived, waiting to break free.[1]

"Harvey," I began, turning to him—but of course he'd already run head-first at the alphas, his fur standing on end and dark mist seething from his body.

"Shit," I breathed. "Em, just jump into the air and yank on your shifting magic. Kai, cover me."

The chances of either of them understanding was slim, but I didn't have time to worry about that. I slashed my left blade in an arc when an eight-foot-tall woman came roaring at me with a mace, the spike at the tip of it as long as my damn forearm. Metal clashed loud enough to make my ears ring, and I knew instantly I had no chance of matching the woman's strength.

"Fuck," I grunted, my arms buckling as her mace pushed against my daggers. Time for plan B.

I crouched and spun beneath her mace, bringing my right dagger up in a gutting slash across her stomach.

Yuck. Gore splashed my face, wet blood sticking my hair to my cheeks and forehead, filling my tastebuds with sharp, bitter copper.

When I got back to my feet, panting, Kai was staring at me like he'd never seen me before. Also, kinda like he used to look at me two seconds before his cock would be buried to the hilt inside me. I raised an eyebrow and turned to intercept the next alpha. My breath caught in my throat as a familiar piercing cry filled the dingy street.

Emlyn.

He soared above my head, the black tips of his long wings brushing my head as he glided through the air. His head was blood-red where a normal eagle's feathers were white, and his beak was the same sanguine colour, his eyes pure ink black.

The alpha who'd raced to attack me paused to stare at my ferocious mate, and I took the opportunity to drag my blade across his turquoise throat from gills to gills.

"Shit," Kai laughed behind me, and the sound was so viciously familiar that my heart twisted into a knot.

I threw him a wry look. "What? Never seen a woman slit someone's throat before?"

"No," he replied.

I grinned, flipping back around when the air around me rippled, warning another threat was close. "Not in a hundred years, anyway."

I sank into the calm of battle, my blood rushing in my ears and a wicked thrill in my belly as I slashed and thrust my knives, blood splashing my arm, alternatively hot and cold depending on what kind of demon I buried my blades inside.

I paused, only once, at the sight of another tan-skinned, black-winged, and grey-eyed woman like me—another Stygian demon. Kai's snakes forced past me in a rush, and the woman staggered back, clutching her throat where two puncture wounds appeared.

"Thanks," I said breathlessly, already throwing up my blades to meet the next threat—a truly *massive* man with a broadsword.

Holding the sword at bay—for now—I allowed myself a rapid scan of the street to check on Harvey. He was ploughing through the lines of alphas, crunching his strong jaws around whatever limbs came close to him, and goring his spiralling horns through stomachs and throats until his fur was slicked to his body.

"Die, bitch!" the broadsword-wielding man growled, baring the massive weapon down on me.

My arms buckled. I slid my daggers free and jumped out of the way—no way was I winning a fight with that thing. Kai was suddenly beside me, flicking an inked hand at the man, the air practically buckling around him. My instincts prickled, screaming *predator, run!*

The giant's face turned purple as he choked, blood bubbling up his throat and exploding from his lips. I didn't know what Kai's snakes had done to the man, but it turned my stomach to hear the deep, gurgling sounds of his death.

A cat demon rushed at Kai's exposed back, her claws

unsheathed and skin covered in striped brown fur that looked so soft and inviting but—I knew from experience—felt like razors when it was touched.

"I don't think so," I hissed and leapt into her path, fingers white around the pink hilts of my knives. I opened a shallow cut on her hip and another on her shoulder to draw her attention to me. "Hi, pretty kitty."

She bared needle teeth. "We're supposed to leave you alive, but I don't see why we shouldn't kill you *all*. A nice, clean job."

"Try it," I challenged, my blood pumping fast and mood calmer, colder with every threat I faced. I felt like the Halwen that got into deadly situations for work and had to fight for her life every weekend, sometimes just for fun. The familiarity was invigorating.

The kitty hissed deep in her throat, her pupils expanding to gobble down light as she eyed me, searching for a weakness. I raised an eyebrow and dove at her, distracting her with a showy move with one blade while the other went for her throat—and missed because she spun, uncannily fast.

Great. She didn't just look like a cat; she moved like one, too. The only demon I'd met like this had been an old man, and he'd been easier to catch. I drove my blades up at the same time, scissoring them when her claws came for my throat. The inscriptions blinked at me, reminding me why I fought.

"Ha!" I barked, grinding the knives together and hacking them through her hand, severing it at the wrist. "That's fun; I've never done that before."

She howled, pain and murder in her eyes, and surprised me by coming at me with twice as much ferocity. Shit, this wasn't supposed to happen. I sucked in a breath when claws tore through my side and punched into my thigh in the same vicious curve. The pain took a moment to hit; I used the tiny reprieve to drive the hilt of a dagger into her knee, forcing her to falter back.

The wounds blazed to life with a vengeance, and I panted, teeth gritted as I kept a close eye on the brown cat currently watching me the same way. I didn't see the small, spiked man barrelling at my left until he was close enough to kill me. I flinched when white light flashed and he staggered back with a scream that made my blood ice over, clutching his face.

Shit, his eyes exploded, gushing blood down his face. If I didn't know better, I'd say it was my own blood power that caused it, but there was still a block between me and my magic.

"What the fuck?" I gasped, shoving the cat demon aside and backing up.

Kai was right behind me, an invisible snake grazing my back. Harvey was still ploughing through the alphas farther down the road, completely feral. Emlyn circled, searching for his next target.

Who made the man's eyes explode?

I knew, even before I felt the slow, taunting stroke down my soul.

"Oh, gods," I breathed, a tremor going through me. "We have to leave. *Now.* Emlyn! Harvey!" I screamed. "We have to go! Tell them, Kai, tell them."

Panic cut off my air, clutching my throat like a cruel hand.

Kai pressed closer, giving me a sharp look. "Why?"

"Wynvail is here," I breathed, yelling my mates' names again, shaking all over.

Em paused in the sky, hearing me. He let out a loud cry and glided down the alley towards us in a rush of red and black feathers.

"Harvey," I breathed, thrusting a blade through the jaw of a man with blue-black wings who tried to get Kai. "We need Harvey. Kai—"

I turned, but a two-headed gemini demon slashed a spiked whip through the air, driving him away from me. *Fuck.* I was surrounded by alphas who wanted to kill me, only Emlyn close enough to swoop down and—

Ten winged demons shot off the ground, broad wings filling the skies above Ulrich Crescent. Cutting him off from me in a perfectly coordinated move.

I shuddered, cold running through my soul and spreading through my body. The last time I felt Wynvail, he was full of heat and rage but this slow-spreading chill was so much worse. It was calculated and intelligent and far more clever than me.

"Come out, you coward!" I yelled, my breaths coming quick as I turned in a circle, searching for him in the crowd of alphas. I knocked a taunting knife aside, and severed the claws of a wicked hand that came close. Where was Wynvail? I didn't see him anywhere.

A shadow blurred in the corner of my eye, and I froze, a memory trying to form. We were in Verrafyn, a mountain town, hunting a harpy who made off with a commander's family jewels.[2] An arrow had flown for me, driving towards my heart and—a shadow knocked it aside. A shadow that was a man.

I screamed, clutching my head as pain split my skull, piercing every bit of soft, vulnerable brain matter. I should have been paying attention to the alpha who grabbed me and threw me against the wall of a weapons shop, but I could barely see his pockmarked face, barely smell the gross, rotten scent coming from his clothes.

I was stuck in that memory, trying so hard to remember even as pain shattered my skull. The shadows were linked to the gap in my memory, I knew they were. But what had Wynvail *done*? Why had I forgotten every memory of him? What was so bad that it needed to be erased?

My head struck brick, but I barely felt it. A hand latched around my throat and squeezed, but the pain pounding from my head in sharp, unbearable waves numbed my skin. The constant ache in my chest flared in response, because apparently I needed more pain. I moaned pitifully.

What happened that day I was nearly shot by an arrow? Who was there? And who didn't want me to remember it?

I screamed as pain mounted, my knees buckling and the only thing holding me up the alpha's hand around my throat. But then the rough hand was torn away, and a loud gurgling snapped me out of the shadow memory and into the present.

I tried to skitter away, but a strong arm was locked around my waist, keeping me on my feet as—as Wynvail slashed a katana-like blade through the alpha's hand, tossed it to the ground, and tore out the alpha's throat with his bare hand.

"No one puts their hands on what's mine," he snarled at the man as he collapsed to the ground, staring sightlessly above—and to the alphas who'd frozen to stare at their master. *"No one."*

His silver eyes dragged to me, scanning me up and down, freezing on the slash through my side and the deep gouge in my thigh.

"Who did this to you?" he asked calmly, his voice carrying powerfully with little effort. He pulled me into his side as my knees tried to buckle again. His grip with ruthless, as hard as iron. Where were my mates?

"I said," Wynvail roared, his temper rearing its ugly head, *"who did this?"*

The cat demon trembled as people cleared a space around her. Wow, what happened to honour among thieves?

"Stay here, honey," Wynvail murmured, scarily gentle as he leant me against the wall of the weapons shop. "And here, consider this an apology for the wounds dealt to you by my alphas."

My breath caught, like broken glass in my chest, when Wynvail plunged his bloody fist through the shop window and grabbed a small, elaborate knife covered in pewter forget-me-nots.

He pulled one of my volcanic daggers from my numb hand and sheathed it at my waist, curling my fingers around my apology gift. His hands were drenched in the alpha's blood, and his own blood wept from cuts on his fingers, glass buried in some. Fear held me in place; pain turned me into a statue.

"I won't be long," he promised, brushing my cheek with a bleeding knuckle like he was just going to the market for bread and not about to slaughter someone who'd hurt me. "Then we can talk about reuniting you with *all* your mates, hmm? I don't think the block is going to last much longer, honey."

I couldn't breathe as he leaned into my personal space, close enough to rip out my throat, too.

Move, I screamed at myself. *Run!*

His lips brushed my cheek, the glimmer in his eye telling me he knew exactly how much I hated this.

When he strode away, I slumped into the wall, shaking all over. My cheek burned, my fingers tingling like they rejected his touch. Like my skin remembered what he'd done in the past even if my mind was blocked, and abhorred him.

Something soft and cold brushed my hip, and I flinched away, my body resuming movement all at once. Blood was all I could smell, all I could taste. My boots slipped on broken glass, and I nearly went crashing through the shattered window. I gasped out a cry, flinging my hands out to protect my face.

But the thing at my hip wrapped around my waist and stopped my fall, and the familiarity made my eyes sting. Relief made my bottom lip tremble. Kai—that was Kai's magic.

My head jerked up when the crowd of alphas sucked in a collective breath, tension wound tight through all of them as Wynvail murmured something to the cat demon who'd cut me. Kai took advantage of the diversion to haul me around the corner of the weapons shop; my legs were too weak to properly navigate my feet around the glass shards, but the soles of my boots protected me.

I stumbled as the snake coiled around my waist tugged me deep into the shadowy alleyway beside the shop, and—

Memories clamoured again. Dominant snakes wrapped around my body, keeping me pinned to the wall as another's careful, hesitant hands explored my body, the brush of finger-tips over my aching nipples enough to push me to the brink of orgasm. When a hot mouth met mine, tongue shockingly fierce, taking full command of me, I tumbled over the edge and—

Someone shook my shoulders, dragging me out of the memory. Oh. I was crying, tears streaming uncontrollably. My chest jerked with deep, heartbroken sobs, the ache worse than it had been in days. I couldn't—I didn't know why—

Fingers bit into my chin, tilting my face up and—Kai. Kai was here, staring at me in alarm, a familiar blaze of worry in his red eyes. His pale face was tight with protective rage.

"I remembered something," I said, my voice scratchy and sore. I fought the wobbling of my bottom lip, meeting Kai's eyes for strength. "A memory that was stolen from me. But I don't know what it means."

Kai flicked a glance from me to the mouth of the alley when a sudden scream whipped through the air, shocking birds into flight. Birds ... where was Emlyn? Where was my Harvey, my sun soul?

"We're leaving," Kai said harshly, sounding so much like himself that I sobbed as he uncoiled his snake. He bent and knocked my legs from under me, sweeping me into his hands. My stomach flipped, but my heart soared. He carefully cradled my wings under me, filling my senses with his amber and firewood scent.

My head spun, my emotions a mix of pain, memories, confusion, and relief that he was acting so *Kai*. I wrapped my arms around his neck, my fingers still locked around the ornate dagger. I should have discarded it.

"Not without the others," I gasped out when he strode to the other end of the alley, his magic wrapping around us in a protective cocoon.

"Look," Kai hissed, picking up his pace, his tattooed hands holding me viciously close to him, like he *dared* the world to take me from him. Or dared Wynvail.[3]

"Look at what?" I snapped, but my voice came out thready and raw, annoyingly soft. Warmth had soaked into my clothes on my left side, but I was trying to ignore it. Pretending I wasn't cut and bleeding with a gaping hole in my leg.

Kai jerked his sharp chin at the sky in the distance and my heart thumped my ribs in a fast beat as I saw Emlyn flying, his impressive black wings carving through the sky in powerful beats. And in his talons, he gripped something huge and black and furry. My shoulders sagged. They were okay. They got away.

It didn't matter that they'd run off without me when they should rather die than leave me behind.[4]

"You came back for me," I realised, staring at Kai as he began to run, holding me tight to him, lines of inked text circling his body.

"Never left," Kai grunted. It was probably the longest conversation we'd had since I resurrected.

I twisted my fingers in the soft fabric of his scarf—he was still wearing it even though blood darkened the tassels—and panted through a feverish wave of dizziness. I held stubbornly to consciousness even though I knew blood loss would knock me out at some point.

I rested my head on Kai's shoulder, pulling his scent deep into my lungs until some of the pain in my soul settled. His brisk steps rocked me, tempting me to sleep as the ground turned from bricks to grass, but I forced my eyes open, refusing to rest until I set eyes on Emlyn and Harvey, until we were all safe.

"Sleep," Kai muttered, casting an irritated glance at me.

"No."

He laughed through his nose, a rough sound that tugged me towards so many memories. But I was done remembering for today; it hurt too much. I just wanted to find my mates and sleep.

I curled my fingers into fists, elaborate iron biting into my palm. I held onto consciousness as Kai led us through the countryside, following some unknown instinct.

"Close," Kai murmured, stirring the damp hairs that clung to my face. I was sweating now, probably because of an infection I'd picked up, but my body would purge it when I actually gave in to the urge to pass out. It was nothing I hadn't healed before.

"Mm," I replied, like that was any real response. At this point, I was mostly unconscious, held awake by the prick of metal biting my palm and sheer bloody-mindedness.

A sudden growl had a weight falling off my shoulders, and relief tempting me closer to sleep. Em was here. Kai replied with a loud hiss, quieting Emlyn's growl, and I tilted my head to see him, my eyes half-mast. The pain hadn't abated from the cut on my stomach and thigh; if anything, it grew worse with every mile we'd crossed.

"You're okay," I breathed when I saw Em storming closer, his wings tucked close to his back and his silver-threaded hair messy, his clothes— "You're bleeding. Why are you bleeding?"

"No," Kai said, striding over to a patch of soft (ish) grass and placing me on it, my back against a log. He jerked his chin towards the ground a few paces away and—the haze over my mind cleared, panic washing the pain from my system like it had never existed.

It wasn't Em's blood; it was Harvey's. My mate lay on his back in his demon form, blood streaking his naked body and his wing at an unnatural angle.

A broken sob clawed up my throat and I crawled across the forest floor to my mate, dragging my heavy wings behind me. I'd lost him. I'd gone to Barnakon to get my mates back, and now I'd lost Harvey.

CHAPTER EIGHT

a hot tear dripped off the end of my nose and down Harvey's tawny cheek, my bottom lip quivering beyond my control. With weak fingers, I brushed a lock of messy hair from his face—and choked on a small sound when his eyes slitted open.

"You're not dead," I whined, and completely fell apart.

I bent over his bare chest, my face to his skin—warm, not cold as the dead—and cried my heart out. My shoulders shook, wings jumping with every broken sob that shattered through my chest, and a blurring mix of terror and relief emptied me of everything I had left.

Harvey made a low, questioning sound, fingertips brushing my arm before darting away.

I sniffled and drew back, struggling to control my sobs as I flicked tears off my cheeks. He watched me with a knot between his brows, and opened his mouth like he'd growl or hiss or—say something. His mouth moved but formed no sound.

I watched, panic beginning to fade now I processed that he wasn't dead. He hadn't been ripped from me again. Gunshots sounded in my memory, and I flinched. Pain cracked through my side at the jerky motion, burning down my thigh, and I hissed in a breath at the sharp reminder of my own injuries.

Harvey touched my arm again and sat up off the ground, opening his wings a few inches for balance before his body locked and he sucked breath through his teeth. I knew those signs—he was in pain. And if my joker, who covered all his hurt and trauma with grins and laughter, was showing pain, it was excruciating. Far, far worse than mine.

"Okay," I breathed, softening my voice. "You're okay. Where are you bleeding, Harvey?"

His throat bobbed. He looked from me to Kai, who replied in a soft rumble.

Harvey tucked his wings tight to himself and skittered back a few inches. I recognised that, too, the knee-jerk reaction to hide any injuries so the weakness couldn't be exploited.

"I'm your mate," I said, and ignored the hot pulse of pain in my side. "I'd never hurt you. If you show me where you're bleeding, I can make sure you'll heal without making it worse. I know you heal quick, Buttercup, but you still need help."

I spoke in a low, calm tone, conscious of the fact he was a wild creature.

"Trust me," I murmured, holding out a hand.

He swallowed again, molten eyes shuttered with pain. But thoughts raced behind those quicksilver eyes, and he must have come to a conclusion because he tentatively opened his right wing. His body froze again, locking down any signs of pain, and maybe he'd rip my throat out with his teeth but *nothing* could stop me leaning close and kissing his forehead.

"Thank you," I breathed, and slowly—so very slowly—reached for his wing. "I'll have to open and close it to see if there's a break," I warned him.

I looked to Kai for a translation. Instead he said, "Don't kill her."

"Oh, that's helpful," I muttered, and gritted my teeth against a sudden flare of dizziness. *Don't pass out, Haley, don't fucking pass out.*

Sweat beading my brow, I gently pulled Harvey's wing open, searching for blood and missing feathers. He snarled, baring his teeth in a clear threat, and the muscles in his throat were so taut, veins stood out.

"I know it hurts," I soothed, stretching his wing and closing it again. "I know, Harvey, I'll be quick."

I gently brushed my fingers over the part of his wing that wasn't moving correctly, and he whimpered so loudly, so suddenly, that both Kai and Emlyn jerked forward—to hold him for my inspection or to rip me off their friend, I didn't know. But Harvey panted through his bared teeth and growled at them to stay back.

I didn't push my luck; I kept the examination quick so Harvey didn't sink his teeth into me. Plus, I was barely clinging to consciousness, so time was running out.

"It's not broken," I told Harvey, sweat dripping off my nose. "It hurts here?"

His high, broken sound twisted into my heart.

"I'm sorry, I'm sorry. That's it, I'm done." I forgot for a moment I was a stranger to him and stroked wavy hair from his face, leaning up to press a lingering kiss to his cheek. "I'm done, Buttercup. But we need to wrap your wing, and you won't be able to fly while it heals."

Kai translated, and Harvey shot me an outraged look. I tried to fix him with a stern look, but I wavered, pain flaring suddenly like fire scorching my side. Oh yeah, that was an infection. *Thanks a lot, kitty demon, I hope Wynvail eviscerated you.*

Ugh, don't think about that tosspot.

Kai barked something at Emlyn, who whipped off his shirt and carefully approached Harvey. To wrap his wing, I realised, feeling a little affronted that they believed I couldn't do the job when I was perfectly—

Dizziness wrenched me sideways and I dropped so suddenly the forest blurred. I landed in Harvey's waiting arms before I could smack teeth-first into the dirt, and I passed out before I could snap at him to be careful.

CHAPTER NINE

" top it," I huffed for the ninth time, giving Harvey a stern look when he itched at his wing. He'd been plastered to my side all morning as we travelled closer to the capital—the only place I had friends who were still alive. I was still processing Foster being dead, the thought like a raw nerve when I brushed against it.

I should have made friends with the dead, or the souls of humans sent here for reward or punishment; at least they'd still be around. Some demons were long-lived like Lucifer and Tali, but most were lucky to reach a hundred. I should have been long gone, even if my mates lived longer as archdemons. I didn't know how long I had now. Didn't know if I was still alive, or undead.

I jumped when Harvey stumbled into me, catching movement on his other side; Kai lowering his hand. Judging by the glare Harvey slanted his way, he'd whacked him upside his head. Probably because he was itching his scabbing wing again.

"If you don't leave it alone, it won't heal," I told him, my eyes snagging on the gold slash of his black leather gloves. He kept flexing his hands and looking at them, a furrow between his brows that I couldn't figure out. He hadn't taken them off all morning, though.

"There," I said, pointing at the city just coming into view, a metropolis of pale spires and lilac towers, with bright greenery bursting between the buildings. "That's Iarlon. Do you remember it? We were there the day we—well, you know."

I glanced at Em, who'd been silent for hours, not a growl or grunt coming from him. "Do you remember any of it? What happened that day?"

Emlyn must have known I was talking to him, or at least sensed my eyes on him because he tilted his head towards me, his blue eyes soulful and deep. He didn't understand the question, but he must have sensed its importance by my tone because he held eye contact for the first time all morning.

"What happened?" Kai asked, breaking the moment.

I swallowed, glancing away from Emlyn, my heart squeezing with a tight pain. I wanted them back. They were right here, but I wanted my mates. I needed the solace and safety of them. Mostly, I wanted to hide from the world in Em's arms; it was one of few places where I knew nothing could hurt me.

"We did something stupid and reckless," I replied, keeping my gaze fixed forward as we followed the curve in the river towards Iarlon, my mood more brittle than it had been when I woke up. "You and I, I mean," I added, looking at Kai. "We were being hunted—we were *always* being hunted—but we'd been safe for years. We had a *home*."

I paused for him to translate it into low, rumbling sounds for the others.

"But the hunter found us, and mercs burned our house down and—I'd had enough. So I snuck out to find the bastard sending killers after us, fully planning to murder him. You came with me, Kai, but we walked into a trap. He set us up so Lucifer would kill us as punishment."

"Shit," Kai hissed, running his fingers over his green scarf, over and over.

"He didn't. Kill us, I mean. He offered us a deal—he'd forgive us breaking into his house if we took on the Damned Realm. He needed someone to keep the souls in line, be a glorified babysitter. So we agreed, and—we thought we were safe again. We thought we escaped."

Em made a low, questioning sound.

I clenched my jaw, blinking fast. The memories of that day were so sharp, they closed around me like knives, opening a thousand little cuts. Feathers brushed my wings when Harvey tussled closer to me, and suddenly I was pulled to a stop and bound up in him. He wrapped his whole self around me, arms and wings wound around my waist, his head settling on my shoulder. I knew if we hadn't been standing, he'd have wrapped his legs around me too.

"Snuggly barnacle," I teased him, ignoring my choked voice as I hugged him back, squeezing carefully, his wing still wrapped. His sun and earth scent overloaded every sense until a pain soothed in my soul, until I could breathe.

I needed a hug so badly, I refused to let go even when Harvey tried to pull away. I exploited a secret weapon and slid my fingers into the hair at the base of his neck, scratching my nails lightly over his scalp, and he melted into another long embrace.

When I let go, I felt every bit as breakable, but at least my chest hurt a little less, the weight on my shoulders a little lighter.

"What happened?" Kai asked, his ruby eyes intent on my face. He wasn't a stranger for a moment; he was my Malakai, my night.

"The man who hunted us—Locke, Harvey's waste of space father—he followed us. He had a shotgun and—"

I shook my head, my jaw tight. I couldn't finish. "We should hurry up; the city's not far now."

Harvey stayed close by my side, and I felt Kai's stare burning my face. He understood everything I said, but did he remember? I hoped he didn't. That day clung to me like a shroud of darkness, nothing like the protective shadow that kept teasing my mind, taunting me of what I'd forgotten.

"Do you—" I began haltingly as we approached the city gates. "Do you remember shadows? Sometimes they're all I can think about, and they're in my dreams. But I can't remember why they're important, and—and it hurts. It hurts so fucking badly."

Harvey stiffened, shooting a look at me when Kai murmured an animal sound.

"Yes," Kai answered with a frown pinching his brow. "We all do."

I swallowed the lump in my throat, my face hot and tight with tears. "What did we forget?"

Whatever it was, we needed to remember. We needed to get it back, because without it, it felt like there was a part of me missing. A part of all of us.

CHAPTER TEN

"*W*hat do you mean you need to check us?" I demanded, scowling when the guards on the city gates stopped me and the guys entering. "I've never needed to pass checks before."

"Yeah, well," the woman muttered, the spike in the middle of her forehead moving as she scowled, "we've never had anyone break into Lucifer's palace before."

"*What?*" My eyes nearly popped out of my head. "How? That thing's guarded better than a prison."

She shrugged, her silent companion—less spiky but far, far taller—glowering at the four of us suspiciously.

"I'm Haley Vakhara. Halwen," I told them with a sigh. "I work for Lucifer—well, technically I work for General Callahan. Grumpy old bastard."

"I trained under General Callahan," the spiky woman growled, her mouth pressing into a flat line.

"Then you'll know how grumpy an old bastard he really is," I replied with a hopeful smile. Her face didn't budge; I groaned. "Come on, I'm serious, I live here. Do you know Tali?

Big, cute, deadly panda? She's my friend. Or how about Renna, the scary, mean purple lady? We're best friends."

At least I'd decided we were when she returned my knives to me.

"Anything you can show me to prove that?" the guard asked, unimpressed. Probably because I'd just listed a bunch of war heroes everyone knew. *And* insulted her old trainer.

I chewed my bottom lip. I had no proof of my job, nothing I could use to get us in the city. "I could show you my boobs?" I offered.

"No," Kai snarled, shoving me behind him as the air shuddered, his snakes bursting into existence.

Ugh, we should have flown over the city limits instead of walking up to the gates. Although, Lucifer probably had the skies guarded, too. I pinched the bridge of my nose.

"Move," the spiky woman grunted. "If you can't prove your reason to be here, you're not coming in."

She gestured a massive bald man through the gates, trying to corral us out of the way.

"Come on," I pleaded. "I need a bath, and a bed—I've been sleeping on the ground for the last week."

The bald man cast a look at me, and paused. His eyes went from my hair to my arm, like he already knew he'd find a tattoo there. "You're the new girl. The bane of Renna's existence."

My heart leapt. "Yes! You know me? And my best friend talks about me! I *knew* Renna liked me."

"She wants to roast your body over an open flame," he replied amiably, a big smile splitting his face as he thrust out a big, pale hand. "Hal. Good to meet you."

I went to shake his hand but Harvey let out a vicious snarl and jumped in front of me, Emlyn pushing me further behind Kai. "Likewise," I said, peering over their shoulders. "Hey, guard lady, can we come in now?"

She huffed an annoyed breath, but moved back to let us through.

"Thank you, Hal," I said as he passed us, no longer able to see me because I was cloistered between my mates. I grinned.[1] "No problem. Nice to meet you too, gentlemen."

"They're not big conversationalists," I told Hal, and nudged my mates towards the gates. "Come on, you three. Stop growling at the man I have no interest in; I'm not going to jump his bones."

That earned me a look from the tall, silent guard.

"*Or* you," I told him, striding through the gates.

Harvey tried to wrap me in his wings as we walked and failed. "Stop it," I huffed at my idiot mate. "You'll hurt yourself."

I checked Kai hadn't run off to murder Hal for daring to look at me[2] but I paused as the spiky guard's words repeated in my head.

"Wait," I breathed, rushing back to her. "You said someone broke into the palace. When?"

"This morning." She scowled. "Why?"

This morning. My ears began to ring. "What part was broken into?"

"The vault," she answered, suspicion darkening her eyes.

"Shit," I breathed, and because she was eyeing me like she wanted to seize me and drag me to the devil, I rushed out, "I need to speak to Lucifer. Now."

It was no coincidence that someone had broken into the vault the day after we evaded Wynvail. He'd be furious. He'd want revenge—and a sure way to kill my mates when he found us again.

"What?" Kai demanded, grabbing my wrist.

"I think Wynvail came to get the tiara."

I'd given him a fake, because the idea of a psychopath like

him having a weapon of ultimate power unsettled me. Now that I'd fought him, it fucking *terrified* me.

What did he want with all that power?

An eerie, paranoid sense told me this was bigger than mates and jealousy. What was he planning?

CHAPTER ELEVEN

*B*y the time we got to my room, my head hurt. All four of us squashed into the clean, gold space with dirty clothes and sour expressions. Thoroughly out of place.

I'd gone over and over what happened in Alphaven with Lucifer, Cerny, Bernard, and even geeky Russ. For now, we were under orders to only tell Lucifer and his immediate family; not even Callahan had clearance for this information.

I wasn't a huge fan of Lucifer's view that something big was coming. One war was over, but he thought another was beginning, right now. With my maniac mate at the heart of it.

And now he had the tiara he'd leveraged me into stealing. *Plus* the bone pin.

"This won't end well," I sighed, rubbing my eyes and tired beyond belief. It was only late afternoon but I was ready to crawl into bed and sleep.

But I was covered in a fine layer of grime that no stream or rainwater could wash off, and I planned to take full advantage of the bathroom down the hall before I passed out.

"Here, hold this," I told Harvey and handed him the memory stone from Ashboren's alchemy shop. *"Do not lose it."*

He looked down at the stone in his hand, Kai repeating my command in a low hiss as he threw himself onto my bed and stripped off his shirt. I tried not to stare at the scars that cut through his tattoos, his pale body familiar and new all at once.

Emlyn grumbled under his breath and stalked to the window, turning his back to us as he stared at the lilac city beyond. He crossed burly arms over his chest.

"Em?" I asked, recognising the signs of a full-on sulk.

"What's up with him?" I whispered to Kai.

He shrugged, stretching his arms over his head. My gaze caught on the lithe muscles in his arms, the long column of his inked throat, the—the smirk on his face.

"Bastard," I hissed, giving him my middle finger. "I'm going to wash this crap off me; you three behave for ten fucking minutes, okay? No fights, no wandering around the palace, no stealing shit, no *breaking* shit."

I pointed a warning finger. Emlyn didn't turn to look at me. I tried not to let that hurt, reminding myself he was prone to silence and brooding even when he knew me.

"I won't be long," I promised, and rummaged through the drawers opposite my bed until I found clean clothes.

I gave them a last look, irrationally scared I'd come back and they'd be gone, and forced myself out into the hallway.

It was just a bath; they weren't going to burn the palace down if I took a bath.

"It'll be fine," I whispered to myself, hurrying down the hallway. "They'll be fine."

339

CHAPTER TWELVE

*H*oly fuck, it felt amazing to be clean. I could see my *skin,* and there wasn't dirt under my finger-nails, and my hair was pale pink not dark with grime and oils.[1]

I dried off and dressed in clean clothes, grabbing my weapons and slinging my dirty clothes over my arm to launder whenever I had the energy. I didn't look too hard at the new addition to my collection, the forget-me-nots moulded into the dagger's handle, but my eyes kept returning to it.

I blamed the distraction of my dagger for me not noticing the sounds coming from my room until I was two feet from the door.

"Fighting again?" I groaned, my mood sinking. I hated seeing them brawl; it was different to watching Kai and Harvey practise the whirling tornado in our kitchen. They never *really* wanted to hurt each other then. But watching them try to cause genuine damage hurt deep in my soul.

I swung the door open. "Guys, knock it—"

Shock blazed as bright and sharp as a star through me. I ...

had no idea what I was looking at. It took me a moment to reconcile the bare skin, sinuous writhing, and deep, masculine grunts. Holy shit.

I hurried inside and closed the door, checking no one had seen. Strangely, fiercely possessive of this moment. No one could see this but me. They were *mine.*

They also hadn't noticed me yet. Emlyn drove himself balls-deep into Harvey's ass while my sun soul bowed over Kai's naked, sweat-slicked body, panting for breath. My body was suddenly scalding, my clean clothes itching. Need pounded between my legs.

"Will you kill me if I join you?" I asked, startling Em rougher into Harvey, drawing a long, deep groan from his throat that only I ever heard.

I should have been jealous but all I felt was a pulsating need.

Malakai leaned back into my pillows, spreading his arms like a cocky prince as he flicked a smug look my way. There was so much damned intelligence in those eyes, it made my heartbeat quicken.

Emlyn bared his teeth and turned his head, his automatic growl simmering to a rumble when he saw it was me. I'd never seen Harvey submissive before; it was intriguing. Enticing as hell.

"They won't kill you," Kai said after a beat.

"I'll fucking kill *you,*" I muttered, giving him a sharp look and avoiding looking at the curse mark on his torso. "You started this. You wanted me to see you all like this."

He tilted his head, amusement glimmering in his eyes and his wine-red hair spilling over my pillow. Gods, he was beautiful. Sharp and deadly, but beautiful.

"You don't remember me yet," I breathed, because I had to say it, had to remind myself.

"No," he agreed, but that didn't stop his gaze gliding down

my body as I dumped my dirty clothes on the chest of drawers. I carefully laid down my weapons, removing the one in my boot before I kicked them off my feet.

Kai raised a dark red eyebrow, making a come hither gesture. "Help me remember."

I scoffed, taking my eyes from him and focusing on Harvey, splayed on top of Kai, panting, moaning. Em gripped his scarred bronze hips, his impatient, frantic pace, one I knew so well.

"You can wait," I told Kai, carefully approaching the bed and staying in Emlyn's line of sight. "Em? Can I join you?"

He replied in a deep, throaty sound, his expression tight with pleasure. I swallowed, biting my bottom lip as I stared at Emlyn's body, re-familiarising myself with his broad shoulders, his soft, squishy stomach, and the groove in his back I'd kissed my way down countless times. My throat ached at the curse mark now branded on his shoulder blade.

I didn't need Kai to translate this growl; Em's eyes fixed on me, smoky, darker blue. I grabbed the hem of my shirt without looking away from him and pulled it over my head, discarding it on the carpet. His eyes roved over my chest and stomach, seeing me for the first time. I swallowed again, my emotional state so damn fragile.

I needed them to touch me, to know me, to be mine again, and I knew this wouldn't fix anything. Their memories wouldn't magically return but—at least they'd touch me.

At least, for a moment, I could pretend things were back the way they were.

So I crawled onto the bed with them.

CHAPTER THIRTEEN

*J*half expected someone to shove me off the bed, for Harvey to snap or Em to snarl. But all Emlyn did was watch me with that same heat, and Harvey was too busy panting, twisting the pale gold covers under Kai into a mess.

I pushed off all my pain, all the memories that made my soul fracture every time my mates flinched from me or watched me like they were waiting for me to hurt them.

Here, now, none of that existed.

I reached for Emlyn, skimming my knuckles down his back and growing bolder when he didn't warn me off. If anything, his low rumble quietened even more, almost like a purr as I leaned over the tangle of legs and bodies[1] and pressed a long kiss to the curse on his shoulder, a new scar slashed below it.

My soul shuddered, bruised but *reaching*, aching to touch theirs. I tried casting myself towards Em, but the bond was shredded in my fingers, nothing but broken threads. For every time I failed to reach him in the bond, I brushed a kiss to Em's heated skin. I didn't know if bonds could be repaired, didn't know if curses could be broken, but I knew my mates were here. Em was *right here,* and Kai was staring at me like he was trying to understand why this felt so familiar.

"You're my mates," I told them softly, swallowing the knot in my throat as I kissed Em's skin again. "You're mine."

Emlyn watched me intently when I drew back, and my stomach flipped at the unwavering stare. But I ignored my nerves and slid my hand along his face, his thick beard rasping over my palm. When he didn't tear himself away, I bridged the distance between us and kissed him.

I meant to be gentle, but there was nothing tentative about the way my mouth crashed into his. The bond that lived in my chest roared at me to claim, to take, to make him mine again.

There was nothing gentle about the growl that rattled Em's chest either, or the way his hand shot out and grabbed my hip, squeezing tight. His hips stuttered against Harvey's ass when I sank fingers into his salt-and-pepper hair and gripped tight, by the roots the way he loved.

He hauled me closer, his teeth closing around my bottom lip as he let out a deep, vibrating noise that made my heart leap. I knew that sound—it was the one Em always made before he growled *you're mine.*

"Yours," I promised against his mouth, my chest hitching when his hand stroked over bare skin. There was something unapologetically possessive in the way he flattened his palm to my back and tugged me closer.

I lost balance, tumbling into his side, my skin pressed to his and my hand grasping for stability. Em's low laugh travelled through my entire body, raising goosebumps all down my back and making liquid heat pool between my legs. Harvey's breath caught on a groan when I flexed my hand, scraping fingernails across sweat-soaked skin, and I realised my hand had landed on him, not Em.

"Come here," Kai ordered.

I lifted my head to give him a narrow-eyed look, and with

deliberate slowness, I reached for Em again and kissed him, taking my time, exploring Harvey's arched back at the same time.

"I told you to *come here,*" Kai hissed.

I dragged my mouth from Em's, my chest heaving for breath, and I groaned when he sucked my bottom lip into his mouth, grazing it with his teeth and making everything inside me tighten deliciously.

"I know you know my name," I told Kai, breathier than I'd intended.

This time Emlyn reached for me first, gripping the back of my neck in a firm hold and tilting my head so he could kiss me thoroughly and deeply. By the time he drew away, I was dizzy and my clean underwear was soaked.

Emlyn's eyes were heavy, the blue darker than usual, and his chest rumbled with a long sound that made me clench deep inside.

"He likes the way you taste," Kai said, impatience a rough burr in his voice. "He wants to taste you in other places."

"Look at you, speaking full sentences," I panted, my eyes rolling a little when Emlyn pulled slowly out of Harvey and drove back in, fastening his mouth to my neck at the same time. It was like he knew all my weak spots; he found each and every one of them, reducing me to a trembling, gasping mess.

"Come here, Halwen," Kai commanded. "I won't tell you again."

I shuddered when I pulled away from Emlyn, his eyes so dark and pinned to me as I crawled away. I paused only to kiss my way up the bowed line of Harvey's spine. He was so beautiful like this, so new and strange in this beautifully submissive position, but achingly familiar. I knew every one of his gasps and choked noises, especially those low, needy moans. They were mine, those noises, but after everything we'd been through, sharing them with Kai and Emlyn was ... special. Significant.

"How long have you been sleeping together?" I asked, recovering my wits now Emlyn wasn't kissing me breathless.

Kai shrugged. "Fifty years. Maybe sixty. It was—dark." His throat bobbed; he didn't elaborate.

When he sat up against the pillows—making space for me between him and Harvey—I slid between them.

"The other way," he huffed, grabbing my shoulder and hip and manhandling me the way he wanted me—my back to his chest, my legs in the tangled nightmare and—ohhhh shit.

"You genius," I gasped, biting my lip as Harvey's hard, weeping cock grazed my pussy through my trousers. "You should've told me to take these off, though."

"We'll just tear them apart," he replied, unworried, and dropped a kiss on my shoulder that made my heart lurch.

"You fucking won't," I growled, my body so hot under all this sweaty, writhing flesh. "Just try and—"

I cut off with a yelp when Kai pinched my nipple hard enough that a sharp sensation stole my breath.

"You can't stop us," he laughed, pushing my hair aside so his lips could trail down my neck. "We can do whatever we want to you. We're beasts, after all."

"Shockingly eloquent beasts," I managed to reply, but with Harvey on top of me, his eyes screwed shut and taut face right above me, his cock grazing my clothed pussy with every one of Em's thrusts, it was difficult.

"Big words for someone at our mercy right now," Kai murmured, cupping my breasts in his hands before—oh gods —his attention moved to my wings.

My whole body locked when he grazed a light touch over my feathers, stroking where they met silken membrane until a guttural sound trapped in my throat.

"I don't know how, but I know for a fact I can make you come by touching these."

"Kai," I choked out, and didn't know if I was pleading for mercy or begging for more.

Emlyn's next thrust made Harvey's cock nudge right over my clit, and my back arched off the bed. I wrapped my arms around Harvey, burying my face in his neck, the feeling of his feathers grazing my sides heightening every sensation until I couldn't breathe. His scent filled my senses until my whole world was sun-warmed earth.

"Something tells me," Kai went on, quiet and arrogant, "this spot right here will ruin you. What do you think, Halwen?"

He might not remember me, but he knew my body.

"Kai," I gasped when his hands glided between me and Harvey, squeezing my boobs at the same time his mouth—*oh gods, his mouth*—found the tender spot on my back where my wings connected. He followed it up and up, grazing his teeth across the membrane until my eyes blew wide and all I could do was pant and cling to Harvey.

Emlyn's broad hands folded around mine where I gripped Harvey's waist, and I choked on every breath, the four of us connected in ways I'd dreamed of since I climbed out of a shallow grave.

Theirs—I was theirs. Nothing would change that, not life or death or anything in between.

My entire body locked, tightened, and I clasped Harvey's shoulder between my teeth without conscious thought, a deep whine in my throat. Kai knew exactly which spot would ruin me. The moment his teeth scraped the ultra-sensitive arch where feathers became soft, velvety skin, I shattered with the hardest climax of my life.

Harvey went feral, thrusting mindlessly against me, frantic to be inside me despite the barrier between us. Every time the head of his cock brushed my clit, it shot me higher.

Emlyn growled viciously, gripping my hands tighter where we both clutched Harvey. Kai's rough teasing softened to slow, adoring kisses scattered down my wing, across my back, and to the other wing, covering me in kisses as I came down hard, shaking between them.

I couldn't—couldn't control my body. I couldn't stop the shaking, and it grew worse, my arms twitching, legs trembling, breath pinching in my chest.

"Halwen," Kai said, his tone shifting to worry in an instant. He turned me in his arms, ignoring Harvey's snarl of complaint, and stroked sweaty pink hair from my face with both hands, pressing a long, lingering kiss to my forehead. "Halwen, Ha—Haley? Come back."

He folded me into his arms, my face pressed to his neck where his scent was thickest, either intentionally or by sheer luck. His amber and firewood scent filled me with comfort and drowned out the vicious instinctual response making my whole body, heart, and soul quake. For a moment, I was back in our home, sitting by the fire with logs crackling on the open fire and my four mates all wrapped around me. Cosy, familiar, safe.

I jolted out of the memory, pushing off the bone-deep ache, the sense that something was wrong, something was *lost*. I shuddered between Kai and Harvey, a sob trapped in my throat.

Kai stroked his fingers through my hair, every touch gentle, and—and he murmured to me in a language I didn't speak.

Tears built in my eyes, clinging to my lashes. "Do you—do you know what that means?" I rasped, my throat so thick I could barely speak.

Kai swallowed when I drew back a few inches to look at him, stroking the tip of a wing over his bare, inked thigh. "Only parts."

I kissed him slowly, giving him enough time to push me away, but he only clutched me tighter and kissed me with devastating emotion. His hands quivered against my back, just under my wings.

"It means *I will always be your shadow and light; you will always be my rose and life."* I kissed him again, adoring and soft. "It's—something you said to me, every year on our anniversary."

Kai's expression froze. His pale throat bobbed. "Anniversary. How long were we together?"

I smiled, a tightness in my chest easing when Harvey wrapped around me from behind his wings overlapping on my stomach, his face resting against the back of my neck.

"Ten years," I answered, pushing through the lump in my throat. "The best years of my life."

Kai's jaw clenched. He tore his gaze from me, glaring at the ceiling. A muscle feathered in his cheek. All signs he was seconds away from emotion ruling over him.

I kissed his jaw until it unclenched, stroked my hands down his sides until he took a shaky breath. "You'll remember. We'll get your memories back. I promise, Malakai."

He nodded once, jerkily. "And then we kill whoever took them?"

"We'll slice them to shreds," I promised, kissing his lips, not drawing away until he was stronger and I was more in control of my emotions, too.

"Ten years," a soft, barely audible voice whispered. Raspy and soft, always quiet.

I whipped my head around, hissing a curse when I almost broke Harvey's nose. My heart thumping, I stared at Emlyn, my Em, my gentle giant mate. It was the first time I'd heard his voice in a hundred years.

"We'll get them back," I promised him too, and kissed Harvey's sharp cheekbone, echoing the same vow. "I swear we will. But they *failed*. They wanted to break us apart forever. It took too fucking long," I choked out, "but we're here. We're together."

I blinked back my tears and gripped the hope soaring through me, pushing it through all of me until it drowned out the aching loss.

"Now, what was your diabolical sex plan, Kai?"

The grin he wore when I looked back at him made me nervous as fuck.

CHAPTER FOURTEEN

HARVEY

*T*heir words swam like underwater noise, senseless and strange, but I clung to other things: the low rumble of the one she called Emlyn, the scent of her wrapped around my tongue—soft orchids and hot blood—and the gleam in Kai's red eyes that promised wicked, pleasurable things.

I needed to come so badly it hurt. I needed that hot, explosive moment where nothing else existed. No pain, no fear, no gnawing hollowness in my chest where something used to belong.

Was it *her*? This murderous, pretty doll who writhed beneath me? Did she fill the hole in my chest? It had certainly fulfilled a base need to watch her fight her way out of the master's pit.

When she touched my injured wing, when she cared for me, it hurt but in a good way. Hurt and soothed at the same time.

That was how it felt to have her under me, to wrap my wings around her as she shook and came apart—it hurt and soothed.

Emlyn's hands, entwined with hers on my body ... that too hurt and soothed.

I didn't know what would fill the aching emptiness. But I knew I wanted her so desperately I couldn't focus on anything else. My cock was hard enough to sink straight into her heat, and I wanted it, *needed* it—

Smirking, deadly Kai turned her beneath me until her black wings splayed across the bed on either side of us, her beautiful chest bared to me again. My upper lip curled back, a guttural sound forcing its way up my throat. Her tanned skin was covered in marks—drawings of flowers and skulls and things as beautiful and harmful as her. And scars, old and healed, carved deep white gouges across her shoulders, ribs, and collarbone. A new, red mark slashed across her stomach, disappearing beneath her trousers. A low, deep sound shook my throat as I stared at it, Kai uttering something in his rare soft, sweet tone.

She—Halwen, Haley, and—another name I couldn't remember—reached for my face, directing my stare to her face. My chest physically hurt whenever I stared into her eyes. I balanced all my weight on one hand so I could touch her, trailing my fingers along her jaw in an experimental touch. She didn't tear away from me, didn't flinch. Her eyes fluttered shut. Her bottom lip shuddered until she pressed them both flat.

I wanted to beg her to look at me again, but I couldn't remember how to shape my mouth right. Instead, I trailed the pads of my fingers over the delicate skin of her eyelids and down her cheek, jolting in surprise when they glided over wet skin. She was—crying.

Don't cry, my lethal doll, my—

The name was so close, slicing through my chest like a scalpel. I swallowed and flinched from dark memories: the fighting pits, the cells, the tunnels. They were always close, stalking me like a shadow.

Shadow...

I needed to remember the shadows. Halwen mentioned them too. I reached into my memories for any whisper of them, but pain flashed through my skull, forcing me away—urging me back to the beauty beneath me.

Emlyn stilled, watching us from behind. I throbbed around his cock as Halwen blinked up at me, the tiniest, saddest smile on her face. Did she see my pain? I saw hers now; sometimes it was all I could see. She wasn't a threat, wasn't someone to kill. She was a doll, cracked and beautiful but refusing to break. Like me.

I wanted to kiss her but I didn't know how. I was too proud to ask Kai or Emlyn.

"Harvey," she murmured.

I knew that word, that name—it was mine. Different to the one the beasts of the pits called me, different to what the master called me. But this name felt *right*. Was it mine, or had she given it to me? A gift from a beautiful, lethal woman?

Kai chuckled, a sound that made even me nervous, and I realised what he planned when he unfastened the ties on her trousers and grabbed each side of fabric. I didn't think he was strong enough, but I was happily surprised to hear the fabric tear and then—the ruined clothes were torn away and she was bare for me.

A low sound rumbled in my throat, soft and sympathetic. *So wet, my doll. You must ache so badly.*

Kai growled deep in his throat. *What are you waiting for?*

I shot him a sharp look and laid her back against him, spreading her out. Her skin scalded my hands; I groaned, the thin wall between me and my beast threatening to snap.

The next moment, my lips were fastened around her nipple, my tongue lapping greedily, desperate for the soft, salty taste of her skin. When her breath hitched and she clutched me closer, I possessively folded the noise into my memory. That was mine; it belonged to me. Only me.

"Harvey," she breathed, faint and needy. Her hands glided over my wings, restless.

You need me here, my lethal doll? I asked in a low rumble, reaching for my cock and hissing a breath at how sensitive I was. I was glad that Emlyn had the patience to stay still so long, so I could have this moment with my—I couldn't remember the word she used. But she spoke it with so much importance.

Haley clutched my hips with a gasp when I brushed my tip through her wetness, the sensation so damn heavenly that my ass clenched around the cock buried inside it, and Emlyn grunted, fingers bruising my hips.

I tried to form her name, but only a growl came from my vocal chords. She panted, staring up at me like she understood, her smoke-grey eyes wide and pleading, ringed with thick lashes that fluttered when I brushed her swollen clit again. I felt it throb against me, and couldn't hold back my beast any longer.

My teeth bared, a vicious snarl tearing from my throat. I gripped her hips, lifting her ass up so I could line my cock with her drenched entrance and sink inside her. I was too frantic to go slow, but she was so slick that my thrust drove me balls-deep inside her. My eyes rolled back. I had just enough control to stop a full shift overtaking my body.

Haley cried out, a high sound that made my balls tight, that made my teeth ache to sink into her, to claim her as *mine, all fucking mine.* She'd bitten me. She didn't break the skin, but it was enough to push me so close to the edge that I'd nearly spilled all over her. I was back on that edge now as her perfect, wet heat sucked me in with demanding throbs, each one corresponding with a quiet little whine from her pink lips.

I didn't know how to kiss her, but the beast in me wouldn't be denied. I slammed my mouth into hers, relief and satisfaction blazing through the darkness that lived inside me. It felt like rays of sunlight on my soul—hot and bright and ruthless —when she kissed me back.

Her lips coaxed mine into shapes that sent shivers down my spine, and I withdrew my aching length from her in a rush, slamming back inside. My eyes rolled all the way back this time, my mouth hanging open as I fucked her, and fucked myself on Emlyn's cock at the same time.

A guttural whine tore from my throat when she sucked my tongue, fucking it with sinuous motions of her mouth until sensations overwhelmed me. Emlyn's hands tightened on my hips, the only warning before he drove into me hard enough that I filled my lethal doll, both of us groaning.

Beautiful—this, her, everything. It was beautiful. I'd forgotten things could have beauty.

Kai stroked a gentle finger down her wing, and she clenched around me with a shudder and a choked noise.

I snarled, the sound coming from deep in my chest, so loud it drowned out her next moan. *Mine*, the growl said.

Kai rolled his eyes and hissed, *ours*.

"Harvey," she panted, her thighs locking around me and her face flushed dark pink, dewy and so stunning it hurt.

"Harvey—" I didn't know what she said next, but her body spoke clearly in the way it bucked up into me, in the way her heat gripped me with ruthless, pulsing pleas.

I tilted her face up for another kiss, and I must have learned from our first kiss because this one made her whine and arch up into me, her pussy strangling my cock as I fucked her with everything I had. The glide of her skin against mine, so fucking soft, was a shock after years of roughness. I never wanted this to end, but I couldn't stop, couldn't even slow.

A bestial growl burst up my throat, a wordless noise without meaning, and I wrapped my hands around her waist, slamming my hips into hers over and over, aware I was being too rough but unable to stop. But Halwen clung to me, gasping, her wide eyes fixed on my face and lips parted on soft, whining words. She didn't want me to stop. She ... loved it. And I—loved her.

I loved her. How did I forget that?

I slid a hand under her ass, lifting her hips to align with mine as I laid atop her, rolling my hips in short, snapping thrusts as I kissed her, my whole body fused to hers, my wings pressed to her sides. Emlyn was behind me, inside me, and Kai was behind her, but in this cocoon of feathers and need, we were alone. She was mine. My—

"Sugarplum," I groaned, the name crashing through my mind like a wave. It was the only word I knew, the only word that mattered.

Her breath caught in a whine, and she clutched me tight like before, burying her head against my shoulder as she gasped and moaned. She was close, and that knowledge made my climax race towards me, pleasure heightening until I could barely kiss her properly. Emlyn picked up his pace, driving deep enough to make pleasure throb through me, hitting my weak spot on every withdrawal.

When her teeth pressed to my skin, I lost it, my hips crashing into hers, my breath cutting out. My hand shot to the back of her head, and I pressed her teeth harder in a wordless plea. She rewarded me with a bite that pierced my skin. I roared, driving her into Kai with my next thrust, burying deep as I came so hard I saw nothing but bright, golden sunlight.

"Harvey," she whimpered, "Harvey. *Gods.*"

Her whole body shuddered, and her pussy latched tight around me, making my eyes cross. That grip tore a choked, high sound from me. *Fuck.* I pressed her teeth deeper into my shoulder, my cock twitching harder, spilling inside her. *Fuck.*

Emlyn roared, burying himself inside me once, twice, and bruising my hips with rough hands when I throbbed around him, forcing an orgasm from him. He bowed over my back, growling hard breaths.

The warmth of him and Haley surrounded me until I was limp and—calm. Not afraid. Not threatened. Not alone.

I hadn't felt like this in ... as long as I could remember. Not ever.

I brushed a soft kiss to the side of Haley's head and gently, carefully, withdrew from her. Ugh *fuck,* Emlyn shifted inside me, making my sensitive cock ache.

The bite on my shoulder throbbed an echoing claim. And I remembered her name now—Sugarplum. She called me Buttercup; I called her Sugarplum.

Remembering that was small, insignificant compared to what I'd lost, but it felt like *everything.*

CHAPTER FIFTEEN

HALWEN

I clung to Harvey as long as I could, satisfaction burning through me, relaxing every muscle in my body even as horror slowly bled through my mind.

Right on the edge, just as I'd been about to come on Harvey's cock, I felt his brother through the bond in a low, predatory stroke. *Wynvail.* It was like he'd stolen my orgasm. Like he'd taken ownership of what should have been a special moment.

It was a taunt and a reminder that he'd find me wherever I went.

I kissed the bite I'd left on Harvey's shoulder, and when he moved back, Em carefully withdrawing too, I slipped off the bed.

"Just going to clean up," I said, swallowing down my rage and unease, and grabbing a dressing robe from the wardrobe so I could duck out of the room.

I wasn't surprised when the bedroom door opened when I'd only taken a few steps. "Kai," I sighed, not even turning.

"What's wrong?"

I shook my head, glancing at him sidelong when he caught up to me. "Not here. I was serious about cleaning up; Harvey came so much I can literally feel him dripping out of me."

He wrinkled his nose.

"Not taken a turn at bottom during the past hundred years?" I asked, catching a glimpse of his body— "Malakai! Why are you naked?"

He gave me a crooked grin and a shrug.

"Someone could see you." My voice darkened when I added, "Someone could see what's mine."

"I'll cut out their eyes if they look," he assured me, his chest rising and falling fast, covered in shifting ink and overlapping scars.

I shook my head, ushering him quickly down the hall. "You don't even have a knife. Turn around!" I barked when a man bearing a tray of clean linens turned into the corridor. "Find another way, or I'll skin you alive and scoop out your eyeballs."

Either my reputation proceeded me, or you learned quickly to not fuck with anyone in this palace, because the man took one look at me and Kai and spun, hurrying back the way he came.[1] "Cover yourself," I hissed at Kai.

"I'm waiting for you to do it for me," he replied smoothly.

In response, I opened the door to the bathroom—exhaling in relief that it was unoccupied—and shoved him inside.

The chilly air pebbled my skin under the dressing gown, but it was worth the cold to bathe in this luxurious room. Gold and white marble formed a wide bath big enough for three[2] and a sink, counter, and an honest-to-gods *toilet*. Parts of Hell were still being upgraded to modern plumbing, but this was a thing of beauty; it even had two flush settings. Say what you want about humans up on Earth, but they were damned good at inventing stuff.

"I felt Wynvail," I told Kai, busying myself with twisting the gold taps until water slammed into the tub. "When we—when I came. I think he was watching, sensing, for a long time before I noticed. He's a sneaky, intrusive bastard."

I pushed the plug into place and stepped back, eyeing the different oils, lotions, and potions. I jumped when Kai fitted his body to my back, his arms wrapping my waist.

"Wynvail is the master of the pit?"

"Yeah, that bastard. He's my mate," I added begrudgingly. "As much as I want him dead, I can't kill him. It could kill me, and then kill all of you. I won't risk that. But he keeps connecting with me, keeps touching my soul and—I'm not sure how I feel about that."

Kai tightened his arms around me. "He's evil."

"Yeah, I figured as much." I muttered, melting into him. His heat spread across my belly through the thin silk. "Well, you know what they say. You can choose your enemies, but you can't choose your mates."

"I've never heard anyone say that."

"I just made it up. What did he do to you—in those tunnels? In that fighting pit?"

I turned so I could see Kai's face, scanning the sharp angles and brutal edges of him. I trailed my stare all the way from the writing inked on his throat, swirling slowly with his magic, up the razor edge of his jaw and the blades of his cheekbones, past his keen crimson eyes to the deadly points of his twin horns. He didn't meet my eyes, staring instead at the bath as water cascaded into it.

"It was never the master himself, but the ones who answered to him ... they tortured us," he said finally, his hands flexing on my hips. "Almost—constantly. It was worse for Harvey. The darkness..."

I clenched my jaw, my nostrils flaring as I fought the sudden need to cry. "That's why he—his other form—"

Kai nodded, his mouth in a flat line. "I don't have another form but it was—I began to lose my words."

I thought he meant his speech but when he drew back, lifting his leg, my heart shot into my throat at the bare, unmarked skin from his ankle to his right calf.

"Kai," I breathed, my heart beating triple time, unable to take my eyes off that unblemished skin even as he put his leg down. "How—? I thought the tattoos gave you power...?"

"No. The power gives me the words on my body, and I can use them to form my snakes."

"Did you lose a snake?" I asked, my voice faint. I was going to be sick. How badly had he been tortured for his power to unravel?

"Eight," he corrected.

"Eight?" I demanded, my shrill voice filling the high ceilinged room. "Kai, fuck, did it—does it—hurt?"

He reached out and shut off the tap before the bath over-flowed, not letting go of my waist. "There's no pain, but I can't feel it anymore. My legs is just ... cold. Empty."

Shit. I grabbed his face, bringing his gaze to mine. "You won't lose any more. I swear to you, Malakai. No one will ever lock you up again."

He stared into my eyes, unblinking, for long moments. "I know," he said finally. "Don't worry about me. Worry about Emlyn."

"Emlyn?" I frowned. "Not Harvey?"

Kai shook his head, tugging the robe off my shoulders and pushing me towards the hot bath. I resisted long enough to dump a pearly lotion into the water, bubbles frothing as I climbed in.

"Harvey's damage is on the outside, where you can see it," Kai said, not satisfied until I was in the bath. I needed to pee, but it was awkward with him here so that would have to wait. "Emlyn's is buried. I can feel it sometimes; my instinct says he's dangerous. I haven't seen what the pit did to him yet."

Tightness gripped my chest, squeezing all the air from my lungs. "What can I do? For Em, for all of you, what can I do?"

Kai grabbed my shoulders and pushed me until my ass slid forward on the tub, ignoring the affronted look I shot him as he climbed in behind me. "You've helped a lot already. I can talk."

"Yeah, now you never shut up," I teased, leaning back into him and sighing when his arms wrapped around me. "I preferred you quiet and obedient."

He pinched my side, making me curse. "I was never obedient."

Wasn't that the truth?

"He made us fight each other," he said abruptly, his breath shivering over the back of my neck. "You asked what he made us do in the pits. I didn't realise why at first, and I didn't really know why Emlyn and Harvey felt like brothers to me. He wanted to destroy that, to turn us against each other. Make us hate each other."

I squeezed his arm where it rested on my waist. "That's why you and Harvey fight all the time. Wynvail trained you to fight."

"To want each other dead," Kai corrected quietly. "I didn't stop wanting to kill them until two days ago."

"What happened two days ago?" I asked quietly, turning to look at him.

Kai shook his head, dark red hair slicked back from his face and something haunted and fragile in his eyes. "I don't know. I looked at them and didn't want to kill them. I wanted to kill anyone who'd ever tried to hurt them. It's ... strange."

I stroked my thumb over his wrist. "The more you remember, the stranger it might feel."

Something sharpened in his eyes. "Why does it hurt *you* to remember things? Harvey, too. I heard him scream in the cells, especially at first, and I thought they were torturing him, but now I can see him..."

"You think he was screaming because he was trying to remember?"

Kai nodded, his throat bobbing.

"There are shadows in my memory, hiding something from me. Whenever I try to see what's under them, it hurts like fuck."

Kai's brow furrowed, his gaze distant. "Shadows...? I've seen them sometimes, when I remember Harvey and Emlyn from before the pit and—"

He inhaled a sharp breath, his arms tightening around me.

"Stop," I warned, reaching up to hold his face. "Kai, leave it."

He gritted his teeth and nodded, exhaling a breath of relief. So it hurt him when he tried to remember the shadows, too.

"Do you remember me at all?" I asked, swallowing my nerves.

Kai filled his lungs with a breath, meeting my gaze. "I remember flowers, little white soulcaps. And drinking coffee by a window in the early morning, watching birds fly from branches in a forest. And—this sounds crazy, but did I ever try to kill you?"

I laughed through my choked throat. "Yeah, when we first met. To be fair, I was hunting you and you felt protective of—" I winced when pain sliced through my skull. "Presumably the shadows. I think it's a person, Kai. The shadows. Too many things don't make sense; it's more than a *thing*. And whenever I try to fit Wynvail into those memories, it feels ... disjointed."

"I don't remember him before the fighting pit," Kai said quietly, massaging a spot on my side—a scar, I realised. He traced it over and over like it soothed him.

"I do," I muttered. "Bastard burned our house down. The

kitchen you remember, where you can see the forest? We lived there for years. And he burned it down."

"Why?"

"He worked for—his father," I realised, putting those facts together. Cassander Locke sent one son to kill another. That was fucked up, even for demons. No wonder Wynvail turned out so twisted. "He wanted … I can't remember what he wanted."

"Neither can I," Kai murmured. "Does he still work for his father? Is that why he made us fight?"

A chill went through my blood, and I turned fully, wrapping my arms around Kai's shoulders, burying my face in his neck. "If he does…" I laughed bitterly, panic clasping around my lungs, squeezing tight. "We never escaped, even in death. We'll never escape him."

Kai's arms tightened around me. "Locke's not an archdemon like Harvey. He never was—that came from Harvey's mother's side."

"So there's a good chance Locke is dead," I breathed.

I'd come to that conclusion myself but hearing it out loud made it sound reasonable, not a desperate delusion. Locke could have died while I was buried in the ground and my mates were locked in the tunnels. That was the only silver lining of the whole thing, but it hinged on that little C word.[3]

"If he's dead, why did Wynvail lock us up and make us monsters?" Kai asked.

I reared back to glare at him. "He didn't. There's *nothing* monstrous about you, Malakai Virex. Nothing."

When he began to argue, I kissed him. I wasn't as soft as it could have been; I kissed him with anger and protectiveness and iron-hard determination to make him believe my words.

"If you kiss me like that, I don't care if I'm monstrous or beautiful," he panted, his eyes dark, dark red. "But you ignored my question."

I ignored it again, kissing him rougher, deeper, because the first one obviously didn't work. By the time I was finished, Kai was bucking his hips under me, breathless and dark-eyed. Better.

"You're mine," I told him, my voice raspy and low. "My night."

"My rose," he replied, blinking in surprise at the name as it fell from his own lips. "You're my rose. *Mine.*"

There was Kai as I knew him—soft and sweet and possessive enough to kill someone for a single glance at me.

"Yours," I promised. But I turned over his question in my mind and sighed. "You're right, it doesn't make sense that Wynvail did all this if Locke is dead. But ... he must have been brainwashed into hating us, to try and kill us so many times a hundred years ago. He still hates us."

Even if he wanted to own me, to break me and make me his, he hated me. There was no denying that.

"What if he found a new master?" Kai mused, a sharpness in his expression. "Or Locke was working for someone else all along?"

I shook my head, knowledge hidden just out of my grasp no matter how hard or high I reached for it.

"No, hunting us, *killing* us was personal. This feels ... different. Did you hear what Ashboren the Terrifying said about the mark on my back? He said we're involved in something big and traumatic. It's no coincidence I'm meant for apparent greatness now I've come back from the dead and found you guys again. And Wynvail is right in the middle of it all."

I inhaled a sharp breath, squeezing Kai's shoulders as I remembered something.

"There was a group of alphas I hunted; one of them told me about Wynvail and Alphaven. He said the Lord collects alphas for someone else, and that's how he had the magic to bind all of you to his command. Whoever he's working for gave him that power."

Kai's jaw clenched. He glared at the bathroom over the top of my head, like the marble tiles bore graffiti insulting his mum. "Then he's been working for this person for a long time. We've been Wynvail's fighters for ... I don't know how long."

"He told me you were reborn not long after Locke killed us. So he's been working for this powerful person for ... a hundred years. Fuck."

"It could still be Locke," Kai pointed out.

Yeah, that wasn't comforting. Cassander Locke was a prideful, manipulative, ruthless bastard who'd throw anyone under the bus to get what he wanted. If Wynvail was collecting alphas—an *army* of alphas—for his father, and Cassander Locke had the power to grant his son control over them ... that was bad fucking news for us.

"I can talk, and I remember the house," Kai said quietly, stroking where the wound on my thigh had left a raised scar. "I'll remember more. Maybe the others can remember too— not just Harvey and Emlyn, but the other alphas."

That was a pretty big maybe.

"He can get into the palace," I said, reluctantly bringing it up. "If Wynvail got in to steal the tiara, he can get in again. He'll come for me."

"He'll die," Kai promised in a lethal whisper.

"You don't even remember me, and you're willing to kill for me?"

"You're mine. No one touches what's mine."

I leaned into him, a smile tugging my lips. He was completely himself, down to his killer promises, but ... I was still a stranger to him.

"I need you to hold the stone for a few hours tonight," I said, swallowing the lump in my throat. "I need—I need you to remember me, Kai. I need *all* of you, but your memories feel so close. It's too easy to forget I'm nobody to you."

"You're not nobody," he growled, so suddenly deep that my heart slammed against my ribs. "Is that what you think? You think the woman who charged through the fighting pit, killing people to save me is nobody? You think the woman who took on our master and *freed* us is nobody? The woman who finds us somewhere to sleep, brings us safe food, and looks at us like we're men, not just beasts—that's the woman you think is nobody? She is *everything* to me. To all of us."

I could only stare at him, my chest cracking apart and heat burning my eyes. Kai felt all that?

He grinned, the severity of his expression breaking. "We'd have slaughtered you by now if you were nobody."

I couldn't stop hot tears falling down my cheeks. That's how he saw me? How they *all* saw me? Even without knowing our history, even with their memories buried?

I brushed tears off my cheeks and kissed Kai, this kiss slow and aching. I practically held my heart out for him to take.

"I love you so much," I breathed, the hitch of a sob in my throat. "I don't expect you to say it back—"

"Why not? I have loved you since you flew me out of that pit."

"Pretty sure you were terrified I'd drop you," I drawled.

He brushed his lips over mine. "And scared we'd kill you. I was scared of both—harming you and you hurting me. The animal in me was wary of the killing mark on you, but you showed me you weren't a threat. And you rescued us from that nightmare. How could I not love you?"

"You're insane for saying it so soon," I told him, but what was new there?[4]

"I'll always be insane," Kai replied, his eyes crinkled at the corners, "but I'll always be yours, too. Now lay back against me, my rose. Let me soothe all your pain."

I gave him a narrow look. "Kai, we're being hunted. The second Wynvail knows where to find us, he'll break into the palace again and—"

He wrapped his warm hand around my throat and used it to turn my body, pressing my back to his chest as his other hand spread my legs, stroking over my slippery skin to my core.

"I told you to turn around," he said in a low voice, catching my earlobe between his teeth at the same time his fingers glided through my wetness and circled my clit.

By the time he was done, I forgot my own name.

CHAPTER SIXTEEN

EMLYN

I woke up before everyone else and glared at the other men for long, long minutes as the sun rose. Harvey slept on the edge of the bed, with Kai in front of him, and Haley was tucked small and warm between me and Kai. She faced *me* though, I noticed with vicious satisfaction. She'd turned over in the night to cuddle close to me.

I wrapped my arm tighter around her now, a quiet rumble in my chest when her fingers flexed against my bare skin and a sigh left her lips.

When I looked at her, peace replaced every other emotion. There'd been hundreds of mornings like these. I knew that, remembered the feeling of them, the comfort and ease, even if I couldn't recall what they'd looked like, where we'd been, or what happened. It was a strange feeling, to know I knew this woman and love being close to her, to want to eviscerate anyone who dared to hurt her, but to not know her at all.

Stranger still was the dark seed of envy in my chest. I

glared over her shoulder at where Harvey slept, dark leather wrapped around his hands. Malakai's green scarf was laid on the chair by the window, arranged with precision and care. Where was mine?

A growl caught in my throat, and I clutched her closer even if I wanted to snarl in her face. Did she want them more than me?

She'd touched me, and kissed me, but she took Harvey's cock, and she spent time with Kai in the bathroom. A muscle fluttered in my jaw when I clenched it, and I ducked my head, pressing my nose into the thick waves of her pink hair to fill my lungs with her blood and orchid scent.

Ten years—that's how long she said we were together. *Ten years.*

Some words were still meaningless, a blur of noise and syllables, but those were clear. Ten fucking years, and I couldn't remember her at all. She belonged to me, she was mine to hold, to protect, to kiss and please and keep.[1]

A disgruntled noise rattled inside my chest, startling another soft sound from Haley. Kai cracked a red eye open to glare at me. I bared my teeth, holding her to my chest. *Mine.* Kai rolled his eyes and went back to sleep.

Good for him. *He* could sleep easily. *He* knew he was important to Haley. Me? I had to prove myself, had to earn her appreciation. I couldn't be separated from these men. I might have fought them for a hundred years, might have scarred them and been scarred by them, but they were my people. Friends? Whatever they were, they were *mine,* and there was an undeniable bond locking us together.

We might have bitten, bruised, and bled each other in the arena, but never by choice. Haley said we knew each other for ten years before their place, but we were bound even tighter now. We were equals.[2]

I sighed hard enough that Haley stirred, blinking sleepy

grey eyes open. All my irritation faded when her mouth curved into a smile.

"Morning, Em," she murmured, her voice raspy and adorable.

Say morning, I growled at myself. *It's not difficult. Morning. Easy. You can think it—just form the same word with your mouth.*

Instead I growled an unintelligible noise. Useless.

Even so, Haley's smile deepened and she let out a long sigh as she snuggled back into my chest. My bitterness faded, sweetened by that smile she gave *to me.* Only me. It was mine —my gift.

I wrapped both arms around her and laid a kiss on the top of her head, the gesture easy and—familiar. She let out another deep sigh, hitching her thigh over my leg and melting into me.

I wanted to hold the stone today, but I didn't know how to tell her that and—she was already asleep, soft puffs of air tingling over my neck. My cheeks curved into a smile, the expression stiff and alien. I buried it in her hair and followed her back into sleep.

I might not have had a scarf or gloves, but I had her. I had peace. And that was more than I'd dared to wish for.

CHAPTER SEVENTEEN

HALWEN

"*S*tealing from us, Halwen?" a smooth voice asked, making me jump halfway out of my body. I shot the rest of the way out when I saw the tall, elegant man staring at me with sharp red eyes and—amusement on his aquiline face. Oh *thank fuck*, he was amused.

"Not stealing, just stocking up," I told Lucifer, dropping three apples into my bag. "We're going into the city to try and find answers about my curse marks. Unless you've got a job for me?"

"I wanted to talk to you again about what happened in Alphaven. Just in case there's anything you've remembered since."

I nodded, less terrified of the devil since I'd seen him with his queen. "With all honesty, your highness, my head was kind of fried when I got back. I've remembered a few things since. I can tell you about them now, if you're not busy."

"I can spare ten minutes," he agreed, although I doubted

that very much. He was the devil, the big guy in charge of all demons, souls, and whatever the hell else wandered through Hell. "Just let me get a coffee."

See, that made more sense. I'd need caffeine if I had to organise billions of souls, too.

"You better not expect me to go back to the Damned Realm now I've found my mates again," I told him, plopping down on a table near the coffee machine and avoiding the looks shot at us from everyone else having breakfast.[1] "Sir," I tacked on the end.

Lucifer shook his head, long dark hair swaying. "Nothing like that. You're a better huntress than a custodian."

"Because I was murdered before I could custode anything," I pointed out.[2]

"So what is it you really want?" I asked, giving the devil a shrewd look when he sat opposite me and sipped his coffee —which was surprisingly milky. I would have expected it black.

Lucifer tilted his head in acknowledgment. "I do want to hear your account of that day again. *But* I also want to know what this Wynvail is planning. And who he's working for."

I straightened in my seat at the way he watched me— intensely, scrutinising. "The only issue is, I don't know. I told you everything I know about him—he has a city full of alphas, and the alpha I interrogated in Kalador said his plan wasn't to kill you."

"We came to the same conclusion," Lucifer admitted, frowning at his coffee. "Which is why I'm talking to you."

"I wish I could tell you something useful. All I know is he's got this collection of alphas, and I remembered Bevan saying he's gathering them for someone else, someone powerful. And he's ... obsessed with me." I winced at that, but I might as well tell him.

Lucifer leaned back in his seat, a shade paler than before.

"You really thought I'd know, didn't you?" I realised. "Because you don't know what his endgame is, either."

Shit, if *the devil* didn't know, the rest of us were fucked.

"Something is happening out there," he replied, casting his voice lower and giving me a hard look that warned me not to tell anyone else what he said. "You know it; there's no good reason anyone would gather that many alphas. And Wynvail is your mate, which means you're the key."

Ugh, I really really hated Wynvail.

"If it helps, I'll kill him the next chance I get," I muttered.

"He's a minor player," Lucifer dismissed, waving his hand. "It won't make a big enough difference."

"This is a really reassuring conversation," I told him, heavy on sarcasm.

He smiled, though it didn't reach his eyes. "We won one war; we can win another." He pushed out of his seat, his cup somehow empty. "I'm not worried."

He was lying. And if Lucifer himself was scared, the rest of us should be absolutely fucking petrified.

CHAPTER EIGHTEEN

"*P*ut that in your pocket," I chided Emlyn when he turned the memory stone over in his hand. He'd been doing it the whole time we walked from the palace and through the city, alternating between staring at it curiously and like the stone had insulted his entire family line.

I hadn't brought up the subject of family, although they must have known after so many years, most people we'd loved were dead. Kai being an archdemon was fluke; both his parents were regular demons and must have passed years ago. Harvey's mum could be out there, but if she was smart she'd be hiding from her other, more insane son.

Emlyn had always been cagy about his past; he dealt out information in rations and only when absolutely necessary. I didn't know if he had an archdemon parent or two, didn't know if there was a chance they were still alive.

I knew everyone in *my* family was gone—they'd all been gone when I was sixteen. But it would be jarring for my mates when they realised.

Emboldened by them letting me touch them last night, I

reached out and caught Em's hand, prising the stone from his fingers and tucking it in the pocket of a jacket we'd borrowed from the unoccupied palace bedroom beside mine. Before he could complain, I wrapped my fingers around his, holding his hand.

My pulse hammered in my throat as I waited for him to tug his hands free, but he didn't. His chest puffed up, his back straighter. I didn't miss the smug look he shot Kai and Harvey, either. I suppressed an eye roll. Now, I'd become a status symbol for bragging rights. It was better than hostile glares, I supposed.

"Don't even think about it," I warned Emlyn when we turned a corner and the silvery-lilac curve of the river became visible. "I don't want a repeat of the fountain in Barnakon."

Em peered at me, all innocence. I couldn't tell if he understood my warning, but if he did, he was a damn good actor. I tightened my grip around his hand when his eyes strayed to the water.

The midday sun hammered down on our backs, burning through the black leather jacket I'd traded a dagger for after Lucifer left the dining hall.[1] I'd forgotten to grab a hat, so my face would be bright red by the end of the day. That was one thing spirits had going for them; they never had to worry about sunburn. At least there was a slight breeze coming off the river when we turned onto the busy street alongside it, fishermen and vendors unloading boxes onto the cobbles. Some of them were fragrant with honey, cloves, and big, overflowing boxes of blooms. Others stank of fish. It was a rich tapestry for the senses, and even worse, apparently, for a shifter.

Harvey pressed close to me and buried his face in my shoulder as we walked, like he could drown out the fishy smell with my scent. I grabbed his shirt so he didn't tumble into the water; the idiot wasn't watching where he placed his feet. Even Emlyn wrinkled his nose, giving the boats full of fish a look of distaste. I released Harvey when we reached a wider part of the street and smacked Em's arm.

"Don't look at them like that; you'll start a fight."

He stared back at me, blue eyes unblinking. If he understood what I said, he didn't give a shit about starting fights. I remembered the quiet burr of his voice when he said *ten years* and swallowed. He understood *some* things.

"No fights," I warned, my voice breathier than a moment ago. Em still hadn't looked away, and the weight of his stare made my heart pound. Emlyn was a quiet man, introverted and thoughtful; his attention was heady and intentional.

"The tattoo shop is just down here," I added, willing my mates to get to the place *without* jumping in the water.[2]

"I want a tattoo," Kai said longingly, his eyes distant. Was he remembering past times he'd been inked, or dreaming about his next design? Most of the tattoos on his body came from magic but not all.

"You have a billion already, buddy. There's not much space left."

Crimson eyes simmered when he looked at me, part heated, part defiant. "I can think of places."

I shook my head, smirking. "You're not getting your dick tattooed. You wouldn't live through that pain."

But that was like throwing the gauntlet down for someone as stubborn and contrary as Malakai. He matched my smirk, a dangerous glint in his eyes. "I would."

I'd created a monster.[3]

I'd admitted defeat when the look in Kai's eyes changed.

"But someone would have to see what's yours," he said. "You don't like that."

"No," I agreed, sending an automatic stroke down a bond

still frayed and nonexistent. I kept waiting to wake up and find the soul bonds repaired. Kept getting jarred by my mates not being there when I reached for them.

I gave Kai a grateful smile instead and spotted the tattoo shop—a small brick house with a black wooden sign decorated with a beautiful sketch of a tiger. Under it hung the old demon word for *ink*. Simple and straight to the point. I liked it.

I suspected I'd like this next part less—showing someone else my curse marks and making myself vulnerable by explaining what had happened.[4]

But I couldn't chicken out if I wanted answers—real, tangible information, not just vague hints and guesswork.

So I pushed the door open—and jumped back when it swung faster than my push warranted. A buff, scary-looking giant filled the doorway, obviously on his way out of the shop. Every available space on his body—and his face—was covered in swirling waves and sea creatures.[5]

"Shit, sorry—" I blurted.

"Not a problem, little lady," he replied in a purr, pale eyes travelling from my face and down my body, lingering on my chest. I didn't even have cleavage on display; most of my chest was covered by a dark button-up tunic and my new jacket.

I opened my mouth to snap at him to keep his eyes where they belonged, but Emlyn tugged me back with a rumble at the same moment Harvey surged forward, his wings taut to his back—agitated. Furious.

I waited for him to break the man's nose, waited for the satisfying spray of blood, but instead Harvey grabbed his skull in two hands and—snapped his neck.

"Harvey!" I gasped, darting forward a step.

My heart skipped, shock making me slow and clumsy. Em caught me before I could walk into the doorframe, and tugged me further out of the door, his whole body shaking and sharp teeth bared.

Malakai strode past him, his tall, lithe body moving gracefully and smoothly enough that my heart didn't just skip; it stopped. That was Kai in full murder mode. If I could see his face, I knew it would be carefully neutral but his eyes would be blazing.

"Holy shit," I breathed when Kai drew a small knife from gods knew where and—and cut out the man's eyes before standing again. He stomped on each eyeball until it burst.

"What?" he asked when he caught me staring. "He looked at you."

My heart sprinted. I wanted to burst into irrational tears. That was such a Kai thing to do that everything felt normal. But we wouldn't be in a tattooist's shop if everything was normal.

My throat bobbed. I looked at Harvey, then Kai. "Thank you."

Kai smiled, the cold killer softening. He brushed the blood from his fingers on his trousers and caught my cheek in his hand, kissing me gently. "We'll always kill your enemies, my rose."

"Not as much an enemy as a creep," I murmured, but I didn't complain when he kissed me again.

Harvey let out a noise between a growl and a whine. I didn't speak sun soul but I knew that clearly. *I want one, too.* I crooked a finger at him and gave him a sweet, lingering kiss.

"Thank you, Harvey."

He straightened, looking pleased with himself, and strutted into the shop. Luckily, there was no one in the first room, so no one had seen us kill a guy.

"You two better clean up this mess," I warned them, pointing a finger. "Go pollute the river with his corpse."

Kai grinned and communicated something quietly to Harvey, whose expression sharpened. "We'll be back soon."

"Make sure no one sees you," I warned them. But the riverside was full of people moving back and forth; chances were as good of going unseen as being witnessed. Hopefully people at these docks knew how to keep their mouths shut. I didn't know how I'd explain this to Lucifer if he found out.

"Let's find the tattooist," I told Emlyn, squeezing his arm and leading him through the quiet, tidy front room. There wasn't much more than a table and four chairs, a fancier leather chair, a tiled floor, and white walls.

Em grumbled but followed, letting go of me. He avoided my gaze when I looked at him, not sure why he'd stopped touching me. I wanted to take his hand and pull him close, but I wasn't sure it was wanted.

"Hello?" I called through the doorway into the backroom. It was dark back here, thick curtains pulled across a window to block out the sunlight. I could just about make out a sofa, a table piled with what looked like someone's worldly possessions, and a bowl of half-eaten porridge on the floor beside the sofa.

I jumped when the sofa *moved*, my hand darting to a knife. A mound of shadows unfolded itself from the sofa cushions, and slammed me into so many memories that I staggered back, my hand lifted to ward them off.

I was safe on the sofa in our home, wrapped in warm arms and velvety shadows; I was running through the forest, threatening someone with bodily harm if he didn't return the food he'd stolen; I was snarling into a brute's face in a dingy inn because he'd stared at the shadows too long, his eyes leering.

Emlyn's growl tore through the memories; he shook me out of them, and I slumped into him with a curse.

"Who are you people, and what are you doing in my

house?" a ready voice demanded, the mound from the sofa resolving itself into a man. Not shadows, not even familiar— he was in his fifties, balding, and had a ring of runes inked around his tawny throat. There were even more on his knuckles and up his arms.

I dragged myself back together, gritting my teeth against the residual pain of the memories. Emlyn rested his big arm across my back, but—there was a distance between us that I didn't remember before yesterday.

Did he ... did he see me differently now we'd been sexual? Was I a casual thing to him, a one-night affair? I'd hoped we might enter a new phase of our relationship, but what if it was meaningless sex to Emlyn, and now everything was awkward and strange because he didn't want me around?

I swallowed the knot in my throat and focused on the short man glaring at us. "Aren't you a tattooist? Your door was open."

Also, a guest just left, but I wasn't about to point that out since we'd killed them.

"No," he replied, rough with sleep. "I'm Oren, the artist. Rudy's the inker; he should be out in the shop."

I swallowed and fought the urge to exchange a glance with Emlyn. "He's not there," I said with a shrug. "Must have popped out."

The artist muttered under his breath but ushered us out of the back room into the brighter space out front. "Hopefully the miserable bastard went for a personality transplant."

I had no idea what a transplant was, but I nodded. "You said you're the artist. Do you know anything about curse marks?"

Oren sighed heavily, crossing his rune-wrapped arms over his chest and glaring at me and Em. "I'll tell you what I tell everyone; if you want to curse someone to suffer for all eternity, have children."

I stiffened. "That's really not funny."

Oren smirked, though. "Clearly, you don't *have* children. I've got eight. Little shits, all of them."

I swallowed, claws twisting into my heart and lower, in my stomach. "I don't want to give someone a curse; I want to understand one given to me. But if you can't help me, go fuck yourself. I'll find someone who can."

I turned, my face hot and expression brittle, and strode for the door.

"Show me," Oren said, stopping me before I could grab the door handle.

I bared my teeth, fighting the compulsion to wrap my arms around myself as I faced him again.

"Here." I tore my jacket sleeve up, the leather snagging on the meaty part of my forearm because jackets honestly sucked.[6]

"Well," Oren said, letting out a long whistle as he scanned the arrows and crescents inked on my arm. "That's elaborate."

"I was told it curses me to kill my mates." Oren nodded, confirming that, and scratched his balding head. "And I was hoping you'd know who gave it to me."

He narrowed his eyes. "It's no style I recognise. No one local, that's for sure."

"There's this one too," I said hesitantly, not wanting to bare my stomach with how breakable I felt. But if Oren could tell me what it meant, or where I could find the bastard who'd inked it on me, I could get the damn thing broken. "It keeps my magic locked away."

"These are brutal," Oren murmured, narrowing his eyes on the mark up the centre of my stomach and nodding. "I don't know whose work this is, but it's unethical as fuck. I can try to break it if you want."

My breath caught. I'd come for answers, but... "You can do that?"

"I can try. I'm no inker like Rudy, but I know how to work the machine."

"Machine?" I frowned. "Don't you use a feather?" Kai got his tattoos by sharpening the edge of a feather and imbuing it with magic and ink.

Oren laughed, giving me a strange look. "That method went out forty years ago."

Of course it did. "Do whatever you need; just break these curses."

"It'll cost you," Oren warned, heading over to the table across the room and opening a drawer in its base.

"I'm cursed to kill my mates; do you think I care about money?"

"Fair point. Sit down in that chair there."

I handed Oren a pile of gold coins and hauled myself onto the fancy leather chair, finally daring a look at Emlyn, who'd been strangely silent, not a single growl or rumble coming from his chest. He wasn't looking at me; his eyes were fixed on the wall, his arms crossed over his big chest and the darkest, grumpiest expression I'd seen in years on his face.

"Em?" I asked.

He gave me a questioning glance, something ... guarded in the way he looked at me.

What's wrong? I asked with a frown. I didn't want to ask with Oren listening in as he prepared the tattoo machine.

Em shook his head, a muscle feathering in his tanned jaw. He glanced away.

He was ... angry at me. And I didn't know what I'd done wrong. Sickness twisted my belly, reminding me too acutely of the day we died. Em had been angry then, too.

"This might sting a bit," Oren said when he'd wiped my curse marks clean and filled the tattoo gun.

"Do it," I growled, my jaw clenched to ward off emotion.

I was already fragile enough with the artist's casual

mention of children, careless of people who'd been trying to conceive for years, who'd give fucking *anything* to have a baby with the men they loved. And now Em was angry at me, it pushed me closer towards an edge I'd been tiptoeing all week.

I swallowed, ignoring the burning in my throat as Oren set the sharp edge to my skin. "I don't care if it hurts."

CHAPTER NINETEEN

*T*his morning, I'd set off into the city feeling hopeful. Funny how the man you love being mad at you can completely ruin your day. I didn't even know what I'd done.

It was worse still when Harvey and Kai returned, saw a man stabbing me with needles, and tried to kill Oren.

"Stop! Don't you dare hurt him; he's helping me," I snapped. "Helping *all* of us. He's trying to break my curse. You know, the one that'll make me kill you?"

Kai froze, catching the back of Harvey's neck.

"Continue," I barked at the artist, ignoring the sassy look he gave us.

"I want extra coin for danger money," he told me, setting the machine to my skin and finishing the line he was etching through the circle at the heart of the mark, disrupting it.

"I don't care," I replied flatly, gritting my teeth against the stabbing sting of the tattoo gun.

"There, that's one done," he said, sitting back and giving me a wary look. "How does that feel?"

"Fine."

"Haley?" Kai asked, releasing Harvey with a low hiss and

approaching me. Violence was there in the glow of his red eyes and the grace of his movements. "Did he hurt you?"

I shook my head. "I'm fine."

His pale jaw clenched, protectiveness in the way he hovered close. "It's okay; if he hurt you, you can tell me."

"I'm *fine*, Kai," I snarled, my shoulders hunching, wings snapping. "Back off and let him finish the other mark."

Kai's frown deepened, concern softening his anger. Damned man could always see through my bullshit.

Oren muttered something about the job getting him killed, but narrowed his eyes on the mark inked up the centre of my torso. He drew several short, biting lines into my skin. By the time he was done, my jaw was locked shut and pain added to the dangerous cocktail of emotions brewing inside me.

Every failure I'd ever made played on repeat in my head. If I hadn't spent nine years thieving and killing my way around Hell, starting fights for fun, maybe my womb would still work. If I hadn't been rash in going after Locke, maybe we'd have lived a long, happy life. If I hadn't—

"That should do it," Oren said, leaning back from me and setting the gun down. "If it's going to do anything, that is. You don't feel any different?"

I shook my head, swinging my legs over the side of the leather chair and setting my feet on the floor. My arm and torso stung viciously, but there was no other sign that he'd broken the curse marks. Until I stood—and blood rushed to my head. My legs collapsed from under me.

Harvey let out a panicked noise and rushed to catch me, his arms slamming into me before my head could smack the floor of the tattoo shop. I gritted my teeth, the stinging of fresh ink moving deeper, slicing through muscle to and prickling through my bloodstream. A moan of pain shook my throat as the prickling built to a fever pitch of vicious, spiking needles, like Oren had inked my insides.

"What did you do?" Kai roared. I was vaguely aware of him throwing Oren against the wall, his magic shuddering through the air.

"Broke her curse marks, like she asked me to," Oren growled back, shoving Kai across the room. A dangerous move for anyone, but especially someone who'd hurt Kai's mate.

I tried to choke out a plea to stop, but all that came out was a guttural groan.

The stabbing sensation in my blood flared until it jabbed my heart, filled my head, and—and I heard heartbeats. Dozens of them. No, *hundreds.* I moaned pitifully as they overwhelmed me, deafening and disorienting, until all I heard was a chaos of *thud-thud, thud-thuds.*

I'd gone through this before, when I was a kid and my magic first bloomed. Dad hugged me and coached me through it then. Now, he was dead. Everyone I loved was dead.

No, not everyone.

I ground my teeth, fighting through the melee of heartbeats, searching for the rhythm of the man holding. It beat erratically, slamming against my body through his ribs, quickening even more when I dragged in a raspy breath and fisted his shirt.

Thud-thud, thud-thud...

I could pull myself through this. If I could do it as a scared teenager, I could do it now.[1]

But when I started to hear the growls and arguments happening in the tattoo shop, another heartbeat surged on the path outside and pulled me back under.

I cried out, throwing my hands over my ears like that would make any difference. Every heartbeat in the city spoke to me, hammered at my senses until I screamed.

Thud-thud, thud-thud...

Thud-thud, thud-thud...

It was endless, disorienting and painfully loud. I screwed my eyes shut, but that made it worse.

Strength and panic poured into my soul, and I grasped onto it, pulling it into me and making it part of myself. I didn't know where it came from, but I had the sense of being gathered into gentle arms.

Hadn't this happened before? Hadn't arms wrapped around me and held me?

Pain of the memory cut through the endless heartbeats, and I gasped, following it up like a lifeline. It hurt so badly I couldn't breathe, but at least I could *think*.

When I opened my eyes, my mates were crowded around me, staring with knotted brows and panic in their eyes. The only arms wrapped around me were Harvey's.

I swallowed, hauling myself out of the never-ending chorus of pumping blood and seizing onto what caused it: the line Oren inked through my curse mark.

"It worked," I rasped, pushing off the floor where we'd somehow ended up. My legs wobbled, but with Harvey's help I managed to stand. The feeling of my soul being wrapped in a hug faded.

Kai shook his head so viciously dark red hair whipped his face. "We're still cursed to kill each other; I can feel it. It's like venom. Looking at your mark burns."

I frowned, trying to remember if my eyes stung when he first showed me his curse mark.

"Show me yours," I told Kai, squeezing Harvey's arm when he let me go. A silent thank-you for catching me, for holding me.

When Kai lifted his shirt, baring the curse mark—identical to mine—I winced and looked away, my eyes prickling so fiercely tears built. The effect was stronger than the last time. When we'd slept together, I'd tried not to look too hard at the curse mark. It was a depressing reminder I didn't want.

I glanced away, finding Oren scowling at us as he cleaned up his face. Oh shit, someone had broken his nose.

"Danger money," I told him. "Lots of it."

He grunted.

"If breaking my second curse didn't work, it won't help to break my mates' curse marks either, will it?"

"No," he agreed, sympathy entering his eyes. Probably because I'd had a screaming fit on the floor of his shop.

"I don't want to see this tattoo anymore," I said, my voice thick and raw. "You said you're not an inker, but you're an artist." I met Oren's eyes. "Cover it up for me. Please. I'll pay you whatever coins I have left."

He pressed his mouth into a thin line, giving me a hard look. I held his stare, pitiful and pained. He groaned, throwing up his hands. "Fine, get back on the table."

When Oren moved towards me, tawny hands lifted, Emlyn stepped into his path with a deep, rumbling growl, and then turned to look at me. There was something entreating in his blue eyes, along with a well of concern.

I laughed bitterly, too many pains overlapping inside me, making me thorny and sharp. "Oh, you're looking at me now? You haven't met my eyes in an hour."

"What?" Kai muttered. "Why?"

"Your guess is as good as mine." I crossed my arms over my chest and winced at the sting on my freshly tattooed lines.

Blood pounded in my ears—not mine. Emlyn's heartbeat, rising faster with every second. My emotional state was too fragile for this.

"Just tell me what I did to piss you off," I snapped, ignoring the break in my voice. "Because I haven't a fucking clue what it could be."

His throat vibrated with a deep noise, anger swallowing the concern in his bright eyes until they were fiery and hot.

"Come on, Em!" I snapped, my wings ruffling, hands shaking. "Tell me. Tell me how I've fucked up this time."

Heartbeats clamoured in my ears. I tried to shut them out, but it was impossible not to hear my mates' and Oren's.

Thud-thud, thud-thud...

Emlyn shook his head, a dark, rumbling laugh in his chest. His brokenness matched my own, and I couldn't figure out what the fuck caused it.

Kai sighed and translated. "You obviously don't want me here. I'm leaving."

"You're the one who doesn't want me," I snarled right back at Em as he pushed past us to the door. "You can't bear to look at me unless it's to stare at my curse marks. You hardly touched me last night, and the few times you did, it was only because Harvey was between us. If you don't want a mate, fine. Leave."

"Don't," Kai growled, shooting me a hard look that cut right through my skin and bone, spearing my fragile heart.

Do not cry. Don't fucking cry, Halwen Vakhara.

I swallowed the knot in my throat, watching Emlyn storm through the door and into the city.

"I'll go with him. Talk to Harvey," Kai hissed, giving me a lingering look of confusion, worry, and anger.

I didn't talk to Harvey. I didn't want to voice the thoughts clawing my mind apart, the insecurity and years' long hurt twisting through my chest. I didn't want to explain the heartbeats that whooshed through my ears, sawing my nerves to shreds.

I climbed back onto the leather chair and told Oren, "I want skulls and flowers everywhere. Make it so I can't see the mark at all."

It would still be there, but it wouldn't glare at me day and night. It wouldn't be the only thing Emlyn looked at, instead of me.

CHAPTER TWENTY

*M*y entire arm stung by the time Oren finished an hour later. That machine must have been enhanced with magic, because there was no way my whole arm should have been tattooed so quickly.

I cast tentative glances at Harvey as we headed for the door after paying the artist. My brittle defensiveness had left, unmasking something shaky and small.

"Buttercup," I breathed when he pulled the door open, casting a look at me—wary and braced. "I—do you remember —when—"

I shook my head, dragging my hands down my face. I jumped when Harvey pulled the shop's door shut and stroked his fingers through my hair.

My face was hot and tight, but I stared at a spot on his stubbled chin and rasped, "When we were together before, we couldn't have children. We tried everything—potions, charms, magic, you name it. Something is wrong with me."

My bottom lip trembled; I pressed my mouth flat to still it. I didn't know how much Harvey understood, but Kai thought I needed to talk to him and he was usually right.

"I can't have children, and it—it fucking hurts. Every time I see a family walk down the street, every time I hear a kid laugh, it's a reminder that I'm so screwed up inside, that I—"

Harvey yanked me into a tight hug when my voice broke.

I managed to squeak out, "Oren said something stupid, a throwaway comment, but it just—reminded me of everything. All my failures."

He stroked my hair again, a low, continuous vibration in his chest. Like a cat's purr but intended to comfort. I sank into it, letting tears fall as I hid my face in his chest.

"I didn't mean to take it out on you, or Em. I don't even know why he's so angry with me. I just—I can't handle you being angry with me right now. Any of you. Please."

Footsteps pounded the riverside road, and I jumped, a sharp gasp in my throat as I lifted my head from Harvey's shoulder and found Kai storming towards us with murder on his face. He barked *move* at a woman carrying a tray of grey fish, and elbowed a man balancing cloth on his shoulders.

"I've looked everywhere but—my rose? Haley?" Kai's hard voice immediately softened when he stopped beside us, panting for breath. Gentle hands cupped my cheeks, devastation written on his face. "What happened? Who made you cry?"

I swallowed and shook my head. "It's fine, I'm just—fragile. Where's Em?"

I glanced over his shoulder, expecting to see my broad-shouldered mate with his wings flared and anger still burning in his eyes. But—there was only Kai.

"Malakai. Where's Em?"

Kai's inked throat bobbed. "I can't find him."

PART II
MARKED

CHAPTER TWENTY-ONE

I threw up in the river. Stress and horror and a brutal emotional strain mounted until I couldn't take any more.

"I'll find him," I rasped, my throat burning almost as badly as my blood magic. "Kai, go back to the palace in case he turns up there. Harvey, stay here in case he comes back for us."

"We're not letting you leave," Kai warned, snagging the lapel of my leather jacket.

"I need to do this alone," I argued, licking my dry lips. "Please, Kai. I—I made him angry. I should be the one to find him."

Tears overflowed; I couldn't hold them back. "I *need* to find him."

Kai swore, sweeping me into a hug, and Harvey wrapped his arms and wings around me too. I didn't care that my arm and stomach stung with new ink or my soul was crushed into tiny pieces. Emlyn was missing. Any healing I'd done this week was undone in a day. But in their arms, everything was okay for a moment.

"Thirty minutes," Kai said, stroking his thumb along my

jaw and giving me a steely look. "Then we're coming to find you."

I kissed his cheek, tears dropping on his skin.

"Thank you for staying with me," I croaked to Harvey. "I'll be back soon, and I'll find Em. I promise."

He was my mate. Even with the bond shredded and dead, I *had* to be able to find him. Ten years of knowing him didn't count for nothing.

Harvey rumbled a warning, his arms flexing, reluctant to let me go.

"Do you—do you know why he was angry at me?" I asked in a small voice, wiping my face and forcing myself to break out of the comforting huddle. Harvey's wing stroked the length of mine, but he let me go.

Kai sighed, his body locking with tension, the tight long-sleeved shirt he wore hugging his taut shoulders. "Because he's an idiot."

Well, I knew that; they *all* were. They were demons, and men, and even more than that—*arch*demons.[1]

"He thinks you want us, but not him," Kai went on, glaring into the river.

My heart stuttered, then collapsed. Em thought I *didn't want him?*

My stomach tightened until it hurt. "Why would he—? I love him more than every sun and star in the sky. How could he—I—"

"Haley," Kai breathed, reaching for me for another hug.

But I was already kicking off the ground, slamming my wings down to shoot me into the air. I soared over boats almost emptied of their wares, fishermen staring up at me.

"I'll find him," I choked out. "Thirty minutes, right?"

"Don't go like this," Kai called after me, holding his hand out to me.

But I had to find Em. Everything was off kilter, everything was *wrong* without him.

So I flew over the river and high above the rooftops of Iarlon. It killed me to leave Kai and Harvey, but it would kill me more to lose Emlyn.

Why did I snap at him to leave?

What had I done?

CHAPTER TWENTY-TWO

*K*ai was going to kill me, but I couldn't stop. I
flew until my wings gave out, until I was
forced to walk instead, dragging my aching, heavy body down
the streets of the capital. The city's beauty blurred, flowers,
trees, and murals insignificant, the cheerful voices that called
to each other little more than dead noise.

My feet throbbed, almost certainly bleeding in my boots,
but I didn't stop walking, scanning every street for a broad
winged body and big, comforting arms. I needed to be
wrapped up in those arms so badly that I sobbed as I walked.

My wings dragged behind me, my exhausted legs moving
sluggishly. Inside my chest, there was a wreck where my heart
used to be. I tried to grasp our bonds, but they fluttered out of
my hands, broken and frayed.

Blood slammed in my ears, filling my head; I no longer
fought my magic. I could take control of every single person I
staggered past, could have killed all of them if I chose. But I
plunged into the chaos of noise and magic and searched for a
familiar heartbeat instead.

I searched for *hours,* until my legs finally gave out and I landed on the flagstones in a deserted alleyway. The buildings on each side towered above me, casting shadows so deep I couldn't see my own hands.

I bent over myself, my wings limp around me, and I sobbed so hard I choked on each cry. My eyes burned, tears scalding down my cheeks, and breathing impossible.

Emlyn was gone. I'd lost him. And he didn't even know I loved him.

Air only trickled into my chest when *something* brushed against my soul, a direct response to my pain. It echoed my suffering, a dark mirror with the same longing, ache, and brutal pain—but sharper, deeper, and ... constant. I didn't know who it was, frankly didn't care if it was Wynvail. I reached back and held on tight.

A soul wrapped around mine like a hug, and my sobs turned to a high, visceral keening. The touch was tentative but strong, and they didn't run from me when my soul collapsed into theirs.

Whoever the dark mirror was, they stayed with me until I was cried out, hollow and raw.

Their grip faded when I stumbled back to my feet and scrubbed my face dry.

Don't go. Please.

I held onto their soul, frantic to keep them close, the thought of losing them *abhorrent*. But the pained, gentle touch of their soul tore away from mine in a rush, and I was left alone. Weak and broken but—just strong enough to resume my search for Emlyn.

CHAPTER TWENTY-THREE

WANE

$\mathcal{T}$he titan wanted my shadows to fall. But he should have known better by now.

Every day for a hundred years, this man—Andryas Revairs, servant of the titan who held me captive—had tried to take my magic from me. My shadows wrapped tighter around me, hiding me entirely.

"Bleeding again, pet?" Andryas laughed, a soft croak that made him sound menacing but only marked him as the same as me—tormented, broken, suffering. He'd belonged to the titan long before I had. "Where did you cut her name this time?"

I levelled a baleful snarl on him from within the cocoon of my shadows, my knees folded to my chest as I pressed my back to the corner. Blood droplets splattered the floor around me, the only reason Revairs knew where I was.

"Pathetic," he sneered, letting the heavy door—made of solid wood and gouged with my scratches on the inside—slam shut behind him as he strode across the room to me. He ground the tip of his boot into the drops of my blood, like he could stamp out its existence altogether. He hated me. It was mutual.

Andryas was a big meathead of a man, with deep brown skin, a shaved head, and features that may have been handsome once but were now crooked, broken, and rearranged by the torturer whose position he'd taken when the titan killed him. Devoured him.

I unfolded to my feet slowly enough that he wouldn't notice the shift in my shadows, curling my hands into fists. He tore out my claws again a few months ago, but they were starting to grow back, enough that they pricked my palm when I curled my hands into fists.

There was little strength left in me, but I wouldn't make it easy for him. My father had made me weak, less a demon than a creature of pain and constant fear. Easily beaten, easily broken. But Halwen taught me to fight. She spent hours in the field behind our house training me to punch, to block, to throw a blade and angle a dagger.

I pressed my fingernails into my hip where I'd written her name this time and blood dripped into my grubby trousers. I had no shirt, nothing to hide the ruination of my flesh. I was a scarred monster, but I was hers. Every overlapping scar, every white mark and red, raw cut marked me as belonging to her.

So when Revairs drew a long, golden severing blade from inside his black jacket—a modified and abhorrent version of the Severance used to cut an angel's wings—I sucked in a breath and used the pain as strength. The cut pulsing on my hip reminded me who I was. I was Halwen's. Not the titan's. Never his.

I caught his wrist when the blade drove down, and dug my fresh fingernails into his wrist, slamming my forehead into his nose until blood sprayed. It didn't stop Andryas wrenching free, didn't stop him driving the vicious edge into my shadows and wrenching a blinding tear in my power, my *shield*.

I clenched my jaw to keep the scream trapped. My voice was a hoarse rasp after years of screaming, but I still tried to deny him the satisfaction. Halwen wouldn't scream; my brother wouldn't scream.

I'm not screaming either, you bastard.

But his forearm slammed into my throat, the cocoon weakening enough for him to glimpse me through them, and I was slammed into the wall before I could defend myself. Light and pain flashed through my head. I gasped, trying to catch the blade before it drove into my body, too.

I should have known better. After all this time, I should have *known* he wouldn't target my body. The titan wanted my shadows, had sent Andryas to cut them out of me. I didn't know why he needed them. He said I was special, my shadows were special.

"I don't know why you bother fighting," Revairs muttered, raking the knife across my shadows in a vicious slash. "How many times have I broken you, Locke?"

I opened my mouth to snarl *that's not my name*, but a scream tore past my lips, and my knees buckled as he opened another tear.

I hit the hard stone floor and released my shadows in a panic, letting the scatter. He couldn't cut them from me if I didn't let them show.

I was Wane van Khama. Not Wane Locke. I would *never* claim my abuser's name as mine.

"Big, big mistake, pet," Revairs sighed, his lips thinning with disappointment.

He could do whatever cruel, tortuous things he wanted to me—and he usually did—but I wouldn't give up my shadows. They were all I had left. No horns, no wings, no claws, no family. Only my shadows and her name.

I dragged my weak nails across the floor, my back bowed as the blade came down again—but cruel, aching heartbreak sliced through my chest before he struck, despair hitting me like a punch to the gut.

Halwen.

I could feel her. Holy fuck, I could *feel* her.

I ground my teeth against the pain that lanced through my back, the blade driving deep into the ever-bleeding wound where a wing used to be. My nostrils flared, nails scratching the ground. None of that mattered; my girl was breaking. She needed me.

I speared my soul across the endless distance between us, another scream slicing up my throat, this one tasting of blood. But even with burning agony in my back, I found her.

A tremor went through me so severely that Revairs laughed, thinking he caused it. I could feel all of her—her soul, her fire, her life, her blood. She was here, she was *alive*. Her soul brushed mine, undeniably real.

Lately, I thought I'd felt her, a few delirious moments of connection I didn't dare to hope were real but *this?* She was tangible and bright, her soul so close.

But it felt like she was ... crying? Breaking, splintering into pieces, losing all hope. I knew that pain intimately.

It was pure instinct to wrap myself around her, to nestle my soul flush to hers and promise everything would be okay.

I'm here, itzaia, I'm right here with you.

How many times had she wrapped herself around me when I was falling apart?

I tried to take her pain into myself, to erase it from her soul. My soul was already twisted up and stained dark, agony a constant through my bleeding back, my broken horns, and my—my broken heart. I could take some of her pain; better that I had it.

But she was *alive;* I could feel her. And if she was alive, my brother could be too. The other two men of our family could be, too.

I hated the titan for stealing their names from me. I should have carved their names into my body, but those were stolen before I could. My twin's name was stolen first.

I gritted my teeth, my eyes shut and all my focus on my mate, but I couldn't block out the impact every time Revairs struck my body, every time he snarled orders to summon my shadows, every time he taunted me with names I hated: pet, freak, monster, Locke.

I tried to keep the worst of it from Halwen, the thought of this poison and suffering touching her soul repulsive to me.

I'm here, I assured her, trying to soothe her pain, holding her like she always held me through my flashbacks. *I'm always here, my Halwen.*

My eyes flew open when Revairs grabbed my shoulders and dragged me off the floor, and my hold on Haley's soul slipped.

"No!" I cried, spearing my soul towards her in a panicked rush. But now my eyes had opened, now I was staring at Revairs, I could see the ragged mess of shadow he grasped in his hand.

Fear made my blood run cold, made the agony in my back bigger, deadlier, and I couldn't hold onto my tether to Halwen. She slipped like sand through my fingers and my soul slammed back into my body so suddenly and brutally I screamed.

Revairs sighed, kicking me onto my back.

The world blacked out, but I had enough just mental strength to reach out for the shadow in his hand, mine but stolen, mine but not mine. I snuffed it out, panting, sweating, crying.

Revairs snarled his rage, his power swelling to fill the

whole cell, pressing on me like an oppressive weight. "Bastard!"

He couldn't take the shadows. They were mine.

But he'd never been able to cut them from me before.

"The titan will hear about this," he spat, but I didn't bother responding.

The titan would hear of it, I would be hauled out of this cell and through the warren, and I would be put through unbearable, world-ending pain.

I would be revived, and it would start all over again. Nothing would change.

But Revairs had cut a shadow free. And if he could do it once, it could happen again.

What would the titan do with my shadow?

Why did he want them so badly?

I shuddered and crawled across the floor when Revairs slammed the heavy door behind himself, and I pressed myself into the corner, my knees to my chest.

It was a day like any other. I would get through it. Even if my bones shattered, my blood drained, and I screamed so hard my vocal chords ruptured, it was just another day.

CHAPTER TWENTY-FOUR

HALWEN

I found Em on the sloped rooftop of a library, little more than an unmoving shadow against the belltower in the middle of the roof. I was drained by the time I reached the top of the building, clutching a precarious drainpipe and swinging myself up. Only years of merc training made the move possible; muscle memory got me onto the roof more than any present skill.

"Nice view," I panted, dragging myself up the tiles until I could sit beside him. The whole city spread around us, dark by now and lit only by street lamps and bright lilac moonlight.

Emlyn snapped his head up and growled, a short, sharp noise I couldn't interpret. Why had I thought this was a good idea? The language barrier was going to ruin any hope I had of mending things.

But his big hand shot out and he grabbed my jacket, hauling me closer to the belltower, and I understood that growl at least. *Are you mad? What are you doing on the roof, Hales? You could get yourself killed!*

Panting for breath, I let him manoeuvre me into a safer position, my legs like jelly and the rest of me not much better. There was a huge park around the library, full of spongy grass, ferns, and night-blooming flowers. Worst case scenario, if I fell, I'd have a cushioned landing.

He didn't let go of my jacket, so I took that as a promising sign. When I could breathe again, I launched into conversation before he had time to leap off the roof to escape me.

"The first time we met, I thought you were insanely hot," I told him. I didn't know how much he'd understand, but he'd understood us being together for ten years, so I had to hope he'd know *some* of what I said. "You were sat in a shitty little pub, and I was there to hunt you, but I couldn't help getting distracted. You looked so fucking good, with your hair curling on the ends and your wings resting in a confident position even though you're uncomfortable in public spaces. And you had this skin-tight grey shirt on that still haunts my dreams." I flicked an amused look at him and added, "Wet dreams."

He didn't smile, but he was watching me, and the furrow between his brows told me he was concentrating hard.

"You're one of the most intelligent people I've ever known," I told him, catching his gaze. "And that is so fucking sexy. There's nothing you don't know, Em, and instead of using that knowledge to take over the world, you use it to keep us safe."

I rested my hand over his where he still gripped my jacket, stroking my thumb over his knuckles—broken and bleeding from getting into a fight with the guys this morning. I didn't even know what this fight was over. I folded my fingers around his, surprised he let me uncurl them from my jacket. He jerked when I brushed my lips to his split knuckles.

"We'd have been caught and murdered at least twenty times without you. You're not just book smart; you're savvy.

That's what I love about you. You're hot as fuck, and clever, and strong—and still, somehow, you manage to be *kind*."

A flurry of wind blew past us, flinging my pink hair into my cheeks, chilling my face. But my skin burned when Em reached out and tucked the hair behind my ear, his touch lingering.

"I wish I was more like you sometimes," I told him, glancing away as my throat bobbed. I fixed my stare on the gardens below instead of the strange blend of confusion and understanding on his bearded face. "I could be kinder, gentler. I could definitely think before I act, too. I'm impulsive; you're thoughtful. It shouldn't work, but we're a perfect fit."

I pushed down the knot in my throat, a smile on my lips despite the cracks spreading through my chest. "Do you want to know when I knew I loved you?"

Em's brow furrowed; he tilted his head, his full attention on me.

"We were in our second safe house, just narrowly escaping the—Wynvail," I realised with a sick twist in my belly. He was always there, just one step behind us. Even now, he hunted us. Hunted *me*. "The place was a single room in a three-storey building in Indraza, on the far, far east of Hell. Paper-thin walls, five to eight people crammed in each room, one communal staircase. A shithole, really. But it was better than being murdered."

I took a tight breath, tasting the wisteria and brimstone scent of the city, along with leather and old paper—the kind that filled ancient books, yellowed and stained and curling on the edges. How did he still smell exactly the same? My chest tightened. Like he sensed it, Em tugged me closer until we fit together, my thigh against his, my shoulder soaking up his warmth.

"We lived on the same floor as three brothers and their parents. Assholes. The kind of stupid that's always starting fights, running their mouths, and taking shit about anything and anyone. Kai broke one of their noses. One of them bruised Harvey's ribs. It was a daily thing. I'd only been with you for four months at that point, but already I was blinding mad whenever one of them insulted you. We'd been—close."

At Emlyn's stare, I bit my lip and amended, "Okay, so we'd had a whole orgy group sex thing one time, and it was epic and mind-blowing and changed my whole life."

Em's chest shuddered with a low growl. I was willing to put money on him understanding the word sex.

"Back to the assholes. One day they were waiting in the stairwell between our rooms, looking smug and punch-able, running their mouths as usual. You always ignored them, and told us to do the same. One of them called you something I won't repeat, and I launched at them, planning to rearrange their entire face, but you held me back." I gave Emlyn a dark look, my lips pressed thin. "I still think you should've let me break his face."

But I grinned, knowing how the memory ended. "But then, when we were going into our room one of them said something crude and suggestive about me, and the other two didn't even bother with euphemisms. Bragging about breaking into our room and fucking me while I slept, shoving their cocks down my throat, up my ass, in every orifice you can think of. I was used to it by that point; I'm a merc in a male-dominated industry. It was nothing I hadn't heard a hundred times. But when the oldest said something about putting me in my place, I blinked and you were across the hallway."

Emlyn made a low sound, surprised or questioning. I didn't know what he wanted to say, so I continued.

"You dropped one of them faster than I could see, punched another in his throat, and shoved your claws into the third brother's eyes, permanently blinding him. When they all hit the floor, you drove your boot into their cocks and made damn sure they wouldn't be putting them anywhere near me *or* anyone else."

I sighed dreamily, recalling the beauty of the violence, the sheer love that erupted in my chest, the unrivalled pleasure of having someone defend me against the vitriol I'd got used to being thrown at me daily. I hadn't had anyone stand up for me since my dad died, and it meant more to me than I'd ever told Em before.

"They were curled up on the floor, crying like babies, and that's when I fell in love with you."

Emlyn was clever, composed, and quiet, but there was a darkness in him like in all of us, and it reared its head to protect his family. He'd claimed me as his that day. And I'd learned never to fuck with my gentle giant.

"I've been in love with you for a hundred years, Emlyn Johahn." I caught his bearded chin, my grip biting and rough, *demanding* he meet my stare. "So you can understand why I'm a little fucking pissed that you think I don't want you. I want you. You're *mine;* that's an irrefutable fact." I paused and added, "You taught me that word. Irrefutable. It means there's nothing you can do to change it."

His brow was still knotted, confusion in his blue eyes but mellowed by warmth and real affection. Oh, fuck it. If he didn't understand words, he'd understand actions.

I dragged his face to mine and kissed him, sliding my fingers into his coarse hair to keep him close. I needn't have bothered; the second our lips touched, Emlyn's chest erupted with a noise like a purr and he yanked me flush to his body, kissing me deeply.

Possessive hands squeezed and roamed, and as if he remembered how I loved to be kissed, Emlyn took control. That purr travelled through his tongue to mine, deepening when I tightened my grip on his hair and kissed him fiercely, a desperate noise clawing up my throat.

He caught my hand when I twisted my fingers in his shirt, my head spinning and need pounding between my thighs. It was like he was in tune with my body, like he knew exactly what I was thinking; he tugged my hand from his shirt and pressed it to the bulge in his trousers. It throbbed under my palm and I groaned into his mouth, a long guttural sound that Em answered with a deep vibrating growl as he tore away from my lips, chest heaving.

"Yours," he grunted, the sound more noise than any intelligent language, but my heart leapt. And I grinned when I understood what he was communicating with both touch and words.

"Yes," I agreed, pressing him back against the brick clocktower and crawling onto his lap, getting a rich purr in response. "This cock is mine. *You* are mine."

I stroked my thumb over his tip through the fabric, and his head fell back against the tower with a groan, heated hands falling on my hips.

"We're outside, on top of a library, near a big public park," I panted, but I reached for the ties on my trousers nonetheless. Emlyn bared his teeth, both feral and carnal, when I shimmied them over my hips, tangling the fabric around my knees. "Anyone could look up and see us."

Em caught my bottom lip with his teeth, and my heart stuttered when I saw the smile on his face. His blue eyes glittered, something settled and soothed between us.

"Why did you think I didn't want you, you idiot?" I groaned, matching his smile.

He narrowed his eyes, like he was sorting through the meaning in my words. I gave him a minute to think, resisting the burning need to take his cock out, to stroke him, to see if his eyes still fluttered, if his cheeks flushed, and the same deep sighs of relief left his lips.

He brushed my lips with his thumb and rumbled an animal noise I couldn't understand.

"You wanted a kiss? All you had to do is ask, Emlyn. Or just grab me and kiss me; I give you permission to take all the kisses you want."

He huffed, the fingers on my hip carefully exploring my new ink, skittering away when I inhaled a sharp breath. It was still sore as fuck over my ribs.

He touched my lips again and—

I groaned. "This is because I kissed Harvey and Kai for killing that perv, isn't it? You felt left out."

I hauled his mouth back to mine to pay that debt, kissing him slowly, taking my sweet time making him hard and throbbing against me. I gave in to the need to touch him, snaking my fingers into his pants and pumping him in my hand. He choked out a wordless sound, fingers pressing harder into my hip.

He didn't utter a word—or a grunt—of complaint when I unfastened his pants and drew his cock out, but he did stop me before I could rise enough to take him inside me.

He flexed his hand, making sure I watched him before miming wrapping a noose around his throat.

"Huh?"

He did it three more times—and I dropped my head on his shoulder with a frustrated sound. "Emlyn Johahn. If you've been in a sulk all this time because Kai has a scarf and Harvey has gloves, I'm going to throttle you."

He frowned, his mouth tugged down.

"I *asked* you," I reminded him. "In the shop. I asked if you wanted anything, and you didn't. You weren't staring at anything like the other two; nothing caught your eye. How was I supposed to know you'd feel unappreciated if I didn't get you anything? I'd have bought you a pair of crappy old socks if I'd known."

His frown deepened.

"I asked you," I repeated, miming it and touching his chest. "You didn't say anything."

He thumped his head back against the clocktower with a hard sigh. Yup. He'd just realised what I was saying. I ran my knuckles down his face, smiling when he began to laugh, a deep thunderous sound that made his eyes crease and teeth poke out, white behind his beard.

"Idiot," I murmured, kissing him. "*My* idiot."

His laughter cut off with a groan when I trailed kisses down his jaw to the weak spot on his neck. His cock jumped in my hand; I resumed stroking, finding all the places that made his breathing hitch.

He grabbed my hip in a demanding squeeze, and that spoke clearer than any words. He needed me. Now.

"I need you, too," I breathed against his neck, kissing the red mark I'd left there and feeling pretty smug about it when I drew back, lining his cock up with my entrance.

Wind tugged at my hair, and fluttered Em's shirt between us, but I didn't feel the cold; I only felt the scorch of lust, the heat of Emlyn's body against mine, and the devastating stretch when I rolled my hips, taking him inside.

He sighed in relief; I swallowed it with a kiss, taking him deeper and digging my fingers into his shoulders when it hovered on that blissful edge of too fucking much and not enough.

"Fuck, Em," I breathed, trying to be quiet so we didn't tempt anyone to look up and see us fucking like horny teenagers on the roof of the Library of Iarlon. Under this roof, in the rooms below, scholars still studied and people were absorbed in their books, oblivious to the way Emlyn grabbed my hips, easing me up his cock and dropping me back down.

I kissed him to muffle my own cry. I was so turned on that it wouldn't take much to push me over the edge.[1]

"Mmm," Emlyn rumbled, his eyes dark and heavy-lidded, cheeks flushed red.

I grabbed his beard and kissed him harder, moving my hips faster, driving him deeper until his thick head brushed a spot that made my eyes cross.

Em growled loud enough that someone would hear. His hands controlled my pace, making sure his cock hit that same spot, over and over until my legs were shaking.

"I'm gonna come. Em?"

He nodded, like he knew what I was asking, and my heart burst full of affection.

"Don't stop," I pleaded, pleasure coiling tight in my lower belly, my inner muscles clutching him, making everything so much more sensitive. "Gods, please don't stop."

Em snapped his wings out, wrapping them around us and shielding me as I whined and shattered so hard I saw stars. When his mouth fixed on my throat, sucking a matching mark to his, I threw my arm around his shoulders, clinging to him as my pleasure shot higher, sharp and impossibly good. Sounds spilled from me beyond my control and my legs shook on the roof tiles.

The rolling, sucking of my pussy must have been too much for Em to endure; he roared in pleasure and drove his hips up, filling me entirely. Clutching me close, he spilled liquid heat inside me, and rewarded me with a familiar husky sigh, drawing out a few more throbs from my pussy.

I dropped my head on his shoulder, panting through rippling aftershocks, hot and sweaty and so fucking happy I couldn't contain a smile. At least until I remembered we were *on the roof of the fucking library.*

"Shit, Em," I laughed, drawing back. My pussy fluttered when I nudged his cock inside me with the movement.

"Hales," he sighed, stroking my face and staring at me with unadulterated love.

My breath caught in my throat. "Say that again."

Was he—did he remember—?

"Hales," he repeated gently.

I whimpered, clutching him as the world twisted under me, panic rising so suddenly that I flinched.

"Move, Hales!" Emlyn roared. "The hunter's here. Harvey's shot. Kai, get the emergency bag, and Wa—"

Pain surged like a sword driven into my heart. A killing blow. It didn't just blast my skull apart, but filled every limb of my body until any scrap of pleasure was obliterated and all I could do was shake, my mouth open on a silent scream.

CHAPTER TWENTY-FIVE

EMLYN

"*H*ales," I breathed, my tone changing. For a moment, I thought she was coming again, but her pussy only lightly clasped my cock—and

Blood began to drip from her nose.

Terror gripped my throat, turning my purr into a stuttering gasp when she shook harder, her body rigid and arched over me.

I withdrew from her heat and gathered her against me, soothing her with a low, comforting murmur and throttling my panic at its core so I could stay calm. A kiss to her cheek didn't slow her shakes; neither did stroking her hair from her face or rubbing her back. Her smoky eyes were vacant, open but unseeing. I was going to be sick.

"Hales," I said tentatively. It was the word that caused this, but it was the only word I knew, the only thing I could think to bring her out of the fit. I reached for other words, shaped them on my tongue, but couldn't give them sound; they emerged as short, uncertain growls.

I did this. I hurt the only woman I'd ever—loved? Did I love her? The emotion strangling my chest, bristling with terror, said I did. The hands that shook as I touched her said I did.

"Hales," I pleaded, crushing her body to mine when she convulsed so hard her wings trembled. Cradling her to me so nothing could hurt her. This was so familiar. I'd held her before, many times. My hands tingled with the remembered feel of her. My mind throbbed, and I kissed her cheek again, my breathing faster with every second her body didn't still.

I waited for her to gasp, to blink, to come back to me, but she didn't.

"Hales." I sank my fingers into her hair, cradling her head to my chest, wrenching on my broken mind for words, any words.

My clumsy tongue formed them reluctantly. "Emlyn. Harvey. Kai. Safe. Wings. Home. Coffee. Five. Zivai."

My mind snagged on zivai, the old world for *my heart.* Why did my head throb, my heart race faster when I said that? I tried to remember, searching the scant, empty memories I had of my life before the fighting pits—and I grunted when pain twisted into my head like a claw. I clutched Haley tighter, summoning a purr for comfort.

When I drew her back to peer at her face, dread clutched my gut and I whined an animal sound. Blood trickled from her nose, ears, and her eyes. I might have forgotten most of the first forty years of my life, but I knew bleeding from your eyes was a sign of death.

"Hales. Halwen. Emlyn. Harvey. Kai. Safe. Home." I purred louder, trying to bring her back, trying to assure her she was safe.

My voice grew gravelly and coarse, but I kept reciting them as I yanked my trousers shut, pulled hers back up her legs, and swept her into my arms as I prepared to descend the building.

A library, she'd called it. I remembered libraries. We'd ... we'd had one, hadn't we? In the home that burned? I remembered ... a sun-facing room full of light and warmth, ringed by bookcases lined with cheap paperbacks. But there were some rare, leather-bound books on the top shelf, in pride of place because ... because they were gifts.

"You," I said haltingly as I pumped my wings and stepped off the roof, forming my mouth around the sounds, the whole thing unnatural after a hundred years of growls and grunts. "You bought—me books."

I didn't remember it, not as a memory, but I *knew* it. We'd lived together for ten years, built a life together, and someone had made me forget. But they couldn't erase the rightness of holding her or the knowledge that I was *hers*. I'd known that for days now, but hearing her speak about our past cemented it, even if I didn't know half the words.

"We ... were happy," I said, angling my wings to carry us to the bright, gilded palace in the distance. The others would know how to help her. Kai would know. "We were safe. I don't ... know what ... how." I knew the house burned; I'd learned that from her and the others. But my memories were a black hole.

I tried to shield her from the worst of the wind as we flew across the river, tucking her face against my chest, my stomach a pit of fear at the blood smeared all over her. That was a lot of blood. We needed Harvey; he could heal her as long as I—

She sucked in a sudden rattling breath, her fingers locking in my shirt and body surging upward like she'd been shocked.

"Halwen. Hales," I blurted, flying us onto the nearest flat roof so I could get a better look at her. Relief made my legs weak, my breathing shaky when she roused.

"Em?" she asked in a small voice, wavering into me when I set her down, my hands roaming over her shoulders, her side, her hips, and back up to her face.

I gritted my teeth, ignoring the flash of pain as I focused my mind. "Hales ... okay?"

Her throat bobbed; she blinked over and over. "I don't know what happened, why I—wait, is this blood?"

She spotted the stains on my shirt and grabbed me in a panic, making my heart so full it hurt.

I shook my head and tilted her head up, swiping my thumb across her cheek to show her.

"Fuck," she whispered, the colour draining from her face.

I pulled her back into my arms for a quick, squeezing hug. "Harvey," I said. "Hale." I couldn't work out how to say *heal*. It should have been easy—I could say *home* and *Haley*. Frustration made my expression flat. "Harvey hale you."

She blinked, pain and anger both shining in those beautiful grey eyes. She leaned into my touch, inhaling a slow breath. I took that opportunity to sweep her back into my arms and kick off the roof, carrying us across the city.

"I need this curse undone," she said against my shoulder, wiping the blood off her face with the sleeve of her jacket. "If I don't, these memories are going to kill me."

I was afraid of the same thing, and without knowing what would trigger her, any moment could be her last. I tightened my arms around her until she grunted. I'd had *days* with her; I refused to lose this life, this love, this strange, new peace I felt around her.

It was mine. I was keeping it. Keeping her.

"Safe," I told her, my lips against her head but my eyes hard on the city, scanning for threats to her life. She was mine to protect. "Emlyn, safe."

I just wished I could protect her from the threats within.

CHAPTER TWENTY-SIX

HALWEN

I drifted in and out of consciousness over the next twenty-four hours, but there were perks to having my brain bleeding out of my orifices. Kai refused to leave my side, watching me with a keen obsession, anticipating my every need. He fluffed my cushions, fetched books from the library, opened the window when it was too hot, closed the window when it was too cold, and remained glued to my side.

Emlyn fought him for space beside me, brushing away whatever blood trickled free with a warm cloth, offering rumbled of reassurance and kisses. Now we'd kissed and had sex[1] he didn't hold himself back from touching me. It soothed my aching soul as much as my body; I luxuriated in every caring brush and lingering kiss.

Harvey went next level. Or as I called it, full psycho-pants craziness. Kai told him to get me breakfast. He returned with a trolley full of bacon, sausages, black pudding, three kinds of eggs, toast, and tomatoes, and not just a single portion—oh, no, my OTT mate brought enough to feed a small army. Plus his pockets were filled with fruits, and a bag around his shoulder brimmed with pastries, bread, and a stolen tub of butter. He'd cleaned out the entire dining hall.

And that was just breakfast.[2]

Of course, my mates had mostly demolished the piles of food, but it was the thought that counted. *And* they'd been locked away for a hundred years, deprived of good food. I couldn't imagine Wynvail serving them toast and fluffy eggs for breakfast. Gruel was more his style.

It was near sunset when I next woke from a shadow-laced dream, feeling like the mangled victim of a woolly yarmouth stampede. My head still pounded, my eyes stung like they'd been stabbed with a thousand needles, and my whole body ached. Memories were a bitch.

Not that I'd remembered anything clearly. But the shadows had wrapped around me in my dream and I knew for certain it was a person. A whole *person* who'd been stolen from me. Someone so important he was in every single almost-memory I had of my life with my mates. So vital that Em, Harvey, and Kai remembered the shadows too.

Someone had been cut from our memories. Not a gradual loss like the guys' memory, decayed by years of madness from our severed bond. No, this felt intentional. I couldn't explain it, but the cut was sharper, like the shadows had been cut from my mind. But imprecisely, with enough half-memories and clues to tell me something had been stolen. *He* had been stolen?

My brow furrowed, but I resisted the urge to probe my mind deeper. My next attempt could be my last.

"Sugarplum," Harvey breathed, making me jump. I thought I was alone, but I should have known better. Kai was intense with my health and protection lately. Emlyn was no less insistent. Bossy, overprotective alpha males.

Harvey let out a soft sigh and rolled his hips against my ass, letting me feel the hard length of him, silently pleading for me. I was surprised to find myself already wet when I turned over, a surprising amount of arousal slicking me. Had I been grinding against him while I slept?

Did I have a wet dream of the shadow man?[3]

When I faced Harvey, he took that as permission to throw the covers off us and crawl down my body, pressing gentle kisses to sleep-hot skin and making my eyes flutter. That felt so good, especially when he nuzzled my ribs and made a soft, pleased sound when I flopped onto my back, giving him greater access.

He took his time kissing his way down my body, like he was remembering the shape of me against his lips. I let my eyes flutter shut, revelling in the softness and warmth of him against me. By the time his lips brushed my pussy, I was pliant and warm with contentment.

My sleep shirt ended up rucked around my waist, but I had no complaints when Harvey settled between my legs, arms tangled with my thighs to keep me spread for him. The soft groan he released almost sounded like the word *beautiful.*

I cracked my eyes open to look down at him and caught my breath at the perfection of Harvey between my thighs, his face flushed, eyes closed, and brown hair fanned across my skin. I reached down, brushing strands off his face so I could see him, and my heart thudded harder when his eyes opened and met my stare.

I couldn't keep the smile off my face. Harvey rewarded me with a slow blink, like he was a contented cat, and licked a long stripe up my centre. He watched my face as he stiffened his tongue, swiping my clit like he knew exactly where it was. Like he'd been doing this for years. Ten years to be exact.

A deep, animal sound built in his chest as we held eye

contact, and my hips bucked, the slow-burning desire shifting to something hotter, needier.

"In our last life," I said, my voice husky, "you used to love this."

I held his stare as I clasped my hand around his throat. Molten silver eyes flashed. He shuddered, hands tightening where they gripped my thighs.

"Sugarplum," he warned in a familiar tone.

I grinned, stroking his thrumming pulse with my thumb. "Yes, Buttercup?"

His gaze darkened even more, until my heart skipped and butterflies filled my belly. Slowly, never looking away, he reached up and unwrapped my hand from his throat, pressing it into the sheets beside me instead, encouraging my fingers to curl.

My whole body flashed with goosebumps when I realised the message. *Hold on.*

"Gods," I breathed when he shot me one last wicked look and dragged his mouth all the way from my clit to my pussy, feasting on me with a demand and fervour that made my head spin.

Every sensitive place, he found it and lavished devastating attention there. Every weakness, he exploited until I gripped the sheets with one hand and buried the other in his hair, holding on as he licked me furiously, a growl accompanying each one.

"Harvey," I panted, inner muscles squeezing around nothing as he swirled his tongue over my clit. "Fuck. Fingers —please."

My whine brought a deeper groan to his throat, but the helpless look he shot me told me he didn't know what I needed.

A cruel tension rode my body, need refusing to release its chokehold until it was satisfied. I grabbed Harvey's hand, my skin whispering over warm leather and hot skin—he refused to stop wearing the gloves.

Panting, I pressed his fingers against my inner thigh. "Please, Harvey. I need—"

A groan swallowed the rest of my plea when he understood in an instant and slid a finger inside me, instantly adding another.

"Faster," I choked out, my eyes rolling back when his lips found my clit again, tongue flicking fast enough to make my back arch. "Harv—"

My breath came strangled. He knew me inside and out, knew how to curl his fingers and how fast I needed them inside me. Tension pulled impossibly tight, my back bowing off the bed, toes curling when he growled against my clit and threw me over the edge.

My hips jerked out of control, my breathing a ruin. I gripped Harvey's hair so tightly I pulled a few strands free, my eyes screwed shut as another wave of pleasure crushed me in its blissful grip.

I thought it was over, but then fingers curled inside me, moving faster, and the shaking began again.

My breath cut off in my chest when another climax tore its way out of me.

When I crashed back to the bed, this time I caught Harvey's wrist, panting for breath.

He murmured a soft noise, pleased with himself as he gazed up at me.

"Don't even think about giving me another. I can't handle a third this early in the morning."[4]

He tilted his head against my thigh, his face soft with a smile and his eyes twinkling. It was good to see him like this, confident and—happy.

When he withdrew his fingers, stroking sensitive nerves, I almost reconsidered and pleaded for a third release. The sight of him licking his gloves clean was erotic enough to make my clit throb.

But the quietness of the room finally hit, and I frowned. "Where are Em and Kai?"

Harvey kissed my inner thigh, in no hurry to move.

"Harvey," I huffed, tugging on his hair. "Don't make me choke you into submission."

He just smirked and raked his teeth over my skin. *Alright, if that's how you wanna play it.*

I wrapped my thighs around his head and surged up, flipping Harvey onto his back. I was tempted to smother him with my pussy but he'd probably enjoy it.

"Where are *Kai* and *Emlyn?*" I repeated, moving down to sit on his chest and—frowning at the sheer delight in his expression. He grinned, dimples appearing in his cheeks. "You're lucky you're cute," I told him, climbing off him and tapping his nose. "Take me to them."

I slid off the bed and hastily cleaned up with a wet cloth I'd left on the side for these exact reasons.[5]

"No," I argued when Harvey's hot hands slid up my stomach to cup my breasts before I could swap my sleep shirt for a tunic. "Harvey. We need to find the others—"

I swear I felt butterflies in *every* part of my body when Harvey caught my hands and pressed them flat to the wall.

Holy fuck. Holy, holy, fucking fuck.

I shuddered violently when hot hands gripped my hips, and he sank into my wet pussy with one smooth thrust.

I groaned, throwing my head back on his shoulder as pleasure rippled through my inner walls.

Okay, just one more orgasm.

CHAPTER TWENTY-SEVEN

our orgasms later, cleaned and successfully dressed, I strode beside a very smug Harveil van Khama down the busy hallways near the dining hall. Harvey had used a dry, crusty bread roll to communicate where my other mates were, and a tiny weight fell off my chest—they were still close, still inside the palace—but the panic wouldn't entirely leave until I set eyes on them.

If they left the palace, Wynvail could get to them. He could lock them back in the tunnels and make me steal another deadly artefact for him.

Or just kill them.

I knew the bastard could get into the palace, but Lucifer had upped security since the break-in and at least here, the guys were surrounded by other demons—including the devil's lethal inner circle.

"No," I warned when Harvey's warm hand drifted from my lower back to the curve of my ass in my leather trousers. "I already came five times."

He seemed to consider that, his gaze distant and hand

returning to my back, hot enough to burn me through my wine-red tunic.

"Six," he corrected, earning a beatific grin.

"You said another word!" I bumped my shoulder into his. "You'll be a wordsmith in no time."

He gave me a strange look, either because he didn't understand or he did and thought I was a weirdo. I was betting on the second.

His sudden eloquence put me in a buoyant mood,[1] and helped ease some of the stress of Em and Kai being out of sight. *Wynvail hasn't got them; they're fine. He'd have made sure to gloat if he'd stolen them by now.*

Volume and voices rose as we neared the dining hall, and I quickened my pace, Harvey making no comment—not even a questioning growl—when I practically threw myself around the doorway.

The hall was full at this time in the evening, so it took me a few seconds to find Em's broad shoulders and grey wings, and Malakai hunched beside him, shovelling food into his mouth like it was an eating competition. Sadness made my shoulders slump as I watched them both cramming food, not even glancing up when people stared and judged with murmurs and whispers.

Alright, fuck everyone in this room.

I scowled at anyone who looked my way, stalking across the room to my mates, holding eye contact with everyone who stared at them. I hoped it made them uncomfortable.

I stroked a hand down Kai's silky red hair and bent to kiss the top of Emlyn's head. They slowed their pace, but didn't stop devouring the food piled high on their plates. If they noticed the judgement from everyone else, it didn't stop them.

"What?" I barked when I caught three too many looks. "Never been starved before? If you've never been in physical

pain from hunger, and not known where your next meal is coming from, you don't get to look at my mates that way."

"Fuck them," Kai muttered between bites of a juicy chicken leg.[2] "I don't care."

But I did. They'd been tortured and neglected and left, essentially, for dead between fights in the pit. They deserved better.

Most people glanced away, guilt in their eyes. Good. A few stares lingered, but they'd shifted to pity and sympathy. It was still five stares too many, but it was better than before. I stroked Kai's and Emlyn's hair, and went to find my own food.

Harvey and I had only been eating for five minutes when a messenger in a gold-edged black jacket and an askew little hat approached us, panting and out of breath.

"Halwen Vakhara?" he asked, ice-blue eyes meeting mine. He was eighteen tops, and thin enough that a stiff wind would knock him over.

"That's me," I agreed warily.

"Her Highness would like to see you. She said she's found something."

My heart leapt. Kai stiffened beside me, a sharpness in his crimson eyes and fangs bared as—as he curled over his food protectively.

"Stay here," I told him, Emlyn, and Harvey who was so absorbed eating his eight steaks[3] that he didn't even growl at the messenger. "I'll go speak to the queen, and tell you what she said. And please, *please,* remember to chew your food."

Emlyn shot me an unamused scowl. It was very scary, very intimidating, a solid eight out of ten. But he had a tiny smear of red wine gravy on his cheek, and it undermined the whole look.

I considered, for a moment, behaving like a well mannered member of society. *Nah.* I leant across the table, caught

Emlyn's chin, and licked off the sauce. Mm, sweet and rich. My favourite.

Emlyn's chest shuddered with a growl. I grinned, rising from my seat and giving the messenger my attention. Actually, on second thoughts, I grabbed a chicken leg off my own plate. "Here, kid, you look like you could use a meal."

He groaned and accepted it. "Thank you, ma'am. It's been so busy today, I missed lunch."

Kai grunted, and I glanced at him to see—he was holding out a hunk of lamb on the bone. I sent a rush of affection down our splintered bond, hoping he felt even an echo of my love. He was willingly handing over his favourite food. Soft, caring, sweet man.

"I won't be long," I told them as the messenger bit into his steak, looking like all his Christmases had come at once.

But what had the queen found? Was it about my mates and our curse—or did she have news about Wynvail?

My stomach knotted around the half plate I'd managed to eat, and I suddenly wasn't sure I wanted to know Lili's news.

CHAPTER TWENTY-EIGHT

$\mathcal{M}$ y head hurt, crammed full of so much information that it was going to burst. My mates had given me a solid five minutes with Lili before they shoved through the door, finding me uncannily.[1] They surrounded me in a protective semicircle, bristling and growly.

It was nice to know I ranked equal with food on their list of priorities. I actually got a little choked up.

Now, we were back in my room, processing, planning— and packing bags full of supplies.

"Haley, hey," Lili breathed, *standing from the chair she'd been sitting in, reading a book with way too many pages for my attention span. "Luc wanted to talk to you, but he's so busy with everything going on. Do you want to sit down?"*

I sat opposite her, a fire roaring in a huge marble monstrosity between us, a table in front of it holding a silver tea set and a plate stacked with pale biscuits. The whole room smelled of books and flowers, every flat surface overflowing with wisteria. It was a little overpowering, but pretty if you liked wisteria, I suppose. I loved soulcaps, but that was because I was soft for Kai.

"Irian said you'd found something," I prompted.

Lili laughed, her brown eyes crinkling in her tanned face. She leaned back in the high-back chair, her wings draped over the top, feathers a shade or two lighter than my own. "Oh, no. He gave you his name."

"He's a good kid," I replied, confused why she was amused.

"Let me guess; he told you it's been mayhem in Hell and he's overworked. Gave you a tragic sob story so you'd feel sorry for him."

"Uh..." Yeah, he told me it was the anniversary of his brother's death. "The kid's having a rough day, and honestly you should cut down his hours. He was starving."

"He was not," Lili laughed, her eyes crinkling when she smiled. "He's always hungry, and he has a silver tongue. A pretty quick hand too; Cerny only found him because Irian tried to steal his sword to sell on the black market."

I sat back, reeling. "No way. He's a sweet kid. He ... he conned me and my mate out of food," I realised, scowling. "I just hugged him."

Lili's chest shook. "He's a little shit."

"Yes," I agreed fiercely. "So—what did you find?"

"It's more something Luc remembered," she replied, leaning forward, her wings rustling. "He's been obsessing over this, to be honest. He's convinced it isn't a coincidence you were reborn at the same time one war ended and another one is starting. You said you were killed, and it damaged your mates' souls. That's why they're..."

"Yeah," I agreed, refusing to give her an adjective. They might have been beastly and primal, but they were mine, and I wasn't going to say a bad word about them. I loved them exactly as they were, however they were. I just wanted them to know me. "That's why."

"Luc thinks if we help you, it could slow down whatever's brewing with the alphas. I think we should do it because it's the right thing to do," she added wryly, "and because you're now my friend. But if this stops you being used to fight us, that's even better."

She was strangely casual for a queen, but I didn't remark on that. I nodded. "I've got no plans to fight my boss."

Lili laughed, her eyes crinkling. That's when my mates broke down the door.

"We'll have to pay for the replacement door, you know," I told them huffily, grabbing a clean shirt and throwing it into a bag along with underthings and a stack of spare weapons. I'd strap most to my body, but it never hurt to be over-prepared. "It's the least we can do if this works."

Lucifer had apparently been skipping sleep so he could think of a way to end our curse—and earn our loyalty, I suspected. We were pretty powerful allies, three archdemons and a woman who'd risen from the dead. I was surprised to learn I was on the same status level as Lucifer's generals.[2]

The devil scoured books, journals, and ancient demon magic tomes, but in the end it was his memory that gave us a solution. There was an ancient woman who existed when the devil Fell; her two mates were killed during the rise of demons, and she went Feral. With a capital F. Good to know what my mates were.

"What if this woman's not even alive?" I muttered to myself, grabbing a bar of soap.[3] "It's been hundreds of years; she might be dead."

But I kept packing, and I couldn't quite kill the hope rising in my chest. According to Lucifer, this woman had gone mad for years, but one day she turned up like everything was back to normal, speaking, functioning, no longer feral.

I needed to know *how.*

If only she wasn't a grumpy, miserable, unpersonable bastard who'd become a recluse and vanished for two hundred years.

"She'll need to be bribed," Lili warned us, watching Harvey attempt to set the door back in its frame. It crashed into the hallway outside, splinters flying off; I winced. To give the queen her credit,

her tone didn't waver. "There's no way we can know what she'll ask for; Luc's best guess is blood or a promise, but it could be as drastic as a firstborn."

I flinched. No.

"We'll pay it," Kai muttered, oblivious to the horror crawling through me. "Whatever the cost."

"Not a fucking firstborn," I snarled, spinning to bare my teeth at him, my wings snapping tight to my back. A tremor went through my whole body—rage carving a home inside me.

Kai didn't argue; he strode around my chair and went to his knees to kiss my forehead, making all my rage scatter. Panic had hidden behind it, a secret even from me. "We'll figure it out. We can kill her after she helps us, my rose."

Lili's eyebrows crawled up her hairline, but her stare was on Kai so I figured it was more shock at his complete sentences than the casual mention of murder.

"Right," Lili breathed, shaking herself out of her surprise. "Luc last saw Adhiti near the South sea, and there's a rumour that she lives inside the Wailing Caves, but that's not confirmed. It's a place to start your search, though."

"Ooh," I breathed, my mood brightening. "I love whales."

"It's wailing, like crying."

"Wailing Caves," I echoed, any excitement curled up and dead. "Like weeeeehhhhh." Emlyn covered his ears at my wail, which was rude. It was pitch perfect. "Why does that sound like somewhere that's going to kill us?"

"Like I said," Lili murmured, a touch apologetically. "She'll need to be bribed. And you'll need this." She lifted an aged map from the coffee table and held it out to me. "Renna would guide you, but the cave only allows people who are willing to trade, and she can't take the risk it will demand her daughter."

"Renna has a daughter?" I demanded, my mouth falling open. "Someone slept with her? And didn't get stabbed? Wow."

Lili's mouth curled at the corners, amusement glittering in her *eyes. "Renna and her wife adopted their daughter. If Renna ever went anywhere near a man, she'd eat him like a praying mantis."*

So now here we were, getting ready for a trip that could demand everything from us, and that might lead to a dead woman—or to our own deaths.

"Are we fools for doing this?" I asked no one in particular.

"Yes," Emlyn agreed, stealing a sword from my stash.

"Comforting, Em. Very comforting."

CHAPTER TWENTY-NINE

*W*e had enough steel to set up an armoury, but something told me knives, swords, and iron wing-tips wouldn't be enough to get us where we were going. At least we had the map, and a truly ancient compass. It was rusted on the edges, but the needle spun and guided us south west, so I kept glancing at it, squinting at the various arrows and dials. This was like no compass I'd seen before, but I was a thief, not an explorer; this was, all things considered, my first quest.

"It's just like any other job," I muttered to myself, my eyes cast down as I navigated the rocky terrain south of Iarlon. Further, the landscape would turn to mountains and grassy plains rife with monsters. I'd never been this far south before. "You're getting paid in your continued existence, not in coin, but how much different can it be?"

"Very," Kai drawled, ignoring the glare I aimed his way. "We shouldn't go this way."

"Tough shit," I huffed, hiking up the straps of my pack. "This is where she lives, so this is where we go."

She—Adhiti, a demon so old she was around before

Lucifer fell and created the realm as we know it, before demons were more than a small collection of beasts with zero brain function. Before we were even called demons. This woman must have seen the rise and fall of thousands of lords, rulers, and assholes who thought the world belonged to them. I didn't know what I'd do to convince her to help us, but I was an enterprising woman; I'd figure it out.[1]

"Don't," I warned Harvey when he dragged his heels, trying to slope off from us. Again. "You can't shift; your wing needs another day to heal, Buttercup."

He grumbled, kicking a stone down the hill we descended, the whole rocky scenery lit by the bright purple of the impending sunrise. Harvey's grumbling growl made clear his thoughts on not shifting.

I gave him another warning look—knowing Harvey, he'd shift, damage his wings more, and leave himself permanently grounded.

I checked the compass again. We wouldn't need the map until we got through the massive swath of grass on the other side of the mountains ahead, but the map would be useless if we ended up miles from the area we were meant to be in.

Queen Lili's instructions were vague, and Lucifer's advice was outdated, but I'd hunted marks on less in the past. We knew she was in the Wailing Caves; we'd find her.[2]

"Hungry," Emlyn muttered, one of his new words. Sweat had soaked through his shirt, strangely alluring and masculine.[3]

"Yeah, me too," I sighed, reaching for the strap of my bag to pull it around the front and hunt down something to eat. I wanted something salty. Gods, *cheese*. Cheese sounded like heaven right about—

With my attention on my bag, I didn't see the hunk of stone in front of me. My foot hit it at a strange angle, pain twisted up my ankle, and I was catapulted several feet into the air.

It happened so fast that my wings didn't even snap out to slow me. I landed hard on a rock the size of Tali, jostling my entire damned skeleton. I let out a long pitiful groan that only rose in volume when I felt the little stones embedded between my feathers.

"Halwen!"

"Haley!"

"My rose!"

Even with pain blazing up my leg and something spectacularly wrong with my shoulder, I couldn't help but smile. They knew me, could speak my name. The progress they'd made this week was incredible. Magical. I needed to return to Ashboren the Terrifying and kiss the grumpy alchemist on his silver-tufted head.

Harvey reached my side first, kneeling on the rock and reaching for my ankle.

"Don't! You need that magic," I panted, gritting my teeth when he ignored me and lifted my foot, jostling pain all the way up my thigh. When a whimper slipped free, both Kai and Em gave him matching snarls of warning, looming above us. "Harvey, you need it for your wing."

The throaty noise he made in response told me he didn't give a shit about his wing. My heart fluttered, emotion catching in the back of my throat. He was a good mate. Even though, for him, we'd only been together two weeks, he was a good mate. An incredible one, actually.[4]

I gritted my teeth when power poured into me, scalding hot and crackling with pain. It burned and broke and twisted as it moved along the fracture in my ankle, and there was no holding back the scream that exploded from my chest.

Emlyn knelt and pressed close to my back, wrapping his arms around me. Kai gripped my hand, linking our fingers.

Invisible magic slithered up my good shoulder to wipe sweaty hair out of my face.

I whimpered, my jaw locked as pain erupted higher, ruthless and sharp. I hovered on the edge of blacking out—but the agony sucked away all at once, and I gasped. Reeling, panting.

I twisted so I could press my face into Em's chest as tears rolled freely down my face.

"Sorry," Harvey murmured, sounding so unlike his cheeky, sarcastic old self that a sob caught my throat. That humour had been beaten out of him, eroded by a hundred years of darkness and fights and suffering. Wynvail had achieved what his father never had.

"No," I rasped, reaching for him, my palm sliding along his cheek. He angled his face into the touch, silver eyes full of misery and—dread. "Don't be sorry. It's not your fault your magic hurts."

Healing wasn't supposed to hurt, but most healers weren't raised in a basement for the first twenty years of their life and—and—

I couldn't even think it, inside the quiet of my own mind. I couldn't give words to what had been done to him. The violence his father partook in but allowed *others* to impart, too.

It took a little convincing, but after a few pointed tugs and a pleading stare, Harvey allowed me to pull him into a hug. My shoulder didn't hurt anymore; it felt numb but back in working order. I tested my ankle—tender but no longer fractured—and pulled Harvey close.

"Don't be sorry. Thank you for healing me." I stroked wild brown hair from his face, and rested my head on his shoulder as I caught my breath.

"Note to self," I murmured, trying for humour, "look where you're walking in the future."

"You're alright?" Kai demanded, his fingers threading in my ponytail.

"I'm fine," I assured him, assured all of them. Sure, I was achy, but a few aches had never held me back before and I wasn't about to let them now. "We should keep moving; the sun will set soon."

I wanted to be on the other side of the hills before it did. And hopefully without any more moronic damsel moments from yours truly.

"That's not good," Kai muttered, touching the small of my back, his body language bristling and tense.

"What?"

But I saw what—far in the distance, a black cloud gathered over the mountains. Almost like someone knew we were coming and sent out guard dogs to keep us away.[5] Almost like we were cursed.

I glanced at my arm. It was covered in flowers and skulls now, but nothing could quite hide the gleam of the curse's ink. I was cursed to kill them, but curses came with other side effects. Shit luck, near-death experiences, and other cursed objects and people being drawn to them.

Whatever was on the other side of the mountains was not good. But Adhiti was there, and she'd survived losing her mates. She recovered herself, despite her soul being shattered. I needed to know how she did it.

Besides, someone as old as her would know a thing or two about curses. We'd kill two birds with one stone.

I just hoped we didn't get killed with the same stone.

"Come on, then," I sighed, getting to my feet and walking —*carefully*—down the hill towards the mountain range. "Unless you *don't* want to remember the life you lived before the pit?"

Kai bared his teeth. "You know damn well we do, Haley."

And all I wanted was my mates back. I wanted to look at them and not be cut apart by longing and heartbreak.

We had nineteen days left before the curse would make us kill each other. Enough time to avert it? To erase the curse? Doubtful. But if they remembered me, maybe they could fight it harder. If they knew me, deep down to my soul, maybe they wouldn't kill me.

It was a fool's hope, but I'd never claimed to be anything but foolish.

"Into the ominous black cloud, then," I said, and led the way into the storm.

CHAPTER THIRTY

*M*y ankle ached, and the climb over the mountains had been exhausting. We were all in a shitty mood when we dragged ourselves across the rolling grassy plains on the other side, each blade so dark a green it was almost black. Of course, it was the perfect time for the heavens to open and dump an ocean of rain on us.

Harvey growled, pulling his jacket over his head. He shot a sulky look at me like I could get it to stop raining. When that didn't work, he scowled at Kai, who glared right back, his red head ducked as rain pummelled us. Em flitted from tree to tree, hiding under its branches like he wasn't already soaked through. I shook my head, smiling at them, but I winced when a twinge went through my ankle.

"When we reach the next hill," I called over the drumming rain, "we need to head more west." I was loathed to take out the map in this weather, but the compass was doing its job, no matter how rusty.

"The storm's darker there," Kai muttered, giving the sky a threatening look.

"Wow, I hadn't noticed," I fired back, as cranky as everyone else. "I didn't see those giant, unmissable clouds there; silly me."

Kai's gaze flattened. "I only meant—"

He cut off with a gasp, and hairs rose all down my arms when a low, rippling laugh swept through the charged air around us.

"Em, Harvey, get here *now*," I barked, reaching for one of my daggers. The pink hilts were reassuring in my hands, but unease grew as the laughter grew louder, low and chattering —demonic but bestial too.

"Hyaeni demons," I breathed, realising exactly what that sound meant.

"It's there," Emlyn growled, pressing close to me, Harvey right behind him.

I followed his line of sight and inhaled a quick breath at the sight of a rangy feline creeping around the curve of a grassy mound. Its spotted, furry body was low to the ground, bristling with predatory anger, and green eyes glowed in a narrow head topped with a dark tuft of hair. Razor spikes of bone ridged its spine and the backs of its legs, sharp enough to slice a body apart.

"It?" I laughed, a hitch in my voice. "Hyaeni move in clans; where there's one..."

My voice died when eight more of the creatures stalked around the curves in the hills, eyes fixed on us. They didn't even bare their teeth; they didn't see us as a threat.

No, they stalked us like prey.

"There's more," Kai finished my sentence, magic shuddering around him and his tattoos scrolling around his arms and throat.

I flung wet hair off my face, searching for a way out, but the hyaeni surrounded us. I considered scaling the hills for a moment, until more hyaeni appeared atop them with glowing eyes and spotted fur slicked to their bodies by the rain.

"No!" Emlyn roared, diving forward—because Harvey had launched himself at the nearest hyaeni.

"Harvey, you can't shift!" I yelled, panic crawling across my skin as I watched Emlyn grapple with him. Harvey was mid-shift, his bronze skin still visible but black fur crawling up his legs, splitting the seams of his trousers. I rushed after him. *"Please,* Harvey!"

He growled so loudly it made the hyaeni take a few steps back, eyeing us more warily.

"We'll fly," I panted, racing to catch up to him and Emlyn. "We can fly. Em, you carry Harvey and I'll take Kai."

My breath stuttered when the hyaeni crept closer, muzzles low to the ground and jaws parted now in an unsettling blend of low laughter and growling. I didn't want to sheath my dagger, but I forced my fingers to unclench from the handle and reach for Kai.

His pale jaw was set, a hard glint in his crimson eyes as he opened his arms and wrapped them around my waist. His magic swelled against my skin, dragging a gasp from me at the force of his power—and his anger.

"Go!" I shouted the second Harvey stopped shifting and Emlyn grabbed him in a tight hold.

I pushed off the ground, my arms like iron around Kai and my stomach dropping when the chattering of the hyaeni demons rose. They knew we were escaping, and they were furious. We'd wandered into their territory, and we were probably fair game, but I didn't fancy becoming a rare demon steak any time soon. Or worse—getting dosed by their venom. A single hyaeni bite could make a person hallucinate for eight hours.

My wingbeats pulled on my aching shoulder as I flapped fast, shooting us off the ground.

We rose five feet, then six. Goosebumps covered my arms as I clung to Kai.

"Haley!" Kai yelled when we banked suddenly to the right, wind driving rain into us so hard that my wing buckled. We tilted precariously above the ground, my left wing scrambling to catch enough air to right us.

"Shit," I gasped when we plummeted fast, cold rain driving through my clothes and into my bones.

My wings were so heavy, armoured with iron, and I was already so tired that it took immense effort to lift them. I screamed through gritted teeth when the ache in my shoulder became all-out pain.

Kai's snakes wrapped around my waist, circling my body all the way to my shoulder where they shored up my weakness like a splint. We rose an inch, then another, a shudder sending us swerving to the left when icy rain sluiced down the back of my neck.

"No," I growled at the sky when thunder rumbled, the air shuddering around us.

"Haley!" Kai yelled right in my ear. "Higher! *Now!"*

"I'm trying!" I shouted back, sweat joining the rain slicking my face as I flapped my wings, hauling us higher, higher until —teeth clamped around my ankle and gnashed, grinding down to the bone.

My voice broke on a scream.

We dropped fast.

My wings moved uselessly, agony rising so suddenly I blacked out the moment of the fall. My sight rushed back in when I slammed into the ground on my bad shoulder, jostling the weakness loud enough to drag another scream up my throat.

My arms fell limply to the wet grass, and I splayed there, every breath wheezing up my throat. Kai landed heavily on top of me, knocking the remaining scraps of air from my lungs with an accidental blow to my stomach.

"Hales!" Emlyn roared, and I gasped as Kai was forcibly

rolled off me, Em's scared face filling my vision. "Are you okay? Say something. Kai, are you—"

"Fine," Kai choked out, but rage shuddered through the air as his magic gathered. Hyaeni whimpered where his snakes struck, but the sounds blurred in my head, and suddenly I couldn't see anything.

"Haley, keep your eyes open," Kai snapped. "Don't you dare sleep. Harvey, get here. I'll handle the hyaeni."

"No," Emlyn rumbled. "I will."

The words drifted in and out of my hearing, meaning attached to some but others completely beyond comprehension. I groaned when I was jostled, pulled against a soaked chest, cold and heated all at once. A sudden growl filled my ears and I jumped.

"She was bitten?" Kai demanded in a snarl. "Shit. *Shit.*"

I whimpered when pain stabbed through my ankle, shock forcing my eyes open and—I gasped when Emlyn bellowed, the noise from deep, *deep* within his chest and strong enough to make Harvey and I flinch into each other.

"What the fuck?" Kai breathed, coming close enough that I could see him as my eyes roved, panic refusing to let my eyes settle.

The hyaeni dropped dead. Literally. They collapsed onto the grass, their eyes wide and unseeing, bodies sliced cleanly in two. Each one was a gruesome cross section, innards and muscle cut with a razor edge.

What did Em do...?

My instinct says he's dangerous. I haven't seen what the pit did to him yet. Was this what the pit did to him?

I tried to keep my eyes open, but they fell shut against my will and consciousness began to float further away from me. At least I couldn't feel the pain anymore.

Harvey rumbled an almost-word, clutching me tighter.

"No, sugarplum," he said roughly, prising my eyes open.

446

But I flinched when the stormy light stabbed into them, Harvey's face swirling above me.

He was—grotesque.

"The venom's taking hold," Kai breathed, leaning over me. He had five eyes and two mouths, both of them hissing with forked tongues. I flinched back with a scared breath.

"We need to leave," Emlyn rumbled. I closed my eyes before I could see the monstrosity of *his* face, too.

"We can't leave; the hunter will find us," I slurred, and wasn't sure why I'd said that.

It was true, though. I could feel him following us, so in tune with my soul it scared me.

"The hunter?" Kai demanded, gentle fingers stroking wet hair off my face.

"He's coming to kill us all. He won't stop until—until—" I didn't know what. "He wants the shadows," I breathed. "But they're mine."

"She's already delusional," Kai murmured, jarring me with a warm kiss to my rain-cold forehead.

"What can we do?" Emlyn asked, his voice tight with a fear I hadn't heard in years. Not since—not since *he* came after us and torched our house, starting a chain of events that ended with us shot dead.

"We need … safe place…" Harvey replied, his words syrupy-thick with effort, "Wane, can you—"

He cut off, but the words echoed around my head, over and over.

Wane, can you—

Wane—

"Who's Wane?" Kai breathed, but there was a soft horror in his voice that made me think the name echoed around his head too.

"I…" Harvey gasped, panic in his tightening arms around me, in the tense line of his body. "I don't know. I think—I—"

A strangled sound of pain tore up his throat, startling my eyes open, and I tried not to scream as one of his eyes melted down his face and landed on my shoulder. I brushed it hesitantly. It dissolved under my touch, making me gasp.

"Your eye..." I cried, sobs bubbling up. "I'm so sorry, I didn't mean to..."

I looked up at Harvey, relieved his face was normal again. But pain crashed through my head like a tidal wave when another face overlapped his, so similar but softer. Anguish cut into the sharp lines of his face, his mahogany hair sleeker, lips not bracketed with smile lines. The eyes were the same, though—burnished, liquid silver. The same eyes as Wynvail, but different. Not hard, not tainted with bitterness and rage. These were eyes that had suffered, that were haunted by unspeakable memories. Eyes that were still kind, almost in defiance,

Wane...

"Where is he?" I demanded, ignoring the slurring quality of my voice. "Where is he? *Where is he?*"

"We need to get out of here before we draw more of those things to us," Kai said, still faint. "Let's get to those trees and find somewhere to hide."

A whimper cut up my throat when Harvey began to walk, jostling me so hard my skull shattered with pain. Memories slipped through the cracks, no longer just shadows but full and clear.

I'd been hired to hunt Wane and bring him to my client, but I walked away without a single coin because I couldn't bear the thought of him being hurt again.

The first night I spent in their safe house, I hadn't been able to sleep. I'd crept out of my room and into the kitchen to find Wane already sitting on the counter, staring at the stars out the window.

Do you have nightmares too? he'd asked, only compassion in his eyes.

I'd sat with him for three hours, until the sun began to rise and we both went to our respective rooms to rest for whatever hours were left in the night.

He was the first person to realise we were mates, the first person to say *I love you.*

He was mine. My heart. Zivai. And I was itzaia—his soul.

How had I forgotten him?

Someone *did* this, cut out my memories of him. Someone stole my mate.

Rage built strong enough to swallow an ocean, and I floated from memory to memory, remembering *everything.*

CHAPTER THIRTY-ONE

KAI

I started, unseeing, as Emlyn strung big, waxy leaves over the makeshift platform we'd made between two branches in a wide oak. How did I forget Wane? He was as much my brother as he was Harvey's. *Mine to protect.* So damn important that he was the heart we all revolved around, like he was secretly the sun instead of a shadow. He was the heart of our family, and we'd forgotten him.

I swallowed, memories trickling back now I remembered his name. Haley was remembering too, laid flat on her back on the branch platform, her head cradled between Harvey's hands to stop her hurting herself in the hyaeni venom's grip.

I'd forgotten her, too. My Halwen. My rose. The name had returned to me, but *her*, my fierce, violent, protective mate? She'd been lost to me.

I shook all over, panic and fury making my whole skeleton rattle.

I tried to swallow it down, still reeling as I knelt beside her and stroked my thumb over her cold cheek. She didn't so much as twitch when I brushed sweat and rain from her face with trembling hands. Pink hair was slicked to her head, making her look so pale and dollike.

"We've got you," I promised her, not looking at her eyes for too long. They were open but unseeing, staring at something we couldn't see. "We're right here, my rose. Nothing bad's going to happen to you."

Sweat rolled off Harvey's forehead too, his jaw clenched as pain ruptured his mind. It crackled through mine, but not strong enough to stop me functioning.

"We'll find him," I swore to them both. "We'll find Wane. I fucking swear it. He's ours; no one gets to take him from us."

Harvey caught his bottom lip between his teeth. He nodded, his throat bobbing.

He might not remember everything yet, but enough was unlocking in my throbbing skull that I didn't hesitate to reach out and cup his head, angling closer so I could kiss the side of his face. It wasn't romantic; it was comfort. And badly needed judging by the way Harvey clenched his jaw as tears gathered in his silver eyes.

"You can cry," I told him, in case he needed to hear it. "Don't hold it back, yeah? Cry as much as you need. No one here's gonna judge you."

"Done," Emlyn grunted, sitting carefully beside us on the platform, his chest heaving. "Is she okay?"

"I don't know," I replied honestly. "The venom will wear off in a few hours, but the memories? I don't think we were ever supposed to remember. There's no way to know how fucked up our heads will be when it's over."

Emlyn clapped my shoulder, his worried eyes saying everything his voice didn't.

"The hunter's coming," Haley mumbled, her eyes moving

rapidly now, vacant and grey. "He's coming to take my shadow."

"No one's going to take anything," I swore to her, pulling her onto my lap when Harvey let go to scrub the tears from his face. I bent over my mate, scattering kisses across her forehead, her cheeks, and laying a soft kiss on her lips. *"No one.* I'll kill anyone who even tries."

She knew I meant it. Parts of our life were returning in a slow, steady stream. I'd always slaughtered her enemies, always made people pay for insulting her or daring to hurt her. I remembered giving her those daggers she was so protective of. Remembered what the words etched down the centre of the blades meant.

I will always be your shadow and light; you will always be my rose and life.

I jumped, jolted out of the memory when Emlyn reached for her hand, bringing her knuckles to his lips. "Remembering hurts," he said, gravelly and quiet, his blue eyes sliding to me and Harvey. "I think—I know him."

"Wane?" I asked, stroking a gentle finger down Haley's cheek.

Emlyn nodded. "Did he ... save us? From an axe woman?"

I didn't know. No memory returned, sparked by his words. I looked at him blankly, apologetically.

"Yes," Harvey rasped, shoving wet, wavy hair off his face and giving Emlyn a look I could only describe as broken. "His shadows..." He moved his arms in an exaggerated motion, miming a hug. "Saved us."

Obviously, I hadn't remembered everything yet because I had no idea what he was talking about. But Emlyn relaxed, a furrow between his brows.

"He's family."

"My brother," Harvey agreed, a fresh wave of tears rushing down his cheeks before he aggressively wiped them away.

"Does that mean you have two?" I asked, looking through the tree canopy and wincing when the pain shattering my head grew worse, dragging with it memories—the five of us getting trashed in a dingy pub; brawling over a flippant dare until Wane's shadows broke us apart; rough mornings soothed by Wane's patient stare, understanding words, and a fresh pot of tea; waking up in the middle of the night to his screams; carefully avoiding any talk of Cassander Locke because even the name could trigger Wane until he shut down, utterly motionless inside his cocoon of darkness.

I panted through gritted teeth, the pain like an anvil striking my skull. I completely missed Harvey's response.

Emlyn gripped my shoulder, squeezing, grounding me more than I knew I needed. I pulled the shards of my head back together until I could think for a minute.

"Thanks," I rasped, meeting his sharp blue eyes. Intelligent eyes that saw and knew too much. I knew that usually pissed me off, but right now I was glad for his wisdom and calm. Glad someone else could take charge, because I wanted to curl up and whimper in misery.

No. What I really wanted was for Haley to wake up, wrap her arms around me, rest her head on my chest, and tell me, in visceral detail, exactly how we'd kill the ones who did this to us.

It had to be Locke, didn't it? Did he kill us and wipe Wane from our memories before he buried us?

And if he did, did that mean he was the one who brought us back, too?

My head pounded worse; I gritted my teeth and decided to stop thinking for a while. It only hurt anyway.

"I don't ... know him," Harvey murmured when I met his eyes. "The master."

"Wynvail," I corrected. "You don't have a master anymore. And never again."

Harvey smiled. Even though his head had to be blazing agony like mine, he smiled, and nodded. "No master. But I remember him … following us. We called him the hunter."

"Haley said that," Emlyn murmured, running his thumb over her knuckles. "When she was bitten. She said the hunter's coming for us."

"Wane is … my brother," Harvey went on, a furrow in his bronze brow as he struggled for words. "I know Wane. Wynvail? No. Only hunter."

"So you think he lied?" I asked in a hiss. My magic spiked, wanting to come out to play, to suffocate the life out of anything and everything in revenge for what had been done to us.

Harvey shook his head, clutching his skull. "Hard … to remember."

Emlyn grumbled his agreement.

"I think—he is my brother," Harvey panted, his silver eyes pained, body locked tight. "I never knew. Only Wane."

"So your dickhead father kept him from you?" I guessed. Maybe he locked him in another basement. Or maybe *he* was the shining, golden child who'd never been locked away to begin with. "How did he find us when we came back? We died, but all I remember is waking up in the tunnels."

They both nodded. It was the same for them; we'd had this conversation a hundred times, but this was the first time we'd used words instead of guttural grunts and growls.

"We need to find that bastard and torture the truth out of him," I snarled, my head filling with pretty, bloody pictures. I didn't know if Haley would let me; he was her mate, after all. Unless he'd lied about that, too.

But he'd found us unerringly in that town. Because he used the bond to find her?

Too many questions made my head hurt. I groaned and bent over again, laying kisses on Haley's cheeks.

"I don't want to hurt her," Emlyn said after a long stretch of silence. His gaze was on her arm where her sleeve had rolled up, her new ink concealing the curse mark but not entirely. And we all knew it was still there.

"We'll find a way to stop it," I swore. The alternative made me want to throw up. "This Adhiti must know something. We're halfway to the fucked up caves—" or whatever they were called "—so we might as well continue. Find out how she survived losing her mates."

Because it felt like I'd *barely* survived losing mine. Now she was back, I could think clearer, but there would always be a base, animalistic part of me that remained. The fighting pits had changed me; the tunnels and darkness and *mistreatment* had changed me. I wanted to inflict my own cruelty on people more than ever. The world deserved to hurt for what it had done to me.

"Haley?" Harvey asked abruptly, leaning forward when she blinked, like she could see us above her. "Sugarplum?"

Her back arched, the only warning before she began to convulse so viciously she almost bucked off my lap and over the side of the platform.

"Hold her close," Emlyn growled, reaching for her. "This happened before. It will stop, but—"

"What?" I demanded, gathering my mate close and trapping her arms against her sides, her whole body jerking against me. Harvey curved his hand around the back of her head, pressing her still against my shoulder. I'd wanted her close, but not like this. Never like this.

Bile crawled up my throat. I really was going to be sick.

"She bleeds," Emlyn finished, rupturing my breathing into a panicked mess.

Bleeding wasn't good. What if she had serious, irreversible damage? What if—what if we lost her?

"Don't even think about leaving me," I gasped to her, my

voice caustic and sharp. "I expressly forbid it, and I can promise you won't enjoy what I'll do to you as punishment." Not like she usually enjoyed my punishments.

She said nothing. My hands shook where I clutched her to me.

"Hales," Emlyn murmured, pressing close so she was surrounded by all three of us. "It's okay. We're right here."

When blood rolled from her eyes, I fucking *lost it.*

Outwardly, I kept as still as possible, my body quivering with visceral panic I couldn't shut down. Inside, I was a cyclone of rage and terror. Whoever had done this to her—death wasn't good enough for them. They deserved far, far worse.

"You're gonna be fine," I ground out through gritted teeth, my magic flaring when she convulsed harder, a choked sound in her mouth. "Emlyn, open her mouth; make sure she isn't swallowing her tongue."

He did as I ordered, and I realised he was shaking too. We all were.

Harvey brushed the blood off her face, murmuring to her in a mix of growls and words, promises to keep her safe, to never let anything happen to her. There were gentle whispers claiming her as his, swearing he was hers too.

I reached out to her with my soul, an instinctual response, and flinched away from the ragged mess that stretched between us. The bond was intact, but *barely.* A single gleaming thread was all that kept it from collapsing, new but frayed already. All the rest had decayed.

I gritted my teeth and forced myself on, not caring how dangerous it was with such a degraded tether.

I couldn't stop until I found her, until I knew she was okay.

When I reached her soul on the other end of the thread, it took all my concentration not to recoil from the blistering heat of her pain. She was here, all around me, and she was breaking.

I'm right here, my rose. I'm here with you. You're gonna get out of this, I fucking swear it. You're not the only one who remembers him; we're gonna get Wane back. But you can't leave us, you hear me? Come back to us, and we'll find Wane.

Outside my soul, in my body, I could hear the roar of Harvey's and Em's panic, but it echoed dully, all my focus on the woman I felt so close but too fucking far. It was her soul around me, cut through with so many cracks it was a wonder she hadn't collapsed entirely. It was rage and stubbornness that held her together. And a violent, defiant love.

I stroked my soul against hers, and jumped when I heard her voice—echoing from far away, like we were shouting across a black ocean.

An ultimatum? Really, Malakai?

If it gets you to wake up and come home to us, yeah, I'll drop a fucking ultimatum.

Only silence answered me, and the echo of my own voice. My hands shook,

So are you coming home or what, my rose? I demanded, unable to soften my storm of fury and panic here with her. She'd always seen me exactly as I was, and I'd always been able to be myself with her. Completely and unreservedly.

I remember him here, she replied, fainter—weak. Afraid. *What if I forget when I wake up?*

We remember him too, Haley. You won't forget. I won't let you.

A shudder went through the soul around me, and even though I was blind, only able to sense her, I felt her approach. I knew her soul as well as my own; I'd sense her anywhere, in any realm.

After you, my night.

Relief erupted so powerfully it was like a silver star lighting up the darkness. I retreated into my own body in a rush, gasping as I came back to awareness. My whole body trembled with barely concealed rage, my teeth grinding so viciously I was in danger of chipping one. Shit, I needed to control my emotions.

My arms were still around Haley; she was still clutched close to me, Harvey bracing her head. The whole exchange had taken moments.

I tightened my arms around her, a silent command for her to make good on her word, and my shoulders slumped when she sucked in a hoarse gasp. She slumped against me, blood smearing across my throat as she panted.

"Haley?" Emlyn demanded, his eyes wide and bearded face drawn. "Are you okay? Please talk."

She groaned, which seemed to be the best she could offer.

Harvey cried again, but this time it was a sob so vicious he couldn't hold it back. I reached out and hooked him closer until I could hold them both; Emlyn took the hint and wrapped his arms around us, too.

"I want," Haley panted, "to slap you—for the—ultimatum. But I'm too tired."

"Noted," I murmured, and kissed her temple, relief weakening me so badly I slumped into Emlyn. It devoured my rage until the only thing left was shaky relief. I remembered her. I *knew* her. She was here, home, back with me.

She tipped her head back to look at us—and screwed her eyes shut. "You've still got too many eyes."

"That's the venom," I murmured, stroking a hand up and down her back, wet hair tickling my knuckles. Well, I stroked as far as my weak limbs would allow, which was approximately three inches. "It'll fade."

"Ugh," she groaned, and tucked her face back against my shoulder.

A moment later, all her weight hit me and I grunted. Emlyn supported us, thank gods, or we'd have tumbled off the platform. I let weakness take hold of me and slumped into him. He was my brother, too. Family, who'd been there for me through good days and bad weeks, through peace and chaos. He'd seen me throw up after a night of heavy drinking; seen me as weak as a kitten, covered in sweat when I caught *demon's fiend;* fuck, he'd seen my cock as we both pleasured our mate. It was a surprise to learn I didn't just trust him because we were bonded by the pit, but because he earned it.

Memories I didn't even know were missing flowed back into me, and I didn't fight the pain this time. I passed out, and knew I was safe with my mate and my family around me.

CHAPTER THIRTY-TWO

HALWEN

*H*atred and longing circled my dreams, taunting me with the truth. Wynvail wasn't my mate. Or at least he never had been before I died. Had someone forced a bond between us, or had I just never realised the hunter who tried to murder us and capture Wane was my soulmate?

I'd never heard of a mate bond being faked, and Wynvail was a cunning, powerful dick but he wasn't *that* powerful. The only reason he was able to compel alphas was because some big, scary bad guy gave him the ability. And it wasn't like I had much chance to feel a mate bond when he was firing knives and arrows at us and setting our safe houses ablaze.

In my dreams, I was in the house, my favourite home. I sensed him, felt the rush and pound of his blood, and felt the hatred and longing too. He'd kept out of reach that time, almost like he knew we'd get away. The sick bastard loved the chase; he probably let us go on purpose.

But it wasn't Wynvail who found us in Iarlon, or chased us to the Damned Realm. That was all Cassander Locke.

"Stop making excuses for him," I snapped at myself. "He kidnapped your mates, locked them in tunnels, encouraged his guards to torment them, and forced them to fight to the death."

He was no hero. He wasn't redeemable. He was a monster.

And I was tired of dreaming of him.

"I want to dream of Wane," I growled at my own subconscious, waiting for the burning house and garden full of assailants to fade. But it didn't.

Wane, my tortured mate, my living shadow.

He'd been traumatised and haunted by his childhood when I knew him. Some days he could go into the basement to grab a bottle of wine; others he stared at it in abject terror, remembering all the ways he'd been hurt while locked away.

Where was he? I knew he was out there. If the others were reborn decades ago, Wane must be too. But why wasn't he *with* them? I was glad he hadn't been trapped in Alphaven too, but something told me where he was was far, far worse.

I remembered the dark mirror that brushed my soul when I broke down trying to find Em. That was *Wane.* I remembered *everything* now; I knew the timid, agonised brush of his soul, and I knew the fire of rage that lived there too. He was with me in my lowest moment. He gave me his strength, and helped me get back to my feet to continue the search.

"Show me Wane," I growled at my dream.

"Why are you making me dream of this *asshole?*" I growled as the scene shifted to one of the first safe houses I'd stayed with the guys. Bricks had come through the window, followed by mercs and assassins and finally *him*, smirking and stunning and repulsive.

He'd had his hands in his coat pockets, not a weapon in

sight. He didn't need them when his smug smile was a weapon in itself.[1]

In my dream, I drew a knife, testing the weight of it in my palm, and looked Wynvail right in his smug silver eyes. I threw the dagger, end over end, and knew it was a sure hit.

I matched his smirk.

When it sank into his chest, driving into his heart, I woke up with a gasp.

"Sugarplum," Harvey said, jumping in surprise when I pushed up from bed—ah, I mean the terrifying leaves and branches strung across a too-high tree.[2]

"Hey," I croaked, making a face at the gross taste in my mouth and rubbing my crusty eyes. "How long was I asleep?"

"Ten hours," he replied, sounding so normal that I didn't notice anything was off for a moment.

"Ten hours!" I yelled, shooting up until I could see him better—and propping my back against the tree because I didn't want a broken neck. "Ten fucking hours!"

"You needed rest," he replied, watching me closely, his expression rapt as he watched me.

He was rumpled and sexy in his blue shirt and leather trousers, damp fabric clinging to his toned body. His long hair was as messy as ever, his sculpted face familiar, but his chin was newly stubbled. I wanted to lick him.

"You might have forgotten, but you were bitten by a hyaeni demon and infected with its venom." His eyes glimmered with a familiar brightness, his voice dry.

"I..." I stared at him. It took me another moment to figure it out. "You're talking!"

His mouth flicked up on one edge and he lifted his arm in an invitation, wrapping it around me when I snuggled up to him.

Fuck, the heat and press of his body to mine was unbelievable, his arm settling heavily around me and making my eyes heavy-lidded.

"I remember some things. Not everything. Some words ... I can't remember."

I tilted my head so I could kiss his stubbled jaw. "It'll come back. You need to be patient with yourself."

"Like you're patient?" he fired back, not missing a beat.

I groaned. He had a point. "How do you feel?"

Harvey paused for a moment, considering his word choice. "Murderous."

I stroked a hand down his wing, resting my head on his shoulder. "Yeah. I know the feeling. We—I—" I sighed, rubbing my face. "As soon as we find Adhiti and figure out how she got herself back after her soul splintered, we need to set a trap for Wynvail."

It shouldn't be hard, given he was obsessed with me.

"Then we torture the truth out of him and find where he's hidden Wane."

Harvey stiffened, a catch in his breath. "He's alive; I can feel him. I don't know how."

"So can I," I assured him, stroking up and down his feathers. "We'll find him, and kill anyone who stands in our way."

A soft breath puffed over my neck, stirring the damp hairs there.[3] "You didn't change. Killing is still your answer to everything."

"Because it *fixes* everything," I defended myself, soaking up his warmth and pushing off the dark dreams. "Name one time when murder made things worse."

"When you killed that guy who scammed you in Jast," Harvey huffed, adjusting me until I was astride him and he could cup my face in both hands. "His sons hunted us for a whole week."

"Until Kai and I killed them, thus solving the problem," I replied slowly, like he was missing the point.

He smirked, resting his forehead against mine and brushing the softest, sweetest kiss to my lips. "No killing unless it's necessary."

"Fine," I agreed. We'd just have differing definitions of the word *necessary.* "So where are my other two idiots?"

I could almost feel them, as if the bond had begun to heal by remembering Wane. Or I could just be deluding myself.

"Checking the ground is clear," Harvey answered, his words brushing my lips and sending a flash of heat through my body. "So we're ready to go back to Iarlon when you're healed."

He paused, waiting knowingly.

I ground my teeth, shaking my head and pulling away from him. "No fucking way."

"I warned them you'd say that," he agreed, amused. His eyes sparkled with some of his old mischief. It was tainted and darker, but there, defiant, all the same. "And I'm with you on this, Sugarplum. We need to know how this woman kept her..."

His jaw clenched when he couldn't think of the word. I kissed the sharp edge until it unclenched.

"If she has answers, we'll find them," I swore to him.

I kissed his cheek and leaned over the platform. It took me a few seconds to spot Malakai stalking through the trees. Emlyn flew high above, his red feathers catching my eye.

"Get back here, bastards. We need to have a little chat."

CHAPTER THIRTY-THREE

I won the debate, like we all knew I would. Mostly because we had no guarantee their feral nature wouldn't return and we *needed* answers from Adhiti, but partly because I was spoiled and they were weak for me.

No hyaeni demons cornered us the rest of the trek across the plains and along the river that fed into the sea on the south-western edge of Hell. The ocean ended abruptly, like water in a glass. I stared at it with a twist in my belly, unease crawling down my spine. It just *ended.*

"Weird," Kai muttered, giving the water a shifty look, curling inked hands tighter around his backpack.

"There," Emlyn said, ignoring the flat edge of the ocean. "That's the cave entrance. There's only one. Good."

Yeah, wouldn't that be typical? There'd be more than one cave in this part of Hell and we'd end up trapped in the wrong damn one.

"We need to stick together in there," Kai said seriously, transferring his glare to the cave, his magic rippling in the air. "No one goes off to do something stupid or heroic."

"Why are you looking at me?" I demanded, scowling back at him.

"Stupid and heroic are in the dictionary under Halwen Vakahara."

I gave him the middle finger. "I'll behave if *you* do."

"What's my incentive?" he asked with a slow grin, taking a fluid step towards me and brushing my hip with a tendril of magic.

"We're about to go into a cave with a dangerous cost to pay," Harvey cut in, raising his eyebrow at us. "Could you save the flirting for later?"

"Depends," Kai replied before I could. He hooked his arm around my back and tucked me into his side, not seeming to care that I was covered in weapons and highly uncomfortable to hold right now. "What's my incentive?"

Emlyn groaned, rubbing a hand down his beard.

"Shut up and get in the cave," I huffed.

"See, even that sounds sexy," Kai muttered. "How could you turn me on at a time like this, my rose?"

"Me? What did I do?"

He gestured fiercely at my dusty leathers, the sweaty hair I'd pulled into a braid, and my scowling face.

"Yeah, I'm still missing the point," I replied flatly.

"You are *devastating* right now, Halwen," he groaned, reaching down to adjust himself.

I gave him a look that certified him insane, and turned my attention to Emlyn. "I'm walking with you, Em. These two crazies can have each other."

He laughed, but there was a pleased glint in his eyes he couldn't hide. I caught his hand as we walked towards the caves. Sure, we'd need to draw weapons soon but there was nothing wrong with a little hand holding.

Emlyn angled a grey wing around me, casting a tense look over the cliff face we approached, the cave mouth dark and uninviting. The ambience screamed, *don't come inside or you'll be murdered, skinned, and turned into a fashion accessory.*

"How's your head?" Emlyn murmured, casting his worried stare over me next.

"Incredible, thanks for asking," I replied quickly. "World-shattering or so I'm told. You'd have a more expert opinion than me, though."

He barked a loud laugh that shook his whole chest, and my heart did a strange little flip-flop.

"When we get out the other side," I added in a purr, brushing my wing against his, "I'll demonstrate so you can verify my claims."

He hooked me closer, his mouth brushing my temple. "I'll hold you to that, mate. And if you're good in these caves, I'll demonstrate my own technique."[1]

"I love you," I blurted, the words too big and demanding to keep on my tongue.

"I love you, Hales," he replied in a sigh, his eyes creasing with a smile. "I remember us now. All the years I lost in the fighting pit—I remember them."

My happiness soared, but there was panic, too.

"What is it?" he asked, missing nothing. He scanned our surroundings and checked Kai and Harvey were following—they were, while bickering amongst themselves.

"I don't want you to forget me again, Em."

"Adhiti will have answers," he assured me, pressing another kiss to my head. "Don't worry; I won't give up a single memory without a bloody, gruesome fight."

My heartrate settled. "Good."

I began to say something else, but a shadow fell over us. The cliff. The cave that would demand blood or a worse, unthinkable price.

When fear tried to take hold, I reached out to Wane, spearing my soul across an even greater distance than before.

But he was there, furious and suffering and—scared. He was *terrified*.

He tried to push me away, but he was too weak, and with all my memories back and no agony splitting my head, I was stronger. I held on, and felt every strike of pain that cut him apart, felt blades carve into his skin, felt his soul flinch as—as someone cut into his shadows.

I gasped, horror making me shudder and giving Wane enough of a foothold to kick me out. I staggered on the rocks near the cave, staring at nothing, gasping for breath.

"What?" Emlyn demanded, grasping my shoulders. "What is it?"

Kai and Harvey raced for us, but before they could catch up—before Harvey could hear—I whispered, "Someone's torturing Wane. We need to hurry, Em. No more fucking about; we get into this place, get answers, and get out. Wane needs us."

CHAPTER THIRTY-FOUR

The entrance to the Wailing Caves was dark and long, and filled with still, ominous water. I couldn't tell if it was just the cave's dim ambience, but the river looked pure black. The last thing I wanted was to go anywhere near that water. It stank, waves of rot and decay choking the cave entrance, like the river was littered with carcasses of everyone who'd been stupid enough to come here before us.

I covered my mouth and nose with the sleeve of my jacket, but nothing masked the disgust in my eyes as I scanned the deep river that led through an archway into darkness. The four of us stood on a shallow ledge that dead-ended a few paces ahead.

"We're supposed to go into the river," Kai said what we were all thinking, his displeasure clear.

"No," Harvey complained instantly, lifting his wings high so the lower feathers didn't touch the damp rock.

I pointed at him, nodding. "Very well said. I could not agree more."

"All he said was *no*," Kai pointed out, shooting me a sharp look. Jealousy?

"And it's a good fucking point. I'm all in with the *no.*"

"There's no other way in," Emlyn rumbled, moving closer to rest his hand on my shoulder. "We need Adhiti; we need to go through the water."

Horror rocked me when he dropped his backpack, reaching for his jacket.

"Em, don't!" I pushed his jacket back up his shoulders with frantic fingers. "Fuck this, it's not worth it. *Anything* could be in that damned river; I'm not letting you risk yourself."

"Wait," Harvey barked suddenly enough that we all looked at him. His voice rang through the cave, so familiar it made my breath hitch. He was talking, he remembered me, he was *back.* "Remember what the queen said. There's a price."

"Which we're not paying," I snapped, my hackles rising and panic swallowing all sentimentality. My wings bristled.

"She said blood," Harvey reminded us, lifting his hand. Before I could stop him or even realise what he intended to do, he raked the sharp claw at the apex of his wing over his palm until blood bloomed.

"Harvey!" I hissed, launching at him, grabbing his biceps. "Are you insane? Do you have any idea how bad it is to cut your palm? Couldn't you cut your forearm like a normal person?"

The stare he levelled at me said, *I'm a healer. I'll heal.*

"Yes, well," I huffed, squeezing him hard. "You're mine, so you're not allowed to hurt yourself."

"I'll be fine," he replied, his voice warming several degrees. He pressed a kiss to my cheekbone and held his bleeding palm over the river, squeezing until it flowed freely.

"Idiot," Kai muttered, shaking his red head.

Harvey flashed him a sharp look—the same glare that had started countless arguments and play fights over the years. Some real fights, too. "I don't see you having any better ideas."

"How is bleeding into a river going to help us cross it? What are you expecting, stepping stones to rise from the—"

He cut off with a soft curse.

"No fucking way!" I breathed, spinning to face the tunnel archway Kai was staring at, his pale face slack. "Oh. That's kind of anticlimactic. You built me up for stepping stones, Malakai."

A small wooden rowboat floated down the black river towards us, minus the rowers. There was a thick layer of lichen all over it, and no reasonable way it should be putting its way towards us.

"That's not creepy at all," I murmured, watching it bob unerringly to the ledge we stood on.[1]

"I'll get in first," Emlyn offered, his big shoulders hunched as he gave us a tense look. It was a mix of *be careful* and *behave.*

"Let me see that," I murmured to Harvey to distract myself as Em climbed into the boat. I caught his hand and winced at the deep gash down the centre of his palm. I had bandages in my pack, but there was no hope of me finding them when it was so full and we had so little time.

I grabbed the vest I wore under my shirt and ripped off a strip at the hem, gritting my teeth at the effort.[2]

"I'm fine," Harvey complained as I bound his hand, tawny wings ruffling and light catching the iron on the tips of feathers.

"Minus all the nerve damage," Kai remarked, brushing my side as he edged past and climbed, carefully, into the boat beside Emlyn.

"Any idea how to steer this thing?" I asked when Harvey nudged me to the boat next. I eyed it warily, half expecting it to zoom away before I could climb inside. But it stayed still as I slid off the ledge, my heart pounding until my feet touched solid wood.

My legs instantly wobbled, my weight lopsided.

"Fuck!" I shrieked, staring into the black, endless river. My wings snapped out at my sides, my arms spread too, and Emlyn threw his arms around my legs.

But gravity refused to be denied.

I screamed, the noise drowned out by my mates' shouting as I plunged into the river.

Icy water bit through my clothes into my skin, and my head dropped under the water for a terrifying moment. I kicked my legs and forced myself back to the surface, my head tipped back as I sucked down air. But my backpack was like an anchor, heavy and deadly.

"Haley!" Kai yelled.

"Take my hand," Emlyn calmly ordered, closer than I expected.

I couldn't see anything but the black water that rocked into my face, let alone where his hand was. I fought the pull of my pack, panting, reaching out blindly.

A rough breath of relief left my lungs when a strong hand gasped my wrist and heaved my chest out of the water. *Thank fuck.* Even without the bag, my wings dragged me down, my feathers heavy and soaked through. I wasn't designed for water. But Emlyn had me; I was okay now.

I threw my other hand up and grabbed the edge of the boat, dragging myself up another few inches. But the moment my chest hit the wood, something slimy and strong closed around my ankle. I didn't get a chance to cry out before it dragged me back down.

CHAPTER THIRTY-FIVE

a shocked scream ripped up my throat as I plunged back underwater, dark liquid shoving through my open mouth until I choked.

Down, down I was pulled, until I couldn't see the bottom of the boat, until pressure made my lungs seize and I had to fight the urge to breathe. I wriggled out of my backpack, hating to give up the supplies, but I had no chance of fighting if I was weighed down by it.

Something swarmed below, at the bottom of the river, blacker even than the water. My heart lurched in my chest, panic clawing at me when gleaming green eyes blinked at me. Ten, twenty, *fifty* pairs of them. Whatever those things were, one of them had grabbed me. And was hauling me to my death.

I don't think so, fuckers.

I sank into the pool of magic I finally had access to, and my awareness *erupted* with heartbeats and noise. It was so brutal that I flinched. I'd been shoving it down all day, the thump of my mates' blood threatening to drive me insane if I let it. But now I welcomed the vibrations, the clamour. There weren't fifty of these creatures, more like thirty. Whatever these things were, they had three eyes.

Three eyes! It was very *all the better to see you with, dear...*

I slashed my hand through the water as the creature dragged me down, down. Power blasted up through my chest and down my arm, my own blood pumping. It felt damned good to have my magic back, to let it tear free and slam into the bodies of my enemies.

I felt like myself again as I made each of their eyes explode, and then sank into their bloodstream, quickening the flow until veins burst and the lights of their eyes blinked out.

Oh, I missed this.

The drowning was less fun, though. My whole chest hurt and fear made me shaky no matter the rush of pleasure killing gave. I tried to wrestle myself out of the creature's slimy hands, fighting so hard that when its grip released—and its eyes and blood vessels exploded—I shot sideways so suddenly I screamed.

But I was free. I was drowning, weakening, but free.

Blood filled the dark water, muddying my vision as I kicked my heavy legs, hauling myself towards the surface. I had no idea where the boat was. I couldn't see anything but dark water and then—a blacker shape, coming towards me so fast I couldn't get out of the way.

I tried to flop out of this new creature's path, but an arm lashed out to hook me closer and—Harvey. It was *Harvey.*

Relief made me slump, my lungs screaming for air and limbs going strangely numb. I didn't fight as Harvey wrenched me tight to his body and swam upwards, cutting powerfully through the water.

This time when I broke through the water, my gasps were frantic and each one hurt as it scraped down my throat. I coughed up water, tasting kelp and blood, and started to shake uncontrollably.

Harvey pushed me over the lip of the boat, and I collapsed into it in a wet, miserable heap. Hands patted my face, words meating my ears in a jumble of sounds.

I panted, my whole chest thumping with a deep pain. For endless minutes I just stared at the dark roof of the cave, processing my near death.

"Haley," Emlyn demanded harsher, stroking wet hair out of my cold face.

"Mmn," I groaned, my throat sore.

Harvey heaved himself into the boat with a grunt—and as if it had been waiting for him, the hunk of possessed wood shot through the water like a throwing knife.

"Never again," I croaked, and tried to remember why I'd ever thought this whole thing was a good idea. I swore the cave pulsed, eager to swallow me back down to its depths where I'd never be found.

For my mates. So I don't lose them again. So they don't forget me.

I shook all over, but I heaved myself off the bottom of the boat and slumped into a spot between Emlyn and Kai.

I clung to Em's big arm, digging my cold fingers into the mix of squishiness and muscle.[1]

A soft sensation brushed my soul, making me jump. I reached for it desperately, my soul crashing into Wane's like a shooting star.

I wanted to talk to him, wanted to hear his voice, wanted to hold him in my arms and know no one could ever hurt him again. Instead, I wrapped my soul around his like he'd done for me when I lost Em, and held on until he inevitably faded from me.

"Fuck!" Harvey screeched, grabbing me in a vicious hold when the boat shot suddenly faster, carrying us into the dark mouth of the river tunnel I'd glimpsed from the ledge. "Slower!"

The boat didn't listen this time, spiriting us through the dark like it was its own stubborn, living beast.[2]

"Duck!" Kai yelled when we sped out of one tunnel and around a bend in the river towards a dangerously low bridge.

I flattened myself to the boat, my teeth gnashing. How was there a bridge and a whole river system inside a damn cliff? Sometimes I really hated Hell.

The scent of blood intensified the further we travelled, until it overpowered even the rotting scent of the river *and* whatever the fuck those things were that had tried to abduct me. Eat me? I shuddered, risking lifting my head a couple inches to take a peek when the boat began to slow.

"Where the fuck are we?" Kai hissed, teeth bared as he sat up.

"Far from the cliff. We're travelling beneath the sea," Emlyn grumbled, hooking me closer as I sat up and stared at the cave we glided into. The only way in or out was the tunnel we just came down.

The cave was a giant, overturned stone bowl covered in bioluminescent moss. It glowed blue and green, casting the wide space in an eerie glow—and rendering the short, curvy woman waiting on the riverbank in gleaming teal.

"Remember the price we're supposed to pay," Emlyn murmured to us. "Give nothing away."

I swallowed, shooting Kai a warning look. If he promised her our firstborn, I'd murder him where he stood.[3]

"Haley, you speak," Em added, ignoring the wide-eyed look I shot his way.

"Why is it always me? I spoke up in the palace, and look how well that turned out."

"We got out alive," Harvey replied, watching the woman—presumably Adhiti—as the boat approached the riverbank. "We'll be fine here, too."

Neither of us reminded him that we'd got out of the palace fine only to be murdered an hour later.

I scanned the cave, paranoid that Cassander Locke was still alive and stalking us. But there were no shadows in this place at all, only the bright silver-green glow from the moss around us.

"Visitors," Adhiti said in a quiet voice when the boat bumped the river's edge. The scent of blood intensified, making me gag. Harvey turned his face away, his wings ruffling in disgust. "Why did it take you so long? I felt you enter the cave an hour ago."

"There was an incident," I answered after a pause, my mates shooting me matching looks, insisting I speak.

Adhiti watched us with eagle eyes, her irises almost glowing a bright gold that was striking against her long lashes and her umber skin. She wore—or rather attempted to wear—two swathes of filmy black fabric embroidered with gold images. Moons in all their phases, swans, and lions. The stitching was delicate, not opaque enough to hide anything. All her bits were on proud display; I tried not to look.

She didn't *look* intimidating, but there was no denying that every single one of my instincts bleated in warning. *She could kill us. Easily.*

"I know why you're here," she said, scanning each of our faces, some sadness churning in her eyes when they returned to me. Unease twisted my stomach. We shouldn't have come here. "Come ashore, and we'll talk about how I endured the curse of losing my mates."

I exchanged a glance with Kai, Em, and Harvey. None of us were eager to get out of the boat.

"I know all about that prophecy on your back, too," Adhiti added, a knowing gleam in her eyes as she offered a smile and beckoned us out of the boat.

Kai practically propelled himself out and reached back for

me. He had his priorities *way* out of order. What was the point in worrying about a grand prophecy when we were all going to kill each other in two weeks? I'd be dead before the prophecy ever happened.

I let out a sigh and clasped his hand, following him. I'd hardly leave Kai alone on the riverbank. Emlyn and Harvey climbed out after me, scowls on their faces and their bodies so close to mine.

"I knew you were coming," Adhiti told us, her golden eyes following the boat as it jerked into sudden motion and drove back the way we'd come.

My heart beat faster.

Unease crawled closer, draping itself over my back.

"I'm his eyes and ears, you see," she told us, her eyes on the boat as it disappeared from view, her voice soft and mournful now. "I never wanted you to come here," she told us, looking directly at me so there was no doubt who she was talking to.

"*Whose* eyes and ears?" Emlyn asked, right on the edge of a growl. He angled himself in front of me, casually enough to look like a coincidence.

A louder, deeper growl answered him and I jumped, spinning towards the source of the sound. Like they'd rehearsed it —or like they remembered the protocol from our past—my mates stepped around me, Emlyn at my front, Kai at my back, and Harvey at my left. There was an empty space on my right, where Wane usually stood. I lifted my hand, reaching for my power to spear it at the woman and—slamming a block instead of grasping Adhiti's blood. My head rattled at the impact, pain snapping through me.

She was immune to my magic. Of course she was.

"Shit," I breathed when I realised the source of the booming growl—not a creature, but a giant boulder.

It rolled across the entrance we'd sailed through, and trapped us in the cave with Adhiti.

CHAPTER THIRTY-SIX

*S*ee, this was why I hadn't felt upbeat about the Wailing Caves. With a name like that, they were *obviously* going to be full of malice, danger, and probable death. We were idiots for coming.

"What do you want?" I demanded, turning to face Adhiti. "And answer Emlyn's question; who the fuck is your big, bad boss?"

Adhiti sighed, batting wavy hair out of her face so she could peer at me. "So much power in you, Halwen, so much potential wasted."

"Fuck you," I hissed, releasing my blood magic and drawing one of my long daggers. I flicked a look at my mates. "Grab her. I'll get my answers the good old fashioned way."

We'd figure out a way out later.

"There's no need for violence," Adhiti sighed, her voice so small and unassuming. "I can tell you everything you want to know."

"Then why lock us in here with you?" I asked, teeth bared. I snapped my wings tight to my back, taking a long breath until calm flowed over me. I was soaked through, freezing, and freaked out, but the calm was always there, waiting to hide all my panic, to help me fight. "Not a very smart idea," I added, my voice flatter, colder. "Given all my power and potential."

She shook her dark head, moving no closer, offering no response. Vague and annoying as hell.

"Fuck this," I muttered, and darted out of the gap in my protective circle, launching myself at Adhiti with the sharp edge of my knife.

I wouldn't actually kill her, but a little slash or two might encourage her to talk. "How did you get your mind back when you went feral?"

She didn't move out of the path of my knife, which was alarming enough that I froze before I could wound her. She made no move to protect herself. Cold sluiced down my spine, but maybe that was just from almost drowning. I took a step back.

"You're not in danger from me," Adhiti said, watching me and only me.

Kai raced past me, his tattoos winding around his body as he drew magic, two daggers in his hands. Emlyn and Harvey flanked me, but I didn't take my eyes off Kai as he ducked low and slashed Adhiti's calves.

She staggered back, but her expression didn't shift from strangely vacant sadness. She wasn't disturbed by her bleeding legs, didn't seem to feel the pain. My blood ran colder.

Blood...

Holy shit! I couldn't grasp hold of Adhiti's blood while it was in her body, but I felt it rush out of her in a torrent, and my breath caught. I tore magic up through me and seized hold of her blood, forcing my magic through the slashes on the backs of her legs and shooting like a disease through her blood stream.

"Now," Kai said, leaping back before she could grab him.

"Answer our questions, or my mate will make your guts explode."

He'd done it on purpose? I fucking loved him.

"You want to know how I survived losing my mates?" Adhiti gazed across the river, light speckling the surface from the glowing roof above. "I didn't. Or rather, Adhiti didn't. This body was feral when I found it, the previous owner completely insane. Possessing her was a mercy."

"In the water," Emlyn growled. "Now!"

I didn't question him. I sheathed my knife, grabbed Kai and Harvey, and pushed them off the ledge, diving into the river after them. The water rushed over my head, forcing up my nostrils, and I had a very unpleasant flashback to being dragged under in the first cave.

But my magic thrummed inside me like an eager fire, and the only heartbeats I felt in this cave were mine, my mates' and Adhiti's. Hers fluttered faster than ours, like a hummingbird's wings, and I tasted relief and despair in her blood. But there were no dark, hungry things waiting in the depths, so I counted myself lucky.[1]

I kicked my legs until my head burst through the water, and tightened my grip on her blood, squeezing, encouraging her veins to implode.

The real Adhiti—the ancient demon Lucifer knew—hadn't survived. She lost her mates, went feral, and then ... got possessed? I'd heard of demons possessing humans, and spirits possessing demons, but demons taking over other demons' bodies? It was unheard of.

What the fuck *was* this woman?

There was no salvation for me and my mates here, no answers. Adhiti—or whoever the fuck she was—was useless to us. So there was no reason to keep her alive.

"Down!" Harvey gasped.

A hand landed on my head, shoving me back underwater.

I spluttered, accidentally inhaling water, and I flipped ass over tit. A scream wanted to tear up my throat, but I locked my lips, holding onto the air, and flailed my wings until I turned right-way-up.

The river rocked like a storm-tossed ocean, a violent wave hurling me away from the bank as magic shook the water. Whose magic? What the fuck was happening?

I swore I heard wailing, low and harrowing, like the water itself was pleading for mercy as I was tossed carelessly through it. Voices cried, pleading for ... no, not pleading. Warning.

The mother ... run from the mother or he'll make you like us...

I shrieked by accident, choking on a mouthful of water. Disoriented, I slammed into a solid body. I knew it was Kai by the viciousness of the arms that came around me, leaving bruises with their grip.

He didn't let go for a second as the river crashed and rocked around us, magic shuddering through every drop of water until I could taste it on my tongue. I tried to kick my legs to carry us back, but Kai's fingers pressed into my stomach, refusing to let go.

I need to breathe, you possessive asshole.

When the water finally stilled and black spots flickered in my vision, unconsciousness close enough that it taunted me, Kai swam us back to the surface. I broke through, gasping down precious air, sick to death of being underwater.

The voices, the *wailing,* cut off instantly, but their effect remained, shaking through me in panic.

The mother. Was that who possessed Adhiti?

I panted, sucking down great breaths, and searched the room for my mates. Harvey crashed out of the river on the other side of the cave, near the giant boulder that had rolled into place and trapped us.

Emlyn ... Emlyn was on the ground before Adhiti.

Kneeling.

"Emlyn!" I yelled, throwing my arms through the water and swimming as fast as I could for the shore. "Hold on, I'm coming!"

Fuck, my throat was sore. Probably all the almost-drowning I'd done in the past two hours. I ignored the burning discomfort and swam harder, hauling my wings behind me, wet feathers and iron tips threatening to pull me back underwater. If the roof hadn't been so damn close, I'd have flown just to escape the water.

Kai swore and followed me.

"Can't ... hurt her," Emlyn growled, like he was fighting to get the words out. His dark head was bowed, his shoulders hunched under his clothes, and every taut line in his body spoke of pain or rage. Or both.

My own rage exploded at the sight of him forced to kneel, and a connection blazed into existence. My arms pumped through the water, but it wasn't the river I saw. It was the riverbank beneath me, the knees of my trousers covered in dust and dirt from the trek across Hell, and my hands—Emlyn's hands, strong and broad with one broken knuckle still healing—clenched in front of me.

From the corner of my eye— his eye—I saw red light stain the water, spreading like blood, and the soft breath Adhiti inhaled drew all my attention to her.

"She has his power," she breathed, almost to herself. "She can do it."

I felt my hold on Emlyn's soul slip, felt water rush up my own throat as I swam. Shit. I pushed strength at him, like Wane had given it to me. I gave him enough to shatter what-ever magical chains she'd used to freeze him, and slammed back in my body in time to hear Emlyn roar and surge up from the floor.

He grabbed Adhiti's shoulders, the woman looking

483

strangely frail. Why wasn't she fighting him? What the fuck was wrong with her? Even when I attacked her, she never hurt me. Never defended herself.

I breathed faster, each breath sharper, and hauled myself from the water when I reached the edge.

"Do what?" I panted, forcing my jelly legs to carry me to Emlyn. I stood beside him, not especially impressive backup. But my arm was glowing, my curse mark lit up with vivid crimson light. I drew my knife with my other hand for good measure, and didn't allow myself to think about the devastating possibility that my weapons might rust after being in the water so long.

"Your mates can't kill me," Adhiti—or whoever she was— replied, giving me a strangely unhostile look. "But you can."

I recoiled, grabbing Em and forcing him back a step. I didn't like the way she was speaking, didn't like her soft-spoken voice or the sadness in her strange eyes. I didn't trust people who didn't stab first, ask questions later.

Water splashed as Harvey and Kai hauled themselves out of the river, both soaking wet and pissed off. They flanked me and Emlyn with mean expressions that would make lesser women piss themselves. Adhiti didn't spare them a glance, didn't take her eyes off me.

"Your potential isn't wasted at all. You're exactly as I hoped you'd be," she said, a new light in her eyes. "I've been waiting for you for so long."

Kai hissed, deep in his throat. I sensed his power lashing out, but Adhiti didn't flinch. She didn't look away from me.

"Let us go," Harvey growled, his body shaking beside mine, the urge to shift too strong.

"Even you can't kill me, sun soul," Adhiti said in that strange sad tone. "If only you could."

I held my arm out, stopping Harvey and giving Adhiti a sharp look. "You want to die? Are you mad?"

"Old and mad and in so much pain," she sighed. I couldn't tell if she was agreeing or disagreeing. "That mark on your back brought you here."

I laughed, low and bitter and scared. "I came here for answers, because you were supposed to be feral and magically cured."

"And your mates are feral," Adhiti guessed, taking a step closer and ignoring the three matching snarls my mates unleashed. She smiled at me, her eyes unsettling as they never wavered. "Are they?"

"What?"

"They *were* feral, certainly," she agreed, taking another step. My hackles rose, wings twitching. "But are they now? Or have you cured them yourself?"

I shook my head. "No, they—"

"They were. But they are no longer. And there's no reason for them to be feral again, because you're reunited. And only death will tear you apart."

"Did we ask for a fucking riddle?" Kai snapped, pointing an iron blade at her. "Unlock the door, roll the damn stone back. Or I'll slit you from head to toe and let Harvey's beast eat your insides."

"Pass," Harvey muttered, sounding disgusted. Or insulted.

"It's not a riddle, it's a prophecy. Like the one on your back, granddaughter."

Silence rang for a moment, only shattered by my mates' explosions of noise.

"What?" I asked, so small it was drowned out. "What?"

"That's why you can kill me. You're my kin," Adhiti explained, taking another two steps, forcing us to back up. But the river rushed behind us, trapping us unless we wanted to jump back in the water.[2] "He makes me wear this, you know? It's hideous. Shameful." She picked at the sheer fabric that hid nothing from view. "He trapped me here, where I could never escape, and he sends men. Despicable men. He made me a whore when I defied him, and trapped me here so I would be killed by my great grandchild. The joke, as they say, is on him. I welcome death."

"I'm not going to kill you," I snapped, more freaked out with every word out of her mouth. My hands shook. The desperation in her voice and the misery in her eyes made my skin crawl, my stomach tight. "We shouldn't have come here."

"You were always going to come here. This is how it starts, don't you realise? This is how the end starts. This is how he dies."

"Enough," Harvey snarled, snapping a wing towards her to force her back.

But Adhiti—or *the mother*—did the opposite of what any sane, rational person would. She raced *towards* me, towards my snarling mates. Her eyes overflowed with apologies.

I threw my hands up to defend myself, to keep her away. My breaths came fast and sharp. I didn't know what was happening. There was a prophecy, we'd almost drowned, she wasn't feral, we were trapped, she was ... my family.

"Stay away from her," Kai hissed, trying to wrench me aside, but Adhiti threw herself at me before Kai could plunge us into the river. Bony fingers clutched my shoulders.

"Make him suffer," she breathed in my ear, her voice raspy but warm. "Make him regret every heinous act he ever committed."

I shook my head. What the hell was she talking about? Who was *he?*

"Thank you," she whispered. "You've ended my eternal torment."

"What? No, I haven't. I *haven't.*"

But cool, dry fingers wrapped around mine and—oh god, I didn't realise, I didn't mean to—

The knife in my hand. I'd lifted both my hands to protect myself. And she'd impaled herself on my blade.

He made me a whore when I defied him, and trapped me here so I would be killed by my grandchild.

"You can't be my great grandmother," I rasped, staring at her face, hating the relief written in every line. "I never knew you, never met you—"

"It's okay," she soothed, drawing her stomach away from my knife, not a flicker of pain on her face as the blade pulled free. Blood spilled down her body, darkening the sheer slips of fabric she wore. "I'm free."

He makes me wear this, you know?

"Who is he?" I asked in a rush, unable to tear my stare from the knife wound she'd inflicted on herself. "Who is he?"

"Did she hurt you?" Kai demanded, throwing Adhiti aside so he could grab me. I pushed him back, shaking my head as the woman crashed to her knees. If she wasn't lying, this woman was my only living family.

And I'd just killed her.

"Who is he?" I demanded, dropping to my knees, catching Adhiti before her face could smash into the ground. "Tell me."

She didn't answer.

I shook her shoulders, biting back a cry when her body slumped into mine, so suddenly heavy.

"No," I growled, ignoring the tears burning my eyes. "You have to tell me. If this is about my prophecy, if I'm supposed to kill this bastard, you have to *tell me!"*

"Haley," Emlyn said softly, kneeling beside me and gently taking Adhiti from my arms, laying her on her back on the riverbank. He closed her eyes and his throat bobbed. "If we hadn't come here … I'm so sorry."

"I don't even know her real name," I croaked, tears flowing freely now. "But I—I don't think she was lying."

"Neither do I," Emlyn replied, reaching for me.

487

I collapsed into him, sharp, broken breaths clawing up my throat. I had no family left. My dad died a hundred years and ten ago. My mother abandoned us on Earth, and was surely now dead. This woman was the only family I'd known in forever. And I killed her.

I threw the knife aside, watched it scatter over rock and sink into the water. I'd never been more glad that I didn't draw one of Kai's gifts. I couldn't bear to hold the weapon that killed my great grandmother ever again.

I killed my own family. Kin-killer. That's what I was, what I'd forever be.

"Guys," Kai said in a tight voice. "Is it just me or is the ground shaking?"

I swallowed the lump in my throat, shaking my head. I couldn't feel anything. Then again, my entire body was trembling so maybe I wouldn't notice.

"Fuck," Harvey breathed. "We need to leave."

"I'm not leaving her here," I snapped, twisting to glare at him. "You heard what she said. Some monster forced her to stay here and wear that outfit because he wanted to punish her. She hates this cave. Hated," I corrected, returning my stare to the woman I'd killed.

I didn't want to kill her. I'd killed so many people, but this? This was unbearable. The only family I had left.

But how did I have her left? If she was my grandmother, she'd have to be over a hundred years old. Either she was extremely long-lived, or the bastard who trapped her here had something to do with it.

"I'm going to find this bastard and eviscerate him," I hissed, breathing fast.

Ruthless hands hooked under my arms and tore me off the ground, trapping my body in cruel, unyielding arms when I fought.

"Stop!" Kai snapped. "Haley, stop. Look! Look around you."

Panting, teeth bared, I twisted my head—and stumbled back into Kai with a gasp. The cave was collapsing. Cracks sliced through the bioluminescent cave, but instead of light breaking through, there was only an empty, gnawing darkness.

"The whole cave's going to come down!" Harvey shouted, the whites of his eyes showing as he threw me a worried look. "Haley, can you use your magic to move the boulder?"

"My *blood* magic?" I demanded, my voice strangely flat.[3]

Something thrummed in my chest, a sharp knife of panic cutting through my soul, followed by harsh, determined reassurance. *I'm coming,* it said.

Now that I was watching the cave crack apart, I could feel the powerful tremors moving through the ground, making each fissure bigger, wider. Whatever was visible through the fissures wasn't a creeping darkness like Wane's; it didn't spill through. But it got bigger, got *closer,* and my heart pounded faster. Awareness prickled over my skin. Without being told, I knew that *thing* was lethal.

"Emlyn!" Kai yelled, his hands covering my ear to protect me from the worst of the shout. But why was he shouting for Em in the first place?

I struggled to free myself from his arms, but only succeeded in twisting enough to watch Emlyn plunge into the water, powerful arms carrying him through the river pool towards the boulder.

Magic shuddered around Kai, ink twisting around the arms holding me as he sent snakes at the boulder too, but it didn't budge. Emlyn growled, using all his strength, but even when more magic surged from Kai, the rock didn't roll out of place.

"I'm coming," Harvey yelled, kicking off the ground. Powerful wingbeats lifted wet hair off my shoulders, fluttering my own feathers. As more pieces of the ceiling fell, taking the glowing moss with it, the cave grew darker and darker.

"What about your other magic?" Kai asked, his lips by my ear. "That red glow from the curse mark isn't your blood magic."

"I don't know how to use it," I rasped, but I closed my eyes and sank into my bonds anyway, feeling for Em. I couldn't concentrate enough to feel his hands where they heaved against the boulder, but I sent a rush of strength at him anyway. He needed it more than me.

The world went strangely light around me, all the heaviness lifted out of it. *Hey, this is nice.*

"Haley!" Kai gasped when my knees buckled. "No, no, Haley, my rose, don't sleep. Stay with me."

I was fine. Wasn't I...?

My body was twisted around like a doll, and fingers pressed to my eyelids, prising them open.

"Very rude," I muttered, my vision hazy but Kai's sharp, pale face as familiar as my own heartbeat. "Pretty, though," I added, and patted his hair.

"It's moving!" Emlyn shouted, his voice distant. "Harvey, push there, yes!"

The grate of stone on stone was louder than I expected, and I flinched, full conscious slamming back into me and clearing out the slurring fuzziness.

"Oh gods," I gasped, watching the stone roll back into the wall and a whole new network of cracks tear through the ceiling, down the walls, and beneath the water lever.

Through the gap in the door, I saw them spread into the next chamber, and the next, and then continue out of sight. This whole *cliff* was going to come down, not just the Wailing Caves.

The screams I'd heard in the water before were louder

now, wailing for mercy, screaming warnings to *run, he's coming, he's coming.*

The cave shook again, a piece of the ceiling knocked free. Right above Emlyn.

"Emlyn!" I screamed, giving him enough warning to throw himself aside. But he didn't make it far, and the impact sent vicious waves through the water. I couldn't see him. Oh gods, I couldn't see him.

"Did it hit him?" I demanded, my voice shrill. "Is he hurt? *Emlyn!"*

"Fuck, I can't see. Can you fly, my rose?" Kai asked, tightening his arms around my waist.

I nodded, flapping my wings to catch air and rising three feet, then another three. But weakness tore through me faster than I'd expected, the world hazy again, and I screamed as we dropped back to the riverbank.

Kai threw out a hand, power making all the hairs on my body stand on end. Instead of hitting the solid ground, we fell into a squishy mound of magic and scales, and bounced, safe instead of broken.

"Sorry," I said in a small voice. Tears gathered in my eyes. I was useless. Em was hurt and I couldn't help.

Kai cradled the back of my head, pressing a kiss to my crown. "Not your fault, Haley. We'll be okay, we'll get out."

But Emlyn hadn't surfaced, and Harvey had dropped into the water to find him, and more of the cave collapsed around us. Huge chunks of stone crashed from the roof and walls into the river, sending ripples big enough to splash us on the banks.

"Emlyn!" I yelled, my voice breaking. "Please, please."

"He's here!" Harvey shouted, his voice distant and weak. I couldn't see them around the huge chunk of ceiling that had fallen. "But I can't carry him."

I tensed my legs, refusing to stay here when my mates

needed me. Even if I was weak and wrecked from drowning, from killing my family, I couldn't just stand here. If I died saving Em so fucking be it.

But I flinched back when the wall behind us exploded, showering bricks and dust around us.

Light flooded the cave, brighter and harsher than the moss's glow, and I shielded my eyes against the sudden stabbing in my eyeballs.

When I dropped my hand, I squinted through the dust in the air. It had fallen everywhere except for a perfect circle around us.

"Kai?"

"Not mine," he bit out, something like rage in his voice. He pushed me behind him, keeping me flush to his back.

"Mine," a familiar voice agreed, making my blood ice over. Cold, cultured, and arrogant.

I didn't need to look to know whose voice that was, but I couldn't stop my eyes seeking him.

"Wynvail," I hissed.

CHAPTER THIRTY-SEVEN

*a*dhiti's words echoed around my head. The man who trapped her here, forced her into revealing clothes she obviously hated, and sent people to do gods knew what to her each month ... was *my mate.*

"I knew you were a bastard, but *this?*" I shook my head, clenching my jaw when a wave of dizziness struck. I was too fucking weak for this. "You're a monster."

"Nothing you haven't called me before, honey. But let's save the insults for when you're safely out of this place, yeah?" There was something tight to his smooth voice, emotion barely repressed. It was there in the angry slash of his dark brows and his clenched jaw, though.

He strode closer, wearing a sharp white shirt and trousers, his shoes shiny and polished, and short, mahogany hair pushed back from his face. Like he could cover his ugliness with designer clothes.

"Go *fuck* yourself," I spat, and turned my back on him, scanning the water for Harvey and Em. "Piece of shit."

"I do love our terms of endearment," Wynvail replied without missing a beat.

"Stay the fuck away from her," Kai hissed, pressing me flush to his back, his body vibrating with rage.

"Oh, keep your hair on," Wynvail sighed. "I'm going to rescue your friends. Unless you'd rather they drowned."

"Don't touch them!" I pushed Kai aside, throwing myself at Wynvail and wishing I had the bone key so I could grow claws long enough to carve his black, rotten heart out. I grabbed his shirt, stopping him leaping into the river.

What would he do? Give us another curse? Trap them here like he'd trapped Adhiti? Or would he kill them, like he taunted he would in Alphaven?

"Really?" he asked, his voice flat. Bronze fingers travelled quickly down the buttons of his shirt, and before I could stop him, he tore himself free and jumped into the water.

I clenched my fist around his shirt, my whole body shaking.

"If they die, you die," he shouted as he cut through the water with broad, powerful strokes. I didn't look at the muscles moving in his back, didn't allow myself to stare at anything but the gleam of Harvey's hair when he dragged Em into view.

"Why isn't he moving?" I yelled, panic clawing through my chest. "Kai, get Wynvail with your snakes."

"On it," Kai said through gritted teeth, power booming through the air, lifting damp hair off my shoulders and sending a violent shudder down my spine. I wavered on my feet, blinking back dizziness.

I *hated* feeling helpless, hated being weak. But the second I kicked off the ground and flapped my wings, I'd fall back to the ground. I was useless. I could do nothing as Wynvail cut through the water towards my mates.

"What the fuck are *you* doing here?" Harvey growled, deep but breathy. Treading water was tiring him out. Would he be strong enough to fight Wynvail?

"Faster, Kai," I urged, closing my eyes and sinking into my own power. Feeling for my mates. But with Wynvail here, our tether alarmingly solid compared to every other bond except Wane's, I couldn't concentrate. All I felt was the deep, all-consuming rage and panic throbbing in Wynvail's soul. What was he scared of? That Harvey would win in a fight? He *should* be afraid.

A loud crack made my eyes fly open, and I snapped my head up, a horrified sound leaving me as a whimper. A massive chunk of the ceiling was about to fall, barely clinging to what stone was left. The moss was still glowing, rich silver-teal, lighting up every horrifying moment. It was right above where Harvey was dragging Emlyn through the water, too slow, too damned slow to escape it.

"Move!" I screamed, lunging for the edge of the riverbank. Kai pulled me back, and wrapped me in his snakes for good measure.

"I can't reach him, my rose," Kai murmured. "I'm sorry. His shields are too thick."

"Harvey!" My voice broke on a shout, my heart stopping as the ceiling cracked apart, baring more unsettling darkness, like it was the mouth to another world. A world of nightmares and monsters, knowing our shitty luck.

Wynvail noticed the falling rock the moment it broke free. *Hit him,* I urged the rock. *Kill him, not my mates, he deserves to die, not them.*

Wynvail threw his hand up, a blinding beam of white light bursting from his palm. I squinted through the vicious bright-ness, my heart thumping, breath cut off entirely. The beam grabbed hold of the rock, halting its deadly fall. I couldn't breathe as Wynvail threw his arm at the opposite wall where the least cracks had formed.

The rock broke apart on impact, crashing into the river and making the water rush and flow.

Harvey and Em were untouched. Not crushed by a falling rock. I resumed breathing.

"Why did he save them?" Kai whispered suspiciously.

I shook my head. I didn't know.

I didn't know why Wynvail summoned another bright beam and caught Harvey and Emlyn in it, lifting them into the air. He deposited them safely on the riverbank.

I threw myself across the space between us, collapsing to my knees and grasping them both.

"I'm fine," Harvey rasped, his tight expression and hoarse voice telling me he was anything but. "Get Emlyn out of here."

"Em?" I asked in a small voice, taking his face in my hands. He was unconscious but warm. Not cold, not dead.

"The water slammed him into the wall," Harvey panted. "He hit his head and passed out. I can heal him, but I don't know how well like this. I'm weak as fuck."

"Back up," Kai snarled suddenly.

I lifted my head, my gaze flat, dead, as I stared at Wynvail hauling himself out of the water, his perfect trousers soaked and shoes ruined. Served him right for not removing them before he—before he saved Em and Harvey.

"What's your game?" I asked, eyeing him warily as he summoned another beam of white light.

"Survival," he replied with enough of a burr in his voice to tell me he was furious. "They're your mates and I'm yours; we're all linked. You saw what happened when they lost you. Going feral is a best case scenario. Worst case? Death."

He explained it in sharp, clipped words.

I laughed hollowly. "I'd rather die here than leave with a man who'd whore out my great grandmother."

Wynvail blinked—and blinked again. "I'm sorry, what?"

"You heard me. Do you seriously think I could ever stand to look you in the eye again after what you did to Adhiti?"

Wynvail laughed, his silver eyes cruel. "If you think *I* did that to her, you're more stupid that I realised. Do you really not realise who the power players are?" He shook his head, water running down his sharp cheekbones and a sneer twisting his wide mouth. "Pathetic."

"Bullshit," Harvey spat, glaring at his brother with so much hatred he could have killed him on the spot.

But the ground shook again, and another chunk of the ceiling crashed into the river. The ensuing wave of water was big enough that it drenched all of us. I lifted Emlyn's head, making sure none forced its way up his nose.

Wynvail smiled, smug and heartless. There was no humanity in him, nothing worth saving.

"Adhiti is dead," I spat, just to spite him. "You failed. She killed herself on my knife to escape you, so whatever you and the 'power players' are planning, you lost. She won."

All the blood drained from Wynvail's face. He spun, staring around the cave, watching it fall to pieces. Darker with every chunk of the walls and ceiling that collapsed. The voices wailing in the water began to scream, awful, gut-wrenching screams that made me recoil, clutching Emlyn tight.

"We need to leave," Wynvail breathed, turning back to us. Paler still. Fear blazed through his soul into mine. *"Now.* You can call me all the names under the sun when you're not about to be killed and eaten. Not necessarily in that order; maybe we'll all be dissolved by stomach acid."

"What the fuck?" Kai asked, his bravado failing. The sight of Wynvail—ultimate bastard and betrayer—unsettled was freaking us out, too.

"Something is coming," Wynvail bit out, throwing a beam of light at Kai, another Harvey, and striding across the ground for me and Emlyn.

The whole cave shook, the voices screaming louder, wordless and terrified.

"Correction," Wynvail bit out, grabbing my wrist and

hauling me to my feet. He swallowed Emlyn with his bright magic and wrenched me against his body, a cold arm banding across my back. "Something is *here.*"

I fought him, but nothing got his grip to relax, and bright light enveloped us too, shockingly cold to the touch. I twisted in his hold, trying to see what he'd done to my mates, but my gaze snagged on the roof of the cave. All the moss and stone had fallen, leaving a jagged hole above the river. It wasn't just darkness, eerie and complete. There was a ring of sharp gold in the middle of it, black inside that ring, and it was only when the gold narrowed that I realised it was an eye.

"Gods," I gasped, shaking hands gripping Wynvail on pure instinct.

"Not exactly," he replied.

If he said anything else, it was swallowed by my scream of surprise when the white light erupted brighter, swallowing even the sight of Wynvail in front of me.

CHAPTER THIRTY-EIGHT

The second my feet landed on solid ground and I could feel my extremities again, I reared my arm back and punched Wynvail in the nose.

He staggered back, giving me a moment to look at where he'd brought us. Kai and Harvey were wavering on their feet like me, struggling for balance. Emlyn was prone on the ground, but groaning, rubbing his head. *Conscious.*

We were on a tiny, cobbled backstreet, but this looked nothing like the Hell streets I was familiar with. The styles of buildings on either side of us were vastly different, there was a beer garden to our left with broad white parasols, there were buildings and shops visible at the end of the sloped road, and—the most telling part—everything was lit in shades of grey and white, not the lilac haze of Hell.

We were on Earth.

"What was that for?" Wynvail spat, cupping his nose as it spewed blood. Watching it pour down his chest was satisfying.[1] "I just rescued you!"

"It's your fault we were there in the first place!" I snarled at him, even if that wasn't quite true. "If you hadn't locked my mates in your fucking tunnel cells, we'd never have needed Adhiti's help—"

"I'm your mate too, but fine," he cut in flatly, silver eyes glaring at me.

"You spent ten years trying to kill us, hunting us from one end of Hell to another, and now you expect me to believe you just *rescued* us? Bullshit." Spittle flew as I spat; that's how pissed off I was.

"If I wanted you dead, you'd *be* dead," he snarled right back at me, perfect white teeth bared and an animalistic rage on his face. Good; I preferred the monster to the cultured mask.

But … he had a point. I swallowed my next words, considering him. He'd had multiple chances to wade in while other assassins attacked us. He could have finished us while we were weak. But every time, we'd managed to get away with scrapes, cuts, burns, or broken bones. Injuries Harvey could heal.

"Fine," I said, curling my hands into fists. "But I know you didn't rescue us out of the goodness of your heart, no matter what you say about survival. This will come back to bite us in the ass. I don't trust you."

"Likewise, honey," he replied, adjusting his broken nose.

"What the fuck was that back there?" Kai demanded, helping Emlyn to his feet. "The thing in the roof."

"The *eye*," I added, a shiver going down my spine.

"And what have you done with Wane?" Harvey growled. "I know you have him."

Wynvail sighed, pinching the bridge of his nose. "You're all imbeciles. Aren't you paying attention?" He shot us a sharp glare. "Both questions have the same answer. I don't have Wane; I *never* had Wane. I barely managed to get *you* bastards."

"I *know* you have him," I argued, my whole body tensing. I reached for a knife, throwing it so fast he couldn't escape it. My finger twitched at the last second, sending it into his shoulder instead of his skull. Fuck, I didn't mean to redirect it. Stupid damned mate bond.

It was there, screaming in my chest, broadcasting his rage and fear. As real as the bond between me and Wane. He was undeniably my mate, and I *hated* it.

"Giving me gifts now, honey?" Wynvail taunted, pulling the knife from his shoulder with a grunt and—stashing it in the waistband of his trousers. Ugh.

"Don't look at her!" Emlyn roared, stumbling forward to shield me. His knee buckled; Kai and I flew for him at the same time, propping him between us. Emlyn's skin was red hot, his breathing dangerously fast. "Don't speak to her. Don't even *breathe* in her direction."

Wynvail snorted, but he was still pale and unsettled. He looked me in the eye and asked, "Are they always this possessive?"

Breaking every rule Em just set. Bastard.

"Where?" I bit out, my hands curling into fists when I should have been gentle with Em. "Is Wane?"

Wynvail cast his gaze to the grey sky with a sigh. "The woman you killed, Adhiti, is better known as the mother. Rhea. She's the eyes and ears—and *wife*—of Cronus. The king of titans."

Kai scoffed. "The titans are dead. The gods killed them."

In the stories. But none of that actually happened. The tales wasn't *real*...

But Lucifer's mother was a goddess. If goddesses were real, were titans, too? Titans were worse, darker, more depraved than even the gods. And if I remembered rightly, Cronus was the worst of all of them. He ate his own kids.[2]

"They *were* dead," Wynvail agreed, dragging a hand through his hair. "But they've been planning their resurrection for a very, very long time. And if *you* can all be reborn, what's stopping someone with a thousand times more power? I'm a pawn on their gameboard. So are you. So is Wane. The titans are the ones playing. Cronus is the one winning. *That's* who has Wane."

Wynvail laughed humourlessly, shaking his head. "And you just made him your enemy."

ETERNAL NIGHT

LEIGH KELSEY

BLURB

Nothing can be worse than death, right?
Wrong.

I knew I had dangerous enemies, but I didn't realise the person who cursed me was a titan. A terrifying, all-powerful being who devoured his own children for power. (He ate them. Not keen on getting eaten myself.)

Now, my mates and I have a target on our backs, and to make matters worse, Wynvail pissed the titan off by saving us from a grisly death. And that all-powerful, god-eating creature has Wane. My mate is being tortured every day, and I don't care how many people need to die to get him back, nothing will stop me.

But when he abducts us and throws us into the mythical Labyrinth, a maze of traps, nightmares, and monsters, it'll take all my strength and stubbornness just to stay alive.

What if we die in the Labyrinth, and there's no one left to save Wane?

For all my babes with praise kinks.

NOTE

This book contains mentions of past abuse and sexual assault that could be incredibly triggering for some readers, and the violence and abuse get very heavy from this book onwards, so please proceed with caution.

Haley is also dealing with infertility, which can be triggering for some people (I love you, you're valid, there's nothing wrong with you.)

Don't hesitate to skip this book if it's safer for your mental health.

This series also contains some spoilers for the Lili Kazana trilogy, which takes place a year before Haley's series, but only minor spoilers for the events of the story (nothing character-wise is spoiled.)

Leigh x

PART I
HOLLOW

CHAPTER ONE

*B*y the end of the day, I was going to commit a murder and my mate was at the top of my list of potential victims.

"Why are we here?" I bit out, glaring at the back of Wynvail's brunette head as he led the way down Princes Street, our more interesting features glamoured to appear human, my wings invisible. We were in Edinburgh, walking from the old town to Haymarket. It didn't escape my notice that Wynvail had brought me to the city where I'd lived for the first five years of my life. Just how much did he know about me? I knew he was obsessed, but this...?

"I have a safe house here," Wynvail replied, his voice biting and tight. He was still thoroughly pissed off that we'd drawn the attention of Cronus. The titan who had Wane captive if my bastard mate was to be believed.

The titans were supposed to be dead. Their age ended when Zeus killed Cronus, with the help and cleverness of his mother Rhea. The woman who, if I dared to believe it, I'd just accidentally assisted with her death.

That's why you can kill me. You're my kin.

I clenched my jaw, fighting back emotion. I'd just killed the only family I had left. My bottom lip wobbled, my chest a wreckage of pain.

If I was Rhea's great granddaughter, that meant *a god* was my grandparent. Which was insane.

Rhea—or Adhiti as we knew her—had been in the Wailing Caves for years. Centuries maybe. All that isolation and trauma probably drove her insane. Not to mention Cronus had sent her men to 'entertain.'

He made me a whore when I defied him, and trapped me here so I would be killed by my great grandchild.

If she really was Rhea—and as much as I hated Wynvail, it fit with those wailing voices calling her the mother—what Cronus had done was abhorrent. Cronus was going to suffer, both for what he'd done to Rhea and what he was doing, right now, to Wane.

What if he ... what if, like Cassander Locke, he was...

I twisted away from Harvey who had his arm around my back and bent over outside a gothic cathedral, vomit exploding over the 19th century bricks. Ugh. I hadn't eaten nearly enough in the past twelve hours; bile burned up my throat followed by the acidic grossness of some horrific invention called a protein bar. The only good thing about what happened in the caves was leaving my bag behind.[1]

All thoughts of the caves cycled back to what was done to Rhea and what could have been done to Wane. What could be happening right now.

Would he plead for me to kill him when we found him? Cronus must have had him for a hundred years. Locke had scarred my mate beyond all comprehension in twenty years; what damage could *a hundred* do?

Would there be anything left of Wane when we found him?

I retched, more acid shooting up my throat. A warm hand rubbed my back until the vomiting stopped, and I straightened with a groan.

Harvey wrapped me up in his arms, still rubbing my back, and I didn't care that we were on the side of the road near a cathedral I'd just thrown up in front of; I held on tight and melted into him.

So many words clustered on the tip of my tongue, but he must have been as terrified as I was, and I didn't want to make his fear for his twin worse. I swallowed every panicked word and sucked in a shuddering breath.

When I drew back, Kai handed me a half-soggy tissue—how did he still have his backpack after everything that happened in the cave?—and Emlyn opened his arms.

"Em, you can barely stand," I protested, wiping my mouth on the tissue and blowing my nose to get rid of the awful burning sensation.

"Get over here, Hales," he rumbled, blue eyes narrowed in concern.

I relented, partly because with my arms around him I could hold him up. Partly because I needed one of Em's bear hugs more than anything.

I sighed, a weight falling off my chest when he hugged me close, his face tucked into my shoulder and big arms a perfect weight around me.

"I'm fine," I muttered, dragging in a long breath, his old paper and leather scent coating my senses

"If you're fine, can we keep moving?" Wynvail asked impatiently. "The house is only three streets away."

"Shut the fuck up," Kai snapped. Judging by the grunt that followed, he'd either punched Wynvail in the stomach or kneed him in the crown jewels.

I kissed Em's cheek and detangled myself from his arms, feeling less sick but no less worried.

513

"Lead the way, asshole," I spat at Wynvail, ignoring the way his cruel silver gaze lingered on my face.

He was a fucking liar, and a clever one. He'd tricked me into accepting he was my mate with the truth—that I was mated to two Locke siblings. I always had been, but one had never been him. It was Harvey and Wane from the very beginning. If he tricked me with that, everything else he said was a lie, too.

The in-denial part of my head said he could be lying about Cronus, Rhea, and the whole titans being back from the dead thing. He'd say anything if it suited him.

The smirk that bloomed on his sculpted face was nasty and slow. "You have vomit in your hair, honey."

"Kai, punch him in the kidney," I hissed without breaking eye contact with Wynvail.

Kai, the love of my goddamn life, didn't hesitate for one moment. He feinted to the left, and when Wynvail moved to defend that side, slammed his fist into Wynvail's kidney. Hard.

"Feral bastard!" Wynvail snarled, the true monster peeking through the cracks in his cultured veneer. "You're dead. I should have put you down when I had you locked in the tunnels—"

He was so focused on Kai, he didn't see my fist coming. I shouldn't have been able to hurt him as his mate, but I was just fucked up enough right now to slam my fist into his jaw. Pain exploded through my knuckles but it was worth it for the second flare of pain I felt in his soul.

"Again," he ground out, taking several steps away. "I just rescued you. You could try being a little grateful."

"Just take us to this fucking safe house," I demanded.

"That's what I was trying to do," Wynvail muttered, pressing a hand to his side as he resumed walking, storming ahead with murder written in every line of his body. He was still bleeding where I threw my knife at his shoulder.

He was lucky he was useful, and had dealt with this titan who had Wane. Otherwise, I'd have left him to rot somewhere.

CHAPTER TWO

Of course Wynvail had an expensive town house with three storeys and a fucking rooftop terrace. Of course he did. Privileged bastard.

I focused on my hatred of him to block out my panic for Wane—unreachable in the bond—and my grief and horror over Adhiti's death. I killed her. Even if she forced my hand, even if she wanted to be free, *I killed her.* Her blood still stained my skin, buried under my fingernails, and every time I looked at my hands, I saw her face, heard the relief and suffering in her voice.

Make him suffer. Make him regret every heinous act he ever committed.

"Sit wherever you want," Wynvail bit out as he led us past the bottom floor and into a wide, front-facing living room. A tall bay window let in light, flooding the quirky furniture. There was a pink rug, an orange three-seater sofa, two turquoise chairs patterned with polka dots, and tiger-print curtains that hung to the floor. Not the decor I would have expected from Wynvail; this was more to my taste.

"Did this place come furnished, or...?" I asked, giving him a strange look.

"No," he replied, frowning when Kai dumped his wet backpack on the rug. "And each piece took time and care to pick out, so I'd *appreciate*," he bit out at Malakai, "if you didn't ruin it with stinking cave water."

Without waiting for a reply, he stalked to the rug, grabbed the backpack, and relocated it to a place on the marble fireplace. And then without a backwards glance, he strode out the door.

"Where are you going?" Harvey demanded, settling Emlyn on the bright orange sofa and glaring at his brother. The brother he hadn't even known existed until Wynvail locked him in the tunnels under Alphaven.

What game was Cassander Locke playing, to keep one son separate?

"Kitchen," Wynvail replied in the same tone.

Kai laughed, a sudden explosion of sound. "So you can warn your boss we're here? I don't fucking think so."

Kai stalked after Wynvail, producing a knife from somewhere. I followed, drawing one of my long, wavy daggers and relieved to see no damage from being submerged twice. Or was it three times? Being drowned will make a girl lose count.

"Imbecile," Wynvail growled under his breath, his shoulders tight as we stalked him down the hallway and into an adjacent kitchen. It was ... lovely. Bright and clean in shades of white and grey, but with accents of soft pastels in the appliances and a matching set of tea and coffee canisters.

"Why would I risk my ass to get you out of the Wailing Caves only to sell you out now?" he muttered, seemingly to himself. "You have no idea how much shit I'm in for assisting someone who *killed Cronus's fucking wife!*"

By the end he was shouting, his shirtless back rising and

falling fast as his breathing escalated. I watched his reaction flatly, not believing a single word of it.

Kai slow-clapped the performance.

Wynvail spun, nostrils flaring and teeth bared. His expression was brittle, his movements jagged. Light gathered in the bastard's hand, and I knew his move before his arm even twitched. With a snarl, I stepped in front of Kai just as Wynvail released the beam of light. My ears hurt when they both shouted at once.

"Haley!" Kai yelled, panic tight in his voice as he grabbed me and spun me around, searching for a wound. The kitchen whirled like a funfair ride. I swayed into him, pain thumping through my chest where the magic had struck me.

"Are you clinically insane?" Wynvail demanded, ripping me out of Kai's arms and scanning my eyes. "I could have *killed* you."

"You could have killed Kai," I snapped, shoving him away and ignoring my wobbling legs. "Don't act like you give a shit about me."

Wynvail just laughed, a sneer curling his lip. "Am I not your mate?"

"Unfortunately," I spat, gritting my teeth as the pain in my chest faded to an ache. The dizziness persisted though, not helped by the fact I still felt sick. I killed my own family...

I leaned into Kai, watching Wynvail's every move, waiting for him to do something sneaky.

Instead, he made a riot of noise opening and closing cupboards, ripping lids off canisters, and slamming them back on. The kettle boiled, so loud it drummed in my ears. When he handed me a baby pink teacup, I just laughed.

"It's poison."

"You just watched me make it," he pointed out, his mouth set in a firm line. "And I'd rather not have you vomit on the couch; it's bad enough this riffraff dirtied the rug."

Kai hissed, his forked tongue lashing the air.

"Don't," I sighed, stroking my hand down Kai's side and watching him melt. "He's not worth it. And anyway, he's right. He kept us alive for some reason; it would make no sense to kill me now."

I took the tea from Wynvail, but made certain he knew this changed *nothing* with the vicious glare I fixed on him.

He rolled his burnished eyes, fingertips brushing over the hilt of the knife sticking out from his waistband. The knife he stole from me.[1]

I took a sip of the tea, rolling it around my mouth, testing for any common poisons and finding nothing but peppermint. Unless he'd used something untraceable.

"I haven't poisoned you," he muttered, shoving past Kai and out the door back to the living room.

We exchanged a suspicious glance and followed, Kai brushing my arm to silently ask if I was okay. I nodded, tilting my head to rest it on his shoulder and sighing when he stroked wet strands of hair out of my face.

"We'll find him," he promised quietly enough that it wouldn't carry to Wynvail. "I promise, Halwen. We'll find him."

I swallowed. "I know. Also, it's weird being called Halwen," I added, trying to lighten the oppressive cloud hanging over us. "I'm a forest now, apparently."

And that was all Wynvail's doing. Unless he'd lied about that, too. He'd conveniently never mentioned Wane, trying to step into the hole left in his absence. It was such a Wane thing to do, to plant whispers so the name spread and became folklore, leaving me clues and hope.

If I'd never met that farmer and he'd never told me I just came from the Forest of Halwen, I might have collapsed. Instead, knowing my mates were out there gave me the strength to drag my ass to Iarlon.

"You're awfully cosy," Wynvail commented in his usual smooth, smug drawl.

I saw why when we strode into the living room and found Harvey and Emlyn sitting thigh to thigh on the bright orange sofa.

"Mind your own fucking business," I snapped, 'tripping' across the rug and 'accidentally' kicking Wynvail. "Oh, I'm *so* sorry. How clumsy of me."

"Careful," Wynvail replied, his voice deeper, darker. "I'm tempted to call this foreplay."

I wrinkled my nose like he disgusted me, and something sharp cut through his soul where it bound to mine. Hit successfully landed.

"Haley," Emlyn rumbled, disapproving but unable to hide his amusement.

I dropped down beside him, snuggling close. Kai remained standing. No, let me rephrase. Kai circled Wynvail like he was his next meal and he was considering how he'd gut, skin, and debone him.

"So what now?" I asked my mates, taking another sip of tea. Motherfucker had even sweetened it like I liked it. It was scary how much he knew about me. Did he have a whole folder of information about me, like General Callahan had on the alphas?[2]

"Now *he* tells us where to find Cronus," Emlyn said in a voice like thunder. He'd put two and two together and come to the same conclusion I did, then. Good.

Wynvail laughed, stalking over to the fireplace and sinking into the chair beside it. There was a kitsch monstrosity of a clock on the fireplace just ticking around to four in the after-noon: a wolf with silver and cerise fur—and it was *fluffy*. I loved it. "You think I can just summon him? A *titan*. Do you really know nothing of their power? It nearly *killed* the gods defeating him—and they're gods!"

"You work for him," I disagreed, swallowing all my rage and panic so I could speak calmly.[3] "He's the one you're collecting alphas for; he's the one who gave you the power to control other demons. Tell me I'm wrong," I challenged.

Wynvail was silent, staring out the bay window. "There's more to this than you think. I didn't wake up one day and decide to make a deal with a titan. I exist because—"

He shook his head, face hardening. I hadn't noticed when his expression changed, and I couldn't put my finger on what emotion I'd seen on his face.

Oh, he was *good*. But if he wanted to lay the bait of vulnerability, I wasn't going to take it.

"And you're all suicidal if you're even entertaining the thought of hunting down Cronus," Wynvail added, his sneer back in place.

A deep, guttural noise tore from my throat in response, and I was surprised to find three others joining me.

"We're not leaving Wane there," Harvey seethed, clenching his bronze hands into fists and physically restraining himself from leaping to his feet.

Wynvail shook his dark head. "It's a death sentence."

I froze. "If it's a death sentence for us, it is for Wane, too. And there's no force on Earth, Hell, or wherever the fuck else we end up that can keep me from my mate."

"He's alive because he's useful to Cronus," Wynvail disagreed. "Your death is more useful to him than your life. He'll kill you. So even if I knew how to contact the titan, I wouldn't tell you."

I got to my feet slowly, my heart hammering fast. "You're lying."

"He summons *me*. I'm his servant."

He wasn't lying; I could hear it, sense the truth in his bitter soul. My stomach dropped, any shred of hope I'd held onto unravelling.

My face was suddenly tight and hot.

I'd got to my feet to break Wynvail's face but instead I rushed out the door and walked as fast as I could down the hallway past the kitchen, heading for a staircase at the end. Anywhere was better than staying in that room and getting crushed by grief.

We didn't know where to find Wane. I would lose him too.

"Haley?" Kai called, hurrying after me. "Where are you going?"

"The roof," I bit out, not turning as I took the stairs two at a time.

I heard the low murmur of Emlyn's voice, and Kai fell back, letting Em take his place. I raced past the second floor, struggling to breathe, and shoved open the door at the top, relieved it was unlocked. I honestly thought I would have cried if it stuck.

The terrace space wasn't big, just a rectangular space with the roof and chimney behind me and an iron fence in front. I grabbed the railing in white-knuckled hands, gulping down air, each breath faster and shorter. Wind grabbed my pink hair and twisted it through the air, but I barely noticed.

Emlyn didn't say a word. He just wrapped his arms around me from behind and held me as I gasped and shook, and eventually the gasps collapsed into sobs.

I turned, burying my face in his chest. One arm locked me tight to his body while he soothed long, comforting touches down my wings. He didn't stop until I could breathe again, until my tears dried. I couldn't have said how long we'd been out here. Longer than ten minutes, I knew that for sure.

"He's being tortured," I said finally, my voice a hoarse whisper. I had almost drowning a few times to thank for that sexy rasp. "I felt it. I felt his *pain*, Em, and I don't know how he's survived this long. If the titan's had him for a hundred years, what if—"

"We'll get him back," Emlyn murmured, fingers gentle on my wings. "And we'll all be there to help him heal. If he has nightmares and scars, well—he's not the only one. We can get him through."

"What if it's worse than how he was before? So much worse? It felt—like someone was cutting his shadows from him."

Emlyn stiffened, sucking in a sharp breath. It took him a moment to compose himself. "He's been through things so dark no one should ever have to experience them. But he was still starting to heal before the assassins found us. I've never seen him hide less than those last few months we had together."

I tilted my head back, my heart aching. "You remember?"

"Most of it," he agreed, brushing a long kiss to my forehead. "Enough to know Wane was broken before, and he began to heal. He can do it again."

But that wasn't a hundred years. That wasn't a titan.

"A titan, Em," I said, my voice cracking. "A *titan* has had my mate for a hundred years. Torturing him. Cutting his shadows and—and doing gods know what else—"

Emlyn couldn't stifle his growl this time, and neither could he hide the pain in the sound. "We'll get him back," he repeated, like it was his lifeline.

I forced a nod.

But a hundred years was a long, long time. Endless if Wane was being hurt every single day. I felt him on the other end of the bond when he let me close. He didn't feel broken; he felt agonised and tired but blazing with wrath. Defiant. Stubbornly strong. But what if this part of his soul was the only thing left?

"What if we find him, and—and he's a shell?" I asked, so quietly.

Emlyn tucked me closer, and I let myself melt into him,

ignoring the cold wind tugging at my hair and wings. "What-ever we find, it doesn't matter. He's ours, and we'll bring him home. He'll have you, and Harvey, and Kai and I will do every-thing we can."

"We can kill Wynvail so he never has to meet him," I added thoughtfully.

"You'd rather die than kill him," Emyn huffed, tugging on a feather. "He's your mate."

"Unfortunately."

"He's going to be useful in finding Wane. He's the only person we know who's had contact with Cronus. Fuck, that's bizarre to say out loud. Cronus is a myth, a story. I used to read stories about him—remember the book of legends I had? With the gold tree stamped on it."

"You were reading it the morning we—*that* morning." I swallowed, shutting out the loud flicker of flames, the heat of the fire, and the creeping feeling along my soul. "That book burned because of Wynvail."

"Hm," Emlyn agreed, dusting my forehead with another kiss. "Don't kill him until after he helps us find Wane."

"Fine," I muttered, hating that he was right, hating that only half of me wanted that asshole dead. I wouldn't even give voice to what the other half wanted to do, though it hadn't fully moved on from seeing him dive into the river, shirtless, to save my mates. Or seeing blood run down his skin. "Only serious injuries."

Emlyn laughed, but I knew his heart wasn't in it. "Halwen—"

I groaned. Whatever he was going to say, it couldn't be good if he was calling me Halwen.

He caught my face in his hand, tilting my head back so he could scan my face. "How are you feeling? About Adhiti —Rhea?"

I swallowed and tried to glance away but he wouldn't let

me. "How am I feeling about murdering my great grandmother?"

"You didn't murder her, Hales," Em murmured, stroking my cheek with his thumb. "She did most of the work; she just used your knife. It wasn't your fault."

"I was going to kill her," I admitted, the shame of it choking me. "I wanted to, when she trapped us in that cave with her. I thought she was going to hurt you, and when she made you kneel—"

"You're my mate; of course you'd want revenge on someone who hurt me," he said reasonably, holding eye contact. "It wasn't your fault."

I laughed, a little twisted.

"Halwen," he said for the second time, waiting for me to meet his patient stare. "It wasn't your fault. You didn't stab her, and you couldn't have stopped her. She was determined to die."

"I killed a titaness," I breathed, a tremble starting in my hands where I gripped Em close. "Oh, god, I killed a titaness. I'll be thrown in jail, and that's the best case scenario. Is there a titan prison? That's where I'll be left to rot. Or maybe they'll throw me in Tartarus."

"They will *not*," Emlyn growled, drawing my attention and interrupting my panic. "I won't let *anyone* touch you. Human, demon, god, titan—I don't care what they are, if they even think about hurting you, they're dead."

My shoulders dropped and I settled back into his chest, his hand relocating to the back of my head and burying in the strands of my hair. Ugh, I needed a shower. I was still covered in river muck; I was pretty sure if I let it dry in my hair, I'd never get it out.

It shouldn't have mattered with my great grandmother dead at my own hand and Wane captive, but—it was the final straw, and suddenly I couldn't stand all the grime on me.

"I need to shower," I said, pulling away from Emlyn, manic energy filling my body. "I'm covered in all this—this—"

"Hales," Emlyn said, so gently.

"I'm fine," I snapped, slamming the door open and jogging down the stairs. "I just need to get clean. You!" I snarled, finding Wynvail with my mates at the bottom of the stairs on the second floor. "Where's your bathroom?"

He raised an eyebrow. "Excuse me?"

"Where's your fucking bathroom, asshole? I need a shower."

He narrowed his eyes, but for some reason he didn't match my aggression. "Staircase at the other end of the hall. Second door on your left."

"I'll come with you," Emlyn offered, brushing the tip of a wing down my side.

"I'll be fine alone," I insisted, turning to give him a reassuring smile. Judging by the way his brows pinched closer together, I did a piss poor job of it.

"I'm ordering food," Wynvail said as I shoved past him, moving too fast, my whole body vibrating. I needed to get all this muck off me, needed to find Wane, needed to stop a titan from meddling in our lives. Nevermind the prophecy of great, terrible power on my back.

"Good for you," I replied to Wynvail, my voice flat. "Enjoy your lasagna."

CHAPTER THREE

$\mathcal{I}$ found the bathroom easily, and let out a long breath when I shut the door behind myself, stripping off my dirty clothes. I felt better with them in a pile on the floor. If I had to be naked for the rest of the day, so be it. I wasn't putting them back on. Not even my beloved leather jacket.[1]

The clock ticking away on the wall said four p.m. I rolled my eyes. Why was I surprised that Wynvail couldn't even get this right? Even his clocks were fucked up; it was four when we got here. It had to be five now.

I wasn't surprised when the door forced open before I could make it into the shower. I *was* surprised it took them a whole minute to barge in on me.

I swallowed, a lump swelling in my throat as Harvey and Kai shut the door behind themselves.

"Fuck," Harvey breathed, staring at my stomach where the biggest curse mark was inked. "Sugarplum," he sighed, closing the distance in a single step and running his hand over the mark. It was still there even if the curse was nullified, even if I had my magic back. Maybe I'd always wear the mark.

Kai slid around Harvey and moulded himself to my left, ducking his head to brush a kiss to my shoulder. "What do you need?"

I'd automatically stiffened, expecting him to ask if I was okay, or how I was coping with killing my great-grandma. I loved this about Kai; he didn't push me to talk, and let me figure things out on my own. Or at least he knew the others would pester me into talking about my feelings.

"Other than a shower?" I replied dryly.

"You're still beautiful even if you smell like a swamp," Harvey assured me, his fingers stroking across my side to my back, guiding over the prophecy marked there, too.

"Aww, thanks, Buttercup," I drawled.

"Any time, Sugarplum."

Kai snorted, gliding a delicate touch over my feathers. Reminding me of his question.

I sighed, my shoulders drooping. "I need you both close. But I don't have the emotional or physical energy to take both your cocks right now."

Harvey laughed, his breath ruffling my wings.

"No DP," Kai agreed, nuzzling my shoulder before laying another kiss there.

"I doubt I could even hold you up," Harvey said with a rueful smile. "I fucked my back trying to drag Emlyn to safety."

My head shot up. "Are you—"

"Fine," he assured me, silver eyes soft and full of love. "I'll heal. Just nothing too heavy for a few days."

"Don't worry," Kai commented, his eyes twinkling as he kissed my cheek. "I'll pick up your slack, Harv."

To prove his point, he unfastened his trousers and kicked them off, stripped his shirt, and picked me up, carrying me into the shower. I hadn't known what a shower was until Lucifer's palace, but now I took them for granted. The hot water that sprayed over me was heavenly, and when Kai set me down, I watched grime wash down the drain with relief.

"Thanks for leaving me outside," Harvey muttered, giving Kai a playful scowl as he pushed into the shower, his clothes discarded.

"Apologies, dear," Kai replied without missing a beat as he adjusted the water temperature. "Should I have carried you, too?"

"It wouldn't have hurt," Harvey shot back, snaking his arm around my waist and pushing me against the cold tile wall. I caught my breath when he knelt before me, kissing a reverent trail up my leg and lingering on an old scar on my thigh.

Kai noticed where his attention had fallen and his crimson eyes darkened, a million threats of murder running through his eyes.

"You killed the guy who gave me this," I reminded him, pushing wet hair out of my face and relaxing under the warmth of the water.

"It wasn't enough," he hissed, his forked tongue flicking out and inked hands balled into fists. Water sluiced his dark red hair to his cheeks, somehow emphasising the danger he posed.[2]

"You dismembered his limbs, sliced his face off, and shoved the skin down his throat," Harvey pointed out, kissing higher on my thigh, each brush slower, longer.

"It still wasn't *enough*," Kai argued, but he wrapped a wet lock of my hair around his finger and some of the rage softened to affection in his eyes.

"What?" I asked when he just gazed at me, intent in a different way, gentler, almost subdued.

"I could have lost you in those caves," he replied, fingers stroking along my jaw to cup my cheek. "You almost drowned, Haley."

"I'm okay," I assured him, my attention torn between Kai's

turmoil and Harvey's kisses climbing higher, brushing the inner seam of my thigh and making me throb.

Kai clenched his jaw, his reply grating but every bit as gentle. "Your voice is burned by the water, you're not breathing right, you're favouring your left side, and there's an ache in your ankle where that *thing* grabbed you. You're pretty fucking far from okay, my rose."

I turned, holding his stare and hoping he didn't see how deeply Adhiti's death scarred me. "I'm also stubborn, and strong, and I've been in a worse state than this. I'm okay, Kai. Promise."

He pressed his mouth into a line, but sighed, relenting. "No more caves," he ordered.

"None," I agreed—and inhaled sharply when Harvey licked a slow line up my centre, swirling around my clit.

"It's nothing a few orgasms won't fix," Harvey murmured, tilting his head to look up at me. Mercury eyes gleamed with a wickedness that didn't quite hide his worry. I sank the fingers of my free hand into his wild hair, slicking it back from his face so I could trace the sharp lines of his features with worried eyes. Weariness was carved into every part of him.

"Harvey," I murmured.

He glanced away and laid a kiss on my inner thigh before burying his tongue in my pussy, effectively silencing our conversation. We were all stressed, all traumatised, and all missing Wane. Harvey especially. He lacked his other half, his twin, but he wasn't ready to talk about that. I knew if I pushed him now, he'd explode, or maybe even break. I couldn't risk that.

And he was probably right; orgasms would fix everything.

Kai ducked his head to kiss my shoulder, his lips burning my skin with a long brush, like he didn't want to pull away. We might have been dragged through metaphorical Hell[3] but we made it out. We *survived.*

"We'll be okay," I promised them both, my voice low and soft, almost drowned out by the slam of the water into the shower cubicle. I couldn't help but notice we all fit into the shower with room to spare, another annoyingly perfect part of Wynvail's perfect fucking house.

"We're cursed to murder each other," Kai muttered against my shoulder, lips dragging towards my wings. "There's nothing okay about it."

"Shut it," Harvey huffed, glaring up at Kai. "I'm trying to make our mate come, and you're being maudlin."

Kai gave him the middle finger and trailed his kisses lower, finding the sensitive spot on the arch of my wing. I stiffened with a gasp, pure electricity shooting through me. I tightened my fingers in Harvey's hair reflexively and he groaned, encouraging me as he licked and sucked me with a deadly, sinuous rhythm.

Liquid heat poured through my veins.

My hips bucked when Kai grazed my weak spot with his teeth. I exhaled a soft moan, reaching for his cock, gliding my fingers over him.

"Can we just—do this?" I asked, shyness making my voice faint.[4]

"Do whatever you want to me," Kai breathed, probably because I squeezed the head of his cock like I knew he loved. I squeezed harder, coaxing a throaty moan from him.

"Haley, my rose, move your hand," he groaned when I kept squeezing. *"Please."*

"Like this?" I asked, and stroked my thumb over his slit with enough pressure to make his hips jolt against my side. I bit my lip, fighting back my own needy sounds when Harvey slid two fingers inside of me so slowly that he must have felt every throb of my inner muscles. His mouth never left my pussy, licking with attention that bordered obsession.

"Or like this?" I said to Kai, stroking up and down his

length and tightening my grip when he throbbed in my hand. Kai's whole body shuddered, his breath hot on my wing when he laid another kiss there.

"Vicious rose," he panted, power shuddering around him. "Faster."

I was happy to oblige, my gaze rapt on his face so I could watch him fall apart. Gods, I loved Kai like this—vulnerable and open and trusting, his pale face flushed and his eyes dilated as he chased his pleasure.

"I love you," he said urgently, catching my mouth in a fierce kiss that made my lips tingle.

His hand glided down my stomach, stroking a scar so faded it was little more than a silvery line, and lingering on the curse emblazoned on my torso among skulls and flowers.

"Here," he grunted at Harvey, spreading my pussy with two fingers and making my clit pulse frantically. "I want to come with my mate; eat her properly."

I sank my teeth into my bottom lip with Harvey flicked Kai an arch look but did as he was told, every sensation so much sharper with the hood of my clit pulled back.

"Touch yourself," I pleaded. "Harvey, please."

He peered up at me, holding eye contact as his tongue circled my swollen clit, making everything inside me clench. He didn't look away as he took his cock and pumped fast, understanding my plea. Love and hot, scalding need burned through our bond, lifting hairs all down my body, and I adjusted my grip on his hair, guiding his mouth in an angle that made my eyes slam shut.

I barely heard the drum of the water, barely felt anything except Harvey's insistent mouth and fingers, and Kai's cock jolting desperately in my hand. I squeezed, and he responded with a needy thrust, teeth dragging up my wing, making slick feathers shudder when he groaned against them.

"Please be close," I whined, my body locking, tighter with

every second. Frantic need coiled in my lower belly, until I shoved my pussy into Harvey's face, riding his tongue and desperate to reach the edge.

"I'm right there with you," Harvey groaned, his words vibrating through my clit. "I was ready to come with the first taste of you."

Fuck. My pussy clenched. I stroked Kai faster, insistent, silently begging.

"Fuck," he grunted, deep and hot as fuck. When his hand covered mine, guiding me rougher, harder, my temperature rose and pleasure wound so tight inside me that I froze.

"Faster, Harvey," Kai ordered. "That's it, my rose, come for us. You're so fucking beautiful, so good for us. Our perfect mate."

"Fuck," I choked out when the coil of pleasure snapped and I shuddered violently, my pussy suffocating Harvey as a brutal wave of pleasure locked my legs around his head.

Kai must have been holding back, waiting for me, because the second I cried out, his cock throbbed erratically in my hand and his power erupted, snakes coiling around my middle in a possessive squeeze, his forehead resting on my shoulder as he panted and groaned and spilled over my hand.

Harvey's fingers pumped faster inside me, matching the frantic pace of the fingers wrapped around his weeping cock. My body locked tighter, pleasure soaring higher, and when Harvey swore gutturally as he found his release, I bit my bottom lip so hard I drew blood.

For a long minute there was only bliss and relief, interrupted only by the drumming of the shower and our rough breaths. For a long minute, there was only peace.

But my brain function returned too soon, and brought all my anxieties back with it. I didn't even get three minutes of calm.

It was official; the universe hated me.

CHAPTER FOUR

"*A*re you done?" Wynvail drawled when we returned to the living room, trays and boxes of food laid out on the table before the fire.

I returned a flat look and said nothing, going instead to Emlyn where he sat in one of the chairs, wolfing down noodles. I kissed the top of his head, echoing the way he'd kissed me on the roof, and hoped he knew it was an apology for excluding him, however accidentally.

"Your clock's broken," I told Wynvail, sitting on Emlyn's lap and smoothing the black shirt and jeans I'd stolen over my knees. We'd raided the wardrobes in the third floor bedrooms and now had clean clothes. I'd stolen a set for Em too, more or less his size. Harvey held them in his arms, but judging by the hawkish way he stared at the food, he might get food all over them. "And I stole these clothes. Who are they for, your girlfriend?"

Wynvail levelled me with a flat look, his silver eyes heavy. "You can't be that dense, honey."

I rolled my eyes. "I'm getting a little sick of you calling me and my mates stupid. What are you eating, Em?"

"Pad thai," he said around a mouthful, and made my heart flutter when he held out the tray to me. "Want some?"

I took a bite of the noodles he lifted on a fork, surprised by the flavour and spice that exploded over my tongue. It was surprisingly hard to find good spice in the part of Hell we lived in. Used to live in.

I stroked salt and pepper hair out of his face before he could try to eat it. "I'll have something from the table; you finish this, Em."

He went back to his meal with a low, pleased rumble, his mate instincts satisfied.

"You won't like that," Wynvail remarked when I reached for a clear plastic box of something brownish. "Eat this."

I glared when he knocked my hand away and held out a container of fried food smothered in a red sauce. When I refused to take it, he smirked and removed the lid. Heavenly smells met my nose, and I barely held in a groan. After our trek to the caves, almost drowning multiple times, and the hollow ruin of grief, I was starving.

"Fine," I muttered, snatching the box from him. The first bite of sauce-smothered chicken, and I couldn't hold back my next groan.

Wynvail sat back in his chair, one foot resting on his knee, looking more arrogant and self satisfied than ever.

"I still hate you," I growled, but devoured another bite. "Here," I told Harvey and Kai, since they hovered close. "Eat this bastard out of house and home."

Wynvail rolled his silver eyes.

"Attention seeking, honey?"

I didn't dignify that with an answer.

He poured a long, sinful look down my body, lingering where tight denim clung to legs and ignoring the three vicious snarls he got from the other men in the room. "The attention I want to give you would make your toes curl. And your voice break. It could break you entirely."

I ignored him, finishing the rest of my life-changing meal. It was the perfect blend of sweet and spicy, and *holy fuck* the chicken was good.

How the fuck did he know what I'd like to eat? Just how deep in my life *was* he? Had he bribed my old neighbours? Paid off landlords in pubs? Tracked down cafés I'd visited?

I waited until Kai and Harvey had demolished a box of food each before stretching and getting off Emlyn's lap, readjusting my knife sheaths. "Well, this has been tedious but I need rest. I hope you have a miserable night and haunted dreams."

"Right back at you, honey," Wynvail purred, his heavy eyelids reminding me of his vulgar promises. I ignored the heat he coaxed from my body, refusing to give into the base response.

"Hope you die in your sleep," I said sweetly, glancing at the time and sighing. "If your clock isn't broken, why has it said four o'clock for the last two hours?"

Wynvail didn't roll his eyes or smirk; his face fell, his skin a shade paler, and he shot to his feet to grab my wrist.

"I thought we'd have longer," he hissed, frantic eyes darting around the room.

He was a liar and a fake, but I believed this panic. Especially since it erupted through his soul, spilling into the bond.

"What's going on?" Kai demanded.

"Cronus is the god of time. And if time has stopped in the house ... he's here."

CHAPTER FIVE

he walls shook, sending artwork and picture frames tumbling to the floor, glass shattering on the hardwood floor. Wynvail gripped my wrist in a bruising hold

"What the fuck is happening?" Harvey snarled, his eyes wide and panicked, jumping from the takeaway boxes as they shook off the table to the doorway when something crashed in the kitchen.

"I spent time and money putting this fucking house together!" Wynvail yelled, his eyes bulging with something close to murder.

The floor shook harder, like Cronus had heard him. I caught my breath when a black spot bled through the rug and grew, too fast for me to process even though my eyes were glued to it.

Wynvail dropped my wrist, his hand slamming into my chest to throw me across the room. I was propelled so hard I had to grab the wall to stay on my feet.

"What the fuck?" I yelled.

"Get out of here," he growled back at me, teeth bared.

I laughed, a frightened, twisted thing. Dark, menacing power rippled through the room—the same wrongness and power I'd felt in the Wailing Caves. "When did you get so selfless?"

I backed up with a sharp gasp when the black spot bled further swallowing the rug in its entirety. Big enough now for me to realise it wasn't just a stain, but a hollow gaping hole.

My panicked stare flicked around the room, quickly assessing. "Em, jump onto the sofa and run over it. Kai, come here quickly, jump over the chair before the black spreads. Harvey—sorry, Buttercup, but I think you're going to have to jump out the window."

Wynvail shook his head, plundering a secret hideaway under a pouffe near one of the chairs. He grabbed jewelled daggers, sharp throwing knives, garrottes, leather straps, and … knuckle dusters. Hey, I hadn't seen any of those in years.

"Here, honey!" he shouted, and threw me a dagger in a sparkly, bejewelled case. I caught it on reflex and frowned at my fingers wrapped around it.

"We need to get out of here!" I growled, relieved when Em jumped onto the sofa and made his way across, struggling to stay upright when the cushions sank but making it to me. Kai wasn't going to make it, though. The black stain spread faster than he moved.

I unfolded my wings and kicked off the floor, the dagger awkward in my hand as I reached both arms out to snatch Kai off the floor.

He realised what I planned and leapt for me without question, outracing the black stain by millimetres. Kai slammed into my body, expelling all my air, but I clung to him and flapped my wings frantically to keep us in place.

"Is that … wind?" Harvey asked, crouching on the windowsill and trying to figure out the latch.

"There's no escape," Wynvail said gravely, strapping weapons to himself.[1]

"Oh, shut up," I snapped at him. His defeatist attitude wasn't helpful.

"He's a titan; we can't outsmart him, we can't outrun him. He wins every time."

I laughed, opening my mouth on a dismissive insult—

"Keep your mouth *shut,* or he'll slaughter you and all your mates. And I mean *all* of them."

That snapped my mouth closed, panic for Wane carving through my chest. I dug my fingers into Kai's back, holding him bruisingly tight as I flew in place. The black spot began to devour the sofa. *Still there, everything out back, weird*

"I'll do the talking," Wynvail added, but he didn't look happy about it. "I've negotiated with him before."

For what? I began to ask, but the wind Harvey had felt whipped suddenly sharper, slicing through my feathers and sending me into a spin. I shrieked, crushing Kai to me and frantically flapping my wings.

The pit in the rug ripped further open, the wind blasting from it like a tornado now. It snatched Emlyn where he hovered by the door, his arms open to catch me. It tossed him right into the pit.

A broken sound ripped from me when he fell out of sight.

"Em!" I screamed so loud my voice broke.

No. Not again. Not again, *please.*

I didn't realise I'd said it out loud until Wynvail repeated, "Let me do the talking. I'll get us out of this, Halwen. It won't happen again. I promise you."

And the crazy bastard leapt willingly into the pit.

I tried to fly across the living room to Harvey, still clinging to the window. But it was like the titan knew my plan, because the wind whipped into a frenzy and the force of it ripped Harvey's hands off the latch. The window flew ironically open. Too late to save him.

He was sucked into the darkness, swallowed so suddenly that I couldn't see him anymore.

Not again. I can't do this again, I can't...

Kai's added weight in my arms must have made us harder prey for the blackened pit, but it tore at us fiercely, forcing us lower.

"I love you," I told him, shaking all over, remembering a moment exactly like this. I'd told Wane I loved him then, and we'd been blasted apart by a shotgun.

"We are *not* dying," Kai hissed, his arms bruising my waist and his expression furious. "Not this time. I fucking swear to you."

Tears gathered in my eyes, prickling and sharp. I barely managed to nod before the wind roared, knocking us out of the air and sending us in a brutal plummet into the hungry maw in the floor.

Blackness consumed everything.

But then a voice shook through the pit, and I felt it down to my trembling bones.

CHAPTER SIX

*Y*ou *betrayed me,* an awful, grating voice filled every space in the blackness around us, tearing through every one of my senses until I wasn't sure if I held Kai anymore. I couldn't see a single thing around us, the pit as dark as a void, but wind battered me from all directions. *And all for your mate?*

I ducked my head, wishing I could slam my hands over my ears but too scared to drop Kai. The voice was as deep as a migraine, but as raw as a touched nerve. Pain tore through my head and I clenched my jaw so tight my bones creaked.

Pathetic.

But, he added, *I'll consider forgiving you if you can overcome your weakness.*

I screamed as the voice sliced through the soft, breakable parts of me. I couldn't feel my face, but I had a strange sense of something rolling down my cheeks. I wasn't sure if it was tears or blood.

Kill the mates of your mate until you are the only one left standing. Then you'll earn my forgiveness. And I'll give you the resurrec-

tion pearl you're so desperate for. Fail, and you know what will happen.

My stomach pitched, and the wind raking cruel fingers through my wings and hair tugged harder, ripping out strands of hair, tearing out a feather. But the brutal pressure lifted from the air, the voice faded into silence, and I felt my lashes sweep my cheeks when I blinked.

I couldn't see a single thing, not even Kai, but I knew we were still falling.

"Kai," I rasped.

His arms tightened around me. Holy fuck, I could feel my body now. I wasn't sure if that was a good sign or a bad one. Kai didn't reply, but he held me fiercely as the wind hammered us from all angles. I tried to catch wind in my wings but we were falling too fast to slow our descent. Shit. I wrapped my wings around him and threw myself backwards, protecting Kai so I would take the brunt of the fall.

Ugh, this was going to hurt.

I couldn't hear my other mates' growls or voices in the void, but they had to be in this vortex, too. That warning from Cronus, still thumping through my head like a migraine ... that wasn't for us.

Kill the mates of your mate until you are the only one left standing.

Wynvail.

I tried to snarl at the thought of him hurting my mates, but wind slammed into my face and down my throat until I choked on it. It crashed into my back, my arms, my wings like a rain of punches. I gasped out a cry when it hit a tender part of my wings, knocking me through the vortex. The jewelled dagger nearly slipped from my fingers; I held onto it by sheer dumb luck.[1]

Empty blackness pressed on Kai and I from every direction, but—there, was that light? I couldn't tell if the spot of grey was real or if I was hallucinating it. Where would this dark tunnel spit us out? Cronus had stopped time in Wynvail's house; were we falling through *time?* Would we emerge a hundred years ago, when the bastard was still trying to kill us?

Would—would Wane be there?

The thought distracted me so much that I missed the warning signs: the grey spot growing bigger, the light brighter, the ground closer.

I slammed into it so hard that I was thrown back into the air with a cry and I bounced twice, each impact snapping something in my arm, my wing, my wrist. I tried to bite back my guttural scream, but the final landing threw me on my damaged wing, and the sound roared up my throat without my permission.

"Haley," Kai rasped, crawling off of me, catching my face in his hands as he stared down at me. At the mess I'd made on the ground, probably. "Hey, look at me. Don't close your eyes okay. *Harvey!* Where the fuck are you?"

Panic made his voice high and piercing. I dragged my gaze to his face, frowning at the smear of blood on his cheek. I reached for it, but the movement pulled on my wing, and I screamed again, blackness closing in for a long moment.

"I'm here, I'm here," Harvey panted.

My eyes must have fallen shut; I had to force them open to see his face. Harvey was so close to me, bloodied hands reaching for my wing. I jumped at the first rush of power, boiling hot shooting past my feathers to broken bones and ruined muscle. Then pain hit so severely that my back arched off the floor of—actually, I had no idea where we were. We could have been back in the Damned Realm for all I knew. Or up in the pearly clouds of Heaven. I couldn't keep my eyes open long enough to see.

"Is she healing?" Wynvail's unwelcome voice asked.

"Why would you care?" Emlyn growled at him, deep and vibrating. "You brought all this on us."

Wynvail sighed. "When will you start listening?"

"When will *you* start killing us?" Kai snarled, getting to his feet in a rush. His magic shuddered through the air around us, snakes brushing my arms as Harvey finally let go of me. I panted, reeling in the aftermath. "That's what your master told you to do, isn't it? Murder all of us so you can get a resurrection pearl? Tell me, asshole. Who are you trying to bring back?"

"That's none of your business," Wynvail replied coolly. "And my plans are not your concern, either."

"Oh, shut up," I bit out on a groan. Now that I wasn't alight with pain, I was just pissed off. We'd just escaped the Wailing Caves, and now Cronus had fucking kidnapped us. Taking my anger out on Wynvail was an obvious outlet.

I leaned my weight into Harvey as I pushed off the floor, testing my wing's movement and hissing at the soreness. No fractures or breaks, though. The rest of me was whole, too.

"Thank you," I murmured to him, catching his hand to squeeze it and frowning at the little stones embedded in our palms. "Ugh, where the fuck are we?"

I climbed awkwardly to my feet, expecting my knees to buckle and send me back to the ground. But with Harvey's help and Emlyn ducking in to support my left, I managed to stand.

"Shit," I hissed when I saw the mammoth walls all around us, steely grey and solid. Formed of pure stone instead of individual bricks. We were sealed in on all sides except for a narrow passage straight ahead. A single route onward.

Unfortunately for us, there was a giant skeleton blocking off the path. Its skull had enormous bull horns on either side, and someone had hewn it clean off their body; it sat a few feet away like a discarded trophy.

"Who the fuck is that?"

"My rose!" Kai breathed, noticing I was on my feet. He halted his inked fist mid-air before it could slam into Wynvail's face, and rushed over to me, clutching my shoulders. "Are you okay? How do you feel? Are you dizzy? How many fingers am I holding up?"

"None," I replied dryly. "You're holding onto me too tight to hold up a single one."

Kai exhaled a harsh sigh, pressing a long kiss to my forehead. "Thank fuck."

"Answer Haley's questions, bastard," Emlyn rumbled at Wynvail, his voice so deep and furious that it shook me back to reality.

We were hemmed in by impossibly high blocks of stone, and Cronus had just ordered his prized pet to kill us.

"Emlyn, come here," I ordered, my voice colder than I planned as I fixed a steely, flat look on Wynvail. He looked a little worse for wear thanks to the fall, his short mahogany hair mussed and smudges of dirt on his cheek and trousers. He was still shirtless. Bastard. "Like Em said. Answer my fucking questions. Where are we, who's the rotted skeleton, and what killed them?"

"That's one extra question," the bastard pointed out, but he rolled his eyes when I only glared, deadly silent and refusing to rise to his quip.

My mates fanned out around me, one scary as fuck archdemon entourage.

"The skeleton is a minotaur. *The* minotaur. And Theseus killed him, so no need to worry about him killing us, too. Theseus is long dead."

"Fuck," Emlyn breathed, his grey wings shuddering and face slack.

"Yeah," Wynvail agreed, his square jaw clenching. "Your mate's already figured it out," he told me with a glare. "If that's the minotaur, and we're surrounded by impenetrable walls, it can only mean one thing."

Wynvail grinned, a vicious, joyless smile. "We're in the Labyrinth."

PART II
CAGED

CHAPTER SEVEN

"**W**hy would Cronus put us here?" I muttered, not fully recovered from having to drag *the* Minotaur's bleached bones out of our path so we could enter the damned Labyrinth. *The* Labyrinth, from bedtime stories that gave little kids nightmares.

My dad used to tell me stories of this place, and all the heroes and gods of the old myths. I never thought they were real. Guess I was naïve for a demon. Even angels up in Heaven knew the gods were real; Em explained everything he knew about them as we walked through the barren stone walkways of the Labyrinth. They had statues of the gods up in Heaven and worshipped them like they were amazing.

If the stories were all true, they were far less worthy of awe than the heroes themselves. Zeus fucked his way through anything that moved, Aphrodite started a war because the world *had* to revolve around her, and Ares was a meathead who started fights to show off his *prowess* and *might*.[1]

Dionysus sounded like a great guy, though. If you ignored the fact he was mostly worshipped by people with their dicks and tits hanging out.

Still, they were *stories*. But now we were in the Labyrinth, the stories were starting to feel very real. And here I thought being an angel-demon hybrid was as interesting as things got.

Gods, titans, myths and monsters—all real. And Cronus had decided to dump us *here?* In a Labyrinth where the old guard was already dead. Why?

"The Labyrinth has been modified," Wynvail said, casting a tight look my way. Probably because we'd only just stopped interrogating him about the resurrection pearl—which did exactly what it said on the tin, and brought back the dead— and who he wanted to return.

Nobody good, that was for sure. He was a villainous, untrustworthy asshole. Anyone he wanted to bring back was probably evil, too. There was an obvious answer, but I was in full denial about it. If he brought back his father…

No. Not happening. Nope.

"Look, you can see evidence of the changes there," the villainous, untrustworthy asshole himself went on, veering closer to the massive stone block on our left and running his hand over the grey surface. "There's a slight difference in the stone colour. This part here must have been an open passage; the stone's less weathered than the rest. Subtle, but obvious if you're looking for it."

And of course he was looking for it. I gave him a flat look. "Modified how? Other than blocking off the exits?"

"I'm not sure yet," he admitted, unhappy about it. "We should expect—"

"If you say the unexpected, I'm going to stab you in the throat," Kai hissed, glaring daggers at Wynvail.

Wynvail looked him dead in the eyes and finished, "The unexpected."

I was ninety percent sure he was going to say something different but changed it just to piss Kai off.

"Choking only," I sighed when Kai threw himself at Wynvail, who only tucked his hands in his trouser pockets and waited for the blow.[2] "And *you,* don't hurt my mate."

Something flashed in Wynvail's silver eyes, his mouth flattening. "I'll do whatever I want, honey."

Kai threw out a hand, lines of inked text winding around his arm, and Wynvail grunted as a snake wrapped around his throat. But his expression didn't change, not even when Kai yelled, thrown back by a sudden flash of white light. It was alarming that Wynvail could push him away without taking his hands out of his pockets.

"Go on, then!" Kai snarled, the whites of his eyes showing. Shit, he was panicking, and I'd been so wrapped up in the Labyrinth and Cronus that I hadn't even noticed. "Kill me. Obey your master like a good little dog."

"Kai," Emlyn warned, his voice low and rumbling as he stepped up on Kai's left, his stare unwavering from Wynvail. His broad shoulders were hunched, arms crossed over his chest.[3]

"You'd love that, wouldn't you?" Wynvail said to Kai, not looking away from him. His expression was as hard as granite, and he didn't spare a single glance for Emlyn. "Killing you would prove you right that I'm evil."

I stalked closer to them, bracing the crackling magic around my volatile mates.

"You *are* evil," Kai laughed, spreading his arms, magic spiralling faster. "Go on. Take the first shot; I'll allow it."

"Malakai," I growled, grabbing the back of his neck in a rough grip. "What are you doing? He's not fucking around; he *will* kill you."

Kai just laughed, bitter and low.

"Don't," I told Wynvail. I went against every instinct to send a brief, tentative brush along the bond between us. He jerked like I'd electrocuted him.[4] "Don't," I repeated, not voicing *please* but projecting it into my voice all the same.

Wynvail laughed, shaking his head. "I'm not going to kill him, honey. He wants it too badly."

"Kai?" My shoulders slumped, a heavy despair crushing my chest. He wanted to die?

"I don't actually want him to kill me," he groaned. "I'd kill him before he ever touched me. I just wanted him to try."

I remembered Kai trying to attack Wynvail when he dove into the Wailing Caves river. Not a single snake had penetrated Wynvail's shields. I wasn't sure who'd win in a fight, and I wasn't willing to find out.

"Trying to put me in my place?" Wynvail drawled, a deadly glint in his quicksilver eyes as he leant back against the mammoth wall. Lazy, cruel, and unbothered. "In the hierarchy of her mates, I'm fully aware of my standing. This—" He removed a hand from his pocket to gesture between him and Kai, "was pointless. And just wasted our time. Well done."

Kai slipped from my hold and launched himself at him, this time with his fists. Wynvail had already had a broken nose today,[5] but Kai seemed determined to rearrange his entire face. Probably because of Wynvail's smug tone.

I reached for Kai's arm to stop the blow, but my hand moved impossibly slowly. Unease pulsed through my heart. It was like pushing through tar; the air resisted me, fighting me back. I growled, but the sound dragged out, sticky and long.

What the fuck was happening? My fingers brushed Kai's arm but he was already swinging forward. He moved insanely fast, like he was a cheetah and I was a snail. I blinked, and Emlyn had yanked him back, Harvey stepping between them and Wynvail, who hadn't even moved.

They spoke, but their words were too fast and high. They were like mice squeaking at each other. I opened my mouth, but my lips moved so slowly I just gave up on speaking.

Emlyn spun dizzyingly fast, scanning the stone corridor. His eyes shot all around the Labyrinth passageway. My stomach dropped.

He looked right through me.

"Em..."

His head swivelled, panic growing. His lips moved rapidly but I knew what he asked this time. *Where's Haley?*

"I'm right here!" My voice was slow, dragged out. Not my voice at all, too deep, too strange. What the fuck?

But I *knew* what—Cronus. He was the god of time, and he controlled this whole Labyrinth. He'd fucked with the time in here, made me slower than everyone else.

"Bastard," I growled and hope he heard me.

My mates flipped from fighting to panicking in a millisecond. Kai went pale, his gaze darting around, nostrils flaring. Harvey raced back to where we'd come from; Emlyn growled and followed him. Wynvail just stared around, his jaw clenched and hands curled into fists.

His lips moved, wide enough that I was sure he'd shouted. *Give her back.*

The unease crawling through me became full-on panic. What if I was trapped like this forever?

A low laugh stabbed my skull with an instant migraine, the pain so brutal that my legs collapsed from under me.[6] I screamed, my hands sluggishly rising to my ears to block out the blinding pain. But the laugh was *inside* my head, rumbling through my skull like a thunderstorm. I dropped my head, tucking it between my knees.

"You ordered me to kill *them,* so why are you targeting *her?*" Wynvail demanded, his voice walking a fine line of control. Barely polite, and not careful at all.

Wait. My breath hitched, a tremor moving through my hands. I could hear him now... Not fast and shrieking but *normal.*

I lifted my head, panting, my jaw clenched on a cry.

"Thank you," Wynvail bit out, and stalked across the stone corridor to me. Murder was written in every one of his features, his rage endless.

Kai got to me before him, scooping me up and pressing me into a hug.

Fuck, it felt so good to be held. My eyes stung. I'd been so scared I'd be stuck that way forever, always separated from my mates.

I gripped him tightly, gulping down lungfuls of his scent and tasting blood, all my limbs shaking.

"What happened?" Kai demanded, his voice strained and sharp as his hands ran over every part of me. Checking for wounds and broken bones. "Where *were* you?"

"Still here," I rasped, squeezing him tighter, my eyes screwed shut as I fought not to fall apart. "Just fucking slow."

"I'll retrieve the others. Don't go anywhere," Wynvail muttered, waiting until I met his eyes. He gave me a long, searching stare, his intensity making my face burn, and nodded.

He took a step—and vanished.

I choked on a cry of surprise, my body jerking in Kai's arms. Is that what I looked like when everything went sluggish and scary?

"What the fuck?" Kai exploded, tightening his arms around me. He bared his teeth like the threat would see him and rethink attacking. Like the threat wasn't a myth come to life.

"Cronus made him slow," I breathed—and jolted again when another, worse realisation hit. *"Em! Harvey!"*

I refused to let go of Kai; I dug my fingers into his arm as I got to my feet and spun, scanning the Labyrinth. Wynvail was here somewhere.[7]

"What are we gonna do?" Kai asked, staring at the empty corridor, arms banded like iron around me.

I shook my head, mentally giving my panic the middle finger. "Find Em and Harvey. After that? Not a clue. Who knows what else Cronus will throw at us."

Hopefully not literally.

CHAPTER EIGHT

*E*m and Harvey weren't by the entrance. And in hindsight, I should have known that flying wouldn't work, but how else was I supposed to see where my mates were in this giant bloody Labyrinth?

Kai watched anxiously from below as I flapped higher and higher, my heart hammering at just how tall the walls were. There was no hope of scaling them; there were no handholds, no grooves beyond the hairline crack between new and old stone, but that was too slight to offer any help.

So up I flew, ignoring the aches that made themselves known, my wings still tender from crashing into the Labyrinth in the first place.[1] The air grew thinner up here, a strange lightness filling my body, buoying my wings.

Holy fuck, this might work.

Kai shouted a question from below, but I was so high up I couldn't hear him.

"Nothing yet," I yelled back, winging my reply.[2] I tipped my head back, the top of the walls swiftly approaching. I wasn't sure I wanted to see this place from above. What if it was as big as a city? What if it was bigger than Iarlon?

Above me was only a flat expanse of grey, what I'd assumed was the sky from below. But there were no clouds. Nothing. Just greyness.

So close now. Only a few metres to go.

I held my breath for the last one, pumping my wings slower and craning my neck. What if there wasn't anything above these walls? What if it wasn't even a maze anymore? Cronus could be tricking us, fucking with our heads.

I rose the last few inches, sweat beading on my upper lip and my fingers stretching for the top of the wall so I could pull myself onto it.

So close, so nearly—there!

I didn't even touch the stone.

My fingers connected with a sharp, crackling field of invisible power, and a charge shattered through me like lightning. Both darkness and light flashed across the grey emptiness above the maze. My wings seized. My body stiffened. Stilled.

I didn't even get a chance to scream before the field of magic sucked me in, like the void had swallowed me in Wynvail's house.

My entire vision flashed black for a long sickening moment, blocking out the Labyrinth walls, the empty sky, and the sight of my mate below. When it released me and light flared back in, my body suddenly mobile, I wasn't ready. I was prepared to be devoured or crippled with pain, not thrown from the sky.

I splayed my wings with a gasp, freefalling backwards and scrambling for control. The thin air and my panic-tight chest made breathing impossible, my scream strangled in my throat as I twisted until I was facing the ground.

A swell of air slammed into me, caught in the curve of my wings, and halted my fall with a sudden jolt. Relief threw my heart against my ribs, and I panted for air, flapping in place.

Okay, okay, I was still alive. Big fan of being alive.

I peered down at the ground to shout to Kai and reassure him I was okay but—the passage below was wider than the one I just ascended. And my mate was nowhere to be seen.

CHAPTER NINE

KAI

"*H*aley!" I screamed, staggering forward when she vanished as if I could bring her back. My breathing spiralled so fast. I threw both hands at the sky, pushing out as much magic as possible. The stories tattooed on my body—tales of my family all the way back through seven generations—twisted around my limbs. Unleashing snakes so powerful that I stumbled in place, dizzy as power built and tore free.

"She's *my* mate!" I yelled at the maze, shouting at the solid walls with a rage I had no control over. "She's not yours! Give her back!"

My hands shook, vicious quakes moving up my arms and shuddering through my ribcage. I turned on the spot, searching the austere passage like Haley would appear, magically gifted back to me.

This fucking maze! It couldn't take her from me. I *couldn't* be without her, not ever again. She was the glue that held my sanity together. She was the only thing that made me feel like Malakai and not the mindless brute who'd spent a hundred years fighting anything and everything that moved.

In our old life, I used my magic to protect, only resorting to violence when my family was in trouble.[1] Wynvail, the absolute cunt of the pit, had made my magic cruel, a blade to be used on anyone, guilty and innocent alike.

Without my mate, that was all I was: a violent beast.

"Give her back!" I screamed, my breathing faster. I spun again, praying I'd find her on my next rotation. Where was she? Where was my rose? I needed her. I *needed* her.

My snakes cut through the air like knives, sinking vicious fangs into a solid roof of magic. That was what Haley slammed into, what stole her from me. I rent the sharp edges of fangs through the sky until holes appeared in the grey expanse, venom eroding its power. I hoped it was torture for the titan motherfucker. I hoped his magic ruptured and his chest cracked open and his heart melted to blood and gore.

The erosion spread, the holes wider, bigger, and I grinned, my own teeth bared. He deserved every bit of pain.

But my heart skipped when the holes knitted back together, so suddenly that the power swallowed one of my snakes and my knees buckled. I grunted, grabbing the wall on my left and hauling myself back to my feet. Shit, that hurt. It throbbed in my chest, like I'd been physically punched.

Back here, now! I ordered my magic, tearing them away from the barrier before it could consume any more of my power. It was *mine.* Like Haley was mine.

"You can't have her!" I screamed, my head tipped back, the words yelled at the barrier, the walls, at the entire fucking Labyrinth. "She's mine!"

A chill went down my spine when dark, low laughter rippled through my head. He was here.

Good.

I curled my hands into fists, absorbing my snakes when they met my skin. They writhed in my chest, furious they'd been denied the blood they wanted so badly.

"Come and fight me instead of watching from the shadows, you coward," I shouted, my nostrils flaring, my whole body shaking. "When I win, you return my mate."

Cronus laughed louder, the sound stabbing the tender place behind my eyes until my whole skull hurt and I gasped at the sharp spike. *You would die.*

Yeah, well. I'd rather be dead than lose my rose. I had no interest in the person I would be without her. Where she went, I followed, even into death.

You're no use to me dead, Malakai Virex, so you will persist.

"Give me back my mate!" I screamed, my voice giving out on the final word.

Anxiety made me shake, make my insides sharp and jagged and fast, so damn fast. I spun and reared back my fist, slamming it into the solid wall beside me. I roared at the pain, at the panic of losing my rose.

I punched the Labyrinth again and again, wishing it was Cronus's face. I didn't care that I was fucking with a titan who'd ruled Olympus, waged war on the gods, and eaten his own children. He was my sworn enemy, worse even than Wynvail.

Wynvail held me captive, made me fight my family, and shaped me into a feral creature, but I didn't give a shit what happened to *me*. Haley, though? That made me so furious that the walls trembled, and my snakes sank their fangs into the ground under me.

Fuck with me and I'd raise my fists. Fuck with my mate, and I'd raise all of Hell.

Best of luck, Malakai, Cronus said with a laugh that told me he didn't rate my chances of survival high.

I was no use to him dead? Yeah, 'cause he'd ordered his

little *bitch* to kill me. For what reason, I didn't know. I got that Cronus was furious because we killed Rhea, his captive/wife. But the Labyrinth hadn't been modified and updated today. No fucking way. He might have been an all-powerful titan but the additions to the Labyrinth were visible, which meant he'd put one of his minions on the job. Magic would have been seamless. This maze had been created in advance.

Because he planned to drop someone else in here? Or because he was always going to come for us? For my girl?

I couldn't forget the prophecy emblazoned on her back—a future of greatness and terror. One I could read because it was written in the same language as my family's stories. What was written there scared the shit out of me. I shut it out.

But Rhea said Haley could kill Cronus. And it was inked right there on her back. What were the chances the titan knew it, too? All this shit was intentional. All of it was to get to Haley.

And that made me insane with rage.

I drew my fist back to slam it into the wall again—I'd punch my way out of this place if I had to—but the ground roared and shuddered beneath me, and I was forced to throw both arms out at my sides for balance.

"Motherfucker," I gasped, still breathing short, my magic rioting inside me as the ground moved *up*.

A square of stone in the floor I'd naively presumed was solid and unmoveable detached and soared up through the maze. I threw out four snakes, anchoring them to the platform to hold me up. Haley would be angry if I returned to her broken.[2]

"Haley!" I screamed as the platform soared, taking me high in the Labyrinth. Was my mate up here, too? I was close to the place where she vanished; I reached up, desperate to touch the barrier and follow her wherever she went.

I needed to crush her body to mine, needed her to hug me

like she did when we dropped into the Labyrinth. She'd wrapped both arms and wings around me, and I'd felt whole for the first time, more myself even than when I was buried inside her.

My fingertips strained for the barrier, my heart pounding fast, hands trembling, but the platform jerked suddenly right, and a square opened up in the wall to carry me away. I was ripped away from the passage where Haley vanished. Taken somewhere new.

"No!" I roared.

My throat burned. I shook harder, energy and anxiety frantic inside me. I screamed wordlessly, my stress erupting as rage. I wrapped power around my fist, coiling the snake tightly to my skin, and drove punch after punch into the platform. Who cared if I fell? It was taking me further from her.

Animal hisses of fury poured up my throat, but it didn't matter that I sounded like the mindless beast of the pits. I couldn't get back to Haley from here. I needed to get back to the other—

The mammoth brick that had slid free of the wall slammed back into place with a resounding crash, and my voice choked off with a gasp.

"No." I shook my head, my shoulders slumped and arms limp. My hand throbbed, bloody knuckles broken.

I was trapped here, locked away from Haley.

All at once, my fury and panic was replaced by despair. At least when we fought through the Wailing Caves we were together. All my family was with me. I hadn't been alone since Haley stormed through Alphaven and claimed us, hauling us to safety.

I didn't want to be alone.

CHAPTER TEN

HALWEN

J'd been walking for years. Every time I reached the end of a passageway, a new opening would grind open, or the floor would sink, carrying me into a dungeon I had to navigate with zero light. Whenever I thought I'd found a way out or heard my mates' yells, the floors shifted, the walls changed, and I was carried further from them.

Now, I walked in a daze, barely paying attention to my surroundings. If I fell off a sudden platform, my wings would act on instinct and catch me. If I missed a new gap in the maze, the walls would shift and switch until they guided me onto the Labyrinth's new path.

Sometimes Cronus taunted me when I ignored a new opening or when I muttered to myself. Or when I walked into a wall.[1]

Foolish, foolish girl, Cronus's deafening voice filled my head now. I didn't know what he was sneering at me for this time. I didn't particularly care; I wiped away the blood at my nose, locked my jaw against the crash of pain in my skull, and walked on.

I sank deep into my mate bonds. Three were frayed, but two were perfect and strong. I'd been walking, dazed, for so long that I couldn't tell whose soul was whose, but I held onto both—kindness and bitterness, frustration and patience, both souls rife with deep, mental suffering. The kind that left scars both outside and in.

The souls tugged me in opposite directions, one straight ahead and one behind. I didn't know which to follow, didn't know which was Wynvail. He was here in this Labyrinth, trapped like me. He could lead me to my mates; he could be with them.

He was the only hope I had, the only bond that could guide me back to them, so I took a guess and followed the soul of bitterness and patience.

The soles of my feet throbbed after another hour, my eyes itchy. At least they'd stopped bleeding—until Cronus spoke next. The walls changed but every passage looked the same: solid grey stone, empty of anything except me.

Where were the nightmares? If Cronus had dumped the Minotaur outside the entrance, where were the replacement monsters? Walking endlessly was driving me mad, but I wasn't fighting for my life. I wasn't battling beasts and bleeding from a dozen places. It unsettled me.

"I need water," I told no one in particular. My mouth was so dry, my lips sore from licking them so often. I'd take being led back to the river in the Wailing Caves over this dehydration. "And a hug."

I wanted my mates, dammit. I hadn't fought through Hell to find them just to be torn from them by an oversized maze. It wasn't fair.

I slumped into a wall and rubbed my face, my eyes sore from staring at grey wall after grey wall.

"I've had enough," I told no one in particular. When Cronus laughed, amusement moving through my skull like thunder, I added, "I'm not talking to you, asshole."

Brave words for someone at my mercy.

I didn't care. I rolled my eyes.

How does your curse glow? Show me, and I'll consider giving you a boon.

"A boon," I mocked, giving another eye-roll because I was in a shit mood and getting damn near disoriented. "What kind of *boon?*"

I can see where your mates are.

A glare slammed my brows over my eyes, and my breathing quickened. Rage replaced the lethargy in my bones, and I bared my teeth at the sky. Was that where he watched us? Looking down on us like a twisted god?

"If you touch them, *I'll end you,*" I vowed, breathing even faster at the thought. Power rumbled inside me, ready to eviscerate this titan even if I was a lowly hybrid and the attempt would probably get me killed. "And I don't *know* how the marks glow. If I knew that, I'd be using it right now to blast through your damn Labyrinth."

Even with blood magic bubbling in my core, nothing happened with my marks. No crimson glow. No power. But heartbeats pumped in two bodies, far ahead but close enough for me to sense them. I was following the right bond.

"Get a real hobby, and stop being a voyeur," I told Cronus, pushing off the wall and resuming my walk. Fuck, my feet hurt. "Watching me walk through a maze? That's just weird."

Experiments need observation, he replied, which was even weirder.

A shudder rippled down my body. It was bad enough being sent into the Labyrinth, but being called an experiment? My blood ran cold. Now I knew how mice felt when they were dropped in little plastic mazes.[2]

But I was a demon, not a mouse, and Cronus had forgotten I had claws.

My aching head swam as I sank into my magic, but I gritted my teeth and powered on. I was surprised I hadn't passed out by now. How long had I been in this place with no water, no food, and no real rest? I'd slept an hour or so, but every time a panel would grate open, I'd shoot back awake. So what was the point? Cronus wanted me on edge, half dead. He was a sadist.

I was just delusional enough to make up a song and start singing to myself as I followed the throb of heartbeats and Wynvail's corrosive soul.

"My name's Cronus, and I'm a giant anus," I sang loudly enough that he'd have no trouble hearing me. "*I bully kickass demons for sad, nefarious reasons.*"

This is tedious, Cronus rumbled.

My knees buckled when pain stabbed through my skull on the heels of his voice. Was he doing it on purpose? Trying to break me with agony? I didn't want to admit it was working.

"I get off on being a raging dick, probably because I have a tiny prick—"

Another flare of pain sent me to my knees, but I fell laughing. The rolling sound was full of madness, truly and utterly unhinged. That was one good thing about me. Take away my weapons, my power, and my mates, but I would always have the infallible ability to piss someone off.

The metre of that song makes no sense, Cronus remarked with an edge of a sneer.

"Nobody asked you for a critique," I muttered, my forehead pressed to the cold stone. "Typical man, offering your opinion when it's not—"

A scream tore through the rest of my words, but he got the point. Pain pounded harder, stabbing until I cried. It echoed the throb of blood through my body—and through the two bodies nearing me.

Please don't be woolly yarmouth. Knowing my luck, it would be two giant, killer octopuses who wanted to digest me slowly so I felt every disgusting, slimy moment. If I'd been in my right mind and not driven mad by days of walking, I could have recognised the beats, could have known if they were friend or slimy foe.

"Piece of shit titan," I slurred, dragging my nails down the wall as I hauled myself back to my feet. I knew, deep down, it wasn't a smart idea to antagonise him, but I'd lost all sense of self-preservation a few days ago. "When I get out of here, I'm coming for you.[3] I want my mate back."

That's assuming there's anything left of him.

Horror made my breathing stop, but fury bolstered it back to life until I was panting. My hands shook, magic pounding faster in my ears. I didn't have any strength left, but spite powered my steps down the cold, stone pathway, wings dragging behind me.

Because Cronus hated me, thunder crashed through the dark sky above, and rain deluged from the clouds. It soaked me through instantly, and I screeched at the icy temperature. He laughed. Psychopath.

Show me your curse mark, Halwen.

I lifted my arm and waved it around. "Not hiding it, dickhead. No glowing magic here either," I snarled, lifting my shirt as I dragged myself onward a few steps. I let the fabric fall back into place, my palm flat to the wall as my steps grew slick and treacherous.

He wanted me to fall, to break. But he should've picked someone far less stubborn.

The heartbeat—Wynvail's heartbeat if I wasn't deluding myself—thumped an angry beat, clearer and closer the further

I slid down the passage. *Please, please don't be a homicidal octopus.*

I stumbled on a few steps, but my boots slipped on the slick floor and the vicious rain driving through my clothes made me swerve into the Labyrinth wall.

I smacked into solid stone with a groan, pain lancing through my boobs and stomach.

"Why is it always the boobs?" I groaned, pushing off the wall and rubbing the ache out of my poor, abused tatas. "Oh, for fuck's sake," I huffed when the drumming rain was drowned out by a loud, grating roar.

Another doorway was opening, the Labyrinth shifting.

"I'm staying here, asswipe," I muttered, throwing wet hair out of my face. "Go into your new chamber yourself. I'm done."

My boobs were sore, I was wet,[4] and I missed my mates. Oh, and my head spun, I was so hungry I would legitimately eat the murder octopus, and I'd had it up to *here* with titans and their bullshit schemes.

Was all this really so he could push me to light up my curse marks? Because he was going to be very disappointed. The scant few times it happened before, I hadn't controlled it.

The wall I was plastered to shuddered, and I was shoved backwards so suddenly that I shrieked like a turkey. My back throbbed where I collided with the wall, and I swore colour-fully, flicking drenched pink hair out of my face.

Fuck. Four solid stone walls were racing towards me, boxing me into a tiny area. Cronus was using his remote controlled walls to position me like a puppet. Well, I refused to dance to the jerking of his strings.

I kicked off the ground, using the space while I had it to rise three feet off the ground. I wouldn't let this bastard trap me. Who knew what he was planning to do? Probably crush me into a smear of blood on the Labyrinth walls.

Use your magic, Cronus said in my head, a sudden stab of pain making me gasp. My wings faltered, but I wrenched hard on my muscles and stayed in the air.

"Go fuck a pineapple," I hissed, throwing a panicked look around me as the walls groaned and rushed for me faster, pinning me in faster than I could rise. Not that I could escape over the top of the walls anyway; I'd learned that lesson the hard way.

Stone brushed my right wing, and I sucked in a sharp breath, tilting away from the Labyrinth walls as they pressed closer. Shit. They closed around me so fast my wings were pressed against my sides and I had no choice but to drop back to the rain-slick ground. My boots slid, but I threw my hands out and latched onto the wall. I wasn't sure I even had enough space to fall; that was the only good news.

"What are you gonna do?" I yelled at the sky. "Squash me out of existence?"

Why would I do that? he replied, making my knees buckle. Fuck, it hurt. I hissed through my teeth, clutching my head. *I don't want to kill you, Halwen.*

Well, I want to kill you buddy, I thought, gritting my teeth.

I jumped up, throwing my hands at the walls and praying for something to grip. I wouldn't stand here and wait to be crushed. The only good part about the walls pressing on me was the adrenaline had cleared my head, and I didn't feel on the verge of a mental breakdown. Just a furious rampage.

The rain stopped without warning, there and gone in a second. Unease tightened my chest.

I yanked hard on the bond rife with stress and cold rage in my chest. *Come the fuck on, Wynvail. You love to stalk me; do your damn job and find me.*

My fingers slid on smooth, solid stone, and I growled through my teeth as I slid back down. Stone pressed on my wings, so close it felt like a coffin. Cronus might have said he didn't want to kill me, but he had a funny way of showing it.

I glared at the sky—and my heart jolted in my chest. My stomach sank all the way to my boots. Where the sky had been rainy and dark, it was now a perfect blue filled with fluffy white clouds. One of which was stretching towards the high walls of the Labyrinth, four long fingers reaching for me. At first I thought fear was making me irrational, but no, those fingers attached to a palm and *there,* that was a stubby thumb. A hand. *A hand* burst out of the sky and dove towards me.

I screamed, pressing my back against the stone, heaving on the walls with all my strength and not caring that a dull ache shot through my wings when I pinned them.

Get me out of here! I yelled at Wynvail, pulling hard on the bond.

I reached for my bond with Wane too, praying for help. His soul rushed towards me, faltering at the fear drenching my entire being. I hoped he didn't know the titan was here. How much trauma must Cronus have given my mate? A hundred years—I couldn't get past it. He'd been the captive of a titan for *a hundred years,* and I couldn't even begin to imagine what had been done to him in that time. When we connected before, his shadows were being cut away from him.

Was that what Cronus wanted to do to me, too? Cut my power away from me? Devour it like he'd devoured his own children?

White filled my whole vision, blocking out the sky as the hand dove for me. Fingers wrapped around my shoulders, my wings, his palm swallowing my head, and I bleated in panic like I was a goat and not an angel-demon hybrid. What would he do to me? A body-wide shudder made my bones rattle, my breathing little more than gasps.

Magic blasted from the inked marks on my stomach and arm, not seeming to care that the curse had been broken on my power. My heart skipped as crimson light cut through the cloud, lighting up the hand with an eldritch glow, and I threw out my hand on instinct. I had no plans, no idea what I wanted to happen, and I didn't connect with my mates this time.

Instead, my consciousness tore out of my body and I saw —myself, but from above. It was only for a split second, but I watched the hand retreat from around me, and a strange bubble of satisfaction and nervousness filled my chest before I slammed back into my own body.

I splayed against the wall behind me, panting for breath. There was no blistering pain in my body, just trembling terror making my chest tight and breathing a ruin.

As I suspected, Cronus's voice rumbled through my head, snapping me out of my shaky terror.

He hadn't killed me. Annoyingly true to his word. I was still hoping to kill the bastard, though. He'd marked himself for death the second he took Wane.

"You might as well have said *aha!* and twirled your evil moustache," I rasped, catching my breath.

You're very promising, Halwen, he told me as if that was a compliment. *You'll serve me well.*

"The only thing I'm serving you is a death warrant," I muttered, pushing off the wall and glaring when the others remained a foot away, not retreating to give me space. I tested my wings—both still in one piece, thank fuck—and my body —bruised but unbroken.

We'll have to work on that attitude, he commented, seemingly to himself. *That shouldn't be too difficult.*

I bared my teeth, a snarl in the back of my throat. "I passed your fucked up test. Let me out of here."

Passed? Halwen, that was barely the first obstacle. You've got a long way to go to prove yourself to me.

"I have zero interest in 'proving myself' to you, asshole."[5]

Cronus said nothing. And the pressure on my skull lifted until I could feel the full impact of the damage he'd wrought. I bit my tongue as pain erupted like an active volcano, my head pounding in three places, and a migraine right behind my eyes.

Cronus was gone. And I was still trapped.

"Fuck," I snarled, and kicked the wall.

CHAPTER ELEVEN

*I*t had taken me two hours to wedge a gap into a crack between two walls with my knife. All I had to show for my work was an inch of space and a very bent blade.[1]

"It'll have to do," I told myself, stashing my bent knife and grabbing the edge of the wall with both hands, wrenching on it with all my strength. "Come—fucking—open," I groaned, muscles straining in my arms and back as I heaved on the solid stone.

The entire thing didn't come open, just a space a little higher than an average door. I couldn't begin to understand how the whole Labyrinth worked, and I didn't care as long as I could find my way back to my mates and out of this damned place.

"Stupid—bloody—*maze*," I grunted, yanking on the stone hard enough to prise it open a few more inches.

It took some creative flapping of my wings, bracing my foot on the opposite wall, but I threw my entire body into widening the crack. My tender head pounded as pressure built in my skull, but I didn't stop until there was a big enough space for me to squeeze through.

I clutched my head, groaning, but I didn't trust the wall to stay open so I flattened my wings against me and shimmied into the gap. Fuck, the Labyrinth walls was thicker than I'd been expecting. They were a whole foot wide; no wonder it had taken so much work to open them.

"Almost," I panted, my head pounding, disorienting me. Cronus had really done a number on my head this time. Damage echoed through my entire skull, throbbing through my face and body as I dragged myself through the tight gap.

The loud, echoing grate of stone on stone made my heart skip.

"No."

He wouldn't...

Cronus wanted me alive; he'd proven that by not killing me when he had the chance. Then again, he'd almost crushed me to get my magic to spark. Who's to say he wouldn't murder me just to see what my curse marks did?

I frantically pulled myself through the opening, but it was so tight I had to take tiny shuffling steps, and my nightmare was confirmed when I felt the wall shift at my back, pressing me into the opposite wall until my ribs burst with pain.

A sob broke from my lips, helplessness and rage making me shaky as I scrambled to escape the walls. I couldn't move fast enough, couldn't get far enough, and my wings dragged on either side of me. Another sob crashed up my throat, tears burning my eyes as the walls pressed all the air out of my lungs.

I was going to die. Here, alone, murdered by a titan with a remote controlled maze.

I threw all my weight to my right. If I couldn't shuffle out of the maze, I could at least fall out. Maybe I'd only lose a leg or a wing. The thought was horrifying, but if it kept me alive, I'd do it.

I tipped, fresh air hitting my tongue, but the walls groaned and shifted, squashing me on two sides and—I was stuck. I couldn't even fall my way out of this thing.

Oh, gods. This is it, isn't it?

Everything I'd survived, and this was how I died. I wanted to go with my mates all around me, peaceful in bed in a hundred years' time.

I tried to throw myself to freedom one last time, heaving my body a few millimetres along, my hand shooting free. I flailed it around, desperate for something to grip onto to drag myself free.

My heart stopped when a cool, rough palm met my own. I sobbed so hard my throat hurt. Fingers wrapped viciously tight, wrenching me sideways an inch, and then two, and then—

I fell free as two big hands thrust the walls further apart to let me out. I slammed into a chest, my body jolting and head lolling on my neck so suddenly that I went dizzy. My head hurt so much, my wings throbbing and chest aching, but cool air caressed my face and I was *free*.

I couldn't catch a breath, couldn't control my body as I started shaking. Arms snapped around me, dragging me away as the walls grated and groaned behind me. No, wait, that groaning was familiar. My heart leapt, tears blistering my eyes. *Em.* Emlyn was here. I was—I was safe.

"He's dead," a low, furious voice hissed in my ear, arms too tight around my bruised ribs. "He's fucking *dead* for this."

I startled, realising in a rush who clutched me so tightly it hurt. Wynvail. He was the one holding me like he'd been terrified to lose me.

"Hales," Emlyn rumbled, his voice reaching into my chest

and soothing my panic like magic. "Talk to me, Haley, tell me you're okay."

"I'm okay," I replied, my voice smaller than intended. I turned my head, inhaling sharply at the pain in my neck, and met his eyes. I slumped, my strength replaced by relief when our eyes locked. "I'm okay now."

"Give her to me," Emlyn growled at Wynvail when he released the Labyrinth walls, his nostrils flaring. It was rare to see Em so worked up, but he had that murder look on his face that told me Wynvail's days were numbered. I was surprised he was still alive. Probably only because he was my mate and it might hurt me.

Wynvail didn't acknowledge that Emlyn had spoken, his arms banded like iron around me and his chest rising and falling fast. Rage and panic filled my chest—both his emotions. I was too weak to know what my own feelings were doing.

"Let go," I rasped, pushing on his bare stomach and surprised all over again at the solid muscle and abs there. "I want to hug Em."

"There's a minor issue with that, honey," Wynvail replied, his voice calm and smooth now, masking the rage in his soul. "The thought of letting go of you is intolerable."

"Em, don't," I warned on instinct. I couldn't feel his soul like Wynvail's, but I knew him as well as I knew myself. And when I sought him with my stare again, he was much closer than before, his blue eyes fiery and mouth set. His hands were raised. One move from ripping Wynvail's arms off his body, and only stayed by my voice.

"Your ears are bleeding," Emlyn told me, his voice gravelly and deep. "We need to find Harvey; I'm worried about you, Hales. You keep bleeding, and that can't be good."

"There could be lasting damage," Wynvail agreed, clutching me tighter.

I gasped out a cry when his arms pressed on my ribs, and the sound started him away from me. Livid silver eyes scanned me, noting the scrapes from the walls and the way I held my wing awkwardly to my side.

I rubbed my face, wetness meeting my fingertips when they brushed the edges of my face. "Where's everyone else?"

I was still processing the fact I wasn't crushed to death. I was *alive*. Em and *Wynvail* of all people got me out. I ... owed him my life. That was annoying.

When Emlyn folded me carefully into his arms, I sank into him, cutting off the sob that wanted to rise. *Enough crying.* I needed my mates, and a way out of this nightmare. I needed *action*.

"We lost Harvey," Emlyn replied carefully, stroking hair back from my face. "He got stuck on the other side of a wall. Kai was with you...?"

I swallowed, resting my aching face against Em's warm shoulder and letting comfort bleed through me. A weak part of me wanted Wynvail to wrap his arms around me from behind and cocoon me between them both. Like he felt my wish, gentle knuckles skimmed down my wings, tucking feathers back into place, pulling out a broken one that had been knocked loose.

"Don't keep that," I warned him, turning my aching head in time to catch him tucking the dark feather into his pocket.

"Keep what?" he asked so convincingly that I almost believed I'd hallucinated the theft.

I shook my head, and regretted it when pressure and pain flared. I dropped my head on Em's chest and focused on my breathing. "I tried to fly up to find you guys, but I touched a field of magic and it zapped me here. I ... left Kai behind."

"Not by choice," Emlyn disagreed, placing a long, soothing kiss on my head. "We'll find them both."

I swallowed, nodding weakly. "Where do we start?"

"If you can't fly," Wynvail said, back to his regular smooth, unruffled tone, "we'll have to follow the path."

I jerked away from Emlyn when a guttural, blood-chilling scream tore through the distance. It echoed in waves, growing louder, rawer, slamming into my soul again and again and again, cutting deep with each blow.

"Harvey," I rasped, shaking all over again. What was making my mate scream like that—like he was *petrified?*

"Cronus," I snarled.

Emlyn dropped his arms from around me and caught my hand. "This way," he growled, protectiveness coming from him in lethal waves. No one got between Em and his family and escaped unscathed. The same went for me.

And Wynvail was apparently on board, or still couldn't put much space between me and him, because he glued himself to my side and raced with us down the wide stone passage.

Another scream made me flinch. I curled my free hand into a fist, pain driving deep through my heart in a phantom of Harvey's.

"He's strong," Wynvail said without prompting as I began to run full out. "He can survive whatever Cronus gives him."

I bared my teeth and growled in the bastard's face. "He's strong because you tortured him."

"He's strong because I trained him to be!" he snapped back, silver eyes flashing. "I kept them all from growing weak while they waited for you."

He knew I'd come back? He had a lot of explaining to do before I killed the traitorous asshole. I began to demand those answers but Harvey screamed again. He was yelling so loudly his voice broke, and I could have sworn the word was *stop.*

My stomach twisted as I thought of what could be happening to him. He'd been through enough already. Too much.

We swung around a corner, almost slamming into each

other with how fast we sprinted. In front of us was a long stretch of grey stone with a flat wall at the far side. A dead end.

And right in front of us was a giant serpent with six necks, six heads, and one impossibly tall body.

"What the hell is that thing?" I breathed, retreating a step.

"Drakon," Wynvail breathed, catching my wrist to tug me back another step. Panic and protectiveness roared through his soul, so severe that I flinched.

"What?" I hissed, my whole body shaking when Harvey screamed again. Power and panic roared through me, pumping my blood faster. He was on the other side of that wall, so close, so far.

"Dragon," Emlyn clarified, and threw himself in front of me when the six-headed creature launched at us.

CHAPTER TWELVE

*T*hree things happened at once.

1. Emlyn shifted into his crimson eagle and cried out so loudly that Wynvail threw his hands over his ears on instinct, letting go of me.
2. The dragon snapped three of its heads towards Em when he soared in front of me, the black tips of his wings grazing the dragon's metallic scales. Its teeth gnashed into Emlyn's wing joint, making him scream louder.
3. And I completely fucking *lost it*.

Magic erupted through me, lighting up both my curse marks and empowering my blood magic until I could hear the *thud-thud* of every heartbeat in the Labyrinth. They drowned out Harvey's screams, Em's high screech, and whatever Wynvail yelled at me. Blood was all I heard, and the fierce thump of my own heart as rage filled it.

I kicked off the ground and threw myself at the dragon,

ripping one of my volcanic daggers from its sheath and driving it into a long, sinuous neck. Scales resisted my knife, but I was on fire with rage and I threw all my strength into it, driving it all the way through. I was lucky this wasn't a hydra, because I cleaved the blade all the way through until the head dropped at the creature's feet. Two heads didn't grow back. It just thrashed and roared, almost as loud as the blood roaring inside my skull.

The glow from my curse marks flared brighter, cast over scales and wings until the dragon screamed and reared back.

Emlyn flew, carrying himself awkwardly, and dropped back to the ground on two feet. He clutched his shoulder, blood slicked all down his chest.

The blood ... that was what I could sense, why my power was growing until my whole body shook with it. Wynvail realised it at the same time I did, and a scary, intense look sharpened his features as he withdrew the knife he stole from me and—stabbed it deep into his forearm, carving open a hole.

My wings faltered when power filled my veins, so sharp and fiery that it almost hurt. The dragon was retreating, trying to get as far away from me as possible. I was the predator now, and it knew it.

But the space dead-ended, and it had nowhere to go.

I couldn't hear myself breathing, couldn't hear what Emlyn shouted at me or the growls coming from the remaining five heads of the dragon.

"You're dead," I told it, and didn't care if I was shouting.

Another wave of power crashed into me, and my eyes flew wide, air cutting off in my chest as magic filled every available space. My wings flared, frozen stiff at my sides, but another force kept me in the air.

I was familiar enough with my blood magic to know it had

locked onto the twin heartbeats of the dragon, embedded itself in every vein.

Kill it, I urged my magic, my glare fixed on the dragon as the creature thrashed and twisted. Trying to get my magic out.

I don't think so. You hurt my mate. Death is the only thing that will save you from this magic.

And even then, I hoped it suffered.

I reached for both pounding hearts in its huge body and clenched my fist in front of me. Instead of the dragon exploding into blood and gore like what usually happened, a blast of crimson power tore from my stomach tattoo, up my chest and down my arm, lighting up that curse mark before it tore from my fist.

A beam of blazing power burned a hole through the dragon and slammed right through the wall behind it, leaving a perfect, burned circle.

For a moment I just stared at the smoking hole in the beast and the wall.

What the fuck...?

This wasn't just my blood magic. The ink on my spine tingled, reminding me of the prophecy. Was this the greatness I was destined for? Blasting apart mythical creatures and mazes?

I didn't want greatness. I wanted my mates.

The dragon fell, its weight dragging it to the ground in slow motion before gravity claimed it all at once. My heart skipped, the vicious power that had pounded through my body ebbing away until it was only my blood magic thumping inside my chest, my head, my bones. But this wasn't normal. How the hell did I *do* that?

The dragon's massive body and five remaining heads crashed to the ground, sending a ripple through the walls around us, and knocking me out of the frozen state that held me in the air.

Ah, shit. I dropped fast, flapping my numb wings like crazy, but before I could come anywhere close to the ground, strong arms plucked me from the air and the loud beating of wings filled my ears.

"Em!" I cried, turning to stare at his rough, bearded face. "Are you insane? You're hurt?"

He grunted, lowering us carefully to a spot that wasn't full of dead dragon. "Nothing's going to stop me catching my mate."

"Insane man," I sighed, kissing his jaw and regaining most of my motor skills. "Thank you."

"Always, Hales," he murmured, nuzzling the top of my head as his feet met the ground. He didn't set me down, though. He clutched me to his chest with a low rumbling sound in his throat. A threat, I realised, when Wynvail came closer, blood running down his arm and trailing across the ground.

I swallowed, my gaze fixed on the blood. So much blood; he'd cut deep. My heart hammered, a haze filling my head. Wynvail was hurt. Emlyn was hurt. Harvey—had stopped screaming.

Oh, god why had he stopped screaming?

"I'm fine," Wynvail assured me, warmth in his voice as I scrambled out of Emlyn's arms.

"You're all psychopaths," I hissed, grabbing his hand and assessing the damage. "Why would you do this? You cut so deep, you madman!"

"I wanted to be sure there was enough blood for you," he replied like that was a perfectly normal thing to say.

I froze when he kissed my cheek, but I threw him a glare when I remembered everything he'd done. He locked up my mates, terrorised them, gave them trauma, and made them fight each other. Made them fight *me.*

I shoved him away from me, shoved *myself* away from *him,* and faced the dragon—and the hole I'd blasted through the Labyrinth wall. The indestructible wall that even *the Minotaur* wasn't able to breach.

How did I burn a hole through it? I wasn't even an archdemon like my mates—as far as I knew—and all I'd ever been able to do with my blood power was explode assassins until their bodies became mush and gore. This? This was so far above my level it was insane.

"I killed a dragon," I pointed out, staring at the massive corpse. Even on its side, it was ten feet high, with five heads splayed out on long necks around us, blocking us off from the path. The one I'd hacked off had rolled a few feet away. Blood rushed in my ears as I stared at it, and the silence on the other side of the wall was deafening.

What had Cronus done to Harvey?

My arm had stopped glowing, no magic blasting from my stomach tattoo either, but my own power bubbled inside me, seething mad.

"Cronus left it here for you to kill," Wynvail pointed out. "Everything in this Labyrinth has a purpose."

"Including you," Emlyn muttered under his breath, settling his hand on my lower back as I began to pick my way around the dragon heads. "You were sent to kill us."

Wynvail shot Em an exasperated look, his eyes sliding pointedly to me. I thought he was trying to say he wouldn't kill them because it would kill me, the woman he was strangely obsessed with.

But nope.

"When a titan tells you to do something, you do it," he replied, icy and baleful as he followed us around the dragon's corpse. "If he wants you dead, you're dead."

But why come to our rescue in the Wailing Caves? He could have grabbed me and left my mates behind.

"So you're his prized bitch?" I asked, hauling myself up over a dragon neck and sliding down the other side. If I hadn't been terrified for Harvey, I might have said *wheeeee*. But with every minute's silence, my magic churned faster and my anger grew to rage, blacking out my terror for the moment.

"I'm whatever he tells me I am," Wynvail replied with a little laugh. "So are you, but you're too dumb to realise it."

I ignored that little dig and hauled myself over another neck, now within five feet of the smoking hole my magic had burned through the wall. It had to be curse magic; there was no other explanation. Whoever had cursed me hadn't just stripped my own magic; they'd given me this devastating force. Probably so it could burn me up from the inside.

Something occurred to me as I rushed to the hole, bending to peer through the other side. More concrete, another corridor. "Did Cronus give me these curses?"

"That would be my guess," Wynvail agreed, throwing a warning glare at Emlyn when he shoulder-checked him to reach me first. "I don't know for certain, though."

"I bet you're not cursed, are you, golden boy?"

Wynvail just laughed, a low, bitter sound, his teeth bared. Whatever that meant.

"I think I can fit through here," I said, ignoring the way my skin crawled where I was marked. I told myself Cronus put the curses on my body with magic and thought-power, not a physical touch. My stomach still curdled though. "Em, support my back," I added, throwing my legs through the hole and trusting him not to let me fall.

"Be careful," Wynvail snapped. "You don't know what's through there. *Or* what your magic will do if you keep using it."

"Don't act like you care," Emlyn growled, his voice so deep. "She's my mate, not yours."

"Ours, in fact."

I ignored them, sliding through the hole awkwardly. Gravity dragged me down on the other side, and I grunted when my ass met solid concrete. But I was through.

"There's nothing here," I called back to them, climbing to my feet and assessing the short, stone corridor. The walls were as tall as the rest of the Labyrinth, but luckily there was no mythical creature waiting to eat us this time.

"Fuck off," Emlyn snarled, so deep and throaty that I jumped, my clit throbbing inappropriately. "I'm going next."

Wynvail didn't reply. He was probably rolling his eyes.

When Em's legs appeared through the hole, I drew up my magic and threw it out in a net, searching for heartbeats and —there, around the corner. I didn't wait for Em and Wynvail to come through; I took off running, my feet pounding the stone. I knew Harvey's pulse by heart, but it was frantically fast, thrumming with fear.

"Harvey?" I called, pushing faster and skidding around the bend in the corridor. I had to grab the edge of the wall so I didn't faceplant the floor.

"Oh," I breathed when I saw him sitting five feet away, pushed into a corner like Wane always was. His knees were to his chest, his arms gripping them tightly, and his face was tucked out of sight. Even from here, I could see he was shaking all over. No longer screaming, but still terrified.

"Buttercup?" I murmured, approaching slowly, scuffing my shoe on the ground so he knew I was coming. "It's Haley. I'm here, you're safe now."

He didn't react, didn't even flinch. I closed the last few steps as slowly as my panic would let me, and knelt beside him. I reached for the bond first, but it was like frayed threads in my fingers. I'd felt Kai, though, at least in whispers of emotions, so I kept trying.

He was breathing, and shaking, but unresponsive. Shit. My face crumpled, but I bit my bottom lip and held it together.

"I've got you," I murmured, throwing a silent snarl over my shoulder when I heard footsteps. But it was only Emlyn, staring at Harvey with the same heartbreak and horror that ravaged my chest. "I'm here, Harvey."

I spread my wings as I crawled closer, wrapping them around my mate and tipping him into my arms, one hand curved around the back of his head, the other stroking slow, careful touches down his back, his wings.

"It's only me and Em here," I told him, my voice a low murmur. "We're not gonna let anything else happen to you. Whatever Cronus did to you, it's over."

I'd kill the monster before I let him hurt my mate again. I shot out thoughts of what could be happening to Kai. I needed to focus on Harvey; he needed me.

Em approached slowly, a low, murmuring rumble in his throat, the same noise he made to me when memories made me black out. Harvey still didn't stir.

I ran my fingers through his hair, rubbing my thumb over the back of his neck, murmuring that he was safe, Em doing the same with his purring growl.

Oh gods. We've lost him. Cronus broke his mind with this twisted, fucked up maze. I'll never see him smile or smirk again, never hear him laugh or tease me.

But Harvey sucked in a breath and shuddered violently. The second my scent hit his senses, his arms snapped around me and he seized vicious hold of my body.

"I'm here, Em's here, you're safe," I promised him, stroking his hair, tightening my wings around his body. My heart stabbed with pain, and I wanted to ask what happened to him, what Cronus *did* to him, but I didn't want to throw him back into that trauma.

"Where's Wane?" he croaked, shaking uncontrollably in my arms. "I want my brother."

I met Emlyn's gaze, more cracks spreading through my heart. My bottom lip caved in. I couldn't speak.

"He's close," Em murmured, sparing me having to answer. "We're going to get him soon. Promise."

I stiffened when quiet footsteps approached, and someone knelt beside us. I knew it was Wynvail without having to look, and I came so close to baring my teeth in a warning hiss. But I couldn't let go of Harvey, and I didn't want to spook him with the sound.

"Don't act like I've spoken," he whispered, so quietly I almost missed it. My brow furrowed. "I might know where to find Wane, but I can't guarantee he'll be there. I've only been once, but—the people there talk about Cronus's favourite shadow."

Harvey flinched in my arms, lifting his head to stare at Wynvail, all the blood draining from his bronze face until his skin was wan. "His favourite?" he breathed so quietly, his lips barely moving.

Wynvail's throat bobbed. I expected a quippish remark, but he just nodded, so small a movement it was easy to miss. So Cronus wouldn't see it?

"That's what our uncle and father called him," Harvey rasped, letting go of me to scrub his face. "Is ... is the titan our...?"

He couldn't voice the fear. I'd worried the same thing, but it was a horrific idea, I shunned it every time it crossed my mind. Knowing everything Cassander and his brother had done to my mates for twenty years was bad enough, but *a hundred years?* It was unthinkable. Sickening.

Wynvail glanced away. "No. Locke is—dead. Cronus killed him."

"Good," Em and I hissed at the same time. His hands rested on my back and Harvey's, offering us both support. I was surprised he hadn't wrangled us into a messy, frantic hug yet.

"You saw it?" I pressed Wynvail, holding Harvey closer to my chest. "You saw him die?"

His eyes fixed on the floor. "I was there. I was tasked with cleaning up his corpse. He's dead."

That was some good news at least. The bad news was my emotions were all twisted up, fear for Harvey making me weak, and sympathy for Wynvail snuck in.

But Cronus could never know. I didn't know how or why but Cronus *couldn't* know Wynvail was helping us.

"You're a sick fuck," I fake-snarled at Wynvail, rearing back like he'd insulted everything I loved.

He flinched, and my heart sank. Oh, gods. Why did he flinch?

He recovered in the next moment, climbing to his feet with a smirk as he realised I was following his own instructions. "That I may be, honey. But I'm the reason you're all alive."

"Until you kill my mates," I spat.

He shrugged, something dead in his eyes. "Strangely enough, it's not my choice to kill them. But needs must." He grinned. "And then I get you all to myself. You'll like that, won't you, Halwen? My undivided attention. A needy, desperate thing like you? You'll climb over your mates' bodies to get to me."

I launched forward, my upper lip curled back and a deep, guttural sound in my throat, but Harvey's wings snapped around me and his fingers hooked in the collar of my shirt.

"He's just goading you," he said loudly, and then in my ear, "It's all for show, Sugarplum. Look at his eyes; he doesn't believe a single word he's saying. He looks practically dead."

I swallowed, glancing away from Wynvail and hugging Harvey close. I hated that asshole; I didn't need to be feeling sorry for him. "Are you okay?" I murmured, my fingers returning to his shaggy hair, stroking with careful movements. I still wasn't sure where he was hurt.

"No," he replied baldly, pressing a kiss to my shoulder. "But none of us are. I'll be fine."

"What happened?" I asked hesitantly.

"I was—back in the basement," Harvey whispered, and he needn't say any more. Images hit me one after another, nightmares conjured from my own imagination and what little details I knew from my mates.

Two metal cots, bare of anything but a thin mattress and dirty sheets, with mould on the walls and a bucket, and scant food on plastic plates—so they couldn't use them as weapons. And above it, a glittering manor house where the mayor put on galas and soirées and apparently paraded Wynvail about like a golden child.

Emlyn had gone to the same mental place I did because his composure snapped and he grabbed both of us into a vicious, sweltering hug.

"*No one* hurts my family," he growled, the sound vibrating through my side, shaking my sore ribs and crushed wing.

A tiny smile flicked up the edge of Harvey's mouth. "Remember when you threw that chaura demon onto a cart full of hay and shit because he called me an inbred half-breed?"

"Threw him," Em scoffed, wrapping his whole self around us, wings overlapping wings, leather laid on feathers. "I gave him a tiny shove. It's not my fault his balance was pitiful. He tripped."

Harvey laughed, a low chuff of sound. "Sure, Em. Like the

time that mouthy bastard *tripped* when you knocked him off a balcony."

"He had wings," Emlyn dismissed, his cheeks rounding with a smile.

"And he called me a cheap, five-silver whore," I input. "Which is rude. I'm a five-*gold* whore at the very least."[1]

"You're worth more than all the gold in Hell," Emlyn said ardently. There was nothing but love in his eyes when he held eye contact, stroking down my wing.

"What about me?" Harvey asked, some amusement colouring his voice.

"One silver," Em replied without missing a beat. "Five on a good day."

He ruffled Harvey's hair and let go, standing to give Wynvail another warning glare. He was handing those out like pigeons gifted shit lately.[2]

"I'll be fine," Harvey murmured when he caught me watching him, unable to hide my concern. He disentangled his wings from mine and helped me stand. "Let's find Kai and get the hell out of this place. I want my brother back."

I gave him a weak smile, covering up how much my ribs hurt when I moved. "Me, too."

"Are you—coping?" he asked, brows coming low over his eyes. "With him being away from you and—"

"At the mercy of a heartless titan?" I finished when he couldn't. "I wouldn't call it *coping*, but I'm alive and angry and that's better than dead."

Warm lips found my cheekbone, the kiss lingering as Harvey pulled me into another hug.

"Sorry, Sugarplum," he murmured, the only warning he gave before fire lanced through my head, my face, my ribs, and every part of my damaged wings.

"Fuck!" I shouted, his healing magic burning me to ash and rebuilding body parts from the ruins.

We both jumped apart at the low, grating roar of walls parting. I exchanged a glance with Harvey and Em. Looked like we had a way onwards. But was Cronus leading us to Kai, or further away from him?

Wynvail didn't hang around; he stalked through the gap in the giant wall without a word. I wanted to leave him to his grisly death or whatever awaited him on the other side, but my damn instincts wouldn't let me.

So I groaned and followed the bastard.

CHAPTER THIRTEEN

WANE

*S*hadows itched over my skin, an early warning I'd developed over the last hundred years. *Pain,* it hissed. *They're coming. Hide.*

I pressed tighter into the corner of the dark room, my knees to my chest. I couldn't stop my hands shaking, even after so many years that pain and suffering was everyday. It was a constant, throbbing from every cut I made on my own skin, each one snarling her name. *Halwen, Halwen...*

"Halwen," I whispered when footsteps came close enough to echo around the endless corridor outside. I knew it was Andryas Revairs from his furious gait, and I pulled my knees tighter to my chest, my ribs protesting the pressure. He broke them yesterday, and left me here to cry and scream. I'd refused to give him the satisfaction of screaming for longer than five minutes, clenching my teeth to keep the noise in my chest instead.

I didn't want to scream today, either, but they would force

it out of me. Andryas and *him*—the titan. My heart beat faster at the thought of him. I prayed to every god listening that Andryas stepped into the room and closed the door instead of barking for me to leave.

If I stayed, it was guaranteed pain, far beyond what I could handle. But if I left? It would kill me. Again.

I didn't want to die again. I wanted it to finally end, but the titan never let me stay dead. I was an archdemon; it took a lot to kill me. And the titan knew exactly how to walk that line between dead and true, irrevocable death. He knew how to break me, over and over.

My heart quickened, hands shaking as I gripped my knees. The door creaked open and Andryas hovered on the threshold, a sneer on his brown face and a trickle of blood coming from a cut on his bald head.

Andryas bleeding meant the titan was in a vicious mood. My heart stopped for a second; I couldn't breathe.

"Get the fuck up. Follow me, and don't fuck around. You'll regret it."

I didn't bother speaking. My voice was a blown-out husk anyway. Sometimes it hurt just to speak my mate's name.

Halwen, I reminded myself, pressing on a fresh mark on my arm and sucking in a sharp breath. She was with me. Even if she wasn't beside me, even if I couldn't remember the sound of her voice or the exact shade of her grey eyes, she was here.

So I got up, and followed Andryas, and neither of us mentioned the fact he was bleeding, too.

THE TUNNELS LED THREE WAYS; ONE WOULD TAKE US TO THE Damned House where Cronus's enforcers lived, one led all the way across the realm and fed out near the fields on the outer ring, and one took us on a long, winding route to the seat of Cronus's power.

Every ache in my body throbbed fiercer, slashing deeper, when Andryas took the third route. I wanted to run, but I'd only ever made it four steps—and that was when I'd had rage and strength in the beginning. I'd be lucky to make a single step now I was so weak.

"Faster," Andryas snapped, ahead of me in the darkness.

I quickened my pace as much as I could, but my ankle had been broken days ago and it slowed me down. So did the lethargy that never left my bones. I wanted to curl up on the floor, go to sleep, and never wake up.

Halwen, my inner voice breathed.

I kept walking.

The tunnels were completely black this far into the realm, and it was impossible to know how far we'd walked, and how close the exit was. There could have been nightmares and beasts snapping their teeth around us. It wouldn't be the first time something had gnashed my hand off. I'd had to begin all over again marking my skin with Halwen's name.

"If he kills you for being so slow, that's on you," Andryas muttered, but the fact he was talking at all gave away his nerves.

"You broke my ankle," I rasped, "and expect me to walk miles. That's on *you.*"

Silence was his only response, and panic closed around my chest, crushing out my air.

Had Andryas left me alone down here? My breathing came quicker, but—*there,* that was the scuff of his boots on the ground. My shoulders drooped, relief forcing a breath from me.

At least until the footstep was followed by the heavy metal *thunk* of a door opening. Oh, gods. We were here.

And I could already hear the titan's roar of fury.

CHAPTER FOURTEEN

*T*he titan's roar brought me to my knees on the black marble floor, pain shattering through my legs but dull compared to the blinding agony splitting my skull in two. I screamed. I didn't want to, but I couldn't help it.

I bowed over, myself grabbing my head, and the titan must have thought I was bowing before him because the pain tore away in an instant. I gasped, tears streaking my face.

See, he rumbled in my head, a voice darkness, nothing like the cool brush of my shadows. These were sharp and scalding, as blistering as an iron poker and every bit as damaging. This was a darkness that could kill. It had before, and would again.

"Apologies, sir," Andryas rushed out—and screamed so loudly his voice cut out. I didn't dare look to see what had been done to him; I couldn't risk it being done to me, too.

The last time I was summoned here, the titan poured so much of his magic into me that my heart stopped and time stopped with it. I still didn't know what I'd done to anger him; I'd bowed deep and not spoken a single word.

Even existing was a cause for death.

Summon your shadows, the titan ordered, and I jumped as

my skull split with a vicious ache. Fear brought an instant refusal to the tip of my tongue, but if I defied him, he'd kill me again.

If I obeyed, what he'd do could kill me anyway.

Questioning him wasn't an option; I'd stopped asking questions half a century ago, when my wings were carved out of my back. They were hung above the titan's grand terrible throne, a trophy to remind his enemies to obey. They still dripped blood, like the wounds on my back still bled. He'd used magic to ensure they would never close.

I gritted my teeth, nostrils flaring with a sudden breath when I reached for my shadows. I had a choice—I could refuse—but the suffering would be worse. I didn't want to die today. So even though it made my whole body shake, I summoned a faint veil of shadows around my hands.

More.

My throat closed. My hands shook harder. But I pulled my shadows further, until my arms were cloaked in darkness and —the titan shifted in his throne and I flinched. Magic slipped out of my grasp, and I cried out, knowing he'd be furious, knowing he'd punish me—

The pain came faster than I expected, and I roared when it scoured through every part of me. My eyes bulged, and my fingers locked where I gripped my head. I didn't want to scream again, but the sound was ripped from the tip of my blistering tongue. More howls poured from my throat until my voice finally rasped to silence. My mouth hung open on empty noise, my body ravaged, skin tearing, blood pouring from my back.

More, the titan ordered.

Claws sank through my shadows, into my skin, and beyond, hooking into the part where my magic lived. I had no control over it, could do nothing but silently scream, my bones locked and my world narrowed to a single point of suffering. I couldn't see the titan on his throne anymore, didn't hear Andryas shifting his weight or my own rattling breaths.

The titan demanded more magic, and I couldn't stop my shadows erupting into the air around me. I couldn't protect my magic. My shadows were all I had left. My shadows and her name.

What was her name?

"No!" I roared, the sound too raspy and weak to reach him. "You can't take her! She's *mine.*"

What was her name? Her name...

I threw myself sideways with a violent wrench, tearing my body back into motion. I hit the ground on my bloody back and held my hands up to my face, scanning the cuts all over my fingers, my palms, and up both my arms.

Halwen. Her name was *Halwen,* and she was my mate, and I was hers, only hers. Not the titan's. Only Halwen's.

Relief weakened me, and I sank against the cold marble floor with a rough breath.

Revairs, the titan ordered.

Tension tightened my body. I tried to roll and push off the floor, but the titan knew what I planned. He was in my head, in my blood, in my magic. He wanted to own me, wanted no part of me left unbroken.

Halwen. He couldn't take her. And as long as I remembered her, he couldn't take *me.* It didn't matter that he'd stolen my name. I knew who I was.

The titan gripped more of my shadows, ripping them out of me until darkness pooled on the floor at the foot of his throne. I could do nothing but pant for breath and try not to choke on my own blood when the titan hooked his power too deep. A pitiful moan came from me, the noise of a broken thing, not even a man.

Faster, the titan barked.

I was too wrecked to even gasp when Andryas knelt beside me, too close to my shadows, almost touching, almost—

I bucked off the ground with a broken scream, my eyes rolling back into my skull and pain twisting into my back, my arms, my—into my soul, where my magic was bound to me.

No!

They couldn't take my shadows. They were mine, not *his*. But the titan's magic pressed me down, froze me in time, and I couldn't even twitch my fingers to stop Andryas slashing the vile severing blade through my shadows.

He cut them away like the feathers of a wing, one by one, and didn't stop even when I blacked out.

CHAPTER FIFTEEN

HALWEN

I should have known better than to expect Cronus to go easy on us. But the Chimera he sent to slow us down or murder us—I couldn't say which he planned to happen—ended up on the business end of Harvey's sun soul form. Wynvail took immense pleasure in pointing out it was a half-breed and not a full-blooded Chimera or Harvey wouldn't have been able to kill it, even as an archdemon and a sun soul. Emlyn elbowed him in the ribs for that comment.[1]

"Malakai!" Emlyn yelled as we walked. We'd been shouting his name for hours now, walking in what felt like circles, following the path Cronus led us on. It was either walk, or try to climb the walls again. That hadn't gone so well for me the first time; for obvious reasons, I was reluctant to get crushed by a wall again.[2]

"Kai!" I screamed, my voice hoarse, straining my eyes at the end of the passage as if he'd be right there. "Malakai!"

"What if he's not here anymore?" Harvey asked, his wing

wrapped around me as he trudged on at my side. He kept pasting a smile onto his face; watching it slip was painful. "Can you feel him?"

I shook my head, hurt arrowing through my soul. "I can't feel any of you anymore. I thought the bonds would start to heal when you remembered me, but..." I shrugged, like it was only a minor concern and not something that kept me up at night. At least it would if I ever slept again. I hadn't slept in … what felt like months.

"They'll repair," Emlyn assured me, turning to give me a look so pure and supportive that I swallowed a lump in my throat and forced a nod. If Em believed we'd be okay, there was a special kind of magic in that.

"Kai!" I yelled, my voice breaking on his name. "Wynvail, can you send up another beam?"

He'd speared the Labyrinth with his bright, moon-silver power four times now, hoping Kai would use it to track us.

"If you say *please*," he replied smoothly, earning a glare.

Whatever genuine side he'd shown when we found Harvey was swept back under his dickhead personality. I'd resisted the urge to punch him in the dick at least twice.[3]

"I'm not saying *please* to you," I sneered, my nose wrinkling and lips pulled back from my teeth.

Wynvail shrugged, his hands in his pockets as he walked casually, like he was out for a stroll between business meetings. At least his perfect trousers were rumpled and stained. I got a kick of satisfaction in seeing every dirty smear marring his perfection. The blood smeared across his chest gave me less satisfaction. Stupid mate bond.

"*Kai!*" I screamed, staring up the walls like I'd spot him perched on top of one, his red tail flicking and a smirk on his face. "Come the fuck on, Malakai!"

"There's another wall moving," Emlyn said, his arms crossed over his chest. It was an intimidating pose, but I knew his arms were wrapped around himself because he was scared we'd never find Kai. And he was probably drained by spending so much time with a stranger; Wynvail might have been related to Harvey and Wane, but he wasn't family. "Can you hear that?"

"Shut up hissing," I spat at Wynvail.

"I'm not making a noise," he snapped, his eyes flashing.

No, he was hissing, scraping something across the ground—

"Shit," Harvey breathed, realising before I did.

I spun, and my breath skittered out of my chest when I saw Kai blazing down the stone corridor to us. His steps scraped the ground, blood spattered his head, his knuckles, and covered his shirtless chest. It dripped down his leg too as he pulled it stiffly along, clearly injured. There was something animal and feral in his expression, and a little shiver went down my spine. There was no magic coming from him, though, only animal brutality.

"Kai," Emlyn warned, angling himself in front of me. Wynvail went one better and shoved me behind himself. I shoved him right back, rushing across the Labyrinth to Kai.

"Where are you hurt?" I demanded, reaching for his face, scanning his bloody body.

My heart stuttered when bloody hands grabbed my waist, and Kai lifted me off the ground. Before I could ask what he was doing, he slammed my back into the nearest wall and looked over me, shaking and intense and very obviously out of control.

"Why did you leave me?" he demanded, guttural and raw. He squeezed my waist until I gasped, the grip too tight.

"What?" I breathed, my hands falling on his shoulders, legs locking around his waist on instinct. I stroked his shoulders, not shying away from the insanity in his glowing eyes.

"Why did you leave me?" he snarled, teeth bared and his breathing fast, frantic. The ground shuddered under us.

"I hit a field of power, Kai. It dragged me away; I didn't want to leave. I'd *never* leave you," I swore, grabbing his face and surprised to feel hot, feverish skin. I pressed my fingers deep into his skin, branding him with their impressions. *"Never,* my night."

His nostrils flared when he exhaled. Something flickered in his eyes, red glowing fiercer. "Never?"

"Never," I promised. "You're mine; I'm never letting you go."

A low hiss rattled his throat, deep and bestial, and a tremor went through him from head to toe. "Who do you belong to?"

"You," I answered instantly, my chest jumping when he pushed me forcefully into the wall, his expression tight, eyes crazed.

"And who do I belong to?" he demanded, reaching between us, tearing at the fastenings on my pants.

He wasn't going to take me here—surely?

"Me," I finished, possessiveness running hot through my blood. "You're fucking *mine.* But Kai, I don't think—"

He wrenched my trousers down, frantically removed his cock, and drove into me before I could finish. I clutched his shoulders, cursing as my pussy stretched around the sudden intrusion.

"Fuck, Kai," Harvey sighed, stalking over to us. "Take a fucking minute to prepare her."

I knew Kai was too far gone when he turned his head and snarled at Harvey, not replying with words but a threat.

"It's okay," I told Harvey in a murmur, the words for Em and Wynvail, too. Both men hovered close, looking inclined to tear me away from Kai. Emlyn wouldn't hurt Kai, but I didn't trust Wynvail not to injure my mate, so I held him tighter to me, my bottom lip caught between my lip when he fucked me like a man possessed.

It wasn't even comfortable at first, but *fuck* it was hot. If I wasn't so worried about Kai, I'd love seeing him lose control, his need for me driving him to a base, animal state.

He hissed, deep and guttural, and sank his fangs into my shoulder. *Fuck.* My back arched, his bite like an aphrodisiac. Within moments I'd soaked his cock, my pussy slippery and his thrusts gliding deeper. I trembled, panting, as he fucked me into the wall.

"I'm right here," I breathed, carefully extricating my left wing where it had gotten pinned behind me. I let the feathers on the ends brush Kai's thighs, soothing him.

"You can't leave," he replied, raspy and raw as he withdrew his fangs. Fingers left marks where he gripped my thighs, fucking me so fast it could only be described as rutting.

"I won't. Not ever." I sank my fingers into his red hair and gripped the strands tight, echoing my promise with a vicious pull. "If anyone tried to take me from you, I'd kill them."

He shuddered, a breath catching in his throat, so I went on.

"If they dared to put their hands on me, I'd peel back the flesh of every finger until there was only blood and bone left."

Kai whimpered, so quietly that only I heard it. His crimson eyes were wide and frantic, scanning my expression, reading the honest truth of my words.

"But I wouldn't stop at their hands. I'd use the daggers you gave me to carve a hole in their stomach." The wavy edges weren't ideal for that precise work, but I'd make it happen. "Even if they begged for their life, even if they apologised for trying to steal me away from you, I wouldn't listen. No one gets to touch me except my mates."

Kai bared his teeth, breathing faster. My pussy rippled around his cock. Pleasure built dizzyingly fast as he withdrew and slammed back inside, never retreating more than a few inches. Like he was desperate to be a part of me.

"Haley," he whined, his tail wrapping around my leg, gripping tight. He didn't look away from me even as Em and Harvey came closer, watching but not touching.

"Even if they screamed and cried," I told Kai, my voice a caress, "I'd make them pay for upsetting you. I'd pull out their intestines, and make sure they saw exactly what I was going to do before I strangled them with them."

"And then you'd fuck me in their blood?" Kai gasped, his whole body shuddering, cock dancing wildly inside me. His skin was feverish where he pressed against me, making mine extra sensitive. My pussy clenched around him, gripping tightly.

"Only when we were covered in it from head to toe," I panted, "with blood dripping from us as you stretch me on your cock, and blood on my tongue as I kiss you, and smeared on my boobs where they press to your chest when you fill me with your cum."

Kai groaned, dropping his head onto my shoulder. His back arched, his cock thrust as deep as it could fit inside me as he came so hard he choked on each breath. He didn't let me fall even as his knees buckled; instead he pinned me to the wall with his hips so his cock stayed buried in my pussy, his cum spilling deep inside me.

I gentled my fingers on his hair, running them through the dark red strands, and circling soft touches around the base of each horn. He grunted, his cock spasming harder, so I kept stroking the ridges of his horns. He was so stressed and afraid he needed the world's best orgasm, and damned if I wasn't going to give it to him. I traced my finger around a sensitive ring of his horn and clenched my inner muscles around him, rewarded with a shout and a curse.

"I'm yours," I told him, a little sad that he'd pull out of me soon. I wanted to keep him wrapped up in me, safe in my arms while I was safe in his. "Always, Kai. I love you."

He groaned, sweaty forehead on my shoulder as he melted into me. He cried out a choked sound when I circled my hips, giving Em a warm look as he hovered, there to catch me if Kai buckled. Fuck, his leg! It looked hurt, blood dripping down it the last time I saw it, albeit for only a second before he threw me against the wall like a sex-crazed beast.

"Haley," Kai moaned, his voice tight. "Killing me. Still —coming."

Wynvail snorted softly. "His balls are going to be wrinkled raisins after this."

"One more word, and I'll cut *your* balls off," I snapped, twisting my head to glare at the smirking, sweaty, rumpled, bloody—oh god, my pussy throbbed around Kai's cock. I carried on, but lost some of my sharpness, "See how wrinkly yours are when they're preserved in a jar."

Kai's fingers pressed into my thighs and he ground his hips against mine, a moan strangled in his throat as he began to throb more powerfully inside me. His bite throbbed on my shoulder, making me so fucking wet for him, pushing me right to the edge.

"Jesus—*fuck*—Haley," he gasped, holding me up as he swiftly withdrew from my pussy, like he was afraid I'd make him come again.

I smirked, pleased with how ruined he was, and especially with the dazed look in his red eyes. I reached up to brush a sweaty strand of hair out of his face. "Feeling better?"

Kai grunted. "You don't need to be so smug."

I kissed his jaw, my smile growing. At least until I remembered the blood covering him. "Fuck, Kai! Your leg!"

"I'm fine," he huffed, setting me on my feet. I tried not to pout at the emptiness inside me as I pulled my trousers back into place. I *ached*, so close to release but so far. "I can handle a bleeding leg, but losing you? Fuck no, I can't handle that."

"How did you get this bloody?" I demanded, able to see the sheer amount of red all over him now he wasn't plastered against me, driving his cock frantically into my pussy. The pussy that was dripping, throbbing.[4]

Kai scratched the back of his head. "You were taken from me and I went a little crazy."

"A little?" Harvey blurted with a laugh, closing the distance between us to grab Kai's shoulder. "Are you alright now?"

"Fine," Kai replied, rubbing his face.

"Except for your bleeding leg," I input, trying to get a better look at the wound on his thigh.

"I just—can't handle being away from Haley, apparently," he went on like I hadn't spoken. Well, he could wilfully ignore his injury all he liked, but I was his mate and it was all I could think about. Well, that and my clenching pussy.

"It'll never happen again," Emlyn growled, as if he was personally daring the titan to incur his wrath.

I glanced up when a possessive hand slid across my back and curved around my hip—and groaned when I saw Wynvail had snuck closer. His mercury eyes were sympathetic but wicked; they simmered with carnality.

"Not you," I huffed.

"You need a cock, honey," he purred.

I groaned at the reminder, my inner muscles quivering. "Not yours."

He lowered his dark head, and it was a sign of how needy I was that I didn't push him away before his teeth could scrape up my throat. I bit back a groan, my clit pulsing, my need spiking so high I couldn't bear it.

"Harvey, heal Kai," I said, breathless and high. "Em—"

Wynvail stroked a finger down the curve of my spine, and I shuddered fiercely, dripping so much arousal that it slicked my trousers. I bit back a whine. "Halwen needs a thick cock in her cunt. Isn't that right, honey?"

"I hate you," I panted, throwing Em a pleading look.

"I'm here, Hales," he soothed, shooting a dirty look at Wynvail before he strode towards me, huge and strong and everything I needed. He was so fucking hot with his silver-threaded hair, his beard, his protectiveness and his big body. I needed him so much I couldn't breathe.

Em soothed me with a gentle *shhh* and ducked low to grip my ass and pull me up against him. My legs had to widen much further to wrap around his hips than Kai's, but the moment I settled against him, his cock pressed against my pussy, and I sighed in relief.

But there were layers of clothes between us, and I was going to go mad. My shoulder pulsed, filling me with need.

Emlyn's lips met mine as he settled me against his hips, the kiss soothing my ruthless need. "Grind yourself against me, my beautiful mate. Find your release. Then you'll have the cock you need so badly."

I moaned, slamming my lips back into his and writhing my hips as he supported me with his broad hands. He was so much bigger than me, soft in all the best places, hard between my legs, and it was so fucking hot. The brush of his beard against my face made me tingly all over, the slick stroke of his tongue pushing me alarmingly close to the edge already.

"I'm fine, stop fussing," Kai barked behind us. "Move. I want to watch my girl come."

"You're still bleeding, you brainless fool," Harvey muttered.

Concern shot through my chest, but Em squeezed my ass and rocked me against him, pressing my clit into the hardness straining against his pants. All thoughts wiped from my head; my eyes rolled at the pressure where I needed it.

I exhaled a curse, locking eyes with Emlyn, my eyelids low. He took control of my body, guiding me up and down the outline of his thick cock, dragging my clit up the whole length.

"Oh fuck," I gasped, throbbing viciously. I'd been so close thanks to Kai's feral fucking, but Emlyn being in control of my release was a whole other level of pleasure. It was heady and addictive, and it only took three more strokes before a whimper broke my breaths apart and my fingernails bit into his shoulders.

"Perfect," Emlyn praised as my hips snapped forward, my body gripped by a long, brutal shudder. "That's it. Come for me, Hales. Come for your mate."

I wanted to kiss him, but I was locked in place, unable to move as I shook and fell apart, my pussy squeezing around nothing. Every throb slammed pleasure through me until I couldn't choke back a breath, until I bit my lip hard, until my body went limp and my hands slipped from around his neck, threatening to drop me. But Em would never let me fall.

"More," Kai hissed, closer than I'd expected. Bright obsession shone from his eyes, his tail swishing, restless, like it wanted to touch me again.

"Give her a moment," Em huffed, laying a kiss on my forehead. "And *you*, turn around. You don't deserve to see this."

"There's not a single force in this realm or the next that could stop me watching her," Wynvail replied, the cold intensity in his tone sending another spasm through my clit.

Em held me for a blissful minute, peppering my face with kisses and murmuring rapturous praises until my heart was full.

I made a noise of complaint when he slid me down until my feet hit the ground, hot hands moulding my body to his liking, pressing my hands against the cold wall and arching my back so my ass was raised.

I bit my lip when Em tugged apart the fastenings on my trousers, pushing them over my knees until I was exposed, so wet that I felt arousal drip from me. Someone groaned, more than one voice.

"Fuck," Kai said, pained.

"You've had your turn," Emlyn chided, stroking a hot hand down my back and squeezing my ass. "How badly do you need a hot, *throbbing* cock, Hales?"

I whined, my eyes screwed shut as I dripped uncontrollably. Emlyn and dirty talk was a deadly combination. My pussy throbbed, my ass squeezing too as his fingers stroked lower, one on either side of my entrance. Spreading me for the others to see. *Fuck.*

"Please. I need it so badly, *please,*" I begged. The orgasm had taken the finest edge off, but he was winding my lust back up to a fever pitch, Kai's bite driving me equally mad as it heightened every sense. "Em, *please,* stop teasing."

He laughed, a soft, rumbling breath. "You know I can't deny you anything you want, my mate. But getting you all needy and impatient is too satisfying." To the guys, he added, "Look at her throbbing. So needy she's leaving a wet spot on the floor. She must be *aching* to be filled."

I made a noise of complaint , my breathing faster, eyes screwed shut. The cold press of stone against my hands and face did nothing to cool me down.

"Em," I pleaded. "Don't be mean."

He stroked my pussy, soaking his fingers. "You think I should give you what you need? Stuff this beautiful hole full of cock until you can't remember how to think?"

"Yes!" I hissed.

"Alright, Hales. My beautiful mate always gets what she wants." He kissed my shoulder and moved back, fingers spreading me again, the head of his cock sliding through my pussy, earning an impatient groan from me.

"Fuck," I swore when he drove into me with slow, powerful strokes. There was no discomfort of stretching this time, only sheer fucking bliss sparking through every nerve until his hips met my ass and the fingers spreading me slipped away.

"Hello, Sugarplum." Harvey's low, amused voice made me clench around him, a violent shudder ripping through me. *Shit.* My toes curled when he glided out and thrust back in, making damn sure I knew who was fucking me. "I missed this so fucking much."

I nodded my frantic agreement, my teeth biting deeper into my lip, the switch-up driving me wild. "Em?" I gasped, Harvey's slow, maddening thrusts making my eyes cross. "What the fuck?"

"I said you'd have the cock you need," Em replied, a smile in his voice. "I never said it would be mine."

I made a low, sulky noise. I wanted Em. And Harvey. And everyone.[5]

"He's getting you nice and ready for me," Emlyn murmured, placating me by stroking his fingers through my hair. That better not be the hand he touched my pussy with. "And then we'll make good on my promise, and wipe every thought from that pretty head of yours."

All these compliments were making me warm, my heart melting.

Harvey bowed over me so he could put his lips to my ear, rolling his hips, his cock hitting *deep.* My whole body jolted, hands fluttering across the wall.

"Trust us, Sugarplum. You're going to love everything we do to you. This pussy—" He thrust excruciatingly slowly, the fat head stroking my inner walls in a loving touch, adjusting the angle as he slid out so my eyes flew open and a cry burst up my throat. "Is going to come harder than ever."

I braced myself against the wall with one hand, reaching back with the other, wildly desperate to touch him. A relieved breath left my lungs when he linked his fingers with mine, squeezing reassuringly.

"Let go, Haley. We've got you."

It was like he knew how tightly I held myself, like he felt every knot of tension in my body, because his words dissolved every bit of it. I exhaled a long breath, and when I relaxed, every gliding thrust his cock made inside me pushed me higher. My head floated. There was something fucking magical in this slow, patient sex, especially when Harvey's free hand caressed from my stomach, up my chest, and clasped my throat. A whine slipped out of me. My skin tingled, so hot that I burned where Harvey's body brushed mine.

"Harvey—"

"I know, Sugarplum. You're so tight, so close. Is this pussy going to come for me?"

"Fuck."

His fingers tightened around my throat, and my whole body reacted. "I asked you a question," he said in a hard voice that made me pant, so close that my entire body was tightening, arching, straining.

"Yes," I forced out, my toes curling. "Oh, god, Harvey—"

"That's my good girl," he murmured as I convulsed, my pussy strangling his cock in violent spasms. The orgasm was so good it made my eyes cross.

Harvey's strokes never turned rough, never quickened; his patience was alarming and hotter than Hell. Who *was* this Harvey, who was calm and controlled enough to make me come before he did? I loved it.

"I—" choked out, gripping his fingers tight where they linked with mine. "Love you—"

He gently pulled me up against him, my back plastered to his front, and laid a kiss on the side of my face as his hips rolled against my ass. "I love you too, Haley. I should have told you every damn day since you found us again."

My heart skipped. My pussy locked around him, fluttering.

I pouted when he slid out of me, his hand releasing my throat. He was done? Before he came? Not fair.

"Ready for us, my Hales?" Emlyn asked.

I was still foggy with pleasure that it took me a minute to catch up. Us—not me. *Us.*

My mouth filled with saliva; I swallowed hard when Em lifted me, my legs around his waist, and Harvey pressed in against my back. *Oh holy fucking gods.*

When he said he'd make me forget how to think, he wasn't kidding.

CHAPTER SIXTEEN

EMLYN

*S*he was the most beautiful woman in any world, and my heart was going to explode. Her lips parted on fast, whining breaths as she stared at me, her sexy body sandwiched between me and Harvey. We should have done this days ago. Weeks ago. The only reason we'd stayed away from her was because the life we lived together had been stolen from us.

The bastard with his filthy eyes fixed on my girl was a big reason why I lost those memories. My teeth itched to rip Wynvail's throat out, but Haley shuddered with aftershocks in my arms, and I fixed my attention on her. She deserved nothing less than obsession.[1]

"Em," she panted when my cock throbbed, caressing through her wetness. I'd thrown my pants to the floor minutes ago, so hard and aching for her that I couldn't stay constricted a moment longer.

"Kiss me," I pleaded, my voice more desperate than I

planned. She answered my plea, her fingers diving into my hair as her mouth met mine. Her lips moved languidly and I matched her slow pace, letting her come down from the orgasm Harvey gave her.

I fought the animal urge to drive balls-deep into her; her arousal and cum dripped all over my cock, coating it in a slipperiness that made me groan into her mouth. Harvey was struggling too, his teeth bared and tawny wings taut as he panted, writhing against her ass, occasionally nudging my cock and accidentally heightening my need. If I'd had two cocks, I would have laid Hales and Harvey on top of each other and taken them both so hard and thoroughly they turned to a sweaty pile of limbs and whining.

When Haley broke for air, her hips circling now, I met his gaze in a clear command. *Patience.* He shot me a surly look, pressing his chest to Haley's back, his hands wandering up her body, pushing her shirt up so he could palm her breasts. I fought a smile. He was more of a spoilt brat than our mate.

"What are you waiting for?" Kai demanded, closer than I expected.

I jumped, giving him a warning rumble. "Unlike you, Malakai, I'm not a caveman who can't think about my mate's needs before my own."

Kai smirked. "My rose? Who's right about what you need right now?"

She groaned, her tongue flicking out to lick her bottom lip as she met my stare. "He's right, Em. The wait is killing me."

I supported her with one hand, stroking her cheek with the knuckles of my other. "I'm big, Hales. And with Harvey in your ass, you're going to be *very* full."

"Promises, promises," she teased, her eyelids heavy over smokey grey eyes.

"I don't want to hurt you," I added, an eyebrow raised pointedly. I knew my mate; if she was horny enough, she'd get herself killed trying to take all our cocks as hard and fast as possible, and she'd love every moment of her death. She was a risk to herself, and it was my job to make sure that didn't happen.

I ducked my head, pressing my lips to her ear; her whole body covered with goosebumps. "There are no baths to soak in afterwards, beautiful. No lotions or tonics to help you heal. Say the word and we'll call this off—"

"Don't you dare!" she hissed, fingernails biting into my back, drawing a smile to my face. "But—I get your point. *Fine*," she relented, sulking, "we'll be slow and careful."

"Good girl," I praised. She'd all but lost her mind when Harvey called her that earlier. She arched into me, a soft breath fanning my hair. I wished our bond was intact; I'd have loved to know what she was feeling right now. "Now stay nice and relaxed for me—and stay *still*. If you try to take more than we give you, I'll be very disappointed in you."

Her bottom lip thrust out, her eyes widening a fraction. I kissed her again, because she was so fucking cute. I'd watched her skin men alive for calling Wane names, watched her pry the eyeballs out of the skull of a woman who leered at me too long. But with her grey eyes big, afraid to let me down, edged with a slow-burning need, she was fucking adorable.

"Arms locked behind my neck, Hales," I gently ordered, and stroked the tip of my cock through her pussy. Fuck, she was scalding hot, and so wet it was like gliding through pure heaven. My dick throbbed in my hand, imagining the euphoria of sinking into her.

Slow, careful, I reminded myself as she followed my order without question. Gods, she was perfect. I kissed her again, unable to help myself, and kept my lips on hers when I slid in the first few inches. Her cries were honeyed on my tongue, mixing with the sweet musk of her natural flavour. My eyes slammed shut when my strokes took me deeper, sheathing me in rippling heat. Fuck. Holy *fuck.*

"Oh gods, Em," Haley gasped into my mouth. "I'm too sensitive for this."

"You gonna come again, my beautiful mate?"

She nodded, fast panting breaths fanning over my lips. Her face stained with a red blush, her eyes glossy and tight with pleasure. Gods, I loved her. I wanted to keep her like this forever, in a perpetual state of blush.

A little whimper escaped her when Harvey pressed a fingertip in her ass, and then deeper, the digit grazing my cock inside her. Haley's cunt went *wild,* milking me with demanding pulses.

I captured her swollen lips, my kisses as tender as my thrusts, stroking my cock over every sensitive inch of her pussy before I withdrew for another thrust.

"No, no, no," she cried, her hand shooting between us to grab my cock and push me back inside. For a moment, panic crossed her face, but the second I gave myself back to her, buried to the hilt, her eyes rolled back and she clamped down around me. When Harvey added another finger, her body shuddered against me and she found her release.

"Fuck yesss," she hissed, her teeth sinking into her bottom lip. The sight made me throb inside her, dragging a gasp from her pretty mouth, but I refused to come yet. I had plans for my beautiful mate, and when she sighed and melted against me I gave Harvey a nod over her shoulder.

An impish grin crossed his bronze face, making him look ten years younger. More like the Harvey he'd been before we were killed, before our memories of Haley faded. The cheeky fucker reached under Haley and squeezed my balls. A grunt choked my throat, the urge to come so much stronger. I growled a warning, but he was already releasing me.

He covered his fingers in Haley's arousal and pumped

them in her ass. I clenched my jaw when I felt them shift inside her as he scissored them, drawing a delicious noise from our mate. He coaxed three more of those sounds and another orgasm from her before he gripped his own cock, lining up with her ass.

"Fuck," someone breathed, raspy and rough.

"If you keep looking, I'll slit your fucking throat," Kai snarled, which meant it was Wynvail who spoke.

"I'll happily die to keep watching her," the fucker replied.

I shut them out, all my focus stolen by the pressure on the base of my cock where Harvey slid inside our mate. She whined, her teeth at my throat as he thrust shallowly.

"Slowly," I warned, breathless.

"Oh fucking fuck," Haley babbled, her fingernails biting deep into my shoulder. "Damn mates—trying to—kill me."

"Stay relaxed for us, Hales," I rasped, my eyes fucking crossing when her pussy rippled around me at the same time Harvey glided deeper, stroking my cock from the other side of such a thin barrier. I couldn't keep my hands gentle on her thighs, fingers biting into soft skin and firm muscle as I fought back the sudden fire of pleasure boiling up in me.

"Look at me," Haley rasped, and I snapped my stare up to hers as she drew back to look at me. A shudder went through me at the love and blazing desire in her grey eyes, my balls tight, cock aching. Every part of me belonged to her. "You're mine. Both mine. All mine."

The claim made me weak. My cock throbbed, each breath shorter, sharper. Harvey didn't help by groaning, the sound so goddamn hot. He thrust into her in slow, steady strokes, fucking both of us. I wasn't used to feeling so out of control, and I wasn't prepared for the way it drove me utterly insane.

"More," she gasped, her restless fingers knotting in my hair. "Em, *more.*"

Oh, shit, she wanted to ruin me. But I could never say no

to her. Haley was a miracle and a gift. I'd lost her, forgotten her, but here she was, clutching me tight, giving herself to me and Harvey. She could have anything she asked for.

But the friction of pulling out of her nearly had me coming, let alone the slide back in. A deep growling sound forced from my chest. I held her tighter, forgetting to be gentle.

"Hales," I grunted.

"Close—" she gasped in reply, reaching a hand behind her to grasp Harvey's shoulder, connecting all three of us. "So, so good."

"That's our good girl," Harvey groaned, voice strained. "Taking our cocks so well. This body was made for us, these perfect holes were made for us."

Haley panted against me, her eyes unfocused. My breathing wasn't much better. All I could do was hold onto her and give her my cock in slow, dangerous thrusts. My eyes slammed shut when she tightened, like a fist around my length, the perfect grip. Oh, fuck, I couldn't take this much longer. Heat boiled up in me, *so fucking good,* and I thrust harder.

"Ah!" she cried when Harvey's next thrust took him deeper, his tip massaging a sensitive spot on my shaft. "Too deep, too much—"

"No, Sugarplum," he replied, strained but in control. "This is exactly as deep as you need me. This tight little ass is gonna come on my cock, and your needy pussy's gonna suck Emlyn's dick until he can't take it."

She whimpered. My next thrust stuttered.

"We're going to fill you with so much cum that it'll still be dripping out of you tomorrow. And you're going to take it all, aren't you?"

She nodded fast, her eyes shut, face stained red. Beautiful.

"Use your words, Halwen."

Her pussy gripped me impossibly tight. *Shit.* My head spun. I forgot there was anything in the world except Harvey and our mate.

My cock jolted inside her perfect pussy. I was gonna come hard, and give her all the cum Harvey promised.

"Yes!" she screamed.

Harvey rewarded her with longer, deeper strokes. Faster, rougher. I followed his example, grunting as heat burst through me.

"Such a perfect little whore for us," he groaned, fucking her faster, desperately. "Taking two cocks at once like a dirty girl. Our dirty, dirty little girl."

I exploded inside her. Haley screamed. Her cunt clamped down on my cock with brutal, sucking throbs. And I lost my absolute goddamn mind.

The only thought I had left was *don't drop her* as I came harder than I had in my life, my cock throbbing like crazy, filling her to the goddamn brim. Holy shit. Holy ... shit.

"Haley!" Harvey gasped, and then his length was jerking in her ass, dragging another flood of cum from me with a deep sigh.

And our poor girl moaned and gasped and shuddered between us, her spine bowed and head thrown back onto Harvey's shoulder as both holes sucked us dry. I'd felt nothing like this before, not even during the group sex before we died. This was hot, sweaty, intense, and fucking world changing.

Disgusting whore, a deep, thundering voice shattered through my skull, making me gasp in sudden pain.

Cronus. He was watching.

I felt sick as I crashed back to Earth, all my peace and pleasure ruined.

"You shut the fuck up!" Kai screamed, losing his mind. "If you say a single fucking syllable about my mate, I'll sever

every single one of your limbs, one by one, until you scream for mercy!"

Harvey and I pressed closer together, shielding her, wrapping her up in us.

White light burst through the space, bleaching even the Labyrinth walls, and I growled threateningly as a shadow nested.

"He can't see you now, honey," Wynvail whispered, his head close to Haley's. "Take your pleasure; you deserve every moment. He won't see a second more."

Haley panted, clinging to me and Harvey, and the fluttering that had died in her pussy renewed when Wynvail's fingers skimmed her neck, trailing to her shoulder before he stepped back.

"We'll kill him, I promise," I breathed to my mate and wasn't sure if I meant Cronus or Wynvail. Maybe both.

"Brutally," Harvey agreed in a whisper. "We'll rip his fucking guts out."

Her pussy gripped us hard, and I stroked my cock inside her, thrusting slowly to tip her over the edge again.

CHAPTER SEVENTEEN

HALWEN

*N*ausea had carved a space in my stomach and refused to leave. The thought of Cronus watching me with my mates left an oily residue on my insides, and Em jostling me didn't help. I clung to his back, too weak and sore to walk thanks to him and Harvey. I usually enjoyed the sore ache after we fucked, the memory of exquisite sex but now I just felt dirty. I wanted to forget it had ever happened, and that wasn't fair.

None of this was fucking fair.

"That corner looks okay," Harvey murmured, subdued like we all were. Even Wynvail had kept the snarky asshole comments to a minimum, and had cloaked us in his moon-white magic long enough for us to dress and clean up.[1] "There are no openings nearby."

"That we can see," Kai muttered, his power writhing on his skin, the text inked on his arms spiralling. Whatever calm I'd given him was thoroughly demolished by Cronus spying on us. "The Labyrinth can change, remember."

"Like I could forget," Harvey snapped. "You didn't face the thing I did, you didn't see the memories I was forced to relive, so don't give me that shit, Malakai."

I reached for their souls to soothe them, a knot twisting in my chest when I found only broken threads. I needed my bonds fixed. I was starting to think this was another curse, and I didn't think a tattoo would break this one. I couldn't escape the fact that I was cursed to kill my mates and time was rapidly dwindling. None of us were talking about it, like it'd go away if we just didn't mention it.

Kai's next laugh was low and broken, the ground shuddering as his eyes flashed, his anger spiking fast.

"Don't," Emlyn sighed wearily. "This is exactly what Cronus wants."

"We're tired," I input. "And hungry, and more than a little angry. We need to sleep, or at the very least rest. If you think that corner's good, Harvey, we'll settle there for tonight."

If it even was night. Who's to say Cronus didn't control the sky above the maze?

"Someone needs to stay awake," Emlyn said, stroking my arm where it draped over his shoulder. "I don't trust the titan not to send something to attack us in our sleep."

"I'll take the first watch," Wynvail offered, his gaze straying in my direction, scanning me.

"Like *hell* you will," Kai snarled, his magic thumping harder, stronger. "So you can slit our throats in our sleep? Don't think we've forgotten your master's death order. *And* you're still cagy as fuck about this resurrection pearl."

Wynvail smiled humourlessly, more a baring of teeth. His perfect, cultured veneer was wearing thin lately. "Because it's none of your business."

"If you told us, we'd be less inclined to kill you," I pointed out, wincing when Emlyn slid me down his back, my pussy twinging and ass sore as fuck.

I waddled up to Harvey, plastering myself to his side and batting my lashes at him.

"What do you want?" he asked, all the irritation leaving his expression when he met my eyes. His gaze softened, lips tilting up in amusement, and his arm snaked around my back.

"I'm sore," I complained, pushing out my bottom lip and giving him a pitiful look. "I know you're almost out of magic after healing me when I got crushed, but can't you give me a little bit more? A teeny bit? You won't even notice it. Promise."

Harvey dipped his head, lips brushing mine when he spoke, and my clit throbbed despite how sore I was. "What if I want you to be sore, Sugarplum? What if I want you to remember how deep we were buried in your needy holes every time you move?"

I groaned and shoved him away. "Unfair, Harvey van Khama."

He laughed and drew me back to him, pressing his lips to my cheek and sending a flash of knife-sharp fire through my skin. I relaxed into him, letting the pain ravage me as it healed, trusting him. When it reached my ass though, I gripped his shirt in a white-knuckled fist and bit his lip. Fuck, my ass was tender. Nope, correction—it hurt. The violent blaze of his power found every painful spot and amplified it until I had to bury my head in his shoulder. I gripped him so hard I left red marks on his skin.

Kai chuckled, stroking long fingers through my hair, his magic making my scalp tingle. "It'll pass in a minute, my rose. You can be a brave girl for us, can't you?"

"Stop—exploiting—my praise—kink."[2]

"Never," he laughed, working his fingers through the knots and tangles of my hair with breathtaking care.

I exhaled a long sigh when the sharp fire faded, leaving behind minimal soreness and strength in my muscles.

"Best I can do, Sugarplum," Harvey murmured, kissing my temple. "I need to recharge."

"You sleep first," I told him, drawing him into a deep hug, squeezing him extra hard so he knew he was loved. "Kai and I will watch the Labyrinth."[3]

"You can sleep over there," Kai told Wynvail, nothing but nastiness in his voice. "That way if something comes down the path, it'll eat you first."

A bolt of alarm went through my chest, and Wynvail's eyes snapped to mine, smugness spreading through the silver depths. "I don't think our mate is too happy with that arrangement."

"Just worried about the monster that'll eat you," I said, my tone sweet as sugar. "You'll probably poison it from the inside."

"Whatever you say, honey," he replied, a knowing look on his face as he settled where Kai had told him to. It completely threw me when he did what he was told, not arguing or threatening us first.

I cast him a wary glance as I settled with my back against the wall a few feet away from where Harvey laid out on the ground. We were going to get so many back problems from sleeping on the floor. I stayed close enough to drape the edge of a wing over his legs, feeling better with some part of me touching him. I did the same when Em laid down, giving Wynvail a suspicious glare even though the man was, to all intents and purposes, asleep. As if anyone could fall asleep that fast; it was unnatural.

Then again, he hadn't spent his entire adult life on the run. Smug, privileged bastard.

"Sleep tight, babies," I told Em and Harvey, rewarded with

sudden laughs. "I'll guard over you. You're safe under my watch, fair damsels."

"You know your ass is going to pay for that, don't you?" Emlyn drawled. The threat was a billion times more heightened coming from Em than any of the others. I swallowed, my ass tightening, my shoulder tingling even though the bite's power had faded.

"I hope so," I replied in a low purr.

Emlyn groaned, rolling over, and I grinned in victory. Good, he deserved a boner for teasing me.

I drew my daggers from my back and set them across my legs, just in case Cronus sent any more dragons for us. Kai lowered himself to the ground beside me with a grunt, catching my hand in both of his.

"This floor's too fucking cold," he muttered, making me laugh.

I leaned my head on his shoulder and let out a long breath. "Use your snakes as insulation."

He snorted, but sobered. "I'm too low on energy; I don't want to waste any. Losing my shit earlier took more out of me than I realised. Now I'm just ... fucking knackered."

I turned my hand over, linking my fingers with his. "Here, lay down. You can watch the bottom of the maze and I'll take the top."

He made a show of complaining but when I pulled him down, shifting my knives so he could lay his head on my lap, he melted into the embrace. If I'd told him to sleep, he would have made a manly show of refusal, but my Kai could never turn down physical contact of any kind. Did I feel bad for tricking him into resting? No. And I'd do it again.

"I'm sorry we were separated," I murmured, running my fingers through his wine-red hair as he relaxed into me, his breaths slowing, more even.

"Not your fault," he replied with a yawn. "Sorry I went batshit insane."

I huffed a quiet laugh. "Don't be sorry for fucking me against the wall. It was so damn hot. I want a replay."

"That can be arranged," he agreed, nuzzling his head against my stomach. "I don't think I can get it up now, though. Too tired."

I brushed hair off his face, trailing gentle touches over his scalp. "Tomorrow, then."

"It's a promise," he agreed.

I didn't need to see his face to know he was fighting the closing of his eyes. Another few minutes and he was limp and unconscious in my lap, breathing deep. I let out a relieved sigh, a tiny part of my worry for him evaporating. At least his body would recover while he slept. His mind, well ... I'd have to work on caring for that myself. And I didn't mind that he'd be clingy and over-possessive for a few days.

A rush of worry filled my soul, making my heart skip. Wane. I reached back, spearing myself down that strong tether until I felt him on the other side. I couldn't give myself to the bond entirely when I had to watch the Labyrinth around me, but just feeling him there on the other side was a comfort that made my eyes blur and my bottom lip wobble.

I miss you, I told him, as if he could hear me. *I want you here. I want to hear your voice and watch you laugh and see your smile. Fuck, I hope you can smile, and Cronus hasn't stolen that from you forever.*

I knew he didn't know the exact words, but my emotions must have reached him because he sent back a wave of love so strong I had to cover my mouth to trap my sob.

I wish Harvey could feel you. I wish you could feel him. He's so strong, but I know he's suffering. He misses you like hell, Wane. We all do.

I just wanted him home. I wanted Wane in my arms where I could keep him safe.

But he wouldn't be able to stand being touched. It was bad enough before, any touch traumatising enough before. But after a hundred years of torture? Touching him might not just trigger him, but cause deep, physical pain. As much as I wanted to hold him, I couldn't.

Concern surrounded my soul, and I swore softly. Wane could feel everything I felt.

I'm fine, I reassured him, my soul ebbing against his in a slow caress. *Are you okay?*

He didn't reply, didn't know what I'd asked. Pain twisted through my chest but I shut it out, not wanting him to feel it.

We're coming for you, Wane. We'll get you out of there. I swear.

I could have sworn the flutter of his emotion in my chest answered, *I know.*

CHAPTER EIGHTEEN

*I*n my dream I was wrapped up in shadows, my head on Wane's chest, and his low, raspy voice in my ear telling me all the plans he had for our future. We'd rebuild our home, put everything back the way it should be, but this time we'd employ security to patrol the woods so no one could sneak up on us. And Kai would scare the shit out of every guard so they didn't dare even *think* about betraying us. We'd be safe, and live happily ever after.

"If anyone tries to hunt us again," he murmured, knuckles stroking down my bare back as I drifted to sleep in the dream, "I'll black out the sun so no one can see anything ever again."

"I love you," I breathed, my eyelids heavy.

"I love you so much," he replied, a kiss feathering over my temple. "Loving you kept me alive. You saved me so many times."

"I'll always save you," I promised, losing my fight with sleep.

But when I fell asleep in my dream, I was yanked awake in the Labyrinth, and a gasp tore up my throat as my eyes flashed open on—a silver-blue ocean. *What the fuck?*

"What happened?" Emlyn yelled, his voice rough with panic and louder than usual. "Where's Haley?"

"I've got her," Wynvail called. An arm hooked around my waist, tugging me up so my shoulders floated above the water. I gasped down air, my head reeling. "Water just poured in out of nowhere."

"I couldn't even wake you before it was filling up," Harvey rasped, coughing up water as he swam, cutting through the water towards us with powerful strokes. "I'm sorry."

"Not your fault," I said, scanning the maze and kicking my legs to stop myself sinking into the rising water. Wynvail's arm helped. Bastard.

There was a chamber open straight ahead, but that was rapidly filling with water, too. And—shapes bobbed in the depths, one black and sleek, another a bright seafoam green.

"Guys, we have company," I warned, swimming as much as I could when Wynvail held me tighter than a clingy octopus.[1]

"Let me go, dickwad," I growled at Wynvail.

He just snorted and held on tighter, threatening to crack a rib. I stretched my fingers down to my knife, but the water flung us suddenly sideways and my fingertips barely skimmed the hilt before I could get a grip.[2]

"Hippocampi!" Harvey screamed, his voice suddenly shrill and fear in the whites of his eyes as he powered through the water to me and Wynvail.

"Fuck," Kai hissed, swimming in place ahead of us, dark red hair plastered to his cheeks. "Em, know any weaknesses?"

"Very few," Emlyn replied, water splashing my neck as he closed in on my right, his eyes narrowed on where Wynvail held me. "They're slower on land, but..."

But we were in a maze rapidly filling up with water, and no way would Cronus be kind enough to open the doors so we could find our way to dry land. The psychopath had filled the Labyrinth with water and unleashed hippocampi in the first place.

I only knew about the creatures because Em read so many books. Hippocampi were like overgrown seahorses, with the head and front legs of a horse and a giant, curling fish tail. From what I remembered, they had killer teeth, could swim at alarming speeds, and drove the chariot of Poseidon. The *god*.

And now two of them wanted to attack us.[3] I wasn't feeling great about our chances against horses favoured by *the god of the ocean*.

"We'll have to swim, and hope a passage opens," Emlyn shouted. "Kai!"

"On it," Kai yelled, rocking the water with a surge of his magic. The wave sent Wynvail and I swerving away from Em and Harvey, and my stomach lurched at the sudden movement. Ugh, I really did not want to be sick right now.

"For fuck's sake," Harvey growled when the skies opened above us, icy, driving rain pounding our heads and shoulders, making the water thrash more treacherously. "Rain? *Now* of all bloody times?"

"It's the hippocampi," Emlyn shouted, pumping his arms to stay afloat on the other side of the passage, his strong legs keeping him afloat but for how long? "They control the weather."

"Anything else they control?" Wynvail barked, his grip slipping on my middle the more the water rocked.

"The sea," Emlyn replied, foreboding heavy in his voice.

"Oh, great," I groaned, straining for my knives again.

The horses glided closer, the gills on the sides of their slick necks now visible, and the transparent frills where a mane ought to be. There was nothing remotely like a normal horse about them; their eyes were milky and opaque, their movements too fast, too smooth to be natural. Goosebumps flashed all over my body.

What the fuck could we do? We were trapped and cornered. My heart raced, stomach knotting.

"They touch you, and they die," Wynvail promised, his cold voice making me shudder even harder.

"You're squashing my wings," I snipped at him. "Let me go."

"No."

I growled in the back of my throat. This asshole was going to get me killed. If I couldn't swim how was I supposed to defend myself?

"Where's Kai?" I breathed, my heart skipping when I searched the frothing waves and couldn't see him. *"Kai?"*

I scanned the chamber again. He wasn't here. He should have been here.

"Shit!" Harvey yelled. "The black one's got him."

My blood ran cold, an unnatural calm spreading through me until my heart beat slower. "Let me go, or I'll kill you to get to that fucking horse."

Wynvail's lips pressed to the sensitive spot under my ear. "Fine. To watch you kill, honey, I'll let go. Just know if you get hurt, I'll be spanking that cute little ass until it's red raw."

I shoved him, ignoring the catch in my breath and the way his fingers glanced across my wings. I hated that they were so sensitive, such an obvious target.

"Kai!" I yelled again, swimming hard and following where Harvey dragged himself through the silvery waters. He was little more than ram's horns and rich brown hair, but I kept close to him while I scanned the thrashing water, the rain whipping it into a frenzy.

I finally spotted Kai and my heart stopped. Gods. The black hippocampus had closed its jaws around his arm, and was dragging him, kicking and snarling, into the other chamber.

Everything inside me went even stiller.

Like *fuck* was this thing stealing my mate.

I let the water carry me for a few seconds, reaching down to grab my volcanic daggers and glad I'd been paranoid enough to sleep with them strapped to me.[4] With a dagger in each hand, I dragged myself through the churning waters, my jaw clenched and murder in my eyes. That cool calm spread even deeper when I saw how hard Kai fought the hippocampus.

"Harvey!" I shouted, drawing his attention. When he swam closer, wet and furious, I said, "I'll distract it; you grab Kai and get him back to the others."

He gave me a look that said I was mad for even asking him to leave me. "I'll get Kai and all three of us can go back to the others."

I groaned, but a sudden rush of water poured down my open mouth and stopped me arguing. More forced its way up my nose until I choked on the taste of salt and water, until I couldn't breathe. It threatened to unseat the killer calm keeping me steady, but I coughed up the water from my lungs and gasped down air.

Now, I was angry. And disoriented. And fucking *cold*.[5]

"Kai, hold on!" I yelled, my voice hoarse now. "And *you*, hippocampus dick, let him go and pick on someone your own size."

"Hey," Kai protested weakly. His snakes cut paths through the water, but they moved sluggishly, and only one of them hit the horse in the neck. It didn't dislodge its jaws locked around Kai's arm. Fuck, the water around them was tinged with red foam—his blood. "I'm ... size," he slurred.

"Of course you are," I agreed, pumping my arms faster and kicking my feet to propel me closer. I gave Harvey a nod, and lifted my wings from the water, flapping them until I rose above the water line.

"I'm what you really want," I called to the seahorse, sinking into my magic until heartbeats throbbed in my ears, muffling the horse's high pitched cry.

I raised an eyebrow in challenge and snapped my wings hard, diving myself at its head, my knives aimed for its milky white eyes. Shit, it moved faster than I expected, raising onto its ... actually I had no idea what that swirly fish tail even was. The sight of it connecting to a black horse front distracted me for a moment until hooves boxed dangerously close to my face.[6]

Something was happening in the other chamber because Emlyn growled suddenly, and pain lashed through my bond with Wynvail. But I was so close to the black hippocampus that I didn't dare turn my head. I had visions of my throat ripped out and dangling from the horse's mouth. I wanted the horse to release Kai, but preferably *without* my vocal chords between its teeth.

"Fuck," I gasped, driving my daggers down when a nasty hoof caught me in the gut, knocking all the air out of me. I snapped my wings out, catching myself before I could spiral through the air, and threw all my weight into driving my wavy daggers into the horse's eyes. I had no issue with hippocampi in general, but this one had stolen my mate, and made the fight personal, so it needed to lose its eyes.[7]

I shot Harvey a quick look. *The second it releases Kai, grab him.* He nodded, fixing his eyes on the beast's jaws. Another wingbeat carried me close enough for the tips of my knives to scratch its eyeballs, and I threw all my weight into the double blow—

And *screamed* when instead of the volcanic steel sinking into gooey eyes, the metal lit up deep, vivid red—the colour of blood and curses. The daggers didn't plunge into its eyes; they rebounded like I'd hit a solid wall, and a blast of power slammed into my body hard enough that my wings faltered and I dropped into the water hard enough to make a vicious wave.

Water filled my ears, bubbles tickling my nose as I frantically fought to find my way back up. Blind panic made me clumsy, and having knives as an extension of my hands wasn't helping. Magic coursed through me, as sharp and blistering as the bone pin that Cerny gave me—that Wynvail *stole* from me —and even kicking my legs didn't keep me afloat as my body struggled to contain it. It was too much power for one body to hold, *too much*. Oh gods, it was going to kill me.

I screamed underwater as the power built and seethed and filled every space of me, pressing against my skin with nowhere to go and *still* swelling, boiling, howling.

Panic cut through my chest, as bright as a star but as dark and velvety as night. Wane.

Fuck. I couldn't die here. I needed to fight my way out of this cursed Labyrinth and find him. I was his mate; it was my job to take care of him, to keep him *safe*. I had a damned job to do.

I slackened my grip on my knives as I sank through the water, ready to swim, but—bright white light split the murky water before I could drop them, and I exhaled a hard breath I should really have saved. Wynvail had me in his moonbeam magic or whatever the hell he called it. It was cold as fuck, icier even than the water, and I shuddered as it ripped me up through the ever-rising water in the Labyrinth and into the air.

My hands shook. No wait, that was my entire body trembling violently. I vomited water and then choked down air, instinct squeezing my body, taking over.

"Don't move!" Kai snarled in a voice so chilling that I froze.

Harvey caught me before I could sink again, the white beam of power flickering and then cutting out without warning. Like Wynvail was struggling to use his power. Like he was weak or in pain. Fuck, why did that fill me with so much panic?

"My rose?"

"I'm fine," I replied, my voice surprisingly hoarse. My chest was tight, my eyes scraped raw by the water. I resumed shaking twice as hard, my teeth chattering as I slumped in Harvey's arms. "You?"

"Angry," he bit out, still slurring a little. Blood streaked his arm where the hippocampus bit him, and I inhaled sharply at the sight of it. I didn't know if Harvey had slept enough to rebuild his reserves. Actually, how long did Kai and I sleep? An hour? Two? We switched the watch with Harvey and Wynvail, and suddenly I woke up floating.

"I told you not to move!" Kai screamed at the hippocampus, his eyes wild and crazy. But the horse had turned to face me, and—lowered its head. Huh?

I exchanged a baffled look with Kai, then Harvey. It was ... thanking me?

"Uh, what's happening?" I asked the horse itself when it lifted its head, water flowing down its mane of gills and trickling back into the water.

The creature blinked bright aqua eyes at me, strangely intelligent—and sad—and a bolt of understanding and unease tightened my stomach.

"Cronus was controlling you, wasn't he?"

The horse dipped its head again, not taking its eyes off me. My stomach flipped.

"And I broke that control," I murmured, glancing at my daggers. "Kai, where exactly did you get these made?"

"I met a guy in a pub," he replied defensively, cutting through the water to place himself in front of me.

"Fucking hell, Kai," I growled. A guy in a pub? All the world's ills could be bought from a guy in a pub.

The hippocampus turned in the water and—swam towards the end of the chamber.

"So it's over?" I breathed to my mates, twisting to look at Harvey. His face had lost its colour, his expression tight and scared, and he squeezed me a little too tightly, but he wasn't bleeding. Thank fuck.

I stared at the daggers in my hands, kicking my feet to stay afloat. The horse couldn't have taken the damn water with it?

A shout from the other chamber made my breath skip.

"No," Kai answered, already swimming back to the other side. "Definitely not over."

CHAPTER NINETEEN

I shot out of the water, flying through the tiny strip of air above the Labyrinth's impromptu ocean. Even with soaked wings, flying was faster than swimming. Harvey shot into the air beside me and did the same, both of us scanning the water below as we flew back into the first chamber. The seafoam green hippocampus was much bigger than the one I just ... defeated? Saved? I was still hazy on what had happened. I didn't let go of my blades, though.

They'd somehow absorbed the magic Cronus used to compel the creature. It no longer burned in my hands, and I could function with the power blazing through me unlike the bone pin's unbearable intensity.

I saw the hippocampus's move before it made it, and I plummeted towards the water with a snarl. *Shit.* I wasn't fast enough to stop it tearing a chunk out of Emlyn's bicep as he hauled his powerful body through the water, salt-and-pepper hair plastered to his skull and his eyes bright with pain. This wasn't the first time he'd been bitten. Or Wynvail, judging by the pain stuttering through my soul.

"Stop!" I yelled, my voice strangely amplified, like a dozen

Halwens spoke at once. My blades flashed bright ruby again, like they still held Cronus's magic inside them. Oh gods, did they still have his magic? What was I supposed to do with daggers empowered by a titan? The titan who wanted me dead, who ordered Wynvail to kill my other mates, and had Wane captive?

Couldn't life ever be bloody easy?

The horse swung around to stare at me as I flew over the water, my heart pounding too hard, too fast, as I assessed the situation. Harvey plunged straight into the ocean to grab Em, Kai swimming not far behind.

We were together; we could get out of this. We'd fought our way out of trickier situations. Granted, those situations weren't compelled by *a titan.*

Oh, fuck, we could really die here. As food for a giant seahorse.

The hippocampus's milky eyes fixed on my glowing daggers, as if it knew what magic lurked inside them, and it let out the loudest, most screeching howl of all time. Pain stabbed through my ear drums and into my skull. I wouldn't be surprised if they bled.[1]

Wane's sudden rush of panic cut through my chest, but I was too distracted to send a rush of comfort. It must have been driving him insane to feel all my emotions, not knowing what made me so scared, not being here to fight alongside me.

The hippocampus kept screeching, violence in its milky eyes as it stared at me.

"Shut the fuck up!" Kai yelled, as if the creature would ever listen to him.[2]

"Stay against the wall," I shouted, adjusting the angle of my knives and dipping lower, assessing the horse's bulky muscle and jerky movements. These things moved too damn fast.

I always knew someone would ignore my instruction, but

I'd have put my money on Kai or Em, their overprotective streaks both over a mile long.

Instead it was *Wynvail* whose expression hardened. He somehow looked even more vicious than usual with his short hair flattened to his bony head, and harsh light cutting into his face, enhancing his cheekbones. Pure defiance radiated from him, along with a healthy dollop of protective rage.

Idiot.

I swung a knife in front of me, shooting down towards the horse with strong wingbeats. But the hippocampus jerked away at the last minute, and my heart skipped when it lurched viciously fast through the frothing water and—

Snapped its jaws around Wynvail's throat.

No.

My heart stuttered, horror making me slow, freezing my blood, my soul.

Harvey exploded into movement when Wynvail's blood curled through the water, his fearsome growl cutting the air in two. It was so loud it shook my ribs, making my whole body quiver as shadows and fur erupted through the water. It had been so long since I'd seen his shadow beast form that my heart lurched at the sight of him. And then it broke when I remembered what Ashboren told us—that this was what happened to a sun soul starved of sunlight.

My emotions were a frazzled mess. Fury and dread clashed with sorrow and love. I wrenched on my numb wings, my eyes fixed on the blood spilling through the water.

Harvey's furry beast form collided with the hippocampus, and added a shot of blinding alarm to my emotions. The horse was close enough to snap his head off. But those vicious teeth remained locked around Wynvail's bronze throat, moments from ripping his life from him.

Please...

I regained movement with a gasp, and dropped suddenly

towards the water at the same moment Harvey roared and swiped wicked claws across the hippocampus's snout. His massive, furry body rippled with darkness, power shaking the air, the water, shaking the entire damn Labyrinth. His eyes had bled from silver to black, and all I could smell was brimstone, thick and cloying and dark. I couldn't forget that crucifying power; I'd screamed until my voice turned hoarse in the fighting pit, and cried until I couldn't feel anything but agony shattering my bones, slicing through my skull until my brain was in little, miserable bits. I'd passed out. He'd almost killed me.

I winced, looking away. It was hard to hear the hippocampus screech and remember just how badly my own mate had tortured me.

But Wynvail made a low moan of pain and snapped me out of it. I tucked my wings and slammed into the icy water, power making me tremble as I sheathed my blades and grabbed the hippocampus's jaws. A scream of effort built as I pulled with all my might, prising the horse's razor teeth out of Wynvail's neck. My grip was the only thing keeping me from drowning but I tried not to think about that.

The creature was weakened by Harvey's attacks, but still dangerously strong. Sweat beaded on my lip as I struggled, but Harvey lashed out with his claws again and the horse's jaws unlocked to bellow an involuntary howl of pain. I ripped its teeth from Wynvail's throat, tears ceiling my eyes as I wrenched him free. My hands shook; he fell into me with a groan, blood sluicing hot over my arms.

"Wyn," I breathed, pulling back so I could see how badly he'd been cut. "Oh, gods, oh gods."

There was a slice about three inches long, and it was pouring blood at an alarming rate, a deep puncture wound on the other side. My hands became slick with it, blood gushing over my chest too.

"Tried..." Wynvail slurred, his eyelids drooping shut over pained silver eyes. "Everything ... to stop him..."

"Wynvail!" I cried, my voice breaking. My soul collapsed, my chest caving in on itself. "Harvey!"

My arm shook as I clutched Wynvail closer, slamming one hand over the mess of his throat, trying to stop blood flow as I swam in place and failing miserably.

"Give him here, Hales," Emlyn said, his calm tone like a rush of oxygen in my lungs. He pulled us further from the hippocampus, Harvey keeping it occupied and Kai attacking with magic and venom. I swam numbly, covered in blood, my chest caving in.

Tears burned my eyes. I couldn't breathe. I hated Wynvail, and I wanted to personally kill him, but the thought of losing him made me want to scream and sob and curl into a ball.

Emlyn pressed his bigger, stronger palm to Wynvail's throat, stemming the gush of blood, and my heart skipped with a mix of panic and relief.

But I felt the weakness dragging his soul, the bond heavier in my chest than it had ever lay.

Arms wrapped around me from behind, Kai's voice gentle in my ear. "You have to stab the horse, my rose. Or try to—whatever you did to the other one. That's the only way it'll stop attacking us."

A broken whine was the only reply I could give, but—Harvey roared, deep and guttural, and hairs rose all down my arms.

Kai was right. The rest of us would get killed unless I did this.

"Em," I rasped, tears blinking free and mixing with the cold droplets splashed on my face.

"I'll do my best," he promised, his face tight with worry. "He won't die on my watch, Hales."

I trapped my bottom lip between my teeth when it

wobbled like crazy, and allowed Kai to guide us through the water closer to the hippocampus. Fuck, the beast and Harvey were evenly matched, each trading blows and slashes, drawing blood and evading hits in equal measure.

"Hey," I rasped, completely missing the *total badass* mark I was aiming for. "I'm the only one who gets to fight my mates."

I lifted my blades, Kai carrying me closer, and sucked in a juddering breath as the hippocampus snapped a hoof at Harvey, pushing him back. My mate snarled and roared like a mindless beast, heedless of the pain he must be in, and a new panic beat through my chest. Would he be able to shift back? Had I lost him again?

Focus on the murderous seahorse, Haley.

I swallowed when the hippocampus swung towards me, but with Kai's arms around me, giving me strength and unwavering support, I kept my trembling arms raised and drove my daggers at its eyeballs. I didn't dare look at the open maw, blood dripping in rivulets down slick green skin. Wynvail's blood. Emlyn's. Harvey's.

Kai carried me the last few inches, his snakes propelling us through the water until the razor tips of my volcanic knives drove into its eyes. My arms jerked, my body recoiling, and Kai tightened his arms around me. The daggers hit the same barrier as before, and even though I was prepared for it, I still flinched when they erupted with bright ruby light.

Power coursed up my arms, making my fingertips numb, my palms burning, and I couldn't keep the scream trapped in my chest even though I knew it would scare the shit out of Kai. Magic shook me like I'd been electrocuted, burning the tip of my tongue until I tasted blood and salt and smoke, and when it finally ebbed away, I hung limp in my mate's arms, panting for breath.

And Wynvail was dying. His throat was torn out.

Tried ... everything ... to stop him...

Not it—him. Wyn wasn't talking about the hippocampus.

"Haley?" Kai demanded, a tremble moving through his body. He squeezed me tighter, his chest moving with rapid breaths. "Talk to me, my rose, tell me you're okay."

"Fine," I replied weakly, tears flowing down my cheeks.

I hated him; why should I care if he died? He was a dick.

I honestly forgot the hippocampus was still in front of us until its mouth opened and *it spoke.*

"You broke the curse on me. Your blades absorbed it." Sharp blue eyes, no longer milky and opaque, gave me and my knives an uneasy look. "I owe you a debt, and so does my god."

"Your god," Kai echoed, because speech was beyond me.

"The king of the sea. Poseidon."

"Oh, okay cool," Kai laughed, a sharp expulsion of sound. "Just casually. Poseidon. Sure."

I groaned, a wordless plea for him to shut the hell up.

"I'll send warning to the gods of what Cronus is doing here. And my apologies that I can't take you with me. The waters I travel by would devour you."

Yeah, that sounded about right. Fit the theme of the day. Or my whole life.

Wynvail was dying. Growing even weaker in our bond, draining all the life and fire from my soul.

Like the other horse, the green hippocampus dipped its head and swam away from us, no longer interested in murdering us. *Unlike* the last one, this seahorse took the water with it. I hardly cared.

I slumped in Kai's arms, my feet meeting the ground again and all my strength sucked out of me. For a moment I just breathed, each exhale and inhale pure effort.

Kai was shaking. Emlyn and Harvey were injured. And Wynvail was dying.

CHAPTER TWENTY

"Oh, gods," I breathed, choking back the raw lump in my throat as I dropped to my knees beside Wynvail. Emlyn knelt on the wet ground beside him, putting pressure on his throat, but unable to stop the blood gushing from his throat even though he was unconscious. "Harvey—"

But Harvey was still a beast of fur and shadows, and when he swung his big head towards me, silver eyes gleaming with violence, my heart actually skipped.

What do I do? Wynvail was bleeding out, the life literally pouring from him.

On impulse, I reached inside my chest and grabbed hold of the bond that linked me to Wynvail, gripping tightly and not caring if it hurt him. *Don't you dare die. Don't you fucking dare.* If I reached him, if it made him hold on, I didn't care if I left fingerprints on his soul. *Stay right here. You're not allowed to leave.*

Not releasing my ruthless grip, I stumbled to my feet, surprised when my legs had enough strength to hold me up, and faced my feral mate.

"Harvey," I murmured, taking slow, careful steps toward him on the slick ground.

"Haley," Kai warned, his voice low. He moved to follow me but I held up a hand. *Trust me.* He expelled a growling sigh. "If he makes a single move towards you, I'm yanking you back."

I nodded, not taking my eyes off Harvey as he snarled, his hackles rising. Dark smoke rippled from his fur, promising pain. I locked down my body so I didn't flinch at the memory of him pinning me in the fighting pit, the agony that flowed through every part of me. I thought he'd kill me. I knew he nearly had.

Wynvail is dying, right now.

I held Harvey's stare even as he bared his teeth, his eyes so dark they swallowed all light and his horns impossibly sharp. It would take very little effort for him to gut me on those.

"Be careful, Hales," Emlyn warned, tension sharp in his voice.

"Harvey," I breathed, freezing when he let out a growl. A warning—or a threat? "Come back to me. I need you. Please."

I slowly lifted my hand, holding it out to him, a plea written all across my face. He towered over me in this form, the malice coming off him in waves making him seem even bigger, but I didn't back down. I swallowed my dread and held my nerve. This was my mate. This was Harvey.

I inched closer, moving so slowly, my heart hammering with every second. If I screwed this up, he'd rip my head off. He'd have to live with that for the rest of his life, and that would be no life at all.

I crept close enough to tangle my fingers in the longer fur over his chest, the darkness softer than I expected. It didn't shock me with pain. Yet.

Harvey's whole body shook, a harsh sound rattling his throat.

"Oh, don't be a baby," I huffed, stroking down his chest.

"It's only me. It's Haley, your Sugarplum. And you're Harvey, my Buttercup."

Gods, they were awful names. It had started as a joke and an insult, but now the names meant as much to me as *my rose* and *itzaia*.

"You don't need to stay in the dark," I breathed when he didn't rip my hand off. I grew bolder with my touches, stroking his massive shoulders, his wide throat. "Please, Harvey. I need you. Wynvail's going to die."

His upper lips drew back, enormous teeth bared.

"I know," I agreed. "I *know* what he's done. But he's my mate, Harvey. If he dies—fuck, I don't want him to die."

My voice cracked, a fresh wave of tears burning my eyes. I flicked them away, looking into Harvey's black eyes. "Please."

His chest shook under my hand, and my shoulders slumped. I didn't know how to get through to him, and when all he could do was growl, we could hardly have a conversation. I swallowed, and tasted tears.

His chest jumped, and I jolted backwards when magic hit me hard enough to make me falter. I blinked back tears until I could see—and honestly wished I hadn't. Harvey in his beast form was impressive and nightmarish, beautiful in a dark, fatal way. Harvey in his demon form was devastatingly sexy, especially when his lips curled in a smirk or he threw his head back and laughed. Harvey halfway between the two? Horrific. He had a man's forehead and messy russet hair, a wolfish black snout, and a pair of sultry lips right below it.

He looked like a failed science experiment, but I loved him and I'd never speak a word about it.

"I'm here," he breathed, his voice gravelly and deep. He reached for me with a hand still tipped in vicious claws. "I'm here, Haley."

I rushed across the space between us, grabbing his face in

my hands and brushing my lips to his in the most gentle kiss I could manage when I was so frantic.

"Can you heal him? *Please.* I know he's a bastard but—"

"He's my brother," Harvey grunted, squeezing my hip and guiding me aside. "Of course I'll heal him."

My bottom lip weakened. I pressed my hand to my mouth as Harvey knelt, wobbling I just-shifted legs but managing not to faceplant the ground.[1]

"How much do you have left?" Kai asked, the bite in his tone telling me he thought we should leave Wynvail to die.

"Enough," Harvey replied in a grunt, setting his hands to the mess of Wynvail's throat. I didn't know how he was still alive; he should be dead. But I felt him weakly through the bond, and I still had hooks buried in his soul, refusing to let him fade away. I couldn't feel his emotions like usual, couldn't really sense him beyond a faint flutter, little more than a heartbeat. My face crumpled.

Em steadied Harvey when he wavered, but he set his jaw, kept his narrowed stare on Wynvail's wan face, and didn't take his hands off his brother until the wound knit back together.

"He might have lost too much blood," Emlyn said gently, his eyes on me. He wasn't sure how I'd react if Wynvail died. Neither was I.

I walked to where they both knelt, my legs less than steady, and rested my hand on Harvey's shoulder in silent thanks. He covered my hand with his, squeezing with reassurance that made my breathing skip.

My eyes burned. What if Em was right, and it was too late? There was so much blood on the ground, and even more in the water that had sucked away. Yet more coated me like a second skin. I swallowed the golf ball in my throat, my whole body shaky.

Come on, Wynvail.

"Don't be a stubborn bastard," I rasped, trying to glare at

his slack face. His eyelids were closed, long lashes casting shadows on his cheeks. I couldn't summon even a hint of a glare. "We went to all this trouble to save your evil ass; you don't get to die."

My hand shook under Harvey's. Fuck, he was really dead, wasn't he?

I pulled frantically on his soul, a brutal, ruthless command to return. I wasn't sure his soul was even fluttering anymore. Had he gone still?

"There's ... something strange about him," Harvey murmured, almost hesitantly. "My magic didn't react to his injury like it normally would. It was absorbed *into* him."

"What does that mean?" Emlyn asked quietly, blue eyes still heavy on me.

I swallowed, not taking my stare from Wynvail for a second. He looked so much younger, so much more fragile like this. No arrogance and wickedness on his face, no glare or sneer. He just looked ... normal. A little broken.

I didn't like to think about the emotions I sensed in his soul most often, bitterness and stress, but there must have been a reason for them. Who was Wynvail, really? If Cassander Locke had done such unspeakable things to Wane and Harvey, what had he done to Wynvail? I should have asked him, should have tried to understand him instead of threatening to murder him all this time.

"Come on, asshole. If you break my girl, I'll come to the afterlife and strangle you back to life," Kai snarled, crouching to shove Wynvail's shoulder.

I flinched when a hand snapped up and grabbed Kai's wrist, and for a moment I didn't realise that bronze hand was Wynvail's.

"You can try," he replied, hoarse and low and *miraculous*. "I'd win you in a fight, Virex."

"In your fucking dreams," Kai snarled, and snatched his wrist free with little to no effort.

"You fucking *bastard*," I yelled, my chest crumpled, my heart wrecked. A sob made me choke on my next breath, but I glared. "You total, fucking—"

"Will you kill me if I try to hug her?" Wynvail rasped.

"Yes," Em, Kai, and Harvey replied in the same threatening tone.

Wynvail groaned, propping himself up so he wasn't prone and vulnerable on the floor. "Well, someone better hug her first, or I'll do the job myself."

"I'm fine," I snarled, baring my teeth, my wings trembling behind me. But when Emlyn swept me into a bear hug, my whole body buckled. "I'm fine," I sobbed, resting my head on his chest, the strong thump of his heart as much a reassurance as the hug. A tear squeezed out of my closed eyes but I pretended not to notice. "Really."

Em didn't even argue, my claims so obviously a lie. He just wrapped me up in him and dropped a kiss on the top of my head. "He's alive."

I swallowed, my throat burning, eyes stinging.

"Harvey!" Kai shouted, startling Em and I apart.

"No," I breathed, jerking forward when Harvey slumped, Kai catching him before his head could slam into the hard stone floor.

Arms shaking, I pulled him close, protectiveness mixing with panic and grief.

"He gave too much," Kai spat accusatively at Wynvail.

"He was mostly dead, Kai," Emlyn sighed, scanning Harvey's body for hidden injuries and finding none. "He had no control over Harvey's actions; you can't blame him."

"But you can blame *me*," I said in a small voice, my breathing sharp knives in my chest. "I begged him to help."

Kai softened instantly, a rough breath leaving his chest. "It's not your fault, my rose. He's been running on practically empty since we entered the damn Labyrinth. This is all *Cronus's* fault."

As if the bastard himself was listening, enjoying watching us suffer, a thunderous roar made us all jump—the nerve-shredding grating a new passage opening in the maze.

I didn't want to fight another mythical beast. Didn't want to endure a new harrowing trial. I just wanted to go home.

But no way would he let us just walk out of this place. So I scrubbed my face dry and straightened my spine. I'd fight my way out. Fuck Cronus.

CHAPTER TWENTY-ONE

"Go fuck yourself!" Kai screamed at the sky, which was probably not helpful, but I agreed with the sentiment wholeheartedly.

"With a cactus," Wynvail added, wheezing as he pushed to his feet, concerned silver eyes on his brother. "I'll carry him."

"Like *fuck* you will," Kai exploded, throwing himself at Wynvail, hands raised to strangle him.

"Kai," I sighed, exhausted as I rose unsteadily, clutching Harvey to me. Fuck, he was heavier than I remembered, all sleek muscle and feral brawn. Or maybe it was all the luscious hair. "Please."

"I hope you know," Kai said to Wynvail in a soft, deadly voice, edging uncomfortably close to him, "the only reason you're still alive is because my rose wants it that way. The second she changes her mind—"

"Which she won't—" Wynvail argued coolly, looking so alive, so *healthy,* that my face nearly crumpled again.

"—you're dead."

"Can we focus on the maze?" Emlyn rumbled, lifting

Harvey into his arms and peering worriedly into his slack face.

I needed my mate bonds back now more than ever, but they were still only whispers and broken strands. What good was I if I couldn't comfort them with the bond? How would they know they were loved and safe with me and I'd eviscerate any threat to their lives?

"What are the chances of us winning another fight?" I asked in a raw voice, turning in the direction of the grating rumble of stone—at the far end of the second chamber. The hippocampi were both gone despite the maze being completely sealed. Did they vanish into the water itself?

"With you and those knives?" Wynvail replied, as if I'd been speaking to him. "We'll win."

"What happened?" Emlyn asked, facing me, a knot between his dark brows. We all ignored the shifting maze; fuck Cronus trying to shepherd us to a new task. "How did they glow?"

I shook my head, clueless. "I tried to stab the hippocampus in its eyes, but I slammed into a magic wall and suddenly my knives were glowing red."

"The same colour your curse marks glow," Em pointed out, his eyes distant.

A slow touch ran down my spine and over my knife sheaths, making me shudder. I turned to face Kai, and saw exactly what he wanted to say but wouldn't with Wynvail listening. This was because of the prophecy marked down my back. Whatever great and terrible future I had involved my glowing curse marks and, somehow, my daggers.

"Do you think it's because they're volcanic?" I asked him, catching his inked hand in mine and squeezing his fingers, the worry in his eyes making my chest heavy. "Can that help them … absorb curses?"

The look in Kai's red eyes was almost pitying. I swallowed, throwing a glare in the direction of the grinding of stone on stone. He thought it was all me, nothing to do with the daggers. I didn't want to admit I suspected the same. Mostly because that meant I'd managed to break someone else's curse but could do fuck all about my own.

"Show of hands," I said, swallowing the knot in my throat. "Who thinks we should ignore the new pathway and just stay here because it's pretty defensible?"

Anything coming at us could only come from one direction, and it would run right into us.

Emlyn and Kai lifted their hands. Kai grabbed Harvey's limp hand and lifted it, too.

Wynvail sighed. "It doesn't work like that. He's the puppet-master holding our strings. If he wants us to go through a passage, we have no choice. You know what happens when you try to disobey, Halwen. You got crushed in the passage."

I winced. I did. But that didn't mean I wanted to jump when Cronus told me to jump. I wrapped my wings around myself, my jaw set. "I'm not his damn puppet."

Wynvail's disdainful laugh said I was sorely mistaken.

"Harvey almost *died*," I hissed, panic beating at my chest and emerging as bared teeth and harsh words. *"You* almost died. And you think we should keep doing what he tells us to? He's a maniac!"

"Yes," Wynvail agreed slowly, one beat away from an eye roll. "That's why we should do what he tells us to."

"*Or* you could keep your filthy mouth shut," Kai snarled, coming to my defence with snakes lashing the air and ink twisting around his arms. "It's your fault we're in this maze in the first place; if we hadn't come to your house, he'd—"

"Have found you anyway," Wynvail argued, cruelty turning his face into something cold and monstrous. The master of the fighting pit was with us. I shuddered.

"And we'd all be dead," Emlyn cut in, smoothing the fight

before it could begin. "And Haley's right; this place is easier to defend. We should—"

Em cut off, his expression freezing. He held Harvey closer, protective.

Cold spread through my body, all my hairs standing on end when the sound of shifting stone came from all around us. From every direction—left, right, ahead, behind. Everywhere.

I was going to be sick.

I turned, scanning the walls on either side of us with wide eyes, my breath catching, breaking.

"Two openings, three, four, *five*," Kai counted, his voice losing its sharp edge. Fear drenched his expression and I hated the sight of it so much I wanted to cry.

"I tried to warn you," Wynvail muttered, grabbing my arm and tearing me away from Kai.[1]

Kai froze for a moment, going entirely still, not a single breath moving his chest. His expression went utterly blank, red eyes blinking once. I knew we were in trouble when his tail lashed the air, the single warning he gave before power fulminated in the maze.

Shit. Magic tore through the whole chamber until snakes writhed against my skin, so powerful I swore I could hear their hissing.

Wynvail barked a sound of pain that slashed the tender flesh of my heart, and I staggered. Not again. Please, I couldn't watch him die again.

"Kai," I gasped, breathing faster, too fast. "Too soon, Kai, I can't—"

He'd been prone on the ground, his throat slit, bleeding out *minutes* ago, and I couldn't cope with the thought of him getting hurt again. Kai's venom would kill him and I'd have to watch him wither away all over again, my soul terrifyingly silent.

White light erupted, so bright I was forced to shield my eyes when what I needed was to grab both of them by the backs of their necks and slam their skulls together.

"The maze is opening!" Emlyn growled, anger deep in his voice. It was such a rare sound that Kai stopped in the act of slashing his hand through the air, probably to deliver a fatal blow to Wynvail. The moon-bright light cut out, too; I had to blink fast so my eyes focused again.

"What *is* that?" Kai breathed, edging closer to me, pressing me between him and Wynvail, two sides of the same psycho coin.

I drew my knives again, my palms slick on the pink handles and my heart sprinting rapidly as I stared at the chambers opening up all around us. We were surrounded. Kai's snakes thrashed in the air, betraying his panic.

I stared at the gaps opening rapidly in the walls, like Cronus had pushed a fast-forward button. The first shadow that emerged was tall and broad, with a massive head, bulging arms bared by a sleeveless leather top and—and one eye. My panicked stare jumped from doorway to doorway, finding the same creature in every opening.

And each of their eyes was milky with Cronus's compulsion.

CHAPTER TWENTY-TWO

"*R*un!" I screamed, and shoved my mates down the Labyrinth passage, towards the first door that had roared open. Panic carved through my chest until there was no space for air, cyclopes lumbering after us with deep, throaty grunts.

The ground shuddered with their footsteps, and fear turned my bones to jelly. Cronus really wanted to scare us into obeying him—or punish us for daring to consider any other route.

My lungs burned as I sprinted, my gaze jumped from Kai, to Emlyn, to Harvey held in his arms, to Wynvail running with white light pooled in his hand, and then to the doors groaning open all the way down the passage. Cronus wasn't taking any chances; he wanted us to go through the door at the end even if it killed us.

If I hadn't been so scared, I'd have been furious.

The cyclopes' heavy grunts followed us from all angles, their footsteps shaking the Labyrinth. They must have been nine feet tall at the shortest. No chance would I win a fight against a single one of them, let alone ten, twelve, more. Fuck, where did they keep coming from? And why did Cronus have an army of compelled cyclopes in the first place?

My stomach dropped when three other doors opened, spilling more cyclopes into the tight stone corridor. They were almost upon us now, could almost grab us with their massive hands. Those things were big enough to crush my skull like a grape. The back of my neck tingled, fear and awareness heightening all my senses until I could smell the sweat and earth scent of them—and the blood soaked into my clothes, drying on my skin.

"Faster," I bit out, terror for my mates' lives making the Labyrinth waver in my vision. I was going to black out, fall, and get trampled by the cyclopes. That was a miserable death. I couldn't stop, had to stay on my feet and keep running.

"Almost there," Emlyn panted, throwing a look behind us. When the blood drained from his face, I knew we were dead.

But Wynvail followed Emlyn's stare. He let out a fierce snarl when he realised the cyclopes were close enough to kill us. My heart skipped when Wynvail reared back his hand and threw the light he'd pooled there, more gathering instantly in his palm. The moment the magic slammed into a one-eyed giant, knocking them back, Wynvail hurled another burst of light at another, and then another. Buying us a few seconds. We couldn't afford to waste it.

"Keep running!" Kai snapped. "Faster!"

That's what I said, I wanted to quip but I didn't have the energy. Every breath I took was a wheeze, every exhale a groan. I didn't have enough space to use my wings to propel me along, which was just typical. Wait—I'd flown down this passage earlier...

"The corridor's shrinking!" Kai yelped, realising it when I did and grabbing my wrist in a bruising grip. "Run!"

"What do you think we're *doing?*" Wynvail snarled, but breathlessly. He threw another flurry of light behind him, knocking back two cyclopes but not harming them. Like he realised they were under the titan's control, too.

But not killing them implied he was a halfway decent person, and that just seemed unrealistic. He probably didn't want to waste the magic it would take to kill them.

My head spun, either at the exercise or because I was having a full-blown panic attack, and my eyes tunnel-visioned on the open doorway at the end of the path. So damn close. Just a little further, and I could collapse.

Kai's snakes surged, almost knocking me down as they raced past me, drawing a deep bellow from a cyclops behind us.

"In, get in!" Emlyn yelled, shoving Kai through the opening into whatever hellish corridor waited beyond it.[1]

I hurtled through the door next, grabbing Emlyn's arm and tugging him through. But he dug his heels in, gripping Harvey tight, my mate sleeping through the whole flight. Em didn't budge until Wynvail threw two more bursts of light and staggered through the passage.

My heart pulled tight, and my bottom lip wobbled. Fuck, I'd really messed up. Now Em saw the bastard as one of us; Wynvail was under his protection.

The second we all fell through the opening, the heavy stone doors slammed shut. Locking the cyclopes on the other side. But trapping us here.

Wherever here was.

I slumped against the nearest wall, struggling for breath, my whole chest sliced apart by sharp pain as my lungs protested the last ten minutes of my existence. This passage was shorter than the last one, but just as tall, and equally grey and depressing. No killer hippocampi or army of cyclopes, though. Things were looking up.

Wynvail collapsed at my feet, breaths rattling his bare, bloodied chest and his forehead resting against my thighs. Kai wasn't any better; only Em seemed to recover faster than the rest of us. Probably because he was the only one of my mates who bothered to run for endurance training; I doubted that part of him had changed in the past hundred years.

"Get off," I panted, weakly shoving Wynvail with my knee.

He wrapped bronze fingers around my calf, breathing hard. "No."

"If I wasn't—exhausted—" Kai rasped.

"You'd kill me," Wynvail finished, too wrecked for even an eye roll. "Same old threats, Malakai. You're getting boring."

Their bickering was so reminiscent of Kai and Harvey's arguments, and the familiarity was comforting. I *just* managed to catch my fingers before they tried to stroke through Wynvail's short, messy hair.

We all jumped when Cronus's voice rumbled through the air. I swore colourfully even pain cracked through my head, every part of me already sore and rife with damage. Any more, and my body would start to shut down. Maybe that was what Cronus wanted; to push me to my breaking point.

You displease me, Wynvail. I gave you one command, and you're such a failure you can't even do that. Why are the men still alive?

Wynvail screwed his eyes shut, his whole body stiffening against me. Almost like he was waiting for an axe to fall. Or like the pain ravaging his body was so much worse than ours, like Cronus was punishing him.

Are you that much of a coward?

A growl rumbled from Emlyn's throat. Even Kai's expression had changed from everyday hostile to downright murderous. Maybe just because Cronus was speaking in general.

"Shut up," I hissed, gritting my teeth against the surge of pain when he spoke again.

Wynvail's fingers tightened on my calf, his breathing fast, shallow. What the fuck was the titan *doing* to him? He hadn't exhibited pain even when the hippocampus gored him; he'd locked it down where we wouldn't see. But now? His breathing was ragged, his jaw clenched, eyes mashed shut, and a vein throbbed in his forehead. Signs of pure agony. I felt it too, like a brand on my soul. I trembled, anger rising.

You, Halwen, have performed beautifully. That's why I'm going to reward you.

Oh fuck you, asshole. Fuck you with zero lube, no prep, and only a giant cactus for a dildo.

Cronus laughed, a low rumble like an oncoming storm, and Wynvail gasped involuntarily, fingers biting into my leg.

My heart shot into my throat, panic muddying my anger when the wall at the end of the corridor began to move, filling my entire being with vibrations.

That grating of stone on stone burrowed through my skull and into my brain, and I flinched so hard I hit my head on the wall behind me. Wynvail held onto me for dear life, his head ducked so I couldn't see his face, breathing quickening even further.

"Is that—" Kai breathed, jerking forward a step when the opening grew wider.

My breath caught when I saw a glade full of wildflowers through the open doorway, not another passage, not a monster or a new trial. An *exit*.

My hands shook; I grabbed Wynvail's shoulders and heaved him onto his feet.

"There's a way out," I gasped, my head still spiking with pain even as I supported him against me. "Come on, we're getting out."

My eyes caught Em's, hope bouncing between us like an echo.

Please. *Please.*

Without a conversation, we all rushed towards the open-ing, Kai ducking closer to help me support Wynvail's other side. With a single remark, Cronus had achieved the impossible, and united Kai and Wynvail. Kai's father had been a piece of shit; he knew the damage vicious words could do. We both saw it in Wynvail's reaction, saw the history of cruel, destructive remarks. Saw the abuse.

Fuck, now I was feeling sorry for him.

I tried to harden my heart, but I was too busy propelling us down the corridor, slamming my wings behind myself to push us faster, further. My knees were weak, my legs not much better, but adrenaline doused my whole body with the sight of freedom so close.

Em sprinted ahead of us, Harvey clutched to his chest, all our eyes pinned to that bright, verdant glade. Freedom. I could taste the fresh air, could feel it slide through bruised lungs like cool relief.

"Haley," Wynvail murmured, his voice thick and clumsy as he staggered, trying to keep up as we pretty much dragged him down the passage.

"Shut up," I huffed. "No talking, only running."

Leave the traitor behind, Cronus ordered, his voice so deep and omniscient that I stumbled.

My shoulder slammed into the wall, pulling Kai and Wynvail with me, and I swore, whispering apologies.

"Do it," Wynvail slurred, his eyes attempting to flutter open.

"Oh, shut up," Kai barked, helping me back up, the three of us running full-out for the door.

I gritted my teeth and endured the spike of a dozen headaches, not letting my gaze shift from that bright glade. I dreamed of flowers velvety under my fingertips, the cool shade of tall trees, the low hum of insects and life that was the total antithesis of the Labyrinth.

The maze was silent; dead. But we were close, we were there.

Three steps. I could taste it now, coating my tongue with promise and hope.

Two steps. Wynvail pitched suddenly into my side, his weight nearly knocking him from my hands, ripping a cry from my lips.

Blood streaked his cheeks, running from his eyes. *Oh gods.*

"Stop it!" I screamed at Cronus. "Stop it!"

He failed my tasks. He deserves to be punished.

"He's mine," I snarled, Kai and I wrenching him back up, forging on.

One step.

Emlyn and Harvey were out, surrounded by grass and flowers, *safe*. Relief choked off all my air. I tightened my grip on Wynvail, refusing to leave him behind.

Kai and I threw ourselves at the opening—

And ground to a halt when three figures stepped in front of us

Cronus's voice shook the Labyrinth with its rage. *Leave him!*

I exchanged a panicked glance with Kai, adamant and scared all at once. *I can't leave him. Please.*

"I know, my rose."

But the people in front of us throbbed with power, obviously mythical—something far beyond demons, angels, and humans. One had snakes for hair and an old, wrinkled face. One was tall with a black dog's head, her teeth bared in a sharp grin. The third had bat's wings and skin as dark as coal, her eyes blood-shot red and a hideous, hungry smile on her face.

Erinyes.

"The Furies," I breathed.

CHAPTER TWENTY-THREE

KAI

I tried to push Haley behind me, but she was having none of it. If it wouldn't have hurt my mate, I'd have thrown Wynvail at the Furies and run while they were distracted. He was a monster, pure, true evil. He'd terrorised us for a hundred years, and not once during those years did he mention Haley's name even though he knew who she was the whole time. Not only did he force us to fight each other, he stood back and did nothing as we lost our memories, our mate, and ourselves.

I was going to kill him; it was just a matter of when, and how I could make it look like an accident. My rose would never forgive me if she found out, but what she didn't know wouldn't hurt her.

The Furies would definitely hurt her, though. They scared the shit out of the most hardened demons, and that was when they were a story, a legend, not standing right in front of you. Snakes snapped at us in the place of hair, making my own snakes shudder in fear; a too-wide smile on the old woman made my feet itch with the urge to grab my mate and run; and the worst of all of them was a tall, slender woman with a dog's head, silver teeth, and a sharp tongue flicking out like she wanted to taste us on the air.

Like she was thinking about tearing into our bodies and devouring our organs. The visceral picture that painted in my head made me edge closer to Haley, gripping Wynvail so tight he moaned in pain. Good. I hope he died of fright; that would save me a job.[1]

"Leave me..." he murmured pathetically.

"Shut up, or I'll sew your mouth shut so you can't talk," Haley snarled, panic making her words flow rapidly. We didn't have time to sew the asshole's mouth, but that was what I admired about my mate; she was so violently ambitious.

My chest filled with buoyant love. Inappropriate when faced with the Erinyes, but I didn't give a shit. I loved my mate. I'd kill for her. I had before, and I would again. Right now, in fact.

I sucked in a slow breath and gathered a new den of snakes from my magic as the dog-headed Fury opened her mouth and garbled something about handing over the bastard. *You're welcome to him. You'd be doing me a favour if you ate him.*

But Haley gripped him tighter, her breathing racing, so I kept the words trapped behind my teeth. On my next exhale, I released ten yellow bellied sea snakes. Only I could see them, their bodies black as a void with vivid yellow undersides, jaws open and fangs dripping venom as they soared through the air.

I sent two at the woman with snakes for hair, two at the one with the petrifying smile, but sent the bulk of the den at the hound in the middle of their trio. I was used to a few snakes missing their target, but most always struck true. I wasn't prepared for all but two to miss and for the Fury's hands to snap out and grip the remaining snakes, squeezing their throats until they choked.

I stumbled back, clutching my chest as an awful gurgling came from me. Pain lashed through my chest, sudden and deep.

Wynvail ended up tipping onto the floor, grunting in pain. It was gratifying as fuck when Haley swung towards me and rushed past his crumpled form to grab my shoulders.

"Kai! What's wrong?" Her face drained of colour, my pain obviously reaching her through the bond.

"She has—my snakes."

The look Haley turned on the Furies was nothing short of murderous. My heart skipped a beat, a swarm of butterflies filling my belly. Who cared if my chest was a mess of pain, and I could barely breathe? My mate was ready to raise Hell to defend me. I was swooning.

When I could stand upright again, Haley took a slow, calculated step closer to the Furies. "Release his magic, and we'll talk about handing over Wynvail."

"Tisiphone!" Emlyn growled, making my jump half a mile. My heart slammed into my ribcage. "Release him."

"You know your legends, boy," the dog-headed Fury said, her voice velvety and deep. A shudder rippled down my body; I gritted my teeth against the pain cracking through my chest and stepped over Wynvail to stand beside Haley.

"So do I," Haley said in a deadly calm voice. My heart swelled when she drew one of the knives I gifted her, her fingers bone white around the pink hilts. "I know even Furies can be killed."

The blades didn't light up, but my breath quickened in anticipation. If she was powerful enough to break a titan's curse on a legendary creature, what could she do to a deadly being like a Fury?

My dick ached, swelling at the violence written on her

beautiful face. And when the snake-haired Fury replied, taunting that the only one who would die here was Wynvail, and Haley cocked her chin up, pure wrath in her eyes, I throbbed for her. A frantic fuck against the wall was nowhere near enough; I needed more from my mate.

Probably best to wait until we weren't being threatened, though.

I yanked on my snakes again, sucking in a sharp breath when the Fury released them and they slammed back into my core of power. *Fuck,* that hurt. Like she'd snapped an elastic band against my eyeball. I gritted my teeth, panting through it.

"Move," Haley growled, her mouth set in a flat line. "I won't tell you twice."

I bit back a groan, licking my lip for some trace of her taste.

Get it together, Malakai. Life or death situation!

"Hand over the traitor," said the third Fury, a crone with bat wings and a smile so hungry and twisted it made me a little sick. Every instinct warned me to turn and run the other direction when I looked into her many-fanged mouth. Worse when I met the hungry blood-red of her eyes. "I won't tell you twice."

"Get your own vocabulary," Haley spat.

"Get your own vocabulary," the Fury parroted.

Haley gave her the middle finger. "Kai, grab Wyn."

Wyn? Fucking *Wyn?* Really?

I was aware of my face narrowing into a sulky expression as I tramped over to the bastard and grabbed him a little too roughly, making sure to squeeze the places he was hurt. He cried out. Oh, dear. So sad.

Wyn.

"She's mine," I hissed in his ear. "Not yours. Never yours."

He just laughed. Piece of shit.

"We're leaving," Haley told the Furies. "Don't get in my fucking way. Unless you *want* to find out what happened to the dragon who tried to stand between me and my mates. It tragically lost its heads."

"You killed the drakon?" Tisiphone demanded, her canine jaws wide. "Impossible."

"Possible," Haley bit out with a mean smile. "Come on, Kai."

She held her dagger in front of her, stalking up to the Fury. I yelled a warning when the air shifted, my magic reacting with a spike, and three snakes shot out of me to grab my mate and pull her back.

The older, bat-winged Fury just *barely* missed Haley when she lurched forward, black claws reaching for my rose. They severed my snakes instead, and I stumbled, choking on a grunt,

The second time I didn't react fast enough. Clawed black fingers tangled in Haley's long hair and wrenched her out of my grasp.

"No," I snarled, rage filling my chest so suddenly that I couldn't breathe, bleeding through every pore until my power filled the air and I was no longer a man but a being of pure, venomous *rage.* I didn't waste time on threats. I released Wynvail and dove after my mate, my heart skipping when I saw movement outside the Labyrinth. Harvey and Em were fighting to get to Haley, too.

The Fury's face elongated, her jaws unhinging. Cold skittered over my skin, unease making me gasp, but I threw my hand out, unleashing a den of vipers on the Fury who dared to touch my mate.

"Megaera!" Emlyn boomed. "I'll make a bargain with you."

"You will *not,*" Haley snapped, slashing with her daggers, fighting like a hellcat to free herself.

But the Fury paused at his offer, her wings stilling. Her elongated mouth was hideous, petrifying. A shiver skated down my spine even as I threw myself after Haley—and right into the path of the snake-haired woman. Fuck.

I really should have paid more attention to Emlyn's books; I might have known their names, their weaknesses. Instead, I cast a horde of snakes out blindly, veering around her, my eyes fixed on my mate as the dog-headed Fury tried to drag her off.

"Stop," Wynvail said pathetically, leaning against the wall and looking pathetically anguished. "Stop fighting. Just leave me, I'll be fine."

I wanted to kick his head in. Haley had just had a breakdown over losing him. Harvey had drained his magic dry to keep the bastard alive. And he wanted us to *leave him here?*

I used my vipers to yank Haley three inches to the left when the Fury's snakes lashed at her. What would their bite do? Paralyse? Incapacitate? Kill?

It was suddenly hard to breathe, and all I could do was lunge towards Haley and push her to safety.

Haley staggered out of Fury's path, splaying against the Labyrinth wall, but I'd left myself open like an idiot. I stiffened when a hand closed around my throat and squeezed so hard I sputtered out a breath.

Haley froze.

Harvey snarled and—Harvey! He was conscious again.

My heart leapt even though there was a hand ruthlessly gripping my throat. I speared my stare past the Furies to find Emlyn helping Harvey to his feet. His eyes locked on mine, the feral edge of insanity in those eyes made me grin. A troublemaker's grin; Harvey matched it.

"Kai!" Haley screamed when I threw my elbow back into the Fury's stomach and grabbed her claws with both hands, fighting to drag them away from my throat. I cut up my fingertips, but I slammed my foot down on the bastard's foot and she screeched. *Yeah, no matter your species, getting stomped on your instep hurts like a bitch.* I followed it up with another blow to the stomach and sent three snakes at her eyes for good measure.

I was able to wrench the Fury's hand away and spin out of her path, a shallow slice on my neck but nowhere near painful enough to keep me down. Unfortunately, I placed myself far from Wynvail. Leaving him alone—with a vicious Fury too damn close.

"Fuck," I groaned, my conscience attacking me, forcing me to go back for him. I was too fucking nice sometimes. *All for Haley,* I reminded myself. I didn't want to see her upset again, didn't want to watch the light leave her eyes. She might have hated Wynvail but she was attached to him, too.

When I was so close I could grab him, the winged Fury stepped in front of me, giving me a smile that made me want to throw up. "He's not worth your effort. Traitor. Coward. Oath breaker."

Wynvail laughed, clawing his way to his feet, slumping into the wall for balance. Haley lunged closer, freezing beside me, both of us staring at Megaera. "Oath breaker? I followed—every damn order."

"But you left her mates alive," Megaera argued fiercely. "You swore a false oath. And all the other times you've lied? You need to pay for those, too."

"Everyone lies," Haley growled, darting forward so suddenly I couldn't stop her. She jammed her dagger all the way into Megaera's side, drawing—black blood. Oh, shit.

I grabbed my mate, pulling her back as she stared at the black blood coating her blade. Yeah, it was freaking me out, too. Were Furies *supposed* to bleed black, or had Cronus poisoned them? My power shuddered, rumbling through the ground until it trembled, too. None of the Furies seemed concerned that the maze was shaking.

"Stay back, Emlyn Johahn," Tisiphone's deep, throaty voice came behind us.

"Get fucked, Tisiphone," he growled back.

I smiled. I was having such a positive effect on him.

"Everyone lies," Megaera mused, clicking her long claws together. The sound sent a shudder down my spine. "But not everyone commits patricide."

Wynvail sucked in a sharp breath, leaning heavier on the wall. We were frustratingly close to the exit, only Tisiphone and the third Fury between us and freedom.

"Patricide?" Haley echoed, not removing her deadly glare from Megaera but her attention sliding to Wynvail. I sensed it, and judging by the way he stiffened, he did too. "You told us Cronus killed Locke."

"He liessss," Megaera hissed, her jaw detaching, hanging open. My stomach turned over. I grabbed Haley's arm, my heart sprinting.

We were so fucking close to the exit. Too close to turn back. And a Fury bled black blood in front of us.

"Get fucked," Wynvail snapped, fire reigniting in him. I hated that I understood him right now, because I *knew* that viciousness was a defence mechanism. "You wanna keep me? Fine. Let my mate go."

"Not on the table," Haley argued, pointing her dagger at him. "It's all or none."

"And *you* Harvail Locke," Megaera snarled, turning towards the glade. "You're no better. You killed your uncle."

Rage filled me until I couldn't breathe. "Because he was an abusive piece of shit!" I exploded, throwing myself at her and not caring when her claws slashed my stomach, the sharp edges of black wings cutting into my thighs. I wrapped her in snakes, sinking their fangs into her over and over, and drew my own blades to stab her with those, too.

The other Furies reacted with screams that made my

hearing cut out. I shook my head, digging the fangs of my magic deeper into the Fury. It wouldn't kill her, but I hoped it hurt her for what she dared to throw in Harvey's face.

"That's not his name," I snarled, my voice deeper, darker, than before. I held on tight despite the stinging cuts, despite the blood. "His name is Harvey van Khama, and he is *ours*. His uncle deserves the death he got, and so does that piece of shit Locke."

I twisted my knife in her belly and ripped it free, kicking her away from me.

"Why?" Haley demanded, grabbing me as I stalked over to her but staring at Wynvail. That was fucking rude; I was right here, bleeding, shaking.

"I found out what he did," Wynvail replied tightly, not looking at her. "To *them*."

Well, that was irritating. He discovered his father was a rapist monster and killed him for it? I admired that. And I didn't want to admire that piece of evil shit.

Movement behind me made me jump, and then the dog-headed Tisiphone spoke in a voice that made my breath short and gasping.

"He doesn't know what it's like to suffer that way," she said, her voice of shadows and velvet. "None of them do. They don't know what it's like to *truly* suffer, to fear every shift of floorboards above, and every creak of a door opening, to know that the rattle of a belt heralds blood and pain so sharp it draws tears and screams—"

"*Shut up!*" Haley screamed, her voice so loud I threw my hands over my ears and ended up shaving off a few strands of red hair with my knife. "Stop speaking!" Her voice was so deep, so resonant, my hands couldn't block it out. "Don't say another word to him!"

Harvey had gone completely still, his gaze distant and— and shadows wrapping around him like they always wrapped around Wane. But his brother was a being of darkness and quiet; Harvey was loud, boisterous laughter, dirty jokes, and defiant sunlight.

Haley stormed past the Furies, none of them reaching out to stop her as she gathered Harvey into a hug I knew was tight and bruising even from this distance.

They'd let us leave, but never Wynvail. I could just leave him...

Walk out of here, stalk into the forest, and wait for the doors to the Labyrinth to slam shut.

But ... he killed Cassander Locke. And he did it because that monster raped Harvey and Wane. My gaze slid from my rose hugging Harvey to Wynvail, inching his way away from Megaera and the snake-headed Fury, hugging the wall because he was so miserably weak he'd fall over otherwise.

I groaned. Fucking hell.

I fixed an eye on the Furies, keeping my knife in my hand in case they tried anything.

"Don't," I grunted when Wynvail shot me a surprised look. I just grabbed him, supporting his back and grinding my teeth when he threw an arm across my shoulder and leant into me. "This is for killing Locke. Once you're out, we're even and I'll go back to planning your death."

He snorted. "I'd expect nothing less."

The third Fury stepped into our path, her snakes reared back, hissing ferociously.

"Oh, fuck *off*, Alecto," Wynvail groaned, slumping into me.

"Do your moonbeam shit," I muttered to him.

"With what fucking energy? Cronus liquefied my insides."

Served him right for—helping us? Ugh, my conscience was getting out of hand.

Alecto, sadly, did not fuck off. Her snakes spat venom; I threw up a wall of my own serpents, protecting us from the spray. I did *not* want to know what that stuff would do if it touched my body.

"You attack us so readily, Halwen," Tisiphone taunted by the exit. Seemed my mate was done hugging Harvey and back to murder mode. I wanted to keep her in my line of sight, but I couldn't take my attention from Alecto. She'd bury her snakes' fangs in our throats the moment I looked away.

Wynvail inhaled through gritted teeth and slashed his brown hand up, a few flickers of light spitting at Alecto.

"That's just sad," I told him.

He snarled.

"Don't you want to know about Wane?" Tisiphone asked Haley in her rough, snarling voice.

I froze. We all froze.

I forgot to breathe for three seconds, and only sucked in air when my lungs howled in demand. Goosebumps rippled down my arms at the look on my mate's face, the back of my neck tingling.

"We all visited him," the Fury went on, not realising her life was numbered to minutes—or seconds. "He sang so sweetly for us. Isn't that right, sisters?"

Tisiphone turned her head, her dog face split by a wicked grin. Bad move to turn your back on an opponent as angry as my Haley.

Alecto laughed, her snakes rippling around her face. "His screams were more beautiful than any song."

The air exploded with enough power that I stumbled back a step, Wynvail falling into me with a curse. Haley's daggers erupted deep blood red as she drew the second, and scissored both around Tisiphone's throat before she could even finish laughing at her sister's vile remark.

Her canine head tumbled to the floor, landing with a thud on the stone. Black blood splashed up from the impact. I swore the whole Labyrinth froze.

Haley kicked Tisiphone's body until it collapsed to the floor and advanced on the other Furies without a single word. My heart skipped a beat.

"God-killers," Megaera whispered, her eyes wide and her claws clicking together at a rapid pace. She was nervous. She should be.

Alecto's snakes went still, her wrinkled face frozen in shock as she stared at her fallen sister. "God-killers," she agreed, darting a glance at Haley's blades as my mate stalked back into the Labyrinth, only murder on her mind.

Alecto turned and ran, racing past Wynvail and I, fear bleaching her face of its colour. Haley bared her teeth, animal fury twisting her beautiful features as she drew back her arm and hurled a long, wavy dagger at the Fury. It wasn't designed for throwing, but whatever magic lived inside it now aimed it true. It sank to the hilt in Alecto's back, toppling her to the ground in an instant. She didn't move, didn't let out a final gasp. Dead.

Megaera spun, staring at her dead sisters, knowing she was next.

"You don't need to do this," she hissed.

"Oh, but I want to," Haley breathed, blood dripping off the knife she passed into her right hand, the movement graceful and deadly. Butterflies danced in my belly.

I sent a long boa across the floor, coiling its long body behind Megaera. Trapping her. When she gave Haley a sneering laugh that failed to hide her fright and turned, planning to run, the boa rammed its solid body into her legs. She hit the ground with a satisfying cry, and my bloodlust throbbed higher.[2]

The Fury kicked up her wings, trying to fly away, but my snake coiled around her legs and kept her grounded. The expression on Haley's face could have frozen lava as she reared her blades back and sank both in the Fury's chest.

The light instantly left Megaera's eyes, and a shudder rushed down my spine. Ordinary demons shouldn't be able to kill a Fury. But my Haley wasn't ordinary; she was marked for greatness, and the great-granddaughter of a titaness.

She didn't just kill Megaera; she loosed herself upon the woman like a Fury herself, driving her knives into her body over and over before she moved to Alecto and finally Tisiphone.

Wynvail and I were silent, awestruck.

She was breathing hard by the time she drew back, the Furies mutilated messes on the ground.

"Shit, Sugarplum," Harvey rasped, breaking the silence with a smile. "Remind me never to get on your bad side."

She'd killed three Furies.

They called her daggers god-killers.

But could she kill a titan?

PART III
LOST

CHAPTER TWENTY-FOUR

HARVEY

*J*f Wynvail was leading us into another trap, Haley
would kill him. Or maybe Kai would get there first.
Emlyn wanted to beat him to a pulp, too, judging by the heavy
slash of his brows over his blue eyes and the shifty glare he
kept shooting at my brother.

My brother. That was fucking weird to think. I had two
brothers, not just Wane.

I should have hated him after everything he did to us, and
a part of me did. But I also knew everything Cassander Locke
was capable of. He and his vile brother inflicted so many
nightmares on Wane and I, and we'd been locked underground for the entire time he'd kept us, only forced to endure
them for a few hours each time. What was Wynvail's life like
above the basement, in the monsters' company twenty-four-
seven?

I couldn't hate him entirely. Not when I knew he'd been
through the same things I had, whether he'd been the perfect

brother paraded around the glittering halls or kept in the basement. Cassander Locke was evil, and there was no chance he'd spared Wynvail. There was a kinship between Wynvail and I, whether he realised it or not—the bond of those who'd suffered unspeakable horrors and lived.

Still, I didn't know if I'd step in to stop my family murdering him if he was leading us from one trap into another. The Labyrinth ... we'd escaped, but it followed us like a ghost. A ravenous ghost with teeth, snapping at our heels.

Locke's voice had been in my head since I got separated from my family in the maze. The Furies' taunts had made it louder, clearer than it had been in years. Even locked in the tunnels under Alphaven, his voice had been duller, quieter. Now, there was no erasing it. It had carved out a home in my head, and burrowed deep.

My gut cramped, tension throughout my whole body as we walked. We followed Wynvail with blind faith as he drew on his memory of visiting Cronus's house, but at least Haley's sense of Wane in the bond pointed in this direction too.

I tried not to envy her that bond; Haley telling me she could feel him, that he was alive, had to be enough. Fuck, I just wanted to see him. I wanted to hug him more than anything else, to grab him and never let go. But I mentally prepared myself for him to be covered in blood, for ... for parts to be cut off, maimed, forever altered.

We'd been tortured in one way under the Lockes' watch, but there were other tortures. Knives, scalpels, water, clamps, blowtorches, pliers—every possibility ran through my head, and my body locked tighter.

The Wane we found might not be one we recognised. But he was ours. He was my brother. And I wouldn't stop looking until we found him.

"Where the fuck are you leading us, Wynvail?" Haley demanded, her voice cutting the silence and making me jump.

A warm hand spread across my back, and some of the tightness left my body. I avoided Emlyn's worried stare, his silent *are you okay?*

No, I was not okay, and I wouldn't be until I found my twin.

No wonder I'd been agitated and on edge the entire last century; there was a part of me missing, a part of me always with Wane. I knew I was missing something, the lack gnawing at me until I couldn't help but snarl and lash out, but when Haley saved us I thought the missing part was my mate. It was Wane, all this time.

"Stop fussing," I muttered to Emlyn, and almost walked into Kai when he ground to a stop.

"This is the Damned Realm," he said, his voice both flat and breathy. "What are we doing here?"

I saw the gate that had given Kai pause and sucked in a breath, cold dripping down my spine.

Wynvail paused and glanced between all of us, missing the significance. "This is where Cronus brought me before. I told you that. The house where I heard people talk about his shadows is here."

"You never said it was the Damned Realm," Haley bit out, brushing her fingers over the pink handles of her daggers for comfort. "This is where we died."

Wynvail's shock was genuine, widening eyes so similar to mine and Wane's, parting his mouth; he didn't know.

"If this is some sick, twisted game—" Kai snarled, jerking forward a threatening step.

"It isn't," I cut in, my heart heavy and the rest of me no better. "Look at him, Kai; he's not lying."

Malakai hissed, his forked tongue lashing the air, but he restrained himself.

683

"I presumed you died in Hell," Wynvail told us, his mouth in a flat line that spoke of anger. "Now I'm wondering if the titan made his home here just to spite you."

"To unsettle us," Haley countered, turning to look at all of us. I didn't know what expression I wore, but she took one look at me and held her hand out. I sped forward to clasp it in mine, a part of my soul settling at the contact. The rest of me screamed in protest at going back into this realm, and howled to be back with my brother.

"It's working," Emlyn murmured, casting a look over all of us, assessing whether we could handle this. He blew out a hard breath, seeming reluctant.

"If we do this," Kai muttered, his arms crossed over his chest, blood still coating him from the Labyrinth, "we go in with shields up. Haley, power up your daggers, Harvey, go in beast form, Em, go as your eagle, and Dickhead, do your moonbeam shit."

"It's moon*light* not moonbeam," Wynvail muttered, bronze hands flexing at his sides.

"Sure it is," Kai agreed tightly, the end of his crimson tail slashing the air. "Show of hands, who thinks we should run home?"

No one put their hands up.

"And who thinks we kill every fucker in this place until we get Wane back?"

Five hands shot into the air.

Kai nodded, facing the iron gate that arched above us, separating the Damned Realm from Hell—as well as a giant swath of Lucifer's shadow magic. In scrolling text, the archway above us read ALL INSIDE ARE DAMNED.

We were already cursed, the clock ticking dangerously low on the time we had left. And we'd found *nothing* to break the curse on us. How long until we killed each other? Two weeks? One?

I swallowed, squeezing Haley's hand.

My stomach knotted when Wynvail led the way silently through the gate. I put one foot in front of the other, carrying me into the realm where my own father killed me. I would have thrown up if it wasn't for Haley's hand keeping me grounded. I focused on the warm, calloused texture of her skin, filling my entire awareness with her touch so the thoughts trying to dominate my mind failed to gain a foothold.

Don't think about Wane, or blood. Don't think about your father and uncle. Don't hear your own pleas for mercy and a reprieve. Don't hear their barked commands to shut the fuck up. Don't hear Wane's sobs—and worse, his silence.

There were moments when I was sure they'd finally killed him.

Haley squeezed my hand, and I was back in the Damned Realm, baring my teeth at the past and digging my heels into the present.

"We'll get him," she promised me, rubbing her thumb over my knuckles. "No matter how long it takes, Buttercup. I swear we'll find him.."

"I know," I murmured, and I did know. I just couldn't shake the crushing fear that it would take years to track him down. "I want to talk to Wynvail."

I tried to pull my hand from hers, but Haley's fingers tightened and she pulled me closer until my side aligned with hers as we walked.

"So, we'll talk to him," she said. I didn't miss the *we* in that statement.

Wynvail slowed, like he'd heard his name, and confirmed it when he threw me a questioning glance. Something moved behind his eyes, an emotion I couldn't place, something like uncertainty or wariness.

"How do you know Wane is here?" I asked him, trying to

sound neutral when inside I was a mess of feelings. I hated him, but he was family and a victim so I accepted him. I wanted to get to know him more, wanted to know how he'd ended up as the master of the pit, but I didn't want to hear about his traumatic childhood.

I wanted to know him and I was scared of it, both at once.

"I've been to this place before," Wynvail replied, casting a look around the realm as the sparse black grassland near the gates became small houses, most barely more than shacks. There was a river of suffering here, I knew. I'd smelled it when we were led in last time, from a different direction. "When I was first—"

"First what?" Haley pressed when he cut off, a muscle feathering in his jaw.

"He doesn't have to tell us," I cut in, my stomach tangling with sickness. I *knew* that pause, that struggle to force the words out. This was confirmation; he *had* been hurt, too. In the same way as us, or in different ways? "Go on," I prompted Wynvail with as much kindness as I could muster.

"I was brought here to Cronus's house, but nobody calls him by name—they're too afraid to say anything other than *him* and *the titan*. It's—I can't describe what it's like inside. You can't breathe properly, and you're scared to even blink wrong or Cronus will have you slaughtered for fun. I saw him ... eat a woman. He grew to ten times his regular size and just—ate her."

"Shit," Haley breathed, gripping my hand tighter.

My stomach turned over. What if he'd eaten Wane, and we were too late?

The small, broken down houses grew closer together. These were two storeys tall, but still ramshackle and bleak, made of grimy wood with open holes for windows and gaps in the roofs. Like whoever made this realm wanted to torture them with the appearance of shelter, but leave them cold and miserable.

No wonder Cronus had chosen this place; it fit him perfectly.

"And I heard people talking about some of Cronus's prisoners—his pets," Wynvail went on, anger threaded through his sleek voice, roughening it around the edges. "One prisoner was his favourite, the most powerful—his shadow."

His pets.

Those two words echoed through my head, loud enough to block out whatever Haley said, to silence the cry of Emlyn's eagle as he shifted and soared above us, scouting our surroundings.

Wane was no one's pet. He was his own damn person, and the thought of anything else made me sick.

My hearing returned in time to hear Wynvail say, "There's no guarantee he's still here. That was a long time ago."

His eyes were on me, heavy silver, rife with an emotion he was trying to hide. I was too scared to dare to decipher it.

But I ran through everything he'd said, his entire horrific story, and paused on one point.

"You said Cronus's house," I breathed, my pulse fast in my throat. I squeezed Haley's hand to brace her. "I think it's the house that was meant to be our home."

Haley sucked in a breath. "You're right. That's exactly what Cronus would do, that heartless bastard."

I wished I could draw some of my old fire, and crack a joke or tease her until she smiled, but I wasn't sure that part of me had survived a hundred years in the dark.

"He's right," Kai said abruptly, letting me know he'd been listening in on our conversation. "I recognise those mountains."

I swallowed bile. I didn't want to return to the realm

where we were killed let alone the *house* where it happened. But if Wane was here...

"We're close," I murmured, squeezing my mate's hand so tight.

Emlyn cried out overhead, a piercing screech as he circled. Probably realising what we just had.

"Harvey," Kai said, throwing me a commanding look and prompting me to shift. As if it was that easy; as if I had any control over it.

"I don't know how," I admitted, my voice quiet so only he and Haley heard.

"It's when your emotions are out of control, right?" she murmured, stroking my knuckles. I nodded. "So ... stop controlling them."

I froze when she stopped walking, leaning up to kiss the spot between my brows.

Stop controlling my emotions. Release the dam on the trauma I'd been holding back since the first day in the Labyrinth. Let it all out—the terror, the hatred, the shame, the bone-deep exhaustion. My next inhale shuddered.

"I'll be here with you," Haley promised, squeezing my fingers. "Hell, if you want me close, I can ride you into battle."

I groaned. "You're not riding me."

She waggled her eyebrows until I laughed. "Not until we get home, anyway."

I hooked her closer with desperate hands and kissed her hard, a small sound catching the back of my throat when she deepened the kiss, her tongue and teeth taking control of me until my panic settled.

Haley had brought me back to myself in the Labyrinth. She could settle my beast. Everything would be fine.

"I love you so fucking much," I rasped against her lips, my breathing fast and short.

"I love you too, my Buttercup," she replied fervently, the name making my heart skip.

"If he's not in the house—" I began

She shook her head hard, flinging dirty pink hair through the air. "Don't think about it. We'll get him."

I swallowed my nerves and nodded, stepping back.

"Might want to back up, my rose," Kai advised, his red eyes shifting between me and Haley—and glaring at Wynvail like he wanted to pull his brain out of his nose with a hook.

The shift happened easily—too easily when I released the lock on my memories.

In my head, I was back there, my skin crawling, pain throbbing through my pelvis, blood in my mouth. I was sobbing silently, conscious that any sound would bring a fist down on me. I was back there, and it was like I'd never left. I would always be in the basement, would never be safe. I was such a naive fool to think I could be safe, or worse—happy.

Fur erupted over my vast body, my roar deep and echoing, carrying far, and claws unsheathed themselves when I flexed my paws, landing on all fours.

"Still with me?" Haley asked, drawing my attention. I could understand her now, but it wouldn't be long before the beast's mind took over, sweeping all my intelligence under primitive needs.

I swallowed, the taste of copper and iron coating my senses. Blood—so much blood. Close by. Too close.

I took off running, not meaning to leave my family behind but unable to stay when terror blacked out all other emotions. Blood and fear—they were so familiar. I knew those scents, knew the taste on my tongue.

In my head I heard sobs and screams, heard him whisper *I can't take it anymore, Harvey, I can't take it.* I heard myself self-ishly beg him not to leave me.

The house rose quickly in front of me as I ran full-pelt, the wide building hidden by a bend in the mountains until suddenly it was there, and gravel crunched under my paws. I'd slammed the front door into shreds begotten I processed being inside.

Don't leave me, Wane. Please, I'm begging you, stay with me.

I sucked in a long breath, faltering in the foyer for a moment. Memories tried to form—tears and hugs and gunpowder, screams, and blood, always blood—but the beast's mind was taking over, and all I could focus on was the smells coming from deeper in the house. Brimstone, piss, and iron —torture.

Where is my brother?

I scanned the hallways as I raced out of the foyer, but the house was empty. No hoards of followers or minions, no monsters, gods, or titans. Why is it abandoned?

A trap, my primitive brain warned, and I feared it was right.

But Wane could be here, my brother could be so close, so I followed my nose, leaving the trampled door behind and skidding down long corridors until I barrelled into another door. This one didn't shatter; it took three slams before it swung off its hinges.

At the sight of a staircase that led down, I froze.

Shut your fucking mouth, or I'll kill your brother. Just shut up and take it. Or do you want me to get your father?

I shook the voice free, a vicious snarl curling my lips back from my teeth. I couldn't escape the memories. I didn't want to go down there, didn't want to enter another basement. The last one...

The tunnels were bad, but at least they didn't remind me of what *they* did to me. My own father and his black-hearted brother. Twenty years I lived down there, with only Wane for strength.

Wane, who was at the bottom of these stairs, where the

scent of blood and excrement was thickest. He had to be here. Even the beast knew that.

I trembled, but I swallowed in the whine that formed, and forged on down the stairs before my courage could escape.

My whole body quivered, air barely filling my lungs before it was forced out, my fur standing on end. I flinched when the wall brushed my side, spinning with a bestial snarl—but it wasn't a threat. Wasn't a threat.

My mate was coming. She wouldn't let anyone hurt me again.

Buttercup? It's Haley. I'm here, you're safe now.

She'd always kept me safe. So I plunged deeper into the basement and—realised it wasn't a basement at all. Not the way I knew it: a single room with two beds, a bucket, and misery sunk into the walls. Below the house was an endless dark corridor, so black even my beast's vision struggled to pick out the shapes of doors and bars on either side of the corridor. Some were rooms. Some were cells.

Had Wane been locked in a cell like I had, all this time?

I took a tentative step, and when I wasn't attacked by shields, I took another. The scent of blood was stronger here, cloying in my lungs until I tasted it with every breath. I prayed Wane wasn't here in this place that stank of death.

The corridor went on for miles, stretching ahead for an eternity. I lost track of time and the only thing keeping me going was knowing the house was too far behind to offer an escape.

I didn't hear a single sound, didn't smell anything but torture and death—until I did.

My steps slowed, my heart slamming against my ribs so hard my fur rippled. I made a low, questioning sound, my beast struggling to form his name. I shook harder, and if this form had been able to sob I would have broken down.

Movement scuffed the ground at the end of the corridor.

Someone was alive down here. I picked up my steps, hoping it was someone else, praying it was Wane—

I froze when another scent wound through the blood and piss and worse things down here. A scent I knew. Sharp, nighttime air and rich woods, but faint, buried under so much filth and pain.

My knees buckled, but Haley's voice had me straightening, urging me to be strong, to not give up now. Wane needed me. Oh gods, he needed me.

This door collapsed when I threw my shoulder into it, and then he was there, folded up in the corner exactly like I remembered but—blood crusted his hair to his face, and his horns were snapped off and his wings—

Where were his wings?

Worse—where were his *shadows?* Only a few flickered to his defence when I stumbled into the room with a whimper.

His head lifted, his expression dead but those eyes, *my* eyes … rage burned within them, limitless and dark. And from one look, I knew he didn't recognise me.

Had he forgotten me, like I forgot Halwen for a hundred years?

CHAPTER TWENTY-FIVE

HALWEN

J'd never flown so fast in my life. What if Harvey reached the house first, and Cronus caught him? What if Cronus *killed* him?

Kai ran as fast as his legs would carry him below, pushed along by a swarm of snakes that made the air tremble around me. Magic shuddered over my feathers as I pumped my wings harder, flying until I could barely breathe.

Emlyn's strident cry made my heart jolt. I might have had wings, but I wasn't avian enough to decipher his cawing. My heart thrummed faster. I couldn't tell if it was a noise of distress, so I angled my wings to carry me closer to him. The vicious wind cut tears from my eyes; I had to blink rapidly to see what he was showing me: the house from above. Our one-day home.

My chest pulled tight, but I exchanged a glance with my eagle mate and swooped towards the ground. If Wane was inside, we couldn't afford to hesitate.

Em had my back; I wasn't alone. It made me brave enough to touch down on the ground and stumble towards the house on wobbly legs.

Holy fuck, something had blasted the front door apart, leaving only shards of wood.

"Harvey," Emlyn said, landing beside me and shifting fluidly back to his demon form. I would have chided him for leaving himself vulnerable, but I didn't know how a giant bird would fly through a house, even one as big as this.

"Harvey," I agreed, and swallowed my dread, forcing myself to cross the threshold even if I was so scared I wanted to throw up.

"Wait!" Kai yelled behind us, his voice distant but loud enough to reach us. I turned, my stomach roiling, and found him racing down the long path towards us. "Wait for me, my rose," he panted, skidding to a stop beside us, grabbing me and Em for stability. "Fuck. I hate running. Is he in there?"

I didn't know if he meant Harvey or Wane, so I just turned back to the house and walked into the foyer, drawing my knives with a soft ring of metal. I was distantly aware of Wynvail's panic as he raced to catch up with us. Was he scared the titan would be here? He wasn't the only one.

Cronus's awareness had covered the Labyrinth like a shroud, but he was a titan, and there was no limit to his power. I bet he could be in two places at once, terrorising a hundred different mazes at once. Who's to say we were his only victims?

Wood crunched under my boots as I crossed the foyer, the empty silence making hairs rise on the back of my neck. Where was Cronus? Where were his followers? The people Wynvail spoke about filling this house were certainly gone and … Wane wasn't here, was he?

A small sound escaped before I could trap it, and Kai pressed closer, his hand on my back. My shoulders dropped, wings dragging across the floor, and I swallowed the lump in my throat so I could tell them Wane wasn't here—

I staggered, clutching my chest when fear cut through it sharper than anything I'd felt in—in a hundred years. Clearer even than Wynvail's emotions.

My knees weakened but I took off running through the dusty house, not questioning where my feet fell, just chasing that knife of fear carving into my chest. He was close. He was *here.* He had to be; his panic filled up my whole chest, swallowing my own emotions until my heart beat even faster, my breaths whistling through my teeth as whines.

Kai and Em hurried after me as I ran unsteadily deeper into the house, my head spinning and hope sharp enough to cut me apart.

Please...

I didn't baulk when the bond led me to an open door, a dark staircase looming beyond it. If the door was open, Harvey had come this way; it was the right direction. Gods, Wane was really here...

I snapped my wings tight to my back and took the steps two at a time, leaping off the last four and running again the second the vibrations of impact left my legs.

"Wane?" I yelled so loudly my voice cracked, sprinting as fast as I could.

This place stank of blood and piss and suffering, abuse and mistreatment thick in the air. I could barely breathe; I choked back a sob and ran faster.

The corridor went on for miles, so dark it was an eternal night. Only our footsteps echoed back to us, the oppressive silence eating into my hope. But fear rose in my chest, thorny and so strong I gasped. He was here, really here. And I was going to eviscerate whoever had made him afraid.

We ran for long, endless minutes, until exertion whipped my lungs and gripped my side.

"Harvey,"Kai panted, keeping pace with me.

I scanned the dark tunnel, a gasp punched from my lungs when I spotted Harvey slumped on the ground at the end of the dark corridor, his black fur barely discernible from the gloom of the corridor. White light cut the darkness behind us, making me jump as the tunnel's ugliness was thrown into stark relief, but I didn't stop. It was just Wynvail; he was family, he was safe.

I ran faster, out of breath and so shaky it was a wonder I didn't collapse to the floor.

Harvey turned his giant head at the sound of my voice, and a pitiful whine flared his nostrils, slowing my pace. No. Was Wane—he couldn't be dead—I could feel him—

But what if I was deluding myself? What if I'd finally gone insane?

My bottom lip wobbled. On heavy legs, I approached Harvey. I ignored the cells and ominous doors around me, not wanting to know what lay behind them, focusing only on the cutting pain in my chest that dragged me to the end of the hall where Harvey lay, hurting. That was what his whine was— misery and sadness and hurt.

The stench thickened, repulsive and so pungent it made the tears in my eyes fall. I faltered two steps away from the room Harvey guarded, my eyes trailing over the door he'd knocked. Emlyn rushed forward to support me when my legs buckled, settling his strong arm across my back. I wasn't brave enough to take those last steps, so Em took them for me.

I struggled to lift my head, too scared to look into the room myself. My throat closed off, blocking out the worst of the smell, but I couldn't breathe.

Pain and fear whipped through my soul, and I clenched my jaw against a wave of emotion, screaming at myself to lift my head, to look inside the dark room.

It took all my courage to lift my head those four inches, to swallow down all the fear slicing through my chest and brave a glance into the room.

My knees weakened.

With Wynvail's brutal light illuminating the space, there was no hiding that it was a cesspit, the grey walls splattered with blood and so many stains in so many places that the floor was five shades darker than the corridor. I was going to be sick.

In the corner, pressed into the juncture of two walls, my mate sat with his knees pressed to his chest and his eyes fixed warily on Harvey. No wings wrapped around his too-thin body to shield him. Only a few swaths of shadow concealed his middle, nothing like the writhing mass he used to possess. My bottom lip wobbled, a cry building in my chest.

I couldn't forget the memory of a blade hacking through his shadows, severing them from him. They were part of him, every bit as essential as his heartbeat. And his wings ... where were his beautiful wings? Where were his horns?

I stumbled forward a step, tears scalding my eyes and my lips quivering uncontrollably. Now I'd been brave enough to look into the room, I didn't dare look away. If I did, would he vanish? Would Cronus steal him from me again?

His body was covered in cuts, so many slices that new scars covered old scars, others bleeding and fresh. What did Cronus *do* to him?

I made a small sound, pain clawing up my chest as I staggered forward another step, and his eyes drifted to mine—silver and molten and haunted. Exactly as I remembered them. But a fire lit in those eyes when he saw me, and he sucked in a sudden breath. My chest cracked under the force of his emotions. Only Emlyn's grip held me upright.

"Wane," I rasped, pressing my hand to my breastbone as shock, weakness, relief and—safety knocked against the inside. Safe? Even in this vile, filthy room, he felt *safe* with a single look at me? My bottom lip wobbled, out of control as tears overflowed my burning eyes. I blinked fast until my mate came back into focus, terrified to lose him.

With Emlyn's help, I took a slow, careful step into the room hovering on the threshold so I didn't box Wane in. I tried not to look at the single bucket in the room, tried not to notice it was full. Bile burned the back of my throat. This was where he'd lived for a hundred years. This was what had been done to him.

I sniffled, my face hot as I cried.

I jumped with a gasp when Wane rushed to his feet in a sudden explosion of movement, too fast for his malnourished, bleeding body; he swayed into the dirty wall, bracing himself there as he stared at me, something fragile and brittle in his expression. Like he was waiting for the trap to spring shut.

"I'm here," I whispered, not brave enough to speak louder. "We're all here. You're going to be okay now."

I gave Emlyn a soft look and stiffened my spine, taking a step on my own. Wane didn't look away, dread and hope and relief mangling his soul. I lifted my arms to reach for him on instinct before I remembered myself, and remembered the horrors he'd been through. My heart twisting, I dropped them to my sides—and jumped hard when Wane threw himself across the room.

His movements were unsteady but purposeful, his eyes bright and ferocious. My stomach knotted.

I braced for claws and knives. I didn't care if he cut me; he was safe, he was here, and we were taking him home. Wherever the fuck home even was these days.

"You're okay now," I whispered as Wane rushed at me.

"Hales," Emlyn warned. I ignored him.

Wane met my eyes, silver irises sparkling with emotion, tears gathering to match my own. I sucked in a breath, prepared for the sharp prick of pain and—he threw his arms around me.

A broken sound choked me. Wane hugged me so tightly I forgot how to breathe, his body quivering against mine, his jagged breathing loud in my ears. He was *hugging* me, clinging to me with a desperation I'd never felt before, and tears flooded my eyes, washing away the Labyrinth's grime.

Slowly, so afraid to startle him, I lifted my arms, first settling one and then the other around his back. He felt so frail in my arms, so breakable, and I couldn't bear it.

He caved in, falling against me. A violent sob burst from him, followed by more and more until he hiccupped gasping cries, his face buried against my neck.

Harvey whined behind us, his heart breaking, and I reached for him even though I knew the bond was frayed and I'd never be able to—touch him. My soul brushed his in a long stroke of reassurance. I—he was—we were—

My breathing fractured. We were whole.

I felt them all then—Kai's all-consuming worry, Em's blazing protectiveness, Harvey's pain and longing, and Wynvail's bone-deep panic. And threaded through them all was Wane's cocktail of relief and fear.

"I've got you," I whispered, my voice too raspy to speak any louder. I didn't dare grip Wane any tighter with the wounds oozing all over his body, but I curved my hand around the back of his head and tilted my face until I could kiss his temple. "I've got you now. No one will hurt you again; if they even try, the only thing left of them will be a smear of blood."

"I never forgot," he croaked, his voice broken and weak, barely audible. "I never forgot your name."

"Shit, Wane," Kai breathed, something vast and unnameable touching my soul as he took a faltering step forward. "You did this to *yourself?*"

Wane lifted his dark head off my shoulder, his eyes filling with more tears at the sight of Kai and Emlyn.

"I couldn't forget," he said, thick with emotion. "He wanted to take her name from me. He—he took—everything else. I'm so sorry, I tried to fight him."

Everything else. Not my name, but Kai's? Em's? Harvey's?

Oh, god, had he forgotten—

"So that's my name," he breathed, so quiet and husky. "Wane. I—I remember it now."

He smiled. He was tortured and bleeding, mutilated all over his body, his wings and horns cut off—and he *smiled.* "Thank you."

"Malakai," Kai blurted before Wane had to ask. "But since you're a good looking bastard, you can call me Kai."

Wane laughed, soft and whispery, and I cried harder, a sob brushing my throat.

"I'm okay," Wane promised, stroking my back like I was the one who'd been locked up and tortured for a century. "I'm okay now."

I needed to let go of him so we could get out of this place, but I couldn't make my arms release him. I couldn't stop touching him ever. But—

"Shit," I breathed, my stomach in knots. "Sorry, that's way too long to be touching you."

Wane swallowed, and I tracked the movement, my eyes glued to the white scars on his throat. They were jagged in places, looping in others, and they almost looked like—words. When I tried to move back, forcing my arms to relax around him, Wane's bronze hand shut out and grabbed my arm.

"Don't," he gasped, panic slicing through my chest hard enough to make my breath hitch. "Don't."

The writing was bigger on his arm, deep enough for me to make out a H, an A, an L—

Oh, gods. I covered my mouth with one hand, dragging him back into a shaking hug with my other.

He wanted to take her name from me.

He'd cut my name into his skin over and over. There wasn't a single part of him that wasn't marked by me. So he could never forget my name.

I trembled violently, teeth chattering as I held him, my eyes oozing trails of lava down my cheeks. "I love you, zivai. I love you so, so much."

"There's—there's a word I call you," he rasped, anger flashing through his soul, as bright as a forming star, not a single wall hiding his emotions from me. Like someone had brutally and meticulously stripped him of every shield. "A name."

"Itzaia," I breathed, stroking his matted hair and trying futilely to stop my tears. "You call me itzaia."

"Itzaia," he echoed, shuddering against me. "My soul."

"And you're my heart."

"We should go," Emlyn murmured in his softest voice, making Wane jump. "Emlyn," he said when Wane blinked at him, tears on his long lashes. "I'm Emlyn, and—fuck." Seeing my gentle giant collapse had my heart crushing into a tiny ball. "I really missed you, Wane."

Wane gripped me tighter. "I missed you. All of you. I never forgot *you,* only your names. He could never take you from me."

Harvey whined again, and I nearly bucked under the weight of his pain. I sent him enough love to drown it out, at least for a moment.

"Harvey is—" I began, stroking Wane's back, my voice choked as I looked between the brothers. "He's a little furrier right now. Still a total badass, though. And I know he missed you like hell. He *loves* you like hell."

Harvey whined louder, getting carefully to his feet—so he

didn't spook Wane, I realised. What happened before we got here?

Wane inhaled a sharp breath and exhaled it as a sob, stumbling out of my arms and into the tunnel. I let him go, wrapping my arms around myself, my chest threatening to collapse under the pain pressing on it. Kai and Em rushed in, shoring me up as I fell apart. Could they feel me now? Did they know how broken I was, deep down in my soul? Seeing what Wane had been through, where he'd lived, what he'd done to himself—I couldn't stand it.

And I knew this was only the tip of the iceberg. Cronus had a hundred years to perfect his torture on Wane.

Harvey's whines landed like knives in my heart as Wane dropped to his knees and fell against his twin, hugging him so tight he ripped out strands of black fur. Something settled in Harvey, in both of them, as they hugged. The world could fall apart, but at least the twins were back together.

"He stole you," Wane sobbed into Harvey's fur. "He stole all of you from me."

Harvey rumbled a reassuring sound, rubbing his head against Wane's shoulder in a comforting stroke. I pulled myself back together while they shuddered and cried. I needed to be strong for my mates; their pain in my chest told me that. I stepped back into the tunnel, ignoring my shaky legs.

"You okay, honey?" Wynvail asked, his eyes on me as he hovered a few steps away, letting us have this moment as a family unit.

"Fine," I rasped, scrubbing my face dry even if my tears wouldn't slow.

Wynvail opened his mouth again, but whatever words he tried to speak never formed.

Wane jerked away from Harvey at the unfamiliar voice, and he shot to his feet with a deep, animal hiss. Emlyn darted forward when he wobbled, supporting him with the tiniest touches. The habit was hard to break when we'd spent so long being careful not to touch Wane.

"You," Wane snarled at Wynvail, and I startled hard, my heart slamming against my ribs as I glanced between them.

If Wynvail had been involved in Wane's suffering, we were *done.* Any shot he had of us not killing him was gone, and I'd murder the bastard myself.

But Wane's scarred upper lip peeled back and he spat, "Why are you here? You're an abomination."

Wynvail flinched.

I recoiled too, his soul cracking with so much shame and hatred that it cut through mine, the only thing I could feel in the mess of my chest.

"What did he do?" Kai demanded in a low hiss, instantly backing Wane up. The air rippled with his magic, snakes writhing.

Wane shook his dark head, pure hatred on his face. "It's not what he's done; it's what he *is.* He shouldn't exist. He's Cronus's creation."

What?

My heart beat faster; I stared at Wynvail and waited for him to sneer and snarl, for his true self to show its face. But he just stood there and accepted it.

"He's my mate," I said tentatively, glancing from his statue-still expression to Wane's bared teeth.

Wane shook his head, his hair so matted it barely shifted. "Barely. He was never meant to exist, itzaia. He was part of the bargain Locke and Cronus made. For me."

"For you?" Kai pressed, a snarl still in his voice. He edged closer to me—or to Wynvail. I didn't trust him not to rip out Wynvail's throat.

Wane's throat bobbed. "Cronus bought me from Locke. He

wants my magic, is obsessed with it. But they—Halwen needed a mate. I don't know why. A secret purpose."

I eyed Wynvail in surprise. He'd been created to be my mate? He wasn't naturally bound to my soul. This had been *done* to us?

I swallowed, tears still close, burning my eyes. "I don't understand."

"He was made," Wane explained, giving me a confused look at whatever he heard in my voice, "from my shadow and Harvey's sunlight. Cronus took parts of each and forged them into a new mate for you, in exchange for keeping me and for —for using my shadows."

"Why did he want the shadows?" Emlyn asked, edging between us and Wynvail. To protect us from the threat?

Wynvail shook his head. He didn't know. *Or* Cronus had commanded him not to say.

"He's building something with them," Wane rasped, his gaze distant and haunted. I felt sick all over again. "But I fought him, I never stopped fighting. He only took them from me this week because—"

He cut off. Silence rang, painfully loud.

"Because I made you weak," I finished.

"I don't care," Wane hissed, silver eyes flashing as he took a step closer. "I don't care. You saved me. You're here. He can take all my shadows; I don't care."

I was definitely going to argue that last point but Emlyn spoke before I could.

"So he's not her mate?" he rumbled, sharp blue eyes pinned to Wynvail and his mouth in a thin line behind his beard.

"I *am*," Wynvail argued, a gleam of obsession returning to his eyes, giving them life. "My soul is bound to hers; she's mine."

"*She's not*," Wane snarled, his teeth bared. His voice was

raspy and quiet but there was no hiding that he wanted Wynvail dead. "You shouldn't exist."

I swallowed. I didn't know what to do with my emotions. I wanted to scream and cry and comfort them both at the same time. But that was impossible.

"Wane," I breathed, my voice shaking. "I can't—deal with this right now. Can we shout at Wynvail later? Please."

His gaze softened. He nodded, and my shoulders sagged, but dread tightened them again when he shot Wynvail a glare hot enough to melt glass.

"He's—still our brother," Harvey muttered, a furrow between his brows and—

"Harvey!" I blurted, throwing myself at my mate now he was back in demon form, hugging him fiercely tight. I needed the closeness, needed someone to hold me together, and he must have sensed that because he clutched me tight, a kiss feathering my cheek.

"Wynvail saved us in the Labyrinth," he told Wane. "He might have been made by Cronus, but that doesn't make him evil."

No, Wynvail was evil because of the things he'd done. But I was grateful Harvey was fighting the bastard's corner.

Wane's gaze shifted between us, and he sighed, frail shoulders slumping. "I guess it's not your fault you were made. But you're still Cronus's creature, and I know you answer to him."

"We all know that," Kai drawled. "And don't worry, Wane, I've got my eye on this asshole."

Wane smiled again. It seemed Kai had a talent for drawing out his smiles now. I cherished every one that softened his eyes and curved his cracked lips. My chest collapsed under the weight of pain. I thought I'd never see that smile again.

Harvey held me tighter, pressing a long kiss in the middle of my forehead.

"Let's get out of here," Emlyn rumbled, scanning each of us

to ensure we weren't hurt. "We need to find somewhere safe to stay."

"You can go back to the safehouse in Edinburgh," Wynvail cut in, his back straight and eyes straight forward. Like he was facing down a firing squad. "Cronus doesn't know where it is; he locked onto my magical signature to open the portal. It's shielded; you'll be safe there."

"You," I echoed, my heart whooshing in my ears. "You're not coming with us?"

His mouth curved into a mirthless smile, his eyes dull and empty. "I'm a monster and abomination, honey. I know when I'm not welcome."

"We'll talk about that later," Emlyn cut in, his expression hard. "You're family, and you're coming with us either way."

Wynvail just shot him a wry smile, and for some reason it made a pit open in my stomach. "Then lead the way, Emlyn."

Wynvail was acting unbothered, but I didn't miss the deep breath he took before he stepped away from the cells, like he dreaded what came next. My eyes stabbed all over. I didn't want to cry again.

"We'll figure it out," I told him, trying to catch his eye. But he walked ahead with Em, and his only reaction to my voice was his shoulders hunching.

"You can't trust him," Wane whispered, sticking close to my side as we hurried down the tunnel, Kai and Harvey at our backs.

"I know," I replied, but that didn't kill the part of me that wanted him to be good, wanted him to be worthy of trust. But did I only want him because our souls were linked? Because Cronus had fucked with my soul and made space for another mate? A sick consolation prize while he planned to devour Wane. I knew that was his next move; steal his shadows, use them in his grand plan, and then snuff out any hint that Wane had existed. By eating him like he'd eaten his godly sons.

I dared to clasp Wane's hand, squeezing tighter than I should have, and my eyes burned at the comfort that erupted through his soul.

"We'll be okay," I promised him.

I lied.

CHAPTER TWENTY-SIX

*T*he light burned my eyes when we reached the house, drawing tears because apparently I hadn't cried enough. Despite the salt on my cheeks, I had Wane beside me, and my bonds were healed. My family was whole again.

It felt too good to be true. I gripped Wane's hand tighter as we retraced our steps to the lobby and found the door Harvey had shattered in his beast form.

Two steps away from freedom, my curse marks flashed crimson, and I spun with a gasp, expecting a monster to be racing at our back.

But the lobby was empty. So was the garden and the path to the gates.

I pulled my wings tight to my sides, unease shuddering down my spine. Wane swallowed, feeding from my fear, but no dark magic roared to life when we approached the shattered door.

"Honey," Wynvail said when we crossed the threshold, the sun watery and dark. Like everything else here, even the sunrise was grey. He paused as I descended the short steps, waiting on the gravel path. "Can I talk to you?"

Wane stiffened but it was Kai who spoke.

"So you can fill her head with lies?" he snarled, rushing past me to put himself between us. "I don't think so, dickhead."

"Kai," I chided, my chest hurting.

"Remember everything he's done. Remember what he is," Kai said harshly, not pulling his punches.

I was too fragile for this right now.

Wynvail gave up on getting close to me, and spoke around Kai, spearing me with a desperate look. "I never had a choice in any of it. It was all a role I played."

"That you took immense enjoyment in," Kai hissed, tongue flicking out in warning.

Wynvail stopped two steps down the driveway, his breathing coming faster. His eyes never wavered from me even when pain chased through them. "I'd change it all if I could—hunting you, getting to the house too late to save you, treating you like shit."

"Making us fight each other," Emlyn put in, his voice deep and disapproving.

Wynvail's bronze throat bobbed. "I had to make it convincing. I couldn't let Cronus realise I only took you three so he couldn't keep you. I tried—Wane, I tried so hard to get you, too, but he wouldn't give you up."

I froze, and even Wane hesitated beside me, confusion spilling from his soul to mine.

"I don't understand," he murmured.

"Cronus only let me take Harvey, Malakai, and Emlyn because I promised to make them suffer. He watched *everything*. I had to make it look real."

"It *was* real," Harvey argued, crossing his arms protectively over his chest, naked as the day he was born. "For us."

Wynvail clenched his jaw and nodded. "I'm sorry. I did the

only thing I could. The arena, the cells—it was *nothing* compared to what he'd do to you."

Questions swarmed in Wane's eyes but he kept them quiet. "He's right," he said instead, though he seemed loath to admit it. "You were better off far away from here."

Wynvail caught my gaze, warmth in the molten silver. No wonder he had Wane's and Harvey's eyes if he was made from them. "And I'm sorry I had to do this. I tried to warn you, but nothing came out. This—" He threw a hand at the house, at the realm around us. "This was my whole purpose. The only reason Cronus created me. This is why he needed me." His eyes drifted to Wane, remembering his warning below. "I'm sorry."

"What did you do?" Kai snarled, launching himself at Wynvail and delivering a punch hard enough to break his nose.

Wynvail landed on the gravel with a wet grunt, and stayed there. A laboured breath lifted his chest, and the bottom dropped out of my stomach as I felt weakness creep through him.

"Kai," I gasped, breaking away from Wane to shove past my mates and collapse beside Wynvail in the gravel. "What the hell did you do to him?"

"Not him," Wynvail rasped, coughing up blood. "Inevitable."

"What are you talking about?" I demanded, grabbing his shoulders. I wanted to shake him, to tell him to start making sense because none of this *made sense*. I wanted to scream and rage and hug him. Why did he feel so weak?

"I tried to warn you," he repeated, fighting back another cough and holding my stare. "But you need your mate. You need Wane."

I didn't understand. I didn't know what was happening.

Something inside my chest began to ice over, going numb. The part of me connected to him.

"Wynvail," I breathed, a warning, a plea. I dug my fingers into his shoulders.

"Taking him out of the house broke the seal on Tartarus. On the titan's prison. That's the whole point of letting you find Wane. I—I was supposed to lead you here."

"You brought us here so we'd break open Tartarus?" Kai exploded, launching forward.

Harvey caught him, stopping him doing more damage.

"Something's wrong with you," he said, staring at his brother. Spawn? I didn't know the terminology.

Blood gushed from Wynvail's broken nose, but it dots from his lips when he coughed again, too. A small, panicked sound escaped me.

Wynvail smiled, an ironic thing that made my eyes burn, tears falling. His hand settled on my thigh, squeezing. "Cronus made me for this—to bring you here, honey, so you'd free your mate and your power would unlock the seal."

"But I didn't do anything—"

The red flash of light as we crossed the threshold. The burst of power I'd felt and couldn't explain. It was so slight I'd barely even felt it, only noticed the glow. That couldn't be enough to free a titan...

"He's been planning this a long time," Wynvail said, pausing when a vicious coughing fit shook him. He coughed up more blood. My bottom lip wobbled, the top of my nose burning as I cried harder.

No...

I held him tighter, like it would hold him together.

"All he needed was someone from his bloodline with powerful magic. He tried it three times before, but it failed. This time, with you... I can feel it. The seal is broken. The house is collapsing, whatever magic held it together all these years coming apart."

I turned to stare at the house, detached and shaky. Would we watch another of our homes be destroyed?

"Fuck the house," I rasped, fighting my nails into his shoulders. "It doesn't matter."

"Wynvail," Harvey murmured, gravel crunching as he took tentative steps towards us. "You—you said this was your purpose. To lead us here and break the seal."

"You've figured it out," Wynvail said with a little smile. "Smart man."

"It's killing you."

I jerked back, staring at Harvey. I felt it, our bond icy and numb, *fading,* but I didn't want to hear it out loud. I *never* wanted to hear it.

"No, it isn't," I choked out. I shook my head hard, staring at Wynvail, at his bloody face. "You're wrong, Harvey."

"You knew it would," Harvey went on, his eyes heavy on Wynvail. Sad. "Didn't you?"

Wynvail nodded. I squeezed my eyes shut, my chest caving in. No. This wasn't real. It wasn't.

"But you did it anyway."

"The order is hooked into every part of me," Wynvail replied softly, his arm snaking around my back to pull me against him, heat bleeding into me, his body so solid and reassuring against me. Safe—it had taken me until this stupid, too-late moment to realise that he was a safe haven, and he'd always protect me.

I sucked down lungfuls of his scent. When would I smell this heady mix of cloves, sugar, and blood again? Would I ever? Tears forced their way past my closed eyelids; I choked on a whine, pleading with every god that had ever existed. *Don't take him. Not my mate,* please. *Please.*

"But self-preservation is as strong as any order," Wynvail

went on, and my soul splintered with pain when he said, "I think I could have fought it."

"Then fight it!" I cried, shoving him. I kept my eyes shut; if I didn't see it, it couldn't happen.

"It's too late for that, honey," he murmured, pulling me back into his arms and drawing another animal cry from me. "The second we crossed the threshold with Wane, it was over for me."

"Then *why?*" Wane demanded, his voice hoarse, low.

"Because she needs you."

"I need you too, you heartless bastard," I choked out, my eyes opening when he brushed a long kiss to my cheek. I scanned his drawn, bloodstained face, suddenly desperate for every last sight of him, and cursing myself for wasting even a second. "I *need* you. We can stop this. I have magic, and Harvey can heal—"

"He tried, just now, honey," Wynvail murmured, stroking my face with gentle thumbs. His face was thinner than it had been minutes ago, his skin sallow and sick. "It's over." But he smiled. "I might have given him what he wanted, but now that he's free? You can kill him. You have your mates all back. You can do it; I know you can."

Wynvail leaned forward and kissed me, so gentle and slow, a direct contrast to our kiss in Alphaven when I stole his knife. A wail tore my chest apart, strangled and low, when he pulled back. "Make him pay, honey."

"Not without you," I argued, holding him tighter, my breathing escalating. "Don't you dare leave. Don't you fucking *dare.*"

He made a quiet sound in reply, little more than a sigh, and dropped his head on my shoulder. Cold—he was so cold.

"After all this shit you put us through, you have to stay and make amends. You *have* to."

Wynvail slumped into me, a bout of weakness making my

soul entirely numb. I couldn't feel him at all. Oh, gods, I couldn't feel him.

"Wynvail?" I cried when his next breath rattled. No. Please no.

"I'm so obsessed with you," he murmured, his head falling off my shoulder, too heavy, too limp.

"I'm obsessed with you, too," I choked out, grabbing whatever magic I had and tearing it up and out of me. "Hold on. I can save you."

My curse marks flashed red in response to my turmoil, and blood power thrashed inside me, too, rising instantly to my call. I threw both into Wynvail, pumped them into his bloodstream, and surged into his heart. The beats were so slow, so faint, but I poured magic into him until I grew dizzy, waiting for his next heartbeat to circulate the magic around his body, waiting...

Waiting...

My hands shook. A shrill, broken sound built in my throat. My entire soul was numb. I screwed my eyes shut and clutched him close.

"Shit," Kai swore softly.

"The house is collapsing," Emlyn whispered, gravel shifting. I jumped at the sound, clutching Wynvail tighter. I refused to accept what Kai's soft breath meant, what my own magic told me as it flowed back into my body. Every drop of magic was laced with pain. He was—he couldn't be—

"Haley," Wane rasped, brushing my shoulder.

I flinched, my eyes flying wide—

My gaze flinched away from the sight of Wynvail's slack, empty face, flying up to the red-stained sky.

"No," I whimpered, rocking him in my arms. "Wyn—"

"We need to go," Kai murmured.

"No!"

"We'll bring him with us," he said gently. "It's okay, my rose."

Nothing was okay. Wynvail was—he—

I howled, my chest cracking in two.

"I'll carry him," Emlyn said softly when my voice cracked. "I'll keep him safe, Hales."

My bottom lip wobbled. I didn't want to let go of him. My fingers dug into Wynvail's arms, but I jumped with a cry when he slid from my grasp. No, he—

His body just ... collapsed, turning to ash in my fingers. A moment later the ash turned to nothing. There was nothing left. I stared at my empty hands, a scream burning my throat.

"What is made can be unmade," Kai breathed, horror stricken.

"What?" Harvey demanded in a snarl.

"That's ... that's part of what it says on Haley's back. The prophecy."

I didn't care. I didn't care about any of this.

The house collapsed behind us with an almighty crash, but I didn't care about that, either. A roar came from its depths, shaking the ground like one of Kai's temper tantrums, and the sky split with a sudden storm, but none of it mattered.

"Oh, gods," Wane breathed. "I heard ... I didn't think it was real..."

"What is it?" Emlyn demanded, pulling me to my feet and binding me in a tight hug when I howled and fought him. My body was numb, my soul icy, but I screamed and kicked and bucked my body like I was made of volatile flame. Em grunted and held on.

"Typhon," Wane murmured. "The father of all monsters. He—Cronus trapped him under the house, I heard his whispers but I thought—I thought I was going mad."

"We need to get out of here," Kai bit out. "Right now."

My mate was dead. Unmade.

Like he never even existed.

"Let him eat us; who cares?" I muttered, empty inside.

I DID WARN YOU THIS SERIES WOULD BREAK YOUR HEART ... BUT when have I ever 100% killed off a harem member with no hope of resurrection?

(whispers) never...

Trust me with this series, babes, things are in motion.

If you want to know what was going through Wynvail's head when he sacrificed himself for Wane, you can read an alternative POV here!

Continue Haley's series with Cursed Dawn which is a doozy (my favourite American word, which I've unapologetically stolen, thank you very much.)

And hey, we've got Wane back. Happy ending, right...?

See you in the next book,

Leigh x

DAMNED NIGHT

A KISSED BY BRIMSTONE STORY

This is for everyone who loves a villain with a strong jawline and a tragic backstory. Sure, there are red flags, but if you squint they could look pink.

DAMNED NIGHT, A WYNVAIL POV

I gritted my teeth so hard a muscle flickered in my jaw, forcing myself to step over the threshold into the Damned House. Cronus's command was built into my very being anyway; it wasn't like I could fight back. I'd been ordered to lead Halwen here, so I had. I'd tried to refuse his orders in the Labyrinth, and his hippocampus had nearly eaten me.

I was alive only because Harvey had saved me. I wasn't sure how to feel about that; I hadn't expected to be beholden to anyone, let alone my 'brother.' I didn't even know what to call him. I was created from a twisted cocktail of shadow and sunlight, like the old gods were made from a spray of blood or a dismembered bollock. I didn't even know what to call myself, if I was even real. Halwen called me a monster; she was probably right.

But ... I was a monster Harvey had saved, and a monster Halwen had mourned, at least until I healed the wound. That knowledge burned in my chest as I crossed the house's threshold and followed the motley crew of archdemons through its disused halls. My skin crawled as I remembered

the last time I was here, when Cronus created me and immediately made me scream in pain so I learned he was my
master. [He burned his orders into my skin like a brand down
my thighs. I would always be marked.]

Not that my life would last much longer if Halwen and her
mates succeeded here. I knew Wane would be in the tunnels.
Cronus had practically gift wrapped him, with a sad little bow
on his head. He *wanted* Haley to take Wane out of this place.

No, I couldn't call her Haley, only Halwen. Haley was
familiar, fond, and I couldn't afford fondness when I was a
monster with a single purpose: to follow a titan's command
and break the prison holding him captive.

If I'd had control of my own life, I'd have exiled myself to a
nice island in the middle of nowhere, hidden away where no
one would find me. Except my violent mate, of course. She
could find me whenever she liked. Sometimes when I was
deluding myself, I thought I saw the gleam of interest and
obsession in her eyes, my own emotions reflected back to me.
She was *mine*. All fucking mine.

Did she realise I was hers?

Kai kept me in his line of sight as we followed Halwen's
frantic path through the house. The place was abandoned,
covered in a layer of dust, but footsteps tracked through it—
Harvey's paw prints and another, smaller and obviously
bipedal. One of Cronus's pets, probably. When he got bored of
tormenting one, he found another and made them his servant,
parading the new pet around for him to torment.

[I knew; I'd been his newest pet at one point, and then led
another to the slaughter. He hadn't lasted long, not like Wane.]

I'd never seen Wane once in the times I'd been around
Cronus, like the titan purposely hid him from me, but
rumours of him trailed from person to person. A shadow
demon locked in the bowels beneath this house, so powerful
that he'd been broken but still lived, who had survived horrors

that would kill even a god. It was probably exaggerated. The thought of it being truth made me queasy.

I fucking *hated* having a conscience. Cronus should have built me without a heart; then I could have sacrificed my mate and her men without giving a shit. I could have saved myself. Instead, I gnashed my teeth, conflicted.

It should have been a no-brainer. Leave Wane here, maybe even kill the others, take Halwen and run. My fingers itched. I could do it and fuck the consequences, but—

"Wane!" she cried, racing down a tall staircase into true darkness, plunging forward even as her voice broke.

Fuck, I was going to hear that crack in her voice for the rest of my short, miserable life. I didn't even think about not following her, even if she *was* unknowingly leading me to my death.[1]

I couldn't see a damn thing down here. Blackness pressed in on either side, making my chest painfully tight. I'd purposely blocked out the memories of my torture at Cronus's hands, but here in the dark it was too easy to remember how his power felt carving through my skin and scorching my bones. His fury had branded me as his, and he reminded me of that every time I was forced to kneel before him.

The marks on my thighs burned, the memory making their sting sharper, deeper. I sucked in a rough breath and tore a blaze of magic from my core, filling my hand with moonlight so I could see the tunnel around me. Doors and cells alternated on each side, all of them empty. Abandoned, like I'd suspected. He'd made an easy path for Halwen to get to Wane.

I exhaled slowly, letting out the tight breath in my lungs. He wasn't here. He wouldn't risk jeopardising Halwen breaking the seal, not now he was so close to getting what he's wanted for hundreds of years.

He's not here.

Halwen's breath grew faster, choppier, the deeper we travelled through the tunnels. I didn't know what room Wane was inside, but she'd find him through the bond. Besides, Harvey had to be down here somewhere so—*what was that?*

I jerked towards the sound, my light spreading further, reaching across heavy doors and thick bars and—Harvey, folded up on the floor in his beast form.

I let out the breath I'd been holding. Fuck, this place was messing with me. Kai cast a suspicious look at me. I gave him a little smile I knew would make him furious; he flicked his forked tongue at me, fangs bared.

Yeah, I'd like to kill you too, asshole.

My attention snapped to Halwen when she let out a small, high sound, staring past a door that had been ripped off its hinges. Harvey could have done that to me—ripped me apart. Instead he'd saved me. It burned fiercer, taunting me.

This place stank of blood and shit and death. Was there anything left of Wane? The sobs shaking my mate's body made me unsure. Maybe Cronus had found another way to free himself, and left the ruins of Wane here for her to find.

The thought made me more than queasy. I nearly threw up this time.

I'd brought them here for nothing, and I would die for it.

"Wane," she breathed, the sound of her voice making something in my chest crumple.

Gods fucking dammit. I shouldn't give a shit about her; she was nothing. Nobody. Just a dead girl who'd been brought back to life.

But she was my mate, and those instincts wouldn't be shut off. She was mine. Mine to claim, to keep, to consume—and mine to protect, to shield, to care for. And *fuck* did I want to take care of her when she tiptoed into Wane's disgusting room, looking so small, so breakable.

I nearly ripped Wane's grimy hands off her when he threw himself into her arms, but I locked my body and remained still, holding back while the others rushed forward. A perfect little family.

Made things like me didn't have families. Why would a monster need a family?

My brands burned as I watched them hug and murmur to each other, the scars reminding me who my master was, who I would always belong to. It was my entire purpose to guide Halwen here, and let her walk out of this house with Wane. And the second she crossed the threshold, I'd have outlived my purpose.

Gods fucking dammit, could she stop crying and making those choked, little sounds? They made me want to grab her from Wane and hold her so no one else could hurt her. I was trying to selfishly save myself here. Let them leave Wane to rot. I wanted to live.

It tasted bitter—the desire to live. Probably because I couldn't listen to Halwen cry and stand by my selfish decision. And that made me *furious*. How dare she stab me and make me obsessed with her? How fucking *dare* she?

And worse. I wasn't just obsessed; I was infatuated.

Cronus had done this by throwing me into the Labyrinth with her, making me give a shit whether she lived or died. I could have happily stayed in the safe house while she almost died, and been blissfully ignorant. But no, I had to be in the maze with her, feeling her fear, growing more and more furious until I was willing to shatter the whole fucking Labyrinth just to get to her.

When she was almost crushed in that passage, something had snapped. A violent before and after. Before was a sickly blend of obsession and indifference. After, there was only rage and possessiveness. And something worse I couldn't name. The same thing that was viciously satis-

fied when she smiled and livid when she was upset.
Like now.

She cried in Wane's arms, her shoulders shaking, clothes
still stained from almost drowning in the Labyrinth, her front
still covered in blood. My blood.

Something to remember me by, the sick part of me remarked.

Halwen's spike of misery drew me out of my morbid
thoughts, and I scanned her face when she turned my way.
Suffering was etched into her tanned skin, a shade paler than
before. I hated the distance in her eyes, hated the feeling that
clawed its way into my soul—she felt lost. Broken and alone.

Wane and Harvey hugged, regardless of Harvey's beast
being able to tear Wane's head off his too-thin neck. And
Halwen stood watching them, completely adrift.

I sent a gentle brush to her soul and caught her eye. The
pitiful look on her face made me want to cry and rage and
hug her. For fuck's sake. I didn't hug people; I scared them,
scarred them.

But nothing in any world could stop me asking, "You okay,
honey?"

"Fine," she rasped, rubbing tears from her face. She was far
from fine, but I didn't call her on her bullshit. I was one
moment from dragging her into a hug when Wane reared
back and glared at me like I'd kicked him in the face.

My heart skipped. Why did he look at me like he hated me
when we'd never met?

"You," he hissed, revulsion filling his silver eyes. The eyes
I'd inherited. "Why are you here? You're an abomination."

I flinched. Shit. *Fuck.* I shouldn't have flinched, shouldn't
have given him a single damned hint of how much I hated
that word. The word Cronus and his followers sneered and
whispered to me. No matter how well I served him, no matter
how big the army of alphas I'd collected for him, I was still a
monster and abomination.

"What did he do?" Kai demanded, itching for a reason to fight me. Let him; we both knew I'd win. Power trembled around him, but if he thought that would be enough to take me down, he was deluding himself.

Wane didn't take his eyes off me. "It's not what he did; it's what he *is*. He shouldn't exist. He's Cronus's creation."

I sucked on a tooth, the words pounding through me, replacing my blood stream with that poison. *Cronus's creation.* And wasn't that the truth? No matter what I'd done, what I'd built, what crimes I'd committed on my own damn merit, at the end of the day that was all I'd ever be. The *thing* he forced into creation. I never asked to be made.

"He's my mate," Halwen breathed, snapping my attention to her. Shit, she looked hurt—and suspicious. What did she think I'd done now? No doubt she expected the worst from me, and had been waiting for this axe to fall all day.

I hated that seeing her close to death had changed me. Hated that I felt anything at all. *Feeling* would get me killed. Literally.

Wane spoke again, probably getting a kick out of telling Halwen my origins, stealing her from me. Reducing me to nothing but a monster in her eyes. And just when she'd started to see some value in me, just when she mourned my almost-death.

It wouldn't happen again. She'd laugh and say *good riddance.*

"He's not, not really. He was never meant to exist. He was part of the bargain Locke and Cronus made. For me."

"For you?" Kai asked.

Wane's throat bobbed. He avoided looking at me now. "Cronus bought me from Locke. But they—Halwen needed a mate. I don't know why. A secret purpose."

So Wane didn't know why this had been done to both of us —why he'd been locked here, left for her to find when everyone else had moved on. And he didn't know why *I'd* been made.

He'd learn. Soon.

My heart hammered faster, a trill of nerves flipping my stomach when I found Halwen's grey eyes on me, stormy and confused, almost blue-green in the light.

"I don't understand."

Her small voice made me want to kill someone.

"He was made," Wane went on, "from my shadow and Harvey's sunlight. Cronus took those parts and forged them into a new mate for you, in exchange for keeping me, for—for using my shadows."

And there it was, the horrible truth of my being laid out for everyone to inspect and sneer at. I wasn't a real person; I was made from threads of their power, bound together into this. This *thing.*

"So he's not her mate?" Emlyn asked, blinking. When he looked at me, I gave him a maddening smirk.

"I am," I argued, possessiveness beating at my ribs. "My soul is bound to hers; she's mine."

"She's not," Wane snarled, hatred turning him from a victim to a monster in himself. "You shouldn't exist."

Tough shit, bastard, I do exist. But don't worry, it won't be for long.

Because like a stupid lamb skipping to its own slaughter, I'd made my decision.

And he was right, bastard that he was. I was made, and I shouldn't exist. I was never meant to be Halwen's mate. She was mine, and I would be hers as long as a single speck of life existed in the universe, but she didn't need me. She needed Wane.

I hated that my heart beat for her. Hated that it roared her name. Hated that I would get myself killed just to see her happy.

"Wane," she breathed, so very close to breaking down into tears again. Rage flared that he'd pushed her to this point, just to get one over on me. "I can't—deal with this right now. Can we shout at Wynvail later? Please."

I stiffened. Of course she'd take his side. She'd called me a monster from day one; she likely rejoiced inside, knowing she didn't have to keep me as her mate.

Little do you know, honey, how soon I'll be gone...

"He's—still our brother," Harvey said, making me jump so violently the light in my hand flickered.

He ... was still claiming me? As family? *Still our brother.* I didn't know how to feel about that. I couldn't think about it *at all* if I was going to go through with this, and let Halwen and Wane walk out of this place. But the knowledge that he still saw me as one of them burned even fiercer than the brands on my thighs, and part of me wanted to scream at the injustice of it all.

I'd gone from a century of hatred, bitterness, and emptiness to having a promise of family. And it would all be ripped away from me.

Halwen threw herself at Harvey with a cry, and I averted my eyes.[2]

"He saved us in the Labyrinth," he told Wane, holding our mate. "He might have been made by Cronus, but that doesn't make him evil."

Shit. My heart pierced with an ache that made it so much harder to breathe. I didn't show how badly I'd needed to hear those words. I didn't dare.

And hey, at least I could march myself to my slaughter knowing someone didn't completely despise me. Silver lining.

Wane's gaze drifted from Harvey to me, distrust swirling like shadows in his eyes, but he sighed. "I guess it's not your fault you were made. But you're still Cronus's creature, and I know you answer to him."

"We all know that," Kai drawled, upper lips curled back from his teeth. "And don't worry, Wane, I've got my eye fixed on this asshole."

Likewise, you snaky piece of shit.

"Let's get out of here," Emlyn said in his deep voice. "Find somewhere safe to stay."

Oh, gods. It was happening now? They were leaving *now?* My stomach pitched; I inhaled a slow breath through my nose, keeping my turmoil on the inside. These fuckers didn't deserve to see my weakness. Even Halwen hadn't earned that yet.

I swallowed my panic, straightened to my full height, and forced my voice even when I said, "You can go back to the safehouse in Edinburgh. Cronus doesn't know where it is; he locked onto my magical signature to open the portal. It's shielded; you'll be safe there."

It was the least I could do, and the only thing I could offer beyond my death—giving her somewhere safe to stay. Giving her somewhere she belonged, that was hers and only hers.

Fuck, I—I loved her.

This was so inconvenient. Why did I have to realise this now?

But it had been there since she first stabbed me. It was there in every violent gift, every snarl and glare etching her on my heart. It was worse now I'd almost lost her, the emotion running deep.

I wasn't just hers. I was impossibly, obsessively in love with her.

"You," she murmured, watching me. "You're not coming with us."

Shit, I hadn't meant to say that.

But I just smiled and said, "I'm a monster and abomination, honey. I know when I'm not welcome."

"We'll talk about it later," Emlyn cut in, giving me a glare that brooked no arguments. "You're coming with us."

I wanted to, and it was strange to realise that. I felt ... bad for deceiving him. "Then lead the way, Emlyn."

My chest crushed out the last remaining sips of air in my lungs when we began the long walk back to the house. *It's not too late to change your mind.*

But Halwen still had tears on her cheeks, and she was holding Wane's hand so tightly her knuckles were white. I couldn't take that from her. I'd give her the whole goddamn world if she asked for it.

You shouldn't exist.

Fuck Wane for being right. Fuck him for having to speak it out loud, for the way his voice replayed in my mind over and fucking over.

I took a deep breath, steeling myself before I took the first step away from Wane's shit-stinking room.

Onward into death, then.

"We'll figure it out," Halwen said, reaching for me through the bond, her soul seeking mine like a sun-starved flower. I couldn't meet her eyes, not anymore. If I let myself pause for even a second, I wouldn't do what needed to be done. So I hunched my shoulders and walked on.

"You can't trust him," Wane whispered behind me, trying to turn her against me.

"I know," she replied, proving there was no point putting in all that effort. She already knew what sort of man I was. Not a man at all. A heartless thing of cruelty and violence.

I trudged on through the endless tunnel, ghosts of memories snapping at my heels but my entire awareness wrapped around the woman at my back. The source of my obsession. The woman I loved, when I shouldn't have been capable of love at all.

I knew what leaving this house with Wane would do. I

knew every breath I took was numbered. I knew my unmaking would hurt like a bitch.

But I walked on, and kept walking until we crossed the threshold that signed my death warrant.

You shouldn't exist.

Then I'd stop existing. Problem solved.

I HOPE YOU LOVED THIS INSIGHT INTO WYN'S HEAD. SORRY FOR all the angst and suffering. The next Kissed by Brimstone book is out now, and the series is complete!

CONTINUE HALEY'S STORY

CURSED DAWN
KISSED BY BRIMSTONE BOOK FOUR

We have ten days to break the curse, or my mates and I kill each other.

Time is running out, and every day we come closer to the end. We finally have Wane back, but with the clock ticking down and grief eating me whole, it's hardly a victory.

Cronus has won, and he knows it. I can't kill him when my world just collapsed. If the Labyrinth broke me, the Damned Realm crushed what was left into dust. Exactly like Cronus crushed my mate when he unmade him. Who cares what the prophecy inked on my back says? Or what great and terrible future I'm supposed to have?

The only thing I want is to keep my mates and I alive. But with monsters freed from Tartarus, vicious gods in our way, and a titan hellbent on devouring me whole, I'll need more than magic to break our curse.

I'll need a miracle.

Read it in Kindle Unlimited and print!

THANK YOU FOR READING!

Haley's series is complete and available in ebook, KU, and print... with maybe a hardcover coming soon! To stay updated with what I'm working on next, come join me in my Paranormal Den on Facebook, or sign up to my fortnightly newsletter! (Links on the next pages, so keep reading, loves.)

If this is your first Leigh Kelsey book, I have lots more books for you to sink your teeth into, and three completed series. I've got vampires, wolves, shifters, angels, and demons - and of course plenty of growly alpha males with tragic backstories.

Reviews make the world go 'round - or at least they do in my world. If you loved this book and you can spare a minute, please leave a review on Amazon or wherever else you like to review. Even the smallest, one-line review has an impact, and helps me reach new readers like you awesome people.

Thank you to everyone who's already reviewed. Your words mean I can keep writing the books you love!

LEIGH KELSEY

WHERE THE MEN ARE *PSYCHO* BUT THE WOMEN ARE *WICKED*

JOIN MY READER GROUP!

To get news about upcoming releases before anywhere else, and early access to my books, come join my Leigh Kelsey's Paranormal Den group over on Facebook!

FREE VAMPIRE ROMANCE STORY!

Hybrid's Curse is a stand-alone paranormal romance.

As a vampire-witch hybrid who can never be killed, Emilio is used to pain and suffering. But when Aislin, an innocent faerie healer, is kidnapped because of him, Emilio will do anything to stop her suffering too. Especially because she's been dreaming of him for seven years, and claims to be his mate.

If you love romantic stories with a healthy dose of suspense, and pairings of dark, gloomy men and sunny, optimistic women, you'll enjoy this happily-ever-after story.

JOIN MY MAILING LIST FOR YOUR FREE STORY

READ QUEEN LILI'S COMPLETE SERIES!

Betrayed by heaven, protected by hell. The devil and his hellhounds will do anything to keep their angel safe.

READ FREE IN KINDLE UNLIMITED

SIGNED LEIGH KELSEY BOOKS!

You can find all my available print copies in my online book store, plus books from my cowrites and pen-names, **and all signed orders come with swag and a dedication from yours truly.**

VISIT THE STORE: https://payhip.com/snarkystabbybooks

ABOUT LEIGH KELSEY

Leigh Kelsey writes about psychos with questionable morals and addictions to shiny, stabby objects, but she's perfectly harmless, she swears. She can be found in Yorkshire, England listening to K-Pop, watching serial killer documentaries, and writing as much spicy paranormal romance as she possibly can in a day.

LEIGH KELSEY

WHERE THE MEN ARE *PSYCHO* BUT THE WOMEN ARE *WICKED*

f

FIND THESE OTHER PSYCHOS BY LEIGH KELSEY!

Feared by Monsters: A stand-alone twisted paranormal romance

Sick and Twisted series

(Twisted Death Gods RH)

All Hallows Night

All Hallows Game

All Hallows Trick (coming soon)

Killers and Kings series

(Complete Twisted Paranormal Demon RH)

Crazed Candy

Sweet Violence

Sugar Rush

Kissed By Brimstone series

(Twisted Paranormal Demon RH)

Hellborn Angel

Midnight Descent

Eternal Night

Cursed Dawn

Shadow Fall: Part 1

Shadow Fall: Part 2

Rebels and Psychos Duet

(Complete Twisted Paranormal RH)

Complete Series Box Set

Killer Crescent

Blood Wolf

Broken Alphas series
(Complete Rejected Mates Dark Paranormal RH)
Complete series Box Set

The Omega's Wolves

The Omega's Mates

FOOTNOTES

CHAPTER 1

1. Ugh, that sounded pitiful even to me.
2. Maybe, and I was just spitballing here, but maybe all the red flags and signs not to take this job were actually trying to tell me something? I was a dumbass for not heeding them.
3. It was disgusting, like drinking fermented paint water
4. It hadn't worked, as you could probably tell.
5. I had visions of my nose being ripped off and almost whimpered. I didn't want to be known as No-Nose Halwen for the rest of my life!

CHAPTER 2

1. It would've been nice to hide in shadows sometimes, like when I was having a traumatic flashback or someone was trying to teach me maths; I envied him that.
2. I couldn't help myself. I wanted to know what he'd do when he snapped. I was hoping he'd do *me*. I'd always had a thing for maniacs.
3. Ughhh, this was a soul mate thing, wasn't it?
4. Not sexually. Definitely *not* sexually.
5. Weird. Very fucking *weird*.
6. Please—*please*—tell me why my chest threatened to collapse at the thought of that.

CHAPTER 3

1. It's multi-purpose. Man attacking you? Knife to the dick. Aggressively hitting on you and won't take no for an answer? Knife to the dick. Stuck his cock in another woman? *Knife to the dick!*
2. And let's be real, if I was going to settle down with a big, strong protector, I couldn't do much better than the woman currently strangling me.
3. Good name for a gang, that. Blanket of Menacing Death. Their minions could be called the Blankies.
4. Ooh. Did he have a pet parrot?

CHAPTER 4

1. Uh-oh. Someone call the Sensible Police because the horny parade going off in my body right now was worrying. I needed someone to remind me of all the reasons why I didn't get involved with anyone. Stat.
2. Despite it being, y'know, a room. Irony was a bitch.

CHAPTER 5

1. That got us this month's rent, thank you very much.
2. But if they watched me being a psycho and thought to themselves *that's the kind of crazy I want,* who was I to question their strange tastes in women?
3. Butterflies. Legitimate butterflies. I fought a swoon.
4. And why wasn't I stabbing Malakai? *Come on, Haley, get it together!*

CHAPTER 6

1. Even the inches I felt throbbing under me. Especially them.

CHAPTER 7

1. She had a point. Books were boring when everyone just stood around chatting. Much better to insert a fight to the death.
2. Like brain matter—heart matter was a thing, right?

CHAPTER 10

1. And by play, I meant murder.

CHAPTER 11

1. Mostly I sensed Wane's; he'd vanished into shadows to protect himself, only his bound hands visible. I wished he'd taken me with him.

CHAPTER 12

1. On the negative side, it was furnished with an *army of the dead* décor theme, complete with cutlasses, axes, and skulls spiked on the wall above the bed in the large, attic room. I was suspicious about the dark staining on the deck outside, too; either it was a cherry red wood staining or blood, and I was betting the latter.
2. If *I'm fine* meant, *I'm a huge mess of emotions and hatred and fear, and I don't know if I'll ever feel safe again.*

CHAPTER 16

1. My face could personally attest to its structural integrity. The builders did a 10/10 job with construction.

CHAPTER 17

1. I just came back from the dead; sue me.
2. Because I had more space to attack Renna in the middle of the road...

CHAPTER 18

1. Do you think I could get away with a rebirth party, like people had birthday parties? I could use an excuse to gorge on cake and drown myself in ale.
2. She was *a queen;* I wasn't about to tell her she had my name wrong. She seemed sweet, but rulers were all the same. One moment it was pleasant chats over tea and cakes, the next it was beheading for treason.

CHAPTER 19

1. Heated, recycled air had to be a demon's invention; it was as bad as brimstone's stench.

CHAPTER 20

1. I didn't even get them halfway. My girl was all grown up now.
2. If I hadn't lost my mates, I'd say it was almost worth dying to get coffee this good because *holy shit.*

3. I had to hand it to the metal box—it certainly knew how to brew a cup of coffee.

CHAPTER 21

1. He was onto something. I'd be trying that as soon as I found my mates.

CHAPTER 22

1. Haha, just kidding.
2. Cock and Claws—whatever. Mine was a better name. Maybe when I found my mates and we were safe again, we could buy a pub.
3. It would be a *tad* alarming if two teenagers had gone out hunting criminals.
4. And by track I mean kill, but you're clever so you knew that.
5. Let's just say my backside would be so red and stinging, I wouldn't be able to sit for *days*.
6. Honestly, this was doing wonders for my confidence. Two days ago I'd been a corpse, but now I was hooking big, burly alphas. *Still got it!*
7. I loved a psycho man, but this was taking things a little too far.

CHAPTER 23

1. Probably not my smartest move, but sometimes you just had to call someone a dick.
2. Other times I thought I was insane, which was *much* more likely.
3. Flying would be awkward as fuck if I was.
4. Seriously. No face. Just a smooth surface where eyes, nose, and a mouth should be. It made my stomach squirmy.
5. Well, minus a hundred or so years.
6. Well, minus a hundred or so years.
7. Great, there went two more knives.
8. I wasn't one to judge but *yuck.*
9. She ate the limbs one by one and left the torso. I really could have lived without knowing that about my friend. Some things were better left as a mystery.

CHAPTER 24

1. If you're thinking I rode Tali, you'd be correct. I couldn't fault her speed but the comfort could stand to be upgraded. Would she let me put a little seat on her back like she was a camel?

2. Definitely not murdered. Nope. No, sir.

CHAPTER 25

1. See, the good thing about being dead a hundred years is no hair growth! I ought to have had an out of control bush, but it was still neatly trimmed. I should die more often.

CHAPTER 26

1. With admittedly better, more wicked senses of humour.
2. What a fuchsia dress was doing in the bowels of Hell, I didn't know, but I wasn't about to complain.
3. Or get Tali to do the honours for me. I still couldn't forget her crunching through that skull.
4. I *did* learn about a gentleman called Scraggy Nave who'd been cursed to have a squid instead of a dick, and his wife Zillah who'd fucking loved it. You do you, Zillah.

CHAPTER 27

1. You guessed it; I wasn't invited to the tea party.
2. Don't ask. Really, don't ask.
3. As long as I had this rage in me, it would never pass. The guy was a grade A moron. Pretty, though.
4. Life hack, my friends, life hack.

CHAPTER 29

1. I shouldn't sneer though; that probably took someone all two of their brain cells to come up with that name.
2. Okay, so some mistakes had been made. This was not my finest hour.
3. Please be unconscious and not brain damage. Please be unconscious.

CHAPTER 30

1. But I wasn't brain dead! Thank Lucifer.

CHAPTER 32

1. Not sexy dominance, but true, powerful dominance that even alphas would bow to. Although now I think about it, that's pretty damn sexy too.

CHAPTER 33

1. Just kidding, they were still urging him to kill me.

CHAPTER 35

1. I loved them no matter what, exactly as they were, but them trying to kill me over breakfast would be awkward as fuck.

CHAPTER 36

1. I could thank Tali for teaching me that gesture, despite her lack of opposable thumbs.

CHAPTER 37

1. Hell, I'd take pushing onto my knees right now; being facedown was not a fun experience. Well, not like *this*...
2. Because yes, he'd invited people to watch me fall to my death.

CHAPTER 38

1. It was bad that I hoped he wanted me for my power and not a light snack.
2. They never did before; why change the habit of a lifetime?
3. No seriously, it was on my list of things to do before I died. First, restore my mates' memories. Second, have insane, mind-blowing mated sex. Third, stab Wynvail in his smug little eyes.
4. Maybe because arrows *had* been driven through me. Fucking Wynvail.

CHAPTER 1

1. They were wilful housecats at this point, with all the sass, violence, and disdain.
2. *Yes,* they were only cupboards, but you try settling down and being all domestic and not caring when your cupboards shattered. It was a big deal, godsdammit.
3. Rain, definitely rain, not tears ... at all...

CHAPTER 4

1. I wondered if it was the demon whose spines I'd made a tiara with. I missed that tiara.

CHAPTER 5

1. Yeah, that phrase had really ticked me off. I would never let this little dweeb hear the last of it.
2. Birds—all the same no matter their size.

CHAPTER 6

1. On the plus side, they'd all followed me to the alchemist's shop. On the down side, they looked eager to smash everything inside it.
2. I wasn't, but he didn't need to know that. And worse case scenario, we had three weeks left to run a few jobs to raise coin.
3. I knew the curse would force us, no matter what, but just let me have this little delusion. After all, a touch of delusion is important for perfect mental balance.

CHAPTER 7

1. Ugh, even when things were okay with us for a few minutes, I found ways to break my own damn heart.
2. His actual family jewels; that's not a euphemism for his cock and balls.
3. Did it make me a bad mate if I wanted Kai's snakes to strangle Wynvail until his face turned purple and blue?
4. Okay, so maybe it mattered a little. A *tiny* little bit. Miniscule really.

CHAPTER 10

1. Nothing ever changed; possessive men were possessive men even if they couldn't remember me.
2. It wouldn't be the first—or tenth—time.

CHAPTER 12

1. Any time I suggested camping again, stab some sense into me.

CHAPTER 13

1. You would not believe how many legs were involved in group sex. I knew, logically, there were six legs, but I could have sworn there were twenty.

CHAPTER 15

1. Actually, now I thought about it, it was probably the sight of Kai's knob swinging around that scared the man off...
2. Definitely not five, though, I'd considered it at length.
3. I meant *could*. Although, there was another C word that sounded very similar which was my go-to name for Cassander Locke.
4. Kai was the kind of crazy to declare undying love and execute grand romantic gestures. Like killing a gang of Illunacorn demons and using their silvery blood to paint KAI LOVES HALEY on the side of a building. I knew because he'd done exactly that four years into our relationship. And they say love fades.

CHAPTER 16

1. Mine to receive gifts from. Why didn't she get me a gift like the others?
2. So why didn't I have a meaningful gift?

CHAPTER 17

1. Apparently having coffee with Lucifer made me a celebrity. If anyone wanted me to sit for a painting though, they'd learn the hard way I didn't like to be stared at. Although maybe mobile phones could paint a portrait; I'd been dead a long time, and the world had changed.

2. I was pretty sure I was using that word wrong, but Lucifer didn't notice. Did that make me smarter than the devil…?

CHAPTER 18

1. I'd had to sacrifice Wynvail's dagger. So sad.
2. There was little chance Harvey would jump in; his beast form looked too much like a big cat for him to go near water without a screaming tantrum.
3. A monster who wouldn't back down until his cock was tattooed. Shit.
4. You know … the murder, being buried, being cursed to kill my mates thing? Yeah, that.
5. He probably had his knob tattooed, like Kai wanted.
6. They looked fierce but having to sacrifice the ability to roll up your sleeves was a bitch.

CHAPTER 19

1. As a scared adult.

CHAPTER 21

1. The more power they had, the stronger their dumbass energy.

CHAPTER 24

1. The edge of my climax, not the roof. *Please* not the roof.

CHAPTER 26

1. Overlooking the entire city, which I was never getting over, ever.
2. Honestly, I should have bled from all my orifices earlier. I could get used to this.
3. Best not tell my mates that, lest they go even more caveman on me…
4. Err, evening.
5. It was cold at this point, but anything beat hurrying down the hallway with cum leaking down my thigh, leaving a trail like a sexy Hansel and Gretel story. Harvey would draw way too much attention by crawling so he could lick up the drops.

CHAPTER 27

1. And let's be honest, all those orgasms didn't hurt.
2. At least I hoped it was chicken, but in Hell you never really knew.
3. Yes, *eight.*

CHAPTER 28

1. Or maybe threatening a guard into coughing up my location.
2. I just hoped he didn't expect me to lead an army any time soon. I'd lead them straight into a pub.
3. Fuck knows where this search would take us, but if I could wash grime off myself instead of wearing it for a week, I'd be as happy as a pig in mud. Wait, shit, wrong metaphor. As happy as a clean pig with no mud in sight.

CHAPTER 29

1. Worst case scenario, I could stab her and Kai could torture her with his snakes. *We got this.*
2. I really didn't want to think about why they were called the *Wailing* Caves.
3. Hey, I told you that soap would come in handy!
4. Five orgasms before breakfast, let us not forget that detail.
5. Was there such a thing as a guard cloud?

CHAPTER 32

1. Or when all the mercs obeyed him like he was a god. Arrogant bastard didn't need to draw *his own* knives, oh no. He was allergic to manual labour.
2. Fuck, I missed waking up in a bed. I'd never take it for granted ever again.
3. You'd think after ten hours asleep, I'd have dried out but apparently the weather hated me.

CHAPTER 33

1. *That* is how you got me to fall in line. Kai needed to take tips.

CHAPTER 34

1. Sure I had blood control, but self-rowing boats? This is where I draw the line.
2. Fuck, how did men make ripping clothes look so easy? My arm burned from the exertion.

CHAPTER 35

1. For safety. For stability. Not because I was enjoying the feel of him under my hand and I was a greedy bitch when it came to touch.
2. Fuck, maybe it was. Had anyone ever heard of a boat demon?
3. Well, where he bobbed in the boat.

CHAPTER 36

1. Plus knowing Harvey, he'd end up getting kidnapped by a sea monster. He was such a damsel.
2. Please fucking no.
3. I could make a joke about getting blood from a stone, but I was too raw for that.

CHAPTER 38

1. And distracting. Oh god, it was distracting.
2. Yup, you read that right. He ate them.

CHAPTER 1

1. My poor spare weapons, though ... they were now rusting in the river of a collapsed cave system.

CHAPTER 2

1. Okay, when I stabbed him, which was fair enough; I'd have kept it, too.
2. He'd forced me to read it; my brain nearly died of boredom.
3. Well, semi-calmly. I couldn't stop baring my sharp teeth at him.

CHAPTER 3

1. I should have told Wynvail I'd traded his 'gift' for the jacket, just to see the look on his face. Not that stealing counted as gift giving.
2. *My* danger, I licked him so he's mine.
3. And *literal* Hell just to spice things up
4. I knew how to beg to be railed in every hole, but asking for something as simple as this? My face burned.

CHAPTER 5

1. I didn't look. I definitely didn't *watch.*

CHAPTER 6

1. What was it with Wynvail and giving me pretty knives anyway? Did he know they were the way to my heart? Nah, why would he care about my heart?

CHAPTER 7

1. If you asked me, he was compensating for something. Starting fights to show he was a big, hard god? Let me tell you what was *not* big and hard...
2. He was still shirtless, in case you were wondering.
3. And very nicely straining his shirt, I might add.
4. Of all the new things I'd learned about since I came back from the dead, electrocution was one of my favourites. I wanted to try it out on my enemies. Cronus was at the top of the list.
5. Courtesy of yours truly, thank you very much.
6. I was going to need a knee replacement if I kept falling...
7. Probably sneering at us for so long, his face developed a permanent *I just smelled cow shit* expression.

CHAPTER 8

1. Oh, and getting bitten by a hyaeni demon, surviving the harrowing Wailing Caves, almost drowning too many times to count, and the trek that took us to the caves in the first place.
2. Get it? Winging? Because I was flying. Fuck, I'm funny.

CHAPTER 9

1. Or when I was bored on a Friday night...
2. Although it would be glorious to watch her unleash her wrath on Cronus...

CHAPTER 10

1. Don't laugh; we've all been there. Raise your hand if you're a member of the *walks into walls* gang.
2. Another thing I'd learned after waking up a hundred years later: plastic was a thing, and apparently everything in the known universe was made of it.
3. Definitely not smart, but I'd lost control of my mouth.
4. Not in the fun way.
5. This was how I would die; talking back to a titan. Mark me down for death by stupidity.

CHAPTER 11

1. Not one of my volcanic daggers, gods forbid. I'd never emotionally recover—and neither would Kai.

CHAPTER 12

1. Five gold coins would buy a cheap dagger, and I was a slut for sharp steel.
2. Often and without care to whether it was wanted.

CHAPTER 15

1. I'm sure he *tripped.*
2. The obvious reasons were my boobs had been through enough, and were only newly healed thanks to Harvey's magic soothing their bruises. They didn't need to get squashed again.
3. And not just so I could touch his dick. But I bet it was huge. Arrogant pricks always were.
4. Five mates and no one was inside me right now, how was that fair?
5. Not Wynvail. I wasn't even thinking about *him.* Standing a few feet away. His eyes fixed on me. Hungry. Engrossed in the sight of me getting fucked by his brother.

CHAPTER 16

1. Besides, I could kill him after.

CHAPTER 17

1. And by clean up I meant use a rag torn off the bottom of Kai's shirt.
2. There was a shocking amount of sex books in Lucifer's palace library. I was a learned woman now.
3. Definitely not snuggle and fool around. No, sir, not us.

CHAPTER 18

1. Definitely a killer octopus, this one.
2. Get a grip on the knife, not mentally get a grip. Although, I couldn't get that, either...
3. Hopefully not eat us.
4. Total psycho behaviour, but look at that—I was justified.
5. Do you think Cronus would give us a fleet of space heaters if I asked extra nicely? If we *survived*, that was...
6. I'd managed to die, be buried, and come back to life with this face intact, and I wasn't keen on losing it now.
7. It had been a while since I gouged someone's eyes out anyway. Like, a hundred years. I was long overdue a gouging. As a treat.

CHAPTER 19

1. Again.
2. Spoiler: it didn't.

CHAPTER 20

1. I gave Em full credit for that; he supported him with a broad hand on his shoulder. Great hands, those. Very safe. 10/10.

CHAPTER 21

1. Never a smart move to take away the only thing keeping a psychopath in check.

CHAPTER 22

1. Although, I'd be over-fucking-joyed to see Hell right now; gods *please* take me home. I'd had enough of god and titan shit to last a lifetime.

CHAPTER 23

1. But a part of me would mourn the loss of killing him myself. I had plans for him, and they involved specialist tools, slow blood loss, and repeated near-deaths.
2. It wasn't the only thing throbbing as Haley wrenched her dagger out of Alecto's back, blood spurting, and twirled both blades in her hands as she advanced on Megaera.

DAMNED NIGHT, A WYNVAIL POV

1. Yes, I was wallowing in misery and bitterness, but I was about to die so just let me have this pity party.
2. Partly because the emotional scene made me nauseated and partly because his cock was just swinging around down there.